Richard North Patterson

FINAL JUDGEMENT

THE OUTSIDE MAN

ARROW

This edition published by Arrow in 2002
an imprint of The Random House Group
20 Vauxhall Bridge Road, London SW1V 2SA

Papers used by Random House UK Ltd are natural recyclable products made from wood grown
in sustainable forests. The manufacturing process
conform to the environment regulations of the
country of origin.

A catalogue record for this book is available from
the British Library

Printed and bound in Germany by Elsnerdruck,
Berlin

ISBN 0 09 188546 9

THE FINAL
JUDGEMENT

Richard North Patterson

PART ONE

Two Women

Chapter 1

Two days after the murder, listening to Brett Allen's tale of innocence and confusion, the lawyer wavered between disbelief and wonder at its richness, so vivid that she could almost picture it as truth.

The lawyer looked at Brett in silence, taking in the oval face, the delicate cleft chin, the curly ungroomed hair, the small breasts and almost too slim body of a late bloomer who, at first glance, looked younger than twenty-two. But what struck her was the bright greenness of the eyes, a gaze so intuitive and direct that it unnerved her.

As Brett described it, the night had been crisp, windless. Moonlight refracted on the still, obsidian waters of the lake and traced the pines and birches and elms surrounding it. The only sound Brett heard was the rise and fall of James's breathing.

They were naked. Brett straddled him, as she had when making love. The cool night chilled her nipples, dried the wetness on her skin. As she shivered, James, flaccid and unconscious, slid from inside her.

She felt a spurt of anger. And then the nausea returned, mingling the acrid taste of marijuana with the torpor of too much wine. All at once, the night burst into shards – images without connection, freeze-frames of color amidst a black jumble she could not remember.

That explained how she had acted with the police, she told her lawyer – pot and wine, shock and paranoia. Dope was really James's thing. As Brett said this, her lawyer saw a sheen of tears, as if the young woman had remembered some fond detail. For days after, as the lawyer grew to believe that Brett Allen was a murderer, the moment haunted her.

3

Before the dope, Brett told her, her memory was sound.

James had called her parents' home, where she was staying for the summer. They had talked a little; then, fearing that her mother might listen in, Brett had suggested that they go to the lake, take some cheese and wine. She had a favorite place, and they would be alone.

Whatever James had to say, she sensed, should not be heard by others.

Brett made her excuses. She saw the tight look in her mother's thin face, the cool gray eyes filling with things she did not say. For a moment, Brett was torn between pity and the desire to confront her, and then she decided that this was pointless. She left the house, its dark mass looming behind her.

She drove to the college for James. In the car, he was quiet, intent. His face was a study in black and white – pale skin, dark ringlets of hair, shadows on his sculpted face. One of his acting teachers, with mingled derision and admiration, had once called him 'Young Lord Byron.' The teacher, Brett pointedly recalled, was a woman.

They drove winding roads, wooded and silent, saw occasional headlights cutting the silver darkness, then the steady glow of a lone car behind them, traveling neither slower nor faster. Abruptly, they turned down a dirt road, hacked so narrow between looming pines that it was pitch black. The car lights behind them passed the trailhead, and vanished.

Hitting the brights, Brett slowed to a crawl, following the headlights as they carved a path between the rough-barked trunks of trees.

Then the path ended.

Brett stopped there. Silent, she opened the trunk of her battered black Jeep, took out the gym bag with the wine and cheese, then tucked a rough woolen blanket under her arm. James followed her into the trees.

Suddenly, there was no sky.

They edged through trunks and branches down a

gradually sloping hill, feet sliding on the hardened ground, the result of two dry weeks after a rainy spring. A branch lashed at her face; in the darkness, Brett felt diminished, like some primitive amidst the mysteries of nature.

'Where are we going?' James murmured behind her. 'To play Dungeons and Dragons?'

Why was it, Brett wondered, that people whisper in the darkness? She did not answer.

And then they reached the clearing.

A glade of grass, opening to a moonlit lake. She stopped there, looking out.

Behind her, James was quiet again.

'This is yours?' he said at last.

Can you leave this? she felt him ask. But she answered only the question he spoke aloud.

'Yes,' she said simply. 'It's mine. If I still want it.'

She did not mean the lake. It was a mile across and nearly that wide; on the far shore were a few fishing camps and summer houses, unseen in the darkness. But since her birth her family had held the parcel where they stood for Brett. It was a fact as certain as her grandfather's love.

Brett gazed out at the water, postponing by her stillness the moment when they would begin to talk.

She could sense, rather than see, the platform where she had first learned to dive. Yet she could have swum there as surely as in daylight. Just as she could remember standing on the rocky inlet between the glade and the water, holding aloft the rainbow trout, speckled in the sunlight, so that her grandfather could see it.

Turning to James, Brett put down the gym bag and held out the wool blanket so that he could help her spread it on the glade. Laying it down, she could feel the dampness of the grass.

They settled onto the blanket, Brett sitting cross-legged, James lying on his side, head propped on one hand. Woods surrounded them on three sides; in front of them was the smooth black sheen of water. Far across the lake, Brett heard the faint cry of a heron. They were utterly alone.

5

'What is it?' she asked him.

James brushed the hair back from his forehead. Brett knew this as a temporizing gesture, a sign of hesitancy.

'I want us to go to California,' he said at length.

Her voice was level. 'I know that.'

'I mean soon.'

It was hard to read his face. But beneath the casual pose, so characteristic of James, Brett felt his anxiety.

'Why soon?'

He was quiet for a time. But in their year together, Brett had learned the uses of silence. She waited.

'That dope I sold,' James said finally. 'I never paid for it.'

Brett despised James's business. They had fought about it for two months: James was adamant that this was the way for him – left without money or family to speak of – to pay his way through what he had sardonically labeled the 'poison ivy league.' It was, he promised, temporary.

'Never paid for it ...,' Brett repeated in a flat voice. 'I didn't know your friends gave credit.'

'I need the money. *We* need the money. To leave here.' James's voice rose. 'Sure as hell your family won't give you any. Not for that.'

'Why should they?'

'No reason to.' His tone softened. 'It's just that I had to do something – start a life.'

He was trying to make her complicit, Brett knew. 'Without asking me?' she shot back. 'You're supposed to do what you want, and I'm just supposed to react to it?'

James sat up now, facing her. 'I owe a little over thirty-five hundred.' He leaned forward in entreaty. 'I made almost forty-three selling the stuff. Enough to drive to the Coast and still have first and last months' rent.'

Brett knew his dream. He would work part time and look for acting jobs; Brett would break from home and family – the stifling effect she felt of too many years of expectations – and write the books she believed she could. But this image seemed more vivid to James than to her.

'I have a life, James. A real one. And not all of it is with you.' She shook her head in impatience. 'My parents are *work*, all right – especially my mother. But I have one quarter of school left, and I owe it to them to finish, owe it to myself if I decide to get a master's degree. And my grandfather – who I love a lot, though I understand it's hard for you to get that – has a heart condition. What I do about them, I have to live with. Just like I have to live with *me*. This isn't about you, okay? Or even me writing the Great American Novel.' She paused, finishing more quietly: 'You never had a family, for bad or good or in between. It's more complex than you think.'

James expelled a breath. Taking her hand, he said softly, 'You're my family.'

It was meant to touch her, Brett knew. But she perceived what James could never admit: that beneath his calculation was the loneliness of a seven-year-old whose mother was dead and his father vanished, his future a series of foster homes that took him in for money.

Conflicted, Brett watched his eyes, searching for the person who lived behind them.

Suddenly, James flinched. He was half standing before she heard the sound.

Underbrush rustling, perhaps the cracking of a branch. James went rigid; in that moment, Brett saw how scared he was.

It was that which raised the gooseflesh on her skin.

'What *was* that?' he said in a low voice.

Watching his face, thin and strained, Brett listened.

Nothing.

Slowly, she turned from him, saw pale branches at the edge of the glade, then darkness.

'Well,' she said with a trace of humor, 'they say the timber-wolves are coming back from Canada. There are all sorts of animals in the woods at night. Everything but people.' When he did not answer, she lowered her voice. 'How much trouble is this?'

James clasped her shoulders. 'He's been calling me,' he said. 'My supplier.'

'And?'

'He wants his money. I said I didn't have it yet.'

Brett felt her eyes close. She was part of a deadline, she realized, that James had created for himself. 'Then give him the money, that's all.'

She heard him exhale. 'Too late. He knows I lied to him.'

To Brett, the phrase had an incomplete sound. When she turned to him, he was still looking over her shoulder. 'They broke into my apartment, Brett. Last night. The place was torn up, and the sheets slashed.'

Brett stared at him. Reflexively, she asked, 'Did you call the police?'

He gave her a faint, crooked smile. With a strange mix of bitterness and affection, he said, 'You really are the judge's granddaughter, you know.'

Her voice rose. 'It *can't* be too late, James. All they want is money. What good does it do to hurt you?'

'That's not how it works, Brett. Please believe me.'

She shook her head, turning away. 'There are too many surprises, too close together. I just can't deal with this....'

Her voice trailed off. He had grown up protecting himself, she thought; he wasn't used to closeness.

Alone, Brett walked to the water's edge.

After a time, she heard his footsteps behind her, then saw his faint reflection in the water next to hers, a slender profile with hands jammed in pockets. He made no move to touch her.

Another part of her, she realized, was listening to the woods behind them.

'What are you going to do?' he asked.

She hunched her shoulders. 'I don't know.'

'We have to decide.'

'You decided without me, James. Now I have to decide what I want. Without you.'

His shadow seemed to slump a little. At length, he said, 'Then just *be* with me, all right?'

Brett knew what James meant, perhaps before he did. It was James's instinct to see lovemaking as a refuge from his insecurity. So that, taking him inside her, Brett never knew whether he was reaching for her or running from himself.

She turned to him. 'Trying to fuck me into submission?'

The crooked smile again. Beneath it Brett saw a flicker of vulnerability – James exposed to himself. 'Not really.'

She felt a first twinge of guilt. 'Good,' she said. 'Because I'm hungry. And thirsty.'

Tentatively, James took her hand. They walked back to the blanket.

They knelt there, James unwrapping the cheese and slicing it with a pocket knife, Brett pouring red wine into a paper cup. There was no sound but their own.

With the second cup of wine, Brett felt the alcoholic glow. A pleasant lassitude crept through her limbs.

She sat between James's legs, back against his chest, in a silent declaration of truce. They shared a cup, James taking it from her hand and placing it back again. Brett was not a drinker; with each sip, the night seemed to close in a little, become a cocoon of warmth. The passing moments were impressions – the rise and fall of crickets chirring, the sheen of water, the rich red taste of wine, the rough-smooth feel of James's face against hers. She tried to push their troubles away, save her decision for the cool, clear morning that would light the lake with silver, then with gold.

'What are you thinking?' he asked.

'I'm just being,' she answered, and drained the cup.

James knew not to push her. Silent, he reached around her and filled the empty cup.

'Some grass?' he asked. 'I brought a joint.'

It was wrong, part of her thought. They should not drift toward lovemaking dulled by dope and wine; whatever happened would have little meaning beyond release. But

9

she needed time to find the answer that might well end them.

When James lit the joint, sucking in the first hit with a low quick breath, she took it from between his fingers.

She did not do this much. The first acrid puff was hot and raw in her throat. But with the second, slower and deeper, she settled in James's arms.

The night changed again. The stars had a diamond clarity, undimmed by clouds or city lights. Brett became lost in them.

They stayed like that, passing the joint back and forth as they finished the bottle of wine. James seemed less a person than a presence; what Brett felt now was a deep immersion in this place – the sky, the water, the rattle of breezes in unseen trees. It was all she wanted.

And then James's hands, tender and tentative, brushed against her breasts.

She wore no bra. Through her T-shirt, she felt her nipples rise beneath his hands, her nerve ends suddenly alive, a pulse of warmth where James had not yet touched. A silent murmur filled her throat.

In this way, at least, he knew her. This way, they worked.

The tips of his fingers touched her nipples now, gently moving. And then she felt the wine and the dope and the shiver of skin exploding in a savage impulse.

She turned to him, balanced on her knees, and raised the T-shirt over her head.

Slowly, as if in a ritual, he untied her sneakers, pushed her to the blanket with one hand cradling her back, then unzipped her jeans and slid them down and off.

That he did not undress said the rest. She lay on her back, watching the stars, as he reached beneath the elastic of her underpants.

Brett opened her legs for him.

James bent his face to her. For an instant, Brett felt it as a silent offering, a plea for closeness. Then all she felt was his face against her thighs, his seeking tongue.

When her hips began to move, she could not help this, nor did she want to. The sounds from her lips were more cry than murmur, becoming quicker, a guide for him. Blood rushed to where his tongue caressed her, swift with the hotness of dope and wanting. Her movements lost all rhythm.

A cry in darkness.

Brett's eyes shut tight as the spasms ran through her body. Only as a tingle reached her fingers did she hear the woman's cries, slower and softer, recognize them as hers.

And then she was still.

She could not seem to move. Beneath the torpor, sex and dope and wine seemed to loop in circuits through her brain.

Awkwardly, Brett got to her knees. She could feel the heat receding from her thighs.

James seemed unreal now, in pieces: eyes wanting her, a hand pulling her close. She felt smoke and alcohol in the pit of her stomach. The night began to spin.

'Jesus,' she murmured.

He did not seem to hear; suddenly his movements had the clumsy concentration of drunkenness. As he pulled down his pants, Brett had the jaded, antic vision of a monster she had seen in an old movie, tottering over Tokyo as he swayed from side to side.

She swallowed, fighting sickness and self-disgust. When he held his penis to her face, she shook her head.

Just don't lie down, she told herself.

'Lie back,' she murmured.

He did that. Clumsily, she turned from him, crawling naked toward the gym bag.

'Where are you going?' he asked dully.

Mute, she fumbled through the bag and then pulled out a foil square. Crawling back, she held it out to him.

'You're on the pill,' he said.

Brett stared at him. 'I'll put it on for you.'

Watching her face, he said nothing more.

Fragments now: sheathing him in latex, its oily slickness between her fingers. Clambering on her knees to mount him. The blunt feeling of him as he entered her. A fever on her skin, too clammy for passion.

As James moaned, urging himself to climax, she thought of two dogs mating.

She rode him out of stubbornness, fighting sickness. He did not come. Desperate, Brett wrenched him upward with her hands beneath his spine. He flinched beneath her; dimly, she realized that her nails had scraped his skin.

His eyes opened wider. 'I love you ...,' he murmured.

Brett stopped moving. Tenderness overtaking her, she touched his face.

James was asleep.

As she shivered in the sudden cool of night, he slipped from inside her. She stared at him, sick and stupid again, fighting the impulse to lift him by the hair. And then, abruptly, anger became sadness.

There was still goodness in him, she knew, much that had not been ruined. He was tender with her, always. When she grew angry with him, he did not lash back; he watched her, puzzled, trying to comprehend. As if listening for music he could not yet hear.

Gently, she laid his head down, turned it to one side. He slept with a child's innocence.

Lost in dope and darkness, Brett had forgotten the lake was there. And then it struck her: the cool water might clear her head.

Rising, she turned to the water.

It seemed opaque, a glassy rock. Brett clambered naked from the glade across the rocky shore, crying out as the sharp stones cut her bare feet.

A splash, shocking coolness as she hit the water.

Swimming felt hard and slow. Suddenly, she was swathed in blackness, swallowed by the lake. In panic, she flailed to keep from drowning, felt herself go under....

And then, shivering and panting, Brett was lying facedown on the rough wooden planks of the diving platform. She felt surprise, then fright that she could not remember how she got there.

Slowly, like a woman half drowned, Brett turned on her back. Her mouth had the brackish taste of algae and still water. Her heart throbbed in her chest.

Gradually, her breathing eased. She had no thought of swimming back.

Time kept slipping. Brett saw an image from childhood: her mother, calm and sure then, teaching her to dive, her grandfather watching with that air of pleased reserve. Brett stared up at the moon, so seemingly close that she could almost touch the craters on its face.

And then the sense was upon her, primal and instinctive, that they were not alone.

Brett trained her eyes on the water. Distances were lost to her. When she turned to the glade where James lay sleeping, it seemed to move away. The faint moonlight on the grass was like the glow of phosphorus.

A sudden shadow rose from the grass.

Brett sat up. 'James ...'

Startled, the shadow turned. Her voice echoed on the water.

'James ...'

Abruptly, the shadow vanished among the shadows of her imaginings....

No.

Brett stood without thinking and dove into the water.

The shock of coolness felt real now. She was less afraid to swim than to stop and look at the glade. She rose from the water's edge, trembling with cold.

The glade was dark and silent. She walked toward the blanket, grass matting beneath her feet.

James was not the shadow. He lay as she had left him, except that he was gazing at the moon.

A sound came from his throat.

Like snoring, Brett thought as she approached. Yet not snoring. In the moonlight, she saw that his mouth was open, heard ragged breaths.

The sound again. A gurgling, Brett thought suddenly. Like the sound of a man whose lungs had filled with water.

James, she thought with horror, was drowning in his own vomit.

With quick, instinctive movements, Brett knelt beside him. As moonlight caught his face, she started CPR.

She felt wetness on his lips, heard her own breath rattle in his throat. Her eyes shut tight. Like a delayed image on the retina, Brett saw his face in the instant before she had placed her mouth to his.

As Brett recoiled, a warm spray rose from his lips, flecking her face and throat and breasts.

His body shivered beneath her in a twitching spasm. His face was speckled, eyes staring at nothing. The last soft spray of blood rose from his severed windpipe.

A knife stuck from his ribs.

Brett made no sound. She stood, trembling, straining to comprehend. Saw the blood on her fingers.

Only then did she realize that she had pulled the knife from his chest.

As her shriek carried across the water, Brett the reasoning human ceased to exist.

All was a nightmare collage: Her hand clutching the knife. His wallet where it had fallen as he undressed. The dark slash through his throat.

She whirled, staring wildly at the woods. The wind, moaning now, was the sound of James dying.

Blindly, Brett ran toward the darkness.

It enveloped her. Branches beat her face and body as she flailed at the darkness with both hands, hacking the leaves from her face. Now the darkness seemed to enter her mind. The flailing became a dream, no moment distinct from the other, the glade behind her no more real than the moon she could not see. Time had no end. And then, in sudden moonlight, the outline of a Jeep appeared.

Brett slowed to a walk. Emerging naked from the trees, she was uncertain of what to believe. Tentative, she rested her hand on the Jeep.

It was real. The keys were still inside.

Brett opened the door, throwing what she had carried on the passenger seat, and turned the ignition.

It worked. Brett locked herself in. She did not know how long she sat there, naked, listening to the low hum of the motor.

She switched on the headlights. When she spun the Jeep around, their beams cut a path between the trunks of trees. Just as before.

Shifting gears, Brett began to drive.

Brett awoke in darkness.

She tasted blood in her mouth, then vomit. Her lip felt swollen.

She was slumped, naked, across the steering wheel. The stench of sickness filled the Jeep. Her stomach felt hollow.

Brett felt a pounding in her head. Stiff-necked, she leaned back in the seat and looked around her.

A wooded roadside. She did not know where she was, how she had gotten there, how long she had been unconscious. She was not sure why she was crying.

A light came toward her.

Brett winced, turning her head. The light filled her windshield.

Behind the flashlight was the shape of a man.

The light circled the hood of her car, moving toward the driver's side. Brett curled sideways, face pressed against the door, arms folded across her chest, eyes and mouth clamped tight.

There was a tap on the window.

No, she thought. *Don't hurt me.*

Fingers digging into her skin, Brett forced her eyes open. The tap of the flashlight stopped. A beam of light crossed her body, captured her hips, a shadow of pubic hair.

As Brett gazed at her own nakedness, a tremor ran through her.

'Open up,' a voice demanded.

15

A young man's voice, Brett thought. She swallowed. 'Open up,' he said again. 'Police.'

Police. By instinct, she reached for the window crank, one arm covering her breasts, and lowered the glass between her and the voice.

He was young, with short dark hair and a pale face. Though he wore the jacket of the local police, she did not know him.

He looked startled, embarrassed. 'What happened?'

Brett shook her head. Words did not seem to come. 'Sick ...'

He thrust the flashlight into the car, jabbing the beam here and there. In a taut voice, he asked, 'Is someone hurt?'

Sudden images. Straddling James in the night. His staring eyes. A knife in her hand.

'Miss?'

A nightmare. She must be stoned, the terrible pictures a dream. James was home in bed.

Her voice was weak. 'Please, take me home....'

His flashlight lit the passenger seat.

A heap of clothes, a wallet. A bloody knife.

'I'm taking you in, miss.'

A convulsive sob ripped from Brett's throat. 'Why ...?'

A moment's pause. 'For driving while intoxicated.'

The beam moved back to her. Brett saw blood on her hands, speckles of blood on her torso.

She curled, elbows on knees, and vomited.

He gave her his jacket.

Their drive to the station was lost to her. The shotgun in his car, the crackle of a radio, nothing else. When she found herself sitting hunched against the wall of a cinder-block cell, it was like awakening from a blackout. The policeman stood over her.

Looking away from him, she pulled his jacket to midthigh, saw specks of vomit on her legs.

In his hand was James's wallet, opened to his driver's

license. Staring from the picture on the laminated card, James looked stiff and frightened.

With terrible vividness, Brett saw the gash in his throat.

The cop's voice was strangely gentle. 'I think there's someone hurt out there, needing our help. If we can't find him ...'

Brett's eyes filled with tears. 'Look by the lake,' she said dully. 'Maybe he's there.'

'Heron Lake?'

Swallowing, Brett nodded.

The cop hurried away. Brett heard footsteps on tile, his voice on the telephone. She waited, drained, until the cop returned.

'I'll drive you to the hospital,' he said.

A blond, bird-faced woman in a state trooper's uniform was waiting by the emergency entrance.

The cop holding one arm, the trooper the other, Brett was led through the bleak corridors. She passed beneath the fluorescent lights as if sleepwalking.

At the end of a corridor was an empty room.

The trooper took Brett inside. Brett stood there, staring at the room – an examining table, two chairs, a metal cabinet and sink and mirror.

She felt the young cop pause in the doorway. 'Is this all right?' he asked.

The trooper nodded. 'For waiting, yes. Until they find something.'

The cop hesitated, glancing at Brett, and left.

The trooper closed the door behind them, stood facing Brett. 'I'm sorry,' she said, 'but I need to take that jacket off.'

Brett clasped it tighter. 'Why?'

'Procedures.' Without waiting for an answer, she unzipped the jacket and slid it from Brett's shoulders.

Brett shivered again.

'Can I clean up?' she asked.

'No. Not yet.'

Brett stared at her. Taking the handcuffs from her belt, the trooper turned one chair to face the cabinet and in the crisp manner of a schoolteacher said, 'Sit here, please. I have to cuff you.'

Suddenly, Brett was angry. 'Tell me why, damn it.'

The trooper shot her a level glance. 'So that you don't touch yourself.'

For that instant, Brett wanted to call her parents, her grandfather. Then the mirror caught her reflection.

Her face was flecked with blood.

Brett walked forward, as if drawn to her image. Dried blood speckled her lips, her throat, her breasts.

Brett sat in the chair.

As she held out her hands, there was blood on her fingertips.

Pulling Brett's arms behind her, the trooper cuffed her to the metal chair.

A plump nurse came. Silent, she took out a needle and punctured Brett's arm. With an odd detachment, Brett watched the plastic tube fill with her own blood. She hardly felt the needle.

The nurse left her with the trooper.

'How long will I be here?' Brett asked.

No answer.

Time passed. Perhaps minutes, perhaps hours.

There was a knock on the door.

Brett turned. The trooper opened the door slightly, speaking through the crack to shield Brett's nakedness.

'What is it?' she asked.

A male voice, new to Brett. 'They found him. At Heron Lake.'

'Is he all right?' Brett asked.

Whispers now. Closing the door, the trooper handed her some papers.

'This is a search warrant,' she said. 'For you.'

'For what?'

A long, slow look. 'He's dead.'

18

Brett began shaking.

Everything changed.

Brett stood there, mute, a magnet for strangers. Another female trooper entered, with a Polaroid, took pictures of Brett's face, her throat and torso, her fingertips.

A knife in her hand …

A nurse in a scrub suit snipped a piece of Brett's hair and then, kneeling, clipped from her pubic hair.

The images came quicker now. A shadow, turning …

The nurse scraped flecks of blood from Brett's skin onto a piece of plastic.

A soft spray rising from his throat …

She turned to the trooper. 'I need to see someone.'

A quick careful look. 'Who?'

'The policeman who brought me here.'

The trooper shook her head. 'First we have to finish this. Then we'll find him.'

At the trooper's signal, a mustached doctor approached from the side. Gently, he led Brett to the examining table, explained that he would take a swab from her vagina.

Brett lay staring at the fluorescent lights. As she opened her legs, Brett remembered the feel of James's tongue.

'It's all right.' The doctor's voice was soothing, comfort for a patient. 'We're almost done.'

Brett stood, unsteady. The trooper held out a jumpsuit. 'You can dress now.'

Brett did not try to clean herself.

When she was dressed, the nurse took one hand, then the other, slipping a scalpel beneath each fingernail.

James wincing as she scraped his back …

She had left him there. For minutes, perhaps hours, she had not told them.

'Please,' she pressed, 'I need to talk now.'

They took her fingerprints and then drove her to the jail.

The sky was purpling with the first thin streak of dawn. Now she recognized the police station.

They led her to a cramped room with two metal desks.

The young cop sat at one desk; somehow he had gotten back his jacket. A stranger sat at another, a tape recorder in front of him.

He was stocky and red-faced, with pale-blue eyes and an air of calm authority. He understood she wished to talk. Hoped she wouldn't mind the tape ...

'You have the right to remain silent ...'

Brett waited until he finished, and then she began to tell them all she could.

When it was over, she searched their eyes, saw nothing. They led her to the cell again, and she was alone.

Voices came from the next room. 'Do you know who her grandfather is?' someone asked.

Only after a time did she see the man standing in front of her cell.

He was tall and almost gangly, his black hair flecked with gray. His work shirt and khakis were wrinkled, and he had not yet shaved. Twin creases elongated his face and made the large brown eyes knowing and a little sad. He seemed kind, somehow familiar.

'Oh, Brett.' His voice was soft with melancholy. 'What in God's name have you done?'

It was, Brett's lawyer reflected, precisely the question she wished that she could ask. But she was a defense lawyer and could not.

'Who was he?' Brett asked her. 'The man at the jail.'

The lawyer hesitated, caught in the scene as Brett was describing it, still wondering how much could be believed. But the tall man's face was very real to her.

'It was the prosecutor,' she told Brett. 'Jackson Watts. Through college, we were friends.'

'And now?'

'I don't know.' The lawyer paused, then finished. 'The last time I saw him was before you were born.'

For a moment, Brett looked at her curiously. But she said nothing.

'Tell me,' the lawyer inquired. 'Did the police ask anything else?'

Brett hesitated. 'I think they asked if James had other girlfriends.'

The lawyer tilted her head. 'To which you answered ...?'

'No.' Brett's voice was angry now. 'No.'

Chapter 2

Two days earlier, the Honorable Caroline Clark Masters had stretched her tan legs in front of her, wriggled some sand from between her toes, and gazed out at the white-capped blue of Nantucket Sound.

It was summer, and afternoon. Sun glistened on the water; a northeast wind tousled the loose black ringlets of her hair. The ocean was dotted with boats, sailing across the northeast winds to Edgartown. Along the beach, stretching to a faraway point, waves broke onto the tawny sand until they seemed to meet a white mist in the distance, sitting lightly on the water. Caroline's mind flooded with memories.

Perhaps it was the boy. A college kid, really – a distant figure now, growing smaller as he walked the surf.

He had looked, she thought, a little as she remembered David. Not the hair so much. Something about the eyes. Perhaps that was why Caroline, disposed to solitude, had spoken to him.

'Hello.'

He stopped on the sand, looking from Caroline to the sprawling house on the bluff behind her. Feeling a little guilty, perhaps, to be walking her private beach.

'Hi.' He shifted from foot to foot, dressed only in cutoffs, lean and brown and not bad looking. With a certain awe, he asked, 'Is this place yours?'

Caroline smiled, shook her head. 'Just renting. For a week.'

He took that in, nodding. Yes, Caroline had thought, a certain pensiveness in the eyes, the same gray blue. But not the same quickness.

'I've been wondering about this place,' he said. 'They say the beach has changed totally, from erosion and storms.' He nodded to the rocks and railroad ties behind her, rising from the beach to the bluff. 'A few years ago they nearly lost this house, someone told me.'

Caroline smiled again. '*Thirty* years ago,' she said, 'you and I would be standing on the lawn. The owner and his family played croquet there.'

'You knew them?'

Caroline nodded. 'Yes. I knew them.'

As he looked at her more closely, Caroline sensed him calculating her age. Then he turned, pointing to a spit of sand some distance away. 'I saw rocks out there, some pilings. Know what that was?'

'A boathouse. But it belonged to the place next door.'

'Know what they used it for?'

'Storage, sometimes.' There was something else, Caroline saw, the way he tilted his head. 'One year, a caretaker lived there.'

'Hurricane got it, I guess.'

Caroline made her tone dismissive. 'I suppose. It was here the last time I was.'

The boy was silent, as if reflecting on the transience of things. 'I hope you haven't minded my asking these questions.'

'Not at all.'

He tilted his head again. 'Do I know you from somewhere?'

Caroline realized, suddenly, that she was not quite ready to have him leave. Smiling, she decided to flatter him a little. 'I think I'd remember you.'

'I don't mean it's like we've met.' Vaguely flustered, he seemed to peer at her. 'Didn't you used to be in the movies or something?'

This tacit reference to her age – which Caroline thought she more than deserved – made her laugh aloud at herself. The grin that came with it had a sardonic quality which was relieved by a dimple on one side of her mouth, a light in her green-flecked brown eyes. 'Not that I remember.'

The boy stepped closer. 'No, really.'

Caroline looked up at him, amusement still playing on her mouth. 'No,' she said firmly. 'Really.'

Now she watched him, growing smaller, until he vanished.

Forty-five, she thought, scraping the wounds of young womanhood. She did not quite understand this: the events that had defined her had made Caroline Masters a distinctly unsentimental woman. Yet she had come here. Sometimes it seemed to her that the central events in her life had not happened in New Hampshire, the home of her girlhood, but in this place, Martha's Vineyard, near the water.

She gazed out at the sound. She did not even know whether David was still alive – a man in his forties who thought of her little or, perhaps, with bitterness. She was past all hope of knowing.

Perhaps it was the nomination that had jarred the past from dormancy.

'Is there anything we should know,' the President's counsel had asked her, 'which might embarrass the White House?'

'No,' Caroline had answered. 'Nothing.'

She had spent twenty years of her life, with rising intensity and ambition, waiting to be asked this question. Perhaps it was inevitable, with the nomination so near her grasp, that she would think about the things that had made her as she was.

The President was down to two choices, Caroline and a fine Hispanic lawyer. At five o'clock, the phone would ring, and Caroline Clark Masters would – or would not – be appointed to the United States Court of Appeals.

A step, though the thought made her superstitious, from the United States Supreme Court.

A giant step, yet perhaps not much farther than the distance she had already come. Caroline had arrived in California at twenty-three, with no friends or family she spoke of. Had put herself through law school, then spent fifteen hard years at the public defender's office, representing murderers and petty drug dealers with more success

24

than the odds allowed; teaching and lecturing and writing articles on criminal justice to spread her reputation; widening her contacts through women's groups and a little politics; yet careful, always, to keep a core of privacy.

And then Caroline was appointed to a minor judgeship, the San Francisco Municipal Court. This much she had planned. But what followed – the Carelli case – was an accident.

The charge was murder. The defendant, Mary Carelli, was a well-known network journalist; the victim was a celebrated novelist. They were alone in a hotel room when, if Carelli could be believed, she had killed him to prevent a rape.

Caroline conducted the preliminary hearing. The medical examiner believed that Carelli's claim of attempted rape did not square with the crime scene or the condition of the body. It was more than enough for a Municipal Court judge to find probable cause for a murder trial in the Superior Court, which – in any other case – would have been Caroline's only job. But then Carelli's lawyer decided to use the preliminary hearing to challenge probable cause, and demanded that the hearing be televised.

For two weeks, Caroline ran the most watched hearing in memory with skill, wit, and, most observers agreed, impeccable fairness. By the end of the hearing Caroline was as much a celebrity as Mary Carelli herself.

Caroline wasted no time. She appeared on television, gave interviews – long on charm and short on biography – to carefully selected journalists. Offers poured in: the one she took, a partnership in a large San Francisco firm, offered her corporate contacts and wider credentials. When the presidency changed hands and the Democrats began dispensing federal judgeships, the people who interested themselves in these things saw the virtue of putting forward a qualified woman who was so widely experienced and so uniquely celebrated. Just as Caroline hoped they would.

The meetings began. First with feminist and other groups whose sympathies Caroline shared. Then with a committee of lawyers who screened candidates for the senior senator from California. Then with the senator herself – a meeting that, after some initial nervousness on Caroline's part, had gone extremely well. The nomination was the President's to make, and the senator was vying with senators of several other states who put forward their preferred candidates. But the senator's letter to the White House had been unusually strong, and the President was in her debt. Caroline permitted herself to hope.

And then, silence.

Months passed. She was convinced that her nomination was slipping away. A law-and-order group wrote the senator, with a copy to the President, opposing her candidacy; a right-to-life organization labeled her 'anti-child' and 'anti-family.' Caroline busied herself in the law, long bike trips, a little hiking.

It really was time, she told herself, to get a dog or something.

And then the senator phoned. 'You're still on the list,' she told Caroline. 'Walter Farris will be calling you – the White House counsel. So be prepared. And call me when it's through.'

Farris himself called two days later, a man with a slow, rheumy voice – white-haired and overweight, Caroline knew from his pictures. There were two candidates left, he told her. He had a few questions.

They went over her background. Family history, education, skimming the surface. Simply a lead-in to his final question: *Do you have anything to hide?*

'I think that's where they are,' the senator told her later. 'The other candidate is a leader in Tucson's Latino community, who is also very qualified, and the senator who recommended him is quite senior on the Senate Finance Committee. If one of you has some problem, it will save the President from having to choose....'

No, Caroline had answered them both, *there was nothing*.

She checked her watch. Three forty-five. In a little more than an hour, Farris would call.

26

She gazed up at the house. No, she decided, she was not quite ready to go inside.

Jutting from the beach was a narrow wooden dock, stretching out into the ocean until it was deep enough for docking. Caroline walked barefoot across the wooden planks to where she had tied her rented sailboat, pulled a bottled beer from an ice chest in the hull, and sat with her legs dangling over the bow.

She sipped the beer – tart on her tongue, cool in her hand – and idly watched the beads of condensation skitter down the sides of the bottle. The beer was left over from yesterday, when she had packed the ice chest with bread and cheese, beer and mineral water, and set sail in the catboat for Tarpaulin Cove in the Elizabeths, as she once had when she was fourteen. Though Caroline had not sailed the sound for years, she did not need a nautical chart: she remembered each bell and buoy precisely.

The morning of her sail had been clear; the day – water and sky – was vivid shades of blue. Caroline had grinned into the wind. She was a nature sensualist, she knew – sun and sea exhilarated her, rain depressed her. In this, she was like her mother had been.

She sailed for the lighthouse where Tarpaulin Cove lay. Docking the boat, Caroline swam to the beach, where she fell asleep in the sun. Only the lapping of the tide at her feet had awakened her.

As she sailed back, a light skein of fog scudded along the water, and the wind shifted in the Middle Ground. Caroline had fought it a little through the choppy waters, edgy. There had been no real danger. But the pull of memory was strong....

Caroline turned to the house again.

It sat near the bluff, a sprawling clapboard dwelling with views on all sides, an amalgam of Cape architecture and gables, surrounded by roses and a white picket fence. The earliest section had been built in the late 1600s, then hauled by oxen two centuries later from the middle of Edgartown to Eel Pond. Her father had added the rest of the house and, somewhat later, the roses. 'They grow well near the water,' he had said to the child Caroline. 'Like you.'

And yet, when she had rented the house from its owners, they had associated the name Masters only with Caroline herself. They did not know her family; Caroline had said simply that she was 'familiar with the house.'

And every room in it, she did not say, *has memories for me.*

When she climbed the steps to the bluff, entering the house, the grandfather clock read four-twenty.

Forty minutes.

She walked through the alcove past the bedroom where Betty and Larry had stayed that last summer; through the beamed dining room, where their family had dined by candlelight, her father at the head of the table; and then into the sunny bedroom she could only think of as her mother's. Entering the master bath, she imagined a makeup mirror that was no longer there, saw once more her last, enduring image of her mother in life – striking and petite, peering intently at her reflection as she applied mascara with her left hand and imagined the evening ahead....

But the bathroom mirror reflected only Caroline, a woman six years older than the woman in the makeup mirror would ever become. A lawyer, perhaps soon a judge, who looked little like her mother.

Except, Caroline allowed with a slight smile, that she had her mother's vanity.

The rest, to Caroline's regret, seemed to come from her father. The height – at five eight, Caroline was five inches taller than her mother. The auburn-tinted black hair, usually subdued into straightness by brush and dryer. An aquiline face that her Yankee forebears might have described as having 'character': a widow's peak, high cheekbones, long nose, full even mouth, her chin cleft and strong. Every feature would have been a little too emphatic, Caroline thought dryly, if they hadn't invented television; it was the media people who began writing, much to Caroline's public indifference and secret pleasure, about her style and aristocratic good looks. After all, Caroline had thought, it was comfortingly better than 'headed straight for menopause, with cellulite lurking around the corner....' Which was not, if you please, a suitable description for a high federal judge.

Four-forty.

Why, Caroline asked herself, was this so very important to her? What would she be if her ambitions turned to dust?

In her heart, she did not wish to know. Her ambition worked for her – it filled her life with interest and challenge. Filled her life, period. Some things should not be tampered with.

Perhaps, Caroline reflected, she had been foolish to come here. Even now, she was impulsive; she had merely learned to stifle her impulses or, at worst, conceal them. Returning here had been an impulse: almost no one but her secretary knew where she was; no one at all knew that this home had once been hers.

Slowly, Caroline walked to the screen porch.

It faced west across the water. Outside, a sea breeze whistled through her father's roses. Near them, on the lawn, was the smooth, flat rock – larger than a table – that her father had ordered hauled there. On his vacations from New Hampshire, he would sit at the rock, facing the water, writing his opinions in longhand....

Nearly five o'clock.

Caroline sat in a wicker chair next to a glass end table with a telephone on top. Lifted the receiver, once and then twice, checking for a dial tone.

Five-ten, then five-fifteen.

Five-sixteen.

The telephone rang.

'Caroline.' The rheumy voice sounded far away. 'It's Walter Farris.'

Caroline composed herself, trying to decipher his tone. 'Walter, how are you?'

'Fine. Dandy, actually. Tell me, do you have a moment to speak to the President?'

Caroline gave a startled laugh. 'Well, I *was* planning to mow the lawn ...'

'Just a minute. He's right here.'

Caroline felt her face flush. 'Caroline,' came the familiar soft drawl.

'Mr. President?'

'Walter tells me you want to go on the Appeals Court.'

A moment's pause. 'I must, Mr. President. I haven't waited this long for a man to call me since the Winter Prom.'

A genuine chuckle, a sally enjoyed on two levels.

'Well, Caroline ... it's yours.'

Caroline felt a sigh run through her, and, with it, all pretense of lightness vanished. 'It's not easy to tell you, Mr. President, everything this means to me.' She paused, voice softening. 'I've worked for this since law school. And I'll work even harder to deserve it once I'm there.'

'I know you will. Anyhow, Walter wants to speak to you. Do stop by and see us when you come back for the confirmation hearings, okay?' A moment's pause. 'Congratulations, Judge Masters....'

'Caroline?' Farris again. 'You'll need to rev up for the confirmation hearings. Jennifer Doran from the Justice Department will be in touch, to help you prepare. She's been through it all before....'

Putting down the telephone, Caroline barely remembered how the conversation had ended. There were tears in her eyes.

So strange, Caroline thought, to want something so deeply for so long that you cannot believe you have it ...

She sat there, tears running down her face now, very glad that no one could see her. At a loss for what to do.

A toast, she thought. A toast to me. She went to the kitchen, buoyant now, and made herself a pitcher of martinis.

The first martini, surgically crisp, went down in two swallows.

To hell with dinner. At a moment like this, anyone gets to be foolish. Tomorrow, no one will know but you.

At seven o'clock, she was still on the porch, watching the ocean fade to gray in evening sunlight. The bitter memories had eased away; for now, at this moment, she had no wish to be elsewhere.

It was dusk when the telephone rang.

She hesitated, trying to arrange her thoughts. A moment passed before she answered the phone.

'Hello.'

'Caroline?'

At first, her mind did not quite absorb it. But she felt it on her skin: a voice she had not heard in twenty years, yet more familiar than any other. A voice that belonged to this house.

Caroline stood, suddenly alert. She found that she could not answer.

'Caroline.' His voice was older now, perhaps rougher with what this call must be costing him. 'There's been trouble here, with Brett. You must come home.'

PART TWO

The Return

Chapter 1

The next morning, Caroline Masters flew to Boston, rented a Jeep, and drove north. An hour later, she crossed the state line into New Hampshire and felt herself – leaden and filled with premonitions – drawn from her future into her past.

Twenty-three years ago, she had left this place for good. She remembered little of that; sitting in the back seat behind Betty and her husband, Larry, as they headed toward Martha's Vineyard and their last summer as a family, she had felt no sense of moment. By summer's end, she had sworn never to return.

And now she had done so.

She had called Walter Farris before leaving the island, explaining only that she had a family emergency that might require a few days. He was gracious and understanding; perhaps Caroline had only imagined the faint undertone of caution, the unspoken question – what kind of emergency could be so serious that it distracted her at a time like this, so sensitive that she chose not to explain it. But refusal to explain herself was the defining choice of her adulthood; she was already fighting the superstition – foolish and egocentric, she chastised herself – that by visiting Martha's Vineyard she had reopened the past, which now waited for both Caroline and a girl she did not know.

But still he knew that she would come.

Driving deeper into New Hampshire, she felt him. The scattered farms and small towns were remnants of the long-ago prosperity that had helped make him who he was. Climbing toward the White Mountains – sheer cliffs, winding streams, and plummeting gorges, miles of dense trees broken by granite faces hewn by time and the harshness of weather – Caroline recalled his belief that New England was a place unlike any other, his admonitions on

35

nature and the virtues of winter: how they built resourcefulness and resolve, reminding man of the challenges ahead and the prudence needed to face them without any help but God's. And she knew, despite all her years and all her efforts, that this man, and this place, had defined the deepest part of her.

Descending from the cloud-swept summit, she drove north and west toward Vermont and into a gray, seeping rain. Yesterday seemed far behind.

The towns had grown sparse, farther apart; the roads were better, some lumber mills seemed to have closed, but little else had changed. It was a place where relationships mattered, Caroline remembered, where lives were private but memories were long, where respect — for a man or for the family he came from — once earned, went deep. For it was not a place where strangers came: the refugees from Massachusetts, the seekers of summer homes, tended to stop short of this corner of New Hampshire. These were the people who had always been there, dwindling a little, their sons or daughters drifting away to look for better jobs, others hanging on. So that life seemed as timeless as the pristine lakes, the rivers, the deep, silent forests.

The country now was undulant valleys, streams, hills rising abruptly against a broad sky. The roads became smaller; at a crossroads by a shabby church, Caroline turned down a tar-and-gravel road where the arrow pointed to 'Resolve Village.' A mile short of the town, she left the road, climbing a gravel path through woods that had once been pasture, until she reached the clearing that was still called Masters Hill.

Caroline was only half aware of how slowly she drove. She was more alert to landmarks — the jagged boulder she once had climbed, the distant blue-gray view of Heron Lake — than to the feeling of the places, so familiar and yet from another life. And then, abruptly, she stopped.

Stiff from driving, she stepped into the mist and rain.

On a hillside, cleared from a stand of birch trees, was a

36

white wooden church. The first Masters had built it one hundred and fifty years ago, to serve his family and those nearby, and its spires and stained-glass windows were from another time. It was where he had taken first one wife and then another; where Betty and Larry had married, with Caroline as maid of honor; where Caroline herself had once imagined marrying. Caroline had spent most Sunday mornings of her youth here, seated with her parents and her sister in the first row, where the Masters family sat by tradition and by right. She could remember the plain wooden benches and sparse furnishings, the unvarnished services of a religion too established for hysteria. But although she knew that, by long practice, the church would not be locked, Caroline did not enter.

Behind the church was the cemetery where the Masterses lay, generation after generation.

Caroline circled the church and went there, face damp and chill

Encroaching birches blocked the light, crowded the weathered stones at the cemetery's edge. The granite markers were worn with wind and rain and dirt. A stone – the marker of an infant long lost to memory – had toppled on its face.

At the center were the markers of her own family. On the largest of them, a granite rectangle rising from their midst, were the names of its members: Channing Masters; Elizabeth Brett Masters; then Elizabeth Wells Masters. At the bottom were the words: 'Caroline Clark Masters, b. June 17, 1950.' Only for Elizabeth Brett Masters did the date of death appear.

In front of this marker was another, set into the ground over the grave of Elizabeth Brett Masters, recording her for posterity as 'Beloved wife of Channing and mother of Elizabeth.'

Turning, Caroline walked to the edge of the graveyard.

The marker here was dirty, covered with leaves. Kneeling in the rain, Caroline cleared them with cold, clumsy fingertips. Saw the inscription, 'Nicole Dessaliers Masters,

b. 1925, d. 1964.' Then read the stark words which were painful still: 'Wife of Channing, mother of Caroline.'

Face wet and cold, Caroline stood there, in silent apology for things she had not then known. Only as she left the grave did she notice that the rain had ceased.

A half mile farther, Caroline stopped at the edge of the road. To her right, beyond a wood that gently sloped away, she could spot distant glimpses of the village of Resolve – a spire, a crossroads, white wooden homes from other centuries. And then only woods again. When she was a child, he would describe for her – until she could imagine it – a countryside of farms and stone walls, cross-stitched with the works of men. A time when New England throve, and the Masters who had lived here was a United States senator.

Caroline turned, facing the house where she was born.

Three stories and twenty rooms, it rose majestically to a domed octagonal cupola, from which the Masterses could see for miles. White-painted wood, arched windows, a massiveness unrelieved by ostentation or the fripperies of architectural fashion. The indulgences were inside: twelve-foot ceilings; seven granite fireplaces; a four-story winding staircase; the floating ballroom.

To him, it was a symbol of his birthright and the obligations that imposed: this house could not be abandoned like other houses but must be maintained and passed on, like the life of the Masterses themselves. Yet within the family he could be droll about its origins. The first Masters, Adam, had fallen deeply in love with a young woman from that cosmopolitan oasis Portland, Maine. Intent that she should marry him, Adam had built this home as a monument to his passion, hoping to surprise and dazzle her. A week after its completion, Adam had received his own surprise: a letter from the young woman, breaking their engagement. The home was, her father told Caroline as a child, an enduring monument to how foolish some women can make some men, a folly which every Masters for generations since had borne the cost of heating. To Caroline, it had seemed quite funny, then.

He still bore the cost, of course. The outbuildings – a barn, the attached garage which had once been a stable – were newly painted. Walking the stone path that rose gently up the hill and beneath the shade of ancient trees, Caroline saw that the grounds were well maintained, the water of the small pond near the barn fresh and clear. It seemed much as it was on the day she had last seen it.

She paused, drawing a breath. Then the front door opened; the instant before she saw who it was, Caroline steeled herself. And then Betty appeared in the doorway, hands shoved in the pockets of her khaki pants, gazing across the years at her half-sister.

Caroline walked toward Betty, studying her face. Comparing her to that last time she had seen her.

Betty stepped onto the covered porch.

'Hello, Caroline.'

She's a middle-aged woman, Caroline thought with foolish surprise. Betty wore wire-rimmed glasses, and the brown had faded to a dull sheen in her short-cut gray hair. Age had brought out the gauntness that had waited beneath the surface of the younger Betty's face; the ridged nose was more pronounced; the hollows of her face were deeper, the gray eyes somehow more intent next to the crow's-feet and pale skin. In the years of their fractious sisterhood, Caroline had thought with a teenager's unspoken savagery that Betty looked like the pictures of her mother, who had at once achieved sainthood and cheated an unflattering middle age through the mercy of dying in childbirth. Now, for an instant, the sight of Betty made Caroline sad, for whom she was not sure.

Without preface, Caroline asked, 'How is she?'

Betty gave her a sharp look. *How do you suppose she is?* Caroline imagined her thinking. Softly, Caroline said, 'You'll remember that I don't know her.'

Another swift look, as if Betty had forgotten this, and

then a nod of concession. 'She's emotional, sometimes willful, but *alive*. The girl of the last two days is a sunken-eyed wreck. At any given moment, she goes from stoic mourning to fear to disbelief.'

Caroline nodded. 'The marijuana won't have helped. Some part of her may not be sure what really happened.'

Another stabbing glance; all at once, her sister looked pinched and afraid. 'She didn't *kill* him....'

Silent, Caroline watched Betty realize that she had answered a question Caroline had not asked, then founder in the complexities of their shared past. Stiffly, Betty said, 'It was Father's idea to send for you.'

Caroline nodded again. 'I know that.'

Betty seemed to blanch. She was off balance, Caroline saw, searching for the meaning of Caroline's words. Quietly, Caroline said, 'We're both out of practice, Betty. And the end was what it was.'

Betty looked down, breathed out audibly. But when she looked at Caroline again, it was with a shade less tension. 'You look well, Caroline. But that's no longer a surprise. Not since we saw you on television.'

'"We"?'

A brief glint in Betty's eyes – the hint of jealousy and irony. *So it still matters to you*, Caroline saw her think, and despised herself for her question. For a time, Betty seemed to study her. 'You're a famous woman, Caroline. You did that alone – without him, or any of us. Is that what you wanted?'

You know *what I wanted*, Caroline thought with sudden bitterness. With a restraint that took all her effort, she said, 'How can you even ask that?'

Betty looked away. After a moment, she said, 'Brett's upstairs, Caroline.'

Caroline shook her head. 'I'm not ready yet. Not for that.'

Betty turned to her in surprise. 'Then why are you here? Don't you understand that they may charge her with *murder* ...?'

Caroline did not bother to explain herself.
'Where is he?' she asked.

Chapter 2

In a jacket borrowed from Betty, Caroline climbed the twisting trail up the side of Masters Hill.

It was where, Caroline remembered, he always climbed to think.

'He wasn't expecting you this soon,' Betty had told her. 'And I couldn't stop him.'

It took Caroline a moment to recall that he was well past seventy, another moment to raise her eyebrows.

'Heart trouble,' Betty said, as if to a stranger. 'An attack last year – mild, but a warning. He won't give up hiking, though, or even talk about it.'

Traversing the steep hillside, Caroline remembered when he would take her with him to the top: the child then, and the woman now, could not imagine him as vulnerable.

But she could tell that he hiked seldom now. The trail – once well trod by the Masters family as they followed his tall, lean frame – kept disappearing in underbrush or beneath a carpet of needles: only the thread of Caroline's memory helped her find it again. It rose between thick pine trees at a steep angle, causing her to walk sideways, sometimes slipping or pausing for breath.

She was out of practice, Caroline thought to her disgust. But that was not the reason her temples pounded. Part of it was Betty; a greater part the unseen girl. But the other part lay moments ahead.

She reached a clearing: a granite-face bare cliff weathered by wind and rain. When she was a child, too young to reach the top, she would stop here with her father. Now she paused, half expecting to find him.

No one.

Caroline sat on the rock, resting. From here, the view went on for miles. There were only a few clearings now;

nature had reclaimed the land, shrouding abandoned farms and old stone walls as the energy of man moved west, out of sight and mind. As land turned fallow, the Masters family had bought it, with a fortune made first in lumber, then by selling their private railroad line – which once serviced their mills – to the Boston and Maine Railroad. This was not an investment, in the ordinary sense. It was a statement, tinged with unspoken hubris: The Masterses were here to stay, as timeless as the land.

But they were not. Years later, they had sold what land they could; Caroline suspected that the prideful look of the Masters home had cost her father dearly and that, in his heart, Channing Masters feared that he would be the last generation to live and die in that same house. So that Caroline, leaving, had abandoned more than a family.

But he would go with pride, and no one outside the family would read its decline on the face of his home. The place was too much part of him, and he part of it.

This hill remained his property. The entire town could be seen from here, a toy New England village in a clearing. Caroline still recalled when they once sat here and she asked how Resolve had been named. She had imagined some stirring piece of history, a stand against Indians or for independence. But when her father turned, his eyes had the light of humor.

'Resolve,' he said, with mock solemnity, 'earned its name by seceding from Connaughton Falls. In the storied conflict over total versus partial immersion baptism. Back then, Caroline, New Englanders took their religion to heart.'

She saw that he was not teasing. 'Which side were we on?'

'The total immersers, of course.' As always, his smile for Caroline relieved a somewhat forbidding mien. 'We citizens of Resolve brook no half measures.'

Even at eight, Caroline heard the ironic undertone. For Judge Channing Masters was Resolve's first citizen, who could speak with confidence for the others.

Later, she understood that Channing – who, as a judge,

could not himself serve — helped pick the selectmen, the police chief, the school board, the vestrymen for his church, and, of course, the minister. He never said this to her; it was simply known. It was not a privilege but a duty; his interest was in finding men of probity and judgement. But the men whom Channing Masters picked treated him differently than they did others. Sitting here next to him, it had seemed to Caroline that her father watched over the town.

Caroline doubted that had changed much. In this pocket of New England, time moved slowly. Channing, with his dislike of fashion in thought or dress, found that right. Caroline's mother had not.

Rising, Caroline gazed up the mountainside, and then she resumed her climb.

At the top of the mountain, Caroline found her father sitting on a fallen log.

Channing Masters looked up at her. Caroline saw him fight several emotions at once — pain, thwarted love, instinctive pleasure in seeing her, anger that she should catch him

him. Quietly, he asked, 'What were you doing on Martha's Vineyard, staying in our home?'

'Sailing.' She paused. 'Why else would I be there?'

Caroline saw him wince at the wall between them. In that moment, she seemed to recover her balance.

She walked to the far end of the log and sat several feet away, gazing out at the sweep of hills and valleys, which seemed less to end than to vanish. When she was ready, she turned to him. 'You summoned me here as a lawyer. In every way but that – and perhaps that too – it's the very worst thing for all of us.'

Channing turned to her. 'Brett is innocent.' Suddenly, his voice was stern. 'You'll think of me as you like. But she won't be just another case to you.'

Caroline studied him. 'You may come to wish that she were.'

He seemed to consider her meaning. With equal quiet, he answered, 'You have better judgement than that.'

Caroline felt the familiar weight of childhood, his expectation stated as certainty. 'Then I should tell you that I don't know if I'm staying past tomorrow. Let alone if I'll defend her, should it come to that.'

His eyes filled with astonishment. 'How can you not …?'

'How can *you* not understand?' Pausing, Caroline spoke more softly. 'I would have thought you learned from me what emotion does to judgement. I won't visit that on her.'

Channing gave her a stoic look. But in his eyes she read both hope and apprehension. 'You've met her, then.'

Caroline drew a breath. 'No. I haven't.'

His gaze narrowed. 'She's been waiting –'

'And *I'd* like to know what the police know. Before I invite her to tell me whatever story leaps to mind.'

His face went hard. 'She'd never do that –'

'Frightened people do that,' Caroline cut in sardonically. 'Even the occasional innocent one. And I'm quite certain that you know far more about what the police know than she does.'

A first faint smile at the corner of her father's mouth,

remembered pleasure at the cut and thrust of their minds. Then the expression vanished, and he was grave, almost respectful. 'Where would you care for me to start?'

'With the first call from Jackson. After he saw that it was Brett they had in custody.'

Channing folded his hands in front of him, pensive. 'Jackson called around dawn,' he said at length. 'Betty answered. She was already up, and worried.'

'Where did she think Brett was?'

'With *him*, I assume.' His voice went flat. 'Long ago, Brett became quite sanguine about staying out all night, without feeling the need to explain herself....'

He paused abruptly; only then did Caroline feel the chill smile on her face. Their eyes met, and then her father continued in a subdued tone. 'Betty was too shaken to make sense of it. Moments later, I had to call Jackson back. He gave me only the barest details: the body, Brett's condition, the blood and knife and wallet, that she'd made some sort of statement. Then he agreed that we could come for her in exchange for her passport.'

'Which puzzles me. Can it be possible that Jackson doubts she killed him? Or is it that he expects she'll make some mistake?'

Her father gave her a sharp look. 'Jackson knows our family, knew Brett as a child, though she couldn't quite remember him. He can't easily believe this.' He paused. 'But, of course, he can tell me nothing.'

Caroline cocked her head. 'And the chief of police?'

He gave a small shrug. 'Told me, as a kindness, that Jackson is waiting for the crime lab results – blood type, fingerprints, and the like – while he checks on this dead boy's background. I believe what bothers Jackson is that Brett waited to tell them what had happened. Or where.' His voice turned cold again. 'But then James Case had fed her wine or marijuana. Neither of which she was used to.'

Caroline found his anger an irritant; it was hard to keep her own thoughts clear. 'That's some comfort,' she answered in an arid tone. 'It also cuts against premeditation.'

He stood abruptly, looming over her. His voice filled with anger. 'Brett did not *do* this, damn you. She's compassionate to a fault, from stray animals to this stray boy.'

Caroline stared up into his face, her own face hard, her tone even. 'I once defended a serial killer, who cut his victims' throats and then raped them while they bled to death.' Her manner became almost conversational. 'After that, he went home and slept with his English spaniel. His biggest fear when they caught him was who would feed the dog.'

There was a tremor in his voice now. 'This is your own flesh and blood —'

'And I'm a lawyer now. That's why you asked me here, I assume. So spare me the childhood stories, please. This is painful enough.' Standing, Caroline faced him. 'When we meet, I'll show Brett all the compassion her aunt Caroline should. In the meanwhile, let's return to the problem at hand. For example, have they traced the knife?'

He turned from her, gazing out at the mountains. The rain of midday had become a mist, Caroline saw, settling into the valleys. 'Not that I know of,' he said at last.

'Did they search the house?'

'Yes.'

'And found?'

'Nothing. At least nothing they took.'

'What about witnesses?'

He turned back to her. 'As I understand it, no one in the area saw anyone come in or go from that trailhead, nor any car or truck. Not even Brett's.'

Caroline smiled a little. 'Your friend the chief is not exactly a sphinx, is he?' she said, and then her smile faded. 'They questioned all of you about the knife, I assume.'

'The state police did. I told them I had never seen it.' He paused for a moment. 'Plainly, they assume Brett brought it there.'

Caroline shrugged. 'For them to assume otherwise would be to assume that someone happened to be in the neighborhood, decided to butcher James Case in a particularly intimate way, and then left his knife as a calling card. Which assumes a great deal, if you're the police.'

Channing stood straighter. 'That's not how it happened. Someone followed them.'

'Into the woods at night? To my old lot?'

His mouth compressed. 'It belongs to Brett now, Caroline, and it's been a long time since you lived in New Hampshire. We don't have random killings here. Someone wanted to kill this boy and waited for a time to do it.'

Caroline's head had begun throbbing. She rubbed her temples. 'That's a tough sell without some evidence. Brett took him there, to an isolated place, owned by our family. To them, it may mean premeditation –'

'If Brett had not gone swimming, Caroline, she might be dead as well. She's fortunate she startled him –'

'Who, damn it?'

Channing slowly shook his head. 'I don't know. Perhaps a vagrant, who picked up the dead boy's wallet and dropped it at the sound of Brett. Perhaps, as she said, it was trouble over drugs.'

'Does she know who his supplier is?'

'Of course not.'

This time it was Caroline who shook her head. 'Professionals don't kill over a few thousand dollars.' She paused a moment. 'Tell me, is there any evidence that someone was there? Other than Brett's word, that is.'

He did not bridle, Caroline noticed; for the moment, he seemed to put anguish aside and accept that they were dealing with facts. 'We don't know yet. The crime scene search was done by Jackson's people – the state troopers.'

'Who found the body?'

'The Resolve police. Two young patrolmen, checking the trails.'

'What do you know about that?'

'Only what the local people told me. The two policemen

happened on the body, promptly searched the immediate area. Finding nothing and no one, they called the EMTs and the state police, both of whom came to the scene. The EMTs pronounced Case dead, and the state police called Jackson at his home in Concord. After which he and the Major Crimes Unit got a warrant to search Brett's property and person – with humiliating thoroughness – and then took her statement.'

Caroline could see it all. 'By which time,' she amended, 'four or five amateurs had been stumbling all over the crime scene, leaving footprints, handling the body, and generally making a mess. Not to mention, quite possibly, blowing Brett's Miranda warnings.'

'True enough.' Folding his arms, Channing paused for emphasis. 'But the state police are excellent, and so is Jackson Watts. Don't assume that he's still the boy you dated.' Another pause. 'Or, for that matter, jilted.'

Caroline did not rise to this. 'How *is* Jackson these days?'

'Smart and unassuming, which is part of his appeal. He's chief of the attorney general's homicide unit, and – prospectively – a judge of the Superior Court. Which, in other circumstances, would please me greatly, as he's a very decent man.' His voice became sad, almost valedictory. 'In fact, I wish he were already on the bench. As, I'm sure, does he.'

He looked ashen, Caroline saw; his thin shoulders had slumped, and the passion had vanished. 'Perhaps,' she ventured, 'Jackson won't handle the case.'

Channing slowly shook his head. 'He's never owed me anything, Caroline. Except, perhaps, to remain the man I always knew that he'd become.'

Caroline searched his tone for second meanings, a mute reproach. But all she heard was the throbbing in her temples. Almost gently, her father said, 'You look tired, Caroline.'

I didn't sleep, she almost said. Instead she answered, 'The flight, and then the drive, made for a long day. And it's not over yet.'

Channing caught the reference. 'You'll like her, Caroline.' His voice was still soft. 'Even under these circumstances.'

She rubbed her temples. 'Tell me, what was he like – James Case?'

'Very handsome.' He paused, then his tone hardened. 'But he was one of the unstable ones, weak and selfish, with that narcissistic self-involvement women seem to find so attractive.'

Caroline's eyes narrowed. 'How often did you meet him?'

'For more than a moment? Twice, perhaps three times.'

She looked at him askance. 'And you perceived all that,' she said in a flat voice. 'As well as how he affected Brett.'

Channing seemed to blanch. 'That's kept you going, all these years, hasn't it? And now it's about to make you a judge.'

Caroline felt her face freeze; something in her eyes made her father hold up one hand, for silence. 'Whatever your differences, Caroline, Betty has been a good mother. And because of it, Brett is a good person –'

'And one is, after all, only as good as one's mother.'

He did not flinch. 'You can be cruel, Caroline. But I never felt that. Not then, and not now.' His hand fell to the side, and then his voice gentled in entreaty. 'You will help her, won't you?'

Caroline gazed at him. 'By staying,' she finally answered, 'or by leaving.'

'Stay, Caroline. Please. I'm asking you for peace. Only for a time, and not for me – or Betty. But for her.' He stood straight again. 'I know my granddaughter, in a way you never can now. Most of all, I know she's innocent.'

Chapter 3

At the door of the house, Caroline paused, picturing the young woman inside. Silent, Channing Masters opened the door, and Caroline entered her father's house.

She stopped in the living room, hands jammed in her pockets, looking about.

All was as she remembered – the antique furniture, the Chinese carpets, even the smell of things from another time. In the foyer was the grandfather clock, made in the 1850s. Oil paintings of ancestors hung in the living room, portrayed in the heroic convention – a general, a senator, a lumber magnate, a clergyman with beetling eyebrows. Her father's books remained in his library: the original Kipling and Poe, complete editions of Dickens and Henry James, Pliny's letters. It was where he had always read to her.

What was she doing here ...?

Slowly, Caroline walked to the dining room.

Her family had eaten every meal at this same polished mahogany table, on china drawn from the beveled-glass cabinet. After Betty had left for Smith, and then Caroline's mother had died, for a few months there had been only the two of them – Channing and his youngest daughter, dining alone, discussing his work or her studies or the news of the day. It was more than conversation, Caroline remembered. It was a tutorial in politics and human nature and how they intersected, with lessons drawn from a scale as large as history – Jefferson, the economics of slavery – or as small as the village of Resolve, the foibles of its affairs and its citizens laid bare by Channing's discerning but not uncharitable eye.

Caroline had basked in it. All that she had wanted then was to settle here as a lawyer, to follow her father's path as far as she could. On the eve of her departure to boarding school, at Dana Hall, Caroline could feel his loneliness, read the sadness in her father's eyes. Grasping his sleeve, Caroline asked him again if she could stay. He shook his head. 'They will attend to your education now,' he said. 'Better than I or any school nearby. Children do not always live to please their parents, or parents to please themselves....'

It was that, more than anything, that had made her wish to please him.

He was standing next to her, Caroline realized. The house felt empty.

Softly, Caroline asked, 'Where is she?'

'Her room's upstairs.'

Caroline did not turn. 'Which one?'

'Yours.'

Alone, Caroline walked to the staircase, still feeling her father's gaze.

She paused, hand on the rail.

Turning her head, Caroline faced the music room, imagined her mother, sitting at a piano that was no longer there.

Even then, before Caroline knew how it would end, her mother had seemed miscast – febrile, high-spirited, too mutable and vivid for this place. Caroline remembered her mother planning trips they somehow never took, until she simply stopped; recalled how her parents began to argue over politics. Nicole had conceived an unreasoning passion for Adlai Stevenson and then John Kennedy, both anathema to her Republican husband. Barely an adolescent, Caroline had sensed this conflict as a metaphor for a conflict too deep to be spoken easily: her mother's desire to leave a life that never quite seemed hers.

She had begun to notice nights when her father grew remote. When her mother, retreating to the music room and the lacquered grand piano, sang Edith Piaf in the breathy French she had never bothered to teach Caroline, that no one in their home could speak or understand.

But even this language, Caroline came to know, was not

quite her mother's own. History had left her without family or country, or any home but this.

Even her mother's 'La Vie en Rose,' Caroline remembered, had the sound of irony. Dark head poised, eyes nearly shut, Nicole Dessaliers Masters would sing with a faint half smile....

Turning from the music room, Caroline slowly climbed the stairs, to Brett's room.

Brett sat facing the window. At first, Caroline could see only her back – the first impression of slimness, brown curls. And then she turned, a quick twist of her body, startled from thought.

Caroline gazed at her for what felt uncomfortably long, though it could only have been seconds. Saw a delicate chin, full, even mouth, slender face and high forehead. Saw that Brett was more than pretty. Saw the smudges above her cheekbones, the hours without sleep. But the green eyes – startlingly alive – gazed at Caroline with uncanny directness.

'You're Caroline, aren't you. My aunt.'

Her voice was soft, yet clear. For an instant, Caroline replayed the sound of it. 'I'm Caroline, yes.' Closing the door, she forced herself to stop looking at Brett, to glance around the room at the mishmash of early womanhood – a red pantsuit slung over a chair; some CDs by the singer Tori Amos; Susan Faludi's *Backlash* on top of a stack of paperbacks. After a moment, she managed to say, 'This isn't quite how I remember it.'

'This was *your* room, wasn't it.'

From birth, Caroline thought, until the day she had left. Every night of her childhood, her father would climb the stairs and kiss her on the forehead. And then there were those much rarer nights, surprising and priceless, when Nicole Masters would read to her, a faint smell of claret on her breath, her lively French-accented English lending each story a touch of the exotic. Turning out the lights, Nicole bent her face to Caroline's....

Caroline found herself staring at Brett.

'What is it?' Brett asked.

Caroline composed an answer. 'Nothing, really. Just a foolish memory – my first childhood act of defiance. At night, I used to listen to Red Sox games. After my mother or father would turn off the lights and my radio, I'd sneak a transistor under the covers and keep listening, rapturous to be getting away with it.' Caroline smiled faintly. 'Looking back, I'm sure he knew. Perhaps was even pleased.'

Brett's eyes showed the faint glint of kinship. 'Grandfather used to take me to Fenway Park to watch the Red Sox.' A quick sideways glance. 'Did he take you?'

Caroline nodded. And then remembered, so suddenly that her forgetfulness shocked her, why she had come.

Crossing the room, Caroline sat two feet from Brett.

What happened next surprised her. For close to half her life, Caroline had sat this close to clients accused of rape, or child abuse, or murder by torture or mutilation. The serial killer whom Caroline had described to her father – a pockmarked man with ferret's eyes – would have raped and killed her for the pleasure of it had there not been Plexiglas between them. So that Caroline had learned to stifle certain images. But as Brett gazed back at her, eyes filling with hope and fear, Caroline imagined the blood on her fingertips.

She touched her eyes. 'Forgive me if I seem more like a lawyer than an aunt. But we've quite a lot to cover.'

Suddenly, Brett looked tense, deflated. Caroline fought back sympathy: she knew too well that the most intense emotions – anguished innocence or the horror of guilt – mimed each other on the faces of her clients.

'Actually,' Caroline said, 'I'm most interested in whatever you told the police. That's what you have to live with.'

Brett sat back. Her voice was taut. 'I told them the truth. Just like I'm telling you now.'

Brett, Caroline realized, had suddenly perceived the working premises of Caroline Masters the defense lawyer. That Brett was guilty. That she would lie. That Caroline's job was not to learn the truth but to keep it from the prosecution.

'The truth is often useful,' Caroline said gently. 'But what you told the police is unavoidable. And they do seem to have questions.'

Brett swallowed. Gazing back at her, Caroline suddenly imagined a child beneath the woman, frightened and alone. And then Brett Allen reached slowly across Caroline's silence and touched her hand. 'Just believe in me,' she said. 'Please.'

Caroline looked down at Brett's fingers, white against the tan of her own skin. She felt the lightness of Brett's fingertips.

By impulse, in the face of years of training, Caroline nodded. 'All right,' she said. 'Tell me everything.'

It was dusk when Brett had finished; the quiet room seemed twilit, a filtered gray that soon would fade to darkness. Caroline felt exhausted.

Softly, she asked, 'Did anyone know you'd be at the lake?'

'No one.' Brett still seemed lost in memory; her response was slow in coming. 'It was a last-minute thing. So we could talk in private.'

'Because you were worried about being overheard?'

A short nod. 'I thought I heard someone picking up another phone. Maybe I just imagined it.'

'Someone?'

Brett's voice was toneless. 'My mother.'

Caroline watched her face. 'Not your father? Or your grandfather?'

Brett shook her head. 'My dad wasn't home. And Grandfather has his own phone line to his room. That's not something he'd ever do.'

Caroline was quiet for a moment. 'But your mother would.'

'Because of James.' Brett turned to the window, added in

a lower voice, 'My mother hated him. She knew he was dealing.'

'You told her?'

'Of course not. But my dad heard rumors, from the campus police.' She looked at Caroline again, paused. 'You know he teaches there.'

Of course, Caroline thought. That was how he lured them back here – a job for a struggling graduate student, a home for his family, a granddaughter to fill the void. And all that Larry had to lose was himself.

'Then your father,' Caroline said, 'must have had some feelings about James.'

'Not like my mom.' Anger crossed Brett's face, and vanished, as if she was too weary to sustain it. She finished in a tired monotone. 'Mom wanted to give me a perfect world, as if that were even possible. So she was afraid of anyone who threatened that. Even now ...'

Caroline sat back. In a few concise words, this girl had described the Betty she had known. There was a quick, bitter memory – two decades old – and then Caroline repressed it. She could deal with her private Betty on her own time; Caroline the lawyer had more practical reasons for drawing Brett's attention from her mother.

'This drug dealer,' she said. 'The one who threatened James. Do you know who he is, or where to find him?'

Brett shook her head. 'James knew I hated what he was doing.' There was another change in Brett's expression, to stubborn loyalty. 'He said he was getting out of it. That he only did it because he had nothing. God knows I wanted to believe it. To believe in him.'

Silent, Caroline sorted through her thoughts. The way Brett spoke of James did not suggest murder. Unless, of course, she was a gifted actress. 'Did James have roommates?' Caroline asked. 'Or friends who might know this dealer?'

'No roommates. Except for me, James pretty much liked being alone.'

'Any neighbors?'

Brett hesitated. 'I met a guy named Daniel Suarez,' she said at length. 'He seemed like a good person. But I don't think he and James were close.'

'What about women?'

Brett looked startled, then defensive. With an edge, she answered, 'We were together.'

Pausing, Caroline wondered what had unsettled her: doubts; some problem with James; the need to sanctify a dead lover; or anger that Caroline might question a relationship that had been so sullied by his death that the police might think she murdered him.

'No girlfriends,' Caroline repeated. 'Just as you told the cops?'

'Not that I know about.' Brett folded her arms. 'You have to understand how beautiful James was. I don't know what he did before I met him. Or who might have been attracted to him whether or not he cared.'

Caroline raised her head, one finger to her lips, contemplating Brett. Softly, she asked, 'Is there anything – anything at all – that might lead the police to believe that you had a reason to kill him?'

Brett rose slowly from her chair, wide-eyed. Her voice trembled with sudden anger and emotion. 'Do you know, Aunt Caroline, what James looked like when I found him? Because *I* remember it too clearly now.' Tears welled in her eyes. 'They'd cut his throat. He was choking on his own blood – when I reached for him, his head fell away from his neck, and his blood spattered my face....' For an instant, Brett stopped, and then she stared down at Caroline. 'Despite his faults, I loved him. If you can't believe that, or respect that, I don't want you here.'

Caroline made herself be still. 'What I asked you,' she said coolly, 'is whether the police might have a reason to believe you killed him.'

Brett stood there, alone in her anger. Caroline simply waited. Anything she said or did now might drive Brett away: with an intensity that surprised her, Caroline did not want this.

Brett raised her head. 'There is no reason.'

'Then sit down, please.'

After a moment, Brett sat. Through her exhaustion, she gazed at Caroline with fresh resolve.

Caroline's temples throbbed. 'There are things I'll say or ask,' she said, 'that I won't like and you won't like. Starting with my next question.'

Brett squared her shoulders. Something in the gesture made Caroline's heart to go out to her. Even as she wondered how much of this girl's volatility – the shifts in mood, the sudden flashes of temper – came from guilt, how much from merely stress and sleeplessness.

'This spurt of blood,' Caroline asked softly, 'how would you describe it?'

Once more, Brett's eyes widened; but for that, her expression did not change. 'It wasn't a spurt.'

'But when they photographed you, there was blood on your face and neck and torso.'

Still no expression. 'Flecks of blood.'

Caroline leaned back. 'So the spurt – or spray – wasn't heavy.'

'No.'

Caroline expected Brett to ask why it mattered. But the girl's anger seemed to have depleted her. Even her eyes held no curiosity.

Caroline stood, reaching for the light switch, and turned on the lamp on a nearby end table. Night was falling fast now. As if awakened by Caroline's movement, Brett turned, gazing through the window at the coming darkness.

'That night,' Caroline asked, 'how much wine did you drink?'

A small shrug. 'We shared the bottle.'

'Before you smoked the joint?'

Brett still did not turn from the window. 'Yes.'

'How many times, roughly, had you smoked before that night?'

'In my life?'

'Yes.'

'Five or six.'

Caroline gave a small smile. 'How could you listen to music?'

Another shrug. Her profile in the light-and-shade, Brett seemed distant now, enclosed in glass. After a time, she said, 'It made my throat raw, and I felt out of control. I didn't like that.'

'Can you describe how it affected you that night?'

Brett seemed to look inward, into some pool of self-doubt. 'It's hard to describe,' she began, and then her eyes narrowed in concentration. 'Have you ever seen a silent movie? It was like that – flickering images, with black spaces in between. I can't remember sound....'

'What do you remember about the cop arresting you?'

Brett's eyes closed. 'The knife.'

'Where was it?'

'On the seat.'

'Where he could see it?'

'Yes.'

Caroline leaned forward. 'Did the cop who arrested you give you any warnings – right to counsel, the right to remain silent, that any statements would be used against you?'

Brett's brow furrowed. 'I don't think so.... All that I remember was staring at the knife. Nothing seemed to go together.'

'Later, why did you tell them to look for James at the lake?'

'It was the way I just described it – the guy who picked me up said someone might be out there, hurt, and it was like I saw James dying. I was still so confused.' Brett looked pale now. 'I know how that sounds....'

'Did he give you the warnings then?'

Brett's throat worked; Caroline was not certain that she had heard the question. Then Brett softly answered, 'I don't remember warnings then. Later, I do – with the two of them and the tape recorder.'

Caroline fell quiet, thoughtful.

Brett turned to her, as if awakened by the silence. 'Why does any of this matter?'

She sounded less curious than tired. It was as if Brett had lost her bearings, so that no event had more weight to her than any other.

For a moment, Caroline wondered how much to tell her. But Brett was bright and, beneath the whipsaw of emotions, Caroline sensed her resilience.

'It's a matter of police procedure,' Caroline answered. 'The first cop probably should have given you the warnings before you told him where to look for James. Which means that a decent lawyer may be able to keep your entire statement out of evidence –'

Brett stood abruptly. 'But I want to say what happened –'

'How,' Caroline cut in, 'do you really know what happened?'

Brett looked startled. 'What do you mean?'

'That drugs and alcohol do funny things to memory. What happens is that there are blanks, which you may never fill in. So people end up confusing primary memory – what really happened – with secondary memory. Which is what they *wish* to remember, or *hope* they did. Or simply believe is logical.'

In the gloom of the bedroom, Brett began pacing. 'It almost sounds like you don't want me to remember.'

'What it sounds like,' Caroline answered with cool emphasis, 'is a warning. Not to remember, with the best of intentions, things that never happened. Because they may hang you for it.'

Brett spun on her. 'How?'

Caroline stood, walked over to Brett until they were face-to-face, and gently grasped her shoulders. She felt so fragile, Caroline thought. Brett looked up at her in weary surprise; something in Caroline's face seemed to keep her there.

'Brett,' Caroline said softly, 'you don't know me at all. But I want you to listen to me, please, for a few more minutes, however hard it may be. Because I've been doing things like this since you were a little girl. And whoever handles this case – if there is a case – will need you to think clearly.'

Brett gazed up at her. '*You* won't do it?'

'I really shouldn't.' The look on Brett's face, fearful and abandoned, made Caroline grasp her tightly. 'We're related. I think that makes this harder than we realized. For both of us.'

Brett turned away. Gently, Caroline guided her back to the chair. When she sat across from her again, Brett was silent, fighting for composure.

Damn him, Caroline thought. *Damn him*.

Her headache had turned to nausea. Since her father had called, she realized, she had not eaten.

'Let me explain,' she said slowly, 'what the police case is. Because I already know.

'There are two cases, actually. The first is premeditated murder.

'In that case, you decided to kill James well in advance. But he was much larger and stronger. So you took him to an isolated place – a lake at night – which you knew and he didn't. You brought the knife and told him it was for the bread and cheese. You encouraged him to drink wine and then smoke dope, knowing that it made him sluggish. And it was you, when making love, who got on top of him ...'

Brett's mouth was half open; she looked stricken. Caroline forced herself to continue. 'You never heard the sound of an intruder. The dope dealer story is preposterous. You never went swimming.' Caroline paused, took a breath, and finished. 'What you did do, before he could reach climax, was cut your lover's throat....'

Pale, Brett shut her eyes.

'Perhaps,' Caroline went on, 'you didn't count on being spattered with his blood. That's why you made up the story about giving CPR to a man who was semi-decapitated. But you planned the rest of it to look like a robbery. Which is why you took the knife and the wallet, meaning to throw them both away.

'But you were stoned, too, and sickened by what you'd done. You panicked and then ran to the Jeep, crazy to get out. But you only got a little ways past the trailhead when you had to stop and throw up –'

'No!' Brett sat rigid in her chair. 'That's not right –'

Caroline made herself finish. 'You were caught with the knife and the wallet, with blood all over you. You needed a new story and were in no shape to give one. So you pretended to be so stoned you were a blackout victim, and spent the next eight hours trying to come up with an alibi that covered those facts.

'And after all that, the best you could do is a dope dealer who followed James Case to Heron Lake at night so that he could slit his throat over a few thousand dollars.'

Brett curled forward, elbows on her knees.

'So are you really sure about taking the wallet?' Caroline asked softly. 'Maybe James left it in the Jeep. That would certainly be nice.

'It would also be nice if the police were barred from using your three different statements – 'nothing happened'; 'he might be at the lake'; and 'a drug dealer must have killed him' – and even better if they aren't allowed to testify that it took eight hours for you to give the last one. So I would hope very hard that the first cop didn't warn you.' Caroline paused for emphasis. 'Because if he blew it, and if you're *very* lucky, they also won't be able to use the warrant they got after you sent them to the lake. And that means no blood spatters, no nail samples, and – essentially – no evidence.'

Hands to her face, Brett neither moved nor spoke. Quietly, Caroline asked, 'Are you listening, Brett?'

Slowly, Brett looked up at her. She was ashen.

'You'd have a clean slate, and all the police would have is you, a knife, and a body. It's not enough. And even if Jackson Watts thinks it is, you can decide *then* whether to testify, knowing that whatever you said before can no longer be used against you.

'That – at worst – is what I want for you.'

Brett seemed to gather herself. 'It's like you're accusing me.'

'Not accusing. Demonstrating.'

Brett's voice rose. 'I had no reason to do this....'

'No motive.' Caroline smiled faintly. 'That *is* a problem with case number one. Which is why *that* case may never come to trial.

'Which brings me to case number two.' Pausing, Caroline spoke to her in a different tone, quiet and compassionate. 'Can you stand any more of this? It's important.'

It seemed to bring Brett back to her. 'I guess I have to,' she murmured.

Caroline settled back. 'Case two,' she said, 'is manslaughter. But in some ways, this will be even harder for you to hear.'

Brett was still, watching her.

'It's very simple.' Caroline's voice was quiet again. 'You never planned to kill him. You got drunk, and then stoned. Quarreled over something. Lost your temper.

'You weren't rational. In a surreal impulse, you simply cut his throat before you even knew what you had done.'

Brett's eyes were open, staring.

Gently, Caroline finished. 'You may not even remember killing him. Or, perhaps, don't wish to remember. So you told the police a story you badly need to believe.'

Brett averted her eyes. 'We never fought –'

'The knife,' Caroline interrupted.

Slowly, reluctantly, Brett turned to her. 'What about it?'

'The knife is critical. If they can trace it to James, or to you, then the case I just described to you may not be the prosecution theory. It may be your best defense. To a charge of murder one.' Caroline's voice became quiet; she reached out, touching Brett's arm. 'Before you answer me, Brett, I need to tell you something else.

'You asked me to believe you. I'm offering you something better.' Caroline's voice became softer yet. 'I don't care what happened. All I care about is that you not be hurt.'

Brett sat straighter, her eyes looking straight into Caroline's. With equal softness, she said, 'I had no reason to kill him, and I never saw that knife before. I'm innocent.'

Chapter 4

Wearily descending the staircase, Caroline was unprepared for Larry.

He turned from the dining room table, a china plate in his hand. As he froze in the candlelight, Caroline saw the young husband she had known, gentle and soft-spoken, beneath the wary gaze of a man of fifty. He was still lean, gray-haired now, the kind aspect of his face tending far less to the amused irony of the graduate student who knew his choice of English lit was feckless but believed that life would somehow reward him for his foolishness, providing the job that he needed and the baby Betty so desperately wanted. For a fleeting moment, Caroline wished that she could stop that summer in midflight, so that she would not now read its end in Larry's face.

'Caro,' he said softly.

She merely nodded. There was really nothing to say.

He moved a step closer, still tentative, as if to verify her presence. Caroline gave him no help. He stopped, looking into her face until he seemed to see what was written there.

'Why,' Caroline said in a low voice, 'did you ever bring her here?'

Larry did not flinch; Caroline saw that he had prepared himself for this. 'All that matters, Caroline, is how she is right now.'

Through his defensiveness, Caroline heard a trace of rebuke, as though the family that lived here was paying a price Caroline would never know. 'Yes,' she said coolly. 'I'm very sorry for you, of course.'

Larry glanced over his shoulder. In an undertone, he said, 'Caroline, please ...'

'The truth, Larry, is that I don't *know* how she is. Only that she's frightened, and smart, and trying to maintain.'

65

The struggle for dispassion, Caroline realized, was costing her: some part of her felt gutted. For a moment, Larry watched her.

'We waited dinner.' Larry's tone held a faint apology. 'You look pale, Caro. It would be good if you ate something.'

Caroline was light-headed from weariness and hunger. Yes, she thought, that was the Larry she remembered – considerate, at pains to empathize. The one she had opened her heart to when she could no longer turn to her own family. She shook her head. 'There's been a lot today....'

As if her admission gave him confidence, Larry reached out, his hand resting gently on her shoulder. 'Stay,' he said. 'Please. We've made up a room for you.'

Caroline looked into his face. Only then did she realize that Betty watched them from the kitchen door.

Following Caroline's gaze, Larry turned to his wife. To Caroline, Betty's face was an inscrutable mask.

Larry crossed the room to Betty. 'I'll help with the pasta.' His tone strained for normality. 'It'll just be the three of us.'

Caroline's mind filled with dark humor, the skewed vision of a television family. *Yes*, she imagined Betty saying chirpily, *Dad's eating in his room tonight. He gets so overexcited whenever he sees Caroline.* She realized that she was studying Betty with a grim half smile.

Betty seemed to stand straighter. At the corner of her eye, Caroline saw Larry give her sister an admonitory gaze, form a few silent words with his lips. They vanished through the kitchen door.

By rote, Caroline sat in the place that had once been hers.

They ate by candlelight, the tradition of Caroline's father and his father before him.

It played tricks on Caroline's memory. The light that danced on the crystal chandelier seemed to come from some other evening; the glow in the beveled mirror from

Caroline's childhood. Gazing across the table at her sister, Caroline remembered her father at the head, Betty and Caroline facing each other, Nicole Masters – small and dark and beautiful – at the end opposite her husband. To Caroline now, more sharply than it had then, the image that struck her was of Betty sitting alone, amidst her indifferent stepmother and the half-sister upon whom her father doted. She imagined that Betty's eyes, meeting her own, still held the jealousy and confusion of the girl who – without knowing why – had lost both her mother and her primacy. But now the cost of her own motherhood was etched on Betty's face.

Larry broke the silence. Quietly, he said, 'Thank you for coming, Caro.'

Caroline turned, slowly, staring at him until his gaze flinched. *I'm sorry*, she imagined him saying. As if to cover this, he murmured, 'We know this can't be easy.'

What I know, Caroline thought, is that neither of you wants me here. Her sister's face was hard. She made no move to join in Larry's grace note.

Caroline put down her fork. 'Perhaps it's best if we try to talk about what happened.'

Betty was silent. After a moment, Larry said, 'I was gone, Caro. Camping in Vermont.' The slightest glance at Betty. 'I'd gone to a trout stream, one a friend at the college put me onto.'

'By yourself?'

A slow nod, and then he shook his head in wonderment. 'I never thought how out of touch it left me....'

Betty's mouth had set, Caroline saw. Caroline picked up her glass of red wine and sipped it, studying Betty over the rim. 'But *you* were here,' she said.

Betty nodded almost imperceptibly. It was more than the strain of her presence, Caroline realized; both Larry and Betty appeared hollowed out by an event they still could not quite accept. When Larry reached to touch Betty's hand, his wife seemed not to notice.

'Who else was here?' Caroline asked.

Betty stared at Larry's hand as if at a foreign object. 'Just Father,' she said. 'Upstairs.'

'When did Brett leave?'

'About eight, I think.' A faint note of impatience. 'I really don't remember.'

'And neither of you went out – you or Father?'

'No.'

'Did you know where Brett was going?'

A sharp look. 'Of course not.'

'"Of course not"?' Caroline repeated.

Larry's hand tightened on the back of Betty's. 'There were strains,' he interjected. 'Over Brett's relationship to James. Betty bore the brunt of it.'

'Meaning …?'

'We fought.' Betty's voice was flat. 'Over this boy's involvement with drugs – I assume you know about that. Over this boy, period.' Betty leaned back, studying Caroline with new frankness. *Did you come here*, the look said, *to judge me?* With an edge, she said, 'Being a parent is *hard*, Caroline.'

Caroline saw Larry's hand clasp Betty's – a restraining gesture. In her most arid tone, Caroline answered, 'So I understand.'

A light flush crept across Betty's face. More evenly, she said, 'James Case was everything Brett didn't need – self-centered and irresponsible, seeing her only as a convenience. There was failure written all over him. Failure and heartbreak. I didn't want that for her, and I couldn't bear to watch it.' Betty slid her hand, slowly and deliberately, from beneath her husband's. 'Brett,' she resumed with suppressed fervor, 'expects the best in people, far more than she should. Instead of a vain young man who aspired to a marginal profession, she saw a damaged boy who could become better if she was only patient. He wanted her to give up everything –'

Betty stopped abruptly, as if she had startled herself.

Larry's anxious gaze moved from Betty to Caroline. But Caroline was silent, her face without expression.

68

Betty faced her directly, retrieving a look of pride. 'What I told her about James,' Betty said, 'is that she had better hope he never became a success. Because then he would leave her. After he changed her life.'

Caroline's throat felt tight. Quietly, she asked, 'And what was Brett's answer?'

Betty seemed to study her. 'That she was old enough to decide what was best for her. And that she would.' Betty's voice grew flinty now. 'What she *believes* is that I'm an overprotective mother who can't let go because my obsession with her is all I have in my narrow and limited existence. And what I *know* is that the line between romanticism and self-destruction is one that she has yet to recognize.'

Caroline gave her a long, cool look. 'Do you really think,' she asked, 'that she understands herself so incompletely?'

Betty met her eyes. 'Do *you* think,' she answered, 'that she's a murderer?'

Suddenly, Caroline felt off balance. 'I don't know,' she said. 'But then I didn't raise her, did I?'

Caroline heard Larry exhale; saw Betty's mouth open again. Caroline continued in a tone of calm she did not feel. 'While you, of course, did. Which leads me to inquire whether you ever listened to her telephone conversations.'

Betty stiffened in her chair. 'What makes you ask that ...?'

'*She* thinks you did. Specifically, that night. When she and James decided to go to Heron Lake.'

Betty seemed to blanch. 'Why does she say that?'

'Because she heard someone pick up a telephone.'

Betty touched her eyes. 'No,' she said.

'No?'

'No.' Betty folded her arms now, staring at the hard gloss of the dining table. 'Why would it matter now? To her or to you?'

'To Brett? Because twenty-two-year-olds don't like being spied on, including this one. To me, because I can't help but wonder if you told someone else.'

Across the table, Betty froze. Larry placed his hand on

Caroline's arm. Voice half anxious, half brusque, he demanded, 'Just what is this about, Caroline? The present or the past?'

Caroline did not take her gaze off Betty. 'The present, very much so. I'd like to know if either of you knows any way that anyone could have found out where Brett was taking him.'

Betty met her eyes. 'No,' she said succinctly. 'I did not spy on my daughter.'

Caroline appraised her. 'And you have no idea,' she inquired, 'how anyone else would have known she was there.'

'No.' A brief pause. 'Perhaps James told someone. Perhaps, Caroline, they were simply followed.'

Caroline shrugged. 'Perhaps.'

Betty's voice rose. '*She did not kill him.*'

Deliberately, Caroline picked up the wineglass and drained it. Betty shut her eyes; Caroline felt Larry's gaze. The wine seemed to numb her.

'This knife,' Caroline said. 'I gather the police asked you about it.'

Betty's eyes half opened. Slowly, she nodded.

Caroline turned to Larry. 'And you?'

Larry shook his head. 'They haven't questioned me yet.'

Caroline leaned forward, her gaze sweeping them both. 'Because it is *very* important that the knife not be traced to Brett. Or to this house.'

Betty stiffened. 'You *do* think she killed him.'

'I don't think anything,' Caroline answered sharply. 'But whoever represents Brett can do without surprises. It's quite important that there is nothing that would lead the police to believe Brett brought the knife.' Her voice became quiet. 'It's not just a matter of you or Father telling the police that you know nothing about a knife, or that no knife is missing. It's a matter of being sure that there is no one in a position to say anything different. Or to be caught in a lie.' Caroline paused. 'Do you understand, both of you, precisely what I'm saying?'

Betty's mouth was tight. 'I understand perfectly. Brett says that she's never seen the knife. You want to be sure that if she's lying, we've thought through whether we can cover it up. Unless we don't know better ourselves.'

'In which case,' Caroline answered mildly, 'you have no problem, do you? ... Incidentally, what you just said was very foolish. Not the thought so much. But to say it aloud.'

Betty stood up from the table, staring down at her sister. 'They showed me pictures of the knife, Caroline. And I never saw it before.' She looked to Larry and back again. 'If you'll excuse me, Brett's alone.'

She abruptly left the room.

In Larry's pensive silence, Caroline heard her sister climb the stairs. She reached for the wine bottle, poured some into her glass, then Larry's.

Only then did she turn to him. In the candlelight, his face was lined, his eyes weary and sad and perhaps ashamed. But he did not look away.

'So,' Caroline said softly.

Larry exhaled, gazing narrow-eyed at the flickering candle.

Caroline simply waited. Given her emotions, it was best.

'For a long time,' he said quietly, 'there were no teaching jobs. Finally, I took the only one I could find – at that junior college in Connecticut.'

'So I recall from your letter. Something about finding a home, just as you told me you would.'

Larry's face tightened. 'I know what I said to you. You needn't remind me.' He turned to her, finishing in a lower voice. 'I wasn't good enough, Caro. I bored them, and they fired me.'

'Yes,' Caroline answered coolly. 'That much I'd worked out.'

Larry raised his hands in entreaty. 'I had no job –'

'You had a child, and a life.' For the first time, Caroline's voice rose. 'How could *you* let him do this?'

'It wasn't like that.' Larry touched the bridge of his nose. 'Your father offered me a job I could believe in – not so hard, coming from someone who's on the board of a college so well endowed by his family that its oldest building is the Channing Library. And Betty wanted – or needed – to be close to him. With you gone, we were all he had –'

'Precisely.'

He turned on her. 'Damn it, Caroline, I had Brett to care for. I know how you felt, and why, but those feelings weren't mine.'

Caroline leaned back, tenting her fingers. 'Are they now?'

'Have I paid, do you mean? Would it make you feel better if I said yes?'

'Better? Nothing would. Especially now.' Caroline shook her head. 'No, the best I can work up is a certain morbid curiosity. About someone I was once quite fond of.'

Larry flushed, turned away. When he faced her again, moments later, it was with a look of silent pain, of mute appeal.

'Really,' Caroline said. 'This is all so unbelievable.'

Larry said nothing. Caroline folded her arms, as if against the cold. 'So,' she said finally, 'how *has* it been for you?'

Larry seemed to study his wine. Then he sipped it, eyes still distant, and slowly put it down. 'Until this happened to Brett,' he said finally, 'I would have told you it was mixed. A life of quiet desperation, quietly examined. But just now, I'm coming to see the truth, if the truth about *me* even matters. And it begins to seem much sadder than merely being the son-in-law with tenure.'

'How so?'

'Because I'm a spectator in my own life. Although Channing lives upstairs now, this home isn't mine – I'm simply the curator. And, in the ways that are most important, this family isn't mine.' He paused, adding softly, 'Just as you predicted years ago.'

Watching him, Caroline said nothing.

'I should have seen,' he said at length, 'how it was with Betty. First he loved your mother and then he loved you.

72

Brett was like a present she gave him, because he would never love her for herself.'

'Jesus ...'

'I know, I know. But I didn't then. It's all so complicated. Betty at once worships him and resents him. A lot of the anxiety that has alienated Brett as an adult – the intrusiveness, the overprotectiveness – began because Betty so badly wanted to give Brett the love she spent her childhood pining for. The all-loving, all-embracing parent ...'

'That's what *I* had, and it nearly ruined me.' Caroline paused, finishing in a lower voice. 'Perhaps, in a way, it did.'

Larry fell quiet, as if unable to respond. 'That's the other thing Betty gave him,' he said at last. 'At some point, I realized she discussed Brett with him more than me. And from the point that Channing retired, when Brett was seven, he always had more time for her.' He turned to Caroline. 'That's how the chain goes,' he finished softly. 'From your mother, to you, to Brett.'

For a long time, Caroline looked at the china, the oil paintings, the silver snifter on the table. Felt the slow accretion of pain.

'This boy,' she said then. 'What was he like?'

Larry watched her face. 'About as Betty described him, with allowances for her intensity. He was too damaged, I think, not to damage Brett if she stayed with him. What worried me – and what Betty and I could never talk about – was that Betty might affect Brett's otherwise good judgment.'

Caroline touched one finger to her mouth. 'Could Betty have been spying on her?'

Larry looked embarrassed. 'I think she could have, yes. Although she'd feel far too ashamed to admit that, and it would be the last straw for Brett.' He paused. 'Betty is angry because she's frightened. And frightened people do a great many harmful things. Including trying to control their world until they've made it perfect. The irony is that Betty desperately wanted Brett to stay in New Hampshire and, in my opinion, made it much more likely that she'd leave this fall, after she graduates, and settle elsewhere.' He glanced beyond Caroline, as if to see whether they were still alone, then asked quietly, 'Did Brett tell you about the fight?'

'With whom?'

'Between Betty and James. After I found out that he was dealing, James came to the house. Betty answered the door. When I came into the living room, she was asking him to leave.' Larry gazed into some middle distance. 'Her voice was low and tight – a sign that she's on the edge of losing it altogether, just hanging on. Before I could do much of anything, James did the worst thing he could do. Which was to smile down at her.

'You would have had to see him. He was dark, good looking, and somewhere he'd cultivated a smile that was superior and faintly derisive. So that when he looked down at Betty, his smile was somewhat like that of an anthropologist who'd happened upon a bizarre form of Pygmy.'

Larry looked at Caroline now. 'It was like a slap in the face,' he said softly. 'Before I could stop her, Betty whirled, grasped a crystal vase, and threw it at him.

'He didn't even duck. Just moved his head a little, and the crystal shattered on the wall.

'I stepped between them – James still with that quizzical smile, Betty with tears of rage. And then Brett came down the staircase, staring at the rest of us.

' "Your mother had an accident," James said carelessly. "Call me." And then he turned around and left.' Larry paused. 'Left a mess on the floor and a mess between my wife and daughter that may take years to fix.' His voice grew low and intense. 'God, Caroline, how I wish that was still the worst of our problems.'

Caroline was silent for a time, caught in the vortex of the scene he had described. 'And you couldn't reason with her?'

'Betty?' Larry stared at his lap, as if pondering how much to say. 'There've been some problems, Caro. Betty's vulnerable right now, and I don't have much capital in the bank. And Channing felt as she did.'

'Yes.' Caroline's tone was as chill as her emotions. 'Habit is such a hard thing to break.'

They sat awhile, quiet again, in the flickering light.

Larry folded his hands. 'How was it with him?'

'Father? The same. All the feelings, as fresh as when it happened. Except that instead of being twenty-two, I've spent twenty-two years living with it.' She shrugged, foreclosing conversation. 'I'm a lawyer now, and I'm here to do a job. If only for a time.'

'For a time?'

'Isn't it clear that I shouldn't be Brett's counsel? At least if it comes to a trial.'

Larry's face looked drawn now. 'Do you think it will?'

'I don't know yet. But I'll try to see Jackson Watts tomorrow. See if I can ferret out what he's thinking.'

'Jackson?' Larry shook his head.

Caroline looked at him steadily. 'As I said, I shouldn't be counsel.'

Larry sat back in his chair. He looked as weary as Caroline felt.

When, she wondered, had his hair become so thin, the lines begun to pull the corners of his mouth, the look of disappointment stolen into his eyes? Once, his smile had been so easy; Caroline had yet to see it today, nor could she imagine smiling herself. His shoulders sagged with the unseen burden of his worry.

'Come on,' Caroline said. 'I'll help you clear the table.'

He looked at her again. And then, as she had wanted, he gave the first faint smile.

Dishes had been their job that summer. Betty was the cook; washing the dishes after dinner, happy in each other's company, Larry and Caroline would argue politics or movies or literature – Larry had admired *Silas Marner*; Caroline had considered George Eliot a life sentence – and watch the setting sun through the window as it spread red across the waters of Nantucket Sound. Five years her senior, with a doctorate in the works, still Larry had taken her seriously, though he had loved to tease and provoke her. One night when they had dried the last dish, finished a particularly hyperbolic argument over George McGovern, Larry had kissed her on the cheek and said, lightly, facetiously, 'I married the wrong sister....'

Twenty-three years later, that same Larry suddenly appeared in the eyes of this middle-aged man. 'Are you sure ...?'

Caroline shrugged. 'You have a dishwasher, don't you?'

He gave another slight smile. In silent tandem, they shuttled dishes to the kitchen.

To Caroline, in some ways this was the strangest room in the house; no longer familiar but instead filled with her sister's curios – bright hot pads, an embroidered sampler, some Hummel figurines, a porcelain rooster – the cheerful artifacts of a mother who wished to make a home. Next to her, Larry rinsed dishes and passed them in the rhythm of two decades before. Except that Caroline now placed them in her sister's dishwasher, in the middle of her sister's kitchen.

Caroline took a dish from his hand. 'Is that it?' she asked.

'Just about,' he said. And then stopped, gazing at her in the track-lit brightness of the kitchen. Almost shyly, as if surprising himself, he said, 'You're beautiful, Caro. Still.'

Caroline met his eyes, smiling a little. '"Still,"' she repeated. 'Don't you think there's something rather sad about that?'

He shook his head. 'For me,' he answered, 'it's about the only thing that isn't.'

Caroline looked down. After a time, she said, 'There's something I have to say to you.'

'What?'

'I wasn't kidding, Larry. About the knife.'

'How do you mean?'

She raised her eyes to his. 'We were brought up around guns and knives – hunting knives, fishing knives, whatever. My father had a collection in the stable.'

Larry stepped back, as if to look at her. 'What are you saying?'

And what are you thinking? Caroline wondered. 'That I want to be very sure that knife isn't traceable. And that you're prepared when the police do get around to asking you.'

'Caroline.' Larry's voice was firm now. 'Think a moment. Brett is five feet three. Maybe a hundred ten pounds soaking wet. James's windpipe was cut through –'

'By the time I was ten,' Caroline interjected, 'I could fillet a fish. So could Betty. With the right knife, newly sharpened, either of us could have cut this boy's throat our first day in junior high school.' She touched his arm. 'Please, don't delude yourself that there's some easy out here. There isn't.'

His mouth was tight. 'I don't think I've been quite clear with you. Whatever our problems in this family, we did not raise a murderer. And with whatever reservations, Brett cared for that boy deeply. Even if she didn't, violence is just not in her. No matter how intoxicated.'

Caroline looked away. 'She has a temper, Larry. I've seen it.'

'All you've seen is someone frayed by shock and tragedy.' His voice rose. 'I mean, wouldn't you be?'

'Of course.'

The concession, stated readily and mildly, seemed to drain Larry's anger. 'What Brett *is*, Caro, is someone with a lot of grit. Grit and spirit and independence of thought – despite all Betty's protectiveness.' He smiled faintly again. 'Some days I look at us and wonder just where it came from.'

Caroline gazed at Larry, and then she asked the question she would never ask her sister.

'Tell me about her,' she said. 'Everything.'

Chapter 5

The next morning, Caroline showered, dressed, and drove two pensive hours to Concord, the state capital.

After Larry had shown her to her room, Caroline, too disturbed for sleep, had tried to channel her thoughts toward meeting Jackson Watts. Part of her felt unready; the other part too anxious to wait. At eight-thirty, she had called Jackson's office from the kitchen phone, edgy not only about Brett but about speaking to him at all.

He was in a meeting, his secretary said. Caroline stated her name and business; there was a long delay, Caroline tautly waiting, and then the secretary returned with the bland message that she could come ahead. Filled with anxiety and relief, Caroline was slow to put down the telephone; in that moment, she sensed, perhaps imagined, a soft click on the line.

Eyes narrow, Caroline paused with the receiver in her hand, listening. The house was silent. Returning to the bedroom, she saw no one.

She began getting ready. The night before, Caroline had hung a red dress in the closet, slightly off for her business but all she had. It was not too wrinkled, she noted; when she caught herself applying makeup with extra care, Caroline reproved herself that there was no problem so grave that it would erase her vanity. And then realized, again, how much of this was seeing Jackson Watts.

Her face and body had been so different then; *she* had been so different. It was more than foolish – perverse – to hope that under any circumstances, let alone these, someone she had deeply hurt would still find her attractive. And yet she did.

What was he like now? Caroline wondered. Wondered if he had a wife, or children; and how he had felt when his secretary delivered this morning's message – that Caroline Masters wished to see him, to discuss the murder of James Case.

Carefully, Caroline finished applying her eyeliner. *Whatever else you are*, she admonished herself – *and you may be little else – you still are a professional.*

She picked up her briefcase and left the room.

What, she asked herself, had she heard on the telephone?

She paused on the staircase, trying to place the others' rooms. One flight above her was Brett's room, *her* old room. She could not help but wonder who had chosen that room for her, what Brett's life had been like in this home. For a moment, she imagined Brett as Caroline herself had been, a young girl running down the stairs to go to school, innocent of the past, oblivious to the future, a smile on her lips....

Caroline started toward Brett's room, to see how she was.

No, she told herself. *That is not your role.* This *is* – *to drive to Concord and see Jackson Watts.* For the next two hours, traveling through sunlight and shadow, Caroline focused her thoughts on the case against Brett Allen.

Concord was little changed. The storefront signs on Main Street were brighter; the brick and stone commercial buildings a shade dingier; the town perhaps was a little poorer. But the side streets were tree-lined and gracious. And there was, of course – as there had been for Caroline the child – the building she still thought of when she heard the word 'capitol.'

Parking the car, she walked across its grounds. A sweep of green lawn, leafy shade trees, a statue of Daniel Webster. And then, behind it, the sculpted building of granite – a pillared federal design, topped by a gold dome. Another reminder of Channing Masters.

When Caroline was barely nine, her father had brought her here to meet his friend the governor. They had begun by touring the marble corridors, Caroline holding her father's hand, then the intimate Senate gallery, and then the vast and ornate House of Representatives – whose four hundred citizen legislators, Channing explained, made up the third-largest representative body in the Western world, yet selflessly served for two hundred dollars a biennium. After this, they had chatted with Governor Powell – dignified but warm to Caroline, easy yet respectful with Channing – in the governor's spacious reception room, replete with oil portraits of early governors, a hand-carved wooden mantel over a black marble fireplace, fourteen-foot ceilings, a long mahogany table. Sitting with Channing in an overstuffed chair as he talked to the governor about matters she did not yet understand, Caroline felt sure that no man was greater than her father, no state better than New Hampshire. She could not imagine another family, another home....

Her thoughts on Brett now, Caroline walked two more blocks to the old bank building that now housed the attorney general's staff. She took an elevator to the second floor, followed the sign that said 'Homicide Division,' and asked for Jackson Watts.

The receptionist rang him. Caroline sat in the reception area, legs crossed, arranging her face in a look of distant calm.

A door opened. 'Hello, Caroline,' a man's voice said, and then she looked up and saw him.

By reflex Caroline almost smiled. The man who stood there was much like the Jackson she remembered – tall and rangy, hair still black, though flecked with gray where it touched the tops of his ears. The ears themselves were still slightly too large, but better now that his face had filled out a bit. His face looked much the same, with the strong cleft jaw, the furrowed cheeks and ridged nose, the luminous brown eyes that were always his best feature. As he studied her, she realized that he was almost handsome now, a handsome Abe Lincoln.

Caroline stood. 'Hello, Jackson.'

Somewhat awkwardly, she extended her hand, one lawyer to another. His clasp was cool.

'Thank you for seeing me so soon,' she said.

A slightly puzzled look. *So soon?* the look said. *It's been twenty-three years since you simply vanished.* But all that he said was, 'I'm sure you're worried. Please, come in.'

She followed him down a corridor with the stark, slightly Stalinist look of modern government, to a neat rectangular office with files stacked on a faux-wood desk. He sat himself behind it, tie askew and sleeves rolled up, and directed her to sit opposite him. Then silent, he looked at her with an air of puzzlement.

'I've been wondering,' Caroline told him, 'what to say to you first. When my niece's file is sitting on your desk and you're now the chief of the Homicide Division.'

Somehow she had hoped to see some connection in his eyes. But she saw nothing she could read.

'There are a lot of reasons, Caroline, for me to be unhappy about this.' He expelled a breath. 'Not only do I respect your father a great deal, but I remember meeting Brett when she was eight or nine....' He shrugged; there was nothing he wished to say.

'Let me start over,' Caroline said quietly. 'How *are* you, Jackson?'

'Fine. Otherwise.' Jackson studied her. 'The basic facts are these — one teenage daughter I love, one dog, no wife anymore. A fishing camp on Heron Lake, a decent shot at a judgeship, and a certain basic contentment. Surprisingly enough, a lot of my life is pretty much what I expected it to be.' Another shrug. 'Or maybe that's no surprise to you.'

Oh, Jackson, Caroline thought, *it was never that — it was so many things that have nothing to do with you.* Quietly, she said, 'I've thought about you a lot. Still do, at times.'

He propped his chin on one hand, studying her with a level gaze. 'I never heard from you. Not since you wrote that letter from Martha's Vineyard.'

Caroline felt a stab of guilt. But it was far too late to

apologize, she knew, and she could never explain. 'I know,' she answered simply. 'No one did.'

'And now here you are. For Brett.'

'Yes.'

He leaned back in his chair. 'It's a bad case, Caroline.'

It took her a moment to catch up with him. Her throat tightened. 'Bad? Or just 'looks bad'?'

'Bad.' He seemed to hesitate. 'I don't have to tell you anything, of course – there've been no charges filed. But the basic facts aren't going to change. I can walk you through what you must already know, or at least guess.'

'Please.'

'All right.' He was crisp now, a prosecutor. 'Let's begin with the idea of premeditation. She took him there, to an isolated place, known to her but not to him. And then got him stoned –'

Caroline held up one hand. 'Intending to kill him? On her own property? With a knife?'

Jackson considered her. 'Her prints were on the knife. And on his throat. No one else's.'

'You've finished the lab work, then?'

He paused. 'Most of it.'

'Because I've never heard of anyone lifting prints off a man's body.'

Jackson frowned. 'For now, all that I can tell you, Caroline, is that they've done it.'

He was not, Caroline sensed, prepared to be pushed. In a muted voice, she asked, 'Did the lab find anything else?'

'Yes. His blood was all over her, in a pattern consistent with arterial spurt. Traces of his skin were found beneath her fingernails. And her prints are on the wallet – again, no one else's.' He paused. 'By now you've met her, Caroline. She's not a fool; even in the worst of circumstances, you can see her mind work. And she seems to have had the presence of mind to take the wallet, the knife, and her clothes – perhaps to make it look like a robbery, or even that she was never there. Yet for hours, she was supposedly too stoned to even tell the police what happened.' He shook

82

his head dismissively. 'That's a tough one to buy. You could argue pretty easily that she never expected a cop to pick her up and then spent the next several hours adapting. So that we didn't get any real story, such as it was, until close to dawn.'

His account was unnervingly like the one Caroline had given Brett. Rather than argue with it, she asked simply, 'Do you have the search warrant papers?'

Slowly, Jackson nodded, and drew a file from his drawer.

She read the papers quickly. 'According to the arresting officer,' she said, 'Brett's hair was wet.'

'So?'

'So if she was wet, and yet had blood on her, it suggests that she went swimming. Just as she said.' She looked up at Jackson. 'There's no sign that James was swimming, right?'

Jackson studied her. 'Not as I understand it.'

'Because I recognize the curly hair he describes here as the family curse – I got it whenever we went swimming, remember? And if Brett went swimming alone, someone else would have had time to kill him. Just as she said.' She paused a moment. 'Tell me, Jackson, what was her intoxication level?'

'Point one six.'

'Impressive.'

Jackson tilted his head. 'Are you saying that cuts against premeditation?'

'I'm saying that it cuts against your case.' Caroline sat straighter now. 'You may not like her story, but it explains everything – the blood, the fingerprints, the skin under her nails, even his failure to ejaculate. And there's not a hole in it. Everything that happened could have happened just the way she says it did.' Caroline paused for emphasis. 'She's either telling the truth or she's an intuitive criminal genius, who not only can plan and carry out the grisly murder of a young man half again her size and twice her strength but can invent the most complex account, covering physical evidence even a criminologist could only guess at, within hours of slashing her boyfriend's throat. All while drunk and stoned. If it weren't for the moral and legal circumstances, I'd be terribly proud of her.'

Jackson's eyes opened slightly. His look became wary, yet intent; something about it suggested more than professional pride, perhaps the desire that the woman sitting in front of him never humiliate him again.

'Within eight hours.' His voice was clipped now. 'More than time enough to sober up.'

'I really doubt that.' How to say this, Caroline wondered, without being patronizing? 'Sorry if I gave my jury argument.'

'No, it was interesting. And informative. So *why* do you doubt it?'

'Because drugs are a huge problem in San Francisco, and I was a public defender there. Which means that a lot of my clients were screwed up on drugs and alcohol. Of necessity, I began to take an amateur interest in pharmacology. For one thing, Jackson, the dope these kids smoke now isn't like the pot *we* tried.'

A raised eyebrow. 'No?'

'No. Today's pot has fifteen percent THC content, three to five times that of our wonder years. If Brett was an amateur doper – and I believe she was – one joint could do things to her that you and I wouldn't even recognize.

'Second, if she drank the wine first – which I also believe – the dope would have had an additive effect. The intoxication is seriously intensified: you get black holes in the memory, some of which never get filled, and there's a kind of surreal dream state, where the images are more like a slide show than real life. So that you doubt your own experience.' Caroline paused, then added succinctly, 'And an experience this terrible is one that you would very much wish to doubt.'

Jackson looked at her skeptically. 'And a single joint would account for all that.'

'It could account for a lot of things. That she at first tried to administer CPR. That she later had trouble remembering – or believing – that this terrible thing had really

84

happened. And the nausea and vomiting are a typical example of the additive effect, which – like the perceptual problems – are also intensified by orgasm. As you may also recall from your youth.'

Suddenly, Jackson looked wary, as if unsure how to answer. *What are you doing?* his expression said. Then a shrug, the barest hint of a smile. 'I didn't know what it was. Maybe the earth moving.'

What were the rules for this? Caroline wondered. She rushed ahead. 'The point is, she wouldn't get over it quickly. The effect lasts not for hours but for days. So that what Brett describes so well – semi-blackout, then flashing on his body, then enough recovery to tell her story – is utterly consistent with the chemistry of memory as affected by drugs. Please, trust me that this is not just defense lawyer's bullshit.' She added softly, almost reluctantly, 'Which does, however, bring me to Miranda.'

'Somehow I thought that it might.' His eyes were keen now. 'Go ahead. I'm listening.'

'You already know, Jackson. In fact, *I* already know when you started calling the shots – when they held Brett at the hospital until they got the warrants to search her person and the property by the lake. That's when they started doing things right. But by then it may have been too late.' Caroline kept her voice quiet, respectful. 'When they called to tell you they'd picked up this naked, blood-speckled girl with a bloody knife, taken her to jail, and then gotten her to point them to the lake, what did they say about Miranda warnings?'

Jackson's watchful half smile was no smile at all. 'You tell me.'

'There were none. Which means there's a good chance that Brett's lawyer – whoever that is – could suppress the first statement about where to find James's body and all the evidence based on that; perhaps the body itself and certainly the search of the lake, the search of Brett, and her later statement about the circumstances of James's death.'

Caroline snapped her fingers. 'Gone, just like that. Leaving you with nothing.'

Jackson's smile had vanished. 'Caroline,' he said in a voice of wonderment, 'of all the conversations I ever imagined us having, this is not one.' His tone became crisper. 'You're also wrong. The bloody knife was in plain view, giving the police good reason to feel that someone else might have been hurt. But they didn't know who or what or why, or even whether Brett and whoever else had been attacked by a third party. And no court is going to punish the police for asking if there's a wounded person out there whose life can still be saved. It's called the exigent circumstances doctrine.' He leaned forward. 'Let me ask you this: Are you willing to advise her to take a lie detector test. Given by one of our people?'

He was very clever, Caroline realized. In a quiet voice, she answered, 'I don't believe in them. And a clever police examiner can use a lie test to interrogate her.'

You don't believe in her, she saw him think. But it seemed to give him little pleasure. 'Then, viewing this as a professional, I must tell you that Brett has real problems. For the reasons you already know, and some that I'm sure you don't.

'Your defense, if you even have one, is that someone followed them to the lake. But look what that requires of your imaginary killer: to start, knowing that she would leave James by himself – after all, who could reasonably expect to hack two able-bodied college students to death? Also knowing that James would be too drunk and/or stoned to defend himself.' He gazed at Caroline intently. '*And* knowing how he -- or she – could then vanish in the woods without leaving a trace.'

Caroline felt a jolt. 'Is that what the crime lab people tell you?'

Jackson folded his hands. 'When she fled the scene, Brett left a trail behind – trampled brush, broken branches, flecks of James's blood on the leaves. If Brett's story is right, there's no way that the killer wouldn't have left the same trail. So far we've found nothing....'

'That just can't be. The local police were there, and the EMTs. You can't tell me that there aren't footprints all around the lake, and all sorts of signs that the cops – or someone – were thrashing about in the woods. I doubt the crime lab people can tell *who* else might have been there.'

Jackson leaned forward. 'There seems to be no escape path except for the one Brett left. The killer would have had to have James Case all over him, just as Brett did. But we've got no trail of blood but hers – nothing else, and no one else. And who else are you going to offer me? Some bum, looking to lift the wallet of a college kid? That's not credible.' Jackson's voice rose. 'This was *personal*, Caroline. The killer butchered this kid like an animal, with a very sharp knife. Name a case you know where someone did that to a stranger.'

Caroline looked at him steadily. 'Charles Manson, for one. And you've got no reason at all for Brett to kill him. Let alone like that.'

Jackson paused, a tacit concession, then parried: 'And *you've* got no one else.'

'You're forgetting James's supplier.'

Jackson raised an eyebrow. 'I may not be up on my THC, but I do know there's nothing in this for a petty dealer.' He appeared to debate whether to say more. 'We searched James's apartment, Caroline. There was no sign of a break-in, let alone torn-up sheets. What Brett told us about someone tearing up his room never happened.'

Caroline felt shaken again. 'Maybe he lied to her. About the dealer ...'

Jackson's half smile was melancholy. 'So who does that leave us? Just a girl who may have been sufficiently drug-addled when she killed him for you to argue this down to murder two.'

Caroline studied him. Softly, she asked, 'You haven't tied her to the knife, have you?'

A moment's silence. 'No.'

'What kind of knife is it?'

'A fishing knife – a Cahill. Quite a fine one.' Pausing, Jackson examined her for a time. 'As you say, Caroline, you've no rights here. But perhaps you'd like to see it.'

'I would, yes.'

Reaching into a second drawer, Jackson withdrew a knife in a glassine bag and placed it on the desk.

The knife was finely crafted. Bone handle, long blade, serrated edge. A knife for a fisherman who cared about such things. The blade was encrusted with blood.

Caroline's stomach felt empty. It was a time before she felt Jackson's scrutiny, wondered how long she had gazed at the knife.

Turning over the bag, she saw the serial numbers on the blade, just as she expected.

The blood obscured them. Caroline had to squint; her reading glasses were in the briefcase. But she did not wish Jackson to know what she was doing. Since childhood, it had been her gift to memorize numbers.

Slowly, she passed the bag to Jackson. 'A fine one. Just as you said.'

He placed the knife on the desk between them, looking into her face. 'Is that all?' he asked. 'Or is there something else you want to cover?'

'Not now.' She hesitated. 'Thank you.'

Caroline stood. Somehow she felt distant, a bit lightheaded.

Jackson rose from behind the desk, hands on hips. 'Did I understand that you may not handle this?'

It brought her back a little. She looked at him directly. 'If there's no prosecution, it shouldn't really matter.'

He did not answer but simply gazed at her, his eyes intent and curious. 'I hear you're going to be a federal judge.'

'So it seems.'

For another moment, he seemed to appraise her. 'Well,' he said at length, 'I'm sorry about this. For Brett, and for everyone involved.'

He held out his hand. Caroline took it, clasped it quickly. 'Thank you,' she said. 'I'll let myself out.'

She turned and left him there.

She hardly remembered her walk to the car, did not look up at the capitol, or anywhere except in front of her. Getting to the car, she sat there awhile.

Her briefcase was on the seat beside her. She reached inside, found a pen and a piece of paper, and wrote down the serial numbers from the blade of the Cahill knife.

Chapter 6

When Caroline returned, she saw no one. It was as she wished. But when she climbed the stairs to the room where her things were, hoping to be alone, there was a message taped to her door.

She stared at Betty's careful script. Bob Carrow had called. From the Manchester *Patriot-Ledger*.

Caroline sat on the bed.

She was not prepared. The one statewide newspaper, the *Patriot-Ledger*, had long dominated New Hampshire; its politics were harshly right-wing – bitterly antagonistic to Democrats, feminists, and judges such as Caroline promised to be – and its stock-in-trade since Caroline's youth had been its crusade for more criminal convictions and longer sentences. There was nothing to gain from returning this call; certainly not for Caroline, whose potential involvement in a criminal matter involving her family – if publicized – would surely get back to the White House. Angry and exhausted, she started to crumple the message into a ball.

Her hand froze. She opened her palm, staring at the crumpled paper.

Who, she wondered, had done this to her?

For there was Brett to consider. If there should be a trial, it would become a major story in such media as New Hampshire had, and never more so than in the *Patriot-Ledger*. For Caroline the defense lawyer, it was important to get her client fair coverage in the press – better than fair, if Caroline could help it. And one did not do that by ignoring the state's largest newspaper.

For another half hour, she thought. About the reasons she had left here. About the twenty years spent trying to become a judge. About a girl she barely knew.

She went to the kitchen to call.

'Bob Carrow.'

A voice such as she had heard in countless newsrooms – edgy, eager, aggressive. Part of her despised him.

She made her own tone polite, puzzled, faintly bored. 'This is Caroline Masters.'

'Oh, yes. Thank you for getting back to me. I hear your niece is Brett Allen.'

'Yes.' More arid now. 'I hear that too.'

A hesitation. 'She may be charged with murder.'

'Really? Who did she kill?'

'Well, James Case …'

'Who told you that? Not, I think, the Attorney General's Office.' Caroline's tone was firm and even. 'This is a young woman who has just lost someone she loved in the most shocking circumstances, including the hideous trauma of finding his body. And no one – no one at all – has any other reason to even *think* about her in connection with his death. Let alone find anything like a motive.'

Caroline broke off. Tomorrow, she chastened herself, the police could find something. It was not like her to go too far.

'So you believe she's innocent,' Carrow said.

'Of what? Brett might well have been killed herself. In that way – if only that way – she's quite fortunate.'

'Then who do you think killed James Case?'

'Someone who wasn't twenty-two and in love with him.' Caroline's voice grew quieter. 'I hope that Brett can look to you for fairness.'

Their talk was over, Caroline's tone suggested. 'One more question,' Carrow said hastily. 'The White House has just announced your nomination to the United States Court of Appeals. Do you feel it's appropriate for a judicial nominee to be involved in a criminal matter?'

At once, Caroline was on edge – where, she wondered, was this coming from. 'I think you may misapprehend my role. I've come here as a member of the family.'

'But you also visited the Assistant Attorney General this morning, Mr. Watts. What was the purpose of that meeting?'

'To express my family's concern. Including that whoever did this be identified.' She permitted herself an edge of irritation. 'Think about it, Mr. Carrow. Not only that someone killed my niece's boyfriend but that someone is still out there. Imagine how frightening that is.'

A long silence. 'Will you be Ms. Allen's lawyer?'

'Lawyer? She doesn't need one. All she needs is her family's support.' Caroline paused. 'I expect shortly to return to San Francisco and get about the business this tragedy interrupted – preparing for the nomination hearings. About which, of course, I'm very honored. Is there anything else?'

His tone combined politeness and a certain sanctimony. 'I know this is a difficult thing. But I really think it would be helpful if Ms. Allen were to speak to us herself.'

Caroline drew a long breath. 'I think you can understand how little Brett feels like talking to anyone. So for the moment you'll have to make do with me. But should she ever feel like discussing this – other than with those closest to her – we will surely let you know.'

'Okay.' He sounded mollified, then eager. 'First, if possible – okay?'

'Yes. If possible.' She took a breath. 'We in this family have great respect for the *Patriot-Ledger*.'

'Good.' In his own hesitancy, she heard the decision not to push. 'Thank you, Ms. Masters.'

'Of course.'

As he hung up, Caroline found herself listening, once more, for the sound of a second telephone. But there was nothing.

The stable was dim, airy, almost barnlike. The sun came from windows high above her, casting shadows in the corners. A white Jeep was parked to one side, dwarfed by the vastness of the space.

The lawyer Caroline knew that she should turn around and leave. Yet she stayed where she was.

At the back of the stable were her father's workbench, his tools, his vise for sawing lumber. Channing Masters believed in self-sufficiency; how many times, his daughter wondered, had she sat with him as he built something, or fixed something, unwilling, she knew, to concede defeat. The standing clock in the foyer was made in the 1850s by a famous clockmaker, Tim Chandler; Caroline still remembered a day when she was seven or so, sitting by her father as he spent half a Sunday with the clock face turned, its complex inner workings exposed, making small adjustments with a jeweler's tools until, suddenly, the heavy chain swayed again, the bell sounded, and she saw the smile of inward pleasure at the corners of her father's eyes.

Caroline walked past the workbench to his gun rack.

Everything was where it had always been – shotguns, for hunting and trapshooting; a revolver; a crossbow; several fly rods. The guns were still cleaned and oiled, their stocks polished; the fly rods and reels were supplied with fishing line. Caroline seemed to recall most of them. Her father cared for his things; out of sentiment and practicality, he preserved what he had, threw little away. He had no taste for the new.

Beside the fly rods was a wooden rack with pegs.

The ten-year-old Caroline had helped him make it, applying lacquer to the wood. She could hardly wait for the lacquer to dry; then they could fix it to the wall and hang his knives there. Later, they had hung them one by one, in leather sheaths.

At the end of the rack, Caroline saw an empty peg. All at once, the stable felt cold and drafty.

Caroline turned, went to the house, and closed the door behind her.

She stood there, leaning against the door. Perhaps she owed Betty and Larry an account of the day – surely she owed that much to Brett. But right now she could not stay here.

She walked to the telephone, reserved a room at the Resolve Inn, and left.

Chapter 7

Caroline started awake in a strange room, her mind dreamstreaked, the window gray with the light just before dawn. It took her a moment to recognize the sparse antiques, the window sash, another to realize that she was in Resolve, the town of her girlhood. She felt adrift; it was as if it had taken twenty years to build a life, and only three days to leave it.

She put on blue jeans and a sweater, went downstairs to the sitting room, and poured coffee into a large mug. After drinking it quickly, black, she drifted out onto the porch and into the main street of town.

On one side was a gradual hill; the other sloped to a rushing creek. The street itself was blacktop now, not gravel, but little else had changed. Caroline took the tree-lined road past white wooden homes from the 1800s, built when the area throve; the spired but austere church where town meetings were held; the yellow one-floor library that, from the sign in front, still kept eccentric hours at the whim of the librarian; the Masonic Hall, its wood frame dingy now, atop a knoll set back from the street. Less out of enthusiasm than from social necessity, Channing Masters had joined the lodge; Caroline still remembered her mother's satirical imaginings of secret Masonic rituals, complete with antlers and women's dresses and blood oaths against non-Masons. Channing had suffered this in silence.

There was only one new structure – a mobile home – and little sign of commerce. The general store was boarded up now, its gas pump closed; Caroline imagined a convenience store and gas station on some more heavily traveled road.

Where the street curved, abruptly crossing a bridge over

the creek, she turned back. A faint air of depression hung above the town.

Caroline returned to the room, called Brett, and asked her to go sailing on Lake Winnipesaukee. She was somehow not surprised when Brett said yes.

The air was warm, breezy; Brett handled the tiller of the rented catboat easily, hair curling in the wind. Sailing seemed to change her. On the drive to Winnipesaukee she had been withdrawn. Now there was color in her face, a brightness to her eyes, and her movements were practiced yet instinctive. It was as though, like Caroline herself, physical action freed some part of her. There was a sensual quality Caroline had not seen in her.

With the Vineyard house sold when Brett was an infant, Caroline knew, Channing would have taught his grand-daughter to sail on Winnipesaukee. She seemed to know each inlet on the span of blue, to gaze at the forested hills around them with deep familiarity. Caroline guessed that the memories were good; when a sudden gust buffeted the sails, shooting a spray of water over Brett as she tacked, she grinned into the sunlight with sudden, surprising pleasure. Caroline decided to let her sail as long as she wished.

It was not until close to two, after three hours on the water, that Brett and Caroline moored near Woodsman's Cove.

The air was humid now, the sun hot; Caroline drank from a can. 'Cheap, watery American beer,' she said. 'Perfect for a day like this.'

They sat across from each other in the stern, gazing out at the water and the hills as the boat rocked fitfully at anchor. Holding her own can of beer, Brett tried to smile. But she seemed to have returned to the realm of fact, and tragedy; there was something muted but alert about her. Caroline waited for her to choose the moment.

'How was it with the prosecutor?' Brett asked at length.

Caroline considered her answer. 'He's short two things.

96

Both critical. He can't tie the knife to you or, more important, come up with a reason for you to kill your boyfriend.'

'There isn't any,' Brett said simply.

To Caroline, she looked fragile again. 'Would you have gone to California with him?' she asked.

There was a flicker in Brett's eyes. And then, to Caroline's surprise, she said evenly, 'I don't think I would have.'

'Was something wrong?'

'Something big.' Brett looked at her directly now. 'Sometimes it was like I never knew what James was thinking, or planning. He grew up protecting himself – he wasn't used to being close. I could understand that. But it's not a way to live.'

Then why did you care for him? Caroline began to ask. But this was not a lawyer's question. She realized that Brett was studying her with new attentiveness.

'Why did you leave?' Brett asked. 'Because no one ever talks about it.' She paused a moment, as if fearing to be tactless, then added, 'Not about you, and not about your mother.'

Caroline smiled faintly. 'How very New England.'

'How very repressed,' Brett said flatly. 'Until you were all over our television, I hadn't heard your name for years. And then there was Grandfather in his room, watching you run that trial and not saying a word to anyone. And my mother, tight-lipped and short-tempered.'

Caroline's shrug was meant to be dismissive. 'Sometimes silence is only that. And absence, only absence.'

Brett's expression did not waver. 'It's not silence, Aunt Caroline. It's something more. For Granddad and my mother.'

Perhaps, Caroline thought, Brett was puzzling through her own relationship to this family, looking to Caroline for clues. She smiled briefly. 'First you can drop the "Aunt Caroline" – it sounds like some menopausal dowager in a dreadful Broadway musical. "Caroline" will do just fine.

About our family, I suppose the best real answer is that I wanted to be independent and was absolutely certain that leaving was the only way. How anyone else felt about that I could only guess: I was twenty-two then and – apparently unlike you – didn't give the feelings of others a great deal of thought.'

'Where did you go?'

'I spent a year on Martha's Vineyard.' Caroline made her tone casual, disinterested. 'Then I went to San Francisco, enrolled in law school, and stayed. That's all there is.'

'But why San Francisco? Had you ever been there?'

Caroline shook her head. 'It just sounded pretty, and it seemed the farthest I could go.'

'How did you get by?'

'I worked. And my mother had left me a little money. From a life insurance policy.'

Brett studied her for a time, as if torn between curiosity and her sense of Caroline's reticence. Softly, she asked, 'I've never even seen a picture of your mother.'

Caroline smiled slightly. 'That's hardly surprising. She's been dead for thirty years.' She paused, disliking her own tone. More gently, she continued: 'She was small and dark and very pretty. To a child, quite exotic.'

Brett seemed to hesitate, perhaps at the look on Caroline's face. 'I'm sorry,' she said at last. 'But you're both this family mystery. All I know about your mother is that she was French and died in an accident.'

Caroline was briefly quiet. But she found it easier to talk about her mother than herself. 'French,' Caroline amended, 'and Jewish. *That* was the first accident, and the one that made all the difference to her.'

It was night; Caroline was nine or ten. Her mother had come to say good night. Surprised and pleased, Caroline had asked her to invent a story: lightly, with mock exasperation, Nicole had answered, 'But I have no stories tonight.'

She had been drinking, Caroline knew. She could tell

from her breath, her levity of mood, an ever so slight increase in the difficulty of pronouncing English. Emboldened, Caroline answered, 'Then tell me about your family. Your parents and brother.'

All Caroline knew for certain was that they were dead. But in the darkness of her bedroom, Caroline felt her mother's silence like a weight on her own chest. Nicole was utterly still.

'Do you really wish to hear, Caroline?'

Her mother's voice was very clear now; the change of mood somehow frightened Caroline. But she could not refuse.

'Yes,' she answered. 'I do.'

The room was quiet. 'We lived in Paris,' Nicole said at last. 'My father taught law at the university. My mother stayed home with my brother Bernard and me.' A pause, then a tone of irony. 'I remember thinking that she spoke French rather strangely – she was Russian, not a citizen, and came to France in her teens. But at the time, my only feeling was a child's embarrassment.

'She was Jewish, as was my father. But his family was deeply French. Yes, we went to synagogue, observed the holidays, but otherwise I did not feel much different from the children of his faculty friends. Oh, a little different, perhaps – but certainly not threatened.' She paused, inquiring softly, 'You understand about being Jewish, don't you, Caroline? What happened during the war?'

She nodded. Something beneath her mother's question made Caroline reach for her hand.

Her mother did not seem to notice. 'When the Germans invaded,' she said quietly, 'I was fifteen, and Bernard was twelve. Marshal Pétain became the head of a French puppet government. And *I* began to know what it was to be Jewish. By the time I was seventeen, I was wearing a Star of David. Under race laws passed not by Germans but by our fellow French.

'My father protested the laws as immoral. When he lost

99

his job at the university, a few friends telephoned to express their sympathy. No one came to call.

'We never saw any of them again.'

Caroline tried to imagine her mother isolated, her own family – Channing, Nicole, and Betty – ostracized. 'What did you do?' she asked.

'My father sold our home and possessions, and we moved to an apartment in the Jewish quarter of Paris. My sharpest memory is of our parents at the table in that darkened room – my father, small and mustached and alert; my brother as dark and bright-eyed as my father. Only my mother seemed gaunt and lost – she was Russian, after all. She had seen it all before.

'Throughout 1942 there were roundups. Foreign Jews taken from their homes by French police or German soldiers, herded to detention points, and then shipped away by rail. To where, we never knew.

'Still I hoped.' Nicole paused. 'I idolized my father, you see. If he felt hope, then I did. We were French, after all. And what Father believed was that no government of France – even this one – would abandon its own citizens. If only out of pride.'

Caroline watched her mother's face in the moonlit room. It was opaque, unfeeling, as if she were reciting by rote a story of which she had grown tired.

'When I was eighteen,' she went on, 'they sent me to university. As if this act of normality would serve as my protection.

'In a sense, it did.

'One night after class, I found my brother Bernard waiting for me. There was to be a roundup of Jews; a former faculty friend of my father's had heard this and sent word to warn him. So my father asked that I stay with a non-Jewish friend, Catherine.

'I begged Bernard to come with me. But he had to go back.' Nicole's tone was quiet with irony. 'To let my parents know that he was safe.'

Without knowing why, Caroline hugged herself.

Her mother did not see this. She seemed hardly to know that Caroline was there. 'I stayed with Catherine that night,' she went on. 'But the next morning, I could not keep away.

'The section in which we lived went back to medieval times – the streets were narrow and dark, cobblestone. I had turned the corner to the street before I saw a uniformed policeman, French, carrying a suitcase in each hand, and crying. I had never seen a policeman cry before. Behind him, with more policemen, were a straggling line of children and adults, dragging their suitcases with them.

'At the end of the line were my father and mother and brother.

'I waited for them to pass.

'My mother never saw me. She looked straight ahead, one hand in Bernard's, the other in my father's. Tears ran down her face.

'As they passed, my father spotted me at the edge of the street.

'I started to speak, to reach out to him. Quietly, his lips formed the word 'no'; he stared at me a second longer, to ensure that I obeyed, and then snapped his eyes away.

'It was then I understood. My mother was not French, and my father would not leave her. Nor would Bernard.

'I watched until they rounded the corner and disappeared.'

Nicole's voice stopped abruptly. In the silent room, Caroline imagined her own parents – Channing and Nicole – vanishing from sight. She found it hard to breathe.

In a muffled voice, she asked, 'What happened to you, Mama?'

In the darkness, Nicole seemed to shrug.

'Catherine's father knew someone,' she finally answered. 'I was sent to Le Chambon, in the Cévennes region. There was a tradition of resistance there – many of the farmers were Protestants, and their ancestors had suffered persecution.

'For the rest of the war I stayed with a farmer family.

They were very kind, as were the villagers. But all that time, I dreamed of my parents and Bernard. Wondered how and where they were. Prayed for them in whatever way seemed best.

'After the war, I returned to Paris.

'I worked as a translator for the Americans, badgered everyone I could for records of deportations, even rumors of my family.

'Finally, I learned of them from a kind American legal officer....'

Her mother stopped abruptly. There were tears in her eyes.

Frightened, Caroline clasped her hand. 'What, Mama?'

Only then did Nicole look at her. Quite softly, she answered, 'Your grandparents died at Auschwitz. As did the boy who would have been your uncle.'

By instinct, Caroline reached out to hug her. But Nicole stopped her, staring intently into Caroline's face until her own tears had vanished.

'You are Jewish, Caroline. There is no government, no person, that can ever really be trusted. Please, remember that.'

For a long time, Brett said nothing.

They sat in silence, beers cupped in their hands, unnoticed. Brett seemed to study her. At length, she asked, 'How was it that she married Grandfather?'

Caroline collected her thoughts. 'After his first wife died, having your mother, I think he was a little lost. So he left Betty with an aunt and uncle, and joined the Army Judge Advocate General Corps. In postwar Paris, his job was investigating war crimes by Germans for the Nuremberg tribunal.' Caroline finished quietly: 'He was the 'kind officer' who told my mother about her parents. After learning that, she must have thought New Hampshire sounded quite safe. And my father had fallen in love with her.'

Brett's face filled with sympathy. 'Do you think she loved him?'

Caroline gazed past her, at the mountains. 'My mother died when I was fourteen,' she said simply. 'Too young for me to truly know.'

Brett's look remained soft, inquiring. 'That must have been terrible for you.'

More than you will ever guess. 'It was hard.' A slight smile. 'But then fourteen is a difficult age.'

Brett was quiet for a time. To Caroline, watching her, it was almost tangible – Brett sorting the missing pieces of her family, wondering what corners of whose hearts she did not yet understand. But Caroline was a stranger to her, and Nicole a marker in a cemetery. Only Channing Masters was real.

'When she died,' Brett finally asked, 'how was it for Grandfather?'

Caroline grasped the unspoken question: *How was it that you could bring yourself to hurt him?* As to this, at least, Caroline chose the truth.

'Oh,' she said quietly, 'I'm quite sure it broke his heart.'

It was perhaps four; the sunlight slanted gently on the blue waters of the lake. Brett had fallen into a moody silence. But Caroline's story seemed to have distracted her a little from the present. For this much Caroline was grateful.

'Have you ever been married?' Brett asked.

Caroline smiled. 'Not even once.'

'Doesn't that ever get lonely?'

Caroline considered her. Part of this curiosity must be Brett working out answers for herself: how much, Caroline wondered, does she talk to Betty now? 'Not really,' she told Brett. 'You get used to being your own companion. Of course, there's still this idea that single women are supposed to feel barren, literally and figuratively. Especially,' she added with a sardonic twist, 'if they compound their misery by being successful.'

Brett tilted her head. 'Then you never wanted children?'

Caroline shrugged. 'As a friend of mine once said, "I love my children too much already to give them a mother like me."' She stopped herself; Brett deserved better. 'Perhaps I would have liked that, Brett. But the things that you can't help, you put out of your mind. It's better that way.'

Brett nodded, watching her more closely. It was clear she would ask nothing more.

There was a first coolness in the air, sun dying. Caroline pulled a windbreaker over her shoulders.

'Once this is over,' she asked, 'what will you do?'

The question seemed to startle Brett. 'I don't know,' she said. 'Nothing's real to me now. Before, I wanted to write. Short stories, novels.'

It might be good, Caroline thought, to get her talking about a future, something outside James Case. 'Why writing?'

'Because I seem to have talent – at least my teachers think I do. And getting a straight job, like in a company, is nothing I can see right now. Though I've thought about getting a master's so I can teach writing.' Brett's voice warmed. 'Writing seems like the only job where what you think and feel really matters.'

Caroline nodded. 'Have you written much?'

'A lot.' A small smile. 'I always have. Even when I was small I made stories up all the time – imagining people, places, things I'd never seen in life. My dad used to say I didn't know real from unreal –' Brett glanced quickly at Caroline.

Caroline pretended not to notice. 'How did your parents feel?'

Brett was quiet for a moment. 'About that they were fine – especially Dad. And Granddad always said a writer needed a place – like Faulkner in Yoknapatawpha County. And that I *had* a place. Right here.'

'Well,' Caroline said mildly, 'it's certainly convenient. For everyone.'

Brett smiled a little. 'I understood that part of it – wanting me here – all too well. But then my grandfather helped raise me: hiking, or homework, or just talking about books or writing. Most afternoons, when I came home, Granddad would be waiting. To do something, or just to hear about my day.' Her smile faded. 'I understand that, still, even if it's not convenient. It was like *I* was the one who was left for him.'

Caroline felt surprise; without warning, Brett could move from ingenuous to acute. 'What do you mean?'

Brett's gaze was direct now. 'That my mother was never his favorite, Caroline. *You* were.'

'I don't think that's true. I don't think it ever was.'

Brett shook her head. 'Once, when we were hiking, I asked him about you. He looked so sad that I never asked again.' Brett hesitated. 'Is that why you came back? For him?'

'The world is not about "him."' Caroline paused, softening her tone. 'Truth to tell, I came back for you.'

Brett looked surprised, then skeptical. 'Why?'

'We *are* related, you know.' Caroline drew a breath. 'I'm a lawyer, and I want to help you. My issues with my family aren't yours.'

'I'm sorry – I didn't mean to piss you off.'

Caroline waved a hand. 'You didn't. Really.' Her voice softened to curiosity. 'Tell me, though, where your dad fit in all of this.'

Brett leaned back. 'Dad and you were friends, weren't you?'

'Yes. We were.'

Brett nodded. 'Dad's an enigma sometimes … he more or less left raising me to Mom.' Brett's voice became sardonic. 'It's a case of the parent with the deepest emotions winning. With the way my mom is, it was no contest – and Dad didn't want the aggravation she'd give him if he tried to make it one.' As if ashamed, Brett paused; Caroline felt once more the quicksilver of her emotions. 'Really, I shouldn't say that. Dad loves me, I know, and he can be so sweet. It's just that he hates conflict, and I think Mom feels things so intensely that it scares him. Sometimes it seemed like Granddad — who, if anything, intimidates Mom — was more my father than he was.'

Caroline remembered Larry of the gentle eyes and slow, warm smile, who first had named her 'Caro,' who still could talk to her when she and Betty could no longer talk at all. Remembered him holding the infant Brett, gazing from Caroline to the sleeping baby with the wonder of sudden fatherhood. Felt sadness and anger that he had receded to a corner of this girl's life, supplanted by Betty's and Caroline's own father.

'Did you ever rebel?' Caroline asked.

A faint smile, and then Brett's voice became ironic. 'Did you see the satellite dish behind the house? *That* was my rebellion. I threatened him — if I couldn't keep up with the outside world, like *Beverly Hills 90210*, I'd go away to boarding school.'

Children do not always live to please their parents, he had said as Caroline left for school, *or parents to please themselves*. Softly, Caroline queried, 'He didn't send you away to school?'.

Neither of them, she realized, had defined 'he'; there was no need.

'No,' Brett answered in the same tone. 'He bought me the dish instead.'

'Not much, as rebellions go.'

'Don't I know it. I even let them send me to Chase College, where my dad teaches, so I could go for a lot less. My mother implied there was trouble with money, and I couldn't bring myself to ask Grandfather. So instead of being like Mom, going off to Smith, I stayed right in the neighborhood.' Brett paused, as if in remembered anger. 'Of course, she said to me that James was a rebellion. Especially after they found out about the drug dealing.'

Caroline fell quiet, caught between her image of the cross-currents of her estranged family and her own doubts about Brett's innocence. And then, to her surprise, she saw tears running down Brett's face.

Softly, Caroline asked, 'What is it?'

'What you asked me before. About whether I'd have gone with him.' Brett paused, fighting to control her voice. 'What I didn't tell you was that now I lie awake wishing I *had* gone, no matter how many doubts I had. Just walked to the Jeep with him and started west that night.' Brett's eyes shut, and then she finished: 'Because we'd have gotten to California today, and James would be alive.'

Caroline did, not reach her room until eleven.

In the car, Brett had fallen asleep. Caroline had driven steadily, glancing at the girl's face against the headrest. Even had Brett awakened, Caroline could not have brought herself to ask about the knife.

Now she stared at the message in her hand – Walter Farris, from the White House. Next to her on the nightstand, the Manchester *Patriot-Ledger* was opened to an article quoting Caroline. *Why*, she asked herself, *hadn't she called Farris this morning?*

A chill breeze blew about the window sash. Caroline stood, pushing down the window – only a crack now, enough coolness to help her sleep.

Caroline reviewed Brett's expressions, her voice, the way she had said things. Caroline the lawyer knew that no one could read guilt or innocence on the face of a stranger. Another Caroline, whose existence the lawyer scorned, pleaded with her to believe that Brett was truthful – that the Brett she had spent today with could not have sliced her lover's throat to the windpipe, no matter how intoxicated. But there was no way, Jackson Watts had told her, that anyone else had been there.

Tomorrow, she would call Walter Farris. And then, to satisfy both parts of her, she would telephone Jackson Watts and ask if she could see the crime scene, the lot her father once had meant for her.

Chapter 8

What Caroline heard first was the new reserve in Farris's tone.

'I should have called you,' Caroline said. 'It's just that things have happened so quickly. As you can imagine, it's extremely trying for Brett, and for the family.'

'I understand that, Caroline. But what wasn't clear, precisely, is whether you're acting as your niece's lawyer here.'

Caroline paused a moment. 'More as an aunt ...'

'Because this meeting with the Attorney General's Office troubles me. Whatever your intention, it could create the appearance that our appointee to the federal bench is trying to use her prospective influence on behalf of a relative. And, even worse, to affect the course of a homicide investigation.'

Caroline felt on edge now. 'Please know, Walter, that it hardly feels like that from here. As for being a lawyer, I'll continue to practice law until the Senate confirms me. That's standard procedure.'

'Of course it is.' His voice aspired to patience. 'But what *isn't* is to represent a member of your family in a brand-new, potentially high-profile murder case. Even without this nomination, it's hardly wise – you can't help but be emotionally involved, which is what no counsel should be. If your niece needs a lawyer, the best thing you can do is help her find one.'

It was, Caroline knew, exactly what she herself would say. 'If Brett should be indicted, that's certainly my intention. We're all hoping that she won't be.'

'And even if she isn't,' Farris retorted, 'your confirmation hearing may involve questions none of us wants.' His voice became crisp. 'We live in a brave new world,

Caroline. Republicans control the Senate now, and – although we have great latitude in our appointments – feminist defense lawyers are not the flavor of the year. All we need is someone like Jesse Helms using this "appearance of impropriety" as an excuse to scuttle you. What I'm saying, to be plain, is that the President has only so much political capital to spend on this. So anything you do up there, other than hold this girl's hand, you do on your own.'

'Of course,' Caroline said with a calm she did not feel. 'And I'll be prudent. As I told the President, this nomination means more to me than I can easily express. As does his confidence.' She paused. 'And yours.'

'I know it does.' As if ready to hang up now, Farris tried to sound reassuring. 'And this isn't a big story yet. All we want is that it not become one.' He paused for emphasis. 'All right?'

In the silence of her room, Caroline nodded. 'All right.'

For a half hour, Caroline lay on the bed and thought.

A faint morning sun came through her window. The town beneath it, familiar from childhood, seemed more alien than yesterday. Yet when she picked up the phone again, it somehow felt inevitable.

'Jackson Watts,' he answered crisply.

'It's Caroline,' she said without preface. 'You didn't happen to tell the *Patriot-Ledger* that I came to see you, did you?'

'No, I didn't. But then that's easy for me. My rule is not to talk to the press, period, unless there's some compelling reason. There isn't here.'

Though his tone was not angry, Caroline felt chastised. 'Sorry,' she said.

'That's all right.' A moment's pause. 'Is that why you called?'

'Not exactly –'

'Because I've been wanting to talk to you.'

It was Caroline's turn for surprise. 'About Brett?'

'No.' His voice was low, almost reluctant. 'About everything *but* Brett.'

Caroline sat back on the bed, stretching her legs in front of her. Softly, she asked, 'Is that wise?'

'I don't plan to violate any code of ethics, if that's what you mean.' Another pause. 'When you left my office, Caroline, it felt incomplete. You were suddenly here, and then gone. With little said that wasn't about Brett.' His voice changed. 'To be reminded of you like that, and be no wiser for it ...'

Caroline touched her eyes. Then she said, 'When. And where?'

'Is that a yes?'

'It's a yes.'

'I'll be driving up to my fishing camp tonight. I'm staying for the weekend.' He sounded relieved, almost boyish. 'So, tomorrow? Maybe I'll take you fishing.'

'Fine.' Caroline hesitated, then added, 'There *was* something else, Jackson.'

'What?'

'The crime scene. I'd like to see it. Today, if possible.' Her voice was soft. 'After all, my father owns it.'

Before going to the lake, Caroline made one more phone call.

It was early afternoon when she reached the trailhead. A state trooper was parked there, and the yellow tape across it had already been cut.

'He's here,' the trooper told her. 'By the lake.'

Caroline drove to the end of the trail and parked by his truck.

She sat in her car, looking around her. Then got out and, facing the dense stand of pines that blocked all sign of Heron Lake, took in the dense pungency of wood, needles, decaying leaves.

The smell, Caroline realized, was implanted in her senses. She could not remember being here since the last spring night with Jackson, twenty-three years ago. Her father had bought this land for her; she was to build a cabin, perhaps a home, own a piece of her past forever. She had left that past behind; because of this, in the unfathomable chain of consequence, Brett Allen had brought her lover here, to die.

Slowly, Caroline stepped into the woods.

Dense trees blocked the sun, filtering sunlight as though in a cathedral. Still it was not hard to find the path of Brett's flight – a random zigzag, marked by strips of yellow tape on branches. Caroline took one in her fingers, saw on a leaf the faint streak of purple. It was blood, she was certain, left as Brett ran from the body of James Case.

The woods felt close and cold. Caroline walked more quickly now. Near the edge of the trees the shafts of sunlight broadened, blue swatches of water appeared among the leaves. She took one deep breath.

Emerging from the woods, Caroline saw him.

He stood by the water, gazing across a mile of lake toward the fishing camp his own father had built in the thirties. He was quite still; what struck Caroline most was how erect he held himself.

She stopped at the edge of the glade. Coolly, she said, 'Hello, Father.'

He turned to her. Without waiting for his answer, she knelt.

For a strange moment, thinking of Jackson and their first inhibited loving, she recalled the stray guilt-stricken thought – haunting and irrational – that her father might watch them. And then she focused on her task.

The grass seemed matted, Caroline saw. From this she could guess the location of their lovemaking and, perhaps, the body. But it had rained since the night of the murder, and there was no way to be certain.

She felt her father standing over her. 'Well?' he asked.

'Jackson's quite impressive.' She looked up from the grass into his penetrating black eyes. 'He claims there's no sign that anyone else was here.'

Channing's eyes narrowed. 'No trail of blood?'

'None. Except for Brett's.'

Stiffly, he knelt across from Caroline, staring down at the grass. 'Of course, they're assuming that *he* was soaked in blood.'

'"He"?'

'The murderer.' Channing reached out one hand, as if cradling an imaginary head. 'Suppose he knelt at the top of Case's head and then –'

With silent efficiency, Channing drew his free hand slowly across the grass, holding an invisible knife, to cut the throat that was no longer there.

'That's it,' he said softly. 'He was here. The spurt of blood never touched him.'

Caroline felt a chill. Quietly, she said, 'Jackson also suggests there were no leaves trampled, no other path of escape.'

'Why would there be? Does Brett claim to have heard anything?'

'She didn't mention it.'

'All right.' Channing's voice was brusque, impatient. 'Then he didn't leave through the woods.'

He rose, unsteady for a moment, grimacing with distaste for his old age. Curtly, he motioned for Caroline to follow.

Single file, they walked to the edge of the lake, silent. Except when it concerned Brett, Caroline realized, they would say nothing.

He stopped, staring down at a patch of silt in front of him. 'This is what I was looking at.'

At his feet were boot prints; near them two sets of shoe prints – different sizes, more widely spaced. 'The shoe prints are the police, I would guess, running to the water to look for a killer.' His voice was quiet. 'The boot print might be the killer. Slipping into the water long before.'

Still Caroline did not look at him. 'Moving along the shore?'

'Yes. Or even to a canoe.'

It jolted Caroline from an imagined world, where she

almost believed his story, to the reality where she felt grounded. 'A canoe? Impossible.'

Channing frowned. 'We used to canoe from the fishing camp to here.' He pointed to the diving platform, his voice rough. 'We had picnics there, remember?'

There was a wound beneath the words, Caroline knew. Softly, she said, 'I remember perfectly. And if someone else had canoed past us, we would have seen and heard him. As Brett would have.'

'Would she? Intoxicated? And at night?'

Caroline shook her head. 'I'm sorry, Father. But this makes no sense – a premeditated murder, by a man who paddles silently through the water, confident that a drowsy victim will offer up his throat while his girlfriend goes for a swim. Please don't ask me to sell that to anyone.'

He fell silent. Caroline turned from him, gazing along the shoreline as it curled away from them. 'No, I like the escape route along the water somewhat better – if only because we don't need to show Jackson any footprints. But how did he get here?'

Grudgingly, her father faced her. 'The same way he left, Caroline. Or are you only interested in quarreling with me.'

It stung her. 'That,' she said, 'is stupefyingly egocentric. What I'm trying to do is find a defense for Brett. Preferably one that works.'

Channing's eyes glinted. 'Then *do* try,' he snapped.

Caroline looked at him steadily. 'That's why I asked you here,' she said, and turned from him to face the woods.

After a moment, she walked toward a patch of dirt near the shore, separated from the glade by a thin line of trees and brush. Reaching the spot, she stopped; even after the rain, the mud was packed hard. She felt her father behind her.

'In theory,' she said, ' "he" could have waited here – no branches to break, perhaps too hard for footprints. At least it's something one could use to cross-examine their crime lab people.'

He was silent for a time. 'Then you're back to that, are

you? The defense lawyer, trying to fabricate a plausible story for a guilty client.'

'Back? I was never there, except perhaps in your own mind.' She lowered her voice. 'It seems quite plain to everyone but you that I shouldn't handle Brett's case, if there is one. Including, interestingly, my friends in the White House.'

'What do you mean?'

Hands thrust in her pockets, Caroline gazed at the lake. In its glassy mirror, clouds skimmed through lapping wavelets, stirred by wind on the surface of the water.

'The White House counsel called today,' she said at last. 'They'd read a story in the *Patriot-Ledger*.'

'Yes.' His tone was indifferent now. 'I saw it.'

'The point is that someone told this reporter about my visit to Jackson.' She paused. 'It's become a problem for me, Father. That is, if I care to ever become a federal judge.'

Channing folded his arms. '*I* had some ambitions once. At least the State Supreme Court, perhaps more. But after your mother died, I forgot them. Because of you.'

Caroline heard him. Softly, she asked, 'Because of me? Or her?'

Channing seemed to blanch. With equal softness, he inquired, 'What do *you* think, Caroline?'

She turned from the look on his face. 'In either case,' she said coldly, 'this is hardly the same thing.'

Channing stared at her now. 'Isn't it?'

'Not to me. I can't stand more publicity.'

'Really.' His voice held faint contempt.

She faced him again. Narrow-eyed, he gazed across the water, as if impervious to her concern.

You *told them*, she realized, *to make me choose*. She stood there, caught between doubt and accusation.

Quietly, he said, 'What is it?'

Caroline paused, irresolute. But when she decided to speak, the question that came to her was different. 'Do you remember the knife I gave you?'

His face froze. 'What of it?'

'It's not where you kept it.'

His eyes widened and then went cold; in that moment, Caroline knew that he understood the question perfectly. But when he spoke, his voice was soft again.

'There was a time, before I grew used to things, when anything associated with you was painful. A reminder of whatever hope I'd had.' His tone became indifferent. 'I gave that knife away, Caroline. Years ago.'

Caroline hesitated. 'Do you remember to whom?'

'No. But then that wasn't the point.' His face grew hard. 'Are we through here, Caroline?'

Without waiting for her answer, Channing Masters turned and walked back to his truck.

Caroline spent the afternoon alone.

Most of this was stalling, she knew – calling the office, checking her mail, returning messages from friends and clients congratulating her on the nomination. To Caroline's ears, her own gratitude sounded oddly hollow, lines recited by an actress in a play. As if to reassure herself, she told her secretary that she planned to return in four days' time.

Even as she said this, she could not take her mind off Brett.

Her purse was on the bedstand. Putting down the telephone, she reached for it.

Inside was the slip of paper with the serial numbers.

She took it out. A ten-minute hunt through long distance gave her the number for the Cahill Knife Company. Another five minutes, and she was talking to the clerk who might be able to help her.

The woman sounded faintly annoyed. 'What was that serial number?'

Slowly, Caroline repeated it.

There was silence. For some reason, perhaps her assessment of Jackson Watts, Caroline had the sense that she was not the first to call. In a cautious voice, the clerk inquired, 'What is it that you want, exactly?'

'To see if you can trace the knife. At least to the point of sale.'

'And this is for what?'

Caroline hesitated, suddenly tense. 'I'm a lawyer,' she said slowly. 'This knife may end up being evidence. In a criminal case.'

'And what is your name?'

Another pause. 'Masters. Caroline Masters.'

'Uh-huh.' More silence. 'Well, I don't know about tracking down the point of sale ...'

'Can you at least try?' To Caroline, her voice sounded oddly pleading. 'Even the year of manufacture might help me.'

'Tell you what. Give me two or three days, and call back. I may have something then.' The clerk paused, as if regretting this. 'Tell me, how would the year help?'

'It's a confidential matter, really. But the year could tell me a lot. Please, it's important.'

The clerk paused. 'Oh, all right,' she said.

Politely, Caroline thanked her, and hung up.

Chapter 9

Caroline and Jackson Watts cruised slowly toward the middle of Heron Lake. Behind the black rubber dinghy, built like a landing craft, the outboard motor made a scudding sound as it beat them through the water. The sky was startlingly blue; sunlight glistened like mica on the shimmering lake. It was a day from Caroline's youth.

They had said little. Jackson had come for her in a green pickup truck with fly rods thrown in the back. They drove to his fishing camp, its spare 1930s rectangle somewhat like her father's own, with a neat and compact kitchen and a view of the lake through trees. He showed her about somewhat awkwardly; Caroline saw a German shepherd sleeping by the stone fireplace and, on the mantel, a framed photograph of a pretty brown-haired girl, perhaps thirteen or so. And then, in a reprise of their past, they had taken the wooden stairs down the hillside to the dinghy, put the two fly rods in, and started up the boat. It was what they once had done when they wished to be with each other and yet feel no pressure to talk until they cared to. There was no one else on the lake.

With a lazy, expert flick of his wrist, Jackson cast a line into the water. Caroline leaned back, arms draped over the sides of the dinghy, taking in the day. Pines and birch and maple trees rose from the shoreline and up steep hillsides, creating the sense of a cocoon around them. The place where James Case had died was too far away to see; Caroline sensed that Jackson would not go near it. The air was cool and still.

Jackson cut the throttle. The dinghy barely moved now; his line floated lazily in the water.

'So you went there,' he said finally.

Caroline gazed at the sky. 'The "crime scene," as it were? Yes. I found the whole thing very strange.'

Jackson nodded. 'So did I.'

They fell quiet again.

He had been so sweet then, Caroline thought. Too eager, of course, but considerate of her; he could not help that it was his first time, any more than Caroline could help that it was hers. Or that, when desire and fulfillment finally met for her, it was not with Jackson Watts.

She watched his face now, two decades later: the crinkles at the corners of his eyes as he watched his line; the hollows beneath the cheekbones, deeper now. Remembering his old smile, quizzical and crooked, Caroline realized that she had yet to see it.

'That letter,' she finally said.

His face seemed to tighten. 'Yes?'

'I've always felt sorry about it.' Her voice was tentative. 'Seeing you, I'm more sorry than ever.'

He looked at her now. 'Why is that?'

'Because I remember how fond of you I was.'

Jackson's eyes narrowed in thought, perhaps in remembered pain. 'I didn't know what to do with it: "Don't call, don't write, don't try to see me – I'm never coming back." I felt helpless.' He shrugged. 'Helpless, and inadequate.'

He spoke the words without emphasis or inflection. But Caroline felt how badly she had hurt him.

She shook her head. 'What's so hard for me to explain is that it wasn't about you – which, I know, only makes it worse. Because *how* I did it wasn't kind. But I wasn't a kind person then. Or, perhaps, now.'

Jackson turned to her with questioning eyes. 'All that you said then was that it was necessary. As if, somehow, you had no choice but to do everything the way you did.' He paused, and said in a lower voice, 'All these years, I've wondered what it could possibly have been. You didn't just leave *me* – you left a place, a family, a life you had all planned out for yourself.'

'Which is why you can believe me, Jackson. It wasn't about you.'

He turned from her, gazing at the bright surface of the water. 'You know,' he said quietly, 'I finally asked your father why. When I couldn't stand not knowing anymore.'

Caroline felt a tightness in her chest. 'And what did he say?'

'That you had your reasons, and that they were your own. And that, in his own mind, there was nothing he could do to ever get you back. It was as if I only reminded him of someone he wanted to forget. After that, I rarely saw him.' He faced her again, voice quiet. 'What happened to change you, Caroline?'

Caroline gave a deprecating smile. 'Please, I don't want to be one of the self-regarding, self-referential singles to whom every tremor of their youth is worthy of a coming-of-age novel. That would be an embarrassment worse than shame.'

Jackson did not smile. Simply studied her for a time and then said softly, 'You didn't ask for this conversation, Caroline. I did.'

Caroline's eyes were grave now. 'If talking about my family made any sense, Jackson, I would. But it doesn't. You'll just have to believe me and, I hope, accept my apology. If it's not too late for that.'

Jackson seemed to consider her. 'No,' he said at last. 'It's not too late.'

In the silence, they looked at each other across the dinghy. 'I think I'll toss out a line,' Caroline said.

They fished together. To Caroline, the moments had a timeless quality, a ritual shared with a friend, that one could slip into within moments after years apart.

'So you want a judgeship,' she said finally.

'Uh-huh.' He paused. 'Trying cases is a young man's game, I'm beginning to think. And I believe – hope – that I have the right temperament to run a trial.' He smiled briefly. 'Not like you, of course.'

Caroline raised an eyebrow. 'Showy, you mean?'

He gave her a first half grin, the one she remembered. 'I was thinking of your admirable fairness. And, of course, your erudition. As so admirably displayed on Court TV.' He looked at her sideways. 'Remember when you decided to be a judge? Tall ambitions for a woman, then. Not to mention for a teenager.'

'Yes,' she said dryly. 'I was much too sure of everything. Including my absolute entitlement to what I wanted.'

'Living on Masters Hill,' he replied with equal dryness, 'would tend to give you that opinion.'

Silent, they shared a moment's remembered amusement, a joke of years past. The son of the Congregationalist minister in Connaughton Falls, Jackson had never had much money; while Caroline went to Dana Hall, Jackson attended the local high school, grinding out the grades to get a scholarship to Williams. So that, on Caroline's return each summer, Jackson would gravely inquire about life among the upper classes. But even as a manager, Jackson seemed remarkably free of envy or rancor – between them, it had been an affectionate game.

'I always wondered,' he said after a time, 'how much of your ambition for a judgeship came from Channing.'

'Then? Perhaps a lot. But a long time ago it became my own ambition. So that I no longer know or care.'

He fluttered his line on the water, hoping to attract some imagined trout. 'It means a great deal to you, then.'

Caroline stared into the distance. 'More than I can tell you,' she said finally. 'So much that even talking about it scares me. Like I'm going to lose it.'

His face was solemn now. 'This thing with Brett. You're serious about not handling it.'

Caroline felt the warmth slip from her. 'Yes,' she answered. 'I'm serious about not handling it.'

Quiet, Caroline gazed at him. After a time, she said, 'You'd be a fine judge, Jackson. You were always fair. And, it's clear, still are.'

Jackson seemed to examine his reel. In that moment,

Caroline felt the absence of a woman in his life; then was embarrassed by how little she now knew about him, how little she had asked. Especially when Jackson, in some ways, had continued to care for her.

'Tell me about your marriage,' she said.

Jackson reeled some line. 'Just like that?'

Caroline smiled. 'Not unless you've thought about it. Though I figure you have by now.'

'Well, I've worked on my rationalizations, at least.' He leaned back against the side of the dinghy. 'Carole is one of those people who light up a party – she has a great smile, a ready laugh, and new places and people are a tonic to her. At first, I was charmed: later, I came to believe it was less an attribute than a symptom.'

'How do you mean?'

'My version of Carole – polished through many trips to a counselor – is that she's a discontented woman: anything in the future will always be better, because in the present there's always something wrong.' He turned to her. 'Do you remember saying something like that about your mother?'

Caroline felt a short, painful memory. 'I believed that as a teenager. I'm not sure that I do anymore.' She forced a wry note into her voice. 'But on the subject of your ex-wife, Jackson, you're a qualified adult.'

He shrugged. 'In any event, we were different. My life pleased me; she thought I was having all the fun. So she decided to go to law school. But once I figured out how to scrape together the money – this was early in our marriage – she decided she despised lawyers. Which I suppose I took somewhat personally.' He half sighed. 'As it turned out, perhaps I shouldn't have. Carole was just like that – charming her way into a job, finding it dreary, finding another, then quitting that one. Which, I'm afraid, became my fault.

'The weekends were like something from Despair Comics – Carole lolling in bed, and then in her robe till noon, completely affectless. Until we went to some party, and she'd light up like a bulb. The more she smiled at strangers, the more I smoldered in silent anger at what a fraud she was. Which I was too afraid to even say. Because, like so many lawyers when they're not in court, I loathe conflict. At least the kind of conflict where you don't have any rules.' He paused, finishing quietly: 'She also had a memorably violent temper. I never learned the rules for *that*.'

'What happened?'

Jackson was silent for a time. 'In a way, it was such a joke,' he said at last. 'Like something from *The New Yorker*. I had food poisoning after lunch one day, came home unexpectedly, and found her in bed with her personal trainer. It was absolutely classic Carole, right on the cutting edge – I mean, she was far too trendy to screw the guy next door, or even her therapist.' His voice filled with remembered astonishment. 'And do you know what I thought? That I hadn't seen her on top like that for years ...'

Caroline began laughing. 'I'm sorry,' she managed. 'I mean, why not the gardener ...?'

'Because we couldn't afford one, what with paying for the trainer. Anyhow, that's when I knew I lacked the energy to try and save the marriage – there was no goodwill left in me.' His brief smile did not quite reach his eyes. 'So what I was left with was a good story. Which, before today, I've never told to a soul.'

Caroline considered him, unsmiling now. 'I suppose it felt like a somewhat hollow joke.'

'"Hollow" is a good word. I felt empty – that I had loved her enough to marry her, and then felt nothing. Not even enough to try for our daughter's sake.'

Caroline fell quiet.

'Do you know what bothers me now?' Jackson said at last. 'Remembering how caught up I was in my own career. That maybe I was so careless that I got Carole – our marriage – all wrong. That at the beginning, when it still mattered, I could have done something. And that *I* was the greatest cause of her unhappiness.'

Caroline considered him for a time. 'I wasn't there, Jackson. But I would guess not.'

Jackson shrugged. 'Well,' he said, 'it's done.'

Caroline held her rod in one hand, facing him. 'How old was your daughter?'

'Eight. Not a good age.' Hand on the tiller, he looped the dinghy in a lazy circle, to keep it away from shore. 'She's sixteen now. Which, for us, also seems like not such a good age.'

'How so?'

He turned to her. 'Really, Caroline, how many bad dinners with divorced men have you suffered through? Listening to these stories about children you don't know and, after you've heard them, don't care to know.'

Caroline smiled. 'Not nearly enough.'

'I'll keep the story brief, then – it's hardly original, so that won't be hard. Carole made Jenny her little confidante, a surrogate adult. I wasn't a strong enough – perhaps a frequent enough – presence to overcome that.' He shrugged. 'Our relationship is more amiable now. But she *is* sixteen – her priorities are school, friends, boyfriend, and, of necessity, dealing with her mother. Which leaves Dad somewhere down the list, understandably enough.' He smiled a little. 'Aren't you glad you asked?'

'Yes, actually.' Caroline paused. 'I've always wondered what I missed, not having children. I suppose it depends on the circumstances.'

His smile was more genuine. 'It depends on the day. Even so, I wouldn't do without her.'

Why? Caroline wondered. For a moment, despite everything, she envied Jackson this feeling. It was not a thought she could express.

They lapsed into silence. Caroline reeled her line in, flicked it again. The instinctive ease of things surprised her. The quiet between them felt deeper, sadder, surer.

There was a sudden jerk on the line.

'Jesus,' Caroline said. 'A fish.'

As the line pulled away, Jackson turned to her, grinning.

'That was the idea, wasn't it? Do you remember what to do?'

'Of course,' she snapped, and jerked the rod to one side, holding the reel tight. From the side, Jackson watched with amused interest.

Whatever the fish was, Caroline realized, it was strong. She remembered the pitfalls – breaking the line, letting her quarry slip the hook – and as the pole bent with the struggle of the unseen fish, she took in the slack, wondering whether it was bass or trout. 'Gently,' Jackson murmured.

The line drew closer, shortened in the water. And then the fighting fish broke the surface of the lake. Its colors glistened in the sun.

Caroline grinned. 'A trout.'

Jackson cut off the motor. The pole bent to the water, Caroline leaning back. A second leap, then a third, as Caroline worked the reel, quickly now.

A sudden jerk of the pole, and then the trout lay at her feet, wide-eyed, sides puffing and trembling with the shock of his defeat, the terrible absence of water.

'A beauty,' Jackson said.

Caroline gazed down at the trout. And then, with still expert fingers, she carefully removed the hook.

For a moment, she held the writhing trout in both hands. And then she half stood, tossing him above the water – a glistening flash of rainbow, silver, and then he disappeared.

Together, they watched the ripples spread across the water.

'I'm glad we came,' she said.

Jackson smiled a little. After a moment, he asked, 'Care for dinner? At the Trout Club, of course. In honor of your humanitarian gesture.'

Caroline was quiet for a time. 'Yes,' she answered. 'I would.'

Chapter 10

The Trout Club was a rambling one-story structure from the late nineteenth century, with canoes and kayaks on its beachfront, Adirondack chairs on the lawn, which faced the lake, and behind that, a screened porch with more chairs, lounges, and tables for cocktails and snacks. Caroline's great-grandfather had put up money to help build it: his picture, complete with fierce eyes and a bristling mustache, was on the wall in the front room. Surrounding him were old bamboo fishing rods and photos of long-forgotten members, many of which celebrated the ancient bond between man and fish – triumphant men and the occasional woman from another era, holding aloft a bass or trout or salmon, some of extraordinary size. Caroline had come here since childhood: in her teens she had once remarked, to her father's amusement, that to be on the wall the people had to be as dead as the fish were. Smiling, he had said that he hoped never to see his picture there. 'Don't worry,' Caroline had answered, 'you won't.'

She stood in the lobby, quiet now.

'It hasn't changed,' she said at last.

Jackson smiled. 'This is New England. Reverse ostentation is a way of life.'

It was true, of course. It took a kind of genius, Caroline thought, for a place always to seem as if it needed paint.

'Do you want to savor the ambience,' Jackson asked, 'or would you like a drink outside?'

'Outside, thanks. What are my choices?'

'Scotch. And Scotch.'

Caroline smiled. There was no bar; members kept liquor in their private lockers, beer and white wine in a giant refrigerator by the kitchen, maintained on the honor system. There was an ice machine on the porch.

'I'll take Scotch,' Caroline said, and picked a canvas chair on the lawn.

Jackson tossed his windbreaker across the back of the chair next to hers, rolled up the sleeves of his cotton work shirt, and went to fetch them drinks.

He came back moments later, with an ice bucket, two dishwasher-scarred milk glasses, and a bottle of Glenlivet. 'Good Scotch,' Caroline said.

When he filled her glass, she did not complain.

They sat there, quiet again. Caroline took her first sip, felt the whisky glow inside her. Took another, gazing across the lawn at the kayaks and canoes, the lake as it turned gray blue with the sun of an early summer evening.

'Amazing,' she said.

'What is?'

'To be here at all.'

He turned to her, as if trying to decipher her tone of voice. 'Does it seem that strange?'

'Yes. It does.' Caroline paused. 'I spent a lot of energy leaving.'

Jackson was quiet awhile. 'Where do you live now?' he asked.

'I have a penthouse.' Summoning an image, Caroline found it unnervingly distant. 'On Telegraph Hill. Very modern, with glass all around and a roof garden on top. On the right day, I can see not only the bay and the city but miles beyond.'

Jackson seemed to imagine this. 'Not much like New Hampshire.'

'Not at all.' She drained her Scotch. 'Have you ever been to San Francisco?'

'Once, with Carole. It seemed quite beautiful.'

'It is, isn't it.' She tried to picture him there, at the opera or a dinner party or eating calamari in the glittering restaurant of the moment; the clearest vision she could manage was of a practical man, looking about him with interest and a certain wry detachment. Somehow New Hampshire seemed very much a part of him.

Thoughtful, Caroline gazed across the lawn.

On the lake, a lone man in a kayak made for shore, stopped paddling, let the kayak drift until it slid onto the rocky beach. He pulled the kayak another few feet and then made purposefully for the club. He was in his sixties, spare, with a white fringe of hair and, Caroline noticed as he approached, bright-blue eyes behind rimless glasses. Seeing Jackson, he smiled and came over.

'Hello, Hugh,' Jackson began amiably, and then, as if interrupting himself on the way to introducing Caroline, stopped.

But the man had turned to her. 'Hello,' he said in a puzzled voice, and then smiled, still hesitant. 'Pardon me, but aren't you Caroline? Channing's daughter?'

Caroline summoned her own smile. 'That's right.'

He extended his hand. 'Hugh Askew. President of the Connaughton County Bank – I've done business with Channing for years.' He paused. 'Sorry for the once-over; except for TV, I'm not sure I'd have known you. I don't think you've been here for a while.'

'No. Not for a while.'

His smile faded. It struck Caroline that he must know – at least suspect – her business here but was too polite to mention it. Even more so in the presence of Jackson Watts.

'Well,' he said in a subdued voice. 'Welcome back. I'm sure your dad is very proud of you.'

'Thank you.'

Briefly, the man nodded to Jackson and went on his way, leaving Caroline self-conscious, her sense of ease diminished.

'Maybe we shouldn't be here,' she said quietly.

Jackson gave her a look of concern, then shrugged. 'These are not judgmental people, Caroline. And you and I have known each other for years.'

She turned to him. 'How has it been for you, living here?'

He seemed to contemplate the question. 'It's the world I know. Perhaps this says something about me, but it always seemed sufficient. Still does.' He sipped his drink. 'If I consume enough Scotch, I can probably spin a piece of philosophy that's downright Jeffersonian – that this is the last laboratory of civility, where people are both decent and restrained, where villages run their own affairs and where even politicians can exist without having to lie too much.' He smiled again. 'But I really *do* need to have been drinking....'

'And where does the *Patriot-Ledger* fit into that theory?'

'Oh, for that I have to drink a lot.' His smile faded. 'Are we leaving, then? Really, whatever feels comfortable.'

What did she want? Caroline wondered. And then realized that Jackson, and then perhaps the Scotch, had dulled her cares for a time.

'Let's stay awhile,' she said, and poured them both more whisky.

They ate dinner on the porch. Jackson found a candle, produced a chill bottle of Chardonnay from the refrigerator, and shuttled two warm meals from the kitchen.

'Trout,' he said. 'The balance of nature continues.'

Caroline smiled, finished her third Scotch, and gazed out across the lake.

Dusk was falling; the last light turned to smoke above the sudden blackness of the water. There was the first sound of crickets; against her will, Caroline imagined that night as Brett described it, wondered again how much of it was true. She wanted to ask Jackson about drug dealers, then – for reasons of both tact and tactics – quelled the impulse: if they came up with nothing, it would make the drug-dealer defense less credible. Far better for Brett's lawyer to chastise some detective on the witness stand for his failure to inquire.

'Penny for your thoughts,' Jackson said.

'Why?'

'Because you had that sort of veiled, intent look you used to get when we'd argue politics, just before you stuck some rhetorical point in my figurative ear.'

Caroline smiled again. 'I was thinking of sticking my fork in the literal trout,' she answered, and did so.

It was fresh, sautéed in butter – perfect with a little lemon. 'This is great,' she said. 'I haven't had fresh trout in ages.'

Jackson poured some wine. Sipping it, oaky on her tongue, Caroline realized that she had well exceeded her self-imposed limit on alcohol. Part of her was troubled by this; the other part was surprised by how good it felt.

'When I asked where you lived,' Jackson said, 'part of it was whether anyone lives with you.'

Caroline shook her head. 'Not even a trout.'

In a cautious tone, Jackson said, 'I read somewhere, I think, that you were never married....'

Caroline gave him a sideways look. As if caught at something, he looked away, and suddenly she began to laugh. 'Why don't you just ask me if I'm still straight, Jackson?'

He gave her an astonished look and then put his forehead in his hands and shook his head, like someone detected in the middle of an unpardonable social lapse. 'I mean, I did consider all sorts of things. If you could turn your back on me ...'

Caroline grinned. 'You mean, did I go to Martha's Vineyard one summer and become a lesbian?'

He held up his hand. 'Please, I surrender. Help me out of this.'

Caroline smiled. 'Whether gay or straight, single women without obvious attachments get used to it. Although usually from total clods. I'm reminded of Martina Navratilova's great line when some idiot sportswriter asked if she was "still gay": "Are you still the alternative?"'

Jackson gave her a sheepish grin. 'Sorry. Anyhow, it was only a passing thought, like rabies or Oliver North.' His look became curious. 'You do sound quite determinedly "single," Caroline.'

She sipped more wine, considering her answer. It had long been her practice, bordering on superstition, not to say too much about the things she held private. Now, for a night, that felt lonely. She looked across the table at the kind face of Jackson Watts, a friend – with whatever fragility and for however long – reclaimed. So that, in this way at least, one part of her past might still feel warm in the present.

' "Determinedly"?' Her voice was soft now. 'I think perhaps what starts as self-protection, for whatever reason, in the end becomes a habit. So that even if you think you want to do better, you find that your emotional equipment is rusted out. That you're no longer used to intimacy, have no gift for the small compromise.' She shrugged. 'Perhaps no longer care …'

He looked at her gravely. 'What do you do, then? Just live alone?'

Perhaps, Caroline thought, it was the wine, the comfort of darkness. Perhaps it was the need to tell him the truth about something. To hope that he would not judge her.

She studied her wineglass. 'What I do, Jackson, is a series of small affairs. Sometimes on vacation, just for a night – the longer term seems always to founder on career or children or whatever.' Her voice became ironic. 'Lately, I seem to have developed a penchant for the long-term married. A couple of them have been good company, and there's no chance they'll become part of my life. Or even, if they're sensible, want to.'

It made him quiet. She gazed at the lake, a swath of black beneath a moonlit ridge, then saw him fill her glass and his.

'Well,' he said thoughtfully, 'we all make do.'

When she looked at him, his face was serious but not unkind. He held up his glass and touched it to hers. 'To you, Caroline.'

She settled back into her chair. Quiet together, they finished their dinner, then the bottle.

When they left, the night was cool and still.

They got into the dinghy, and Jackson started the motor; its low thrum as they crossed was the only sound on the darkened lake.

Caroline sat back, feeling the night air on her face. The glow of wine was receding a little, her sense of time returning; whatever respite she had enjoyed was coming to its end. She watched Jackson pilot them across the water, searching keen-eyed for his camp.

'There,' he said.

A moment later, they cruised up to his dock. Jackson jumped out; Caroline tossed him the line, and he hitched it to a spile. Reaching out, he took her hand as she stepped onto the dock.

To her surprise, he did not let go. He looked down at their hands, as if surprised himself, and then let her fingers slip away.

He stuck both his hands in his pockets. 'Can I get you something before you leave? Coffee, brandy …'

After a moment, Caroline nodded. 'Brandy.'

'Good.' Jackson turned and climbed the stairs up the hillside, Caroline coming after him. A wind stirred the trees, and there was the deep aroma of pine; Caroline remembered sleeping at her father's camp, the comforting sense of woods around her. The stars, she saw, were bright.

They entered the cabin. He went to the fireplace, threw in wood, knelt, spread tinder, and then struck a match. The fire leapt to life. Caroline stood in the kitchen, quiet, watching the first tongues of blue and orange as they rose from the burning log.

Jackson stood, turning to Caroline. 'I'll get that brandy now.'

He walked through the kitchen without looking at her, opened a cabinet, and reached for two snifters and a bottle of cognac. Carefully, head bent, he poured a measure in both glasses.

Turning, he passed one to Caroline, raised his own glass. 'To what, this time?'

Caroline cupped the snifter in both hands. 'I don't know, really.' She paused for a moment. 'I just didn't want to leave without saying something. Like "thank you."'

'For what?'

'For forgiving me, a little. For making me feel like you were still a friend.'

He gave her a funny look, vulnerable and surprised. Almost under his breath, he said, 'Jesus, Caroline ...'

Her chest tightened. As if without thinking, she went to him, took the brandy from his hand, and put it with hers on the counter.

She turned to him again, hesitant.

'What is it?' he asked.

Caroline took his face in her hands, looking up into his eyes. Her blouse grazed his chest.

Jackson gazed down at her, as if to make certain that he understood. Softly, he said, 'I think I remember ...'

She was still smiling as he kissed her.

His mouth was warm, somehow familiar. She closed her eyes, leaned against him for a while. Silent, gentle, he held her, kissing her hair.

How do we do this? she wondered. Her nerve ends tingled.

Jackson leaned back now. When she looked up at him, his head tilted in inquiry.

Quiet, Caroline nodded.

Slowly, he unbuttoned the top of her blouse.

She looked at him steadily, eyes not moving from his face. When he had finished, she reached behind her, and then her bra fell to the floor.

The rest of it she did herself.

'You're beautiful,' he said. 'Still.'

Smiling a little, she began to undo his shirt.

His body still. Still lean, not quite as taut, but still his. When their skin met, it felt warm to her.

He led her to the fire.

There was a couch there. Still holding her hand, Jackson angled his head toward the couch, inquiring. Caroline shrugged.

They lay together, finding their place.

Jackson kissed her forehead. 'I don't have anything,' he murmured. 'But I'm all right.'

'Me too.'

Gently, his mouth moved to the hollow of her neck. She slipped beneath him.

He was still careful now, but knowing. Knowing in the touch of his mouth, his hands, his fingertips. Caroline felt her hips move without her thinking. She grasped his neck, suddenly hungry for him, pressing her mouth to his.

When he entered her, it was different.

Caroline thrust against him. They had never had this, then; the warm, confident leisure, the sureness that all would be well. She lost track of anything but the warmth of his body, hers, the slow insistent surge as he moved inside her, she moving with him – quickly now. More quickly …

She called his name, and then she exploded with the feel of him.

Fingertips numb, the world dark and close, she clung to him as he came inside her.

Afterward, she lay beside him, not wanting or needing speech. Watching the dance of shadows from the fire.

The seniors league, she thought fondly; what we lose to youth, we make up in grace and comfort. At least so it seemed with Jackson.

Still quiet, she gave him a kiss of tenderness and approval.

He smiled at her. 'Better?'

'Better.' She kissed him again. 'Good old Carole.'

It made him laugh. The next time they made love, an hour later, Caroline was on top.

In the morning, she woke in his bed. Her temples throbbed with Scotch and wine.

'Hello,' he said.

'Hi.'

He propped his head on his elbow, as if gauging her mood. 'Are you okay?' he asked after a time. 'I didn't turn into a pumpkin, did I?'

She did not smile. 'No. Not at all.'

He raised an eyebrow. *Talk if you want*, his expression said, *but I won't push you.*

Suddenly, Caroline disliked herself intensely. 'Last night,' she said, 'I was selfish – I liked being with you, and I didn't want it to end. But in the clear light of morning, I'm Brett's semi-lawyer. Who's compounded her ethical confusion by fucking the prosecutor.'

His eyes were serious. 'Think of me as an ex-boyfriend, Caroline. If that helps.'

For Caroline, the reality of Brett had filled the room. 'I wish it did.'

'Whether or not you represent her?'

Caroline touched her eyes. 'I don't know, Jackson. Please, I have to think this all through.' She stopped. 'That is not, by the way, a reference to Brett's guilt or innocence. But that I even have to tell you that illustrates the problem.'

He was quiet now. Caroline sat on the edge of the bed. 'Really,' she said quietly. 'I think I'd better get back.'

'All right.'

They dressed in silence.

'Ready?' he asked, and walked briskly to the door.

She stopped him there, a touch on the elbow. He turned to her.

Caroline tried to smile. 'What I thought,' she said, 'is that I'd kiss you goodbye. Here, where no one's watching.'

He paused, looking seriously into her eyes.

Slowly and firmly, Caroline kissed him. 'I really wish,' she said, 'that you weren't the prosecutor.'

He smiled a little. 'I really wish,' he answered, 'that you had a different niece.'

They walked to his truck together.

For the ten minutes to town, they talked about small things. What he would do today. How Resolve had changed. Anything but Brett.

When they stopped in front of the inn, Jackson did not get out.

He leaned on the steering wheel. 'I'd like to see you again,' he said. 'Before you leave.'

Caroline touched his hand. 'We'll talk, at least.'

Slowly, he nodded.

Caroline made herself get out. She was through the door of the inn before his truck disappeared from view — a lawyer again, beginning her day.

Chapter 11

But it was several hours before Caroline the lawyer resolved what to do, and another hour until she drove to Chase College, Jackson Watts still too much on her mind.

The campus was wooded, rolling, nestled in hills. A creek, spanned by a covered bridge, meandered past the spired clock tower, brick Gothic buildings, and a wide green commons surrounded by trees. But the building James Case had lived in, a two-story apartment house outside the town, was a remnant of the Eisenhower years. Even the brick was veneer.

Daniel Suarez lived on the second floor. She took the stairs, found room 203, and knocked on the door.

The boy who opened it – he could not have been more than twenty – was tall and slender, with luminous brown eyes and a sensitive, slightly brooding aspect that was somehow quite appealing.

'You're Brett's aunt?' he asked.

'That's right. She mentioned you to me.'

He waved her in. To Caroline, the cinder-block room was reminiscent of other, long-ago rooms at Harvard or Radcliffe: clothes thrown about, stacks of books and magazines, stale cooking smells from the kitchen. Even the posters – the Stones and Led Zeppelin – had not changed much.

Caroline found herself smiling faintly at a gray-haired Charlie Watts. 'Like them?' Daniel asked.

'Used to,' she said carelessly. 'Now I'm more into Sheryl Crow and REM. These days, nostalgia hurts.'

A glimmer of amusement. 'Especially for my dad. He's a real Deadhead.'

'Oh, well.' Caroline shrugged. 'Anyhow, thanks for seeing me.'

'Sure. Can I get you anything?'

'Have a Coke?'

'I think so.' He went to the kitchen, prowled through the refrigerator, and returned with a cold can of Pepsi.

'Good enough,' Caroline said.

She sat in the kitchen. Daniel took a chair across from her, his expression tentative.

'So you saw Brett here,' she said.

'Uh-huh.' He nodded toward the next apartment. 'With James next door, and her over a lot, sometimes we'd borrow things back and forth – milk, food, whatever. Two or three times we'd end up talking.'

'What was she like?'

A cautious nod, as if affirming something to himself. 'She was really nice, easy to be around, and seemed squared away. You could talk with her about pretty much anything.'

'And James?'

Daniel paused, directed a hooded look at the stained rug in front of him. 'Different,' he said at length. 'He was smart, too, and pretty talented, I think. But he seemed more into himself than she was.'

'Who were his friends?'

A moment's reflection; whether on the truth, or merely on his answer, Caroline could not tell. 'Brett, mostly.' His liquid eyes rose to meet Caroline's gaze. 'Do the cops really think she killed him?'

'I don't see how they can, in the end.' She looked at him closely. 'I gather they were here.'

His shrug was more a twitch. 'Oh, yeah.'

'What did they want to know?'

'A lot of the same things. Who James's friends were. Whether I knew Brett. What their relationship was like –'

'And whether he was dealing drugs?'

'That too.'

'And what did you tell them?'

'Not to me.'

'Did James ever try?'

'No.' He paused. 'About that stuff, I mind my own business.'

His eyes were steady. But Caroline was morally certain that a thorough search of this apartment would produce a bag of marijuana in the sock drawer, and that Daniel Suarez did not wish to say so.

Caroline simply looked at him.

He folded his arms, fidgeting as she tried to hold his gaze. 'Why does the drug stuff matter, anyhow?'

The truth, Caroline knew, might drive him further inward. But there was little choice. 'Suppose,' she asked, 'he was in trouble over drugs. Stiffed his supplier, somehow.'

Daniel seemed to consider this. 'That,' he said, 'I wouldn't know about.'

Their eyes locked. The answer was truthful, Caroline was suddenly sure, just as the tacit admission in its phrasing – that James Case was dealing – had been a deliberate signal. Briefly, she considered the notion that, for dramatic effect, James Case had lied to Brett about his vandalized apartment but not about his problem. And then she had the sudden jarring thought that she could read Daniel Suarez far more easily than she could Brett.

In Caroline's silence, Daniel leaned forward, an unspoken appeal forming in his eyes. 'If I could help Brett,' he said quietly, 'I would.'

The best tack, Caroline decided, was to shame him. In a tone of skepticism, she responded. 'Oh? And why is that?'

'Because I didn't like the way he treated her. Though I guess she figured she could deal with it.'

Caroline felt herself tensing with surprise. Casually, she said, 'What do you mean?'

Daniel looked at her hard, and then shrugged. 'Maybe Brett didn't know.'

'That he mistreated her?' Caroline stopped herself and then, almost against her will, asked, 'How could she not know?'

Daniel folded his hands. *So*, his brown gaze said, *you*

138

don't know, either. 'There was this girl from school who used to come here – blond. The only name I got was Megan.'

' "Here"?'

'To see James.'

'Probably a friend.' Caroline paused, affecting a carelessness she did not feel. 'How often did she come?'

'A few times.' Daniel's voice was soft now. 'One morning, she came to my door in James's T-shirt. To borrow milk.'

Caroline sat back. It was a moment before she asked, 'Did this girl say anything in particular?'

Daniel's face was serious. 'It was more how she was – wired, smug, a little in my face. Like she wanted someone to know that she was screwing him. Even me.'

Think, Caroline ordered herself. She paused, phrasing her next inquiry with care. 'When the police asked about Brett's relationship to James,' she said slowly, 'what was your answer?'

Their eyes met; the sense of a silent understanding, suddenly shared, ran through Caroline like a shock.

'I told them it was fine.' A first, faint smile. 'As far as I know, it was.'

Caroline was pacing her room when the telephone rang.

She snatched at it. The nasal drone of a secretary announced that the senior senator from California was calling Caroline Masters. There was a click, and then the senator came on the line.

'Caroline?' Her voice was brisk, professional. 'Your office said I could find you here. How are you?'

Caroline inhaled. 'I've been better, I'm sorry to say. We have something of a family problem.'

'That's what I understand.' A moment's pause. 'Walter Farris called today. To touch base and, I detected, in the hope that I'd underscore his concern. So here I am.'

Caroline closed her eyes. 'Thank you,' she said, although it did not sound quite apt.

'Oh, of course.' Pausing, the senator adopted a sympathetic tone. 'I'm sure that it must be terrible for you, for all of you. And that you'll want to do everything appropriate to help your niece.'

Caroline did not miss the inflection. 'I will, naturally. But there's only so much I can do.'

'I imagine that's true. Hopefully, though, this won't come to anything, and your niece will end up in the clear.' Her voice modulated to the casual. 'So when will you be able to come back?'

Caroline reflected. 'Three or four days, I think.'

'Good.' Another pause. 'After all, a number of us have worked very hard for this nomination. No one more than you.'

'Thank you,' Caroline said. 'I appreciate that.'

'Then see you soon,' the senator said, and got off.

Chapter 12

The next morning, the woman at the front desk called Caroline's room and announced that Mr. Watts was in the parlor.

It surprised her: she was not prepared for him. Distractedly, she checked her hair in the mirror, then went downstairs.

He was seated in a wingback chair. When he saw her, he stood, but he did not give her the smile she half expected. His eyes were somber.

Quietly, she asked, 'What is it?'

He glanced toward the front desk. 'Let's go outside, all right?'

They went to the porch, sat next to each other on the love seat. Except for a young boy on a bicycle, the street was deserted.

'You were supposed to be back in Concord,' she said.

Jackson gave her a sideways look of deep unhappiness. 'I should be,' he said. 'I wish I were.'

Caroline felt numb. 'Brett,' she said softly.

'You'll need to find a lawyer for her, Caroline.' He exhaled. 'We're getting an arrest warrant. As early as this afternoon.'

'For what?'

'Murder one.'

Yesterday, Caroline thought, she had awakened with him. 'Something happened,' she said.

Jackson gave a slow nod. 'A new witness contacted the state police yesterday morning. I met with her last night.'

Caroline felt a premonition. 'What did she say?'

Jackson stood, gazing out at the street. 'She claims to be James's lover. According to her, James asked her to go with him to California.'

The sentence had an incomplete sound. 'And?'

'Brett was obsessively jealous – obsessed with James, period. She watched his apartment for other women.' He paused, speaking in a monotone. 'One night, James brought this woman home. Her story is that Brett got in with a key and found them in bed together. Then threatened to kill them both.'

Caroline rose from the love seat, stood next to him. 'Does that really sound right to you?'

Jackson still studied the street. 'This woman makes a good impression. She's not an obvious flake.'

'Then what took her so long?'

'It hasn't been that long.' He turned to Caroline. 'How eager would you be to become a principal witness in a very public murder trial?'

Caroline placed her hands on the porch rail. Softly, she said, 'I don't see murder one here. Even if you believe this woman.'

'If you believe this woman, Caroline, Brett threatened Case well before he was murdered.' He lowered his voice. 'It's one of two things. Either Brett drove him to the lake with an intent to kill or, high on drugs and wine, she hit a flash point of jealousy and slashed his throat without thinking. Which I imagine will be Brett's lawyer's argument.'

Caroline closed her eyes. 'What's this girl's name?'

Slowly, Jackson shook his head. 'I have to protect her privacy. When Brett's lawyer wants this woman's statement, I'll hand it over at the appropriate time. But not now.'

Standing straight, Caroline folded her arms, fought back a sense of helplessness. 'And bail?'

Jackson frowned; his voice was a prosecutor's now, well prepared and matter-of-fact. 'I'll have to oppose it, and I'll win. In New Hampshire, first-degree murder is virtually nonbailable.'

Caroline tried to imagine Brett in jail, found her mind

resisting the image. 'For God's sake, Jackson, she's no flight risk.'

Jackson turned to her. 'Really,' he said quietly, 'there's no point in arguing over this. Please accept that I'm sorry.'

'Is that what you came to say?'

He looked at her directly. 'I came to make arrangements, for Brett to come in on her own. And, however difficult, to tell you in person.'

'What arrangements?'

'We won't arraign Brett until tomorrow afternoon, so that she can have some time with family. As long as a police car follows, I'll let you bring her to the jail at Connaughton Falls, where people can visit easily. And I'll try to keep the press away.'

That, Caroline knew, was as decent as he could make this. 'Is that it?'

For a moment, he simply looked at her. 'That's it.'

She nodded. 'Thank you.'

Jackson began to leave and then stopped close to her, touching her elbow. She stared down at his hand until it fell to his side.

'Goodbye, Caroline.' And he walked to his truck and drove away.

Caroline drove to Masters Hill through a light drizzle, not unlike that on the day of her return.

Larry was in the library. Without preface, Caroline demanded, 'Is Brett here?'

'She's out for a walk.' He studied her expression. 'Is something wrong?'

'Go find Betty.'

He stood, alarmed now. 'Should Channing be here?'

'Just find her, for God's sake.'

When Larry returned with her, Betty's face was pale. 'What is it, Caroline?'

'Please, sit down.'

They did that. Caroline regarded her sister and brother-in-law; they looked diminished, shrunken, in the overstuffed chairs. Larry struggled to maintain calm; Betty's face was sallow.

Caroline's voice was softer now. 'There's no good way to tell you this,' she said. 'I just saw Jackson. They're charging Brett with first-degree murder.'

Betty's lips parted, but she made no sound. 'Why?' Larry managed.

'There's a witness – a woman. Her story is that she was involved with James; that Brett found out; and that she threatened to kill them both.'

Betty's hands balled into fists. 'That's ridiculous. Brett would never threaten anyone.' She stopped herself, and Caroline saw the gray eyes move from anger to anxiety. 'Who is this woman, Caroline?'

'I don't know.' For a moment, Caroline considered asking Larry if he knew a student named Megan, and then did not ask: the risk was too great that Betty – or even Larry – might do something unwise. 'Jackson wouldn't say –'

'Because she's a liar.'

There was something pitiful, Caroline thought, in Betty's anger. Caroline had seen it before: the look of a mother who has just learned that her child is ensnared in a legal system she cannot control or even comprehend. But always, before, the mother had been a stranger, the child just a client.

Quietly, Caroline said, 'Brett's lawyer will find out soon enough.'

Larry, Caroline saw, caught her meaning as she spoke. She watched the dawn of comprehension redden Betty's face.

'You won't help her?' she demanded.

Caroline forced herself to be calm. 'I didn't think you wanted me to. And I shouldn't. For Brett's sake.'

'For Brett's sake.' Betty stood, shock and derision mingling in her voice. 'Is this what you call selflessness?'

Caroline folded her arms. 'Yes,' she said coolly. 'For lack of a term we can agree on.'

Larry crossed the room and took Betty by the arm. 'It's Caro's decision. We have to look ahead now.'

'What I'd suggest,' Caroline said in more even tones, 'is someone from in-state, who knows the laws here – written and unwritten. Father will know who's good.'

Betty stared at her. 'And what will *you* do for her?'

'Other than give her lawyer the best advice I can?' Caroline paused, expelling a breath, and finished in a lower voice. 'Go home. For everyone's sake, and for all the reasons I haven't been part of this family for over twenty years.'

Caroline watched a range of emotions cross her sister's face – irresolution, dislike, and then so much fear for Brett that it erased all else. 'Betty,' Caroline said softly, 'it's the decent thing for me to do now. That was decided when I decided to leave. No matter what you've done, or how I may feel about it.'

Betty sat back in the chair, heavily and gracelessly, face dull with fear and confusion. Larry rested his hand on her leg. Neither looked up at Caroline.

'There is one other thing,' Caroline said. 'Which, for Brett's sake, I'd very much like to mention.'

It took a moment for Larry to raise his head. 'Yes?'

'My father had a fishing knife – a bone-handled Cahill that he kept in the garage. Where is it?'

Larry's face clouded. 'What are you saying?'

'Betty?' Caroline waited for Betty to look up. 'Our father says that he gave it to someone. Years ago.'

Betty's upward stare was sharp. 'What *are* you saying?'

'That the question may come up.' Caroline's tone was neutral. 'And that if it does, it would be very much in Brett's interest if the family memory is consistent. Or, at least, that no one gives a careless answer.'

Larry's expression grew hard. 'Caroline, I have no answer. I leave Channing's things alone –'

'Damn you,' Betty burst out. 'You think Brett killed him.'

Caroline kept her face blank, her voice calm. 'I don't "think" anything. I'm suggesting that *you* think.'

Betty's mouth compressed. 'Whatever Father says, Caroline, is true. If that's your question.'

Caroline watched her for another moment and then spoke to both of them. 'I'll tell Brett myself – there are things I need to say to her. I'm sure you won't mind if I wait for her on the porch.'

Chapter 13

Caroline first saw her as a distant, hooded figure in the drizzle, walking with downcast eyes.

Caroline paused, glancing at the sky. And then she rose from the porch and went to meet her on the gravel road. Until she was close enough to hear the crunch of Caroline's footsteps, Brett did not seem to notice her approaching.

She stopped, watching Caroline's face, hands thrust in the pockets of her yellow slicker. 'What are you doing, Caroline? Trying for pneumonia?' That she did not smile betrayed her anxiety.

For a long time, Caroline simply looked at her. Quite softly, she said, 'Clients lie to lawyers all the time. I should be used to it.'

Brett gave her a funny, trapped look, equal parts guilt and surprise. Her lips parted, but no sound emerged.

'No,' Caroline went on. 'I should put you out of your misery. Who, pray tell, is Megan?'

Brett looked down. Then she stood straighter, facing Caroline, and said, 'A woman James was involved with.'

Caroline nodded. 'So she tells Jackson.'

The green eyes locked on Caroline now. 'It was over, Caroline.'

'Was it? Perhaps you'd care to tell me about that.'

Slowly, Brett nodded. When she spoke again, her voice was thick.

'James was so attractive – with him, it was a weakness. This girl, Megan, began looking for him around campus – the library, the student union, after class. Almost like she'd figured out his schedule.' Brett's face took on an unsettled look. 'There was something creepy about it –'

'And how did James feel?'

Brett began to answer and then looked at Caroline as if

147

one thought had interrupted another. Quietly, she said, 'I'm sorry, Caroline. I wish you weren't so angry with me.'

Caroline tilted her head. 'Am I?'

'Yes. In that way you seem to have.'

In Caroline's silence, Brett's green eyes seemed to fill with challenge and vulnerability. Tersely, Caroline answered, 'My emotions, whatever they are, don't matter. Yours do. And his.'

Brett folded her arms. After a time, she said, 'I think James was attracted to her at first. Something about being stalked was flattering.'

'Is that how you saw it – she was "stalking" him?'

Brett nodded. 'I could forgive that much. I mean, he wasn't the aggressor....'

Her voice fell off. Caroline felt the damp in her hair, the wetness on her face. The mist of her breath hung in the air. 'What was it,' she asked softly, 'that was harder to forgive?'

Brett swallowed, looked down, then quickly up at Caroline. 'I went to his room one night, to pick up some notes I'd left there. I thought he was going to be out. Instead I found Megan.'

'Found?'

'Yes.' Brett's voice was toneless. 'In bed with him.'

'What happened?'

'I just stared at both of them. James looked ashamed and caught, somehow. But she was almost smiling at me, with the strangest glint – like she'd won some contest. I've never hated a woman so much.'

All at once, Caroline registered that Brett's reaction to Megan reflected that of Daniel Suarez. Sharply, she asked, 'So what did you do?'

Brett exhaled, then said, 'I knew I couldn't stay there – I'd scream or cry, make a fool of myself in front of him and this woman. So I pulled the key off my chain, threw it on the bed, and told him in the calmest voice I could, "If you want to tell me about this, you can call." ' Pausing, her voice was soft with hurt. 'Then I left.'

'Did you say anything else? To him, or to her?'

'Lots to him. But I never said a word to her. Then, or ever.'

'No?'

'No. Why give her the satisfaction?'

'And James?'

'Came to my room that night.' Brett shook her head, and then her voice fell. 'He promised me it would never happen again, told me she'd just kept after him. And then he seemed to realize that sounded so pathetic that he began to cry....'

'What did you do?'

'Just sat there, I think, shaking my head. I said maybe he had a problem, one I couldn't live with. That I didn't even want to try ...' Her voice filled with wonder. 'He wanted to make love with me.'

Despite herself, Caroline gave a short laugh, harsh to her own ears.

Brett looked at her. In a tone of remembered scorn and anger, she said, 'I told him not without a rubber.'

Caroline placed her hands on her hips. 'Which is why,' she said, 'you brought a rubber that night. And why you weren't going to California.'

'Part of it. Yes.' She paused. 'Maybe other women could live with that kind of doubt. But I don't think I could have.'

Caroline looked at her closely. 'Why were you even with him?'

Brett seemed to collect herself. 'Because he promised me, and because I cared for him enough to try.' She looked away. 'As far as I know, he kept his word.'

Caroline watched her. 'How long ago was this?'

'April.' Her voice was soft again. 'I remember because it was two days before my birthday.'

Caroline was quiet for a time. 'Did you ever threaten him? Or her?'

'Threaten?' Brett looked at her sharply, and alarm filled her voice. 'No. Never. Who says I did?'

'Megan, I think. Though Jackson won't tell me who –'

'That's bullshit.'

Caroline simply gazed at her. 'You want to know,' Brett said quietly, 'why I didn't tell you. And why you should believe me now.'

It was time, Caroline thought, to tell her. 'It hardly matters ...' she began.

'No,' Brett interjected. 'I want to explain.'

Caroline felt tired. 'I already know,' she said tonelessly. 'Because you thought that you'd look guilty.'

'That's part of it.' Brett's eyes filled with apprehension. 'But there's something else I didn't tell you ...'

'What?'

'We fought that night.' Brett stopped, and then said, 'It was over her....'

Facing James in the darkness, Brett shook her head, as if to clear it. 'There are too many surprises, too close together. I don't know what I'm doing anymore.'

'What do you mean?'

There was pain on his face, and somehow this made her angry. 'What do I *mean*? Besides this latest thing?'

James studied Brett with new intensity. 'Her? It's over.'

She stood straighter. 'Do you have any idea how much you hurt me? Do you think me finding you fucking that bitch was something sad that happened to *you*?' Her voice filled with wonder. 'Do I even exist for you outside of what you need from me?'

He stretched out his hands. 'Brett, please. Will you stop punishing me?'

Her voice went cold. 'I didn't punish you enough. That's why you're able to feel so picked on. And why I still feel so much pain and anger that I wake up at night and see you in bed with her.'

Her voice carried on the water. James looked around them, as if they might be overheard. More quietly, he said, 'I know I hurt you. I saw it on your face. When I started crying that night, ashamed of what I'd done, did you think it was just for me?'

It did not seem to help. Tonelessly, she said, 'Who knows.'

James came toward her. 'I know.'

'Well, I don't. I can't. Not yet.' She shook her head. 'I need time, all right, to know if I can trust you again. And now you tell me I'm out of time. Because of something else I have no say in. Just a little problem involving drugs that has you jumping at every noise in the woods. Or so you tell me …'

Turning from him, Brett walked to the water's edge.

After a time, she heard his footsteps behind her, then saw his faint reflection in the water next to hers, a slender profile with hands jammed in his pockets. He made no move to touch her.

'What are you going to do?' he asked.

She hunched her shoulders, helpless. 'I don't know.…'

Even in the rain, Brett's face was tear-streaked. 'I was afraid to tell you,' she murmured. 'About being so angry at him.'

'Because you thought it would look bad?'

Brett shook her head. 'Because it was like I'd done something bad.' Her voice seemed to fill with superstition. 'Like I'd been so angry that it somehow killed him.…'

Caroline was suddenly shaken. Carefully, she asked, 'Is that what you think happened?'

'No.' Brett's voice was fierce now. 'But when you said they might think that drugs made me lose my temper, it scared me. Like I could never admit we fought.'

Caroline faced her. 'Well,' she said softly, 'you don't have to admit that. Even to your lawyer.'

Brett stared at her. Before she could ask, Caroline said, 'They've decided to arrest you, Brett. For first-degree murder.'

Brett seemed to take a backward step, face filling with shock. 'Why?'

'Because of Megan. She claims that you stalked James

out of jealousy and threatened both their lives. From where Jackson sits, he may not have much choice.'

There were no tears now, no protest. In a dispirited voice, Brett said, 'She must truly hate me....'

Caroline gazed at her, trying to decipher the meaning of that. Then she made herself say, 'Jackson wants you to come in voluntarily, by tomorrow afternoon. He'll keep you in Connaughton Falls. I think you'll have to stay there.'

Brett closed her eyes. 'Brett,' Caroline said gently, 'your parents already know. Before you decide anything, all of you will have to talk this over. I'll try to help find you a lawyer.'

Slowly, Brett nodded. There was something in the gesture that Caroline found wrenching; it was as if Brett had lied and thus earned Caroline's abandonment.

Swallowing, she opened her eyes. 'Tomorrow,' she asked simply, 'will you be there?'

Caroline hesitated and then saw the look on Brett's face. 'Yes,' she said softly. 'Of course.'

Silent, they turned, hands in their pockets, and walked together to the house.

The next afternoon, when she came for Brett, seemed to Caroline incongruously bright.

Brett was waiting on the porch with a duffel bag. In an awkward clump beside her were her parents and her grandfather.

Channing looked shaken, haunted, and much older; it was as if, Caroline reflected, his own mortality had seeped to the surface of his skin. Betty and Larry were grim, uncertain of what to do or say. Betty had the wounded eyes of someone who has received a shock too heavy and sudden to absorb; she looked at Brett with such inarticulate fear and love that Caroline could not watch it.

Facing Brett, she spoke to her quietly. 'We should go.'

Brett nodded. As she turned to her family, Caroline edged away. She watched Betty hug her stiffly, kiss her dry-eyed on the cheek, then fold her arms and look at the porch. Saw Larry's wan smile as he clasped Brett's shoulders. And then Channing, the one with tears in his eyes.

His voice was rough, strong. 'Don't worry,' Caroline heard him say. 'I'll have you out soon. Believe that, Brett.'

An old man's useless promise, Caroline thought, in a time that has outlasted his power. As if knowing this, Brett pulled her grandfather close.

Awkwardly, the girl turned from them, walked to Caroline, and nodded. As they turned to leave, Betty gazed at Caroline as if she had stolen her child.

In the car, Brett said, 'I told them not to come. It would only make things worse.'

Caroline nodded. 'Did you bring books?'

'Yes.' As Caroline started the car, Brett turned to her. 'What will this place be like?'

'Somewhat bleak.' Caroline tried sounding matter-of-fact. 'The good thing is that it's a converted county hospital, so it wasn't designed as a prison. An economy move in the great New Hampshire tradition.'

For that moment, the misery in Brett's eyes eased. Calm, Caroline guessed, was what Brett needed. So for the twenty-minute drive, Caroline was calm. It was the longest twenty minutes in her recent memory.

The arraignment itself, quick and quiet, was a blur to Caroline; her clearest impression was of Brett's stoicism. And then, as promised, Jackson let her come with Brett to the county prison.

The converted hospital in Connaughton Falls – a three-story red-brick building from the late 1800s – also served as the police station. Caroline and Brett crossed its shaded grounds, flanked by two police officers, Brett gazing at the windows in the upper floors.

'I'll be up there?' she asked.

'Yes. They'll have a separate cell for you.'

Brett's steps slowed. She turned, looking at the sunlit

grounds. Caroline waited, hand on the double door, until Brett went inside.

The booking desk waited in a stark green rectangle. Next to the young patrolman at the desk waited Jackson Watts, with a short-haired female trooper. All that he said to Caroline was, 'They're ready for her.'

The young cop booked her, printed her, input the bare facts of her life on an old computer. Jackson stood in a corner, Caroline close to Brett. The stoic look Brett fought to maintain pierced Caroline's heart.

Was it possible, Caroline wondered, that she had not killed him? Or had Caroline simply crossed the line between lawyer and someone else.

The policeman, she realized, was looking at her. 'We're done,' he said.

Startled from thought, Caroline turned to Brett. Softly, she said, 'It's time now.'

It changed something in Brett's face. As if to brace her, Caroline clasped her shoulders. 'You'll be all right.'

Brett's pleading eyes were her sole answer; by now, Caroline knew that Brett would not ask her to stay. Silent, Brett turned her head.

'It's all right,' Caroline murmured again, and pulled her close.

'I didn't kill him....'

She felt so slight, Caroline thought. Over Brett's shoulder, she mouthed to Jackson, 'Wait.'

He nodded, eyes intent on Caroline.

She held Brett as the girl wept without sound. For this, at least, Caroline had nothing but time.

A few moments passed; Brett seemed to have wept herself out. But it was Caroline, now, who did not know how to leave.

Slowly, Brett looked up at her. Her eyes showed both fear and resolve. 'It's okay....'

Caroline felt Jackson watching her, the last monitor of reason. And then, against her will, she took Brett's face in her hands. 'I'll stay,' she said gently. 'Until you don't need a lawyer.'

Beyond Brett's expression of surprise and gratitude, Caroline saw Jackson's look of astonishment. When the deputy took Brett away, her eyes were still on Caroline. Jackson watched them both.

Caroline turned and left through the wooden doors.

It was done.

Alone in her room, Caroline did not call Masters Hill. She did not speak to anyone.

On the bed beside her was the number of the Cahill Knife Company.

In what felt like a final loss of will, Caroline reached for the phone.

'Cahill,' the operator said.

Caroline read the name she had written, asked for the clerk. When she answered, Caroline sounded quite calm. 'This is Caroline Masters. You may remember I called the other day. About a serial number on a Cahill knife.'

A moment's silence. Coolly, the clerk told her, 'Like I thought, we can't tell you where we shipped it. Not who bought it, or even who sold it to them.'

'I understand.' Caroline paused. 'You thought you might know the year it was made.'

'Yes.' The voice was more patient now. 'I can tell you that much.' A brief shuffling of papers, muffled by the phone. 'Here it is. From what I've written down, it was made in 1964. Early in the year.'

Caroline kept her voice steady. 'Nineteen sixty-four.'

'That's what I said.'

'Thank you,' Caroline said politely, and put the phone down.

With an odd detachment, she held her hands in front of her and saw that they were shaking.

PART THREE

Summer 1964

Chapter 1

When Nicole Masters proposed to take her to Martha's Vineyard three weeks earlier than planned, Caroline had been surprised.

'It will be the two of us,' her mother said with a smile. 'A little time, perhaps, before we exile you to boarding school.'

Caroline adored her father and would miss him. But she loved the house at Eel Pond, the days spent sailing in the Crosby catboat her father had bought the summer before. And her mother's excitement pleased her. Nicole was often distant, her moods so mutable that Caroline was never quite sure how her mother felt about her, or about Channing himself: as she moved toward young womanhood, Caroline had become preternaturally sensitive to the growing silences between her parents, divining some intricate scheme of cause and effect – in her father's affection for her, Caroline felt her mother's withdrawal.

To Caroline, the signs of this withdrawal were, as so often with her mother, unspoken. Her occasional trips with Channing to New York City – which had seemed Nicole's greatest pleasure – no longer occurred, though Caroline did not know why. Nicole's response was to take less interest in their home and village. She spent long days in her room; with the other women of their class – the wives of lawyers or doctors or bankers – Nicole maintained a polite acquaintance, the by-product of their husbands' prominence, which now lacked all pretense of intimacy. This spring, Caroline had noticed that her mother, who loved small things of beauty, no longer planted the bright flowers she once maintained in the rear garden. With instinctive caution, Caroline did not ask her why.

The trip to Martha's Vineyard happened suddenly. The three of them were at the dinner table; Caroline's father was describing, as if to Caroline alone, how his grandfather had come to have their summer home pulled by oxen to Eel Pond. Across from her husband, Nicole listened with a politeness so unvarying that Caroline could feel the minutes passing in her mother's mind.

As if to compensate, Caroline said to her father, 'I can't wait to go back. When will we?'

Her father smiled. 'July. Only a month now.'

'Perhaps you can go sooner.' Her mother had not spoken for some time; as Nicole turned to her, Caroline felt surprise. 'I may be able to discard my many obligations, Caroline, and leave early. With your father's consent, of course.'

This cool touch of irony made Caroline glance at Channing. But his fathomless gaze was fixed on Nicole. Her look at him was steady; perhaps only Caroline would have felt this as a challenge. In her own discomfort, Caroline said to Channing, 'Do you think we could, Father? I could sail the new boat.'

For another moment, Channing considered his wife. Then he turned to Caroline with a small, reflective smile. 'Of course, Caroline. It was rather a long winter. For both of you.'

Watching him, Caroline realized that the thought of having Nicole to herself, away from here, felt like desertion and yet came as a relief. And that her father knew all this.

They left one day after Caroline finished school.

They stopped in Boston, bought some summer dresses, had cocktails and dinner at the Ritz-Carlton. The next day, eyes alight, Nicole presented Caroline with a gold bracelet and her first set of expensive earrings. 'We've become so provincial,' Nicole said lightly, 'that we're both at risk of becoming like the heroines of an English Gothic novel, so earnest and unadorned that no one will read our pages. A tragedy for us and the world alike.' By the time they got to Martha's Vineyard, the trip had begun to seem like an escapade, a high-spirited rebellion against a dreariness that only her mother felt.

But Caroline was happy to sustain the mood. One afternoon, they played tennis at the Edgartown Yacht Club and then had dinner at that bastion of Republicanism and plaid pants; after much laughter and perhaps too much champagne, Nicole had wondered aloud why Barry Goldwater had so much compassion for Southern blacks that he would not burden them with the difficulty of voting. If a few heads had turned, Nicole did not care. 'These people,' she murmured on leaving, 'will forever wonder why everyone can't be more like them, while *I* will forever wonder why they wear such foolish clothes.'

But beneath this, her mother's feelings were more serious. The island was alive with civil rights ferment – church services, rallies, speeches by young summer residents now working in the South. The next Sunday, a somber Nicole took Caroline to a memorial service for Medgar Evers, the murdered civil rights leader. Though her mother had said nothing, Caroline could not help but wonder whether she was thinking of her own family. When she touched her mother's hand, Nicole squeezed Caroline's fingertips.

Yet much of their time was light, almost airy. When they went to the movies, Nicole chose a Taylor-Burton romance over *The Longest Day*, just as she chose a Beatles album for the record collection. When they played croquet on the lawn above Nantucket Sound, Nicole poured another glass of wine and began changing the rules: their contest became so antic, the antithesis of Channing's geometric game, that Nicole and Caroline forfeited competition to laughter and shared the rest of the wine. But Nicole followed the presidential race with an intensity that brooked no humor: the night the Republican convention shouted down Nelson Rockefeller, she shook her head and murmured, 'Frightening. And to think that last year there was Kennedy.' Then, a short time later, she said, 'Now Americans will have their own racist war.'

'What do you mean?'

'Vietnam. So murderous and yet so provincial – to learn

nothing from the one thing the French truly have to teach ethnocentrism.'

To Caroline, it was like discovering a stranger, mordant and despairing, who lived below the shifting surface of her mother's moods. Caroline found this sudden window on her mother's soul both exciting and disturbing, as if discerning the distance that Nicole had moved from them, her family, beneath the cover of her silence. Not once in their first days together did Nicole refer to her husband.

It was this realization that most unsettled Caroline. But it did not truly strike her until the night the telephone rang and, as Nicole answered it, Caroline knew that the call was not from Channing Masters.

Perhaps it was a rise in her mother's voice, the slightest change in her slender body, now catlike in its stillness. 'Who was that?' Caroline asked.

They sat on the screened porch as sunset spread across the water. Nicole put down her wineglass; the veiled, considering look she gave Caroline seemed imported from New Hampshire, so different was it from their last few days. 'Oh,' she said casually, 'a friend – you remember Paul Nerheim. He hopes to see us sometime.'

'All of us?' Caroline asked.

A second's pause, her mother's look keen, then vanishing with a wave of her hand. 'I suppose it depends on the time.' Her voice became dry. 'But I will give you plenty of notice.'

So she knows how I feel, Caroline thought. She was not sure that this was a comfort.

Caroline had disliked Paul Nerheim's smile before she sensed her father's feelings.

There was something about it that Caroline did not care for – perhaps, she thought now, the way it seemed to linger on her mother.

'You're very tall,' he had said to Caroline. 'Like a dancer or an athlete.'

It had been the summer before, when Caroline was thirteen. She was not yet used to being taller than Nicole;

162

her breasts had not filled out, and she was afraid of looking too much like her father. Knowing this, her mother had answered, 'More like the runway model I could never become,' sparing Caroline the necessity of saying anything. As if in sympathy for Caroline, Channing Masters did not smile.

Their family – Channing, Nicole, and Caroline – stood in the entryway of Nerheim's summer home on Martha's Vineyard. Caroline felt their presence as the kind of arbitrary social act peculiar to adults: for some reason, Nerheim had asked them here; someone – her mother, Caroline assumed – had accepted; and Caroline could not understand why anyone had bothered. In a vague way she knew that Nerheim was an investment banker from New York; that he had met her parents on the night when Nicole had inveigled a reluctant Channing into a summer dance in Edgartown; and that Nerheim was an acquaintance of John F. Kennedy. But what she sensed most keenly was that this man would never be her father's friend.

They even looked different: Nerheim with his even tan, white tennis sweater, gold-coin watch; Channing with his slacks, plain shirt, comfortable hiking shoes. Even Nerheim's thin face, mobile eyes, and lively gestures seemed the opposite of Channing's quiet dignity, his air of watchful judgment. Nicole stood smiling between them, lightly touching Nerheim's arm.

'You were so kind to ask us, Paul. And your "country place," as you put it, is lovely.'

And it was, in a way. They had taken a twisting dirt road through the woods of Chilmark, close to the unseen bluffs of the Atlantic, which opened unexpectedly to an acre of green manicured lawn, fronting a mansion so eccentric that Caroline found it startling. It was a sprawling, almost gingerbread structure with chimneys, windows, and dormers everywhere, and a glassed-in porch with panes shaped like waves, so that they seemed to flow and ripple across the porch. Nicole contrived to be enchanted.

'This is wonderful,' she said. 'So many people live as if they're communing with their ancestors.'

Caroline glanced at her father, who was studying Nicole with a faint half smile. 'This would drive my ancestors crazy,' Nerheim said, and gave Nicole a smile of complicity that seemed to exclude Channing. 'If I even knew who they were. Come, I'll show you the attic.'

Trailing after them, Caroline fell in next to her father. The attic was made of polished teak, shaped like the prow of a ship. In spite of herself, Caroline was impressed.

'The original owner hired a shipbuilder and then ran out of money,' Nerheim explained. 'It wasn't finished for years, until I did the rest last summer. A masterpiece of the shipbuilder's art.'

'Does it float?' Channing inquired mildly.

Nerheim gave a short laugh. 'Perhaps we'll see,' he said. 'During the next hurricane –'

'But where's the ballroom?' Nicole interjected. 'You, Paul, who seem to like dancing so much.'

'Oh,' he said. 'I'll pour some champagne and show you.'

Glasses in hand, her parents followed Nerheim across the grass to a carefully laid stone path that meandered artfully through the woods. At its end, a clearing suddenly opened to a clay tennis court.

They stopped by the net. Surrounded by woods, they could not be seen or heard from the house. Nerheim gave a mock bow.

'The ballroom?' Nicole asked.

Nerheim smiled. 'Of course.'

At a dinner served by two silent servants, Nerheim turned the table talk to the opera season in New York, the symphony, the jazz clubs he knew here or there. Nicole listened appreciatively; her questions sent him on knowing tangents, which, Caroline saw, seemed of interest only to her mother. What inquiries Nerheim addressed to her father seemed so studiedly polite that they underscored Channing's inability to speak to what seemed to engage his wife. To Caroline, Nerheim said almost nothing.

'Can I go for a walk?' she asked before dessert. 'I'd like to see the ocean from here.'

'Of course,' her father answered, excusing her from Nerheim's table without glancing at their host.

Outside, in the cool of early evening, Caroline breathed deeply.

The sun was falling behind the trees. Caroline walked the darkening path through the woods until she reached a fork; she stopped, confused for a moment, and then chose the path which she guessed must lead to water. But the woods were thick and gnarled; it was not until she climbed a steep rise, toward a sudden swatch of evening sky, that she found herself on a sheer cliff above the blue endless sweep of the Atlantic.

The surprise of it caught her in a moment of vertigo, left her pulse racing. Two hundred feet below her was a sandy beach; the orange sandstone cliff, scarred by wind and rain, was so precipitous that it seemed to drop beneath her feet. Down the face of the cliff, stairs crisscrossed to the bottom; beside them were strewn the skeletal remains of other stairs, destroyed by storms.

Caroline sat, gazing across the water.

It was strange. She had always viewed the ocean with a respect close to awe, but never with fear. Yet beneath the gray-blue surface of the water she felt the savage roiling of a storm she could not see, save on the ruined cliffside. It was some time before she rose, a little unsteady, and backed away.

When she returned, the adults were in the living room, still chatting about opera. Her father glanced up from his chair. 'Tired?' he asked pleasantly.

To her surprise, Nerheim summoned a look of deep courtesy for Channing, a smile for Caroline that was close to rueful. 'She should at least be bored,' he said. 'I've been so alone lately that I ramble on about whatever interests me, without a care for my guests. My apologies, Caroline.'

Caroline did not know what to say. But her mother's expression changed, as if this last remark had engaged her more than what had gone before. 'What may seem boredom,' she said gently, 'is, in Caroline, self-sufficiency. As for us, there is very little opera in Resolve. You are kind to remind us of the larger world.'

As he turned to Nicole, Nerheim's smile became warm; perhaps it was only to Caroline that his humility seemed too self-assured. 'Thank you, Nicole. I'm sure Resolve has other charms. Next time – and I hope there will be – I'll leave room for you to tell me of them.'

Nicole's returning smile was oblique and ambiguous – to Caroline, it could have meant anything, from *Of course, all of us know that we'll never do this again* to *Please give me a few days to consider what Resolve's charms are*. As Channing put down his coffee, contemplating his wife, Caroline sensed an unspoken humiliation.

'I am kind of tired,' she said to her mother. 'If you don't mind.'

'Of course,' Nerheim said with a tolerant smile, and rose from the table.

At the door, Nerheim clasped her father's shoulder, one friendly man to another. Knowing that her father disliked being touched by strangers, Caroline winced; Channing's expression did not change. 'Channing,' Nerheim said, 'thank you so much for lending me your family. As I said, I've spent too much time alone.'

As Channing extended his hand, the gesture put distance between them. 'Thank you,' he said with civility. 'It was good of you to have us.'

The corners of Nerheim's eyes crinkled, and then he turned to Nicole, clasping her hand in both of his. 'Nicole,' he said. 'I hope I see you again. All of you.'

Her mother tilted her head; what this suggested to Caroline was that, were it not for Channing, she would have proffered her cheek.

'Oh, you will, Paul.' She gave a wry look at their surroundings. 'Solitude in such a place must be a trial for you.'

Nerheim laughed. 'Oh, it is,' he said, and released her hand.

The ride home was quiet. Leaving, Channing stopped at the fork in the road, beam lights catching a gnarled tree. 'To the left,' Nicole said softly. Otherwise, she was silent.

Later, Caroline went to the kitchen for orange juice, heard raised voices from her parents' bedroom. The last voice was her father's.

Despite herself, Caroline crept to the bedroom door.

'The man is cheap and insinuating,' she heard her father say. 'And you played to him.'

'The man is polite, Channing. As was I. For both of us.'

'You're my wife.' The thick anger in her father's voice was something Caroline had never heard. 'You needn't compensate for me. I'm sure that there are other women who can give Paul Nerheim the admiration he so clearly needs.'

There was silence. When her mother spoke again, her tone was so quiet and weary that Caroline barely heard. 'Admiration,' she said softly, 'is all that's left to me.'

In the darkened hallway, Caroline felt herself flush with the shame of listening. She turned away.

The next day, they left the island, four days earlier than planned. Now, a year later, the memory fell like a shadow between Caroline and Nicole.

'I don't feel like seeing him,' Caroline said to her mother.

Nicole finished her wine. 'You don't have to,' she answered in a careless voice. 'I'm not sure that I do, either.'

Chapter 2

As the days passed, Nicole Masters seemed restless.

She took less interest in their tennis, did not come up with new excursions, retreated into books. She encouraged Caroline to contact the daughters of other summer people, friends from past years. Yet for two nights running, Nicole walked the beach alone; Caroline watched her, hands in the pockets of her white cardigan sweater, gazing out to sea. Caroline felt a loss.

When her mother returned from the beach on the second night, Caroline was waiting. With new directness, she asked, 'Are you all right, Mother?'

Nicole looked startled, as if awakened from her thoughts. 'Have I not been?'

Caroline hesitated, afraid to articulate her instincts. 'I don't know....'

Nicole gave her a faint smile. Gently, she said, 'It's not you, Caroline. If that's what you're sensing.'

Caroline felt relief, the tenuous renewal of their bond. 'What is it, then?'

Her mother shrugged. 'Does "it" have to be anything? Other than me?' Her voice was dispassionate but not unkind. 'I have my moods, that's all. Perhaps you notice them more without your father to distract you. If so, I apologize.'

It was less apology than statement of fact; it was as if Nicole had accepted her own apartness, and thus that others should. But Caroline did not wish to.

'I've been thinking – tomorrow, let's go for a day sail.' Caroline's voice quickened, as if to impart excitement to her mother. 'We'll sail over to Tarpaulin Cove, where Father took me last year – have a picnic on the beach and go swimming. Really, i would be fun for you.'

Nicole's smile did not quite hide a sadness in her eyes. 'Would it?'

'Sure,' Caroline answered. 'I'll make the sandwiches and sail the catboat myself. All you have to do is go with me.'

Nicole considered her, still smiling a little. 'All right, then. You make it hard to argue.'

Before Nicole could change her mind, Caroline went to the kitchen and began preparing for their picnic. When the telephone rang, her mother answered it in another room.

Caroline emerged from the kitchen. 'The picnic's ready,' she said. 'Was that Father?'

Nicole seemed to study her. 'Your father would have asked for you. But you may call him if you wish.'

The tacit rebuke silenced Caroline. She found that she did not want to speak with Channing.

But when morning came, Nicole did not wish to sail.

'I'm sorry, Caroline.' Her voice was soft. 'I find that I don't feel well.'

In her mother's eyes, Caroline saw a silent plea for understanding – of what, she did not know. But Nicole said nothing more.

Caroline's anger burst out unbidden. 'It's a beautiful day,' she said. 'I'm not going to mope around the house all day or hang around that goddamned yacht club, talking about boys.'

Nicole looked at her gravely. 'Such language, Caroline. But about the "goddamned yacht club," I understand. So what do you propose?'

'Sailing. If I have to go by myself, I will.'

Nicole glanced down, as if knowing that what Caroline most wanted was a change of heart. Softly, Nicole asked, 'Would your father let you do that?'

Caroline folded her arms. 'He told me I could last summer. Whenever I felt ready.'

'And you are?'

'Yes.' Caroline hesitated, still hoping for a sign that

Nicole would go with her, saw none. In a flat voice, she finished, 'Can I go now, Mother?'

For a long time, Nicole turned to gaze at the weather, eyes hooded. 'When would you be back?'

'By six o'clock.' Caroline made her voice indifferent. 'There's no point in getting back any sooner.'

Nicole's eyes were sad again. 'All right,' she answered. 'You can go.'

The day was brilliant.

It lightened Caroline's heart, braced her defiance. For a moment, she forgot that her father, knowing the sudden treachery of oceans, never would have let her sail alone. She walked swiftly to the catboat without looking back.

The boat was handsome and beautifully maintained – a twenty-foot Crosby, built in 1909. When her father had first shown it to her, a present for Caroline's thirteenth birthday, she fought back tears of surprise.

'Your birthday is special to me,' Channing said gently. 'Sail this with the care you deserve.'

Warmed by the memory, guilty at her willfulness, Caroline set sail.

The sky was cloudless, the breeze stiff and constant. She did not check the weather.

The sail to Tarpaulin Cove was brisk and sure. Caroline felt a sense of her own mastery. Running before the wind, she headed toward the lighthouse.

At the head of the cove, Caroline moored the catboat, turned to measure the expanse of ocean she had crossed with such ease. On this sparkling day, she still could see the Vineyard.

She would take her time, Caroline told herself, do everything she would have done had her mother not deserted her. She ate her sandwich, drank her Coke, legs dangling over the bow. Only when she had finished did she jump into the bracing water and swim confidently to shore.

The beach was empty, the sand warm. She lay there lost in her own thoughts, the ocean lapping at her legs and feet.

She should not be angry at her mother, Caroline decided. Things that Nicole could not avoid or help had happened well before Caroline was born. Caroline would take the good days as they came, fight the disappointment when her mother slipped away. She wished it seemed that simple for her father.

When at last she looked at the ocean, a long finger of fog crept the line between sky and water.

Caroline sat up, surprised. Knew at once that she must leave long before she had planned.

Forgetting her parents, she swam quickly to the catboat. As she clambered up the stern, the fog was darker, a dense bank rising from the water between Caroline and home.

She set sail toward the fog. The varnished deck of the catboat still glistened in the sunlight; she would sail through the fog, Caroline assured herself, and see the Vineyard through the sunlight on the other side.

Sails creaking, Caroline reached the first seeping mists. The water was suddenly gray, and then fog and solitude closed around her.

Her face was damp and chill. The catboat plowed forward, knifing the water Caroline could scarcely see. But she was on open sea, she told herself; unless someone rammed her, there was little danger.

Suddenly, the fog was no longer sitting on the water but whistling past her, breaking up before her eyes. Startled, Caroline tried to remember what Channing said this meant.

Just before she saw the black line of clouds racing toward her on the horizon, she knew.

A squall.

She had only minutes. Now she remembered clearly what her father had told her – with the thunderstorm would come a driving rain, savage winds from every direction. She saw no sailboats on the water.

For an instant, Caroline was paralyzed. Then the other thing that Channing had said came back: the winds could capsize her. Panicky, she crawled along the ledge toward the bow, one hand over the other, clawing at the handrail.

171

As the storm swept toward her, she loosened the rigging and let the sail drop.

Then the squall hit.

The first wave threw her from the bow, grabbing at the halyard as she fell on her side. She cried out; rain lashed her face. In a moment, the seventy-mile-per-hour winds would be upon her: already the boat bobbed like a cork, waves swamping the cockpit.

Caroline threw herself onto the deck, and then the next wave covered the catboat.

As Caroline grasped the wrought-iron tiller, the surge of water ripped her seaward, turning the boat on its side. Her muscles screamed with pain. There was a quickening surge beneath her, and then the boat righted itself in a spasmodic shiver.

Blinded by seawater, Caroline felt the primal ocean envelop her. The next fierce wave would tear her hands from the tiller and sweep her out to sea.

She clenched the tiller in both hands, eyes stinging with salt and tears from the pelting rain that scoured her face. Through half-open slits she saw the rope swirling in the flooded cockpit.

In her mind, Channing Masters ordered Caroline to lash herself to the tiller.

She grasped at the line with her right hand. The boat knifed into the air. Caroline fell back, head striking the floorboard. The cracking sound filled her ears, and then everything was black and lost and nauseous in the pit of her stomach. With a will of their own, the fingers of one hand still grasped the tiller.

Water pounded her face, seemed to throw the line into her hand. She sat upright; from a great distance, her father's voice told her again to coil the line around her waist and lash her body to the tiller.

In the whirling boat, she snaked the rope between the spokes of the tiller and around her waist. A knot – the work of instinct – and Caroline and the boat were one.

A wall of ocean hit. Caroline wrenched upward, was

caught by the rope, ribs cracking against the wheel. She prayed that her knot would hold, that the catboat would not capsize and trap her beneath the ocean, a captive, lungs filling with water until she drowned. A bolt of lightning struck the mast, the roar of thunder deafened her. Caroline shut her eyes and prayed to no one. The boat surged and plummeted at random, wind singing in her ears, rain driving sideways into her face.

And then it stopped.

Caroline opened her eyes.

A last thin darkness passed over her, and then the air was crisp and sparkling. Caroline began to cry.

No, she told herself. With clumsy hands she freed herself. Her head throbbed, her rib cage felt raw.

Then she could not seem to move. It was as if, in some deep trauma, she was helpless.

Straining, she rose from her paralysis and moved haltingly to the rigging. As the sails rose above her, a fresh wind made the canvas crackle and then fill. She could see the Vineyard ahead of her.

Numb, Caroline took the tiller again. Her eyes were swollen with salt.

A second fog was seeping across the sound.

Caroline sailed toward it in the southeast wind. The fog moved slowly, spreading across the water. This time, Caroline sensed, there would be no storm, no sound.

Breathing deeply, she made the most of her last ten minutes in sunlight, and then entered the fog again.

It was different. Silent, still, windless. Her sail flapped and withered on the mast.

Blindly, Caroline drifted with a tide she could only feel.

The tide could sweep her to shore, she knew, break the catboat on the rocks. Through the fog came the haunting toll of the first bell buoy. She was not sure where she was.

Bearings lost, she drifted.

All that she could do was listen to the eerie sound of the buoys slowly clanging, nearer and nearer, until she knew that she was inside them, closer to shore. She sat at the helm in the rear of the cockpit, trying to keep the catboat from the shoals of West Chop, hoping for the breezes that came in midafternoon.

She could sense the cliffs coming closer, feel the choppiness of shallow water. And then – it seemed on schedule – her sails flapped with a gust of wind.

Caroline grasped the tiller. Tilting leeward, the catboat sailed into sunlight, clearing the promontory of West Chop.

It was as though the Vineyard had appeared by magic through a sheer curtain. She could see the mansions of West Chop, the distant masts spiking the harbor at Vineyard Haven. Faint and exhilarated, Caroline grinned as if she would never stop.

She could not wait to tell her mother, to *see* her mother. All memory of anger had been swept away by the storm, the wind, the enormity of survival. The sail home was endless, a blur.

Docking, Caroline forced herself through the rituals of seamanship, bursting with all that she would say to Nicole. Then she hurried stiffly to the house, sore and bruised and filled with love and gratitude.

'Mother,' she called out.

The house was silent. 'Mom,' she called again.

Perhaps she was asleep. Turning, Caroline crept down the hallway to her mother's bedroom. It was only as she turned the knob, too late to stop, that Caroline suddenly knew what she would find.

Next to her mother's face, wide-eyed and startled, the head of Paul Nerheim stared at Caroline.

Their bodies were frozen. Nerheim on his elbows, sheets to his waist; Nicole beneath him, legs apart, the tips of her breasts still touching Nerheim's chest. Their stillness seemed so fragile that Caroline could not move.

'Please.' Nicole's eyes were pleading. 'Leave us now.'

Caroline's legs felt weak beneath her. 'My father ...'

Nicole's eyes shut. '*Please*.'

Caroline backed slowly from the door.

Wandering to the living room, she slumped in a chair

and waited. She did not know whether the nausea she felt was for herself or for her father.

In front of her stood Paul Nerheim.

His hair was mussed, his clothes not right. His voice was soft, tentative. 'I'm sorry, Caroline. And so is she.'

Caroline simply stared at him.

He shrugged, helpless. 'Your mother wants to see you.'

Caroline straightened in her chair. With a coldness she did not know was hers, she said, 'Get out. Now.'

Their eyes met. Slowly, Nerheim nodded, and then he turned and left the house.

Chapter 3

Moments later, Nicole appeared.

She was wearing a silk bathrobe and an air of composure that, to Caroline, seemed fragile. Her mother sat across from her, studying her closely, and then Caroline's disarray seemed to register in her eyes.

'What happened to you, Caroline? Your face is bruised.'

Caroline folded her arms. She said nothing; it was too late for Nicole's concern, and the idea that she could be so cheaply bought filled her with contempt and anger.

Nicole seemed to know this. 'All right,' she said softly. 'You wish me to explain myself.'

Caroline was unsure of this: what she wanted most was for the last half hour to vanish like the nightmare that it seemed. But she had no words to say this.

Nicole crossed her legs, arranging her robe with a distracted air. In the light through the window, her face looked thin and pale. 'What I did was wrong,' she said at last. 'More than anything, because you saw it.'

Caroline's voice was cold. 'I'm sorry I surprised you, Mother. I know you weren't expecting me.'

Her daughter's words seemed to strike Nicole like a slap. Her eyes flew open, and then she sat back, folding her hands. 'Do you expect me to flay myself, Caroline? Would that make things better?'

It left Caroline without words again.

'No?' Nicole's voice held gentle irony. 'Then perhaps I can trouble you to listen.'

Caroline shrugged. But she felt her heart race.

'I did not expect this moment,' Nicole continued softly, 'and I have no speech prepared. Especially for a daughter who loves her father as much as you love Channing. So if I am tactless, or inartful, please forgive me.'

Caroline filled with a kind of dread. Her face was stone.

Pausing, Nicole seemed to swallow. 'There is nothing wrong with Channing, Caroline, but that he married me. Perhaps it was his mistake to ask. Certainly, it was my mistake to accept.'

Caroline stiffened in her chair. 'He gave you a *life*, Mother.'

There was a first glint of passion in her mother's eyes. 'He gave me *his* life –' She stopped herself abruptly, forced her voice to lower. 'I saw a gentle man, Caroline. Perhaps paternalistic, but kind. What I did not see was the frightened man. Frightened of women. Frightened of whatever he could not control –'

'Father's not frightened.' Caroline felt her mystification become anger. 'People look up to him. Everyone I know.'

Slowly, Nicole nodded. 'In his world, yes. That is his strength.'

Caroline gave her mother a look of cold rejection. Nicole's voice was soft again, as if she was willing herself to ignore the evidence of Caroline's eyes. 'I was the choice, Caroline, of a frightened man. Young and rootless, an alien in my own country, shattered by what I had lost. Not just a family, but a world that once made sense to me. I no longer had any world of my own....'

Nicole paused. Her voice was stoic; it did not ask for sympathy. But part of Caroline, just by listening, felt dirty and complicit. She watched her mother in silence.

'Channing,' Nicole continued quietly, 'believed in his own kindness. But he also believed that I would never defy him, or leave him, or even question him.' Nicole looked down. 'As a man, or as a lover.'

Caroline stiffened, and then Nicole gazed at her directly. 'On all counts, Caroline, I have been a disappointment. So perhaps you could say Channing healed me.'

Buried in her voice was a trace of bitterness so faint that Caroline could not detect whether it was directed at her father or at Nicole herself. But Caroline seized on it. 'Quit trying to turn me against Father.' Her voice rose. 'You don't deserve him –'

'Don't I?' Nicole burst out. 'With his fear, possessiveness, and anger? I would think you would find me more than deserving.'

Oddly, the sudden outburst changed the balance between them; Caroline felt her confusion become a chill self-control. 'I would never have said that, Mother. Not until I saw you in bed with him. So I guess Father has always understood you better.'

Nicole seemed to flinch. 'I know,' she said in a husky voice, 'that I've been no great mother to you. But please take the good from your father without letting him control you. Because the danger is that he will – your life and your thoughts.'

At once, Caroline felt the sudden desire to lash out so that her mother would stop. 'Damn you,' she screamed. 'Do you think I need Father to tell me that I just found you fucking Nerheim –'

'Caroline, please.' White-faced, Nicole stood. 'If this is what we must discuss, at least understand me as a woman. I know you must have begun to feel these things yourself.'

Caroline felt herself flush. Pausing, Nicole looked down at her intently. 'I have little that is my own, Caroline. But I remain a woman, with a woman's needs.' Her voice was calm now. 'It is a fact in which, as a man, your father has little interest. Whatever his flaws, Paul Nerheim does. And that, to Channing, is the mirror of his own inadequacy.'

The sound of her mother speaking Nerheim's name made this dispassionate shaming of her father unendurable to Caroline. 'Don't talk like that. Not about my father,' she cried out. 'He *saved* you. Do you think what happened to your parents is some kind of excuse? It's like "They were murdered, so *I* get to hurt anyone I want to hurt –"'

Abruptly, Caroline caught herself. The look on her mother's face was too terrible to watch.

Folding her arms, Caroline looked away. Her mother's

voice, soft and clear, seemed to come from far away. 'So I've wounded you that badly....'

Caroline could not answer, or even look at her.

There was a long silence, and then she felt Nicole's fingers rest gently on her shoulder. Her voice was softer yet. 'I know that you will never tell your father, Caroline. But I won't make you my accomplice. Paul Nerheim will not set foot inside this house again.'

Caroline did not answer. It was a moment before she realized that her mother was gone.

Alone, Caroline went to the porch overlooking the water, and wept until she had no tears left.

For the next three days, they barely spoke.

Caroline had no wish to be near her mother, or with friends. She left the house early: on the first day, she willed herself to sail to Tarpaulin Cove and back; for the two days following, she hiked and cycled alone. Nicole made no approach to her.

Caroline did not know, or wish to know, how Nicole Masters spent her days. From their silent dinners, Caroline had the sense of a woman who seemed to have gone somewhere far away, until she would suddenly catch her mother watching her with veiled curiosity. At night, Caroline could hear her pacing the house.

In a week, Caroline knew, Channing Masters was due to join them.

Caroline found the thought unbearable. She could not imagine them dining together, every silence laden with Channing's ignorance, her mother's guilt, and the knowledge that Caroline devoutly wished she could erase. But the only person she could say this to was Nicole.

Finally, Caroline could not stand their silence. On the fourth afternoon, returning from a bike ride, she went to her mother's room.

At the moment Caroline saw Nicole, she froze.

Her mother sat at her dressing table, her fine-boned face reflected in a makeup mirror. With her left hand, she carefully applied eye-liner to the corners of her bright-green eyes.

Caroline's voice was flat. 'Going out?'

'Yes.' Her mother's expression did not change. 'Until midnight or so, perhaps. So you needn't wait up for me.'

The moment was strange to Caroline: the irony in her mother's voice; the intent look in her eyes; the light on her face. Nicole did not turn; to Caroline, it was as if her mother was lost to her.

'What are we going to do?' Caroline asked abruptly. 'When Father comes.'

Nicole moved the eyeliner a fraction, gazing narrow-eyed into the glass. 'I haven't considered it. What we always do, I suppose.'

To Caroline, this did not ring true; even Nicole's tone had the sound of an evasion. '"What we always do,"' she said in desperation, 'won't be like that for me anymore. I don't think I could stand it.'

For the first time, Nicole turned to her, asking softly, 'But what can I do, Caroline? Now that you know. Tell him for you? Or simply leave him?' She paused. 'Which would mean, once Channing was done with me, that I must leave you as well. For he would never let me take you.'

Caroline felt a tremor in her body. 'Then don't go out, at least. Please.'

Nicole studied her. 'I must,' she said finally. 'At least for tonight.'

Caroline could say nothing.

Nicole regarded her and then turned to the mirror, more intently than before. It was as if she did not care to look at Caroline's face.

Caroline drifted to the sun porch.

She gazed out at the waves, swelling, lapping, dying on the beach beneath them. There was something hypnotic about water, Caroline realized; as frightening as the ocean could be, its timelessness soothed her.

Her mother's footsteps sounded on the porch.

Caroline turned, looking into her mother's face. For a

moment, Nicole's eyes were soft, and then she bent to kiss Caroline on the cheek.

Caroline froze, silent, neither welcoming nor resisting. Nicole's lips were light, fleeting.

Her mother stood, walked away. To Caroline's surprise, she stopped, turning in the doorway.

'I'm sorry,' she said simply, and left.

Chapter 4

Caroline waited up for her.

She could not help this, could not sleep. She imagined her mother's evening, prayed that her father would not call. The house was dark and still.

At one o'clock, her mother had not returned.

Caroline went outside, stood on the bluffs, listened to the slow, deep surge of the purple waters against the cliff. The night was black, moonless.

The wind in her face was stiff. Caroline felt a chill; folded her arms against the cold; listened, vainly, for the sound of tires on gravel, the white Porsche that Nicole treasured and Channing found ostentatious.

Nothing.

Caroline tried to envision her mother, found it painful. Perhaps, she told herself, Nicole had drunk a little more than normal, forgotten her promise to return. Perhaps they had made love more than once.

The luminous dial of her wristwatch read one o'clock.

At two, Caroline promised herself, she would do something. What, she did not know; it was as if by setting a deadline she could induce Nicole's return.

Sometimes her mother drank too much.

She said this to herself, curtly and baldly, as she had not before. It made her feel the change in her, the clear-eyed sorrow.

Yet she shrank from calling Nerheim.

Deeply lonely, Caroline returned to the house.

She went to the kitchen. In the pale light, she gazed at the schoolroom-style clock.

She would hate it, Caroline told herself, if her parents ever did this to her, keeping watch. The thought of her parents made her sad again.

Damn Paul Nerheim. He had no right.

Yet at two o'clock, she found that she could not call him.

There was nothing magic about two, she told herself. How would she feel if she interrupted them from lovemaking, like a child with her face pressed against the window? Worse, a child who could not understand the world of adults, who simply needed their attention ...

Caroline made herself tea.

There was a noise outside. Caroline stood, walked quickly to the front door, cracked it open so that her mother could not see her.

The drive was empty.

Caroline closed the door, leaning against it. Then she went to the kitchen and opened the telephone book.

For long minutes, she stared at Nerheim's number, until she knew it by heart. Then she stood, forcing herself to turn the dial.

'Hello?'

It was Nerheim, dull-voiced, puzzled. Caroline drew a breath. 'Is my mother there?'

'Caroline?'

'Yes.'

A moment's silence. 'She left.' Nerheim's voice was clear now. 'Hours ago.'

Caroline felt her chest constrict. 'When?'

'A little before twelve.' His tone was oddly kind. 'She wanted to get home to you.'

Caroline felt her eyes close. Quietly, she said, 'She's not here.'

Nerheim's silence seemed endless now. When he spoke again, his voice was low; Caroline heard both concern and efficiency. 'I'll call the Chilmark police. And the state police.'

Caroline was silent; it took her a moment to realize why she did not wish him to do this.

'No,' she said. 'I will.'

An hour later, the telephone rang. Caroline jumped up to

snatch it.

'Miss Masters?'

Caroline sagged with disappointment. 'Yes?'

The man's voice was quiet and level, with a distinct Massachusetts accent. 'This is Sergeant Mannion of the state police. The locals say your mother may be missing. Or at least that you don't know where she is.'

'No. No one does.'

He seemed to hear the despair in her voice. 'They told me she was leaving Windy Gates in Chilmark. Is that right?'

'Yes.' Caroline paused. 'She was visiting a friend.'

'Do you know where else she'd go?'

'No. Just here.'

A tentative note entered his voice. 'Is your father there?'

'He's in New Hampshire.' Defensively, she added, 'At our home.'

'I see.' His voice was careful, neutral. 'She hasn't been gone that long –'

'Please,' Caroline interrupted. 'Can you just look for her? I'm afraid she's had an accident....'

Saying this, Caroline felt her stomach wrench. Wished to tell him, *If it weren't for me, my mother would be home.*

He could not have known this. But when he spoke again, more gently, it was as if he had heard her. 'What does she drive?'

'A white Porsche.'

Caroline heard the quiet of thought. 'All right,' he said at last. 'I'll look for her. By the time you hear from me, she'll probably be home.'

For two hours, the telephone did not ring and no car came. Caroline wandered through the empty house, defenseless against her imaginings. She had never felt so alone.

A little before five, the first thin dawn turned the darkness of the ocean blue gray. Gazing out the window, Caroline realized that night had kept her hopes alive. In the chill light of morning, she knew that her mother would not return.

Caroline heard the spit and crunch of gravel, tires stopping on the drive.

Filled with sudden excitement, she ran to the door. In her mind, Nicole Masters was alive again, stepping from her low-slung Porsche as Caroline opened the door.

When she saw the black patrol car, Caroline froze.

A uniformed man emerged. As he came closer, part of Caroline registered his reddish hair, pink scalded face, mild blue eyes. He was slightly pigeon-toed, she noticed; perhaps that was why he seemed to walk so slowly.

'You're Caroline, aren't you.'

It was the voice of the state policeman, softer now. She nodded, numb.

'I'm Frank Mannion.' His tone was muted, but his eyes would not leave her face. 'There's a car been spotted – a white Porsche. I should call your father now.'

Caroline blocked the doorway, as if to keep him from the phone. 'Where is it?'

A shadow crossed his face. 'On the beach. Below Windy Gates.'

Caroline's heart stopped, and then she felt herself shudder. 'How …?'

He seemed to inhale. 'Caroline,' he said, 'there's a body near the car. A woman.'

She felt her eyes shut, her head bend forward. Heard Mannion say, 'Please, let me call your father.'

Slowly, eyes still closed, Caroline shook her head.

'Someone should identify her.' His voice was still quiet. 'And your father should be here for you.'

Caroline opened her eyes. 'No.'

'Caroline, I'm sorry –'

'I won't give you his number.' Her voice was tight. 'I can't let him find out.'

Mannion shook his head. 'He has to know …,' he began, and then something like comprehension appeared in his eyes.

Quietly, Caroline said, 'Take me there.'

The ride was impressions. Dawn breaking over the Vineyard, as fresh as creation; the white homes and picket fences of Edgartown; then woods and farmland; telephone poles; stone walls; fields as open as the Scottish moors, rolling toward the sea. As they neared Chilmark, Caroline could feel Mannion's reluctance, the leaden silence between them.

'Did you always live here?' she asked.

She felt his surprise, a moment's hesitancy. 'No. I'm new. Until me, they never had state police on the island before.'

Caroline was quiet for a time. 'Do you like it?'

She felt him turn to her, as if to appraise what she needed. 'The islanders aren't so sure about me,' he said finally. 'They've had their own way all this time. But my wife likes it, and it's good for the kids.'

Caroline nodded. 'How many do you have?'

'Three.'

They turned off the road, down the dirt path toward Windy Gates. Caroline could say nothing more.

Trees enveloped them, thick and ancient and overgrown, hanging over the path so that only patches of morning sun dappled the red clay. Caroline felt the tightening in her chest and throat; with sudden clarity, she imagined her mother the night before, dancing with Paul Nerheim on the tennis court to music no one else could hear, their bodies close, a bucket of chilled champagne nearby....

As they neared the fork in the road – one path leading to Nerheim's estate, the other continuing straight to the water – Mannion slowed the car. His mouth was pressed tight.

Turning, Caroline looked toward the house. Imagined her mother driving down the twisting road, as they had the night Caroline had come with her parents. Saw her mother squinting as the headlights struck the trunks of trees, guiding her on the pitch-dark path until she reached the gnarled tree that marked the fork: toward the ocean, or toward home. Remembered her voice, softly saying to Caroline's father, 'Left ...' Saw her in the darkness alone, this time turning toward the water.

Quietly, Caroline murmured, 'She knew the way....'

The look Mannion gave her had a touch of superstition, as if he were afraid to speak. And then they passed the fork, rose slowly upward on the twisting path Caroline had walked until she could go no farther.

They went more slowly now. The twists grew more abrupt; there was a chill on Caroline's skin as the memory came to her, just before they reached it – a final bend to the right, as if to turn a corner, and then a rise breaking from the trees to an open sky....

At the edge of the cliff was an ambulance.

As Mannion stopped the car behind it, Caroline said softly, 'They should close this road.'

Mannion could not look at her.

They got out. He stood by the car; alone, Caroline walked to where the road simply vanished, like the end of the world.

She inhaled. And then, by an act of will, she gazed down at the beach, two hundred feet below.

What she saw first was the white Porsche. It was upside down near the water, its nose dug into the tawny sand as glistening waves lapped against the hood. Near the car, the small figures of three men walked in a desultory manner, sometimes gazing at the water like lovers of nature who had awaited the dawn. Swallowing, Caroline watched one of the figures break away and slowly cross the sand.

He stopped, gazing down.

A tiny figure lay there in her mother's dress, arms outflung, her black hair strewn across the sand like seaweed washed up by the tide. There were patterns in the sand around her, lines and arcs, darker where the crest of the last wave had touched.

Caroline could not breathe. She felt Frank Mannion behind her.

Slowly, Caroline walked from him to the stairs. Saw her mother as she left the earth, free-falling in darkness.

I sent her here, she thought.

Caroline took the last steps to the stairs.

She descended them with her head bowed, Mannion behind her, not looking at the beach. Perhaps it was not her mother, she told herself in silent prayer; from above, the woman looked too small and frail to be the woman Caroline knew. The stairs behind her groaned beneath Mannion's plodding steps.

She took a tier of stairs, then another and another, until her feet touched sand.

Before her were the scattered ruins of other stairs. She stopped there, looking back up the cliffside. Saw the scarred clay near the bottom where her mother's car first hit.

Cool water lapped at her feet. The tide was rising, she realized; as she turned again, slowly walking toward the body, the first wave swirled her mother's hair away from the white face.

Like an automaton, Caroline walked the last few yards to the body of Nicole Masters.

Her face was china. There was a delicate line of blood from her mouth, and her neck was strangely angled. Otherwise, she seemed untouched. But the spirit that once animated Nicole Masters had left her; to her daughter, this waxen figure in the sand had ceased to be her mother, the woman whose clean profile she had last seen in the mirror, who had kissed her goodbye.

Tearless, Caroline sat by the body. 'Leave her,' she heard Mannion murmur to the others.

Caroline stayed there, gazing at her mother, wishing to unsay the things that would hurt Nicole no longer.

After a time, she felt Mannion standing next to her.

Caroline did not look up. 'That's her,' she told him. 'My mother.'

He knelt by her then, empty hands cupped in front of

him. Quietly, he said, 'She hit the brakes, Caroline. There were skid marks up above.'

Caroline's eyes shut. Only then did the tears run down her cheeks.

'So,' Mannion said gently. 'You see.'

Dully, Caroline nodded. She could not speak.

His voice was still soft. 'We need to take her now.'

After a moment, Caroline stood. She drew sea air deep into her lungs, gazed up at the cliff from which her mother had come. At its edge, she saw the figure of Paul Nerheim.

Next to Caroline, Mannion said, 'I'll call your father.'

Caroline still stared at the man above them. 'No,' she said. 'I will.'

They buried her mother at Masters Hill, some distance from where her husband would someday lie. The service was brief and spare: no one mentioned that she was French, or Jewish, or how she had come here. The details of her death were unspoken.

But Caroline had spared her father nothing. When he had come for her, he put his arms around her and said in a hoarse, gentle voice, 'Fathers protect their daughters, not the other way around. Why did you think I needed that from you?'

Caroline could not answer. When she turned from the look on his face, it was no longer to protect him but to protect herself from the knowledge of her father's pain.

In the days after the funeral, they were alone; at her father's urging, Betty returned to her interrupted tour of Europe. Her father treated Caroline with haunted kindness.

Once, sleepless, she found him in the music room at midnight.

'Do you want to talk?' she asked.

'No, Caroline.' His voice was harsh. 'Not to you.'

In that moment, Caroline felt his solitude, knew that his sternness was directed not at her but at himself. They never spoke of Nicole again.

Nor would he hear of Caroline staying. They had

enrolled her in Dana Hall; nothing, Channing insisted, should change their plans. When she thought of leaving him alone, Caroline's heart ached. She wept for her mother where Channing could not see.

In the weeks remaining, they made themselves the semblance of a life.

Channing's birthday fell three days before she left. In secret, Caroline picked a present for him; when the morning of his birthday came, she pressed him to take her fishing on Heron Lake.

There were scattered clouds; sunlight sparkled on the lake, vanished, fell again. Caroline faced her father in the rowboat.

'I love it here,' she said. 'I wish I weren't leaving.'

Channing smiled a little. 'You've not leaving, Caroline – this is your home. You're simply going away.'

Caroline looked at him: the black hair, deep-set black eyes, strong face on which only Caroline could read hurt. Impulsively, she said, 'I wish I could take care of you.'

There was a brief wound in his eyes, and then he smiled again. 'I'm not nearly old enough, Caroline. You'll have to wait your time.'

Caroline felt awkward, knew that she should not have acknowledge what she saw. As if to cover this, she told him, 'I've decided what I want to do.'

'Oh? And what's that?'

'Be a lawyer. If you're not a judge anymore, I can practice law with you.'

He tilted his head. 'And after that?'

She hesitated; perhaps it was foolish, but she wanted him to know. 'I'd be a judge. Woman or not.'

For a long time, he simply looked at her. 'Caroline,' he said in a soft voice, 'that would please me greatly.'

Caroline felt a catch in her throat. For a moment, she almost forgot his present.

Awkwardly, she reached into her backpack, pulled out the slim black box with the ribbon she had tied around it.

'What is this?' he asked.

Caroline placed it in his hands. 'Happy birthday.'

He gazed at the box with a funny half smile. 'Shall I open it?'

'That's why I brought it.'

Carefully, Channing untied the ribbon. Inside the box was a handsome Cahill fishing knife.

He held it in front of him, admiring the leather sheath, the bone handle, the slender steel blade.

'Caroline ...' He paused; at first, Caroline thought he could not finish. And then he said, simply, 'It's the finest knife I've ever seen.'

She tried to smile. 'It's so you can fillet a fish without me.'

Channing Masters took her hand and covered it in both of his.

At Thanksgiving, when Caroline returned from school, the knife hung on their rack in the old stable. Her father had kept it spotless.

PART FOUR

The Witness

Chapter 1

Caroline stood at the foot of her mother's grave.

The morning was bright, beginning to warm; only in this corner of the cemetery, shaded by woods, did dew remain on the grass. The edges of Nicole's headstone were covered with moss.

Two days before her father's call, bringing her back to Masters Hill, Caroline had returned to where her mother had died. The trail at Windy Gates was overgrown now, fit only for walking; the stone wall was barely visible beneath a tangle of vines and shrubs. At the end of the path was a wooden barrier, and then sheer cliff. One hundred feet or more had been eroded by time; the cliffside seemed to crumble beneath her feet. Staring over the edge, Caroline had been surprised to see no car, no body, so strong had been her memory. She did not walk the beach.

Turning, Caroline had taken the path to Nerheim's mansion. It was dark and dank and half ruined. There were trucks outside; a rock singer from California had bought it, Caroline had learned, to restore it to its days of pleasure. But the tennis court was overgrown with weeds....

Gazing at her mother's headstone, Caroline heard footsteps behind her.

She did not turn. 'What is it?' she asked.

'We need to talk, Caroline.'

'Then you could have picked a better time. And place.'

Her father was quiet for a moment. 'For the twenty years you were away,' he answered, 'I've come here. The memories, of whatever kind, belong to both of us.'

Turning, Caroline walked a few steps, away from the grave, and faced him.

The shock of Brett's arrest was written on his face, and

his black eyes had the intensity of fever. 'I knew that you would stay, Caroline.'

The instinct to escape, the deep imperative to leave this place and this man, returned to Caroline across two decades. She folded her arms. 'Is that what you came to tell me?'

The light in his eyes dulled. 'Betty says that you're going to Concord, to review the prosecution files. I want to go with you.'

'No. Thank you.'

He stiffened. 'Brett is my granddaughter.'

Caroline felt a rush of anger. 'Is that what it always comes down to? What's yours?'

'Is this about me, Caroline? Or about you?' His voice mixed pride and desperation. 'No one is better equipped to advise you. Are you forgetting – after Nuremberg, I had Jackson's job, then twenty-five years on the bench. I know the law, the lawyers, the judges, all the things that no one ever writes down. If I weren't your father, you'd be begging for my help.' He stopped himself, framed his last words with the softness of a plea. 'There was a time, Caroline, when you wanted nothing more.'

Caroline watched his face. 'So that's what this means to you,' she said coldly. 'Through Brett, you'll win at last. All that she needed to do was kill someone.'

A patch of color stained his cheeks. 'How can you say that?'

'That she killed him?' Caroline shrugged. 'True, I can't be sure. But now that I'm her lawyer, whether or not she murdered this boy is of no particular interest to me. And your feelings about it interest me somewhat less.'

Channing walked over to her. For a moment, it seemed that he would reach out to her. His hands were stiff and awkward at his sides.

'Please,' he said in a rough voice. 'I could die soon. I want to see her vindicated.'

Caroline felt suddenly weary. 'That won't be easy, Father. You may have to live for a while.'

He seemed to slump. 'How is she?' he asked softly.

'Under the circumstances? All right. She's frightened, of course, and her moods change. But she seems to have a certain resilience.'

Channing looked away. 'Do you think she can hold up?'

'Yes. For a time.'

Channing turned to her. Quietly, he said, 'I know that I've put a lot on you.'

'You? I stayed for her.'

He did not answer. 'This judgeship,' he said at length. 'Where does it stand?'

The inquiry surprised her. For an instant, she felt her ground slipping from beneath her. 'Really, I can't think about it now....'

'I can help, Caroline.' His voice gained strength. 'Tim Braddock is on the Senate Judiciary Committee, in line for the chairmanship. I could call him....'

Caroline shook her head. 'That's the last thing I need. Or want. Can you understand that?'

Momentarily, her father looked more frail. 'Yes,' he .nswered with dignity. 'I can.'

'That part of our life is over, Father.' Looking into his face, Caroline drew a breath and then finished: 'But if you want to think Brett's problem through with me – without emotion – I'm willing to put all that aside. At least for now.'

He raised his head. 'Thank you,' he said simply, and left her there.

From the photograph, James Case stared up at her.

The fatal slash through his throat was a dark line, and his head twisted at an angle impossible in life. His eyes looked dry, glassy. His face was flecked with blood; from his lips, slightly parted, came a red bubble.

Caroline placed the photograph next to the others on the conference table.

The crime lab technicians had been thorough. There were close to twenty color prints – the stations, Caroline thought, of James Case's agony and death. His nude body sprawled on the blanket. His torso dappled in blood. His flaccid penis sheathed in a condom. The gash in his chest. A shot of his throat so close that Caroline could see his vocal cords.

She could not help but think of Brett. 'Your killer,' she said, 'left no room for chance.'

Behind her, Channing studied the photographs with a faint distaste. 'Some people,' he murmured, 'aren't meant to live long lives. How could she have ever slept with him?'

Silent, Caroline turned from him.

They were in a sterile conference room at the state police headquarters in Concord, both reviewing files. Her father let a moment pass. Then, as if nothing had happened, Channing said, 'Jackson has no answer for the idea the killer could have come on water. Or along it.'

'And who would that have been? The killer, that is.'

'Case's supplier. Perhaps even a vagrant.'

'I've checked the police reports. No homeless reported in the area — no robberies, either. As for James's angry drug dealer, his break-in story looks bogus.' She paused, studying a picture of the dead boy's torso. 'No, we're better off keeping bums and dealers a shadowy threat that the police did not take seriously. The more we investigate, the more we prove they shouldn't have.'

Channing stood, restless. 'You need a suspect, Caroline.'

Without answering, Caroline picked up an envelope and removed a sealed glassine bag. Her father's eyes froze.

Wordless, she passed the bag to him.

He held it between his fingers, staring down at the bone-handled Cahill knife. Its hilt was still crusted in blood.

Softly, Caroline asked, 'Do you know where Betty was?'

Channing looked up at her face. His face was cold. 'At home,' he said. 'With me.'

Their eyes met, and then Caroline gave a slight nod at the bag. 'Messy, isn't it. But, as you say, Jackson will never trace the knife to Brett. Given that she's innocent.'

Without answering, her father turned and placed the knife back in its envelope.

'So,' Caroline said softly. 'We can turn our attention to other things.' She passed him the photograph of James's torso. 'What, for example, is wrong with this picture?'

Distractedly, Channing took it from her and held it in front of his face. 'Not much blood,' he said at length.

Caroline nodded. 'It's too light – he should be blood-soaked from arterial spurt. Particularly if the killer cut his throat from behind James's head, as you suggest, so that he or she didn't absorb the spurt.'

Channing studied the picture. 'And if Brett were on top of him,' he asked, 'as the police suggest?'

'Then she'd be blood-soaked, which their own pictures and report show she wasn't. And we can assume she was on top – they lifted her fingerprints from his throat and from the blood on his chest.' Caroline paused. 'Jackson will disagree, of course. I'm going to need experts.'

'A serologist?'

'Possibly. Certainly a criminologist, a forensic patholo-gist, and a detective. Also – critically – someone who can testify to the effect of drugs and alcohol on memory.'

Channing sat down. 'How much will all this cost?'

'If we go to trial? A hundred thousand. Perhaps more.'

Channing stared at the table. 'Caroline,' he said slowly. 'Except for my pension, I've very little money.'

It startled her; she remembered young Caroline Masters, who never wanted for anything. 'How can that be?'

He folded his hands in front of him. 'It's "been" for a long time. I just never told you.' His voice was tired. 'There was a time when I thought you might keep Masters Hill alive. Then you were gone –' Catching himself, he finished with an air of fatalism. 'What investments I had grew worse, and Betty and Larry have no money of their own. Leaving us with our home, and what's left of our good name.'

The last, Caroline knew, was said without irony. In

profile, her father's jawline was set, his face prideful. He did not care to look at her.

'Is that,' Caroline asked, 'why you didn't send Brett away to prep school? Or college?'

His eyes narrowed. 'We did what was best. At whatever cost.'

Caroline studied him. Softly, she said, 'Aptly put.'

Channing stared straight ahead, silent. 'If it comes to it,' Caroline said at length, 'you can mortgage Masters Hill.'

His eyes were still. 'I already have. And the property values have fallen here....'

It was as if she were tormenting him, Caroline realized.

'All right,' she said. 'I can raise some money from my place. But I'll need twenty thousand now. From either you or Betty.'

'For what?'

'The probable cause hearing.' She paused. 'I've demanded one from Jackson, and it's in only ten days from now. Assuming I decide to go through with it, I'll require some expert help.'

Channing turned to her. 'As the defense did in the O.J. Simpson case?'

'Precisely, and for the same reasons. Like Simpson's lawyers, I'll never win – the court will find probable cause. But if the court lets me get away with it, I can examine Jackson's witnesses before they're prepared – like the pathologist and the crime lab people – and lock them into a story.'

Channing considered her. 'Or,' he said pointedly, 'encourage Brett to consider a plea bargain when she sees the evidence against her.'

Caroline felt herself stiffen. 'Of course, I may not succeed in bludgeoning Brett into submission in time to save my judgeship – she's somewhat willful.' Her voice was sardonic. 'But there are other benefits. Such as winning the battle of pretrial publicity or – better yet – so drowning the public in the evidence against Brett that they no longer find it shocking. As you know, it's somewhat easier to sell reasonable doubt to a jury that's already bored with the worst.' She shrugged. 'After all, if I have to practice law again, an unexpected victory could keep me in demand. It might even help me cover the expenses of Brett's defense.'

Channing flushed. 'I won't let you pressure her into a plea –'

'You won't "permit"? Then you might consider that a life sentence for Brett would run appreciably longer than a life sentence for you.' Caroline's words grew softer. 'Don't ever tell me, Father, what *you* will or will not permit. Because *I* will do or say whatever I believe to be in Brett's best interests. Including – though I've not quite decided – putting Jackson through this probable cause hearing.'

Channing seemed to study her; for a strange moment, Caroline thought she saw the faintest smile cross his face. 'I can raise twenty thousand,' he said quietly. 'In three or four days.'

Caroline did not answer. She waited briefly, to clear her head, and then put on her reading glasses.

She had saved the statement of Megan Race for last.

She read it once, for meaning, trying to detach her feelings from the words on the page. The second time, she took careful notes.

When she had finished, Caroline slid it down the table. 'Read this.'

As if to imitate Caroline, Channing put on horn-rimmed reading glasses. It surprised her; she could not remember that he had ever needed them. He read in silence.

When he was through, Channing put the papers down. His face was pale. 'She's lying.'

'Why?'

'She has to be.' He turned to her. 'Without this girl, Jackson lacks a sufficient case. At least if your experts do their job.'

'Just so.'

Channing looked uneasy. Quietly, he asked, '*She's* why you want a preliminary, isn't she?'

Caroline smiled a little. 'Suppose Megan's the obsessive

one. Suppose *she* followed them, spied on them.' Watching his face, she added with a touch of irony, 'Suppose, Father, that she even killed him.'

Channing stared at the pages in front of him. 'What if she was with friends that night – assuming that you're remotely serious.' His voice fell. 'Or, more realistically, that her reputation is good.'

Caroline's smile grew cold. 'Then I'll have to destroy her, won't I? For all our sakes.'

Chapter 2

'I've got everything I need,' Jackson told her, 'for murder one.'

Caroline had found him at his fishing camp. He stood on the pier in a gray morning light, sunlight refracted through a thin layer of clouds. The lake was still.

She put both hands in the pockets of her blue jeans. 'Except proof that the knife was hers.'

Jackson gave her a look of irony. 'They don't register knives, Caroline. I don't have to know where it came from.'

Caroline felt her nerves tighten. 'You overcharged this one,' she persisted. 'If you really think this looks like premeditation, then I've a wonderful insanity defense – Brett coolly planning to run naked through the woods, covered in blood, then make her escape still disguised as a hysterical naked woman. All after neatly disposing of the body by leaving it in plain view on her property.'

Jackson gave her a look somewhere between compassion and curiosity. Then he sat on the pier, legs over the edge, and motioned for her to join him.

Silent, Caroline sat next to him.

'You're feeling me out,' he said softly. 'Specifically, you're hoping for manslaughter. With Brett getting out before she turns thirty.'

He was good, Caroline thought. Or perhaps, now, she was less good.

'It never hurts,' she answered, 'to define the real world.'

Gazing at the lake, Jackson slowly shook his head. 'In your world – San Francisco – real is maybe two hundred murders a year: the prosecution has to plea-bargain, or the system will just break down. But this is New Hampshire, where we have less than forty murders statewide, and the pressure on us is to try them.' He looked at her directly. 'I won't play games with you, Caroline. Under our guidelines, manslaughter is out. The best I can do is second-degree murder with a twenty-year minimum.'

Caroline sat back, speechless for a moment. 'That's absolutely medieval,' she said. 'She'd be inside until she was forty-two.'

Jackson looked defensive. 'It's absolutely New Hampshire,' he shot back. 'And James Case never reached twenty-four. You're expecting me to sell him out.'

'Is that what I'm doing?' Abruptly, Caroline turned on him. 'Or are you overcompensating?'

'By asking twenty years for a life?' A sudden anger, controlled yet intense, showed in his eyes. He forced himself to finish slowly, softly. 'Just what, Caroline, am I compensating for?'

Caroline went silent, regretting her words, unsure of what to say next. She watched his anger die, replaced by the sense that he had withdrawn from her.

'All right.' He folded his hands in front of him, staring straight ahead. 'If you're referring to my prior relationship to Channing, the other lawyers in my section are no better off – he helped the two senior lawyers get the job and knows the two remaining through Republican politics.' His voice became almost casual, as if conveying a minor point of information. 'As I said, I haven't spent any real private time with Channing since shortly after you left. It was a little painful for us both.

'Which brings me to you.'

He turned to her with a look so cool she found it hurtful. 'If I have a problem, it's trying a case with you on the other side. And it's you who shouldn't be here, presuming on whatever there was – or is – between us.'

His last words, flat and passionless, hit Caroline like a slap. She forced herself to sound calm. 'As it happens, Jackson, that was a very nice day for me. But it has nothing to do with why I came here. Which involves nothing more than seeking fairness for a client.'

He crossed his arms. 'I offered you a lie test.'

'No. For all the reasons I gave before. And because she may well have been too confused by drugs to have any accurate memory.'

He raised his eyebrows. 'How about one simple question, then. Like "Did you kill James Case?" What's she going to say – "I don't remember"?' He shrugged at his own question, dismissing its absurdity. 'Like it or not, we both know that Brett killed him and that the only question is degree. And you're at once too close to this and too far away: a lawyer from California, who – with all your gifts – knows next to nothing about how things work here.'

It stopped her for a moment; the comment came far too close to Caroline's unstated fears. 'I can learn, Jackson. With all my gifts ...'

'Why are you doing this?' he demanded. 'I mean, you haven't seen her for twenty years and plainly didn't give a damn –'

'That's not for you to say.'

'No?' He shook his head in wonder. 'What are you trying to prove here, and to whom? I thought you'd left this place behind –'

'Christ.' Caroline leaned back on her palms, staring at him, and finished in a low voice. 'Don't try to psychoanalyze me. You don't know enough.'

His lips compressed. 'Forgive me, Caroline, but there are a lot of very good defense lawyers in this state who don't carry whatever baggage you've returned with and who don't have a judgeship at stake.' He paused, tone softer now. 'This is already a tragedy for Brett and for her family. I don't want it to be a tragedy for you. Or – and this is my weakness – to be any part of that.'

Caroline felt the emotion drain from her. 'I promised her,' she said simply.

He studied her for a moment. 'No manslaughter, Caroline. If you want that, you'll have to try the case.'

Slowly, she nodded. 'Then count on a hearing, all right?'

He cocked his head. 'Is that all?'

'That's all.' Caroline got up. 'Thank you for your time.'

They stood there, silent, looking at each other. Then Caroline smiled a little and turned away. He did not walk with her to the car.

'Megan Race,' the detective repeated, and wrote the name at the top of a lined yellow pad.

They sat in the office of Caroline's new local counsel. Carlton Grey, a bespectacled veteran of the local courts, sat at his walnut desk; Caroline and the detective from Concord, Joe Lemieux – dark, ascetic looking, and thirtyish – in guest chairs facing Grey. Lemieux had turned to her.

'What is it you need?' he asked.

'Everything,' she answered crisply. 'In less than ten days. Where she's from, what jobs she has, what courses she's taken. Her family. Whether she's ever seen a therapist or is seeing one now. What friends she has. And, critically, former boyfriends. That one's a priority.'

Lemieux looked curious. 'What are we after, exactly?'

'Anything that I can use to destroy her credibility.' Caroline paused for emphasis. 'She'll have something, Joe. Everyone does.'

He nodded, silent.

'Then,' Caroline went on, 'there's her relationship to the dead boy, James Case.'

Carlton Grey leaned forward. 'As I understand it, Caroline, you want to know when it ended.'

'According to her statement, Megan and James were lovers unto death – so much so that he asked her to go with him to California. But according to Brett, James broke it off in April – two and a half months ago. Did anyone, I wonder, see them together since?'

Lemieux noted this on his pad. He had long fingers, Caroline noted, an air of delicacy. He would not put people on edge. 'And the former boyfriends ...?' he asked.

'First, were there any. If so, then we'll want to consider approaching them.' She looked from Lemieux to Grey and back again. 'What would help is for someone to say that she's malicious, spiteful, or – best of all – unbalanced.'

Grey nodded. 'You need a reason for her to lie.'

'Precisely. It would very much help to have it for the probable cause hearing. Whether I use it or not.'

'She won't be there,' Grey put in. 'Jackson would never call her.'

Caroline smiled. 'But I can subpoena her, can't I? Assuming that the judge lets me.'

Grey raised an eyebrow. 'You've been reading our statutes.'

'Oh, yes, I do that.' She still smiled faintly. 'It's one of my gifts.'

'My niece has asked me to do this,' Caroline said slowly. 'To my surprise, I find that I can't turn her down.'

It was night; she had called Walter Farris at home. At first, she heard only static, a faulty connection. Then Farris said, 'That poses a problem.'

Caroline forced herself to sound calm. 'But should it? There's no realistic question of my using influence here. Really, Walter, in the age of family values, I'd hope that people – including senators – might sympathize a little. What good is twenty years defending strangers if you can't help your own niece?'

The answer, carefully prepared, silenced Farris for a time. When he spoke again, his tone was neutral. 'You're quite close, I take it.'

Caroline considered her answer. 'We've become so,' she said, and returned to her carefully wrought appeal. 'If it will help things, I'm prepared to write the chairman of the Judiciary Committee, explaining my difficulty, confirming my continuing interest, and expressing the hope that confirmation hearings can be held promptly after completion of the trial.'

In the silence, Caroline felt herself tense. At length, Farris asked, 'How long might that be?'

Caroline hesitated. 'Maybe six months.'

'I think that's too long.' His voice was brisk. 'Once we get near the election, the Republicans can hold things up, see if they can elect a President. You're too obvious a target.'

Tense, Caroline forced herself to think swiftly. 'Because I'm a woman?' she asked. 'Or, as you put it, a feminist? Then that *is* a problem.' She made her voice sound tentative, musing. 'But I suppose there may be another way to view this – as a chance for the President to remind them that he'll stand by his appointments. Unless there's a better reason than Jesse Helms's displeasure, as you once put it.'

Her tone was so mild that Farris could not confront her. 'What would you like me to do?' he asked with muted annoyance.

Caroline held her breath. 'Just to tell the President,' she said, 'that I'll do whatever he wishes. After all, I'm the nominee only at his pleasure.'

Farris fell quiet again. Caroline could imagine him – cornered, unable to say so, wondering how much of this she had calculated. 'All right,' he said at last. 'I'll run this by him.'

Alone in her room, Caroline closed her eyes. 'Thank you,' she said.

Chapter 3

A woman deputy brought Brett to a stark interview room with yellow walls and a pressboard table that, to Caroline, seemed passed on from some county office. Brett sat across from her; the deputy stepped outside the room, occasionally peering through a wired-glass rectangle in the metal door. A certain light replaced the dullness in Brett's green eyes.

'Thanks for coming,' she said to Caroline. 'I've gotten to count on it.'

Caroline smiled. 'Oh, it's pure self-indulgence – a place like this puts my company in a new and attractive light. Quite heady for a neglectful aunt.'

Brett's own smile was slow to come and, when it did, perfunctory; Caroline could see her imagining endless days like this. 'Have you worked up some sort of routine?' she asked.

'A little.' Brett gave a fractional shrug. 'It reminds me of something my philosophy prof said once – that life is a way of killing time.'

She looked somewhat removed, Caroline thought, almost detached. 'What kinds of things do you do?' Caroline asked.

'Yoga, a little reading ... The people who watch us are nice enough, and in the cell there's still only me.' Brett shifted in her chair. 'A couple of friends came by – high school friends, 'cause the college people are mostly gone. But they don't know what to say to me, or me to them.' She shrugged again, helpless. 'I mean, I can't tell them about nightmares, or missing James, or this fantasy I have where we're in California now. It would be too weird for them, you know.' Brett gazed at the table. 'It's not their fault, I suppose. Not many people have this experience. They can't exactly say things like, "I know how you feel."'

Brett paused again. 'Do you know what's really weird,' she went on. 'This is the first time I can remember being alone – without Grandfather or my parents, or a roommate, or maybe James. That was another reason I wasn't sure about going with James. It was time for me to be on my own.' Her voice filled with wonder. 'Now I'm finally alone....'

It was as if, Caroline thought, Brett were musing to herself, in Caroline's presence. She felt a strange intimacy between them.

'There was a time in my life,' Caroline said at length, 'around your age, when I decided to spend time alone. It lasted for a while – a period of months, actually – and I even wrote a little. And when it was over, I found that I had come to some conclusions about the future I would have, for worse or better. And about the price I'd pay for that.'

Brett studied her, curious. And then she simply said, 'You're saying that I should do that – take this time to think. And maybe write.'

Caroline shrugged. 'What else is it good for?'

The fingers of Brett's left hand idly stroked a tendril of brown hair. 'All that *I* can think about,' she said at last, 'is how I got here.'

Beneath this statement, uttered with the simplicity of truth, Caroline felt a challenge. *I think about it*, the girl was saying, *because I'm innocent*.

Caroline's own gaze was steady. 'Think about whatever comes,' she answered softly. 'But here you can talk – or write – about anything *but* that. Or James.'

Brett's look grew cool. 'Because they'll read it.'

'Or hear it. And, perhaps, misinterpret it.'

Brett sat back, appraising her before she spoke. 'Why did you stay here, Caroline? When you don't believe I'm innocent.'

Taken by surprise, Caroline flashed on the bloody knife. She kept her own voice calm. 'Lawyers don't believe anything. Because belief is pointless. I, and the law, presume your innocence. My job is simply to preserve that presumption.'

'That seems so cold.'

It was strange, Caroline thought, that a simple word from this girl could hurt her. 'Sometimes "coldness" is merely a point of view. And *you* should presume that some lackey may try to curry favor by reporting something you said. Real or imagined.'

Brett folded her arms. 'We're in different places, aren't we? And not just now. When you were my age and needed to think, you chose the time and place and subject.' Her voice turned bitter. 'I'm not free to do any of those things. Unless you get me out of here, I may never be.'

Caroline looked down, accepting the rebuke. 'What I said was foolish. We're not the same, and this isn't the same. I was only trying to tell you to be careful.'

'Fine. And I'll try not to tell anyone that I cut James's throat.'

When Caroline looked up, there were tears in Brett's eyes. They regarded each other, silent.

Caroline drew a breath. 'There's something else we need to talk about.'

Brett seemed to clasp herself tighter. In the pallid fluorescent light, her eyes had a vivid sheen. 'Whatever.'

Caroline rested her cheek on the fingers of one hand. 'I spoke with Jackson,' she said slowly. 'He won't take manslaughter.'

Brett's face hardened. '*I* won't take manslaughter. I already told you that.' She leaned forward, looking into Caroline's eyes. 'That might sound crazy to someone who only "presumes" my innocence. But I won't plead guilty to something I didn't do.'

After a moment, Caroline shrugged. 'Well,' she said, 'that makes it simple, doesn't it.'

Brett stood, pacing. Then, abruptly, she turned on Caroline. 'This probable cause hearing you told me about – when is it?'

'Eight days. Assuming we go through with it.'

Brett stared down at her. 'I want that hearing. And I want to testify.'

Caroline pushed her chair back from the table. 'No,' she said tersely. 'Absolutely not.'

'Well, I'm going to.' Brett's voice rose. 'I sit here, day after day, with no one to say I'm innocent. So I'm going to say it.'

Caroline kept her own voice quiet, sympathetic. 'I understand your feelings – at least as much as I'm able. But my whole purpose in forcing this hearing is to catch Jackson's witnesses unprepared, Megan Race – who refuses to even speak with me – being the most critical of all. I won't let him catch *you* like that.'

The mention of Megan seemed to silence Brett, as Caroline had intended. She tried to seize the moment. 'Trials are like theater, Brett. You have to know your lines or, at least, know the play well enough to improvise. I don't have a firm grasp of their evidence yet. And there's not nearly enough time to get you where you need to be.'

'Theater?' Brett gave her a look of disbelief and anger. 'The truth is the truth, and I'm testifying.' Her eyes were bright now. 'Whose trial is this? Yours or mine?'

Caroline stood, facing Brett across the table. 'This is not negotiable. I refuse to help you commit suicide. Jackson will cut you to shreds before you even figure out that he isn't Jimmy Stewart –'

'Did you hear me, Caroline?'

'Yes.' Caroline paused, steeling herself. 'Now you hear me. If you insist on this, I quit.'

Brett stared at her, lips parted. She was suddenly pale. 'Then quit. I'm sick of not controlling my own life.'

'This is a poor time to decide *that*,' Caroline snapped. 'You'll know you've grown up when your first decision isn't quite so stupid.' She caught herself. 'Don't make the wrong choice for the sake of making one. Please.'

Brett's gaze seemed to waver, then her mouth set in a

stubborn line. 'You can leave now. Grandfather will find me someone else.'

With what money? Caroline wanted to say. But the girl she saw stopped her for a moment – vulnerable, with pride and fear fighting for control of her face. 'I'll leave,' she said at last. 'Though not before we do this.'

'Do what?'

'Sit down,' Caroline said curtly. 'I'll be Jackson, and you be you. Just like in that glorious scene in court you so vividly imagine without my interference, a mere eight days from now. And don't forget to write.'

Pale, resolute, Brett sat stiffly.

Caroline stood, watching her. 'The rules are simple. I ask the questions, you answer within ten seconds. So that your audience can see how forthright you are.'

Brett stared at her, defiant. 'Not quite so hostile,' Caroline said in an advisory tone. 'Remember that I'm Jackson and that the truth is the truth.'

Brett flushed. 'Will you start?'

'All right.'. Pausing, Caroline could feel her own pulse. 'You've described the murder, your own shock and horror, and everyone watching is incredibly sympathetic. Now you're in the police car – all you have to do is explain what you did next.'

Caroline saw a first glimmer of uncertainty, perhaps self-doubt.

'When the policeman stopped,' Caroline began, 'you were naked, correct?'

Mute, Brett nodded.

'You have to speak up for the record. I'd recommend a clear, steady voice.'

'Yes.' Brett's tone was flinty. 'I was naked.'

'And covered in blood.'

Brett hesitated. 'There was blood on me, yes –'

'Eye contact, please – you'll make a bad impression.' At once, Caroline slipped back into her role. 'Where did you think James was?'

Brett's eyes narrowed, as if straining for memory. 'I was stoned.'

'But you weren't "stoned," were you, when you picked him up?'

Brett squared her shoulders. 'No.'

'Couldn't you remember *that*?'

'I think so. Yes.'

Caroline placed her hands on her hips. 'Then did you also "think" that James had simply vanished?'

'I didn't know.' Brett closed her eyes. 'I had flashes, like a nightmare.'

'There was a bloody wallet in the car, wasn't there?'

Brett's eyes shut. 'Yes.'

'Did you think *that* was a nightmare?'

Slowly, Brett shook her head. 'All I had was fragments. I didn't want to believe them.'

'Oh, it's not quite all you had. There was also a bloody knife on the passenger seat, was there not?'

Brett's face was haunted now. 'Yes.'

'And did you think that had arrived from a dream?'

'No.' Brett looked up in silent appeal, as if seeing Caroline and not her tormentor. 'You have to understand. Nothing seemed more real to me than any other thing. I couldn't remember what happened.'

Silent, Caroline sat across from her. She said, softly, 'You mean you can't remember whether or not you killed him?'

'No.' Brett's body went rigid. 'I couldn't have.'

Caroline paused; the pit of her stomach felt hollow now. Quite calmly, she said, '"Couldn't have"? I thought you couldn't remember.'

'I did.' Brett's eyes fell. 'But later on.'

'Eight hours later?'

'I don't know. Whenever it was that my head began to clear.'

'Before that, where did you imagine all the blood on you had come from?'

Wearily, Brett shook her head. 'I didn't know.'

'So that, two hours later, you were only able to recall that James "might" be at the lake.'

'Yes.' Brett's voice was husky. 'I thought he might be.'

Caroline leaned forward. 'And why did you think that?'

'Because I remembered taking him there.'

'But you *always* remembered, didn't you – just like you remembered picking him up. Because you weren't stoned then.'

'I don't know.' Brett's voice rose. 'Maybe it was the knife in the car.'

Slowly, Caroline shook her head. 'No, Brett. Because you knew all of this – James, the blood, the knife, the wallet – two hours before, when you were still in your car.' Her voice became quiet. 'When you told the patrolman absolutely nothing.'

Brett touched her eyes. 'I didn't remember.'

Caroline placed a finger to her lips, contemplating the girl. 'Tell me,' she said in a tone of mild curiosity, 'does your memory always work like that? Where it only comes back to you after hours, or even days.'

Brett stared at the table. 'It was the drugs. What I wasn't stoned for, I can remember.'

Caroline composed herself. 'Such as the night you found James in bed?' A lethal pause. 'With a naked girl named Megan Race?'

Brett's head fell slightly. 'Megan ...' she began, and stopped.

Caroline leaned forward. With terrible quiet, she asked, 'Were you stoned then, Brett?'

'No.'

'But when the police asked you about girlfriends, you somehow didn't mention that.'

'No.' Caroline saw a throbbing in Brett's temple. 'I didn't want to think of it. Or remember it.'

'I understand.' Caroline's voice was gentle now. 'Just like you don't want to remember killing James.'

A tremor ran through Brett's body. When, at last, Brett

raised her head, tears ran down her face. Her silent gaze at Caroline was her last, tenuous show of defiance.

Caroline wanted to comfort her. But all that she said, voice matter-of-fact, was, 'Your lines need work.'

Brett swallowed, still silent. Caroline waited until she was certain the girl would not be sick, and then went on. 'Of course, that was off the top of my head. Jackson will be much better.' Her voice was level now. 'Unless, of course, I can keep your statements out of evidence – something I mean to set up through the probable cause hearing. In which case, Jackson will never get to ask any of those questions.'

Brett could not seem to move or speak; it was as if, Caroline thought, she was staring into the abyss of her own doubt.

Caroline reached for the girl's hand. 'Listen to me, Brett.' Her voice was soft again, her own. 'The only thing I can promise is that you'll get the best that I can give you. And that I won't let anything or anyone – even you – ever get in my way.' She paused for a final moment. 'Please, let me do this.'

Brett looked down at their hands. After a time, she asked, 'Can I go now?'

'Of course.'

Through the glass window, Caroline watched her leave. Brett's movements were weary, drugged. She did not look back.

Outside, Caroline sat in her car, alone. It was a while before she felt like going anywhere.

Arriving at the inn, she went to her room and called Joe Lemieux. When he answered, she asked her question without preface. 'The girl,' she demanded. 'Do you have her schedule yet?'

Chapter 4

From the edge of the quadrangle, Caroline watched the young blond woman leave her job at the student union and start across the campus with purposeful strides.

Unaware, she walked toward Caroline. There were few people there – a trickle of summer students and their teachers, a group of shirtless boys near Caroline, playing Frisbee in the noonday sun – and the lone figure of the woman somehow seemed apart from them. As she approached, too deep in thought to notice her, Caroline saw that she was pretty – a strong jaw, a snub nose, even features – and that the blond came from a bottle. Her eyes were on the ground in front of her.

Fighting back her tension, Caroline stepped forward. 'Megan?'

The woman stopped, eyes flying open, a wary blue-gray. Her gaze narrowed as if she was trying to place the tall woman in front of her on some sliding scale of risk. Comprehension crossed her face; the slight smile that followed, less welcoming than a warning, did not change the guarded look. 'You're Brett's lawyer. The woman who called me.'

'Yes.' Caroline made her tone mild, unthreatening. 'Actually, I'm her aunt.'

All expression seemed to leave Megan's face. 'Who told you to come here? Her father?'

Caroline shook her head. 'I asked around, and came on my own –'

'This is like harassment. I already told you, Mr. Watts said not to talk with anyone.' Megan placed both hands on her hips. 'Look, if you think this has been easy for me ...'

Caroline held up both hands in front of her, a plea for understanding. 'No, I'm sure it's been quite awful for you.

Losing someone is bad enough without having to relive it all in court.'

Megan stared at Caroline, then folded her arms and looked at the ground again. She pressed her lips together; her eyes closed, and then she slowly shook her head. 'It's like she ripped my heart out but my body still keeps moving....'

Megan's voice trailed off. She frowned at the stone path in front of her. 'Really,' she said in a dubious tone. 'I'm not supposed to talk to you.'

'But I *need* to talk to you.' Caroline paused. 'Megan, part of what I need help with is deciding whether Brett should even go to trial. It would be less than honest not to admit that you're the biggest part of that decision.'

Megan seemed to stand a little taller; her natural posture, Caroline realized, was straight-backed, athletic. 'And you think I can help you.'

Beneath the doubt, Caroline sensed a lessening of resistance. 'If there's no trial,' she said quietly, 'wouldn't that be best for everyone?'

Megan's eyes narrowed. 'Let me think about it. I'll call Mr. Watts.'

'Oh,' Caroline said, 'you already know what he'll say. If not, I know Jackson, and he loves to try cases – for prosecutors, it's really not the same.' She softened her tone again. 'While you think about it, there's no harm in not talking with me over coffee, is there? I've been waiting here for a long time, and I wouldn't mind just sitting.'

Megan thought a minute and then shrugged. 'I guess not.'

Together, they started back to the student union. The campus of Chase College was a classic piece of New England – sylvan and quiet, with old brick buildings at its heart. They crossed the white wooden bridge that spanned the brook, lazy with its summer ebb. 'Have you liked it here?' Caroline asked. 'At least until now?'

'Before James? I don't know. People here are pretty unaware.' She gave a sardonic smile. 'You know – let's go skiing and drink a lot of beer. Most of them don't know Günter Grass from Kurt Vonnegut.' Her smile vanished abruptly, and her voice became almost fierce. 'James did.'

She had a certain manner, Caroline thought, that suggested they were peers. Instinctively, she decided to pursue it. 'It's so hard,' Caroline observed, 'to really find someone. So many times I feel like what passes for conversation is just making noise, and I end up listening to myself like I were someone else, chattering at a bad cocktail party. It's tough to live on autopilot.'

Megan peered at her sideways, as if deciding whether to accord trust. 'It's worse at my age,' she said finally. 'I believe in serious friendships, really intense, with no thoughts held back. But how can you be that way with people who are scared to think?'

'Do you think it gets better,' Caroline asked, 'just because they're older?'

'I hope so. I mean, I can't stand the idea of dating if all it means is a lot of traffic.' Megan stopped, speaking in a lower voice. 'At least older men have had a chance to grow up, face a few things about themselves. But James changed all that.'

For a time, Caroline chose silence. They got to the door of the student union, a cement Bauhaus structure badly out of keeping with its surroundings. With respectful curiosity, Caroline asked quietly, 'Did you ever try that – older guys?'

Megan glanced at her sharply, then nodded. 'Except for the sex part, it was better. That was where James had it all.'

It was said with a stubborn pride, as if to remind Caroline that James belonged to her and she did not care who heard her; from a nearby table, a boy in glasses looked up from his newspaper. Megan led Caroline to a table at the center of the room.

It was sterile and cavernous, with glass on all sides. Caroline looked around them. 'Who was the architect?' she asked in tones of wonder.

Megan waved dismissively. 'Awful, isn't it? Like Le Corbusier done by a computer.'

They sat, facing each other. Megan flicked back her straight blond bangs, crossed her legs, and sat upright in her chair, looking fixedly at Caroline. 'I think architecture is like politics. The nineties aren't about anything, except maybe pushing women back down where they "belong." And neither is this building.' She gazed about her with a vaguely scornful look. 'To me it says two things – "engineer" and "penis." There's nothing spiritual about it.'

Caroline nodded her understanding, careful not to study Megan too closely; beneath her new animation, Caroline sensed a warier, second Megan watched her. 'Of course,' Caroline said, 'it's not a spiritual age. The things we used to believe in, we don't anymore, and nothing has taken their place. Not even kindness.' She softened her voice. 'This meeting is very hard for me, Megan. Because I'm deeply sorry about what happened to James, and to you.'

Megan looked down; furrows appeared in her high forehead, and her mouth seemed to quiver. 'We were a couple,' she murmured, 'and then we weren't. Because of her.'

Caroline folded her hands. 'I don't really know Brett,' she admitted. 'I'm not close to any of them, actually, and now I have to make sense of this....'

'It makes no sense.' Megan's voice was angry now. 'Unless you understand what Brett Allen is really like.'

Caroline shook her head. 'I'm not sure that I do yet, and there isn't much time.'

Megan looked up. 'Jackson said something about a hearing.'

The use of "Jackson," Caroline thought, was the assertion of some new intimacy – adult talking to adult. 'In seven days,' Caroline said. 'But I'm still deciding whether I want one.' She paused, as if reluctant, then added, 'Brett keeps saying she's innocent –'

'Wouldn't you' – Megan's voice was etched with scorn – 'if you'd cut someone's throat?'

'But that's what I have a hard time believing. Even with all the evidence.'

'You don't *have* all the evidence.' Megan leaned forward, looking intently at Caroline. 'She used to threaten us, follow us. She's sick – sick and obsessive.'

Caroline inhaled audibly. 'It may well be, Megan. But you're the only one who knows that.'

'Only because James is dead,' Megan grasped Caroline's sleeve. 'Don't you sense it by now – there's something feral about her. I see those green eyes in my dreams.' Sudden tears appeared. 'That's what's so awful – already, I can see her face more clearly than his. Like I'll live with her for the rest of my life.'

Caroline lowered her eyes. 'This is none of my business,' she said softly, 'but you have to keep him alive somehow. Have some part of it that stays a part of you.'

Megan shook her head. 'What can you do when you were with someone so much, looking toward a future, and suddenly all you've got are mental images – the same ones, running over and over, with all the surprises stolen from them?' Her voice caught. 'I remember him acting scenes for me, from his play....'

Caroline touched her arm. 'I'm sorry ...'

'We made love all the time, he wanted me all the time. Would ask me to undress for him, to turn around just to see how beautiful I was.' She looked at Caroline with sudden vividness. 'It wasn't exploitative – just intense, like everything we did. Every moment was so *conscious*.'

Caroline looked puzzled. 'But what about Brett? Where did she figure in?'

Megan seemed to bristle. 'Oh, she was still there – do you know she threatened to kill herself if he ever left her?' Her voice filled with anger. 'I wish she had. Instead, she killed James. I guess that was the only part she meant.'

'But weren't you afraid?'

'Anyone would be. To have your lover inside you, and then he's suddenly standing at the end of the bed, naked, wrestling with a woman who's trying to scratch your face.' Megan shook her head. 'After that, we both were careful – it was almost like we went into hiding. Maybe, in a strange way, James was keeping his options open by treating me more like a mistress than a commitment.' A faint note of scorn entered her voice – for whom, Caroline was not sure – and then vanished. 'But we had what we had. In the end, James decided to be with me.'

Megan was bright-eyed now; Caroline felt a sudden warning on her nerve ends. In a tone of bemusement, she asked, 'Then why was he with Brett the night he died?'

Megan gave a haunting smile of bitterness and triumph. 'Because we'd decided to leave her and this place behind, to go to California. That was the night he was going to tell her.' Suddenly, her voice grew quiet. 'And when I found out that she'd killed him, I knew that he had.'

For a long time, Caroline simply stared at her. She could think of nothing to ask.

It seemed to bring Megan back from anger. 'I don't know how you make these decisions,' she said evenly. 'But whatever you do, don't put these people through a trial. Because their daughter is a murderer.' She paused, studying Caroline until compassion seemed to enter her face; lightly, her fingers touched Caroline's wrist, and her voice became almost confiding. 'I know that she's your niece, Caroline, and how hard this must be for you to face. But you'll come to see what James did – that beneath that China-doll look is a selfish and demented woman.' She paused, finishing quietly, 'And to see the one thing James never saw: that, if he left, she'd kill him.'

Chapter 5

Brett sat in front of her. The metal door whispered shut, and they were alone.

Brett's eyes were swollen from sleeplessness. She gave Caroline a certain bleak scrutiny; it was as if their conflict yesterday had stripped her of illusion. In a flat voice, she said, 'What is it now?'

Caroline placed her arms on the table, struggling to master her emotions.

'I caught up with Megan Race. It's far worse than her statement suggests. According to Megan, she and James were lovers to the end. They'd decided to leave for California. And the night James was to tell you was the night he died.'

Brett seemed to have lost the capacity for surprise; the only sign that she had even heard was the stillness of her eyes. Softly, she said, 'That never happened. Any of it.'

Caroline studied her. 'At best,' she responded, 'you can't know whether he was seeing her or not. And Megan's story is that you stalked them.'

A first flash of anger, although Brett's voice was calm. 'I didn't need to "stalk" him. After I found them together, he was with me almost every night.'

Brett's self-control, Caroline found, drew her more than protestations. 'All night?' she asked.

Brett stared at her now. 'I don't go for hit-and-run. If someone wants to make love with me, I want him to stay with me.'

Somehow Caroline found this affecting – the remembrance of a code, the reassertion of Brett's pride, in the face of terrible news. 'Perhaps Megan's rules were different.'

Brett shook her head. 'James may have been an actor, but he wasn't a good liar. I could always tell.'

It was said with a tinge of fatalism; there was something clear-eyed about Brett, Caroline realized, when she was faced with things she could not change. It was strange that in this moment of extremity – her final acceptance of Brett's guilt – the girl seemed so real to her.

'Then where,' Caroline asked, 'does the part about California come from?'

For the first time, Brett looked away. 'I don't know,' she said at last. 'Somehow she must have invented it.'

'But how? And perhaps more to the point, why?'

Brett looked up again. 'I don't know "how." But the why is obvious.'

'Jealousy?'

Brett stared at her. '*I was jealous*,' she said slowly. 'But Megan Race is mentally ill.'

Caroline sat back. 'Because she "invented" all this …'

'Because she invented *me*.' Suddenly, Brett looked haunted, as if grasping what she faced. 'I cared for James. At times I loved him passionately. But I wasn't obsessed with him – however hard it might have been, I was willing to let him go.' Her eyes held a new intensity. 'Caroline, when this woman tells you about me, she's talking about herself.'

Caroline watched her. 'But you don't really know her, do you?'

Brett's body grew taut. 'I know her the same way she knows me. Through James.'

Caroline leaned forward. 'How do you know,' she asked softly, 'that James *didn't* tell you he was taking her to California? And, please, *think* before you answer.'

'I already have, damn it.' Brett stood abruptly. 'Listen to me. Last night, I couldn't sleep. I just lay there, going over it all, horrified because you'd torn me apart until I felt as if I *had* killed him. But everything you asked me was about how I acted *after* I was stoned, *after* I found him. Because you were right – the things that happened *before* we smoked the dope, I remember perfectly.' Her words were a torrent now. 'He asked me to go to California, we fought about him

224

screwing Megan and this dope-dealer thing, and then I said I didn't know what I'd do. He was ashamed about Megan, all right? There's no way we both got stoned and then he told me he was taking her to California instead of me. We were making love, not fighting – doesn't that mean anything to you?' She paused, as if interrupted by a sudden thought, and then softened her tone as she gazed down at Caroline. 'I know I lied to you about the fight. But I knew I was lying. Just like I know that I'm telling the truth to you now. No matter what you think.'

Caroline sat there, silent, staring up at her. There were too many things that she could not say. That she knew about the knife. That, at best, Brett might never know what she had done at the moment of James's death. That Megan Race fitted neatly with the evidence. And that the first hard lesson learned by Caroline the lawyer, when Brett was a faceless child in a faraway state, was that given enough time, a guilty person may come to believe the story of her innocence.

As if challenged by Caroline's silence, Brett demanded, 'What did *you* think of Megan?'

The question was asked in anger. But beneath it, Caroline felt a plea: Believe in me, not her. And then something came to Caroline, wings beating against the windowpane of her subconscious. It was simple enough: the memory of having loved.

'What I think,' she answered finally, 'is that Megan never loved him. The James that she describes is a mirror for herself.'

It took several hours for Joe Lemieux to return her message, and when he called, from a pay phone, she had fallen asleep from exhaustion.

'Sorry,' he said, 'but I've been busy on this. Talking to whatever apartment neighbor is willing to talk with me.'

Caroline fought for alertness. 'And?'

'And most of them aren't college students, so I've had some luck.'

'So did I, in a sense. I met Megan today.'

'What did you make of her?'

'Quite smart, it's clear. But mercurial, perhaps somewhat narcissistic – she's plainly someone who likes, even needs, attention. Of course, that could describe a lot of people.' Caroline paused. 'The big questions, in order of importance, are: Did anyone see Megan with James after early April? And can you find any other boyfriends before or after?'

'It's a little thin, on both fronts.' Lemieux seemed to organize his thoughts. 'She did see Case, all right, and early April doesn't mean anything to her neighbors – they weren't keeping track of her affairs by date. But James's picture has been in all the papers, and the two folks who can remember seeing him at Megan's place think that it was quite a few weeks ago. Which is the same thing that kid Daniel Suarez said. Anyhow, they all agree they hadn't seen them together for over a month. Which gives us at least a couple of weeks before the murder.'

'*Her* story is that they were hiding out. Making beautiful love, of course.'

'Must have been, is all I can say. 'Cause no one saw them come up for air.'

Caroline considered that for a moment. 'Keep digging. I need anything that suggests the presence – or absence – of a relationship at any time close to the murder.'

'Okay. Now, about the boyfriends, there's even less.'

'Less, or nothing?'

'One thing. Months ago, Megan cornered one of her neighbors in the laundry room – a middle-aged lady who wasn't that up for it – and started carrying on about her relationship with an older guy. Something about how much better it was.' A note of humor entered Lemieux's voice. 'I took awhile to get this lady to admit that "it" was sex, and that Megan's not very bashful on the subject. Even without meeting her, Megan sounds a little quirky, although even this lady described her as "charming" and "vivacious" – just a little too emancipated for her taste.'

226

'The word,' Caroline said dryly, 'is "liberated." Which took place somewhat later than the end of slavery. But I'm wondering if Megan isn't something more.'

There was silence. 'If you mean unstable,' Lemieux said dubiously, 'no one seems to think that.'

'Does anyone purport to know her?'

'Know her?' Lemieux thought for a moment. 'The impression people gave me was that Megan could be pretty voluble. But I don't think they mean the same thing, and I really don't have a handle on how she might be with her peer group.'

'No girlfriends visiting?'

'Not that I heard of.' Another pause. 'Actually, I didn't meet anyone who mentioned being inside her apartment.'

'What do you have about her family?'

'A little, and it's not a pretty picture. Her father died in a boating accident when Megan was roughly twelve. Which apparently left her mother so depressed that she became very withdrawn, and stayed there. She's been in and out of institutions.'

Caroline was quiet. 'Find out more about the mother,' she said finally. 'Dates of institutionalization, if possible. Also, I'm still interested in any therapy for Megan. And do you think you could get me her class schedule?'

'For what?'

'For ever since she got there.'

Lemieux considered this. 'Without breaking the law?'

'That would certainly be preferable,' Caroline answered in an arid voice. 'For both our sakes.'

'I agree. Anyhow, I'll see what I can do.'

Caroline thanked him, and hung up.

She went to the window. Twilight was settling over the white houses, the rolling countryside. An older couple strolled slowly beneath the window of the inn until they disappeared from view; oddly, it made Caroline wonder how many meals in her lifetime she had eaten by herself.

She should eat something now, Caroline thought without

227

enthusiasm; she felt weak from hunger. She was wondering where to go when the phone rang.

'Hello?'

'Caroline.' Betty's voice was strained. 'I'd like to see you. Please.'

Caroline sat on the edge of the bed. 'Can we make it tomorrow?' she asked.

Chapter 6

'Thank you for coming,' Betty said.

They sat on the porch; the morning was clear but cool, and steam rose from Caroline's cup of black coffee. In profile, her sister was pensive; it was as though the enormity of Brett's problems had dwarfed their estrangement.

'You asked me to,' Caroline answered. 'So I did.'

Betty did not look at her. 'I know how much you hate me. You think that I betrayed you – twice.'

Caroline suppressed a bitter smile. What was of interest was not Betty's insight – it was hardly that – but the fact that she expressed it. Softly, Caroline answered, 'Not just me.'

Betty's eyes narrowed; for a moment, Caroline wondered if she had caught her meaning. 'For years,' Betty said at length, 'I told myself that I was acting out of love.'

'And now?'

'I know how jealous I was – of you and of him. Of you, I always had been.'

Caroline gazed across the gravel road and down the swiftly sloping hill toward the village of Resolve. Remembered those few grades when she and Betty, five years apart, would stand beside the road until the bus came. Together, Caroline thought, and yet separate – sisters, and yet not. 'I was only a kid,' Caroline said. 'No one at all, really.'

Betty shook her head. 'To me, you were his dark-haired princess, with a beautiful mother who'd taken my mother's place, just like you'd taken mine.' Her voice went quiet. 'Pathetic, I realize – even then, you didn't think of me at all. But maybe that was the worst of it.'

It *was* pathetic, Caroline thought. 'If only I'd known the

price for it,' she answered, 'I would have been more sensitive. But then seven-year-olds so seldom are.'

Betty turned to her, gray eyes almost accusing. 'Do you know how terrible it is to see you now? It's like seeing all my failure and guilt, everything I've done wrong, trying to right what I did then.' Her voice softened. 'You even blame me for this, don't you?'

So she *had* understood, Caroline thought. She sipped her coffee, coolly studying her sister over the rim. 'At the risk of being insensitive yet again, I find that I lack the energy to care. But then we each must form our own ideas about what – and who – is important to us. Especially at a time like this.'

Betty turned crimson. 'You have a talent for cruelty, Caroline.' She paused a moment, and then continued in a halting voice, 'I asked you here to talk about Brett, not my feelings. But I thought it might help if first we confronted what happened, as honestly as we could.'

Caroline considered her. 'What would it help?' she asked quietly. 'Sometimes the fact of something overwhelms the reasons for it. Do you think it really matters to me that you didn't intend what happened? Even assuming that it's true.'

Betty looked down; in the haggard face of this aging woman, Caroline could see traces of the young Betty she had known – watchful, a little afraid, as if something would be taken from her. It was a measure of all that had happened between them that compassion felt beyond her. 'Betty,' she said softly, 'this does no good. It never will. Perhaps, for both our sakes, we should concentrate on Brett.'

Betty closed her eyes. 'I did what I thought was best for her, too,' she said finally. 'And if I hadn't, and she had gone away, perhaps there would never have been someone like James Case.'

Caroline said nothing; the knowledge of irony, plain in Betty's eyes, kept her from responding.

'I thought I was being a good mother,' Betty continued, 'keeping her close, watching over her – everything I used to wish I had a mother to do.' She turned to Caroline. 'The precious mother that I knew *you* had, and that you and Father loved in common.'

Caroline watched her closely. But there was no awareness on her sister's face. *He never told you*, she thought with grim amusement, *just how and why my mother died*. It was as if they had lived in different families, their understanding of each other defined by the one common member, whom, in turn, they had come to see so differently. The thought made Caroline quiet and still.

'Didn't *he*,' Caroline asked at length, 'also want Brett "close"?'

Betty straightened in her chair. 'We all did. Perhaps I wasn't the best mother, or the wisest. Perhaps I've pushed her away. But I tried.' She paused. 'This may be cruel of me, Caroline. But you've never had to face the moment where you're holding this baby and suddenly you know that with all your shortcomings and blindnesses, you more than anyone will make her what she becomes.' Her voice lowered. 'There was only one moment that felt as awesome, and as frightening: the day I sent Brett to kindergarten and it came to me that there was so much in the world which would touch her, and which I couldn't control at all.'

Caroline held the coffee cup, cold in her hands, sorting her own emotions. 'But that's inevitable,' she said softly. 'And at some point, when the child is older, the inevitable becomes fitting.'

Betty's jawline seemed to tighten. 'This world is different than the one we grew up in. The drugs are worse, the random violence is worse, the random sex – rape included – possibly fatal. Who would hurry to push a daughter into *that* world before her judgment is fully formed –'

'But how,' Caroline snapped, 'does she form it? By being tied to her parents? Or, more accurately, to a rigid old man who's frightened of anything or anyone he can't control –'

Betty spun on her. 'Do you think James Case was better? Would you have liked your daughter to be with a worthless, selfish boy who had turned her on to drugs, who had 'promiscuous' written all over his smug face, and who didn't give a damn about anyone but himself? Would you want her to throw her talents and her past away for a promise that had no future?'

Caroline kept her temper in check. 'But who makes these decisions?' she asked. 'Brett, or you? Because from experience, I can tell you just how well the last works out....'

'And you think *this* worked out?' Betty's own voice was quiet now. 'You think Brett made *this* decision, don't you? That she was capable of murder – at least with the help of James's drugs.'

Caroline considered her answer. 'For someone else to have killed him,' she said at last, 'he or she would have had to follow them to Heron Lake. Or, at least, to know where they were going.'

Betty's eyes met Caroline's. 'Are you at least considering that?'

'I'll consider anything that might help. But there's little sign that they were followed – no tire tracks on the trail, no other cars spotted.' Caroline watched her sister's face. 'As for knowing they'd be at Heron Lake, the question becomes "who?" And, I suppose, "how?"'

Betty stood, walking to the edge of the porch. Silent, she gazed out at the distant village. 'What about this girl?' she said. 'The one that claims James was breaking it off with Brett that night.'

'It seems far-fetched to me.' Caroline remained in her chair, unable to see Betty's face now. 'Did Brett ever talk about her?'

'No. She wouldn't have.' The weariness of failure entered Betty's voice. 'I still don't even know her name.'

Caroline stood, moving next to Betty. 'In some ways,' she said, 'the less you know the better. Because nothing Brett or I can say to you is privileged.'

Betty turned to her. 'They wouldn't call me to testify against her, would they?'

'As to what?' Caroline put an edge in her voice. 'Is there

something else I need to know? At least that the police are capable of knowing?'

Quickly, Betty shook her head. 'No ... Of course not. It's just how they can twist things, like the fights we had about James –'

'But how would that hurt Brett?'

'It wouldn't, I suppose.' Betty paused. 'Except if they tried to make her seem – I don't know – more volatile.'

Caroline was quiet for a moment. 'I wouldn't worry,' she answered. 'I doubt that Jackson would want to give the jury too much time with Brett's agonized mother. Regrettably, he has better things to do.'

The front door opened behind them. But when Caroline turned, expecting her father, it was Larry who appeared.

His face was grave. 'Hello, Caroline.'

Betty went to him. 'Have you checked Father?'

'Yes. He's up now.' Larry turned back to Caroline. 'This has been a strain on him. He's usually up at six, but he's seemed so tired. Still, when it's close to nine, and no one's seen him ...' He paused, shrugging.

Caroline nodded. 'I'm sorry,' she said to Larry. 'But there's something I need to ask you.'

Larry turned to her, his face tired and wary. 'What is it?'

'This student – the witness against Brett. Her name is Megan Race. I was wondering if you knew her, or have a faculty friend who does.'

'Megan Race?' Larry repeated. He shoved his hands in his pockets, staring down at the porch as Betty watched him intently. 'That's the woman James was seeing?'

'Yes.'

His eyes seemed to narrow. 'Do you know what her major is?'

'Not offhand. Is there any way I could get my hands on her file?'

'No legitimate way ...'

'I'm not asking you to do that. Just for any information you can come up with.'

Larry seemed to exhale. 'I'll have to think about it,' he said. 'Very hard.'

When Caroline returned to the inn, there were two messages.

The easiest to return was from Walter Farris. She placed the call, waited on hold for ten minutes, pacing the room. By the time that Farris took her call, she was certain that he would tell her the nomination had been withdrawn.

'Caroline,' he said brusquely. 'I've spoken to the President.'

She felt herself tense. 'And?'

'And we reserve the right to withdraw the nomination if this trial goes on too long, or if there's any problem in what you're doing up there. By that I mean any problem as we down here define it.' Farris paused for effect. 'But, as of now, your nomination is still alive.'

Caroline sat down on the bed. 'Thank you.'

'Thank the President, who has more compassion than I would.'

His voice grew softer. 'Please, Caroline, don't misunderstand this. You're on your own now. Any misstep, and I'll pull the plug myself.'

The second message, from Joe Lemieux, required two calls to his beeper.

'I have her schedule,' he said. 'No grades, but at least you can see what she was taking. For whatever it might be worth.'

'It's a start. We can see what professors might know her, who else might have been in her classes. How did you get it, incidentally?'

'The school's computer system – the student can punch in for class schedule, registration, and a bunch of other stuff.' Lemieux laughed softly. 'The computer age presents an unlimited potential for invasion of privacy – in this case, all I needed was Megan's student number, which wasn't that hard to come by. But I wouldn't mention this to anyone.'

Caroline took a deep breath. 'I won't, believe me. And please, check with me before you do anything else like this I'm not interested in coming up on ethics charges, thank you.'

'I understand.' He sounded faintly nettled. 'Look, do you want this stuff or not?'

Caroline paused for a moment. 'Yes,' she said. 'I want it But don't fax it over. Drop it off by hand.'

She hung up and went to Carlton Grey's office. For the next two hours, she read statute books and talked by phone to experts – a serologist, a criminalist, and a doctor who treated drug and alcohol addiction. So that it was perhaps three-thirty before she returned to the inn and found the manila envelope beneath her door.

Caroline opened it. Megan was a senior now; Caroline reached the first trimester of her junior year before she stopped, staring at the schedule with what she wished were disbelief.

The telephone rang again.

She was slow to answer. 'Caroline,' Larry said, 'there's something I have to tell you.'

'Yes,' she replied. 'I know.'

Chapter 7

Caroline found him in his office at the English Department, sitting at his desk. He seemed too distraught to look away.

Caroline sat facing him and then said softly, 'You should have told me sooner.'

Larry stared at her. 'What must you think of me?' he asked with a certain dignity. 'I didn't know who the witness was until this morning, and I thought my confession could do without Betty. Given that your presence would complete her humiliation.'

Caroline's eyes met his. 'She doesn't know?'

'Not to a certainty, and definitely not who.' He stood abruptly. 'There's something wrong with her.'

'Megan, you mean?'

'Of course Megan.' His hands gripped the chair. 'First getting involved with Case, and now as the key witness against Brett. It's like she's had a plan to destroy my daughter ...'

'Somehow, Larry, I doubt she counted on James Case dying.'

Larry stiffened. 'How do you know Megan didn't kill him? This can't be some coincidence –'

Caroline held up one hand. 'I'm not saying that, either. Only that you brought this woman to Brett's doorstep.'

He blanched. 'But wouldn't that mean Brett's innocent?'

Caroline tilted her head. 'No. But what it may mean is that the key witness against her is damaged goods.' She paused for a moment 'In addition to whatever it does to your marriage.'

Larry's gaze was bleak. 'There's no help for that,' he said at length. 'Like so much else, Caroline, it's far too late.'

Slowly, Caroline nodded. 'Then tell me about you and

Megan. Considering that you're the only one who seems to know her. Besides James Case.'

Eyes averted, Larry walked to the door of his office, closing it tight, and then went to the window. He stood there, watching the late-afternoon sun fall softly across the red-brick buildings and rolling campus.

'It's been good here,' he said. 'All in all.'

Caroline studied his slender frame, the sunlight catching the silver in his hair. She said nothing.

Larry seemed to steel himself. 'My only excuse, Caro, is that I wasn't looking for her, at least not consciously. This woman came to me.'

Caroline considered him. 'I don't believe in Kismet. In my experience, people like Megan Race always know who to find.'

'Perhaps.' Larry turned from the window. 'But in the classroom, I was the one they heard. Not like at home.'

There was a faint undertone of self-contempt, as if Larry saw both versions of himself – the admired teacher, the deposed husband – as risible. 'And Betty?' Caroline asked. 'Where was she in all this?'

'Silent, in the great tradition of your family. Which slowly became mine.' He faced her again. 'In my experience, all those sex manuals miss the point. It isn't a matter of putting tab A in slot B. It's all the things that are unspoken and unresolved.' Briefly, Larry looked away. 'A kind of gray depression seeps into your soul, almost by stealth. So that you're so taken by how vivid someone like Megan Race can seem that you're blinded to the obvious – that whatever it is she sees in you is not about you.

'As first, she didn't seem that remarkable: a blond girl in the front row, asking questions, listening to your keenest points with her body leaning forward, her face open, straining to get it all. Then you notice the way she'll sit there for a moment when the lecture ends, a thoughtful, almost fond, half smile at the corner of her mouth. Until you begin to look for her and then, in an odd way, to count on her. Without either of you having said a word.'

Larry paused for a moment. The sadness in his eyes seemed to go with the creases in his face and neck, the sag of a persona that had lost its vitality with the loss of illusions. 'When she started coming to my office,' he said quietly, 'something inside me knew.

'It all began to fit. The way she moved the conversation from T. S. Eliot to things outside the class. The way she shut the door behind her, showed no interest in having coffee, or being in a public place. The almost reckless candor about herself and, after a few times, her sex life.

'I watched us with a kind of fascination, like a spectator to my own seduction. The married professor, listening with placid interest to the pretty student while she segued from Dylan Thomas to things like, "I think sex is spiritual, don't you – I mean, a mind that is uninhibited is more sexual than a well-toned body...."' He stopped himself, shaking his head.

'I've met her,' Caroline said quietly. 'You've developed some gifts as a mimic, Larry. She does have a certain breathless way of speaking.'

Larry's eyes shut. 'Jesus fucking Christ,' he mumbled. 'How could I have done this?'

'Because, as with several other things, you didn't see the consequences. At least not all of them.'

He turned from her. 'I never imagined, Caro, that I was endangering my daughter. Merely that I was risking my marriage and perhaps my job.' His voice held a musing bitterness. 'Later, I wondered if I didn't have some wish for self-destruction. To end my life, figuratively speaking, as I knew it.

'Whatever, I'd crossed the line. By the time Megan came to my office, to say she wanted an affair with me, I was past surprise.

'I sat there while she proposed the rules, with this strange light in her eyes. We would only meet at her apartment. She would no longer come to my office. She'd never mention my name to anyone. She wouldn't cause trouble in my marriage or take any more of my classes. All that she wanted was time with me.' Larry's voice grew quiet again. 'When she reached across the desk and placed the key in my hand, I could already imagine us.

'The next afternoon, I went there.'

Part of Caroline, the girl who had teased with her sister's husband over twenty years before, had heard enough. But the lawyer Caroline had no good use for her own sensitivities, or the remnants of his pride.

'Please, don't spare me the details,' she said. 'I need a picture of this woman.'

Larry leaned against the wall. As if to himself, he murmured, 'I'm late for dinner.'

Through the window, the fading light caught the hollows of his face. Caroline did not answer.

'The first time we were alone,' Larry said softly, 'she asked me to lie on the bed, and watch her.

'There was a full-length mirror on the wall. Slowly, she took off everything, a piece at a time....

'Just before she was naked, she turned to see herself.'

Larry paused, shaking his head. 'Do you know what I remember? That when our eyes met in the mirror, she mouthed "I love you."

'After a moment, she bent over.

'I understood it as she meant me to. When I was inside her, she masturbated until she came. And when *I* came, my eyes still open, she smiled at her own reflection.

' "I'll do anything you ask me to," she whispered.

'Suddenly, Caro, I was God. There was nothing I couldn't have from her – nothing. And when we had done whatever I asked, she would tell me that I was the best lover she had ever imagined....'

Larry's voice became tired, empty. ' "Imagined" was the word – I'm sure that my new prowess happened only in her head. But it also happened in mine.' He searched for words. 'Part of me knew that this "relationship" was arbitrary, of her own invention. But I was a sexual person again. I felt myself walk taller, smile more easily, a great lover within my secret world. Even as I lay next to Betty, frightened to death …'

Caroline watched him steadily. 'That was all there was? This meld of *Intermezzo* with *Fatal Attraction*?'

He winced. 'No. I also listened to her.'

'About what?'

'There were recurring themes. Her social views – which turned out to be some weird hybrid of Camille Paglia and "the politics of meaning." Literature, of course: sometimes she'd ask me to read to her.' He reflected. 'And, more and more frequently, her childhood. Mostly trauma, loneliness … Her father was killed in an accident.'

Caroline nodded. 'Did something strike you about that?'

His eyes narrowed. 'Less then than now.' He faced her now. 'When I broke it off, I gave Brett as a reason. What I remember now is Megan saying that I'd chosen Brett over her.' He shook his head, chagrined. 'In retrospect, it was like she'd lost a father.'

Caroline's eyes changed. 'I thought all she wanted was a little piece of your mind. And body.'

'At first, yes. There were rules for that too: Monday and Thursday, from three to five-thirty. Until she came to my office by surprise.

'That was the first breach of the rules.

'She was talking before I could protest.' Larry stopped, pensive. 'What I haven't conveyed to you is any picture of her energy – the excitement, the intimacy with which she looked at you, this incandescent smile. It was like she took you over….'

'Yes. I've seen some of that, too. I sensed a tinge of desperation about it.' Caroline considered him. 'I assume that she wanted, or needed, something from you.'

'To go away for a weekend.' In profile, Larry looked ashen, unable now to face her. 'And then she slipped a white envelope in my hand and asked me to open it before I answered.

'Inside was a Polaroid picture. One she had taken of

herself, in front of the mirror. She had only one hand on the camera....' His voice fell off.

'Yes,' Caroline said evenly. 'I think I get it. Do go on.'

Larry crossed his arms. 'There was also a note, making me a promise. The one thing I hadn't dared ask her to do.' He paused again. 'I don't know whether it was that, or the smile on her face when I looked up.

' "You see," she said, "I know you." '

Caroline felt a kind of dread. 'So you went with her.'

'Yes.'

'And Betty?'

'When I said I was going camping, she became very quiet.' Larry gazed out the window. 'I hadn't done that since Brett was small, and Betty has this instinct for anything that threatens her, or hers. The week before I went away, we hardly spoke.

'Megan and I drove to the White Mountains. With every mile, I felt more haunted, less safe. We had hardly pitched the tent before I made her keep her promise. But all that it meant to me was an escape from my own thoughts....

'To Megan, it meant something more.

' "We're different now," she told me. "No boy has ever done that to me. I was waiting for a man." '

'Something in her voice made me cringe. Part of it was the feeling – suddenly quite clear – that she had cast me in a fantasy that was far too comprehensive. But the worst part was the contrast between the 'man' of her imaginings and the real man, filled with the regret and memories of a twenty-five-year marriage, fearful of being caught before he gave that his due.' He paused. 'And then – and this was eerie – she started asking about Betty.'

He shook his head. 'I'd had this illusion, Caro, that I'd kept my worlds separate – that all I had to do was spend a few hours in one, and lie a little in the other. And then suddenly Megan wanted to know everything: about how Betty and I met, what she liked, what kind of home we had and what kind of mother she was, what we did in bed together....

'It was so bizarre. I was willing to violate our marriage vows, but to violate our privacy was too great a betrayal.' His voice grew quiet again. 'It was like whatever there was between us – our disappointments, our failures, our understandings, and even our silences – was Betty's and mine. And that I could never cheapen it to feed this girl's needs.'

'And after that?'

Larry turned to her. 'Two more weeks, and it was over.'

Caroline put a finger to her lips. 'Did anything else happen?' she asked.

Silent, Larry nodded. 'The whole balance changed,' he said finally. 'She began to fantasize about her role in my life, to advise me about my career and how to relate to Betty. She even spoke of befriending Brett....' He paused, shaking his head. 'I couldn't imagine what Brett would think of her –'

'*I* can,' Caroline said coolly. 'Tell me, did Megan ever approach her?'

'Not that I know about – if Brett had ever learned about us, I'm sure I'd have gotten more than a piece of her mind. But I felt Megan coming closer to the core of my life.' Larry shoved his hands in his pockets. 'Just before I broke it off, there were calls close to dinner-time, two nights running. The first one Betty answered; she said whoever it was waited for a moment, and then hung up. I just shrugged it off. But in my heart, I was afraid I knew....

'The next night I made sure to answer.

'We were in the kitchen. When I hurried to the phone, Betty looked up from the sink. So that she was watching my face when Megan began to speak....

' "I just wanted to hear your voice," Megan said.

'Betty had turned to me. ' "I think you have the wrong number," ' I managed to say.

' "Thank you," Megan whispered, and hung up.'

Larry lowered his eyes. 'When I put down the phone, Betty watched me for a moment. She didn't ask me anything at all.

'That was when I knew that *she* knew. And that I had to find my way out of this, any way I could.

'For the next two days, until our Monday, I tried to frame my excuses. Something, anything, to dampen the explosion I had begun to fear.

'Megan sat there on the edge of the bed, hands folded in front of her, while I told her. I tried to dwell on the person with whom I thought Megan might sympathize most – Brett.' His voice turned harsh. 'The whole time I listened to what a fraud I was – this cipher, inflating my role to what a real father might have. But the odd thing is that my story had been true, once – when Brett was six, before I was trapped by tenure, I imagined leaving Betty, the job, the looming omnipresence of your father and that house.' His voice softened. 'Do you know what stopped me, Caro? That I'd be leaving without Brett. Because they'd never let me have her.'

Caroline folded her arms, head bowed. For a moment she could think of nothing to say.

'And Megan?' she asked at length.

'Defied my expectations. There were no tears, or threats, or rage. All that she said, as if she had expected it, was, "You've chosen your daughter over me."

I left as quickly as I could.

I was on edge for days – jumpy when the phone rang, or the door to my office opened, afraid it would be her.

There was nothing. Just one sad, simple letter, which, in its own way, frightened me as much. Because it described a relationship that we had never had.' He exhaled. 'A meeting of souls, she called it.'

Caroline looked up at him. 'Did you keep the letter?'

'Of course not.'

'Because I was hoping that you'd have some proof that any of this ever happened.'

Larry stared at her. 'I'll have to testify – show how this woman must have said and done these things to get at me....' The thought stopped him, for a moment, and then

243

he finished with calm resolve. 'I'll need to tell Betty, of course. As soon as I get home.'

Almost absently, Caroline rubbed her temple, still gazing up at Larry. 'Did you tell anyone about Megan at the time?'

Larry's eyes widened slightly; with a kind of fascination, Caroline watched as understanding dawned. 'No,' he said in a flat voice. 'I was very careful.'

'So no one saw you?'

'I don't think so.'

'No gifts, or pictures?' Caroline's voice softened. 'Not even a Polaroid?'

Larry flushed. 'No.'

Caroline sat back. 'So now you know, Larry, how Megan expects to get away with this. Because, it appears, *you* did.'

Larry lowered himself heavily into his chair. They sat there in the half-light of early evening, silent.

'Why would anyone believe,' he said at last, 'that I would concoct a story like this, and destroy my marriage in the bargain.'

'Oh, I believe you – the whole thing sounds right to me. But the reason you'd "concoct" this story is simple: to save your daughter by claiming that the key witness against her is acting out of spite. And even your version can't explain Megan's relationship to James, or her quite lethal claim that she was the one James was taking to California.' Caroline's voice grew quiet. 'For all Jackson Watts knows, Betty may be part of your conspiracy.'

Larry's mouth formed a stubborn line. 'They'll believe me.'

'Will they? Because it's clear that Megan was involved with James – for however long and for whatever reason – and you can't prove that she was ever involved with you.' Caroline paused.

'When did it end, by the way?'

'Late last fall.'

'A nice cold trail, that.' Caroline raised an eyebrow. 'Then I take it this mythic camp-out with Megan was not the one you were on the night that Case was murdered.'

244

'No.' Larry looked away. 'Ironically, I really was alone. To think.'

Caroline smiled without humor. 'Well,' she said, 'at least you're not Megan's alibi.'

Across the desk, she watched as Larry's eyes closed. Softly, he said, 'How badly that summer has ended, Caro. For all of us.'

For a long while, Caroline was silent. When she spoke again, her voice was gentle. 'I'll try to use this without calling you as a witness. Let me speak to Jackson first. If he's afraid Megan is flawed enough, he may dismiss the case while he looks for more. Including more about Megan.' Her tone grew quieter still. 'So you needn't tell Betty yet, or Brett. I'll let you know if you have to face that.'

Larry's eyes opened. 'And Channing?'

Caroline sat straighter, and her voice became brittle. 'There's been quite enough running to Daddy in our annals, don't you think?' She caught herself, finishing in a level tone: 'I refuse, unless I must, to leave this family even worse than I found it. That might be more than even I could bear.'

Chapter 8

'So,' Caroline said, 'your defendant's father was fucking your prize witness. Who strikes me, by the way, as more than a bit unstable.'

Jackson sat next to her on a park bench near the station house. He rolled up his shirtsleeves, expression quite calm, as if she had said nothing at all remarkable. 'Too bad,' he said finally. 'Megan spoke so well of you. Better, it seems, than you do of me.'

Caroline gave him a level gaze. 'You have to get on this, Jackson, and you know it. The defense has come to you with critical information, which it could have used to sandbag you in court. If you go forward without an inquiry, it's virtual misconduct.'

Jackson turned to her. 'All right,' he said. 'What would you have me do?'

Caroline looked at him intently. 'For openers, send the Major Crimes Unit to interview Larry and then check out his story – there must be someone, somewhere, to whom Megan said something.' She drew a breath. 'But if there isn't anyone, I'm asking you to search this girl's apartment.'

'A warrant? For what?'

'For anything that would confirm her relationship to Larry. And to explore whether she had any relationship to the victim after April.'

Jackson stared at her. 'So that's why you came. You want the prosecutor to alienate a prosecution witness by doing what the defense has no power to do – get a search warrant to turn her place upside down.' His voice became incredulous. 'Tell me, Caroline, have you had any luck with this one in San Francisco?'

'I haven't had this one in San Francisco.' Caroline felt herself losing any pretense of dispassion. 'Megan has such obvious potential bias that she may have made this whole thing up –'

'Not about going to California,' Jackson cut in. 'And you damned well know it. Please, don't insult my intelligence.'

Caroline folded her hands. 'You might be able to explain even that. If you'd simply look in her apartment.'

'If I simply treat this girl like a criminal, you mean.' His study of her face became lingering and comprehensive. 'I know this involves your family. But I've got no basis for doing what you ask.'

'Perjury *is* a crime, you know.'

'Only if proven.' Jackson paused. 'Look, I'll talk to Larry myself, without you. I'll also have our people sniff around. And then I'll confront Megan with these charges.'

Caroline stood. 'With what, damn it? She'll deny it and – like a fool – I will have prepared her for the hearing.'

'Not like a fool.' His gaze grew pointed. 'If you honestly thought you could salvage Brett by destroying Megan Race on cross, you'd have done it in a heartbeat – her parents' marriage be damned. But you don't have anything, do you, and you don't think you're getting anything, either. Unless you have my help.' His tone became even. 'You're just as well off having me surprise this girl. Because if there's any real problem, you know that I'll act on it.'

Caroline considered him. 'Yes,' she said at length. 'That much I do know. But I think I've made a terrible mistake and that you're about to make one too. At whatever cost to Brett.'

Jackson stood. 'I truly hope not,' he answered. 'Because this hearing you want so badly is in five days now, and it would be nice if it produced some semblance of the truth. Which, as I continue to believe that you believe, is that Brett Allen killed this boy.'

He turned and walked back to his office.

Leaving the car, Caroline faced the stand of trees alone.

It was night, twelve hours since she had driven from Concord, the image of this moment slowly forming in her mind. So that now, entering the trees, she imagined herself as Brett.

Deadwood crackled beneath her feet; branches struck her face, her body. Arms raised for self-protection, she could see almost nothing. Only her senses knew the way.

The darkness seemed interminable. Amidst towering pines, no moonlight came. There was no sound but Caroline.

And then, a first thin light, the trunks of trees appearing. More swiftly now, Caroline walked to the edge of the stand. Her face was damp with sweat.

In front of her was the glade.

She knelt there, next to where James Case had died, and gazed at the lake.

The moon was crescent, half of what it had been for Brett, and the water was an obsidian sheet. She could not see the platform to which Brett claimed to have swum.

In the woods behind her, something crackled.

Caroline whirled, heart suddenly racing. The woods were black, silent.

She stood there, facing the dark, a chill on her skin.

Slowly, reluctantly, Caroline turned back to the lake.

She was still for a moment, remembering where the platform must be. And then she pulled off her jacket and jeans, and stepped from the glade toward the water. Through her running shorts and tank top, the night air felt cool.

With halting steps, she moved to the shoreline, rocks hurting her feet. Just, she realized, as Brett had described.

The first shock of cold water as she dove jarred her from the thought. She was Caroline now, swimming for the platform her father had built when she was small, borne by a memory that crossed the fissures of her life.

Her strokes were long and smooth, as they had been since she was young. She found that she knew – almost to the moment – when her hand would touch the platform she could not see.

She pulled herself up, sat on the edge, breathing deeply in the cool night air.

The light was better here; on the lake, trees did not block the moon. But the shoreline was a rise in the darkness, formless trees. Only the glade seemed light.

Motionless, she listened.

Nothing.

Slowly, systematically, she scanned the shoreline for movement.

But she saw nothing, heard no one on the water. Felt cold and dampness, the wet tendrils of her hair, her eyes straining for light.

Something had changed.

As she turned, a shadow crossed the glade, silver in moonlight.

Caroline froze. Only when the shadow knelt, still and silent, was she certain it was there.

Caroline dove into the water.

Her strokes were choppy, panicky, as Brett's might have been. Her body strained in the water, nerves tingling as she struggled to shore. Her pulse sounded in her ears.

When she reached the shore and stepped from the water, the shadow was still.

Her breaths were ragged. As she walked toward the glade, grass beneath her feet, the shadow stood to face her.

'Hello, Father,' Caroline said.

Channing Masters stepped into the moonlight. His deep-set eyes were shadows.

'You could see me, then.'

'Only in the glade. Not before.' Caroline paused, to ease her breathing. 'Where did you come from?'

'The trail past Mosher's place. It ends perhaps a hundred yards from here.'

In the moonlight, she could see that his boots were wet. 'And then along the water?'

'Yes. Just as I suggested.' His voice was firm. 'You couldn't see me, Caroline, or hear me – just as Brett couldn't. Until I reached the glade.'

'True. But then your killer, whoever that might be, would have to know the way. And know, somehow, where Brett and James would be.'

Silent, Channing sat, staring at the lake. 'Just that they would be here,' he said finally. 'The sign at the head of Mosher Trail says "Heron Lake."'

His voice was quieter now. Caroline put on her jacket and knelt on the grass beside him. 'Tired?' she asked.

'A little, yes.' He still looked at the water. 'Do you know what was strange for me, Caroline? That for a moment, as you came toward me in the darkness, your face was like Nicole's.'

Caroline folded her arms. Softly, she answered, 'I'm no more like her than I ever was. I look at my face, Father, and I see you written there.'

He was quiet, still. She stared at the grass in front of her.

'Hasn't it occurred to you,' she said at last, 'that a knife is the wrong weapon for your killer? How could he, or she, count on slashing two healthy young people at once?'

Slowly, Channing nodded. 'He'd use a gun, I think. But suppose he saw that Case was alone, and asleep.' His voice became thoughtful. 'A knife has the virtue of silence. Which, in turn, could mean escape without detection.'

Narrow-eyed, Caroline picked at a blade of grass. 'That means bringing a gun *and* the knife. A very nice knife, at that.'

When Caroline turned to him, her father would not look at her. 'All that I'm saying,' he said at last, 'is that it's plausible. And that, for a jury, plausible might do.'

Caroline said nothing.

He stood up, still gazing at the water. 'This Megan. Could she be a suspect? Just as you suggested?'

'A "plausible" suspect, you mean? As opposed to just a liar?'

Channing hesitated. 'Yes.'

'I don't know yet.' For a moment, Caroline watched him. 'But your theory surely needs one. As does Brett, quite desperately.'

Chapter 9

Caroline pored over her notes and began to outline her examination of the police witnesses – the arresting and interrogating officers, the medical examiner, the crime lab technicians. Carlton Grey's spare office was quiet; the first light of dawn came through the window. It was four days before the hearing.

The press had begun calling. Caroline had been courteous; quietly, she intimated that the hearing would expose deep problems in the prosecutor's case. But Jackson had refused to fuel the stories with any comment of his own. Caroline did not know the status of Megan Race.

She rose from the desk, staring out the window. Brett was facing matters with a new composure; though she was clearly tired and afraid, she treated Caroline with a certain courtesy, as if sensing that self-control was something Caroline needed from her. It was as though they had exchanged roles – Caroline herself was short-tempered, her nerves frayed. She had passed the point of exhaustion without noticing.

When the telephone rang, Caroline flinched.

She turned, saw the phone on an end table she had never noted. She gathered herself, walked across the room, and answered.

'Yes?'

'Caroline?' Jackson said. 'I tried the inn, and they said that you were gone. I know it's early, but I also know how concerned you've been.'

His tone was so polite that Caroline's hopes began to fade. 'This is about Megan, I imagine.'

'It is.' Jackson spoke quickly, as if his speech was well rehearsed. 'If it were simply a matter of Larry's demeanor, I would have found this easier – what he told me sounded persuasive, and seemingly quite painful. I came out wanting to believe him....'

'But?'

'But he couldn't give me any corroborating evidence, and our investigators couldn't find a scrap of it – no one who saw them together, or even heard Megan speak his name outside class. Beyond some vague statement Megan made to a neighbor about the virtues of an older lover, there's nothing that even suggests that Larry might be telling the truth –'

'So give him a lie detector test.'

She had said it on impulse. But Jackson's civility was too complete, she realized, to throw her own refusal regarding Brett back at her – sufficient answer in itself.

'Once I do that,' he said evenly, 'I have to test Megan too. Which transfers the task of assessing witnesses – none of whom are charged with a crime – from the courtroom to a machine, one that a fair number of experts don't accept. We don't run our cases that way and, with respect, I can't start now. Even granting your concern.'

Caroline stood straighter. 'Quit treating me like I'm some emotional cripple at the deathbed of a relative, all right? I'm a lawyer whose client was indicted because of a witness who may well be a pathological liar.'

For the first time, Jackson hesitated. 'I've spoken with her, Caroline. Quite angrily – and also quite persuasively – Megan says that Larry was nothing more to her than a moderately interesting professor she had for a single class. And she reminded me, as if I needed it, that her testimony involves a proven relationship with James Case, which was discovered by your client. Another fact that, unless and until Brett testifies, no one has disputed. Not even you.'

Caroline was silent for a moment. 'Jackson,' she said at length, 'there's something wrong with Megan Race. Her whole performance the other day was aimed at persuading me to plead Brett guilty. Every instinct I've got tells me she's afraid of testifying.'

'Then she's got a poor way of showing it. Because once

she came forward, she had to know that testifying is a real possibility. And – assuming Larry's story to be true – that he would be a central subject of any cross-examination –'

'All that she assumed,' Caroline interjected, 'was that no one would be able to prove it. Which you haven't.'

At length he said, 'Then that's become your problem, hasn't it.'

Caroline's fingers tightened on the telephone. 'Please,' she said, 'get a warrant. Look for calendars, datebooks, scraps of paper – anything with Larry's name on it. Or James's name.'

This time Jackson did not hesitate. 'I'm sorry, Caroline. I won't harass this witness – not unless you've got something more. Do you?'

Caroline paused. 'No. Not yet.'

'Then please call me once you do,' Jackson said politely, and hung up.

With the office door shut, Caroline listened to Joe Lemieux's report on Megan Race. It was past noon, and Caroline had not eaten.

'There's no therapy we can find,' he said in summary. 'No history of strange behavior – at least nothing really bizarre.'

'What about merely eccentric?'

'Maybe that. She does seem a little short of friends – which may be why she treated that poor neighbor lady, and you, to lectures on her sex life. The one roommate I found said that she sort of glommed onto her, like she was trying to take over her life. The way she put it was that Megan wore her out.' Lemieux shrugged. 'Since then, Megan's lived alone.'

Caroline nodded. 'All that fits with Larry's story. There's something obsessive about this girl, Joe. Which is exactly how she described Brett.'

'Meaning?'

'That if you're disturbed enough, you project your

disturbances onto other people. Megan saw in Brett all the threatening qualities she herself had.'

Lemieux frowned; with his thin face and thoughtful eyes, he looked less like a detective than a doctoral student, lost in his own private specialty. 'Maybe,' he said dubiously. 'But if you're right, then Megan's pretty good at maintaining. There's no evidence, for example, that she's ever been in therapy. She was a high school honor student, and she's gotten through three years of college with good grades and no obvious problems – let alone being caught baying at the moon.' He looked at Caroline more closely. 'There is this, Caroline: You know that job she has at the student union – noon and night?'

'Uh-huh.'

'For whatever reason, and for whatever it's worth, she called in sick the night Case was murdered.'

Caroline cocked her head. 'We can confirm that?'

'With time slips, sure.' Lemieux scowled. 'The problem, of course, is that there's no good reason to believe that she had any reason to hate the guy, or was anywhere near Heron Lake. Let alone that she walks around with – what was it? – a knife and a gun.'

Caroline studied him. Softly, she said, 'Anyone can get them, Joe. It's the American way.'

'So it is; But you're a long way from putting a gun in this girl's hands. Or even that knife.'

Caroline was quiet for a time. 'I also wanted her current schedule,' she said at last.

Lemieux looked at her hard now. 'Can I ask why?'

Caroline shrugged. 'Curiosity.'

Lemieux's eyes narrowed. In a flat voice, he said, 'Same schedule – noon to two serving food, and eight to ten running the coffee bar. Some nights, when it's slow, she closes early.'

'Thanks.'

Lemieux considered his fingernails. 'No luck with the prosecutor?'

'None.' Caroline folded her hands in front of her. 'What kind of security does Megan's building have?'

Lemieux looked up at her. 'It's a fifties apartment,' he said slowly, 'like the one Case lived in. A buzzer at the front door is all.'

For a moment, Caroline was quiet. 'Dead bolts?' she inquired.

Lemieux's eyes met hers. With equal quiet, he answered, 'I can't do that, Counselor.'

Caroline's stomach felt empty. She kept her face expressionless. 'You can't tell me if there are dead bolts?'

Lemieux's eyes did not move. 'I didn't see dead bolts,' he said at last.

At two o'clock, restless, Caroline left the office. She was dressed in jeans and behind the wheel before she knew where she would go.

She drove past Masters Hill, hardly glancing at her father's home, and did not get out until she reached the foot of the trail she had climbed two weeks before – before she had met Brett Allen and begun unraveling the self-creation of more than twenty years, until she was no longer sure what it meant to be Caroline Masters.

Slowly and steadily, Caroline traversed the side of the hill, climbing between the brush and trees. As she reached the top, she half expected to see her father on the fallen log, surveying Resolve and the country beyond. But Caroline was alone.

Though the day was overcast, she could see great distances – the roofs and spires of the town from which she had driven, mountains undulating westward until the last peaks met the sky. But nothing else was clear to her.

For twenty years, Caroline had lived by the law and its rules. Perhaps not the rules as lay people understood them – Caroline the defense lawyer accepted the hardest truths of justice: That the presumption of innocence must protect the guilty. That when police and prosecutors break the rules, sometimes an evil person must go free. That it was

Caroline's job to enforce these rules at whatever cost. Sometimes this had haunted her: police without rules were an injustice waiting to happen, but where was the justice in freeing an incorrigible criminal – a murderer, a rapist, a molester – to harm yet another victim? The fact that she might also have protected the innocent was, on certain nights, too theoretical to allow for easy sleep.

But she had always obeyed the rules as she understood them. Just as, she insisted, the police should.

Closing her eyes, she imagined Brett's life.

This was far too easy for her now. Caroline knew Brett's daily routine – loneliness, too little exercise, reading until the words swam in front of her, writing in a diary she must censor to protect her deepest thoughts. And then, in her mind, Caroline followed her through the twenty-year sentence that Jackson Watts, with the prosecutor's pitiless sense of duty, demanded as the minimum. Knew the terrible apartness, yet the loss of all her privacy. Felt the absence of friends or lovers or children, the withering of sexuality as twenty-two became thirty-two, and then forty-two. Saw the pallor as Brett at last left prison, her face lined from the passage of empty years, the richness of her youth behind her. All because of a single witness and the darkness of a single night.

All at once, a memory came to Caroline. She was young again, a lawyer for perhaps a year. A client, out on bail, had come to her office. He did not deny his guilt, hoped merely for a lighter sentence. He was scruffy and slight, and wore a slightly aggrieved expression. 'They made it so easy,' he complained – like so many of her clients, Caroline realized, he blamed a nameless 'they' for the actions he had taken. And then, to prove his point, he closed the door to her office, produced a thin plastic credit card, and slid it through the slit near the door handle.

The door seemed to spring open in his hand. 'See,' he said in an accusatory voice. 'No dead bolt.'

'Yes,' Caroline had answered dryly. 'What else can "they" expect?'

What they could expect, Caroline thought now, was that a judge would honor the law. At whatever cost.

Caroline gazed at the distant town. When she was done, whatever happened, she would ask them to withdraw her nomination.

Chapter 10

Caroline sat in her car, a half block down the twilit street.

Her watch read 7:50. Edgy, she scanned the rearview mirror. No one passed through the front door of the apartment building.

Perhaps, Caroline thought, Megan would not work tonight. She waited, poised between tension and relief.

In the mirror, the door to the building opened.

Caroline did not turn. There was a flash of reflected movement; in the dusk, the figure of a woman was a tiny shadow in a piece of glass. Caroline could not tell who she was.

The passenger window was cracked open. Caroline waited, utterly still, listening for footsteps on the other side of the street. Hoping that twilight and the shade of trees hid her inside the car.

The sound of wooden heels on cement came faintly through the window.

Still Caroline did not turn. Only after another moment did she see the tall, stiff carriage of Megan Race as she passed beneath a tree.

A streetlight came on. Caroline last saw Megan as a shadow, moving from light to darkness, heedless of anything.

Looking about her, Caroline stepped into the silent street.

It was tree-shrouded, empty. Dressed in a light jacket and jeans, Caroline crossed the street. Her running shoes made no sound.

The half block to the apartment seemed vague, unreal. She reached the door with a sense of disbelief.

The building was a sterile rectangle with four floors.

Megan was on the fourth, Caroline knew, which increased the difficulty of entrance or escape.

She stood there, irresolute.

This was no good – someone might see her. She fought her imagination: the thing to do was to go one step at a time. Knowing that these moments, however fatal to her spirit, could pass without detection.

Stiffly, Caroline pushed all ten buttons for the second floor.

Silence.

Caroline breathed in, waiting. Then some trusting soul above her pushed the door buzzer, and she was inside.

She stood in a bare lobby – an elevator, a stairwell with a green neon exit sign. Caroline opened the door to the stairwell and then closed it behind her.

The stairs were dark. Soon apartment doors would open on the second floor and tenants would peer into the hall, wondering who had buzzed them. Caroline hurried up the stairs.

At the second floor, she whirled, saw a lone woman in the hallway through the glass window of the exit door. It was only as she reached the fourth floor that she realized this reminded her of Brett, and prison.

Breathing rapidly, Caroline peered through the window. The corridor was empty; there was no sense of the disturbance two floors down. Once in Megan's apartment, Caroline could disappear.

With an air of calm she did not feel, Caroline stepped into the corridor. It was not long, just five doors on each side.

Megan's apartment was on the left.

Don't think, Caroline told herself. *Just do.*

She went to Megan's door.

In the pocket of her jacket was a handkerchief and the thin plastic card that Caroline used to enter her office building after hours. It was the one card that did not bear her name.

Looking over her shoulder, she saw no one. The hollow

sound of voices on a television came through the door next to Megan's.

Caroline slipped out the card and placed the handkerchief on the metal doorknob. Her forehead felt damp. No longer would anyone mistake what she was doing; suddenly, she regretted again that wearing gloves would make her conspicuous, that buying them would make her memorable. She slid the card through the crack –

It slipped from her fingers.

Caroline caught her breath. The card hit the tile with a slap and lay at her feet, glistening in the light. Taut, Caroline knew that she could have lost it through the crack.

Quickly, she picked it up.

With every hesitation, the inevitable moment when the next person entered the hallway was that much closer – perhaps the manager, following up the unexplained ringing. Caroline's watch read 8:17.

Slowly, she reinserted the card, eyes narrow. Slipped it above the latch, then at an angle, to catch the indentation of the lock.

Breath held, Caroline slid the card between the lock and the door and pulled gently on the door.

There was a soft click. The knob had moved in her hand.

Opening the door, she slid into Megan's apartment and softly shut the door.

It was pitch dark. It took Caroline a moment of blind fumbling, handkerchief covering her fingertips, to find the switch on the wall.

She stood there, blinking in the light.

The apartment was simple – a living room with a kitchen to one side and, next to that, the door to what must be Megan's bedroom. As Caroline stood there, irresolute, footsteps sounded in the corridor.

She froze.

The footsteps were heavy, a man's. They came closer; for an instant, Caroline imagined that they had stopped at Megan's door. Then the next footstep fell, and another. After a moment, she could not hear them.

For a time, Caroline told herself, she was safe.

Caroline looked around again.

She had expected color, vivid posters, perhaps pictures of Megan herself. But the apartment was bland, impersonal – the furniture looked institutional, the walls were bare cinder block. There was little sense that anyone lived here, Caroline thought – young or old, man or woman.

She went to the bedroom, handkerchief still draped across the fingers of her left hand.

Inside, on the door to Megan's closet, was a full-length mirror.

Just as Larry had described it, the mirror faced the foot of Megan's bed. All at once, Caroline was certain that Larry had told the truth.

Her watch read 8:25.

Swiftly, Caroline went through the drawers of Megan's dresser. She found nothing but slacks, T-shirts, bras, and underpants – all thrown together in a chaotic mess. Wiping clean the drawer handles, she went to the closet.

It was generous in size, with sliding wood doors. One door was off its tracks; arduously, Caroline pushed it to the side and then peered into the closet.

There were dresses, a parka, boots and shoes. But what stopped Caroline abruptly was a large open box.

On top of the box was a Polaroid camera.

Caroline knelt, carefully putting the camera aside.

Beneath was a spiral notebook. Written on the cover was the name of Larry's course.

Caroline opened the notebook. The notes she read were detailed, less the practical jottings of a college student than something almost reverent, as literal a rendering of lecture upon lecture as the hurried scrawl could make it. But nothing more.

And then Caroline saw the calendar.

It was from the year before. The months of October through November, the time of their affair, had been ripped out as if in rage.

Wedged to the side was a map of the White Mountains.

Caroline opened it. Toward the bottom, circled in pen, was the campsite that Larry had described to her.

For a moment, Caroline was still.

She was right, Caroline now knew – at least about what Megan was, as well as who she had been to Larry. But none of what she had found so far would prove anything in a court of law. Even if she could leave with it.

Carefully, Caroline placed each item back in the box and closed the closet door.

It was 8:43.

Caroline turned, facing the bedroom.

The sole piece of distinctive furniture was a light oak rolltop desk.

There were a few books on its shelf. All dealt with psychology, Caroline saw: the family, dysfunctional or not; only children; the relationship between fathers and daughters. But there were no clues – here or anywhere – to Megan's real family.

Caroline slid open the desk drawer.

Inside were two expensive pens and a red leather-bound journal with a green ribbon coming from between its pages.

The journal fell open in her hands.

The entries were dated from the beginning of Megan's sophomore year. Hurriedly, Caroline began reading. The first pages were an unsettling jumble – vague spiritual yearnings, descriptions of sex acts without names or faces, a paradoxical hostility to men as a group. The entries seemed to gain in extravagance, or vehemence, as Caroline worked toward the middle. And then Caroline turned a page and found the ragged remnant of a ripped-out entry.

The months of September through December were missing.

Without much hope, Caroline resumed in February.

The handwriting seemed jagged now, the sprawl of emotion on the page. But Caroline saw no mention of Larry.

She turned another page and then stopped abruptly.

She read the page, read it again. With trembling fingers, she scanned the entries, until she got to May.

Caroline stopped again, staring at the page.

'Jesus Christ,' she said aloud.

Caroline read again, more carefully, sitting cross-legged on the floor. She could feel her heart race.

When she had finished, she sat with the journal in her lap, trying to collect her thoughts.

Her watch read 9:15.

There was no way to copy these pages, return the journal to its drawer as if she had never been here. The only conceivable place to Xerox was the library at Chase College, and there were too many traps: that she would be seen there; that she might not be able to reenter the building or Megan's apartment; that she would be caught if she tried; that Megan herself could find her. Caroline stared at the journal in her lap.

Whatever the consequences, she could not leave without it.

The time was 9:22.

Fighting her nerves, Caroline systematically reviewed where she had been. Then she put down the journal, went to the living room with her handkerchief in hand, and began to retrace her steps.

At every point – the light switch, the inside knob, the door to Megan's room – Caroline wiped the surface clean of fingerprints.

Sometimes she leaves work early, Lemieux had said.

Hurriedly glancing at her watch, Caroline saw that it was 9:31.

There was still much to do.

She went to the bedroom, wiping the dresser drawer handles and then the sliding door to Megan's closet.

The biggest problem, she realized, was the box.

Pulling it from the closet, Caroline wiped all that she could remember touching: the camera; the cover of the notebook; its edges; the corners of the map; the box itself.

As she did this, she listened for sounds. But all she could hear was the faint sound of the television in the apartment next door.

It was 9:51 when Caroline shoved the box back inside with the toe of her shoe.

Turning, she gazed at the journal on the floor.

It was the moment of decision, she knew, the final chance to return the journal to its drawer and leave. She could feel her own hesitancy, the premonition of ill consequence.

Caroline walked across the bedroom and wiped away the final fingerprints on the rolltop desk.

It was 9:54.

Within fifteen minutes, Megan would return.

There was no more time to decide.

Caroline went to the center of the room, picked up the journal, and turned to leave.

There was a sudden sound, the rattle of keys outside the door.

For an instant, Caroline froze. She did not know what saving instinct told her, just before the door opened, to scramble to the wall and switch off the bedroom light.

As Caroline faced the darkened room, Megan closed the door behind her.

Caroline sensed, but could not see, the door to the closet. Her pulse pounded in her ears.

Quickly, Caroline moved forward, hoping not to trip on something. She found the crevice of the closet door as Megan's footsteps crossed the living room, coming closer.

Pushing with one palm, Caroline forced open the reluctant door. As she stepped inside, the door softly squealed, then slid into place.

With crabbed steps, Caroline turned.

Megan's footsteps entered the bedroom.

The light switched on.

Megan stood there, peering about. In profile, she looked wary and unhappy, consumed by secret thoughts.

If she faced the closet, Caroline knew, Megan would see her.

Caroline was utterly still.

Walking to the middle of the room, Megan pulled off her sweatshirt.

With a kind of fascination, Caroline watched – afraid, as Megan slipped off her blue jeans, that she would hang them in the closet.

Megan left them in a heap.

When she was naked, Megan turned to the mirror.

She studied herself intently, critically. And then she tilted her head, eyes opening wider, as if imploring the mirror for compassion. One finger grazed her nipple; she stood there like a statue, caught in her aloneness. Caroline held her breath.

Megan turned from the mirror.

For a moment, she gazed at the floor, pensive. Caroline could see her full face now; all that Megan needed was to look up, and her eyes would meet those of the woman who watched her.

Slowly, Megan turned from the closet and moved toward the dresser, slipping from Caroline's view.

There were only sounds now – a drawer sliding open, hands sifting clothes. And then Megan, wearing a T-shirt, crossed the bedroom and disappeared again.

Caroline hesitated. If she stayed here, Megan would surely find her; even if she did not, Caroline could not chance crossing the bedroom later in the hope that Megan slept.

Megan's footsteps grew lighter.

Please, Caroline begged her, *go to the kitchen*.

Caroline slid from the closet and stole across the bedroom, holding the journal. Her feet made no sound.

At the bedroom door, she peered into the living room. No one.

As Caroline stepped into the living room, she heard the rattling of silverware.

Caroline tried to remember the layout of the kitchen. The sink and cabinets, she recalled, were on the wall; to use them, Megan could not face the living room.

Caroline took a deep breath and headed, swiftly and silently, for the door.

A few feet farther on, Megan would be able to see her.

Caroline reached the space. As she swiftly turned, half expecting to hear a cry, she saw Megan bend over the sink, a tea bag in her hand.

Soundless, Caroline crossed the living room.

She paused at the door, hearing Megan stir a spoon inside a cup, and took the handkerchief from her pocket.

Fingers draped on the handkerchief, Caroline turned the knob.

The door groaned slightly.

Abruptly, the sounds from the kitchen stopped.

Panicky, Caroline peered into the hallway, saw no one. She slid quickly through the door.

It shut behind her, of its own weight, with a soft click.

Caroline hurried for the stairwell.

She did not care about noise now. Heart racing, she pushed open the door, jerking it closed behind her. Through the glass window, she saw Megan peer into the hallway.

Caroline ran down the stairs, through the above, and into the cool night.

The drive was surreal. The mundane became the mirror of Caroline's fears – headlights were police cars; the old man sitting on the porch of the inn had peered at the journal in her hand. She hurried to her room.

She sat on the end of the bed. *Now you know*, she told herself, *how it feels to commit a crime*.

There was nowhere, Caroline knew, that she could hide the journal.

In her briefcase was a flat manila envelope.

As the idea took form, Caroline saw that there was no choice: by now, quite possibly, Megan had called the police.

From the briefcase, Caroline took the Magic Marker she used to red-line pleadings.

On the face of the envelope, she printed her own name. Beneath that she wrote 'c/o Betty Allen,' the address of Masters Hill, and the words 'personal and confidential.' Her painstaking block letters were not Caroline's own but those of a child.

She took a roll of stamps from her purse and applied six stamps to the envelope.

For a last moment, she looked at the diary. Then she placed it inside the envelope, licked the flap, and sealed it tight.

When she left her room, descending the stairs, the man no longer sat on the porch. The main street of Resolve was dark and empty.

Alone, Caroline wandered the streets of her childhood. In the quiet, a flash of memory came: Caroline and Jackson Watts in a convertible he had borrowed, careening through the streets on a warm summer night, a six-pack of beer in the back. In that moment, the years vanished, and her life was new again.

But now only Brett's life was new. There was no sound but crickets, the soft fall of each footstep on asphalt.

At the bend in the street was the old general store. As Caroline approached it, she could make out the dark shape of a blue postal box.

Caroline opened the metal lid. For a last minute, she considered her choices. Then she dropped the envelope down the chute, consigning Brett's future, and perhaps her own, to the mercies of the U.S. mail.

There was one more thing to do.

Caroline walked to the bridge. Beneath, she could hear the soft murmur of the brook, see her outline reflected in the moonlight.

She took the Magic Marker from her pocket and gently dropped it in the water. It made no sound at all.

Chapter 11

'I thought I'd deliver these,' Caroline said, 'in person.'

She had found Jackson on the dock of his fishing camp, repairing an outboard motor. He wiped the grease on his jeans.

'What are they?' he asked.

'Subpoenas – five, actually. For your various people and, of course, for Megan Race. Unless you'd prefer that I serve her myself.'

Jackson hesitated. 'No. I'll make sure she's there.'

Caroline studied him. 'Somehow you don't sound confident of that.'

Jackson took the subpoenas from her hand. He perused them, eyes narrow, and then gazed at the lake, glistening with midmorning sun.

'Megan called me yesterday,' Jackson said at length. 'She believes that someone broke into her apartment. The night before last.'

Caroline raised her eyebrows. 'Believes? Either someone did, or they didn't.' Her voice turned arid. 'Tell me, is there any sign of a break-in? Or is this a particularly rich chapter in Megan's fantasy life?'

Jackson turned to her. 'She thinks you sent someone, Caroline. A professional.'

Caroline gave a short laugh. 'I didn't "send" anyone.'

Jackson looked at her hard now. 'I assumed that, Caroline, even without your saying so. But I couldn't help pondering how intently – and how recently – you were pushing me to search her place.'

Caroline considered him. 'Why do you even believe her? Is she missing anything?'

Jackson frowned. 'I don't know. But whatever she thinks happened seems to have spooked her quite a bit.'

'Perhaps it's a guilty conscience. Rather like Lady Macbeth.' Caroline smiled faintly. 'If Megan starts mumbling "Out, damned spot," I'd commence to worry.'

Jackson placed his hands on his hips, staring down at the dock. 'Caroline,' he said softly, 'what do you know about this?'

'Is that an accusation?'

Jackson looked at her sideways. 'Then let me put it another way,' he said at length. 'As one professional to another, is there something more that I should know?'

For an instant, Caroline wished to talk with him. But this was now impossible; the impulse died, leaving a residue of sadness. 'As you so succinctly told me, Jackson, Megan is my problem now.' She paused a moment, and then finished softly, 'Just have her there, all right? I'd hate for Megan Race to miss her moment in the sun.'

'I have a plan,' Caroline said quietly, 'to deal with Megan.'

Brett tilted her head. 'But you won't tell me.'

Caroline looked at Brett intently. 'You asked me once to believe in you. Now I'm asking you to believe in me – at least that I've done everything I can. And that there's a good reason I can't tell you what that is.'

Brett slowly shook her head.

It was strange, Caroline thought, how isolated she felt; it was as if she had crossed into a place she could share with no one. 'I don't want you to go to prison, Brett. For that to happen is unacceptable to me.'

Something in Brett's face changed, showed a quality of openness.

'I believe that,' she said at last. 'Maybe it's a choice I've made, like people who decide to believe in God. But I've had endless time to think about you, Caroline. I don't believe that you'll ever think I'm innocent. What I feel instead is this incredible acceptance – as if whether I killed James doesn't matter to you, that all you care about is what happens to me now.' Brett considered her for a moment. 'Is that how lawyers are?'

Caroline smiled faintly. 'That's how defense lawyers are – the last redoubt of unconditional love. Other than your parents, of course.'

Brett looked at her. 'My poor parents,' she said finally. 'My father acts as if *he's* guilty, and my mother just sits here, trying to say something when there's nothing to say, helpless when I need help most.' Her voice took on a resigned bemusement. 'It makes me sad for her, in a way.'

Caroline was quiet for a moment, and then shrugged. 'She really can't do anything. Except, perhaps, figure out some entertainment for prison visits. Which is harder than you may think.'

Brett still watched her. 'Why is it,' she said at last, 'that you dislike her so much?'

'Do I?'

'Of course you do. You talk about her with this awful detachment, like she's a slide under a microscope. It's so much worse than anger.'

It's so much deeper than anger, Caroline thought. 'Betty and I are different, that's all. Our lives went different places.'

Brett gazed steadily at Caroline. 'So different that no one can be close to you?'

Caroline felt it again – the strange power Brett had to wound her. 'Well,' she said dryly, 'we just have different gifts.' And then Caroline realized how much she had sounded like her mother, Nicole.

'I'm sorry,' she said tiredly. 'I think I missed the confessional part of the eighties – sometimes I suspect that it does more harm than good. But as to your mother and me, we're the only ones who own the problem.' She smiled again. 'With luck, you can develop new problems of your very own. Which, of course, is what I live for.'

Brett was quiet for a moment. 'You sound more optimistic than you have.'

Once again, Caroline thought of the knife she would never mention. 'I feel better,' she said at last. 'At least in certain ways.'

Pensive, Brett brushed back her hair; something in the distracted gesture interrupted Caroline's own distraction.

'You're left-handed, aren't you?'

Brett gave her a quizzical look. 'Why – are you?'

'Not at all.' Pausing, Caroline wondered at herself. 'It's just something you'd think I'd notice.'

For some reason, Brett seemed to find that amusing. As if in condolence, her left hand covered Caroline's. 'Don't worry,' she said with mock solicitude. 'You've had a lot on your mind.'

For a moment, they smiled together.

For two days, Caroline waited.

She worked in her room, making notes from her memory of Megan's entries. Sometimes she would stop, imagining that the manila envelope had ripped open, that the red journal had become separated and then lost.

The afternoon before the hearing, she drove to Masters Hill, stopping at the cemetery.

The afternoon was clear and bright. Caroline stayed for some time, standing near her mother's marker.

What would you think of all this? she asked.

The cemetery was quiet, still. Smiling faintly at herself, Caroline shook her head.

Leaving, she went to her father's house.

Betty was on the porch.

'Are you all right?' she asked.

Caroline stood awkwardly on the lawn. 'I'm fine.... All that I want to say is that I'll do the best I can for her. And that nothing's going to distract me.'

Slowly, Betty nodded. 'I believe that. We all do.'

Caroline stared at the grass. *Please*, she thought, *say that it arrived.*

'The hearing starts at nine,' she said. 'I'd suggest you be there by eight-thirty, sitting in the front row. Suit for you, jacket and tie for Larry – the media, you know.'

'Of course.' Betty paused, as if at a sudden thought. 'There's a package for you. For some reason it came here.'

Caroline felt her shoulders slump with weariness and relief. 'Can you get it?'

Betty disappeared inside. When she returned, she held the manila envelope, eyeing the childish printing with a wary curiosity.

She handed it to Caroline. 'Unopened,' she said in a flat voice. 'As you can see.'

Their eyes met. Caroline said nothing, glanced at the package. 'Odd,' she murmured. 'Thank you.'

Turning, she crossed the grassy lawn, feeling the weight of the journal in her hand.

Betty's remark, laden with meaning, had triggered something. It took a moment for Caroline to grasp it – the memory of a summer, so many years before, when another woman had filled a journal with the secrets of her heart.

Walking slowly to her car, Caroline drove away.

PART FIVE

Summer 1972

Chapter 1

The first time Caroline saw him was the day before her twenty-second birthday.

The course of her life seemed settled – Harvard Law School in the fall; practice in New Hampshire after that; a tacit understanding with Jackson Watts, with whom she shared such comfort that much between them needed not be said. If there was a certain absence of passion or surprise, Caroline took pride that she was so unlike her mother, the servant of mood and impulse. Caroline knew what her future would be and was content with that.

A part of this contentment was the expectation that, after some suitable time on her own, she might practice law with her father. He had talked of stepping down from the bench at sixty, using his name to draw clients and his experience to counsel Caroline as she spread her own name and reputation. With his network of friendships among Republicans, Channing could advance an ambition of his which was also becoming hers – that some governor a few terms down the road would appoint her to a judgeship. True, Caroline and her father had their differences over politics: Radcliffe and her own maturation had not left Caroline untouched, and her views on Vietnam and the women's movement were at odds with his. But these fissures lacked a personal edge: to Caroline, her father was a man she deeply loved, and their arguments were a form of mental exercise. She felt fortunate to have him.

It was her father, oddly enough, who had encouraged her to summer on the Vineyard.

He had not sold the house. But the remaining Masterses had never returned: for the seven summers since her mother's death, they had rented the house to strangers. Caroline had never spoken of Martha's Vineyard.

And then, to her surprise, her father did.

'What would you do,' he asked, the Christmas before her graduation, 'if you could spend next summer any way you liked? Go back to Europe?'

Caroline shook her head. 'I'd spend it sailing.' She thought for a moment, 'Maybe I can go to the Caribbean for the summer, work a charter boat, and sail on the side.'

Her father sat back in his chair, sipping a glass of wine. 'Why don't you go to Martha's Vineyard?' he asked quite casually. That's where you learned to sail, after all, and you'd have a real home.'

Caroline studied him. It came to her that her father wished, by some tacit understanding, to place the past and her mother behind them both forever. But the cost of such a summer – confronting yet dismissing the memory of what had happened – struck Caroline hard.

'I don't know,' Caroline said. 'I mean, what about making money?'

Her father put down the wineglass. 'Caroline,' he said, 'you've worked hard at Radcliffe. Now you're about to graduate with great distinction and enter a career that will require even more of you. It would please me if you were free from work for one last summer.' It was as if his eyes, Caroline thought, were saying what he refused to put into words. 'Besides,' he finished with new firmness, 'Betty and Larry could use a respite from academia, and Larry needs a place to write his thesis. I'm sure that a summer there would please them too.'

Of course it would, Caroline reflected – the house holds no memories for them. But to say this seemed both childish and selfish. 'Let me think about it, Father.'

'Of course.' He smiled slightly. 'By the way, I'll have your catboat sent there from Winnipesaukee. If you like.'

A few weeks later, Caroline decided that she would not run away – that she would take her summer on the Vineyard and enjoy it. None of this was spoken between them.

'I'm pleased,' her father said. 'I'll come down to visit

you, of course. But what's best is how good this will be for you and Betty.'

It was, Caroline assumed, a reference to something that she did not think her father cared about – that in the unspoken calculus of her family, the phrase 'half-sister' captured her relationship to Betty. Neither Caroline nor Betty had known Betty's mother, Elizabeth Brett; Nicole had treated Betty like the stepdaughter she was. Separated from Caroline by age and looks and temperament, Betty seemed to see her as the interloper whose rapport with their father foreclosed any need for an older sister. Five years after Betty's marriage to Larry Allen, Caroline and her sister were less antagonists than strangers.

'I'm sure it will,' Caroline said with indifference.

Curiously, this seemed to be true.

Perhaps the key was Larry. Within days of their arrival on the Vineyard, he and Caroline fell into an easy, joking relationship. Betty did not seem to mind – it was as though Caroline's liking for Larry conferred some approval on her. Which was right, in a sense; Caroline could see how devoted she was to him, how much Betty wished for them both to be happy. And there was about Betty a sort of painful honesty, a lack of pretense or vanity – in looks or manner – which Caroline knew she did not possess. The absence of her father, Caroline realized, might free them to be friends.

To Caroline, the one source of tension in those first weeks was Betty's obsessive desire to have a child.

With the detachment of the cocktail party psychologist, Caroline sensed that Betty needed to lavish on some son or daughter all the care she felt she had missed herself. To say this to Betty would too cruelly expose her deepest insecurities. But Caroline saw it as the source of pressure on Larry: they could not truly afford a child; it was plain that Betty was insisting that they try; and, for whatever reason, no Allen baby was forthcoming. To Caroline, the whole subject hovered in some realm between the painful and the comic, with Larry laboring nightly in the field of

Betty, some silent part of him praying that the crops would lie fallow until his tenuous career took root.

'Well,' Larry murmured to Caroline one evening, drying the last dish, 'back to the salt mines.'

He said this good-naturedly enough; with his boyish looks, scoop nose, and nimbus of brown hair, there was an air of blithe optimism about him. So that Caroline grinned before answering, 'I just hope you're not overdrawn at the bank.'

Larry rolled his eyes in mock exhaustion. 'This kid – should she ever be born – will be the only baby in history who allows her parents to sleep *more*.'

Caroline raised an eyebrow. ' "She"?'

'Oh, yeah – that's part of the deal. "No boy sperm need apply."' Larry smiled again. 'Don't stay out late, Caro. For lack of a suitable offspring, Betty and I consider ourselves *in loco parentis*.'

'Stay out late?' Caroline asked innocently. 'With whom?'

Larry's smile was ambiguous. 'I don't know yet,' he answered.

The ironic memory that came to Caroline, recalling that particular day, was that it seemed so much like any other.

She was sailing back from Tarpaulin Cove, at peace. Her skills were returning quickly, and the afternoon southeaster was steady and benign. She could not sail this route without remembering her mother. But a little discreet checking had told her that Paul Nerheim no longer owned Windy Gates; it struck her that this summer on the Vineyard, in slow, unnoticed increments, had swollen in contentment.

She missed Jackson and her college friends, of course. But she accepted that her college world was gone, and two of her friends had promised to visit in late August. As for Jackson, she was used to being apart from him, often for weeks or even months. She was, she now knew, something of a loner: unlike many of her friends, she had never lost herself in a man. Nor did she ever plan to.

She first saw him at the end of the Masterses' dock – a slim figure, dark-haired from a distance, his hands in his pockets. Though nothing about him looked familiar, he seemed to be waiting for her.

As she docked, gliding perfectly, she tossed him the line. 'Mind doing that?' she asked.

He caught the line and tied it expertly to the dock. Caroline glanced at him; his head was bowed, and Caroline saw only curly hair as jet black as her own.

'Thanks,' she said.

He looked up at her then. With something like shock, she saw a young man in his mid twenties with a trace of the beauty that had belonged to Nicole Dessaliers – long lashes, ridged nose, a face of angles so clean that it was like cut glass. His eyes were a startling blue gray.

She turned, unfurling the sails. When she had finished, he was still there.

'Nice boat,' he said.

She stepped on the dock, turning to inspect the catboat. 'Do you sail?' she asked.

'A little.' He paused. 'Where did you go?'

Caroline still did not face him. 'To Tarpaulin Cove.'

'Have you sailed there before?'

'A few times, seven or eight years ago.' She hesitated. 'I had a bad sail there once, so it seemed like something I should do again.'

Next to her, he nodded. 'They say these waters are tricky.' Pausing, he seemed to study the ocean. 'There was a famous sailor from the Vineyard, Joshua Slocum, who sailed around the world at the end of the last century. Then he came back home, went for a sail on a clear day, and vanished. No one ever saw him again.'

Caroline turned to him now, her expression sardonic. 'I hadn't heard that one, actually. But it's really inspirational.'

He grinned; the smile was crooked and, for Caroline, leavened his prettiness with something boyish and engaging. But it did not change the look in his eyes, observant and a little wary.

He extended his hand. 'I'm Scott Johnson. I live at the Rubin place next door, caretaking.'

His hand was firm, cool. 'Caroline Masters,' she said.

He nodded again. 'I've seen you.' He angled his head toward the house. 'Do you come here every summer?'

Caroline looked at him more closely; there was about him some combination of reserve and presumption that did not quite seem to mesh. 'Not for years,' she said finally.

Scott smiled a little. 'The Rubins aren't here much, either. But as Fitzgerald once said, the rich are different.' He turned to look at the Masterses' white gabled house, perched on the bluff above the beach, soft with the sun of late afternoon. 'It's hard to imagine not wanting to be there. At least whenever you could.'

Caroline felt a moment's irritation; how, she wondered, had she gotten involved in this conversation? 'My mother died here,' she said tersely. 'Several years ago, in an accident. My family found other places to go.'

He shoved his hands back in his pockets. 'Sorry,' he said. 'Ask too many questions, and sooner or later you'll ask a dumb one. It's just that I saw your place was occupied, then saw you and got curious. I guess I've had too little to think about.'

It was a fair enough apology and had the effect, Caroline realized, of making it seem rude to just walk off. 'How long have you been here?' she asked.

'Since January. Winters are quiet, I found out.'

'You're not from here, then.'

'No.' He smiled. 'I just came, and then answered an ad. Never even been before.'

There was a carelessness in the way he spoke, Caroline thought. Yet something about him did not match the feckless image of a rolling stone with nowhere he cared to be and no clear place he wished to go.

'Why the Vineyard?' she asked.

'Seemed like a place to sort things out.' He checked his watch. 'I'm supposed to call the Rubins now. Give them a report.' He smiled again. 'The rich *are* different, you know. They expect one to be on time.'

Abruptly, he left her there – her curiosity a little piqued.

That night, a windstorm rose suddenly.

It battered the house, rattling the doors and the glass in the windows. Awakening, Caroline thought of the sailboat, imagined it slamming against the dock or drifting out to sea. She had not tied the knot herself.

Restless, she put on blue jeans and a down-filled jacket and went out to check the boat.

The howling wind almost knocked Caroline off balance. But the night was brilliant, the stars bright and close in a black endless sky. The world seemed magical and awesome.

The mast of the catboat spiked above the dock. As Caroline walked toward it, reassured, she saw a still, silent figure at the dock's end.

He was gazing out to sea, his hands in his pockets. The wind seemed not to affect him.

Her footsteps were muffled by the wind sweeping toward her. She stopped by the catboat, about twenty feet from him. Though whitecaps thudded against the boat, someone had used a second line to lash it tight to the dock. It hardly moved at all.

'It's safe enough,' he said.

He had turned to her; Caroline felt that he had sensed her presence for some moments. 'Did *you* secure it?' she asked.

'Yup. I heard the wind and wondered about damage.'

It was a sailor's concern, delivered in the impersonal tone of someone who cared more about boats than their owners. The thought dampened Caroline's gratitude. 'Thanks,' she said.

'Oh, sure.'

His face was in shadow, and he came no closer. To Caroline, who owned the dock, it was as if she had invaded his private space. But some courtesy seemed required. 'Can

281

I make you a cup of coffee?' she asked. 'Seeing how we're up?'

From the stillness of the shadows, he seemed to watch her for a moment. 'No,' he said. 'But thanks yourself.'

He began to walk, less toward her than past her. Then he stopped, facing her, and Caroline saw again how beautiful he was.

'The boat'll be fine,' he said quietly. 'Have a good night, okay?'

Once more, he left her there.

Chapter 2

For several days, she did not see him.

The weather was poor for sailing, rainy or windless. When a fine morning came – bright and crisp and breezy – Caroline packed a cooler and eagerly left the house.

He sat on the beach near the foot of the dock, a mug of steaming coffee cupped in both hands. It was as if, Caroline thought, he knew she would go sailing. But he did not turn to her.

She stopped beside him. 'Hi,' she said.

He looked up at her, a hint of humor in the gray-blue eyes. 'You're a stone fanatic for sailing, aren't you?'

Caroline heard a certain admiration, or, at least, an understanding. She was not used to this – Jackson, with whom she shared so many things, had no great love of sailing. So that she asked without thinking, 'Want to go out?'

His eyes became hooded, as if torn between disinterest in her company and the desire to sail. When, once more, he looked directly up at her, there was a smile at one corner of his mouth. 'Think I can take the helm a little?'

Suddenly Caroline thought of her lost solitude, spent making conversation with a stranger. But now it was too late.

'Just remember Joshua Slocum,' she said.

He seemed to learn the boat quickly, noting its quirks with interest. He sailed with such skill and confidence that not even a certain modesty, in speech and in movement, could conceal how routine this was for him.

To Caroline, it seemed that she was invisible. For minutes, he would run before the wind, wordless in the bright exhilaration of the day. The sense of his enjoyment gave Caroline silent pleasure.

Just when she thought he had forgotten her altogether, Scott turned to her. 'Thanks,' he said with a smile. 'It's been a while.'

Caroline took the helm. 'Where did you learn to sail like that?'

'On Lake Erie.' Scott's smile broadened. 'You've heard about the Great Lakes, right? They noticed those at Radcliffe?'

Caroline felt her annoyance sweep *politesse* aside. 'Oh, come off it,' she responded. 'This middle-class boy meets Daisy Buchanan thing.' She softened her voice a little. 'It's like bad Fitzgerald. And Fitzgerald was bad enough.'

Scott did not answer. But she felt his level, reflective gaze, turning toward the water, as a silent acknowledgment. He never tried it again.

They sailed across the Vineyard Sound to the inlet of Lake Tashmoo, mooring in its sheltered waters. Caroline shared her sandwich and a beer.

'Do you ever go into town?' she asked. 'Places like the Black Dog or the Square Rigger?'

'Hanging out with college kids, you mean? Drink beer and listen to music?' Smiling, he shook his head. 'Already done that, I'm afraid. For four long years.'

Caroline studied him. 'You didn't just get out, did you?'

'Oh, no.' The smile grew smaller, and the hooded look returned. 'No, it's been a while since college.'

Something in his tone and manner did not welcome further inquiry. But Caroline found that she did not care. 'So what have you been doing?' she asked.

He gave her a sudden look of such directness that Caroline felt she had crossed some invisible line. Softly, he said, 'Not much of anything. At least anything that's useful.'

She was, Caroline realized, determined not to be buffaloed. She met his gaze, raising her eyebrows in silent inquiry.

After a moment, he seemed to sigh, as though she had cornered him. 'I may not look it,' he said finally, 'but I'm a casualty of our nation's foreign policy. I sacrificed so that others might die.'

Caroline's eyes narrowed. 'You went to Vietnam?'

Scott smiled slightly. 'That's just it. I didn't go to Vietnam. Staying out took all I had to give.'

Caroline heard a certain irony, directed at himself. 'Let me guess,' she said. 'You're psychotic, in love with a wonderful guy, and suffering from hay fever.'

'Hadn't thought of the last one.' Scott slowly shook his head, no longer smiling. 'It's such a waste, really. Although all *I* had to waste was time.'

'How so?'

Scott seemed to collect his thoughts. 'I was sliding through Ohio Presbyterian, secure in the knowledge that the worst form of conscription in my sheltered life was compulsory chapel. 'Cause I could always go to graduate school in something ...

'But 1968 was a magical year. King and Bobby Kennedy got shot, the Russians invaded Czechoslovakia, and, with his last political breath, LBJ took away our grad school deferments. Enabling the class of '68 to occupy a unique wrinkle in time – the first class to lose their deferments, the last class before the lottery. Which has since saved so many lives that it's put new flesh on the old saying 'Life is a lottery.''

Caroline thought of Jackson. 'I know,' she said. 'My closest friend got number 301.'

He gave her a brief, sharp look. 'Well,' he said, 'your friend's a lucky man. One roommate of mine was killed. Another friend went to jail for draft resistance and had a nervous breakdown. As for me, I was forced to discover my passion for teaching.' His voice became ironic. 'Kindergarten, in an inner-city school. A meeting of minds.'

Caroline shrugged; there was something in his flippancy she did not find attractive. 'I guess it got you a deferment.'

'Only for a year. My predecessor preempted me by miscarrying. The next September, she was back.

'I briefly considered pregnancy myself. But there was no one I really wanted to make pregnant, and I couldn't act alone. So I fell back on more traditional disabilities.'

He gazed out at the ocean, wind ruffling his hair. Caroline's sense of him kept changing; beneath the cynicism, she suspected, lurked some deeper feeling. Abruptly, Scott shrugged. 'Anyhow, it worked. After two years of trying, I was saved by a hiatal hernia. Fortunately, it doesn't affect my sailing.'

'Then that's good, isn't it?'

Scott slowly shook his head, seemingly less in disagreement than in bemusement. 'It was – it is. But I no longer had a purpose. I'd been trying to beat the draft so long I no longer knew who I was. Or what I wanted.'

He fell silent. A cool wind kicked up; a seagull passed overhead, circling above them. Hands on hips, Scott stared at the gull with a small smile of puzzlement.

Watching him, Caroline wondered about what she had heard. People, she reflected, are seldom immobilized unless they want to be, and the reasons they give for not doing something are so often illusory. This one, Caroline sensed, was much smarter than he pretended. And then she made her first judgment of Scott Johnson – no ambition.

Caroline hugged herself. 'I'm getting cold,' she told him.

He gave her a sideways look, somewhere between amusement and understanding. 'Let's go back,' he said.

They docked the boat, Caroline tossing him the line. 'Have time for a beer?' he asked. 'You're buying.'

There was one beer left in the cooler. With the same underhand motion, Caroline tossed him the cool brown bottle. He caught it in one hand.

They sat on the dock together, legs dangling over the side, passing the beer back and forth. Caroline felt ready to go in.

'So what are you going to do,' he asked, 'now that you're out of school? Marry number 301?'

Caroline gave him a sharp look; she had mentioned Jackson only as a 'friend.' 'Why? Is that what I'm supposed to do?'

The corner of his mouth turned up, as if this trace of annoyance amused him. 'Only if you want to.'

'What I "want" is to have a career in law.'

He tilted his head, interested now. 'Why law?'

No one, Caroline realized, had ever asked her that. She was suddenly not quite sure if she had ever asked herself. 'My father's a judge,' she finally answered. 'I've grown up with it.'

The answer sounded shallow, inadequate. But Scott, who seemed to have a certain edge, surprised her by not showing this. 'What kind of law will you do?' he asked.

Caroline hesitated; she could not yet summon a clear picture. 'I'll probably start as a prosecutor. Just for the experience.'

Scott turned back to the water. 'Well,' he answered, 'it's nice to know what you want.'

This time it was Caroline who left.

Chapter 3

'Did you see the thing about Eagleton?' Larry asked at dinner.

Caroline poured herself more claret. 'What thing?'

'He's admitted to undergoing shock therapy.' Larry pulled a wry face. 'Nothing major – just a little jolt whenever he got depressed.'

'Are you serious?'

'He is,' Betty put in. 'But it was only two or three times, in the sixties. The press is making a big deal out of it.'

Caroline stared at them both. 'McGovern's screwed,' she said finally. 'All the Nixon campaign will have to say is that McGovern wants to put this guy one heartbeat away from the atomic button, and people will wonder what happens the next time Eagleton gets his synapses rewired. I mean, does he wake up all optimistic and decide that Tuesday's a terrific day to nuke the Ukraine? And if McGovern dumps his vice-presidential choice, he looks incompetent.' She shook her head. 'Politics has gotten so depressing. At least to me.'

Larry sat back, wineglass cupped in both hands. 'What are Jackson's politics, anyhow? I've never gotten a handle on that.'

'That's because Jackson's not big on what he calls extremes.' Caroline paused. 'When someone works his way through school, politics seems like a luxury. He hasn't had a lot of time for sit-ins.'

Larry nodded. 'I was just curious, that's all. He and Channing seem to get on so well.'

Betty, Caroline noticed, had begun watching Larry closely. 'Why shouldn't Father like Jackson?' she inquired.

'No reason,' Larry answered, still looking at Caroline. 'I like Jackson. Best of all, Caroline likes Jackson.'

'Well,' Betty said finally, 'that makes it unanimous. At least in our family.'

Betty's remark was meant to be warm, Caroline knew, perhaps defensive of Caroline herself. But something in the conversation made her edgy; perhaps, she reflected, it was simply the sense that she was a surrogate in some buried argument between Larry and Betty.

'Well,' she said dryly, 'I'll let you know before I marry Jackson. So we can put it up for a vote.'

Larry gave her a keen look. As if in diversion, he said, 'I wonder what would have happened if Betty had put *me* up for a vote.'

'Simple,' Caroline answered with mock imperiousness. 'I'd have vetoed you before Father even got his chance. You're far too impoverished to be so obnoxious.'

Larry grinned, raising his glass. 'To all the little people,' he intoned, and then glanced at Betty. 'Present and future.'

Smiling, Caroline touched her glass to both of theirs. Her sister's smile seemed a little forced.

'What was that about?' Caroline asked Larry afterward.

They were alone in the kitchen, washing dishes. Through the window they could see Betty begin one of her solitary walks on the beach. With dusk descending, she was a lone figure framed against tawny sand, darkening water.

Absently drying a wineglass, Larry watched her. 'What was what about?'

'The undercurrent at the dinner table. And I'm not referring to our discussion of Eagleton.'

Larry smiled. 'Or Jackson?'

'That, either.'

Larry was quiet for a time. 'Your father has floated a trial balloon,' he said at last. 'To Betty, if not to me. Help in finding me a teaching job somewhere near him. There's a college or three nearby, and some prep schools.'

Caroline turned to him. 'How do you feel about that?'

'I'm really not sure. Betty and I've done pretty well with our families at a certain distance.' He shrugged. 'In fairness to Channing, he's only trying to help. As he put it to Betty, his influence pretty much ends at the state line.'

'So what do you think you'll do?'

'Oh, it's way premature.' His voice came to life again. 'My TA job at Syracuse is going pretty well, I think, and my thesis too. Maybe I can hang on at Syracuse or even find something better.'

It was an aspect of Larry that Caroline liked – his optimism, a certain generosity of spirit that seemed to encompass others as well as himself. 'I can guess,' she ventured, 'what Betty is thinking. That you could support a baby.'

Slowly, Larry looked away. 'Just before we left, Caro, Betty and I went in for a battery of tests. They were pretty thorough – I even got to jerk off in a jar. Which I'm sure was better for the jar than it was for me.' He paused. 'It took them a while, but they got back to us this morning. Looks like there may be a problem.'

Caroline put down her dish. 'What, exactly?'

'Low sperm count. Not impossibly low, but definitely substandard.' He smiled without humor. 'When you made that joke about being "overdrawn at the bank," you got it right. I may have fucked myself into a negative balance.'

All at once, Caroline felt the pressures bearing down on Larry. 'But don't you think that's part of it?' she asked. 'If people treated getting pregnant like it was some sort of lab experiment, no one would ever have babies. You and Betty have become this pair of hamsters.'

'That's kind of what the doctor said. So my new marching orders are to save myself for prime time.' He smiled again. 'Betty and I should be free for Scrabble tonight, if you're up for it.'

Caroline laughed. 'Anything to help. As long as it's all in the family.'

'Thanks a million.' Larry shook out his towel, wiped another dish. 'Anyhow, I figure my count will skyrocket once I get a real job. It's all a question of how many sperm

290

you can afford.' He paused, as if at another thought. 'This guy next door, Caroline. What's his story?'

Caroline felt her eyes narrow. 'How would I know?'

'Well, you did take him sailing the other day. So I thought you two also might have conversed.'

Caroline handed him the final dish. 'He's late-sixties fallout, that's all. Nowhere to go and nothing to do.'

Larry gave the dish a few perfunctory wipes. 'Seems like kind of a loner. Nice-looking kid, though.'

'He's not a kid, Larry – he's only a couple of years younger than you. It's just that he lacks your driving sense of purpose.'

Larry considered her a moment, a smile at one corner of his mouth. 'So you did find out something about him.'

Caroline gave him a long, cool look. 'I don't know what's on your mind. But I know what's on mine – nothing. I was just being charitable.' She began drying her hands. 'Think you can concentrate on Scrabble now? Because I'm absolutely going to kick your ass.'

Larry's smile broadened. 'Caro,' he said, 'you're so beautiful when you're annoyed.'

Chapter 4

It was several days before she saw Scott Johnson again, and then only because she refused to let Larry tease her out of every casual impulse.

She had returned from sailing, determinedly alone, dismissing any idea of asking him to join her. The sail had been so good that the memory of his enjoyment made her feel a little selfish. Docking the boat, she paused and then went to find him before she gave this more thought than it was worth.

He lived in the boathouse at the end of the Rubins' narrow pier. From the outside, it was a one-floor layout with a deck that faced the ocean. Beneath her, water slapped at its sturdy cement pilings.

Caroline knocked on the door.

She waited for a moment, restless: perhaps she only imagined soft footfalls inside the boathouse. She had begun looking back toward the Rubins' place when the door opened behind her.

She turned to face him. 'Hi,' she said.

He peered at her through the half-opened door. Caroline realized that she had prepared herself for his reaction – wariness, or indifference, or even amusement. But what she saw was pure surprise.

'I thought I'd give you one last chance,' Caroline went on, 'to drink beer with college kids.'

The door opened a fraction wider. His expression seemed to go through several changes – hesitancy, puzzlement, distress at being caught off guard. But the last look he gave Caroline told her how alone he was.

'Where?' he asked.

The Square Rigger was on the outskirts of Edgartown – a

dark, smoky room with a wooden bar and walls, and tables jammed with college students working on the island. Scott seemed to have regained the persona she had seen most often – amused, somehow apart. He took in the ambience and people with a single sweeping glance.

'The future leaders of America,' he said, 'getting plastered on Budweiser. Somewhere among us may be our forty-third President.'

His voice was half sardonic, half bemused. 'I don't mind that he's plastered on Bud,' Caroline retorted. 'I just mind that he's a man.'

Scott smiled. 'Now that you're here, maybe the odds have evened out a little. Shall we find a table?'

They seized one in the corner, just as the live entertainment came on – two guys and a long-haired blond woman, who appeared, like Scott, to be in their mid twenties. Both men had twelve-string guitars; the woman stepped front and center on a low wooden platform and began to belt out 'If I Had a Hammer' in a throaty voice almost as good as it was loud.

'Holy shit,' Scott whispered to Caroline. 'It's Peter, Paul, and Mary.'

With a fractional smile, Caroline braced herself for an evening of sarcasm, beginning to regret that she had roused him from his self-imposed exile. And then she saw the brightness in his eyes.

'Drinks are on me,' he said. 'What can I get you?'

'Scotch.'

He seemed to have no trouble catching the eye of the waitress, a southern-accented brunette with a smile, Caroline told herself, that she could never match this side of a lobotomy. When Miss Congeniality came to the table in record time, to be greeted by a dazzling smile from Scott that Caroline had not known he possessed, she was sure that their service would be excellent.

Gazing down at Scott, the waitress bit her lip, as if reluctant to deliver bad news. 'I'm sorry,' she said, 'but I'm going to have to card y'all. The manager says no exceptions.'

Scott pulled a face. 'Caught with a minor again,' he said, and turned reproachfully to Caroline. 'I knew you could never pass for twenty-one.'

To Caroline, this burlesque was an- abrupt, surprising change of character. She smiled politely and produced her driver's license.

The waitress scrutinized it. 'Thank you,' she said, and turned expectantly to Scott.

'Scotch,' he said firmly. 'For both of us.'

The waitress hesitated. And then Scott produced a smile more incandescent than the first; forgetful of her duties, the girl smiled into his eyes. Glancing back at him, she went to fill their orders.

Somehow Caroline found this both curious and amusing. 'Don't you feel a little embarrassed,' she whispered to Scott, 'encouraging her like that?'

Scott made himself look innocent. 'Who says I was encouraging her?'

'I do. I mean, I was only watching, and *I* felt a little bit encouraged.'

Scott's smile, directed at Caroline, became that of a coconspirator. 'I'll smile,' he said, 'and we'll drink. It'll help the music some.'

They did that, for one round, and then two more.

The ersatz Peter, Paul, and Mary were not too bad, Caroline thought; Scott watched them faithfully, first with what seemed like courtesy, then with a certain interest and even sympathy. No matter how their waitress smiled, he hardly seemed to notice her.

'It ain't easy,' he murmured, 'singing to a bunch of drunks. Particularly horny drunks.'

The fingers of his right hand, Caroline noticed, had begun keeping the beat.

The room was almost sensual now – the laser voice of the blonde, the thrum of guitars, the smell of smoke and bodies close together, swaying or whispering or smiling at each other. Scott ordered a fourth Scotch. His face was becoming almost careless; he seemed to be partly with Caroline and partly in some other place, perhaps ten other places, bars and parties and student apartments in a time when he had, Caroline found herself guessing, liked himself a little better. On the platform, the blonde was getting into it, twitching and swaying with the beat until each song seemed more sexual than the last.

'I'd love to watch her,' Scott murmured wryly, 'doing "Onward Christian Soldiers."'

His expression was amiable and not unkind. This was not sarcasm, Caroline realized – more an amused acceptance of the singer's humanness that somehow embraced everyone in the room. It struck Caroline that, unlike many people, Scott might actually become nicer when he drank. The thought surprised her.

When she turned to him again, he was still keeping the rhythm, a half smile on his face. He seemed oblivious to everything but where he was. All at once, Caroline was glad to have invited him.

They stayed until the place closed up.

They found Scott's car in the parking lot, a beat-up VW bug with scrapes in its black paint job.

'Want me to drive?' Caroline asked.

It seemed to interrupt Scott's mood, make him conscious of himself again. He paused to contemplate the question. 'I'm okay,' he said.

Caroline hesitated. It was not too far to Eel Pond, she told herself, and Scott did not have the truculence of someone from whom she should grab the keys. She got in without argument and buckled her seat belt.

Scott started the car, whistling soundlessly to himself.

They took Beach Road in amiable silence, the shadows of trees by the road vanishing behind them. He was driving a little fast, Caroline thought – not out of control, but braking and accelerating to a kind of inner rhythm, taking the feel of the bar home with him like something he did not care to lose.

The car gained speed.

Caroline felt her tension grow, separate them. She did not need to ask herself the reason.

Five more minutes, she told herself. The road was empty; his driving – if fast – seemed good enough to get them home. It was clear that he knew the road.

She saw him flinch just before the first swirling stab of red flashed in the rearview mirror.

His reaction, she thought, was almost otherworldly. He did not curse or speak or even show emotion; instead there was the sense that he had become someone else again, a sober man, a series of orderly thoughts marching through his brain as he slowed the car to a perfect stop. Only Caroline could see how pale he had become.

The patrol car stopped behind them. Still Scott said nothing.

The beam of a flashlight cut through the rearview mirror. Narrow-eyed, Scott took a deep breath, straightened in his seat, and then got out to meet the cop. He seemed to have forgotten that Caroline was there.

Instinct told her to get out with him.

The cop was a faceless form behind a flashlight, aimed at Scott's intent eyes and still body. As Caroline circled the car, the cop said evenly, 'I'll be needing your license, son.'

There was something familiar about the voice, the way the cop's dark figure held itself, heavy in the shoulders. Scott made no move to take out his wallet.

All at once, Caroline thought of the waitress, asking for identification.

The cop's voice was harder now. 'Hand over your license, please.'

Scott glanced toward the car. Suddenly, Caroline felt a delicate balance, seconds from being broken.

Instinctively, she stepped between them.

The cop's flashlight made her blink. 'Hello,' she said.

She saw his head tilt, peering at her from behind the beam.

'Caroline? Caroline Masters?'

'Yes,' she answered. 'I'm Caroline.'

The cop stepped forward, face suddenly caught in his own headlights. His voice was hesitant. 'I'm Frank Mannion.'

The memory came swift and strong; the image of her mother's dark hair, swirling in the water, hit Caroline in the pit of her stomach.

'I remember,' she answered quietly.

She saw his shoulders relax. In the light, his face was a little pouchier but still pleasant, his red hair gray at the temples. He took off his patrolman's hat, wiping his forehead, and stood closer to her. His voice became gentle. 'I always wondered what happened with you.'

'Nothing, really.' Her own voice, Caroline was grateful to hear, seemed close to normal. 'My father and I made it through, and I'm going to law school next year. Things turned out all right.'

Slowly, he nodded. Caroline could feel Scott's gaze; something in his stillness made her throat tight.

'And you?' she asked Mannion. 'How did your family adjust to the Vineyard?'

He looked surprised. 'You remember that too?'

'I remember everything about that day. Including how nice you were.'

Mannion glanced toward Scott, awkwardly shifting his weight. 'Well, we're all fine, thanks. My oldest just graduated high school, and soon he's off to Boston College.' He interrupted himself. 'It's been good here.'

Caroline stuck her hands in her pockets. 'I'm glad it worked out.'

Mannion nodded, and then he seemed to remember Scott. 'Mind coming over here?' he asked.

Scott hesitated and then walked toward Mannion. His movements seemed strangely weary – the loss of adrenaline, Caroline thought.

'Do you *have* a license?' Mannion asked.

Scott did not answer. Caroline felt herself tense.

Mannion's tone was soft now, an inquiry. 'Son?'

Slowly, Scott slid his wallet from the back pocket of his jeans. He fumbled with it and finally produced a square of paper.

Mannion gazed at it and looked up at Scott. 'You're a ways from home,' he said at last. 'Where you living now?'

Scott's own voice was a murmur. 'Eel Pond. I watch the Rubin place.'

Mannion appeared to study him. 'Then do me a favor, *and* yourself. Don't drive like you've been drinking.' He angled his head toward Caroline. 'Not with her, or without her, either. Now give me your keys.'

As if in a trance, Scott held them out.

Mannion took the keys and gently placed them in Caroline's hand. 'Are you all right to drive?' he asked her.

'I'm fine.' Caroline felt a surge of relief. 'Thank you.'

Mannion did not acknowledge this. 'Drive carefully, Caroline. And good luck in law school.'

Silent, he returned Scott's license and walked back to his car.

Caroline and Scott got inside the VW, not talking. She worked the clutch until she had its feel, and drove cautiously away.

Mannion's patrol car followed them until they reached the turn for Eel Pond. Its headlights flashed past, then the red taillights, and the policeman was gone.

In the passenger seat, Scott touched his eyes.

They passed the Rubins' house, parking at a turnaround above the water. The windshield filled with black ocean, black sky. Caroline could still feel the pounding of her heart.

Softly, Scott asked, 'What happened back there?'

'I think I saved your ass.' Caroline glanced at him sharply. 'From a speeding ticket, at least.'

Scott was quiet for a time. 'It was something about your mother. The accident you mentioned.'

Caroline stared through the windshield. 'She was driving.' Her voice was flat, emotionless. 'When it happened, only the two of us were here. Officer Mannion took me to identify her body.'

'And she'd been drinking.'

'Yes.' Caroline exhaled. 'It was eight years ago, all right? I got over it.'

Her tone was more curt than she'd intended. 'No, it's not all right,' he answered. 'With you or with me.'

His voice was soft with self-disgust. 'Do you want to feel sorry for yourself by yourself,' Caroline said at last, 'or do you feel like making me coffee?'

For a moment, Scott seemed to hesitate. His eyes studied her with an intensity she had not seen before.

'Come on in,' he said. 'Please.'

Chapter 5

Hand on the knob, Scott seemed to hesitate, and then he opened the door.

Inside was a single large room with a hardwood floor and wainscoting and a kitchen along one wall. Glancing around, Caroline saw that the room conveyed no sense of him.

He kept it neat and spare – a couch, a coffee table, a seascape on the wall, everything picked up. The one thing that must be his – and now this did not surprise her – was a battered guitar leaning in one corner.

'Do you play that?' she asked.

'A little.' He smiled. 'Not well enough to match this evening's entertainment.'

Caroline turned to him. 'The bar? Or the police?'

'Take your pick,' Scott answered, and went to the stove.

He would not explain himself, Caroline realized; perhaps there was nothing to explain. From over his shoulder, Scott asked, 'How do you like your coffee?'

'Strong and black. Like for final exams.'

Caroline drifted to the window. Beneath them, she heard the ebb and flow of Nantucket Sound; the sensation was not unlike standing on the prow of a ship. She remembered Scott on the night of the storm, gazing out to sea.

'Where do you sleep?' she asked.

He bent over the coffeepot. 'On the porch. There's a screen to frustrate bugs, and it gets the breeze at night.'

He filled two mugs of coffee. As he gave her one, his hand brushing the back of hers, Caroline's skin tingled. It startled her: the shared tension with the police seemed to have created a current that did not exist before. She was keenly aware of standing close to him.

Caroline turned away. 'Can I see the porch?'

His small smile seemed part inquiry, part amusement. 'I

'guess it's all that's left,' he answered, and opened a door near the stove. Caroline stepped out onto the shadowed porch.

The steady soughing of the wind and the sea came through the screen. The air was warm and heavy and smelled of salt.

Caroline paused, breathing deeply, and then Scott switched on a lamp.

She turned. Out of the darkness materialized a cot, a nightstand stacked with books, a chair facing the water. There was a pen and what appeared to be a half-finished letter beneath the books, the first two of which, somewhat to Caroline's surprise, were *One Day in the Life of Ivan Denisovich* and Jack Newfield's biography of Robert Kennedy. She found herself wondering just who it was he was writing to.

He waved her to the chair. 'Have a seat – I'm used to being horizontal.'

She had a sudden image, Scott lying on the bed, and then the few things that were his own seemed to ache with his aloneness. Scott stretched out on the cot, mug cupped in his hands. 'I didn't really thank you, did I?'

'For what?'

'For trying to protect me from the law.' He seemed to watch her. 'Funny work for a future prosecutor.'

Caroline shrugged. 'It just seemed like too good a night to end with getting busted.'

Scott smiled a little. 'Except for that, it *was* good. My debut in Vineyard society.'

Caroline paused, a question forming, and then decided not to ask it. 'Except for your driving,' she said wryly, 'it was a real success. I even know where you can find a date.'

Scott watched her over his smile. 'Not interested,' he said.

'Oh, well.'

There was an awkward silence.

'Speaking of society,' Scott said, 'who else is over there? So far I've counted a skinny guy who doesn't come out much, and a woman who walks the beach alone. But no one who looks like the patriarch.'

This somewhat cavalier summary made Caroline bridle. And it struck her how much he had seemed to glean from very little – the predominance of her father; her relationship to Jackson.

'The "skinny guy,"' she answered tartly, 'is my very nice brother-in-law, Larry, who's working on a Ph.D. The woman is my sister, Betty – who happens to like nature. As for the "patriarch," as you put it, he's coming to inspect his holdings later.'

He grinned, refusing to be discouraged. 'So what do the three of you do all day?'

'Oh, we perform weird and secret rituals. Play Scrabble, argue about the election.' Her tone grew solemn, hushed. 'Sometimes Larry and I wash dishes. In the dark …'

His grin became a smile, perhaps a little chastened. 'Sorry. Families interest me, that's all. I haven't seen mine in a while.'

This snippet of biography sounded genuine. Her sense of him kept shifting; at one moment he was flippant, the next, a lonely person with people he seemed to care for.

'What does your family come with?' she asked.

'The all-American package.' He gazed at his mug. 'Two parents who still like each other. A brother in college who's not too bad. And a sixteen-year-old kid sister, who was born so late that I never got over the fact that she was cute. Still is, unless she's eaten too much junk food.'

Beneath the observation, offhand and affectionate, Caroline heard an undertone of regret. 'So why don't you go home?' she asked. 'You don't have to live in exile just to feel lost.'

For an instant he gave her a funny look – vulnerable, caught – and then his gaze grew veiled. 'Losing yourself,' he said, 'is not as simple as you think.'

The comment puzzled her. Scott looked away; she found herself studying the unfinished letter on the nightstand,

and then the book on Robert Kennedy. She nodded toward the book. 'Did you work for him?' she asked.

'Uh-huh. I sacrificed a few weeks of college to the Indiana primary.' He seemed to study his mug again. 'The night he was shot was the worst thing I've experienced that didn't happen to me personally. Sometimes I wonder how many other people died because of it. Or just lost hope.'

Scott was not looking for a response, Caroline saw – he could have been talking to himself. It made her quiet: as wrong as this might be, as lacking in what her father would call perspective, Scott seemed to feel, as Caroline sometimes did, that something irretrievable had been lost.

'I was a little young for that,' she said at last. 'Later, it hit me that maybe our best leaders are dead and without them all the rest of us are slowly drifting apart.'

Gazing at his coffee cup, Scott did not answer. And then he looked up, giving her a faint smile that mingled irony and kinship. 'We're a sad pair, aren't we. Nothing to look forward to but the rest of our lives.'

'Like sailing trips and graduate school. If you can ever figure out which graduate school you want.'

Scott shrugged, silent. Perhaps, Caroline thought, he was simply glad to have backed away from seriousness. But the moment had left something behind that was not there before; once more, she was aware of the ocean sounds, the smell of salt, of him. And that, until tonight, he had pretended to be someone nowhere close to who he was.

As if sensing her thoughts, he shifted subjects again. 'Your brother-in-law,' he said. 'What's his Ph.D. in?'

'English. From Syracuse.'

'And Betty?'

'Wants to have a baby.'

Scott's look was quizzical. 'Is your father paying the freight?'

'Not that I've heard.'

'Ouch.'

Caroline pondered whether some explanation was more, or less, fair to Betty. 'Betty's nice, really. But I think somehow she felt displaced, and now she's got an image of family that goes deeper than for other people.' Caroline paused. 'The problem is that it's making her a little crazy. Like everyone from here to Mongolia is pregnant except for her.'

Scott gave a comic wince, and then inspiration crossed his face. 'Wait,' he said, got up, and went inside.

He came back with his guitar.

'What's this?' Caroline asked.

He sat on the edge of the bed, assuming a pose of great seriousness. And then, eyes suddenly limpid, he gazed at Caroline and began to sing in a mock-soulful voice.

' "*She's having my ba-by* ..."'

Caroline grinned. 'Oh, no ...'

Scott seemed undeterred. In a parody of blissed-out rapture, he closed his eyes. His features in the pale light looked sculpted, fine.

'*She's having my ba-by.*

What a lovely way to tell the world she loves me ...'

Caroline burst out laughing.

With a look of wounded dignity, an artist misunderstood in his own time, Scott sang each heartfelt line.

'*Could have swept it from her life but she wouldn't do it ...*

She's having my ba-by.'

The lyrics, Caroline thought, were preposterous. What silenced her was how good he was.

Only when he was finished did Scott open his eyes again.

His sudden gaze startled her. 'My favorite song,' she told him. 'It captures my whole worldview.'

Scott grinned, giving her a mock bow.

Caroline sat with her elbows resting on her knees, face cupped in her hands, looking at him. Quietly, she said, 'You're really good, you know?'

He tried to make a joke of it. 'Just good enough to become a bad lounge act. "Scott Johnson, coming to a Holiday Inn near you."'

He said it lightly, smiling. And then their eyes met, and they both no longer smiled. In that instant, Caroline sensed that he was more than lost or sad or sweet, felt that something in each of them called to the other, and that he felt it, too.

Caroline did not know what it was. She knew only that — in a fleeting, imperishable moment — something changed for her.

Scott put down the guitar. He stood, gazing at her, silent. There was only a few feet between them.

Walking toward him, Caroline saw nothing but his eyes, felt nothing but her own pulse.

His mouth was warm.

Where had she been? some part of Caroline wondered. *Who had she been?* Her arms went tight around him.

Slowly, gently, Scott pulled back, forehead resting against hers. Only then did she think of Jackson.

'Jesus,' Scott murmured.

So he felt it too. This strange pull, yet the instinct to resist.

Her voice was quiet. 'I'd better go.'

She went to the door, hardly aware of her own movements. He did not try to stop her.

She turned in the doorway. Scott stood by the bed, gazing at her as if at something he could not have.

As though in consolation, Caroline said, 'Tomorrow we'll go sailing, okay?' And then, hearing herself, she softly added, 'If you want to.'

He watched her, not moving. 'I want to,' he said at last.

Chapter 6

They went sailing the next morning, and the two days after that.

It was different now. There was a new gentleness between them, an unspoken affinity, although, for Caroline, something about Scott remained elusive, just out of reach. At odd moments, she felt them try to read the other's thoughts. But neither crossed their unspoken line. He never touched her.

He was always ready for her company. They hiked in the hills near Menemsha; went to hear Tom Rush sing and play guitar; swam in the freshwater pond at Long Point, the rough surf of the Atlantic a mere hundred feet away. Sometimes it seemed close to effortless; Scott knew the grace of silence, of letting Caroline think her own thoughts. His sarcasm now was sparing, turned solely on himself; he treated Caroline with respect, as if coming too close might harm them. The days fell gently, one upon the other, until time seemed not to matter. There was nothing to tell Jackson.

Perhaps, Caroline later thought, Scott knew more than she did. But for her – almost to the moment when it happened – the night that changed this seemed like any other.

The idea of eating lobster on the beach was hers.

Scott had smiled. 'You mean like Faye Dunaway and Steve McQueen in *The Thomas Crown Affair*?'

Caroline shook her head. 'Did you ever wonder how they got the lobster pot in his dune buggy? I'm talking take-out lobster. From the Homeport.'

Scott rolled his eyes. 'Take-out lobster? Where's your New England work ethic?'

'Dead and buried,' she answered firmly. 'Come on.'

They drove to Edgartown for bread and a bottle of chilled wine. Caroline found bread; looking for Scott at the package store, she saw him eyeing the California Chardonnay with a certain practiced leisure, as if such a grave decision should not be rushed.

'Hard to choose?' Caroline said from behind him.

He turned to her, surprised. 'Only when you don't know wine,' he said, and seemed to pluck a bottle at random. 'Let's take a chance on this one.'

By some unspoken consensus, Caroline always drove now, taking her time. They reached Menemsha a little before eight.

The fishing village was quaint and quiet – the trawlers were in, the beach was almost deserted, and the sun was slipping beneath the distant line where ocean met a darkening sky. The gentle putt of an outboard motor echoed in the harbor.

All that was open was the Homeport restaurant. People wandered in and out of the wood-frame building, a few tourists on the deck watched the sunset over dinner. Caroline led Scott to the take-out window and ordered two lobster dinners. Patient, he waited with the wine and a woolen blanket tucked beneath his arm until their food was ready, and then they set out to find the right spot on the beach.

There was no hurry. The night felt close and warm; the moon, slowly replacing the sun, cast a first glow on the waves. Caroline felt the luxury of time.

They walked the beach until the lights of Menemsha were far behind, and they were alone.

Scott broke their silence. 'I was looking at your catboat the other day. The dinghy's sprung a leak – you should have it fixed pretty soon. And one of the ribs in the hull looks weak.'

Caroline smiled at this: among the bonds between them, she sometimes thought, was the proprietary interest he had taken in the catboat. 'After I leave,' she asked, 'would you look after my boat for me? I might decide to keep it here.'

Scott stopped, facing the water. 'If I'm here,' he said at length. 'But I don't think I will be.'

Caroline turned to him, puzzled by her sadness. Perhaps it was the impermanence of things: as days went by, and the summer grew more precious to her, Scott and the Vineyard had come together in her mind. She could not quite imagine this place without him.

Together, they spread the blanket.

Caroline laid out the bread and the lobster; Scott took a corkscrew to the wine, filled two glasses, and handed one to Caroline. He seemed about to propose a toast, and then looked at her again.

'Is something wrong?' he asked.

Caroline made herself busy with the blanket. 'Oh, I don't know,' she said at last. 'I think in some stupid way I imagined you still here when I came back. Like I'm entitled to arrange every corner of my world just the way I want it.'

'And populate it too?'

'I suppose.'

Scott studied her. 'I guess that happens when things seem good. But they always change. It's a little hard to imagine you, your husband, your kids, and me all going sailing together.' He smiled, as if to remove any sting. 'For openers, you'll need a bigger boat.'

Caroline smiled back. 'How many kids do you think I want?'

Scott grinned. 'Don't know. Just more than I think I want.' He raised his glass. 'To population control.'

Caroline touched her glass to his and sipped. The wine, she realized, was the best she had ever tasted.

She settled back on her elbows. 'So what will you do?'

'I don't have a clue – I just know I can't stay here.' He gazed out at the water. 'Maybe it's the flip side of what you were saying. That when you go off next month, to begin your real life, the island will seem a little lonely.' He gave a dismissive shrug. 'There are other places – I'm not that big on nostalgia.'

She turned to watch him. There was something very still about him, as if he were holding some moment in his mind. And then, with the sudden realization that she knew parts of him by instinct, came the certainty that he was lying to her but not to himself: that he carried pieces of the past within him, and that this summer would become one.

'Well,' she said, 'we've got the time we've got. Which hasn't been so bad.'

He turned to her, smiling. 'Not bad at all. Unless the lobster's cold.'

She spread out paper plates and drawn butter. The lobster shells were already cut; all they had to do was eat.

The night was calm, peaceful. The water lapped at their feet; a faint breeze carried the smell of sea and salt. Neither of them spoke, or needed to.

'Remember when you were a kid,' he said at last, 'and camped out?'

Caroline smiled to herself. It was just right, she realized: the sense of being away from things and yet quite safe, with night closing around you. She knew that Scott required no answer.

All at once, Caroline's senses opened.

She felt everything come together. Felt the breeze on her skin and hair. Saw the moon-streaked ripple on the water, the stars grow bright and close. Felt Scott lying next to her, as lost in the night as she was.

Time seemed to stop.

She did not know how long they lay there, not moving. She knew only what the night had become, and would not have been without him. Until, finally, she found a way to say this.

'Have you ever had a perfect day?'

Scott did not turn. 'No,' he said at last. 'But I've had a perfect hour. Now.'

Hesitant, Caroline reached to cover his hand with hers.

He turned to her then, looking into her face. Slowly, he

reached out and touched her hair.

There was no mistaking what she saw in his eyes.

'Yes,' Caroline heard herself murmur.

He could not seem to move. And then, gently and firmly, Caroline kissed him.

She felt his lips against her face, her neck. Closing her eyes, she held him.

Now it was all feeling. His mouth, slow and unhurried. His lean, hard body against hers. The way his hands seemed to belong wherever they touched. The beating of her own heart.

He slid back from her, and then Caroline felt his fingers on the top button of her blouse.

She opened her eyes.

As he undid the first button, they gazed at each other.

She lay there, silent, as he did this. His eyes did not move until the blouse lay beside them.

Caroline wore no bra.

Gently, she took his head in her hands and cradled it between her breasts.

After a time she felt his mouth on her nipples, her stomach. Felt him unzip her jeans.

She arched her back, helping him.

When she was naked, she lay there uncovered, watching as he undressed. His body was slim, muscular.

He knelt, bowing his head. His mouth grazed her thighs, moving toward the center of her.

Caroline closed her eyes again.

Now it all felt new to her. His tongue. The feel of his body, different from Jackson's, as she opened her legs for him. The wanting as he entered her. The urgency as she moved with him, this strange, blood-rushing need ...

She could not stop now.

With the first tremor of her body, Caroline cried out his name. For there was no one to hear her but him.

She lay in his arms, weak and shaken, the warm feel of his own release inside her.

310

Neither spoke. It was as if their minds were absorbing what their bodies already knew.

What does this mean? Caroline wondered. *Anything? Or everything?*

'Was this just another perfect hour?' she asked.

Silent, Scott pulled her close.

They could not stop.

Sometimes all it needed was for Caroline to look at him. They would go to the boathouse, hardly saying a word, and stand inches apart as they undressed. She spent each night with him.

Each time only fed his hunger for her.

It was as if, some part of Caroline thought, he wished so desperately to talk to her – about what, she was not sure – that he could bear his silence only by making love with her. Sometimes, at night, she would hear him pacing in the next room, so as not to awaken her. Her senses were alive with some unspoken thing.

But when she tried to say this, Scott merely smiled. 'I just wish I were that interesting,' he said.

She could not bring herself to call Jackson – the thought of lying, or the truth, were both too painful. And the only truth she understood was that she had a lover who could make her feel what Jackson could not.

If wasn't that she did not try to understand: the Caroline who wanted Scott so desperately was not some other person. But her accustomed world seemed far away. In this new world, Caroline was alone: not even Scott – especially not Scott – could help her. Even the world of Martha's Vineyard was divided: quite deliberately, it seemed, Scott deflected any suggestion of spending time with Betty and Larry. His only interest was in Caroline herself.

Why did she want him, Caroline wondered, and what did she want from him?

That Betty and Larry said nothing only increased her isolation: their silence told her that the change in her, her nocturnal comings and goings, was so marked that it made them cautious and confused. Perhaps only her mother, Caroline told herself miserably, might have understood.

And yet with Scott – moment to moment – Caroline felt happy.

One morning, she awakened to find him still asleep, the smile of some pleasant dream playing on his mouth. She watched until he awoke.

'You were smiling,' she told him.

The waking Scott smiled again. 'Was I? I must have been teaching you how to sail.'

She kissed his forehead. 'No,' she said. 'I was teaching you how to drive.'

Caroline was still smiling when she crossed the threshold of her father's home.

On the kitchen table was a note in Betty's coiled cursive.

Father called, it said. *When you get the chance, please call him.*

Chapter 7

When Caroline called her father, his tone was careful, neutral; he asked about her sailing, her plans for the remaining weeks, what she had heard from Jackson. Only at the end did he mention that he was coming earlier than planned – the next day, to be precise.

When Caroline put down the phone, she went to find Betty.

She was sitting on the porch, drinking coffee. Glancing up at Caroline, she studied her expression and then said, 'So he told you he's coming early.'

Caroline stared at her. 'What's this about?'

Betty exhaled. 'Caroline, we haven't said a word to him. He's called several times lately, asking to talk to you, and each time one of us covered for you. But Father's not a fool.'

'I am twenty-two.'

Betty nodded in acknowledgment. 'I understand. But you have to imagine this from his point of view – a daughter who's been stable and predictable, with a boy-friend at home, suddenly can't be found at pretty much any hour of the night. Don't you think maybe you'd be a little concerned?'

'It's my life, isn't it?'

Betty's brow knit. 'Even Larry and I have worried a little – we don't know this boy at all, you hardly seem to know him except to spend the night with, and even when you're with us now, you're not.' Betty paused, voice softening. 'Would you mind terribly, Caroline, telling me a little about what's going on?'

Caroline felt her defensiveness die. She sat in the canvas chair next to Betty, gazing at the morning sunlight on the water. 'I wish I knew.'

Betty sipped her coffee. 'Well, he is attractive.'

Caroline shook her head. 'It's not just sex.' She paused, trying to find words. 'It's like I know so much more about him than what he tells me.'

Betty seemed to reflect. 'Has it occurred to you,' she said finally, 'that maybe there's nothing more to him than what he tells you – a rudderless guy without any deep interests but sailing? And that for reasons you haven't coped with, you're projecting your own needs on someone who's a pretty blank screen?'

Though Betty's voice was not unkind, Caroline found that the words stung. 'I don't think I need a shrink, Betty.'

'Really.' Betty's voice was level and unimpressed. 'How are things with Jackson?'

Caroline looked away. 'I don't think I can talk about it now.'

Betty considered her. 'Then let me make one request, as your older sister: that you think about it. And that, while Father's here, you cool things off with Scott a little. There's no point in upsetting Father over something you don't understand yourself.'

It was good advice, Caroline knew, and Scott did not disagree.

'Do what you need to do,' he said. 'Honestly, I understand.'

'But we've only got four weeks left. And he's staying for a week.'

Scott shrugged. 'He's been your father for twenty-two years. And, pretty clearly, the main influence in your life.' He took her hand. 'I don't expect you to rock that boat, and I really don't want you to. Certainly not on my account.'

Why, Caroline wondered, did his understanding make her feel so diminished?

Perhaps, she reflected, it bespoke the limits of her importance to him. Or perhaps it was simply that – like Betty – Scott accepted so easily that Caroline's first obligation was to put Channing Masters at ease.

She did not take Betty's advice.

For the first few days, Caroline spent most of her time with her father, doing many of the things – sailing, hiking, riding rented bikes – that she usually did with Scott. Even in his early fifties, Channing Masters was vigorous and fit, and he took keen pleasure in being outdoors in the company of his youngest daughter, his unspoken favorite. Whatever his concerns were, he kept them to himself, as if the time that Caroline gave him was reassurance enough. Her occasional absentmindedness seemed not to bother him. He was himself sometimes distracted by memories of Nicole, Caroline sensed; when he lapsed into silence, gazing at the water, Caroline could almost feel the hurt her mother had inflicted on him. As for Caroline, her pretense of normality seemed to satisfy him that nothing was so wrong that she need confront it.

Caroline found that she disliked herself for this. But not nearly as intensely as she missed Scott.

On the third night of her father's visit, she came to the boathouse.

As she approached the porch, Scott startled awake. He sat bolt upright, staring around him. And then she saw him freeze.

'Caroline?' he asked.

His voice was tight. 'It's me,' she answered.

In the dark, she saw the shadow of his body relax.

She went to the side of his bed, placing the kit that held her diaphragm on the nightstand. 'I just missed you,' she said.

Gratefully, Scott reached for her.

But it was not the same. Caroline was used to bringing the rhythm of their days to their nights alone; now their lovemaking felt furtive, hurried, something divorced from the rest of her life. Some childish part of her imagined her father breaking in on them: in an odd, chilling moment, she recalled the image of her mother turning to face Caroline as she lay beneath Paul Nerheim.

Scott seemed to sense this. Gently, he said, 'It's a little

315

like high school, isn't it? Sneaking down to the family room after the folks have gone to bed.'

Caroline lay in the dark, listening to the waves splash beneath them, feeling the cool breeze across her naked skin. 'Have you missed me at all?'

Scott was quiet for a time. 'Quite a lot, actually.' He paused, as if trying for a certain fatalism. 'It's just that you've got a father to pacify, and I can't treat that like a tragedy – "Romeo and Juliet at the Beach." Especially when all that's at stake is your time until law school.'

Why, Caroline thought, did she imagine a bitterness buried beneath the offhand realism? And who might he be bitter at?

'What do you want me to do?'

'Nothing.' He kissed her neck. 'Don't worry about me, Caroline. I've got no need to be a character in your family minidrama. Even if it's a bit part.'

In the darkness, she could not see his face.

The next morning, she told her father that she would be sailing with a friend.

Channing raised his eyebrows in pleasant inquiry. 'Oh,' he asked. 'Who?'

'The caretaker from next door. He's quite a good sailor.'

'Does he have a name?'

Caroline smiled. 'Yes,' she said, and went to find Scott.

When Scott opened the door, he did not smile at all.

'How did you explain me?' he asked.

'There's nothing to explain. Are you coming, or am I going out alone?'

Scott gave her an inscrutable look, hesitant, and then took his jacket from the peg beside the door. With a kind of rueful affection, he asked, 'Are you familiar with the term "willful"?'

Why, Caroline wondered, did so many moments – even words – now summon images of her mother? Seeing her expression, Scott's smile vanished.

'I guess you are,' he said.

For the next two days, without explaining herself to anyone, Caroline spent time with Scott.

He seemed almost to stand outside their time together, watching her. 'Has it occurred to you,' he said softly, 'that you're using me?'

They were drinking beer beside the boat, after a long day's sail. 'Using you for what?' she said.

'To define your own territory.'

Caroline gave him a long, level look. Quietly, she said, 'When you can think of something better I can use you for, Scott, please let me know.'

Their time, Caroline thought with sudden pain, was running out.

That night, she came to him again.

She left before dawn, lost in the feel of him, the chaos of her own thoughts. And then she noticed the dim light on the porch of the Masters house.

She stopped on the beach, gazing up. Her father's shadow stood in the semidark, still and silent, watching her.

For a moment, in unspoken acknowledgment, neither moved.

And then Caroline resumed her walk, crossing the beach and climbing the stairs to the bluff, to face him. She could feel her heart race. But when she reached the bluff, the light was off, and he was gone.

Chapter 8

The next morning, at the breakfast table, her father was silent.

Caroline sipped her coffee, trying to look composed. She had not slept.

Larry seemed quite oblivious, chatting on about his thesis. But Betty, Caroline saw, kept looking from her father to her.

When Caroline rose to help clear the dishes, her father raised a hand. 'Caroline,' he said. 'A word with you, please.'

Larry glanced at him, newly aware. Betty touched Larry's arm and motioned him to the kitchen.

'Yes?' Caroline said.

Her father folded his hands in front of him. His voice was quite calm. 'I couldn't help but notice that you spend a good deal of time with the boy next door, as it were. Before I go, I rather think I'd like to meet him.'

Their eyes locked. 'Why, Father?'

'Because it seems polite to acknowledge your friends. And because, curiously, Betty and Larry claim not to know him.' His gaze grew pointed. 'Which strikes me, whoever is at fault, as more than a little uncivilized. Wouldn't you agree?'

Caroline felt cornered; her father knew, or guessed, who was 'at fault,' and she had no excuse for Scott's reclusiveness. The subtext of the night before lay silently between them.

Caroline shrugged. 'All that I can do, Father, is ask....'

'Dinner?' Scott raised his eyebrows. 'What are this man and I going to say to each other? And why does it matter to you?'

'Because he knows how it is with us.'

Scott shook his head. 'But aren't you the one you have to answer to?' he asked.

Caroline crossed her arms. 'You'd think you were crossing the Rubicon instead of facing one middle-aged man across the dinner table.' She paused, hearing herself, and then said softly, 'Sometimes people just do things for other people. Please, don't embarrass me.'

Folding his hands, Scott propped them beneath his chin and stared out at the ocean, pensive. 'All right,' he answered. 'If it really means that much to you.'

The first hour had a deceptive calm.

To Caroline, Scott seemed another person – respectful to her father; amiable and pleasant to Betty and Larry; attentive to Caroline without overdoing it, so that the impression left was that he valued her. He helped Betty in the kitchen, talked to Larry about academic politics.

He seemed wholly at ease, as if a polite dinner with a privileged family was second nature to him. Caroline saw Larry and Betty warm to him, and him to them. If he minded Channing Masters' inquiries about his background – and Caroline was somehow certain that he did mind – he gave little sign.

With cocktails over, they sat down at the dinner table. 'Is it true,' Scott was asking Larry, 'about publish or perish?'

'Depends on the school.' Larry smiled. 'Think there's a spot for me at Ohio Presbyterian?'

Scott seemed to reflect. 'There should be. My last English course was more like a séance than a seminar. Even the dead dropped out.' His voice turned wry. 'The professor had published extensively.'

From the end of the table, Channing watched him. 'Were you an English major?' he asked.

Scott shook his head. 'History. Twentieth-century European, mostly. It wasn't very cheerful.'

Channing did not smile. 'History seldom is. And seldom will be. It's in our nature, I'm afraid.'

Caroline turned to her father. 'That's rather Hobbesian, isn't it?'

Channing seemed to consider her. 'I don't believe in the infinite perfectibility of man, Caroline. If I ever did, I stopped. In Germany.'

Caroline looked to Scott. 'Father served with the Nuremberg tribunal. As an investigator.'

'Out of which,' Channing said to Scott, 'I came to believe in law. But not in men. People are, in the end, who they are.'

Her father's eyes had fixed on Scott. 'But men make laws,' Caroline interjected. 'And write history. Like we're trying to do in Vietnam.'

She saw Larry surreptitiously cover his eyes and emit a silent groan. 'The *V* word,' he murmured.

Channing gave a slight smile and raised his eyebrows at Caroline. 'You were saying, Caroline?'

'That if the Vietnamese wrote history, and convened their own tribunal, Nixon and Kissinger might be condemned as war criminals.'

Channing frowned. 'I think that's much too facile. What our government committed were not crimes of war but acts of war –'

'They bombed civilians, Father. Thousands of them, and for what? To save face in a war we'll never win and now don't even plan to win. Because human beings are only pieces on their geopolitical chessboard.'

Channing shook his head. 'With respect, Communism is a form of tyranny which has killed at least as many people as the Nazis did. With whom you so blithely compare Messrs. Nixon and Kissinger.' His voice became gentle. 'Forgive me, Caroline – you're more than entitled to your own ideas. But I hardly think your maternal grandparents, who died at Auschwitz, would grant your comparison. Or even your own mother.'

Caroline felt herself flush. Through her shame, she remembered that Nicole had felt much as she now did and that her father knew this. But it was beyond her now to say so.

In the silence, she saw Scott gaze at her with deep surprise, and then compassion. Channing turned to him. 'Tell me, Scott, do you have a view on this? Perhaps I've been too harsh.'

Caroline saw Scott fold his hands. He paused, gazing at her father quite openly, as if coming to some decision.

'I wouldn't know,' he said quietly. 'But then I haven't just been trumped with the death of six million Jews. Two of whom were my own grandparents.'

Channing looked at him fixedly. To Caroline, everyone else were figures in a painting: Betty with her eyes downcast, Larry quite pale.

'Do you believe,' Channing asked softly, 'that the Vietnamese are our Jews?'

Scott's faint smile did nothing to his eyes. 'What I'm saying,' he answered with equal quiet, 'is that if the same platoon of Americans had marched into a German village and begun killing and raping everyone in sight until there was pretty much no one left, they wouldn't have put out a record called "The Battle Hymn of Lieutenant Calley." They'd have strung him up –'

'And quite legitimately, I'm sure. But it does point out a larger problem with your reference to My Lai.' Channing's voice took on a lethal quiet. 'Because the young people with, shall we say, the "finer sensibilities" have claimed the right to select their wars. Sensibilities so fine, in fact, that they left *this* war to those with so few advantages that Vietnam looks like a career opportunity. And to, as you put it, the war criminals. Whom the absence of their moral betters, safely deferred, deprived of so many good examples.'

For a moment, the room was silent. 'Yes,' Scott said. 'I'm lucky that I haven't had to die to justify my position. Which leaves me here, free to argue, among the living. Unlike my college roommate, who died there, uselessly.'

Channing's face hardened. Then, as if remembering

himself, he looked suddenly embarrassed. 'Please forgive me, Scott. I've become so used to argument and advocacy that I forget my role as host.'

Scott seemed to study him. 'No need to apologize,' he said. 'My dad and I used to do this all the time. Before we stopped speaking.'

In the nervous laughter that followed, Caroline saw that her father barely smiled.

'Why haven't you ever told me,' Scott asked an hour later, 'about your mother?'

Caroline did not face him. 'It's not the kind of thing that comes up.'

They stood on his deck, hands on the railing, watching the Nantucket Sound at sunset. He turned to her. 'But it's important, don't you think?'

She tilted her head. Softly, she asked, 'Do I know everything that's important about you?'

He did not answer. Caroline was quiet for a time. 'Anyhow,' she said, 'I'm very sorry. For starting that whole argument about Vietnam.'

Scott's eyes narrowed. 'That wasn't about Vietnam, Caroline. It was about you. And me and you.' He paused for a moment. 'Do you really think there's ever a time when your father doesn't know exactly what he's doing? And what he wants?'

She touched his hand. 'He's been a good father, Scott. By his own lights, he wants whatever seems best for me.'

Scott's hand closed around hers. 'I always thought the test of a good parent,' he said softly, 'was to raise adults.'

Withdrawing her hand, Caroline felt herself stiffen. 'Are you saying that I'm not one?'

Scott's eyes were still and serious. 'What I'm saying,' he finally answered, 'is that he may force you to choose. But the choice isn't the one he imagines – between him and whatever bad stuff I or anyone else may symbolize for him.' He paused, ending quietly. 'It'll be between him and *you*.'

She found her father on the porch, sipping a brandy. In the dusk, his eyes looked deep-set, shrouded.

Caroline did not sit. 'That was unforgivable,' she said flatly.

He looked down. 'Yes, I suppose it was. Especially when I insisted that he come.'

He sounded genuinely contrite. 'Why did you do that?' she asked.

'Because I believe that ideas matter. That rigorous thought matters.' He looked away. 'Perhaps it was more than that, Caroline. I find that being here, I think of Nicole.

'I remember all she went through during the war, and what I thought I meant to her because of that – that I could somehow save her, when her own people could not. And then I think about Paul Nerheim.' He paused, finishing softly. 'And, in spite of myself, I feel the anger of her betrayal. Which I inflicted on all of you at dinner, without meaning to. It was as if the two of you had cheapened what I felt. For which, of course, I'm quite ashamed.'

It was painful for Caroline to hear this, to know how little the years of silent restraint had healed him. She felt her anger deflate, become the sadness of her own memories. There was, she thought, nothing more she could say.

Caroline went to Channing and kissed him on the forehead. 'Good night, Father.'

She turned to leave.

'Do you want to know what I think?' he asked mildly. 'About Scott.'

Caroline faced him again. After a moment, she said, 'All right.'

Her father put down his brandy, as if gathering his thoughts. 'There's something wrong with him, Caroline.' His tone was still soft, reluctant. 'A real person is integrated – they're simply the sum of who they are and what they've done. They don't have to think about it.' He looked up at her. 'Haven't you noticed this boy thinking? Not so much about his ideas – the passion is real enough. But about who he is. Or pretends to be.'

323

'Just what are you trying to say, Father?'

'I don't know yet.' His eyes narrowed. 'It's the sense you'll have, perhaps a decade from now, after you've cross-examined a hundred witnesses. You watch their eyes and see that split second of calculation. And you know that they're thinking just a little too hard. Just as this boy spent the first hour of our dinner pretending to be less clever than he is.' He paused again. 'I don't know where you and Jackson stand. I'm not sure I want to know. But Jackson is a real person, and a fine one.'

'Who never disagrees with you.' Caroline's voice rose. 'Isn't that your trouble with Scott? That he stood up to you?'

'How can you think that? This is about character, not ideas.' Her father's gaze grew distant. 'I don't want to be intrusive, Caroline. I like to think I haven't been − at least no more than any only parent with basically good intentions. But bad character is a rot, and there is no cure. The only thing you can do is resolve to avoid the taint yourself.'

With sudden intuition, Caroline sensed that this conversation, too, was not simply about Scott Johnson, but about her own mother.

'There is no taint,' she snapped. 'Except in your mind.' Before he could answer, she turned and left the room.

Chapter 9

But the confrontation with her father ran like a fault line between Caroline and Scott.

With him, she felt joy and passion, yet the undertow of doubt: all her instincts told her that, in some sense she could not identify, Channing Masters was right. Alone in her room, she would add up the discrepancies – between Scott's air of carelessness and his deeply ingrained caution; his supposed unsophistication and his evident worldliness; his studied unsociability and his ease with the few people they had met; his persona of cynical purposelessness and the incisiveness of his mind. Their time was running short, and Caroline might never know him.

Some part of her felt that to penetrate Scott's veneer was dangerous – if there were certain things he did not wish to share, there must be a reason for it. But as each day passed, and Caroline knew only that she wanted to be with him every moment she could, the sense of something between them that they could never say, never reach, ate through her until she feared his silence even more than the reason for it.

'There are things you haven't told me,' she said. 'Things about you. I want to know why.'

They were sitting on the deck after a long day on the water, enjoying wine and cheese and a sunset that stained the wispy clouds orange red. Caroline had broken a pleasant silence; her question, sharp and sudden, so at odds with the mood of their day, startled her.

Yet Scott did not look surprised. With a veiled, wary look, he asked, 'Where's this coming from, Caroline? Your father?'

'Quit sparring with me, all right? You're playing at being someone you're not, and I'm supposed to sit on everything

I think or feel.' She stood, feeling the depth of her anger. 'I spend every minute I can with you, like it's life and death, and all I've really been doing is fucking you for the summer. Because I can't reach you.'

He put down his wineglass and faced her. 'It's you who's going away, Caroline. I don't expect you to drop out of law school. So don't expect me to open up a vein.'

Beneath the chill words was an undertone of emotion. Caroline placed both hands on his shoulders, looking up at him. 'All the time I'm planning to go on with my life, I feel like you've turned me inside out. Please, doesn't this summer mean anything to you?'

She saw him blanch at her intensity. Suddenly, Caroline felt naked and exposed, without any defense between Scott and her emotions.

'Look at me,' Scott said softly.

Slowly, she did that. The tears ran down her face.

Seeing this, his own eyes shut. Caroline saw him swallow. And then his eyes opened; as he touched her face, tracing her tears with his fingertips, he looked at her with a tenderness so open that it was hurtful.

'Why are you doing this?' he asked. 'Don't you know by now how much I love you?'

Caroline felt stunned. Mute, she shook her head.

He seemed to slump. 'Why do you think I stayed here, Caroline? I should have left weeks ago.'

Caroline clasped his shoulders. 'Why?'

Shaking his head, Scott put his arms around her. He seemed to hold her with a desperate longing.

'Make love with me,' he murmured. 'Please.'

His voice was hoarse; Caroline felt her body tremble. They went to the bed like children drawn to a flame.

Now they were fumbling, desperate, tearing the clothes from each other, hands and mouths seeking each other's bodies, like two lovers meeting after weeks apart. Yet they had never been like this – lost, heedless, their bodies from the moment he entered her moving with a frenzy so deep that Caroline no longer knew herself.

They cried out together.

Afterwards they lay in the dark. Stunned, defenseless, Caroline pretended to sleep. She felt ripped open.

Beside her, Scott stirred, restless, rose from bed. Caroline said nothing.

She lay in the dark, alone. Scott did not return.

Naked, Caroline stood.

The air was cool. She felt her skin rise, her nipples. Picking through the clothes on the floor, she found his T-shirt and slid it over her head.

He was on the deck, wearing only his jeans, staring out at the water.

She walked behind him. From his stillness, she knew he was aware of her. But he did not move.

'What is it?' she asked.

He turned to her. In the moonlight, she saw him pause.

'My name,' he said quietly, 'is David Stern.'

It was almost as if, Caroline felt, he were talking of someone he had lost. She took both his hands in hers. He gazed down at their fingers, laced together. 'The funny thing,' he said, 'is that I chose Johnson as a joke, because of Lyndon. But Scott was because I always liked Fitzgerald. I guess you and I will never agree on everything.'

Caroline stared at him. 'But why pretend like this?'

'Haven't you figured it out?' His voice was low and bitter. 'I gave myself my own exemption, Caroline. I'm a draft dodger.'

It made Caroline quiet; she felt both shaken and relieved. She looked at him, waiting.

'I'm from California, not Ohio,' he said at last. 'I went to Berkeley and was going to Stanford law.' He gazed at the deck. 'I was also 1-A.

'I absolutely opposed the war. My father screamed at me about World War II; my mother begged me to go to Canada; my draft counselor told me to work on becoming a conscientious objector.

'Nothing was right.

'I hated the war, and I didn't want to die there. Canada's not my home. And I would have fought in my father's war.

'For two years, I tried for a medical deferment. Until my appeals ran out.

'The only principled thing, I told myself, was to go to jail.' He paused and then looked directly at her. 'Your father had me pegged. At the last minute, I couldn't face it. The day before I was supposed to report, I just took off.'

His tone was laced with self-contempt. As if to encourage him, Caroline squeezed his hands. 'My mother gave me some money,' he finally said. 'My father never knew. One morning, I just lit out with my guitar, a suitcase full of stuff, and a plane ticket to Miami under the name Scott Johnson.

'I picked Miami because I'd never been there.' He shook his head. 'All I had was two thousand dollars and a California license that said I was David Stern.

'I got myself a crummy room in a hotel that didn't care who I was, and made contact with a draft resisters group I knew about from law school. Some of them had a side business – turning birth certificates for dead people into a new identity. So I gave them some money and waited in my room, working on my interim story.'

His voice softened again. 'Day by day, what I'd done sank in....

'I was no one anymore. I had no friends. I couldn't tell anyone the truth. I couldn't call my folks or write them – the FBI could tap their phone or read the mail, which happened to that friend of mine who did end up in jail. And I wasn't sure that my dad wouldn't do something stupid, like come look for me, or that my brother or sister wouldn't blow it somehow.'

Caroline watched his face. 'So they're real. Your family.'

'Oh, they're real.' He looked at her sharply. 'That letter you were looking at, the first time you came over, was to my aunt in Denver. She burns the envelopes and reads them to my mother on the telephone. I can never say where I am.'

Caroline tried to imagine herself adrift, cut off from her own family. But David was lost in his memories now. 'Before I could get my new ID,' he continued, 'the FBI busted the people who were working on it.

'I took off before anyone could find me.

'I couldn't rent a car, which would put my name in a computer. So I bought a bus ticket to Boston, the only place I could think of where there are so many students that one more would just blend in. But there were too many people to lie to, and too many people who wanted ID – for jobs, to buy a car, even for drinks. And now I was short of cash and afraid to buy another identity.

'I'd come face-to-face with what a luxury it was to have been David Stern.' His voice was soft again. 'So I came here – the end of the world, or at least of the United States.

'Vineyarders are used to transients. And they leave you alone.' He paused. 'I scrounged a job, bought a car without registration, and hoped no one would find me until I figured out what to do.'

Caroline watched him. 'So the night we went to town ...'

'I'd let myself go out with you, and now you might see my license. How could I know who you might talk to?' David shook his head. 'But that was nothing compared to how stupid I was, forgetting myself like that. All your cop friend needed was to put me through a computer or check my registration or even just get curious.' His tone turned wondering. 'If it weren't for you, I might have ended up in the local can, waiting for some FBI guy from Boston to come around whenever things got slow.

'That was when I knew I had to leave.'

In the silence, she touched his face. 'Where?'

'Canada.' His voice was quiet and sad. 'I meant to leave here weeks ago. But every week I made another excuse to stay. Until I knew I'd only leave when you did.'

Caroline stepped back from him, trying to absorb it, fingers touching his now. 'All those things you told me ...'

'Were lies, pretty much. Except the part about Bobby Kennedy. Only that it was California, not Indiana. I was there the night they shot him.' His voice slowed. 'We were going to *win*, Caroline. We were *that* close ...'

He did not finish the sentence. In the silence, his fingertips curled beneath hers.

It was the smallest of gestures, and it brought his world down on her. The depth of his loss. The fear in which he lived. The weight of her responsibility, suddenly clear, to protect him from whoever, out of carelessness or malice, might choose to turn him in.

'Can't you fix this somehow?' she asked.

His smile seemed knowing but not unkind; it was as if he saw that, in the numbness of first comprehension, she could get no farther than the desire that things be different.

'Short of jail? This is not a forgiving government, or a forgiving time – too many kids far younger than me have gone there and died for most people to feel sorry for a draft dodger. I'm afraid that job's been left to me.' He paused for a moment. 'And after jail, what would I do? I couldn't practice law here. I don't think I'd even get to vote. I just made a bad decision. And every night I go over it, and over it, and over it....

'I'm tired of it, and sick of myself. At least in Canada there are law schools, and I can be David Stern again. Maybe after a few years I can even figure out who he is now.'

It came to her then: his loneliness; his fear of others; his knowledge that – in a moment of fear and indecision – he had damaged himself in some way that would always be part of him. And then, quite softly, he said, 'It isn't much to offer you, is it?'

Caroline sat down in a deck chair. 'I want a life,' David said softly. 'I want a life with you. But I can never have one here.'

Caroline felt sick. 'You're asking me to come with you.'

'Yes.'

It was as if, Caroline thought, she'd been transported to someone else's life. She had never felt so lost.

He touched her hair. 'If I leave here now, not knowing

what you'd say, it would be the one thing I could never live with.'

Caroline shook her head. 'There's just so much ...'

He withdrew his hand. 'I know. You have your father. You have this life....'

'I have the life *you* used to have.' Caroline's voice rose. 'It's not fair to lay this on my father. Until two years ago, you had my life. Now I find out that most of what you've told me is a lie, that your life as an American is over, and that maybe I can turn mine in and go somewhere I've never been and never cared about. All right, and leave my family behind.'

He turned away. 'That's why I tried not to fall in love with you. Because loving you isn't fair to either one of us. Certainly not to you ...'

'Just let me be here, okay? Alone.'

He turned to her for a moment. And then, without a word, he stood and left.

It was too much to absorb. For a time, she could only see the places that were part of her and, she had believed, would always be – Masters Hill; the town of Resolve; Harvard Yard; Boston; Heron Lake; the streams and mountains of New Hampshire. And then the faces of her college friends; of Jackson; of Betty and Larry; of Channing Masters, the parent who had been with her, and guided her, since the first dawn of her consciousness.

And in none of them, with none of them, had she ever felt as she felt with David Stern.

David.

He was a real person. Beneath the harm he had done himself, he was the person she had sensed he was. For an odd, almost giddy moment, Caroline felt elated. It was possible; *they* were possible.

Because Caroline Masters was in love with David Stern.

Happy and sad, filled with love, terrified by her confusion, Caroline went to him.

He was lying on the bed, staring up at the ceiling.

Quietly, she said, 'You have to be David to me, okay? That's at least a start.'

He gazed up at her, eyes filled with hope and doubt. 'I really do understand,' he said. 'If you can't go, it's for a good reason.'

Caroline stood by the head of the bed, watched him in the moonlight. And then she slowly pulled his T-shirt over her head.

She stood in front of him, not shy. As David looked up from the bed in silence, wanting her, Caroline wished that she could freeze this moment forever.

'I love you, David.'

Silent, he reached out to her.

She went to him. Slowly and sweetly, David Stern made love to her.

Afterward, they lay together in the dark.

There were minutes without speaking. And then, still quiet, David ran his fingers down her spine.

Perhaps he wanted her again, Caroline thought. She touched his face.

'Tell me about your mother,' he said softly. 'Everything.'

Chapter 10

It was insane.

They would lie there, looking into each other's faces, bodies damp with lovemaking. Caroline could not imagine life without him.

But her life before had been perfectly fine, the steady accretion of steps, one upon the other, down the only path she had ever imagined. The Caroline Masters she had always known was not a woman who lived in a vacuum – she was a New Englander; her father's daughter; a graduate of Radcliffe; a person with a career ahead; even Jackson Watts's girlfriend. Without these things, there *was* no Caroline Masters – there was this passionate creature, defined solely by her love for a man she barely knew, and whose real name felt strange on her lips. Who could not imagine her life *with* him.

It was insane.

She could not sleep, lost her desire for food, felt nauseous in spite of that. There were circles beneath her eyes.

And yet each night she went to David.

She could not decide, and there was no one who could help her.

More deeply than in the months following her death, Caroline missed her mother.

Her father would call, and Jackson. At the times that she was there to answer, Caroline sounded to herself like a chattering stranger. She hardly noticed their reaction.

The only person to whom she could truly speak was David.

In the middle of the night, he listened to her doubts and fears. 'Caroline,' he told her finally, 'if I'd known I'd put you through such hell, I'd never have asked you. I should have just gone away.'

He looked so sad that when she left, Caroline was suddenly afraid she would never see him again. So that when she looked out the window the next morning and spotted his curly head as he sat on the corner of his deck, her eyes filled with tears.

There was one week to go, and she was headed for law school like an automaton, spiritless and irresolute.

The morning after Caroline canceled her college friends' visit on the feeblest of excuses, she walked alone on the beach. She felt like a prisoner in her own skin.

Caroline sat on the beach, fighting tears.

Gazing along the edge of the water, she saw the distant figure of her sister, searching for shells.

Instinct told her to get up. But some deep exhausted part of her no longer cared how she appeared. All that she could manage, as Betty approached, was to stop crying.

Silent, her sister sat next to her.

For a time, Betty sifted sand through her fingers, narrowly watching the grains spill on the beach. A cool mist touched their faces.

'Please, Caroline, talk to me.'

'There's nothing to say. Really.'

Betty was quiet. 'Then I have something to tell *you*,' she said at last. 'I think maybe I'm pregnant.'

Caroline turned to her. 'How do you feel?'

'Fine, so far.' Betty smiled. 'But I'm way late.'

Forcing a smile of her own, Caroline touched her shoulder. 'I hope it's true. Then I get to be "Aunt Caroline."'

'You would be, wouldn't you?' The thought seemed to give Betty sudden pleasure, and then her smile faded and she rested her fingers on Caroline's arm. 'I know we haven't really been sisters always. But I wish you could talk with me.'

Caroline felt too drained to speak. Tears came to her eyes again.

'Please,' Betty implored. 'You can't go on like this.'

For a long time, Caroline stared at the sand. Out of wretchedness and exhaustion, she said, 'His name isn't Scott.'

The words, raw in Caroline's throat, felt like a betrayal. Betty's lips compressed. 'Is he in trouble ...?'

Caroline grasped her shoulders. '*I* can't talk about this. *We* can't talk about this.'

'What *is* it?' Betty's fingers tightened. 'Larry and I are worried sick about you, all right? And so is Father.'

Caroline swallowed. 'They can't know,' she murmured. 'Just you.'

After a time, Betty nodded.

Caroline felt her eyes shut. 'They're after him – he didn't report for induction.' She paused and then looked directly at her sister. 'He's asked me to go away with him. To Canada.'

Betty paled. 'My God, Caroline.'

The hushed shock in her voice seemed to run through Caroline. Of all people, she thought, Betty might understand. 'I know,' Caroline said. 'It would change my whole life....'

'Then how can you even think about it?'

'Because I've never loved anyone like this. I never even knew I could.' Her throat felt tight. 'Do you know what that's like?'

Betty gave a first, faint smile. 'The feeling you can't get close enough, that he can't get deep enough? That you'd dredge your soul for him?' Her voice sounded husky, rueful. 'The world of a new love affair is like insanity. And part of the delusion is that you think you're the only one it ever happened to....'

'I don't think that,' Caroline said sharply. 'It's just that it's happened to me.'

'Just like it happened to me – with Larry.' Betty paused. 'But he never asked me to throw away my family and everything I knew. And after a few weeks or months, I wouldn't have. Because I was able to put Larry in the context of a life I wanted and see that he was part of a whole. And that – fortunately for me – he fit.' Her hands grasped Caroline's shoulders. 'You have a whole life planned, Caroline. Scott – or whoever he is – doesn't fit that. And this person whom I'm looking at now isn't you.'

'But is it my life,' Caroline burst out, 'or just the life our father gave me?'

Betty looked astonished. 'Is Canada your life?' she retorted, and then her voice softened. 'I know he feels like the love of your life. But he isn't – if he were, he wouldn't be asking you to change your life. Because that's not how love is supposed to work....'

'But you have so many rules for things – how love is supposed to work; how families are supposed to work. David's not pushing me –'

'David?'

Caroline hesitated. 'Yes.'

Somehow this seemed to deflate Betty. Her voice was quiet again. 'I'm so sorry, Caroline. I never imagined this happening to you.'

Caroline felt her sister's sadness. 'What do you mean?'

Betty looked down. 'That you always seemed so smart and strong to me – that you'd never need anyone the way I need Larry.' She tilted her head. 'Here I was wanting to help you, and now it's me who's shaken. I guess even more for Father than for me.' She paused, then finished quietly. '*I* can't replace you for him, Caroline. No one can.'

It was a hard concession, Caroline knew. Silent, she squeezed her sister's hand.

'Since your mother died,' Betty said at last, 'he's been so alone. Sometimes I've thought that the hope of practicing law with you is the main thing in his life.'

It was as if, Caroline thought, David had numbed her to this painful truth. 'I know,' she finally answered. 'But does that mean I should do it?'

Betty looked at her again. 'It hasn't just been Father,

336

Caroline. It's been you. He didn't get you into Harvard Law School – you did.' Her voice grew sharper. 'You're saying you can't define yourself for Father. How can you define yourself by a decision made by someone who, two months ago, you didn't even know existed. And such a bad decision.'

It was nothing more, Caroline silently acknowledged, than she had told herself.

Betty watched her face. Quietly, she said, 'Talk to Father, Caroline. It's the least you can do. For him, and for yourself.'

Caroline touched her eyes. 'I can't,' she said miserably.

'David may have a deadline. But you don't. You can go to Canada anytime.' Once more, Betty's voice was soft. 'Let him go, then talk to Father. Because I couldn't stand to watch what you could do to him.'

The thought of Betty, the neglected one, trying to hold the threads of their family brought tears to Caroline's eyes.

'Please,' Betty said. 'For both your sakes.'

Caroline took her sister's hands. 'What I do, and how I do it, has to be *my* decision. Please, promise me.'

Betty watched her, and then her gaze broke. 'All right,' she said.

'I'm going to Boston,' Caroline said. 'To Cambridge, really.'

In the darkness, David was quiet. 'To see your old stomping grounds? Or your new ones?'

'I don't know yet.' She touched his arm. 'Part of it's that I can't seem to think here.'

He brought her close. A little sadly, he said, 'That was the idea.'

She flew to Boston the next evening.

In the afternoon, on a crisp, fall-like day, Caroline aimlessly strolled the Harvard campus. She barely saw it.

For a time, she sat on the steps of the law school. Summer students came and went; she could almost have been one of them. But now, Caroline knew quite clearly, she might never be.

She forced herself not to call him.

That night, alone in her hotel room, Caroline slept badly. She had not eaten lunch or dinner.

In the morning, Caroline gazed out her window toward the Public Garden.

It was green and pastoral, a piece of London amidst a much younger city. The skies were darkening, Caroline saw; with the instinct of a sailor, she sensed that the Vineyard was in for stormy weather.

Caroline closed her eyes. In her mind, David sailed the catboat with the wind on his hair, smiling at her across the wheel.

She went to the phone and called him.

The phone rang, and rang again. She did not hang up. Finally, he answered.

'Hi,' she said. 'It's me.'

'Hi.' Her spirits lifted with his voice. 'I miss you.'

'I miss you, too.' Caroline took a breath. 'I'm ready to talk about this, okay? I'm flying back this afternoon.'

'Shall I pick you up?'

'I'll find you.' She paused. 'It'll give me that much more time.'

There was silence for a moment. Quietly, he said, 'Can you give me a preview?'

She sat on the bed. 'I think it's better just to talk things through. Okay?'

'Okay.'

He was trying to sound stoic. Softly, she said, 'I love you, David.'

'And I love you, Caroline.'

Slowly, Caroline put down the telephone, not knowing that it was the last time she would ever hear him say this.

Chapter 11

Caroline flew to the Vineyard in a driving rainstorm, which buffeted the twin-engine prop plane. There was the crash of thunder, a sickening jolt; the tiny plane took a brief, vertiginous drop, and then a second bolt of lightning lit the roiling seas below. Caroline gripped the arm of her seat and tried to think of David.

As it dipped for a landing, the plane lurched from side to side. And then the wheels hit the ground, circling to a stop, and the handful of stunned passengers straggled out like refugees into the pelting storm. Caroline was last.

In front of the airport, a wooden outpost that dated from the Second World War, she found a battered taxi. Inside, she shivered; her hair and face were wet, and a sideways rain spattered the windshield like hail. Once she had given her destination, neither Caroline nor the taciturn gray-haired cabbie spoke at all.

She was going straight to the boathouse.

Her life might be about to change, she thought. How foolish to wish for better weather.

The cab turned down the road to Eel Pond.

Caroline tried to compose herself. In the darkness, all that she could see was the cabbie's fleshy neck, the low shrubs and trees of the moorlike fields as the headlights caught them. And then they passed the Rubins' place, and the terrain opened to the bluff above a black, pounding sea.

The cab stopped. Hastily, Caroline fumbled loose some bills from her purse and got out with her suitcase into the rain.

She stood atop the bluff for a moment, gazing at the silhouette of her father's house, perhaps two hundred feet away. A bolt of lightning struck nearby. Caroline started: as the thunder exploded, she imagined in her mind's eye that she had seen the outline of her father's car. But this could not be.

Turning, Caroline ran down the bluff and across the beach.

Her boots labored in the wet, heavy sand; by the time she clambered to the pier, suitcase still in hand, she was panting, half blind from rain. She ran for his door, footsteps hammering the wooden planks.

His light was on, Caroline saw. He was waiting for her. She sprinted the last four steps and burst through the unlocked door.

She stopped, blinking in the light. David's clothes were pulled from drawers and strewn near his suitcase on the floor.

Caroline turned, stunned and frightened, looking for him.

He stood in the passage to the porch, white-faced. The tension building inside her drove Caroline across the room to him. She clutched the front of his shirt. '*What happened to you, David?*'

He stared down at her. 'Your friend came to warn me,' he said tersely. 'Frank Mannion. He didn't like draft dodgers much, he told me, but he didn't want you hurt anymore.' He paused. 'The FBI's coming tomorrow, Caroline. Someone turned me in.'

Caroline felt herself freeze.

David watched her face. 'You were the only one I told. The only one, including my own mother, who even knew that I was here.'

Caroline's eyes shut. Silent, she laid her head against his chest. He did not move, or hold her. Quietly, David asked, 'Who did you tell?'

Miserably, she whispered, 'Only my sister.'

Gently, firmly, David pushed her away. When he knelt to close the suitcase, his face was taut and his eyes were narrow slits.

Caroline trembled with cold. 'She wouldn't do that.'

Snapping the final latch, David looked up. Voice still

soft, he answered, 'But your father would, wouldn't he?' He paused. 'The rich *are* different, after all.'

All at once, Caroline went numb. 'His car ...'

'Oh, he's back.' His tone was bitter now. 'I'm sure to "inspect his holdings," as you once put it. Of which you're one.'

Tears came to Caroline's eyes, and then the weight of betrayal overwhelmed her – her betrayal of David, Betty's betrayal of her. Her father's ...

'But I was going *with* you.' Her voice filled with anguish. 'After we talked, if you still wanted me, I was going *with* you.'

David turned pale. 'Don't do this. Please. You never would have gone, not really. You're much too tied to all of them.'

His voice was flat, final.

Caroline folded her arms, staring at the floor. In a few terrible moments, she realized, her life had changed forever. Despairing, she asked only, 'What are you going to do?'

He looked at her and then gave a faint sardonic smile in which, Caroline hoped, she might have seen a glimmer of affection. 'Think you can keep a secret?'

'Tell me, damn it.'

There was another flash of lightning. David glanced out the window, then said, 'I'm stealing your boat.'

Caroline stared at him. 'That's crazy.'

'Is it?' David pulled on his jacket. 'The only other ways off this island are the airport and the boat from Vineyard Haven. Both places will be watching for me. The only ticket they'll give me is to prison. And I refuse to go there on account of your family.'

Caroline was seized by despair. 'You'll never make it. Not in a catboat.'

He looked at her steadily. 'I've sailed through much worse. And once I do, I'm halfway to Canada. Just a pleasant sail up the coast of Maine.'

Wordless, Caroline clutched the front of his jacket, shaking her head.

'I'm taking the boat,' he repeated. 'You can help me, or say goodbye here.'

Caroline fought back tears. In a muffled voice, she said, 'I'll help you.'

Gently, David removed her hands from his jacket.

He went to the doorway. Standing there, irresolute, Caroline saw his guitar in the corner.

She walked across the room to get it.

Caroline turned to him, guitar in hand. Framed in the doorway, he looked at the guitar, then at her, and a second faint smile crossed his face.

'Let's go,' he said.

They walked down the pier in the driving rain, David carrying his suitcase, Caroline his guitar. Not looking at each other, and yet not hurrying. Struggling across the beach, they left twin trails of footprints.

At the end of the Masterses' dock, the catboat bobbed in the storm. Caroline stopped abruptly.

'I never fixed the dinghy,' she said. 'Or the rib.'

'I know.'

David paused for a moment, gazing at the boat, and then kept walking.

Slowly, she followed him. Beneath the wind and rain, his footsteps sounded hollow.

Turning, David looked at her, and then he tossed his suitcase onto the catboat.

As Caroline leapt onto the boat, guitar in hand, the rain came down in sheets.

She went below. Carefully, she placed his guitar in one corner.

Above, David had begun to unfurl the canvas. His curly hair was rain-soaked.

Caroline went to help him, a catch in her throat. Together, they raised the sail aloft, flapping in the punishing wind.

Numb, Caroline moved from one task to the next. Just as

342

they had done in so many days of summer – silent, knowing their routine so well that there was no need to speak.

In the rain, Caroline's tears were nothing.

David had turned to her. Softly, he said, 'I think we're ready, Caroline.'

She could not seem to move.

He came to her then, taking her face in his hands. 'No,' he said. 'You can't.'

The boat lurched violently beneath them. Tears ran down Caroline's face.

David placed both hands on her waist and looked intently into her eyes. It was as if, Caroline thought for a moment, he wanted to remember them.

Perhaps he would change his mind.

Gently, he lifted her over the side and placed her on the dock. She started to reach out, realized she could no longer touch him.

'Think you can toss me the line?' he asked.

Caroline knelt, freeing the line from the spile that secured it. For a last moment, she held it in her hand. And then, underhand, she tossed it to him as he had asked.

'Please,' she said, 'at least let me know that you've made it. Somehow.'

Silent, he gazed at her and seemed to force a smile. 'Don't worry. I'll remember Joshua Slocum.'

Wind flapped in the sails above him. David gave her a last long look and then turned quickly to his task.

Caroline watched, hands in her pockets, as the catboat slipped into the storm.

Soon it began to merge with the dark. Caroline strained to see him. He was a slim figure at the helm; perhaps in her imagination, in the last moment before he vanished, David turned to wave.

As far as Caroline knew, they never found him. She never heard from him again.

Later, when she came to California, Caroline tried to find

343

his parents. But she could not. Perhaps it was best; she was not sure what she would have said.

She made her own life. At odd times, Caroline the defense lawyer imagined a man named David Stern, in Canada. She hoped he had forgiven her, for she had so much to tell him.

PART SIX

The Hearing

Chapter 1

Amidst a throng of reporters, Caroline Masters ascended the steps of the Connaughton County Courthouse.

The crowd – the outthrust microphones, the cameras, the reporters jockeying for position – was largely Caroline's doing. Two days before the hearing, she had told the *Patriot-Ledger* that she would expose weaknesses in the prosecution case and singled out Megan Race by name. She repeated this challenge on television, to ensure that Megan would not miss it. Now the hearing had become an event, its centerpiece Megan's testimony, perhaps three days away.

'Do you expect to vindicate Brett Allen?' a woman reporter called out.

Caroline paused, gazing straight into a hand-held camera. She had sacrificed sleep to preparation, and the circles beneath her eyes had required more work than usual. But in her sleekly tailored blue suit, with her hair freshly cut, she looked crisp and in command.

'What I intend,' Caroline answered, 'is to show that the prosecution case against Brett Allen should not satisfy anyone who comes to this courthouse with an open mind. I hope the prosecution meets that description.'

Caroline turned away, making this challenge to Jackson her sound bite of the morning. It also hid her own discomfort; after all, she thought grimly, only she could guess the origin of the murder weapon, only she knew that Brett and James Case had quarreled in the moments before his death. Her stomach felt hollow.

At the top of the courthouse steps she turned, waiting for her family.

Dressed in a three-piece suit, Channing Masters was a figure of judicial rectitude, head held high as he climbed the stairs toward Caroline. Betty clasped one elbow, Larry the other; their faces, as Caroline had schooled them, were open and hopeful. They met Caroline, forming the tableau of a family come to seek justice for its youngest member.

Minutes before, Jackson had arrived.

With a certain restraint, he said only that what mattered was the evidence. As for Megan Race, she was in virtual seclusion: two nights before, a television camera had caught her leaving the apartment, straight-backed and angry. She would not speak at all.

The previous day, Jackson had appeared at the inn unannounced.

They had gone to her room. In a voice much colder than usual, Jackson asked, 'What have you done to Megan Race?'

With feigned indifference, Caroline had answered, 'What does Megan think I've done?'

Jackson gazed at her across the room. His eyes looked puffy; Caroline knew that he was as tired as she was.

'She wants me to investigate you,' he said finally. 'She still thinks someone broke into her apartment.'

Caroline sat back. 'Any more proof of a break-in?'

Jackson hesitated. 'No. Not that we can see.'

'Then it never happened, did it? Just like a drug dealer never broke into James's apartment ...'

'Don't play games with me. Megan's jumpy as a cat now – you did something to intimidate her.'

'Maybe she's trying to intimidate *me*. Or maybe you are.' Caroline's voice was brittle with strain. 'If you want to investigate me, go ahead. But not until this hearing's over.'

Jackson folded his arms. 'Save it for the cameras, Caroline. I've been watching you ratchet up the pressure on this girl for the last two days. If you've got some reason to believe she's not reliable, tell me.'

'I already did,' Caroline snapped. 'And yet you insist on calling her.'

'She denies any relationship to Larry.' Jackson stood,

hands on hips. 'Look, if you've got something else, tell me. But don't try to set me up.'

Rubbing the bridge of her nose, Caroline was silent. 'This is a capital case,' she said at last. 'It's about Brett, not you and me, and you've chosen to base it on Megan Race. I'm entitled to cross-examine her without giving you a preview.'

'You did do something, didn't you?' Jackson's tone was sharp now. 'Hasn't it occurred to you that whatever it is will come out too? What about your judgeship?'

Caroline looked at him wearily. *And what about* your *judgeship*, she wanted to ask; all at once, she understood what public embarrassment might do to him as well. It made her sorry for them both.

'I'm a defense lawyer,' she answered. 'Brett comes first.'

'Just what do you plan?' her father had asked.

They sat in Carlton Grey's office a few hours after Jackson's visit. Perhaps it was fatigue; Caroline felt the full weight of her memories, the deep despairing wish never to have returned. It took an act of will to address her father as a lawyer.

'Several things,' she said. 'First, to show that the physical evidence, in which Jackson put such stock, is ambiguous. I've been over this with our experts – on serology, on drugs, on pathology, and on forensics – until the lab reports are swimming before my eyes.'

'Yes.' Her father's tone was suddenly gentle. 'You look tired.'

Caroline did not want sympathy. In a flat voice, she said, 'I've had a lot on my mind.'

Channing was quiet for a moment. 'Being tired is no good,' he said finally. 'For you or for Brett. And from the way you've dealt with the press, you've staked a lot on this.'

'Yes,' Caroline said with some asperity. 'I've considered that.'

Channing turned to the window. The office was shadowed, but outside it was brilliant summer; in the half-light, the skin of Channing's face had the translucent look of parchment. 'You're still my daughter,' he answered softly, 'and Brett is my granddaughter.'

There was nothing Caroline wished to say.

After a time, Channing spoke as if her silence had never happened. 'Judge Towle is a friend, Caroline. He's hardly pro–defendant, but he does have a certain libertarian streak. I think he'll give you latitude in showing that Brett was too intoxicated for the police to question, or that they didn't warn her properly.'

Caroline raised an eyebrow. 'Even if it means that everything – her statement and the warrants to search her person and the property – goes out the window? Leaving Jackson with next to nothing?'

Channing shrugged. 'As a district judge, Fred Towle won't have to make that ruling – the Superior Court judge will, if Fred otherwise finds probable cause. But I believe that Fred will let you call Jackson's principal witnesses and tie them down on that and other points.'

Caroline raised an eyebrow. 'Even though under New Hampshire law I'm not allowed to ferret out Jackson's case? After all, in theory, the sole purpose of this hearing is to establish probable cause.'

'Fred may find that a hard line to draw.'

Watching him, Caroline found herself wondering if her father had spoken to Judge Towle: the integrity of New Hampshire judges was a matter of great pride, but Channing Masters had helped Towle secure his judgeship. And who could know what might be said in some passing conversation over bourbon at the Trout Club.

'I hope you're right,' Caroline said at length. 'I want the sworn testimony of Jackson's witnesses before they're as well prepared as Jackson will have them at trial. If we can show how drunk Brett really was, the pressure will build for Jackson to knock the charge down to manslaughter.'

Channing's mouth compressed. 'She's not guilty, Caroline.'

'Oh, I know. You've already said that.'

Channing straightened in his chair. 'You may have become so jaded that guilt or innocence doesn't matter. But it should.' His voice turned hard. 'Now that you've made this hearing such an event – for reasons I don't completely follow – nothing will do but that you destroy Jackson's case if Fred Towle lets you try. Because if you don't do Jackson real damage, Brett will be worse off than ever. Not simply because you'll have lost the battle of publicity, with the attendant effect on prospective jurors. But because we'll have given away to Jackson, and his witnesses, your best lines of attack at trial.'

Caroline frowned; she knew all too well the perils of the decision she had made. 'This isn't helping me. Assuming that's what you came for.'

Her father folded his hands in front of him. 'Caroline,' he said at last, 'what will you do about Megan Race?'

His voice mingled apology and concern; more than antagonism, Caroline found, this made her edgy. She did not want to feel the burden of her father's sleepless nights.

'I'm going to destroy her, Father. Just as you suggest.' She smiled faintly. 'After all, how do I know that *she* didn't kill him? How do Jackson and the police know, when, as I intend to show, they were so quick to latch onto Brett that they never even looked for the real killer?'

Her father studied her. 'You still believe she's guilty.'

Caroline no longer smiled. 'We're all guilty,' she said quietly. 'Brett no more than the rest of us.'

Her father gave her a complex look of inquiry and comprehension. 'And you won't tell me what you mean to do to Megan.'

Caroline folded her hands in front of her. 'No,' she answered. 'Over the years I've learned to keep my own counsel.'

Her father blanched and then looked down. After a time, he said, 'You never will forgive me, will you.'

It took Caroline long to answer, but when she did, her voice was steady. 'All these years, and you've learned nothing. You think that feelings are an elective – that I elect

351

to feel this way to hurt you. But all that I elected was to survive.' Her tone grew quiet. 'You say you look at me and see my mother. But when I look at you, it's David's face I see. No matter how hard I try.'

He gazed up at her, stricken. Softly, she finished: 'That is far more painful to me than I can ever tell you, Father. And it will never change.'

With her father beside her, Caroline entered the courtroom.

She faced him, pausing a moment. And then, for the press who watched them – for Brett – she touched him on the shoulder, then Larry, and turned to Betty.

Betty looked away. To cover this, Caroline clasped her shoulders, and kissed her softly on the cheek. Her lips barely touched her sister's skin.

Turning, Caroline drew a breath and walked to the defense table.

The courtroom was small and plain, with the American and the New Hampshire flag at each side of the judge's bench. The press began to cluster in the back, and the slow gathering of a courtroom reaching critical mass began – Jackson shuffling papers at the prosecution table; a bailiff coming through the judge's door at the back of the room, the court reporter sitting at her machine in front of the raised bench where Judge Towle would sit. The murmur of onlookers grew quieter.

Caroline folded her hands beneath the table. At the back of the courtroom, a second door opened, and then Brett appeared with a deputy.

She wore the simple blue dress Caroline had selected for her, and her hair was pulled back from her face. The effect was demure; Brett's eyes seemed to widen at the courtroom, and her bright green gaze sought out Caroline. And then she smiled a little and came to her directly.

Feeling strangely light, Caroline stood. This was what she was here for.

Brett gazed up at her. 'Hi,' she said.

Her voice was close to normal. 'Are you all right?' Caroline asked.

Brett smiled again. 'Anything to get out of there.'

The joke did not quite work; for a moment, Caroline wished that she could hug her.

'Well,' she said in her calmest tone, 'I'll see what I can do.'

They sat together. Caroline squeezed Brett's hand beneath the table. Then Carlton Grey joined them, and she let go.

'All rise,' the bailiff called out.

District Judge Frederick Towle appeared. He was plump and brown-haired, no older than Caroline and no taller. He took his time, his round, amiable face solemn and a little abstracted, as if he was aware of being watched. Assuming the bench, he looked at Jackson.

Jackson did not look happy. Caroline knew why: at seven-thirty that morning, Judge Towle had brought the lawyers in to take care of preliminary motions. Carlton Grey had moved Caroline's admission for the purposes of the case; graciously, Judge Towle had welcomed her back to New Hampshire, and then he set the rules for the hearing. His sole purpose, he went on, was to determine whether the prosecution had probable cause to pursue a charge of murder in the first degree: Jackson would be allowed to put on hearsay evidence, asking the police to testify as to knowledge gained from other witnesses. But after argument from Caroline, Towle ruled that Jackson could not show probable cause solely through the lead investigator. Instead he must himself call four of the prosecution witnesses whom Caroline had subpoenaed – the arresting officer; the lead investigator; the medical examiner; and Megan Race.

Jackson had protested vigorously – this, he said, would present the defense discovery not permitted by New Hampshire law. But Towle held his ground: the purpose was not discovery, he responded, but establishing probable cause in a matter that relied on the credibility of Megan

Race and on medical evidence – including photographs –
too complex for hearsay testimony from lay witnesses.
Jackson had looked astonished; watching, Caroline could
feel her father's presence, though he was nowhere near the
courtroom.

Now, still facing Jackson, Towle nodded. 'Mr. Watts,'
he said, and the hearing began.

Chapter 2

Watching Jackson rise, Caroline wondered if this would be her last appearance in a courtroom. The sense of emptiness frightened her – who would she be if not a judge or lawyer. And then she felt Brett beside her.

Get a grip, Caroline told herself. What Brett needed now was for Caroline to be as good as she ever had been.

Passing before the cramped spectator section, jammed with media, a young policeman in uniform took the stand.

Officer Jack Mann of the Resolve police was much as Brett had described him: stocky, well built, barely in his twenties. His brown hair was cut short on the sides, Marine-style, emphasizing his square chin and prominent nose. But his face seemed hardly written on, and his eyes were guileless: the effect was of someone decent, striving to fill his role and almost painfully sincere. Caroline could see why Brett had trusted him.

Jackson stood near the witness box in his prosecutor's outfit: navy-blue suit, white shirt, subdued tie. The sober spokesman of law and order, soberly examining its first line of defense.

Quickly, Jackson disposed of the preliminaries and got to the critical facts. 'That night,' he asked, 'when did you first encounter Brett Allen?'

'I saw her Jeep.' Mann glanced quickly at Brett. 'It was stopped by the side of the county road, with the headlights on. I thought someone might be needing help.'

Next to Caroline, Brett sat with her head bowed. She made herself look up at Mann; in Caroline's line of vision were two young profiles – Brett gazing at the policeman; Mann facing Jackson.

'So you stopped?' Jackson asked.

'Yessir. And went to the car.'

Jackson shoved his hands in his pockets. 'And what did you find?'

'At first I couldn't see anyone. So I went to the driver's-side window with my flashlight.'

'And?'

Mann stared straight ahead now. 'There was a naked woman inside. She was hunched down behind the wheel, face pressed against the car door.' His voice carried the memory of puzzlement. 'Sort of curled up in the fetal position, like she was trying to hide.'

Brett's face reddened. Caroline touched her arm.

'I called to her through the window,' Mann went on. 'After about the third time, she opened it.' He paused a moment. 'She tried to cover herself. But I could see the blood and vomit on her.'

'Did she say anything?'

'Only that she was sick. I could smell it too – along with marijuana and maybe wine.'

Caroline glanced about. An odd decorousness had settled over the courtroom: Judge Towle studied nothing in particular, and reporters soberly scribbled notes. But Betty and Larry were rigid in profile, and her father's stare was fixed.

Caroline turned back to Jackson.

He was moving closer to Mann. 'Did she tell you how she'd gotten that way?'

'No.'

'Nothing about a boyfriend?'

'No.'

Eyebrow raised, Jackson skipped a beat. 'Or a murder?'

'Nothing like that, sir. She didn't say anything about him.'

On Brett's eyes was the sudden film of doubt – all at once, Caroline sensed that Brett herself was not sure of what had happened. She wondered if this was better, or worse, than the settled knowledge of one's guilt.

'Did you search the car?' Jackson asked Mann.

'No, sir – I didn't have a warrant. But there were certain items on the passenger seat, in plain view.'

The young cop's voice was stiff now – he wanted to show how well he had stuck to the rules. As if to affirm this, Jackson nodded before asking, 'What were those items?'

'A wallet and a knife.' Mann's voice lowered. 'The knife had blood on it. From the looks of it, the blood hadn't dried yet.'

The process had begun, Caroline thought: the slow accretion of fact upon fact to establish Brett's guilt. Brett herself was still, attentive.

'Did you ask her about that?'

'I asked if anyone was hurt.'

'And what did she answer?'

'I don't remember, exactly. But what it amounted to was "no."'

'And how was her demeanor?'

'It was like she was so scared she was numb. But her eyes followed me – I could see she understood my questions. When I asked her name, she told me.'

'And what did you do then?'

'Told her I was taking her in, for DWI.' Mann's voice turned defensive. 'I didn't know what else had happened, but it was pretty clear she was drunk or maybe stoned.'

The next question, Caroline knew, was critical. Jackson paused before asking it, and each word was slow and distinct.

'At the time you arrested Ms. Allen, Officer Mann, did you believe that a homicide had been committed?'

Mann fidgeted in his chair, but his voice was firm. 'I had no idea what had happened, except that there was blood in the car, and someone might be hurt. At first, I thought it might be *her* blood. But she wasn't telling me a thing.'

'So you took her to the station in Resolve.'

'Yessir. I gave her my jacket and drove her in. Then I booked her for DWI and put her in a cell.'

'What did you do then?'

'I went through the wallet and found a driver's license with a man's picture and a name – James Case. That was the first time I was sure the wallet wasn't hers.'

Jackson nodded. 'Did that concern you?'

'Yessir.' Mann's shoulders hunched together, and his forehead creased; with a certain detachment, Caroline watched the young policeman gather himself to give the answer he and Jackson had rehearsed. 'I was worried that someone might be hurt somewhere and needing help. I mean, that's one of the reasons you take this job – to help protect people. You have to consider all sorts of things, like maybe there's a killer out there who might hurt someone again if we didn't find him, who even might hurt Ms. Allen. But the first thing was this guy on the driver's license, and was *he* hurt and still out there.'

It might even be true, Caroline thought; at least Mann was young enough to believe it. Next to her, Brett stared at the table.

Caroline whispered, 'Keep looking at him. No matter what.'

Brett did that. But she could not look at Caroline.

'So at the time,' Jackson was asking, 'your concern was public safety?'

'Yessir. And maybe saving a life.'

'And you did not believe that a homicide had been committed, or that Ms. Allen had committed it?'

For the first time, Caroline rose to address Judge Towle. 'Objection,' she said in a calm, clear voice. 'To both questions, actually. I don't want to interrupt Mr. Watts's testimony, but he shouldn't be telling our nominal witness what his answers should be. After all, these proceedings should have at least some spontaneity.'

Towle's owlish look at Caroline said that he understood perfectly: that Jackson, unsure of his witness, was steering him through a trap Caroline wished to spring – that he had waited too long to read Brett her rights for a charge of murder. And that Caroline must cut this off.

'Sustained.' Towle turned to Jackson. 'Let's have this in Officer Mann's own words. And thoughts, if possible.'

Jackson looked unruffled; his question had already provided Mann with the answer, and Caroline's objection had underscored how central it was. 'Did you show the license to Ms. Allen?' he asked.

'Yessir.'

'And what, if anything, did you say to her?'

'What I just said – that I was afraid someone out there might be hurt, might get worse if we couldn't help him.'

Jackson nodded in approval. 'And did she answer you?'

'She did. She told me to look out by Heron Lake.' Turning to Brett, he finished quietly, 'When they found him, his throat had been cut with a knife.'

Brett's face was white. Beneath the table, Caroline touched her knee.

Jackson let a moment pass. 'Between the time of Ms. Allen's statement and the time James Case was found dead, what did you do?'

Slowly, Mann's gaze returned to Jackson. 'I called the state police. At their instructions, I took her to Connaughton County Hospital and then drove back to the station.'

'And when did you next see her?'

'After they'd found the body, and we'd called the Major Crimes Unit of the state police. They called from the hospital and said she wanted to see me.'

'What did you do?'

'Waited for Sergeant Summers from Major Crimes in Concord. When he got there, he had them put her in a room with both of us.'

'And at that time, did you give Ms. Allen her Miranda warnings?'

'Sergeant Summers did. It's all on tape.'

'And how did she seem to you?'

'Pale and upset. But sober – anxious to talk.'

'Did she seem to understand her rights?'

'Yessir. On the tape, she says that doesn't matter – that she wants to talk.'

Jackson paused a moment. 'How long,' he asked slowly, 'had it been since you picked her up?'

'It was nearly six. I'd picked her up at approximately eleven-thirty.'

'Did she seem coherent?'

'Yessir.'

Jackson nodded. 'We'll introduce the tape through Sergeant Summers. But could you describe the essence of her statement as to how James Case had died?'

Mann nodded. 'She told us that someone else had killed him. And that she found him like that.'

'And in the course of her statement, did you ask Ms. Allen about her relationship to Mr. Case?'

'Yessir.'

'And what did she say?'

'He was her boyfriend.'

All at once, Caroline could see what was coming. She had an objection – that the tape spoke for itself. But to raise this would only make things worse.

Pausing, Jackson gave Mann a long, considering look. 'And did you then ask her if Mr. Case was involved with any other women?'

'Yessir.'

'And what did she answer?'

As he turned to Brett, Caroline saw the girl brace herself. 'Ms. Allen said, "Of course not."' Pausing, Mann seemed bemused. 'It was the only time she sounded angry.'

Caroline felt the implications in the pit of her stomach: that Brett was sober enough to lie. And that she had needed to lie about Megan Race because she needed to lie about everything.

In an involuntary reflex, Brett looked down.

Turning to Caroline, Jackson said with grave politeness, 'Your witness, Counsel.'

Chapter 3

Walking toward the witness, Caroline took a moment to gather herself. She saw her family watching her, her father's grim inspection. Most of all, she felt Brett waiting behind her. 'Let's take this from the beginning,' she said. 'You found Brett Allen in her Jeep, by the side of the road. Naked.'

Mann gave her a wary look. 'That's right.'

'Spattered with blood.'

'Yes.'

'Specked with vomit.'

'Yes.'

'And, it seems fair to say, disoriented.'

Mann shook his head. 'I don't know if I could say that.'

Caroline appraised him. *Take it slow*, she told herself. Quietly, she asked, 'You had no doubt she was intoxicated, right?'

'Not really, no.'

'And what did you base that on?'

'Like I said, I thought I could smell wine and marijuana. Plus she'd thrown up.'

'Is that all?'

Mann leaned back in the witness stand. 'I think so, yes.'

Caroline raised an eyebrow. 'She was naked, wasn't she?'

'Yes.'

'How many other naked drivers have you arrested?'

Mann hesitated, and then shrugged. 'None.'

'And yet you testified that at the time you picked her up for DWI, she seemed to understand you. Was that based on anything she said?'

'No.'

'Because she didn't respond at all, did she?'

'Not that I remember.'

Caroline moved closer. In a flat voice, she said, 'Indeed, after you told her you were taking her in, the next thing she did – the very next thing – was throw up.'

Pausing, Mann looked troubled. 'She did that, yes.'

'And on the way to the station she said nothing, correct?'

'Correct.'

'So your entire basis for believing that this naked, bloodspattered, nauseous, and intoxicated young woman was nonetheless not 'disoriented' was that she could tell you her name. Oh, and that her eyes 'followed' you when you asked questions.'

Mann glanced toward Jackson. 'I guess so,' he said at length.

'But how do you know that she understood you?'

Mann's brow furrowed. 'I can't *know* that.'

'Or even that she knew what had happened to her?'

Mann glanced at Brett. 'She told us she did later. She gave a whole statement about what happened.'

It was a good answer. Caroline felt it break her rhythm; in that moment, she knew why Jackson had let this go.

She drew a breath. Quietly, she asked, 'Have you ever been intoxicated, Officer Mann?'

Jackson was on his feet at once. 'Objection, Your Honor. Officer Mann's personal experience in this regard – if any – is irrelevant to Ms. Allen's conduct here.'

Caroline faced Judge Towle. 'Your Honor, Officer Mann has offered an opinion – at least a surmise – on Ms. Allen's state of mind from the moment of arrest until she finished her statement. Unless he has a medical background, that opinion is based solely on practical experience. Perhaps including his own.'

Towle propped his chin on one hand, glancing quickly toward Channing Masters. Almost absently, he said, 'I'll allow it.'

'Have you?' Caroline asked Mann.

Mann flushed. 'I would say so, yes. A few times – always whiskey.'

'Ever get so drunk that you didn't know where you were?'

Mann looked down; a painful attempt at honesty seemed to tighten his face. 'Once. After a bachelor party.'

'And do you remember everything that happened that night?'

'Most of it ...' His voice trailed off, and he looked at Caroline with sudden comprehension.

Quietly, she finished for him. 'But not until later.'

He nodded slowly. 'That's right. And not everything.'

That last comment, Caroline realized, was far too close too home.

'At the time you arrested Ms. Allen,' she asked abruptly, 'was her hair wet?'

Mann blinked, surprised. 'I think so, yes.'

'On what do you base that?'

Mann thought for a time. 'Like I said, I gave her my jacket. When I put it over her shoulders, her hair felt wet.' He scrutinized Brett briefly. 'Her hair was curlier and tighter than it looks to me now.'

Caroline paused. 'So that later, when she gave her statement, there was at least one part you believed. When Brett told you she'd gone swimming.'

'I guess so, yes.'

'That must have been before James Case was killed, correct?'

Mann hesitated, and then spread his hands. 'How would I know?'

'Because when you arrested her, Officer Mann, her face and neck and torso and hair all were flecked with blood.'

Mann looked surprised. 'That's true ...'

'So that it's quite possible that – just as she told you – Brett Allen was in the middle of Heron Lake at the time James Case was killed.'

There was a first murmur from the press. Instantly, Jackson rose to object. 'Your honor,' he said. 'That may be counsel's argument. But how and when Ms. Allen's hair got wet is well beyond the knowledge of this witness.'

363

That, Caroline knew, was utterly correct. 'Not so,' she answered tartly. 'Not when there was blood on Ms. Allen's skin and in her admittedly wet hair.'

Towle permitted himself a smile. 'It's not the 'wet' part Mr. Watts objects to. It's the 'lake' part. Objection sustained.'

Caroline did not argue; she had made her point. Turning back to Mann, she asked, 'Would you characterize the blood spatter on Ms. Allen's skin and hair as heavy?'

Mann seemed to search his memory. 'No, I wouldn't say "heavy."'

'Then how would you describe it?'

Mann folded his hands, glancing again at Jackson. 'It was more like spray – dots and a few drops.'

'So the surface of her skin was hardly blood-soaked.'

Mann shook his head. 'It was more like a spray on her face, and then spots on her breasts and stomach. Pretty far apart.'

Caroline wondered for an instant how hearing this felt to Brett. And then Jackson was up again. 'Your Honor, we have photographs of the spray pattern on Ms. Allen. I suggest that these exhibits are the best evidence of what Ms. Masters is trying to elicit here.'

Caroline still faced Judge Towle. 'With a few more questions, Your Honor, I believe that I can demonstrate that Mr. Watts's pictures are not "best evidence" of anything. May I proceed?'

Towle nodded briskly. 'Go ahead, Ms. Masters. But quickly – otherwise, I'm inclined to agree with Mr. Watts.'

Caroline faced Mann again. 'You gave Ms. Allen your jacket, correct?'

'Yes.'

'And she zipped it up?'

Mann hesitated. '*I* did, actually.'

'And she wore it to the jail.'

'Yes.'

'How much of Ms. Allen would you say the jacket covered?'

Mann looked down. 'Maybe to midthigh.'

'And did Ms. Allen pull the jacket down around her, trying to cover herself?'

Mann seemed to flush. 'I remember that. Yes.'

'So that, inevitably, the jacket touched her skin?'

Mann looked down. In a slow, reluctant voice, he said, 'When I got the jacket back, there were spots of blood on it. So I'd have to say yes.'

Caroline felt briefly sorry for him; for perhaps the first time in his life, Mann was learning what the most thoughtful – or thoughtless – act might become in the hands of a defense lawyer. 'Did you send your jacket to the cleaners, Officer Mann?'

'Yes.'

'And you never discussed this with the medical examiner or anyone from the state police?'

Mann raised his head. 'No, ma'am,' he said formally. 'I did not.'

'All right. Then let's move to your conversation with Ms. Allen after you got to jail. You did not advise Ms. Allen of her rights – such as the right to counsel and against self-incrimination.'

Mann's face hardened. 'That's right,' he said firmly. 'We didn't even have a body, ma'am. All I was after was protecting public safety and maybe finding someone who'd been hurt.'

Caroline placed both hands on her hips. 'And how did you think this unknown person might have gotten hurt?'

Mann gave a fractional shrug. 'I didn't know.'

'Maybe with the knife? After all, it was bloody, and there were no stab wounds you could see on Ms. Allen.' Caroline paused. 'And you'd pretty much seen everything.'

Mann flushed again. 'I thought it was possible that it was the knife, yes.'

'Possible? Except for the knife and the blood on Ms. Allen, you had no reason to wonder if anyone had been "hurt," correct?'

'I guess not.'

365

Caroline mustered an incredulous look. 'And how did you think that this person had gotten "hurt"? By falling on the knife?'

Jackson stood at once. 'Objection, Your Honor. There's no reason for counsel to badger this witness. If she has a question, let her ask it straight out.'

'I accept that, Your Honor.' Caroline turned to Mann again. 'My apologies,' she said quietly. 'But in all candor, didn't you consider the possibility that this unknown person had been "hurt" by Brett Allen?'

Folding his hands again, Mann took a long time to answer. Caroline became aware of the dampness of her palms. Then, in a soft voice, Mann said, 'Yes, ma'am, I suppose I did. But all it was was speculation.'

'So when you asked Ms. Allen if someone was hurt out there, you'd considered the possibility that Ms. Allen might have committed an act of violence?'

Mann drew a silent breath. 'Yes.'

'And after Ms. Allen told you that you might want to look at Heron Lake, you called the state police.'

'Yes.'

'With whom did you speak?'

'Sergeant Summers. The one who came here after we found the body.'

'And what did you tell him?'

Mann hesitated. 'That we might have some sort of actual or attempted homicide. Maybe involving someone named James Case.'

Caroline nodded. 'Did you tell Sergeant Summers about Brett, the knife, the wallet, and the blood? To get his advice on what to do?'

'Yes.'

'And when Sergeant Summers told you to take her to Connaughton County Hospital, it was to preserve the evidence on her body, right?'

'Yes.'

'Until you could get a warrant to search her person.'

Mann's voice was softer now. 'Yes.'

'Because she was a potential suspect, correct?'

'Objection.' Quickly, Jackson moved forward; for the first time, he looked angry. 'What Officer Mann may have said or been told after Ms. Allen's initial statement is irrelevant to what he thought before. Ms. Masters is trying to turn good police work into something sinister.'

Ignoring him, Caroline faced Judge Towle. 'Not at all, Your Honor. Officer Mann is entitled to take reasonable measures to find a theoretically wounded person, including inquiries of Ms. Allen. But without Miranda warnings, Mr. Watts is not entitled to use the statement of an intoxicated, disoriented young woman in police custody as evidence for a charge of murder. Or as a basis for warrants to gather yet more evidence – dubious as the evidence may be.'

Towle held up a hand, gazing from Jackson to Caroline. 'That question,' he said to them both, 'will be resolved by the Superior Court should this court find probable cause. It's not the purpose of this proceeding. But while we're here, I'll allow Ms. Masters to ask the questions, as they may also relate to probable cause.'

'Thank you, Your Honor.' Caroline glanced at her father. His gaze was inward, his face quite composed; perhaps Caroline alone could have read the satisfaction in his face. She turned to Mann again.

'The question, Officer Mann, was whether, at the time you sent Ms. Allen to the hospital at Connaughton Falls, she was a potential suspect in some possible crime of violence.'

Mann's jaw worked. 'Yes.'

'Based on her statement regarding where to look for James Case.'

Mann hesitated, formulating his answer. 'That,' he said, 'and the knife and blood and wallet.'

'But without Ms. Allen's statement, you wouldn't have known where to look, would you?'

Mann's face had closed now. 'Not right away.'

Caroline tilted her head. 'Prior to Ms. Allen's initial statement, did you test her for intoxication?'

'No.'

'How did she seem to you?'

Mann glanced at Brett again; his expression softened a bit. 'Slow. Kind of stunned.'

'Did she have a hard time speaking?'

'A little.'

'Have you ever arrested someone who was under the influence of marijuana?'

'Yes.'

'Was Ms. Allen's demeanor like that?'

Mann paused. 'She seemed to have a hard time remembering words, and her speech was slurred.'

Caroline moved closer. 'Tell me, Officer Mann – about how long was it from your arrest of Ms. Allen until she arrived at Connaughton County Hospital?'

'Maybe two hours.'

'And was she then tested for intoxication?'

'Yes.'

'Did you see the results?'

'Yes.'

'Was Ms. Allen intoxicated?'

Mann folded his hands. 'According to the report, Ms. Allen was at nearly twice the legal limit.'

'So that it's fair to say that she was intoxicated the whole time she was with you?'

'I would say so.'

Caroline nodded, satisfied. Not only was it clear that Brett had been intoxicated at the moment of the murder, but if the Superior Court followed the law, what Brett said before her trip to the hospital might be kept out of evidence. Even the evidence obtained through the two search warrants, secured because of her initial statement, could possibly be suppressed.

It was time to address Brett's final statement.

'What is your understanding, Officer Mann, as to when Ms. Allen was tested for intoxication?'

Mann's eyes narrowed. 'Pretty quickly, from the report. Maybe thirty minutes after getting there.'

'So about two o'clock?'

'I'd have to see the report again. But I think that's pretty close.'

'And you and Officer Summers started questioning her around six-fifteen, correct? At least according to the tape.'

'Yes.'

'And before that, Sergeant Summers read Ms. Allen her Miranda rights?'

'True.'

'Did you also retest her for intoxication?'

Mann hesitated. 'We did not.'

Caroline made herself sound puzzled. 'So you don't know whether she was still intoxicated?'

Mann frowned. 'She was a whole lot different by then — coherent, eager to talk.' His voice rose. 'Before we questioned her, we called Dr. Pumphrey at the hospital — the one who tested her. He said that by four hours the effect should have worn off.'

'But the doctor didn't see her before questioning, right?'

'No.'

'Or test her?'

'No.'

'Do you know when Ms. Allen had last eaten?'

'No.'

'Or slept?'

'No.'

'Did you give her any food?'

For a moment, Mann looked chastened. 'No.'

'Are you familiar with a chemical known as THC?'

Another pause. 'I know it's in marijuana.'

'Do you know how it affects memory?'

'Not really, no.'

'Or how long it stays in the bloodstream?'

'No.'

'Or the extent to which the potency of marijuana may be affected by the prior use of alcohol, followed by sexual intercourse?'

369

Mann's mouth formed a stubborn line. 'I'm not a doctor, ma'am.'

But Caroline's expert was, and he was prepared to say at trial that Brett could not have been sober and that her memory was inevitably confused. Quietly, Caroline responded, 'I appreciate that, Officer Mann. Thank you.'

Mann looked toward Towle, as if hopeful that this was over. His demeanor was different now – less conviction and idealism, stubbornness seeming to alternate with confusion. Still, Caroline was not quite done.

'Tell me,' she asked, 'during the time you spent with Ms. Allen, did you form an impression as to whether she was right- or left-handed?'

Mann leaned back in his chair. 'Left-handed,' he said finally.

'And on what do you base that?'

'I remember she was always brushing the hair back from her face, like she was nervous or distracted. She'd use her left hand.'

Caroline nodded. 'Thank you, Officer Mann. No further questions.'

Chapter 4

'You're really good,' Brett said.

Caroline felt anything but good; the adrenaline of the courtroom had evanesced, leaving only weariness and a certain vague depressions. But Caroline did not believe in false modesty, and it was better to place more pressure on herself if it helped Brett through the hearing.

'Yes,' she answered. 'I am. And I did better than I'd expected.'

They sat at a beat-up desk in a spare room at the Connaughton County Courthouse; court was adjourned for the day, and an officer waited outside to deliver Brett back to prison. But they needed to talk, Caroline knew, though perhaps Brett just needed time.

Brett was quiet for a moment. 'I felt a little sorry for him, though. The cop.'

'Maybe he wanted to help you, in a way. Or maybe he'll just learn to lie next time. In San Francisco, he already would have.'

Brett considered her. 'Is that hard for you? Embarrassing someone like that?'

Caroline shrugged. 'You just don't think about it. Lawyers can't – if I did, where would *you* be?'

Brett looked curious. 'It's like you can turn your feelings off. Like flicking a switch.'

It was odd, Caroline reflected, how little she minded this girl's probing now. 'Is that so interesting?' she asked.

'It's not *usual*. At least not for a woman.' Brett shook her head, as if bemused. 'You're so unlike my mother it's ridiculous.'

'We had different mothers. Genes count for a lot.' For the first time, Caroline smiled. 'You don't have to understand everything, Brett. Or everyone.'

Looking at Caroline, Brett's face became softer. 'It's just so childish. Three weeks ago, I didn't even know you. And now I depend on you completely, and I'm so damned scared.'

How best to answer? Caroline wondered. 'Being on trial does that to people,' she said quietly. 'It's part of the reason I am the way I am. Or, at least, try to appear that way to you.'

Brett tilted her head, as if to see her from a different angle. 'Who worries about you, Caroline?'

Caroline gave a wry smile. 'Why should anyone? I'm only the lawyer here.'

Brett studied the desk. 'Someday,' she said, 'I hope we can just be friends.'

Caroline smiled again. 'That's why I'm trying to spring you, of course. Because you've never come to San Francisco.'

Brett's face seemed to relax, and Caroline watched her imagine a place she had seen only in pictures. At another time, Caroline would have been content to sit quietly in her company. But there was far too much to do.

'There's something we've never really gone over,' Caroline said at last. 'That telephone call to James. Just before you went to the lake.'

Torn from fantasy, Brett looked down again; the memory led to a vortex of confusion, Caroline could see — or, perhaps, guilt. In a quiet voice, Brett asked, 'Why is that important now?'

But Caroline could not answer. 'Just humor me,' she said.

Hours later, Caroline cracked open the window of her room. The air of a fresh summer night felt cool on her skin.

She could not sleep yet.

On her desk, next to a mug of coffee, were police reports and transcripts of interviews — of Brett, Betty, Larry, her father, Megan Race. On top of that was Megan's diary.

She sat at the desk, reading the entries yet again.

Even as she studied them, mentally extracting her cross-examination from Megan's coiled script, this invasion made Caroline queasy. Too clearly, she remembered her own diary. Could recall across the years the entries after David vanished, in the months she stayed on at Martha's Vineyard, estranged from her family, hoping still to hear from him: a litany of loss, longing, guilt, regret, rage -- at her father, at Betty, and, most of all, at herself. Until the hope faded and, with resignation and resolve, Caroline forced herself to imagine a new life. The diary stopped one page from the end.

The day before she left for California, Caroline had burned it.

Rising now, she returned to the window. Saw again the church, the white frame houses, the rolling hills. A snapshot from her memory.

She had never thought to return here. Never thought that the decision she had once believed essential to that new life might, in the end, undo it.

She had lied to Brett. With a longing as deep as it was pointless, Caroline wished that she could talk to someone. But it could not, in fairness, be this girl. And, in open court, Caroline would ruin what remained of her friendship with the other person who might understand.

Three mornings from now, Megan Race would take the stand.

Caroline returned to the desk and began making notes.

Chapter 5

Caroline's first image of the morning was Jackson, bending over the rail between lawyer and spectator, murmuring to her father. The moment was awkward, formal: a civil handshake; a few words from Jackson; her father's slight nod; Larry and Betty pretending not to notice. And then Judge Towle assumed the bench, and Jackson called Sergeant Kenton Summers.

From his first moments on the stand, Caroline saw that Summers would be difficult: as Jackson quickly established, he had sixteen years' experience with the state police and an expertise in forensics, and had been lead investigator in twenty-seven homicides. The experience of court was stamped on his ruddy face – in the heavy lids, the calm cobalt eyes, a certain absence of expression. With his chestnut hair and still youthful face, Summers could not be much over forty, but he had the air of someone who was beyond surprise or anger. He gazed at the tape machine in front of Jackson.

'Prior to your interrogation,' Jackson was asking, 'how would you describe Ms. Allen's behavior?'

Before responding, Summers seemed to consider each response; it was a trick, Caroline sensed, to cover those moments when he was truly surprised. Now, quietly, he answered, 'She was sober, coherent, and clearly followed our questions. As the tape will show.'

As if on cue, Jackson punched a button, and the tape began playing.

Summers' voice filled the courtroom, calmly reciting the Miranda warnings. Next to Caroline, Brett listened, intent and pale, as she waived her rights. She sounded quite lucid.

Save for Brett's voice, the policeman's soft questions, the courtroom was silent.

As she approached the facts of the murder, Brett's tone moved from hesitancy to dread. Perhaps only Caroline heard the pause as Brett recounted her conversation with James, omitting their fight. But while Brett listened to herself describe finding the body, voice trembling with a surprise and horror that seemed quite genuine, anyone could see the convulsion of her throat. And then the tape reached her incontrovertible lie.

'Did James have other girlfriends?' Summer asked.

'No.' Brett's voice was shocked and angry. 'There's no way.'

Listening, Brett was still. *When?* Caroline wrote on her pad, and then the tape ended.

Someone coughed, and Jackson spoke again. 'Did you begin by placing credence in Ms. Allen's statement?' he asked.

Summers nodded. 'It was the only clear account we had. In fact, one of our main objectives was attempting to confirm what she told us.'

It was clever, Caroline saw: Jackson would use Summers to show how much they had wished to believe Brett's story. 'Could you describe your efforts?' Jackson asked.

'To start, there was the crime scene. We used six investigators, including two from the crime lab, to cordon off two hundred square feet around where the body was. Then we divided the area into tenfoot sections. For one week, we went through each section inch by inch.'

'What did you find?'

'That we could follow Ms. Allen's path from the body clearly – there were broken branches, trampled underbrush, specks of blood on the leaves. But we found no such signs of a second person. With as much blood as Mr. Case lost, it would be almost impossible for the killer to leave the scene without traces of blood on leaves or shrubbery.'

Judge Towle watched Summers intently. 'Did you take other steps,' Jackson asked, 'to explore Ms. Allen's claim of an unknown killer?'

'We did.' Raising a thick hand, Summers ticked them

off. 'We talked to neighbors and other people in the area, looking for sightings of strange people or vehicles anywhere near the lake. We found none.

'We checked for reports of vagrants or break-ins, searched for signs that anyone had been living in the woods recently. Again, nothing.

'We looked for evidence that James Case, as Ms. Allen claimed, was in trouble with some unknown drug dealer. But we found no evidence of a break-in at his apartment, or any stolen money.

'We interviewed his neighbors, his landlord – anyone we could find who knew him. And we came up with no one who, as far as we could tell, had any motive to do what someone had done to this boy.' Summers paused. 'Which was cut his throat so deeply that his head was more off than on.'

This last was delivered with such matter-of-fact authority that, even for Caroline, it took a moment to register. 'And on what basis,' Jackson asked calmly, 'did you conclude that it was Ms. Allen who had done this?'

Summers stroked his chin. 'To start, there was the physical evidence. Other than Officer Mann's, the only prints on the knife were Ms. Allen's.

'We found her fingerprints on the neck of the victim – but no one else's except the EMTs.

'Her prints were on the wallet – again, no others.

'The only path from the scene, leaving traces of the victim's blood, was hers.

'The only hairs on the victim's body were from Ms. Allen's head and pubic area.

'There were no signs of a struggle, and the only marks on his body – other than knife wounds – were scratches on his back. Which were accounted for when we found traces of his skin beneath Ms. Allen's fingernails.

'A search of Ms. Allen showed the victim's blood spattered on her hair and body, and established that they had had sexual intercourse.' For the first time, Summers looked directly at Judge Towle. 'And yet the victim had never climaxed.'

'Were there other factors?' Jackson asked.

Pausing, Summers frowned. 'The nature of the homicide. In my experience, drug dealers don't go around killing other drug dealers with knives. Too dangerous.'

This was right, Caroline knew; next to her, she saw Brett's eyes shut. 'This had the look of a very personal killing,' Summers continued. 'Driven by passion and anger, and not done by a stranger.'

'Keep looking at him,' Caroline whispered to Brett, and stood. 'Move to strike,' she snapped. 'This witness's opinions on what the mode of death must mean are the sheerest speculation, as in all the business regarding the mode of investigation. And, as I once pointed out to Mr. Watts, neither Charles Manson nor his friends knew the people they butchered.'

Jackson faced Judge Towle. 'Your Honor,' he said, 'this is not a jury trial, and the court is fully capable of weighing any piece of testimony in assessing probable cause. Moreover, we are about to show that the nature of the killing seems consistent with the motive for the killing.'

'I'll hear it,' Towle said promptly. 'Overruled.' But when Caroline sat down, Brett was composed again.

At once, Jackson turned to Summers. 'You'll recall, Sergeant Summers, that Ms. Allen told you James Case had asked her to go to California, and that – at least as far as she knew – the victim had no other romantic involvements. Did there come a time when another witness came forward to shed light on that statement?'

'There did.' Pausing, Summers seemed to draw the courtroom closer: as reporters paused, pencils over pads, Towle leaned forward. Next to Caroline, Brett seemed not to breathe. 'A student at Chase College,' Summers went on, 'who told us that she and the victim had a continuing and intimate relationship, and that he had asked her to go with him to California. And that he had promised to break this to Ms. Allen on the night he was murdered.'

There was a stirring in the courtroom. With a cold, channeled anger, Caroline resolved to make Jackson pay for this. 'Were you able to confirm that such a relationship existed?' he asked.

'Yes. Through neighbors.' Summers faced the judge again. 'And according to our witness, Ms. Allen knew about it.'

Amidst the sound of stirring, Jackson nodded. 'Based on this new information, what – if anything – did you conclude?'

'Conclude? Nothing. But it was a motive, jealousy and anger, and it helped make sense of how Ms. Allen acted.' Summers gathered himself. 'In my view, Ms. Allen used wine and marijuana to place James Case in a position of extreme vulnerability – sexual intercourse. And then cut his throat before he climaxed.' His voice was soft, uninflected. 'Which may also explain why she took his wallet afterward. Because her imaginary drug dealer, the one that she invented, wanted back his money.'

Chapter 6

Summers' eyes were pale-blue chips, Caroline thought — opaque and unimpressed.

'You placed considerable emphasis,' Caroline began, 'on Brett's taped statement. But her initial statement was made to Officer Mann, wasn't it? When she suggested the police look at Heron Lake.'

'Yes. That's why Officer Mann called me.'

'Did he express concern that there had been an act of violence?'

'Yes.'

'After which you told him to take Ms. Allen to the hospital?'

'Yes.'

'So that the police could get a warrant to search her?'

'If it seemed justified.'

'And did you subsequently determine that a warrant to search her person was justified?'

'Yes.'

'Because you found Mr. Case's body?'

'Yes.'

Caroline paused. 'Based on Ms. Allen's prior statement?'

A first stubbornness in the blue eyes, the instinct to resist. 'We would have found him,' he said finally. 'It might have helped us find him quicker.'

It was a good answer: Summers understood the trap — that much of the evidence against Brett was based on her initial statement — and was trying to avoid it. Caroline made herself look puzzled. 'The location of the body is fairly inaccessible, isn't it?'

'Yes.'

'Making it unlikely you would have found it before daylight.'

Slight hesitation. 'Maybe.'

'By which time you were questioning Ms. Allen for the second time.'

'Yes.'

'After you'd already obtained a warrant from Judge Deane, at three a.m., and searched her body.'

Once more, the minimal answer. 'Yes.'

'And searched Mr. Case.'

'Yes.'

'And Brett Allen's property.'

'As best we could, in the dark.'

'Searches based on a warrant application which cited Ms. Allen's statement and the body, correct?'

Summers frowned. 'Yes.'

'And you understood that Brett Allen's statement – the one to Officer Mann – was obtained without Miranda warnings?'

Summers sat back. 'When Officer Mann called, that was what he told me, yes.'

'During that conversation, did you and Officer Mann discuss whether he should interrogate Ms. Allen further?'

Summers' lids dropped slightly. 'Yes,' he said at length.

Caroline felt a moment's relief: at least they were honest. 'And did you,' she ventured, 'advise Officer Mann not to question her?'

Summers folded his hands. 'At that time, yes.'

'For what reason?'

Summers considered her. 'It was a matter of experience.'

'And intoxication?'

'That too.'

'So that you were concerned not only that Ms. Allen hadn't been Mirandized but that she was too intoxicated to make sense.'

Summers shrugged, a slow shifting of shoulders. 'I wouldn't say concerned. When in doubt, it's better to test someone.'

'And, when tested, Ms. Allen proved to be intoxicated, correct?'

'As of roughly two o'clock.'

'And at six o'clock, when you interrogated Ms. Allen, what was that based on?'

Summers gave her a level gaze. 'Her request.'

It was a splendid answer, and quite wounding. Caroline stood very still. 'I meant the interrogation,' she said evenly. 'It was based, was it not, on finding the body, searching Ms. Allen, and searching her property?'

Summers hesitated. 'In the main.'

'All of which was based on her initial statement to Officer Mann, telling him where to look?'

A longer pause: Summers knew quite well that, if Caroline was lucky, she could suppress almost every piece of evidence obtained through the initial statement. 'We would have questioned her,' he said, 'as soon as she was sober – body or no body. Which we'd have found in daylight. But she came to us.'

Another damaging answer. 'Sober?' Caroline shot back.

'Sober.'

'According to whom?'

'Dr. Pumphrey.'

'Who never saw her, correct?'

For the first time, Caroline watched Summers fight himself: he wanted to argue with her but was too experienced to do so. Watts, he knew, would handle this. 'Dr. Pumphrey saw her at the hospital,' Summers answered. 'At six o'clock, I just described her to him.'

'So the people who did see Brett at six were you and Officer Mann?'

'Yes.'

'And you, like Officer Mann, cannot offer a medical opinion as to her sobriety?'

'No. Just an eyeball opinion....'

'On the effect of THC on memory?'

'No.'

'Or personality?'

'No.'

Caroline put her hands on her hips. 'Do you also have no

medical opinion on whether marijuana and alcohol can have the effect of inducing what is commonly known as paranoia?'

Annoyance, she saw, expressed itself through a certain deadness in Summers' eyes. 'No,' he said tersely.

Caroline paused a moment. 'So based on your assumption that Ms. Allen was functioning normally, if she gave you any information you perceived to be misleading, you thought this was deliberate?'

'Not necessarily.' Summers' voice rose slightly. 'After all, she *had* been intoxicated....'

'Precisely. But now she was a suspect, right? Had to be, or you wouldn't have given her Miranda warnings.'

Summers folded his hands again. 'If someone is even potentially a suspect, we'll warn them.'

'Perhaps you,' Caroline retorted. 'But not Officer Mann.'

'Objection,' Jackson said. 'Asked and answered.'

'Sustained.' Towle glanced at Caroline. 'Your point is taken, Counsel. Move on.'

In the moment Caroline took to compose her thoughts, she was aware of everyone around her and everything at stake – for her and, most of all, for Brett. And then, as at other moments of her life, a blessed calm came over her.

'Isn't it true,' she asked, 'that from the minute you first questioned her, Brett Allen was your prime suspect?'

Summers shook his head. 'Prime, no. An obvious possibility, sure. As I said, we looked for others – like this drug dealer.'

'But you dismissed that, right?'

'No evidence – no money in his apartment, no sign of a break-in.'

Caroline looked bemused. 'Does it seem logical to you that someone who wanted to hide stolen drug money would stick it in his apartment?'

'Objection,' Jackson interjected. 'Calls for speculation.'

'No more so than that drug dealers are too genteel to cut throats.' Caroline turned to Judge Towle. 'I'm calling on

Sergeant Summers' extensive knowledge of the drug culture, Your Honor. As did Mr. Watts.'

Towle smiled faintly. 'Overruled,' he said, and looked to Summers.

'It is speculation,' Summers answered finally. 'But no, your own apartment might not be the best place to hide money.'

Caroline paused a moment. 'It is also true, is it not, that Mr. Case's door lacks a dead bolt?'

Summers gave her a long, hard look. 'That's right.'

'And based on your knowledge of the criminal element, one desiring to enter an apartment can take a mold and have a key designed, correct?'

'Yes.'

Caroline could feel Jackson's gaze now; her pulse was rapid. 'Or even, with sufficient skill, enter by using a credit card?'

Summers put a finger to his mouth, tapping it lightly, still appraising Caroline. 'True,' he said at length.

'After which, to the extent the apartment was disordered, James Case could simply have cleaned it up. If not the intruder himself.'

'I suppose so.'

Motionless, Jackson stared at the table. 'Now,' Caroline went on, 'can you say whether or to what extent James Case was dealing drugs? Because, among other reasons, it's something college kids don't chat with cops about.'

'Sometimes,' Summers retorted quickly. 'But there's no evidence that this drug dealer ever existed, let alone found his way to an isolated spot in time to murder James Case with a knife. The physical evidence all points to Ms. Allen.'

It was the answer Caroline had hoped for. 'Let's take that evidence, then. You say, for example, that you found Brett's fingerprint on the victim's neck. Would you call that print important?'

A small shrug. 'It's one among many pieces of evidence. I wouldn't want to classify it.'

383

'Isn't it true that, at least in the reported literature, no one has ever lifted a print off the body of a man?'

Summers emitted a soundless sigh, as if reaching for calm. 'I wouldn't know.'

'Are you personally aware of any?'

'No.'

'Because, among other reasons, the hair and roughness of a man's skin make lifting prints more difficult.'

'True. But in this case, Ms. Allen left a print on the skin surrounding the wound. Where there was blood to reflect a print.'

'That's hardly surprising, is it – she says she touched him *after* his throat was cut. Tell me, didn't you find other prints in the blood?'

Summers considered her with chilly eyes. 'One. It belonged to an EMT who was called to the scene.'

Caroline raised an eyebrow. 'Is he a suspect?'

'No.'

'And, in truth, there are no prints on the skin other than those found in the victim's blood?'

'No. There are not.'

Caroline nodded. 'Brett's prints on the knife are also found in a deposit of blood, are they not?'

'Yes.'

'As are Officer Mann's?'

Summers tapped his lips again and then, quite consciously, placed both hands in his lap. 'Yes.'

'Who made them, just as Ms. Allen did, by touching the bloody knife?'

'Yes.'

Caroline tilted her head. 'Are there any clean prints on the knife? Ones not imprinted in blood?'

'Not that we found, no ...'

'Nor,' Caroline pursued softly, 'can you link that knife to Brett Allen.'

'No.'

'What about the wallet? Was Ms. Allen's print there found on a deposit of blood?'

Another pause. 'Yes.'

'Any clean prints?'

'No.'

'Not even James Case's? It *was* his wallet.'

'No.' Summers examined his hands. 'Leather usually won't take a print.'

'Then all this could have happened just the way Brett told you, correct? She found the body, tried to administer CPR, and got blood on her hands.' She paused. 'And, therefore, left bloody prints on the victim's neck, the knife, and the wallet. Just like the EMT and Officer Mann.'

'Whose prints we can explain.' Looking up, Summers finished in a chill voice. 'There are no other prints, Ms. Masters.'

'And a thousand possible reasons why.' Jackson, Caroline saw, had remained quite still. 'For example, might the killer have worn gloves?'

Summers assumed a certain calm again. 'Counselor,' he said patiently, 'there's not many ways to tell if someone was wearing gloves.'

'Precisely. But if Brett had her hands on the knife, about to slice Mr. Case's windpipe, wouldn't she have left at least one clean print on the handle of the knife?'

'The handle's bone. Not an easy print, either.'

'But the sole print Brett Allen left on the hilt is a bloody one, correct? Clearly made sometime after Mr. Case's throat was cut.'

Summers lowered his eyelids, studying her closely. 'That's true.'

'So it couldn't be the prints that caused you to opine that Brett Allen must be a murderer.'

'Not in themselves, no.' Summers' patience sounded strained. 'You have to look at the totality of the evidence.'

'Let's do that, Sergeant. Pick a piece – any piece.'

'Is that a question?' Jackson interjected.

Caroline ignored him. 'All right,' she said to Summers. 'I believe you mentioned Mr. Case's failure to ejaculate.'

Summers nodded. 'I did.'

'And what did the tests show regarding Mr. Case's level of intoxication?'

'That he was intoxicated.'

Caroline smiled slightly. 'In your observation, does intoxication in the adult male sometimes lead to, shall we say, incomplete sexual performance? Or is impotence inevitably the result of death?'

From the back of the courtroom, someone coughed, suppressing laughter. 'Maybe,' Summers said mildly, 'I should leave that one for the medical examiner.'

'But you don't insist, do you, that violent death is the only explanation for Mr. Case's failure to ejaculate?'

A first grim glint of humor. 'No.'

'And, in your pantheon of evidence, would you say that this failure is more or less important than *your* purported failure to find evidence of an escape path other than Brett Allen's?'

Summers hesitated. 'Less.'

'Much less?'

'I would say so.'

'We'll get to that in a minute, then. But let me ask you this: Do you have any reason to quarrel with Officer Mann's belief that Ms. Allen's hair was wet?'

'I've got nothing on that, one way or the other.'

'So you also have no belief as to whether Ms. Allen went swimming?'

'No.'

Caroline raised an eyebrow. 'The police photographs do show a bare footprint by the beach, do they not?'

Slowly, Summers nodded. 'One. But it could be anyone's.'

'And did you attempt to determine whether the print might be Ms. Allen's?'

'Not specifically, no.'

'Wouldn't that have tended to confirm Ms. Allen's claim that she went swimming? And thus was nowhere near Mr. Case at the moment of his death?'

'Objection,' Jackson called out. 'Compound. And either question calls for speculation.'

'Only because the job wasn't done,' Caroline shot back. 'Which makes this whole proceeding speculative. I'm entitled to show that – contrary to the prosecution claim – no one pretzeled himself to believe Brett Allen.'

Towle looked from Jackson to Summers, and then nodded. 'Overruled,' he said.

Summers shifted in his chair. 'It might have,' he said finally. 'But there's no way to tell.'

'Not now there isn't.' Caroline crossed her arms. 'According to the police photographs, wasn't there also an unidentified boot print twenty feet further down the lake? Along the water toward Mosher Trail?'

Summers frowned. 'Again, it could have been anyone's. The police were there and the EMTs.'

'Any of them wearing boots?'

'I don't know.' A trace of asperity. 'For all we know, it could have been some fisherman.'

'Or the murderer?'

Summers threw up his hands. 'Because of one print, maybe forty feet from the body? There's no reason to connect the two.'

Caroline folded her arms. 'Describe for me, if you will, the terrain between the body and that footprint.'

Summers went quiet; the pauses were no longer feigned. Caroline's throat felt tight. 'Grass,' Summers said at last, 'near the body. Then small rock along the shore.'

'No way to get footprints off grass, correct?'

A reluctant nod. 'We couldn't have.'

'And the rocks on the shore were knocked about?'

'True. But it could have been the police, or anyone.' Another pause, then a concession. 'No way to get prints there, either.'

'So that it was possible for someone to walk from the body, all the way to the muck that captured this boot print, without leaving any other print?'

Summers seemed to appraise her. 'A theoretical possibility, yes. But there was also no sign of blood.'

'And no branches or bushes to leave blood on, correct?'

Another pause. 'That's right. But there was grass and rocks.'

Caroline looked astonished. 'Grass and rocks? Is it your belief that this 'theoretical' killer crawled away from the scene?'

Summers nodded. 'I don't believe in this killer at all, Counsel –'

'Answer the question, please. Why would a killer who – in your version – was sitting on James Case's chest have blood on the soles of his feet?'

Summers folded his arms. 'I wouldn't know.'

'A judicious answer.' Caroline cocked her head. 'Did you also consider whether the killer might have other means of approaching the lake? Along the water, for example, or even by boat?'

Summers looked annoyed and then visibly reached for calm. 'We didn't consider helicopter, Counselor. But we did consider other means of approaching the lake than by going through Ms. Allen's property. And in no instance did any resident report seeing an unknown person or vehicle.'

'Let's take an example, then. Mosher Trail is the next-closest path to the crime scene, true?'

'I would say so, yes.'

'And it goes to the edge of the water?'

'Yes.'

'Did you attempt to determine whether there were fresh vehicle tracks or footprints?'

Summers gave her a level stare. 'The ground was packed hard – dried mud from spring – and that trail's pretty well traveled. So there was no way to tell who might have come there, or when.'

'So that, again, it would be possible for a killer to walk or drive to the end of Mosher Trail, walk along the water, and approach the place where James Case was lying. All without leaving footprints.'

'I suppose so. Assuming that no one had seen this person.'

'It was night, wasn't it?'

'Of course.'

'All right,' Caroline said equably. 'Have we adequately reviewed the 'physical evidence' that you say points to Brett Allen's guilt – the knife, the wallet, the fingerprints, the supposed lack of an exit path, and Mr. Case's lamentable failure to ejaculate?'

Summers' mouth and eyes seemed smaller now. 'You can't compartmentalize it like that. Among other things, there's the pattern of blood on Ms. Allen and the victim, as attested to by the medical examiner.'

'Oh,' Caroline said carelessly, 'we'll take that up with him. But tell me, Sergeant Summers, when did you and Mr. Watts receive the ME's report?'

'About four days after the incident.'

'By which time you already had the lab results.'

'Yes.'

'You didn't run right out and arrest her, did you?'

'No. We didn't.'

'So when, relative to that report, did you determine to charge Brett Allen?'

Another faint smile, a small acknowledgment that Summers knew where she was going. 'About five days after.'

'Really?' Caroline made herself sound curious. 'What happened in those five days to make your case so compelling?'

Summers paused for a moment. 'We had time to put it all together –'

'Come now, Sergeant Summers. Wasn't that when your witness came forward? Mr. Case's supposed lover – Megan Race?'

Summers' mouth opened, then shut. In that moment, it was plain to Caroline that Summers knew to be careful on the subject of Megan, but that neither he nor Jackson knew why. 'Yes,' he said tersely.

'Who claimed, among other things, that the night James

389

Case died, he was to tell Brett that he and Megan were taking off for California?'

'I said that this morning.'

Caroline cocked her head. 'James sure had a funny way of getting his message across, didn't he? Of course, maybe that's why he couldn't climax – the guilt was just too much.'

'Is that a question?' Rising, Jackson gave Caroline a look of annoyance. 'Because if it's a statement, perhaps Ms. Masters should leave it to the only living person who was there.'

Jackson, she could see, was at the limit of his patience; the challenge for Brett to testify showed that she had damaged him. 'There were two people,' she answered mildly. 'Brett and the killer.'

For an instant, Jackson gazed at her, eyes steady now. Softly, he repeated, 'Do you have a question, Caroline?'

He had broken her rhythm, Caroline knew, and now her concentration. 'Yes,' Towle interjected. 'Please find a question to ask.'

Caroline nodded to Jackson and then turned back to Summers. 'From the evidence at the scene – including a condom – does it appear that they were having consensual sex?'

'It does.'

'And is there anything to support your theory that this was Brett's idea? Or is that just theoretical?'

'I'd have to say it's theoretical....'

'Indeed, Sergeant Summers, is there anyone other than Megan Race to say that Mr. Case meant to leave with her at all?'

Summers paused. 'They *were* seen together, Ms. Masters.'

'That wasn't my question, Sergeant. But I'll take your answer and ask this – is there any evidence that Ms. Race and the victim were seen together after early April?'

Summers considered her. 'We didn't specifically ask that, counselor.'

'Do you have an answer?'

'No.' Summers paused; suddenly, he looked relieved. 'But how would Ms. Race know to talk to us about the same subject Ms. Allen did – that he had asked her to go to California but somehow wound up dead?'

From the stand, Summers seemed to watch her face for signs of alarm. But Caroline simply smiled. 'So you considered it important that Ms. Race knew the victim wished to go to California?'

Summers paused; it was as if, Caroline thought, he sensed the trap but could not see it. 'Yes,' he said at length.

'And this enhanced her credibility.'

A curt nod. 'To me.'

'As well as, according to this morning's testimony, providing you with a motive? A promise to drop a bomb on Brett that would surely make her angry?'

'Yes.'

'Indeed, for you, it explained why Brett Allen had killed him.'

Summers gave her a look of veiled defiance. 'I already said that.'

'Is it also fair to say, then, that Megan Race is a critical part of the case against Brett Allen?'

'There's lots of other evidence,' Summers began, and stopped himself. 'But she's a significant witness.'

Briefly, Caroline imagined Larry behind her; when she turned, glancing at him, he looked away. Turning back to Summers, she asked, 'In fact, didn't the appearance of Ms. Race cause the decision to charge Ms. Allen with the crime?'

'Calls for speculation,' Jackson said evenly, and turned to Caroline. 'As Ms. Masters knows, it wasn't his decision.'

Towle nodded. 'Sustained.'

But Caroline was already facing Summers. 'Prior to charging Ms. Allen with murder, did Mr. Watts ask your opinion?'

A reluctant nod, late in coming. 'Yes.'

'And what did you tell him?'

'That we had enough to charge her.'

Caroline touched a finger to her lips. 'And before Ms. Race came forward, did you express an opinion to Mr. Watts on whether to charge Ms. Allen?'

For the first time, Summers glanced at Jackson. 'I did.'

'And what was that opinion?'

'That we should keep looking.'

Silent, Caroline considered him; she could see Summers hope that she would be satisfied with this concession of Megan's importance. But Caroline was not quite done. 'How long was it,' she asked, 'between the time Mr. Case was killed and the time that Megan Race first came to you?'

'About six days.'

'Didn't you suggest to Mr. Watts that this was curious? After all, according to Ms. Race, they were so in love that they were going away together.'

Almost absently, Summers glanced at his cuff. 'We discussed it, yes. But according to Ms. Race, she was afraid of what Ms. Allen might do.'

'Did you accept that?'

A small shrug, watchful eyes: Caroline imagined him wondering why she had not raised the affair with Larry. 'I'm not Ms. Race,' he said.

Caroline let him sit there for a moment. 'Isn't the major reason you believed Ms. Race that, in your view, Brett Allen lied to you about her very existence?'

Summers leaned forward to answer, as if she had thrown him a life raft, and then his head snapped back and his glacial eyes turned faintly puzzled, probing her for a motive. 'Could you repeat that?' he asked.

Moving closer, Caroline said curtly, 'Did you believe Megan Race because you thought Brett had lied about her?'

Summers hesitated, then came to a decision. 'That was a factor, yes.'

Caroline smiled down at him. 'But according to the tape, you didn't ask Brett about James's past involvements, did you?'

Summers put one arm on the rail and propped his chin

in his hand, ostentatiously weary of a hair-splitting lawyer. 'Not explicitly,' he said, and then added, 'I guess I expected her to answer the question reasonably.'

Caroline's smile turned sardonic. 'Because you assumed that Megan's alleged relationship with the victim continued to his death?'

'Yes.'

'Then perhaps you should have made that assumption clear to Ms. Allen.' Caroline paused a moment. 'Before you suggested indicting her for lying to you.'

Summers flushed. 'I know *that's* not a question,' Jackson snapped.

Caroline turned to him. 'Do you? Then I have none.'

Facing Summers, she thanked him and sat down. As with her first, her last image of that day in court involved Jackson and her father, now both facing her – Jackson's look of wariness; Channing's cool, appraising eyes.

Turning from them, she focused on Brett's smile for her, filled with relief and gratitude.

Chapter 7

Caroline cut herself another piece of Gruyère, washed it down with a deep red Chianti, raw in her throat.

'Thanks for bringing this,' she said. 'And for the information about Megan's mother.'

Joe Lemieux smiled. 'Was your day productive? Or just long?'

Caroline did not answer; perhaps the hardest part, she thought, was pretending to everyone – herself included – that she felt nothing. She sipped more wine. 'That may depend,' she said at last. 'What else have you got?'

They sat in Carlton Grey's office. It was nine o'clock, and Caroline's lamp cast shadows in the corners. Lemieux shifted in his chair.

'I can't say for sure. It's already been three weeks since this guy was murdered, and now no one remembers seeing her. But then they've got no reason to – that night was nothing special to them.' Lemieux seemed to watch her. 'All I can really tell you, Counsel, is what we knew before – that she called in sick to her boss at the student union.'

Caroline shrugged. 'Keep looking, then.'

'I have been. No one near the lake remembers seeing her, or her blue Honda.' Pausing, Lemieux made a steeple of his fingers. 'Are you serious about trying to place her there, or will it do if no one saw her?'

Caroline considered him. 'Near the lake is better, obviously.'

'Because all it takes is for her to be watching TV with a friend, and you're out of luck.' He gazed at her with curiosity. 'Unless you believe ...'

Caroline gave him a wintry smile. 'I don't know what I believe. But then, in my job, it's not essential.' Abruptly, her smile vanished, and she asked in a quiet voice, 'Did you show them *all* the pictures?'

Lemieux looked at her hard now. 'Every one of them.'

'Is there anyone we missed?'

Lemieux studied the tips of his fingers. Softly, he said, 'You *are* serious.'

Caroline simply stared at him.

'There's a gas station left,' Lemieux told her. 'By the head of Mosher Trail. The kid who works nights took off for Florida the next day, to see his mother. He won't be back till two nights from now. Thursday.'

Caroline reflected. 'She'll take the stand on Thursday, I think. I'll try to keep her there until Friday. Somehow I doubt that will be too hard.'

Lemieux's eyes asked a silent question. 'I'd better get going,' he said at length.

Caroline leaned back in her chair. 'By the way,' she asked, 'is Megan right- or left-handed? I never noticed.'

Lemieux gave her a faint, puzzled smile. 'Right, I think.'

Caroline nodded. 'Good.'

Chapter 8

Dr. Jack Corn, the medical examiner, had lank gray-blond hair, wire-rim glasses, and the amiable half smile of a small-town banker. Little about this mild appearance suggested that – as Caroline well knew – he was a nationally recognized pathologist who had brought the New Hampshire Medical Examiner's Office to a place of professional esteem. His manner was courteous, his voice soft and faintly midwestern.

Methodically, he took Jackson from his appearance at the crime scene through the trip to the morgue in Concord – Corn and two assistants assessing and photographing the body; inspecting it for trace evidence; measuring the width and depth of the wounds; taking blood samples; searching for prints on the body. The reality of this, Caroline knew, was not pleasant; it was part of Corn's gift to make the process sound clinical, thorough, and scientific. Which it clearly was.

'And in the course of these procedures,' Jackson was asking, 'did you determine the cause of death?'

Corn nodded slowly. 'The victim died from a deep wound to the throat, severing the jugular vein, the carotid artery, and the victim's airway. As a result, the airways were filled. So that, quite literally, Mr. Case drowned in his own blood.'

Next to Caroline, Brett folded her hands on the table, took a deep breath, and kept on looking at the witness. 'Could you describe,' Jackson said, 'the nature of such a death?'

Corn's face had lost its semi-smile. 'It would not be instantaneous, Mr. Watts. There would be a gurgling sound, perhaps with the victim thrashing in agony, for as long as three or four minutes. What Mr. Case would have experienced was the quite horrific knowledge that he was drowning and that there was nothing he could do.'

Caroline saw Brett's eyes shut. Jackson moved forward. 'This gurgling sound, Dr. Corn – what would account for that?'

'Asphyxia. The victim would be unable to speak. Instead he would suffer what we call agonal breaths, spewing blood from his mouth for approximately ten to fifteen seconds.' Corn paused, as if imagining the moment. 'Eventually, he would suffer hypovolemic shock: the absence of sufficient blood to the brain. I should add that with respect to movement, there does not seem to have been much. But then the wound was so grave that Mr. Case's head was partially severed.'

Touching Brett's arm, Caroline felt a spasm pass through her. Caroline's fingers tightened around her wrist.

'Was there also, Dr. Corn, a second wound?'

'There were three, actually. I believe that the first in time was also a throat wound, but much shallower, from which we concluded that the fatal wound was a second and more successful effort to sever the victim's throat. The last wound, we believe, was the stab wound near the heart.'

Corn's narrative, calm and uninflected, somehow conveyed the picture of a determined killer, a butchering both intimate and passionate. 'And did you determine the type of wound?' Jackson asked.

Corn folded his hands. 'It was a knife wound. From the tearing of the skin, it appeared that the knife had a serrated edge. From that, and from our measurements, we determined that the wounds were consistent with the Cahill fishing knife found in Ms. Allen's possession.'

'And did you photograph the body and the wounds?'

'My assistant did. Yes.'

Jackson produced a sheaf of photographs from an envelope on the prosecution table. Reluctantly, he turned to Caroline, glancing at Brett as he did so. 'Would you care to review these again, Ms. Masters?'

Briefly, Caroline turned to Brett. She had her own

copies. But it had been Caroline's judgement that seeing the photographs would only haunt Brett's nights. 'Don't look,' she whispered. 'There's no point to it.' Pale, Brett nodded and turned away.

'Yes,' Caroline said evenly. 'Thank you.'

Looking down at Caroline, Jackson hesitated. Then he handed her the photographs and went back to his table.

Caroline took them one at a time.

By agreement, they were premarked for identification: the first, prosecution exhibit number twenty-seven, was an overhead shot that captured the staring eyes of a man for whom death was the end of agony.

Next to her, Caroline felt Brett flinch. Caroline wondered if this was the horror of discovery, or of memory.

'Don't' she murmured. 'They get no better.'

Caroline reviewed the photographs as quickly as she could. 'Thank you,' she said to Jackson.

Taking the exhibits, Jackson shot a quick, opaque glance at Brett. In that moment, Caroline saw in close-up the deepening lines at the edges of his eyes, the bruises of weariness.

Within minutes, a blond assistant from Jackson's office had pinned the photographs to a bulletin board. Even from a distance, Caroline could see the spatters of blood on James's face, the gash in his throat.

Glancing at her family, Caroline saw Betty and Larry looking down; only her father, face impassive, seemed to study the photographs. Next to her, Caroline heard the slow intake of breath. 'It was dark,' Brett murmured. 'I couldn't see him.'

Caroline turned to her. Staring at the pictures, Brett's face had filled with something close to awe. 'How could someone do that ...?'

Jackson stepped forward. 'Dr. Corn,' he asked, 'were these the photographs taken as part of your autopsy of Mr. Case?'

'They were.'

'And are they consistent with your opinion with respect to the cause of death?'

'Yes.' Corn left the witness stand and stood before the photographs; Caroline saw the judge's gaze, intent and narrow, follow him. 'For example, Exhibit Twenty-seven shows the pattern of blood on the victim's face – large spots in some areas, spatters in others. For lack of a more felicitous description, the airway wound sustained by Mr. Case creates a pattern similar to a can of spray paint that is running low, where spurts and spatters alternate with the degree of pressure.' Pausing, Corn adjusted his glasses, and then he concluded: 'After a time, ten to fifteen seconds, the pressure subsides altogether. But this pattern was already here.'

Caroline knew what was coming now. Within moments – a few brief exchanges between Jackson and Towle – a second bulletin board of premarked exhibits stood near the first. Next to Caroline, Brett was still.

In the photographs where Brett's eyes showed, they were dull with shock. Her breasts and face and torso were flecked with blood.

'I'm sorry,' Caroline said softly. 'But there's no help for this.'

Brett's eyes had frozen. Perhaps, Caroline thought, it was simply humiliation; more likely, it was the shock of seeing the masks of James's dead face, her shocked one, twinned by specks of blood. Even Judge Towle seemed transfixed by the imagery.

'Did you also,' Jackson asked Corn, 'examine the pattern of blood on Ms. Allen's face, neck, arms, and body?'

'I did.'

'And are these photographs consistent or inconsistent with the conclusion that Ms. Allen killed Mr. Case?'

'In my opinion, they are consistent.'

Brett stared at Corn, her body rigid with anger. But Jackson sounded quite calm; it was as if, Caroline thought, he preferred this case in someone else's hands. 'And on what, Dr. Corn, do you base that opinion?'

'The pattern of blood.' Pausing, Corn pointed to a photograph of Brett's neck. 'The pattern in Exhibit Thirty-nine, for example, is consistent with the spraying from the first infliction of the wound. It's the spray I would expect when, in the alternating force of pressure, it lessens.'

'Could it also be consistent with the administration of CPR, which Ms. Allen claims to have attempted?'

'Not in my view. For instance, there's no contact pattern of blood on Ms. Allen's mouth, as one might reasonably expect. And, while CPR might possibly cause the pinpoint spray one sees in Exhibit Thirty-seven, it would not account for the teardrop pattern on Ms. Allen's stomach. As shown by Exhibit Thirty-nine, for example.' Corn turned to the judge, as if conducting a seminar for one. 'You'll notice the teardrop pattern of the spatters here: slender at the bottom, much wider at the top. That would not be caused by CPR on the victim after the immediate spurt from his wound had abated – it's much too heavy. But it could be consistent with the agonal breaths of the first few seconds.'

He was quite impressive, Caroline thought. 'It's all right,' she murmured to Brett, and scrawled a note – *cast-off pattern*? – on the pad in front of her.

Jackson's voice was firm now. 'Are there other factors which are consistent with the commission of a homicide by Ms. Allen?'

'There are.' Corn turned to the picture of James's stomach. 'As I understand the prosecution theory, Ms. Allen cut the victim's throat while sitting astride his torso, perhaps during intercourse. You will note from the photographs of Mr. Case's chest that there is a void – a distinct lessening of spatter – on the area of his chest and stomach. Suggesting that the spray was blocked by Ms. Allen's chest and stomach.'

Watching, Judge Towle seemed to nod. 'In sum,' Jackson said, 'the pattern on both Mr. Case and Ms. Allen is consistent with the belief that she cut his throat and then stabbed him?'

'It is.'

Slowly, Jackson turned to Brett, eyes a little melancholy. 'How could a woman as slight as Ms. Allen inflict such grievous wounds?'

Facing Brett, Corn's expression was somber. 'Quite easily.'

'On what do you base that?'

'The murder weapon, to begin with. The blade was razor sharp.' Pausing, Corn retreated to the professorial. 'A number of years ago, a famous pathologist, Bernard Knight, established that it takes just a little over one pound of force to stick a sharpened knife into the human body. Which, when one thinks about it, we know from our own experience. After all, how much force does it take for a nurse to give you a flu shot?' Folding his hands, Corn finished quietly. 'The knife was quite a fine one, and it was well maintained. With a knife like that, Mr. Watts, a woman like Brett Allen would have no trouble killing this boy at all.'

Chapter 9

Walking toward Corn and the bloody photographs, Caroline took her time. Her face was as serene as she could make it.

'Are you familiar,' she asked, 'with Ms. Allen's account of the murder?'

Corn gazed at her, neither welcoming nor defensive. 'I believe so, yes.'

'Specifically, that she and Mr. Case had wine and marijuana. That afterward, while making love, Mr. Case passed out. That she went swimming. That she saw a shadow over Mr. Case. That when she returned, she heard a gurgling sound. That in the belief that Mr. Case might be choking in his own vomit, she got on his chest and administered CPR. That this caused blood to spray on her face. And that, in horror and shock, she pulled out the knife she discovered in his chest.' Abruptly, Caroline's voice softened. 'You *are* aware of all that, aren't you?'

Corn folded his hands; the effect was of someone bracing himself. 'Yes, Ms. Masters. I am.'

'Well, what's wrong with that? From your review of the medical evidence, couldn't it have happened just as she says?'

Corn frowned. 'I don't believe so.'

'But it is consistent with the lack of struggle, is it not?'

'It could be.'

'And with the agonal breaths you describe.'

'Possibly.'

Caroline put her hands on her hips. 'By the way, you're not asserting here that Brett Allen did kill Mr. Case, are you? Only that she could have.'

'Yes. Who killed this man is beyond my province.'

'And the entire reason that you prefer Mr. Watts's story

to Ms. Allen's is that, in your view, the spatter on Ms. Allen is inconsistent with CPR?'

Corn pursed his lips, forming a small *o*. 'It's the totality of the circumstances. But sticking to the spatter pattern, it's at least two things. First, the appearance that the blood on Ms. Allen's torso accounts for the void on Mr. Case's. Second, the fact that the teardrop pattern of some spatter on Ms. Allen is inconsistent with what CPR would cause.'

Caroline nodded. 'All right, Dr. Corn. Let's take CPR first. You're not saying that all the blood on Ms. Allen is inconsistent with CPR?'

'No. CPR could have caused a brief spray from Mr. Case's throat, resulting in the light spattering found on Ms. Allen's face. But it could not, in my opinion, explain the teardrop spatter.'

Caroline looked puzzled. 'But as you described the fatal wound, at least in its first seconds, a spray would alternate with a spewing pattern – almost a gushing. Correct?'

'Yes.'

Turning to the first bulletin board, Caroline gazed for a moment at James's dead, staring eyes. 'Indeed, on Exhibit Twenty-three, the streaks of blood on Mr. Case's face reflect that spewing effect.'

'That's true.'

Walking to the second board, Caroline stood next to a picture of Brett's face. 'But there is no such pattern on Ms. Allen's face, is there?'

Corn paused. 'There is not. But that could be the result of distance.'

Caroline turned to him. 'Forgive my indelicacy, Doctor, but does "spray" travel farther than "spew"?'

'Not necessarily. But you're assuming that, through those first seconds, Ms. Allen kept her face equidistant from Mr. Case's throat.' Corn examined the board. 'I also point out Exhibits Thirty-five and Thirty-six – the heavier spatter on Ms. Allen's breasts and stomach.'

For a moment, Caroline simply looked at him. With a

hint of asperity, she asked, 'Are you familiar with the term "cast-off pattern"?'

'Of course.'

'Could you define it for us?'

Corn gave her a glance of oblique annoyance. 'It's the blood spatter made by the entry of a sharp object into the human body.'

'Or exit?'

'That too.'

'What are the characteristics of a cast-off pattern?'

For a moment, Corn gazed at the photographs of Brett. 'It can have a teardrop effect,' he conceded. 'As you see on Ms. Allen.'

'And can that effect result from the *withdrawal* of a knife?'

'It's possible. Yes.'

'So that it's also possible that the medium-velocity splash pattern on Ms. Allen's face resulted from her administration of CPR, and the teardrop pattern on her torso from the withdrawal of the knife?' Here Caroline paused for emphasis. 'And not from the agonal breaths you ascribe to Mr. Case?'

Turning to Caroline, Corn seemed to study her with the interest of a professional. 'Yes,' he said at length. 'That's also possible.'

'Which leaves Mr. Watts only with the void in the pattern of blood on Mr. Case's chest.'

Corn's small brown eyes were watchful. 'If you're referring to the pattern of blood and not to the prosecution's entire case.'

Caroline nodded briefly. 'You've already told us that the void would have been caused by the murderer sitting astride Mr. Case. From the pattern of blood on the victim's face, what pattern would you expect on the murderer?'

Corn removed his glasses, polishing them with a handkerchief. 'Hard to say, Ms. Masters. Again, it might depend on distance.'

Turning, Caroline pointed to the spray on Brett's

shoulders and breasts. 'Wouldn't you expect a pattern heavier than this?'

Corn studied the photograph. 'All that I can tell you,' he finally answered, 'is that it's possible....'

'So that it's also possible that the killer, not Brett, absorbed a heavy spray of blood. Thus creating the void on Mr. Case's chest and leaving Ms. Allen with the far lighter spray caused by CPR?'

'Again, that's possible. But what about the absence of a contact pattern on Ms. Allen's mouth?'

Caroline raised her eyebrows. 'Do you happen to know, Dr. Corn, how long it was between the murder and the time these pictures were taken?'

'In my understanding, about two hours.'

'More than long enough, in other words, for Ms. Allen to lick her lips. Or, as we know she did, to vomit and then wipe her mouth.'

'I suppose so.' Rising, Corn walked to the second bulletin board. 'But as we talk, Ms. Masters, I should note the existence of a spurt of blood on Ms. Allen's neck. Which is neither spray nor teardrop, but similar to the kind of spewing pattern I might expect from an agonal breath.'

'One spot?' Caroline stood next to him. 'Are you familiar with Officer Mann's testimony that he lent Ms. Allen his jacket?'

'Yes.'

'And could the single spot you note be a smear? Caused by contact between the jacket and Ms. Allen's skin?'

Narrow-eyed, Corn considered the photograph. 'Yes,' he said tersely. 'At this point, I can't tell.'

Turning, Corn headed for the witness stand. 'While you're here,' Caroline interjected, 'there's something else I'd like to ask you. About this picture.'

Corn turned back to her. 'Yes?'

Caroline rested her index finger beneath a smudge mark on James Case's neck. 'What's that?'

Corn studied the mark. 'On the body,' he said dryly, 'it looked like a bruise. Left by a finger, perhaps.'

'Could you lift a print?'

'We could not.' Corn's voice remained dry. 'As I believe you pointed out yesterday to Sergeant Summers, that's quite difficult on the body of a male. At least in the absence of blood.'

Towle, Caroline noticed, was leaning forward from the bench. Quietly, she asked, 'Could it also be difficult, Dr. Corn, because the person who made this mark was wearing gloves?'

Corn angled his head. 'Impossible to say. At least from this.'

'Then hang on.' Quickly, Caroline walked back to the defense table and produced a photograph from her brief-case. 'Subject to proof,' she said to Towle, 'this is a blowup of the area on Mr. Case's neck. With the court's permission, I'd like to ask Dr. Corn about it now, rather than recalling him.'

Towle looked toward Jackson. 'Mr. Watts?'

Jackson stepped forward, took the photograph from Caroline, and studied it for what seemed quite long. When he gave it back to her, his expression was blank. 'Subject to proof,' he said to Towle.

'Thank you,' Caroline responded, and gave the photograph to Corn. Standing next to him, she indicated with a finger a faint line at one edge of the bruise.

If he's honest, her expert had told her, *the* ME *can't say no. At least not for sure*.

'Do you see that line?' Caroline asked.

Slowly, Corn nodded. 'I see it, yes.'

'Could it have been made by the seam of a leather glove?'

For a long moment, Corn squinted, silent. 'Yes,' he said at last. 'That's possible.'

'And yet we know, from her fingerprints in Mr. Case's blood, that Ms. Allen was not wearing gloves.'

Corn appeared troubled now; though whether by doubt, or by being cornered, Caroline could not tell. 'We know that, yes.'

He looked up at Caroline, expecting her to drive the

point home. Instead she passed the photograph to Judge Towle, and said simply, 'Thank you, Dr. Corn. You may sit down now.'

Corn gave her a brief, querying glance, and then resumed the stand.

Standing in front of him, Caroline permitted a moment's silence. 'Are you quite certain,' she asked, 'that whoever killed Mr. Case did so while sitting astride him?'

A look of surprise, and then renewed confidence. 'Yes. I am.'

'And why is that?'

'There are several reasons. The void on Mr. Case's chest, the angle of the chest wound – suggesting a thrust down and in – and the presence of spray on the grass behind him all suggest as much.'

Caroline nodded. 'All right, then. Could you demonstrate the motion with which you believe the murderer slashed the victim's throat?'

Corn hesitated for a moment. And then he raised his right arm and cocked his wrist; with a blunt downward-slashing motion, he cut James Case's imaginary throat. 'Like so,' he said. 'That would be the motion.'

'Thank you.' As if puzzled, Caroline paused. 'But shouldn't you have used your left hand? Assuming, that is, that you were imitating Brett Allen.'

Corn looked surprised and then gave her a slight smile. 'I guess so.'

'And the reason you agree with me?'

'Her fingerprints on the hilt of the knife – the ones in the victim's blood – were made with her left hand.'

'Just so.' Caroline moved to the bulletin board again, standing next to the photograph of the gashes in the dead man's neck. 'You measured the depth of the victim's neck wounds, correct?'

'Yes.'

'And was the depth of the wound uniform?'

'Of course not. As you would expect, it was deepest at midthrust.'

'But were the wounds deeper at one end than the other?'

At the edge of her vision, Caroline saw Jackson stir. 'As I remember,' Corn answered, 'they were deeper on the right side.'

Caroline nodded. 'Tell me, Dr. Corn, are you familiar with a phenomenon known as the tailing effect?'

A brief pause. 'Yes.'

'And could you describe it to us?'

Corn glanced at Jackson and then faced Caroline again. 'As a very general rule, the blade of a knife is presumed to enter the throat more deeply – assuming a horizontal slash wound – than it exits.'

'And here, in both cases, the right-side wound was deeper.'

'Yes.'

Pausing, Caroline folded her arms. 'And what, assuming the tailing effect, does that suggest about the person who killed James Case?'

'Objection.' Quickly, Jackson came to the bench. 'The question not only calls for speculation but piles one piece of speculation on the other. Starting with the motion with which the murderer wielded the knife.'

'With which,' Caroline retorted, 'Mr. Watts was perfectly content – as long as the killer was Ms. Allen, sitting on the victim's chest. Which is also the foundation for my seeking Dr. Corn's expert opinion.'

Nodding, Towle turned to Jackson. 'I'm going to allow it, Mr. Watts. And weigh it for myself.' He turned to Corn. 'You may answer, Dr. Corn.'

Corn looked steadily at Caroline. 'It is speculative. But if I'm correct about how the wounds were inflicted, and the tailing effect holds true, the murderer is more likely to be right-handed.'

Behind her, Caroline felt a stirring in the courtroom. 'Thank you,' she said crisply. 'I have nothing more.'

Chapter 10

'So,' Jackson said, 'are you going to offer us the real killer? Or do you prefer a nameless phantom?'

Caroline shrugged. 'I don't know yet.'

It was six o'clock, and they stood beneath the trees on the lawn of the Connaughton County Courthouse. The press had gone to file their stories – that Caroline had called for Jackson to dismiss the case. Brett had returned to prison, and the rest of Caroline's family to Masters Hill. So that now it was only the two of them, in the light of early evening.

Caroline kicked off her shoes.

Jackson was in an edgy humor, she decided – he treated her with a mixture of familiarity and distrust, and his tone was sardonic. But he had approached her for a reason, and she could guess what it was.

Caroline breathed in deeply, face raised to the failing sun, waiting out his silence. 'It's weird,' she said. 'Being locked up like this all day. You forget there's a world.'

Hands in his pockets, Jackson looked around them. Connaughton Falls was in the heart of the valley that embraced Resolve, and the vista of hills and forests was familiar to them both from childhood. 'Did you ever miss this?' he asked.

'Some. Because I knew I'd never come back.'

Jackson glanced at her sideways. 'Well, you're back,' he said finally. 'And you're the best I've seen. There's capable – like me – and then there's something more.'

His tone was one of detachment; because he could acknowledge her gifts, this said, he was also smart enough to beat her. 'You make it sound,' Caroline replied, 'as if Brett's defense is a matter of talent. Perhaps you should consider that it may be something more.'

Jackson turned to her. 'Brett's defense so far, Caroline, is possibility upon surmise, 'could be' upon 'should be' upon 'might be.' What impresses me is your ability to assimilate what is obviously a slough of expert advice, all in ten days, and find some black hole in each witness's testimony from which to extract yet one more "possibility".'

Caroline shook her head. 'The holes are there, and the possibilities are real. Your problem – your witnesses' problem – is that when Megan Race came along with a motive, she made all of you assume too much. So that you believed you had the practical equivalent of a locked-door killing: no other suspects need apply.'

Jackson shoved his hands in his pockets. 'Yes,' he said sharply. 'Megan. Tomorrow's witness.'

This did not call for an answer, and Caroline gave him none.

After a time, Jackson took off his suit jacket, unknotted his tie, and sat with his back against a tree. 'So who is Megan the biggest problem for? Brett, or me, or you?'

Caroline sat next to him, gazing out at the lawn. 'One of *us*,' she answered quietly. 'Brett's not even in the running.'

'And you won't tell me anything.'

'I can't. For Brett's sake. Unless you dismiss the case for good.'

'Which I can't, as you damned well know. Not without reason.'

Caroline shrugged. 'So there we are.'

Jackson turned to her. Softly, he said, 'Even if an inch-by-inch survey of Megan's apartment turns up funny fingerprints?'

Caroline's face closed. 'If I understand you,' she answered coolly, 'you're assuming a conflict between Brett's interests and mine. Or, perhaps, my ambitions.'

Jackson shook his head. 'I'm trying to understand *you*, Caroline. And I can't.'

Caroline tented her fingers, placed them in her lap. 'Then perhaps it will help,' she said at last, 'to know that

I've put ambition aside. You're now the only one of us who still wishes to become a judge.'

His silent gaze was without comprehension: it was as if Caroline watched them both, trapped in a moment only she understood. By instinct, she touched his arm. 'I'd have taken anyone else for a prosecutor, Jackson. But that's really all I can say to you.'

He gazed at her hand. 'Because of Brett?'

'Yes.'

Slowly, Jackson slid his arm from beneath her fingers. 'Then let's set aside Megan and discuss where we are right now.'

Caroline felt awkward. And then she felt the reflex of her adulthood: the withdrawal of feeling in exchange for thought. 'You want to offer me manslaughter,' she said.

Jackson smiled without humor. 'How did you ever guess?'

'Is there a recommended sentence that goes with it?'

'Ten years.' His smile vanished. 'It's open for one day only, Caroline. Let me know before court tomorrow.'

Caroline felt herself go cold. 'I thought this wasn't about your star witness. And whatever I may have in store for her.'

Jackson's eyes narrowed. 'And I thought *you* had no conflict.' He paused for a moment. 'I don't know what you've got for Megan. But it can't change the case we've built already, and Fred Towle isn't going to bounce me. Because your questions have been about reasonable doubt, not probable cause. And you'll have to offer a New Hampshire jury more than some song and dance about a righthanded drug dealer in gloves who paddled in by canoe while Brett was swimming, cut James's throat, and paddled out again. In the end, it just won't wash.'

This, Caroline feared, might be true. 'Then why the offer?'

'Because between intoxication and jealousy, I expect you can entice a jury to believe that Brett acted without thought. That might even be a just result. But what you can't guarantee her is ten years.' Jackson's voice became soft again. 'Out by age thirty-two, Caroline, with the rest of her life back. Not much of a price for what we saw in those pictures.'

'Those pictures,' Caroline retorted, 'may never get into evidence – at least not the ones of Brett. Because most of what you have is a direct result of her first statement to Mann, which I'll suppress for sure. That makes a whole lot else – the pictures, the search of Brett's person and property, her second statement – the proverbial fruit of the poisonous tree.'

Jackson rested his arms on his knees, regarding her quite calmly. 'I can tell you what'll happen. You'll get Brett's first statement tossed and, if you're very lucky, the second. But all the physical evidence resulting from finding the body comes in because we would have found him without her help. And at trial, Brett will have to tell her story, anyhow, and give me or my successor a shot at cross-examination. Because no reasonable jury will forgive her for not explaining herself in the face of all the evidence.'

Caroline stared at him. 'Or your successor?' she repeated.

'That's right. I find that I'm not enjoying this case quite the way I should.'

Caroline sat back. Was this distaste or prudence? she wondered; the deeper stress she sensed in him could be dislike of what he was doing, fear of losing a judgeship, or the ascendancy of doubt over zeal that comes with middle age. From her own experience, it was probably all of these.

'Back in high school,' she said at last, 'could you have imagined this conversation?'

'Jackson gave the small, lopsided smile that had hardly changed since then. 'Even if I could have, Caroline, I couldn't have guessed how it would feel.'

Caroline became quiet, without quite knowing why. Then it came to her: this was likely the last civil conversation she would have with Jackson Watts.

Turning, she gazed at the lawn, the trees, the deepening shadows.

'I'll talk to Brett,' she said. 'But if you're still calling Megan, I'd have her ready to go.'

Tonight, everything about Brett – the vivid green eyes, the coils of brown hair, the quick movement of her hands – seemed to quiver with suppressed anxiety. She looked far more real than Caroline felt, standing on the precipice of doubt. So that Brett's long silence startled her.

'I must not be explaining this well,' Caroline said.

'You explained it fine.' Brett's gaze was steady and penetrating. 'Ten years and out. I'm just trying to read what you're not saying.'

Caroline felt one thought intersecting with another. And then she remembered the moment in a famous murder case, in which a celebrity was accused of cruelly butchering his wife, when Caroline had known that he was guilty – the day two months after the killing that the accused, prompted by his public relations expert, had offered a reward for the 'real' murderer of the beloved mother of his two young children. 'I was wondering,' Caroline said at last, 'what you would say if I asked who you think murdered James. A drug dealer?'

'No. I don't believe that now.' Brett's eyes did not waver. 'Any more than you do.'

Surprised, Caroline hesitated. 'Then *who*?'

'That's what scares me.' For a moment, Brett was quiet. 'All day I looked at those pictures. I've thought about them ever since.' Her words became low, intense. 'There's memory, and then there's the things you just know. That's nothing I could ever have done to him. I don't know anyone who could.'

In the bare yellow room, Caroline studied her: the moment carried echoes of other talks in other rooms, risks being bartered for years. And yet it was so different.

'But what do *you* think, Caroline?' Brett's voice became

ironic. 'I get so hung up on being innocent I forget that you're my lawyer.'

Inwardly, Caroline winced. 'Perhaps I'm not as detached as I should be.'

Torn from her own concerns, Brett gave her a brief, curious look, and then her voice grew softer. 'The last three days have been horrible. Sometimes it's hard to imagine how anyone else feels about it. Or to care much, either.'

'No reason to. But is my advice so important to you?'

'Yes.' Brett's voice was quiet. 'Now, it is.'

Caroline inhaled. 'I wouldn't take Jackson's deal.'

Brett's eyes probed hers. 'Why?'

'Because any capable defense lawyer can get this deal later – even Jackson's case screams manslaughter.' Pausing, Caroline felt the weight of her last words. 'Of course, that's easy for me to say. Take ten years now, and you'll cap your risk forever. No more trial, or waiting, or fear. You just start serving your time, hoping that when you get out you'll still have some sort of life – a career, kids, who knows. And maybe Jackson's successor will be a real hardass, and you'll never get this deal again.' Finishing, Caroline felt shaken. 'But I can't tell you to do this, Brett. Because – although it scares me to say so – I think that I can make things better for you.'

Brett looked at her in hope and doubt. After a time, she asked softly, 'Because of Megan?'

For a long moment, Caroline was silent. 'Yes.' she answered. 'At least because of Megan.'

Chapter 11

There are days in the courtroom that have a deeper texture, Caroline thought. Sometimes this is felt only by the lawyers; at other times, those watching know it also. But Megan Race brought with her something more: the sense that, for her, this was a defining moment.

She seemed conscious of everything – the reporters, the Masters family, the import of her testimony – in the way that an actress, pretending to ignore her audience, shows her awareness through her bearing, the specificity of her gestures, the inflection of a word, a telling stillness. From the time that she walked to the stand, tall and straight and proud, Megan drew a particular quiet.

Caroline was quite certain that she alone felt the potential for the rarest of courtroom events, a psychic meltdown that would not be pleasant to watch. But this was merely the smallest reason, among several, that made her wish this morning had never come.

She had told Jackson privately, and briefly, in a corner of the lobby. 'Brett can't do it,' Caroline said. 'Among other things, she insists she's innocent.'

Jackson looked at her in silence; he seemed as subdued as Caroline felt. 'Can I ask what you advised her?' he said at length.

'The same, I'm afraid.' Caroline shrugged. 'So there we are.'

For another moment, Jackson watched her. 'I keep trying to understand you,' he said. 'You can't seriously believe her, can you?'

'I've begun to actively consider it, Jackson. As should you.' Caroline paused. 'I really wish we could talk about Megan. But it's not in Brett's interests.'

Jackson smiled without humor. 'Oh, well,' he said, and

turned to enter court. To Caroline, watching, the moment was sadder than he imagined.

Now, sitting next to Brett, she knew why she had come.

Brett, of course, understood none of this. Her focus was on Megan: she watched her with a cool anger that, to Caroline, was bracing.

'What kind of person,' Brett murmured, 'gets pleasure out of this?'

That was it, Caroline thought, and Brett had caught it: there was a narcissism about Megan, and the courtroom fed it. Worried about Caroline as she might be, Megan would not, in the end, be able to hold back.

'Prepare yourself for a long morning,' Caroline murmured to Brett. 'But after that, things will get better.'

Head raised, eyes straight ahead, Megan swore to tell the truth.

For a last moment, Caroline turned to watch her family. Her father had fixed Megan with a gelid stare, as if she were an insect. Somehow Caroline found this more chilling than anger; perhaps it was the memory of her first horrified awareness, the night that David had vanished, of the way Channing Masters could dismiss the claim of another human being to any shred of sympathy. For all that she was like him, Caroline thought, this was the difference that had made her a defense lawyer; that made her, in this way at least, Nicole Dessaliers' daughter.

As if by reflex, Caroline glanced at her sister.

Betty, she thought grimly, lacked her father's resources: her face was pale, distorted by fear and anger. The anger, Caroline knew, was far deeper yet no more complex than the outrage of a mother whose child is picked on by a bully. But it was the fear that never left her – that whatever Betty most valued would be taken from her, for reasons she could not comprehend. It was fortunate that she did not know that it was Larry, by violating her trust, who had helped place Brett at risk; not even Caroline could take pleasure in what this would do to Betty.

Next to her, Larry clasped Betty's hand, unable to look

at Megan. With a certain lack of charity, Caroline made sure that he saw her. It was not until his gaze broke that Caroline turned away.

Damn all of you, she thought.

Beneath the table, she touched Brett's hand, and felt the girl's fingertips close around hers. Softly, Caroline said, 'Don't worry.'

On the stand, Megan was a portrait of grief and dignity.

She wore a suit, blue and severe, such as one would wear to a job interview. Which was how Jackson treated her first moments in the public eye.

'And what, to this point, is your grade point average at Chase?'

Megan folded her hands. 'Three point seven,' she said. 'Straight A's would be a four point.'

Her air, Caroline thought, was a touch supercilious. Quickly, Jackson moved to the most appealing part: that Megan, a high school honor student, was at Chase on partial scholarship; that her father had died when she was twelve; that she worked to help pay for school. With a certain fascination, Caroline watched Jackson gild Megan's character, wondering if he suspected that the one detail of importance was the loss of Megan's father.

'And you and your mother are close?' Jackson was asking.

'Very. Since Dad died, it was just the two of us. But his dream was that I go to college, and we've dedicated ourselves to that.' She paused, looking down. 'Until now, going to Chase was his dream come true.'

'Here we go,' Caroline murmured.

Jackson paused, as if permitting Megan to regain her bearings. 'Are you acquainted with the defendant, Brett Allen?'

For the first time, Megan turned to Brett; her quick glance at Caroline was both surreptitious and defiant. 'Yes,' she said. 'I am.'

Her answer was given with a catch in her throat. So far,

Caroline acknowledged, Megan showed close to perfect pitch. 'Don't take your eyes off her,' Caroline whispered to Brett. 'Make her feel you.'

'And do you know any other members of her family?' Jackson asked.

At the edge of Caroline's view, Larry looked down. 'Her father.' Megan folded her hands. 'But only as a professor for one class, or to visit his office if I had a question.'

'And what grade did you receive?'

'An A.'

'Do you have any animosity toward any member of the Allen family?'

Megan raised her chin, displaying a long, elegant neck. Her blond hair, Caroline noted, had been carefully trimmed, so that it barely touched her shoulders. 'Only one,' she said at last. 'Brett Allen.'

It was a good answer, Caroline thought; whatever else, Megan had been carefully coached.

'Can you tell us, Ms. Race, the reason for this animosity?'

Her eyes seemed to widen in shock, suddenly recalled, at the loss she had suffered. In a quiet voice, she said, 'Because James Case and I were in love.'

It was a demure answer, Caroline thought, reflecting Jackson's advice. His own voice softened to match Megan's. 'And how long was that relationship?'

Megan raised her chin again. 'It began in February. And continued until the day he died.'

'And your relationship was an intimate one?'

'Yes. It was very intense.' Megan's voice took on an assertive pride. 'Physically and emotionally.'

Brett's jawline tightened. But what Caroline felt was a *frisson* of unease; what she heard was not Megan's claim of intimacy but the need for it, the sad secret of the young woman whom Caroline had witnessed in a lonely, unguarded moment, touching herself in the mirror.

As if she had read her thoughts, Megan turned to

Caroline. Caroline smiled faintly. When Jackson spoke again, Megan seemed to flinch.

'How often did you see each other?' Jackson asked.

A hesitancy, distracted. 'At least twice a week.'

'Why not more often?'

'I have to work at night, as well as study – my scholarship depends on maintaining a certain GPA, and it doesn't cover everything.' Megan's voice fell. 'And James was trying to make up his mind.'

'About what?'

Megan touched her collarbone; to Caroline, the gesture had a certain widowed sensuality, the feel of a lover recalled. 'Between Brett,' she answered softly, 'and what he had found with me.'

Brett's face showed anger and distaste; for all that she appeared volatile, Caroline sensed that she had the New Englander's dislike for self-dramatization. But Caroline's second thought went deeper than reason could justify – that Brett seemed too real for there to be a second Brett, waiting beneath the first to be summoned by drugs or wine.

'So, in your understanding, James was involved with Brett at the time you began dating?'

'Yes.' Megan's voice became sententious and a little sad. 'He was obviously looking for a way out. But like a lot of men, he had this misplaced sense of guilt.'

Caroline did not bother to stand. 'I wonder, Your Honor, if we might stick to what Mr. Case did, as opposed to how Ms. Race cares to imagine him. Assuming that she knows the difference.'

Caroline's tone, while mild, was so unsympathetic that Jackson – clearly expecting Caroline to tread more carefully – gave her a look of genuine surprise which was mirrored in Towle's raised eyebrows. 'Well,' Towle observed, 'it's probably best to let events speak for themselves.' He turned to Megan, adding courteously, 'If you could, Ms. Race.'

But Megan was staring at Caroline, and the prideful look had become rigid. *You can't take it*, Caroline thought, *can*

419

you? 'Thank you, Your Honor,' she said to Towle, but never took her eyes off Megan.

'In any event,' Jackson said promptly, 'there came a time when James was seeing both you and Ms. Allen?'

Megan's head snapped back toward Jackson. 'Yes. There was.'

'And was Ms. Allen aware of this?'

'Yes.'

'How did you know this?'

Briefly, Megan looked unsettled. 'At first, I almost couldn't believe it, what James said – that she was following us.'

It was nicely done, Caroline thought: a bizarre story that, in retrospect, had become horrifying because of James's death. This time Caroline stood. 'Move to strike,' she said. 'Ms. Race's account of James's supposed knowledge is clearly hearsay.'

'Of course it is,' Jackson retorted. 'But it's admissible under a standard exception – that it is offered not for the truth of the assertion but to describe Mr. Case's state of mind –'

'Then what good is it to you?' Caroline snapped.

'Because, among other things, it helps explain Mr. Case's later conduct toward both Ms. Race and Ms. Allen.'

Towle nodded, and turned to Caroline. 'I'm going to allow it, Ms. Masters.'

Caroline sat down. As she had expected, the smallest reinforcement lent Megan a sense of triumph; her eyes seemed to glint, and she looked briefly, imperiously, around the courtroom. And then, head bowed, Megan slipped back into her role.

'Did there come a time,' Jackson asked her, 'that you gained personal knowledge that Brett Allen was following you?'

A slight, reluctant nod. 'Yes.'

'And when was that?'

Megan looked into a middle distance; once more, there

was the glaze of shock remembered. 'She burst into James's apartment and found us together.'

Next to her, Caroline saw Brett grip the edge of the table. 'What were the circumstances?' Jackson asked.

Megan's eyes half shut; her voice was a curious mix of reticence and pride. 'We were making love. In James's bed.'

'That's a relief,' Caroline whispered. But Brett did not seem to hear her. She had the concerned look that Caroline had seen before – someone trapped in a courtroom, listening to a version of her life she could not challenge, reduced to wondering how her reaction appeared to others.

Silent, Caroline touched Brett's hand.

'I know this is difficult,' Jackson said, 'but could you describe what happened?'

Megan paused, looking away. 'James was on top of me. So that I was the one who saw her first.'

'Go on.'

She shook her head, as if in disbelief remembered. 'Brett's eyes were wide and staring. And then she got this kind of crazy smile, but filled with hate.

'I think I screamed then – I'm not sure. What I remember is James's eyes becoming frightened, and then him turning to face her.

'At first, she was after *me*. Calling me a bitch and trying to scratch his face so she could get to me.' As if by reflex, Megan touched her face. 'I was so stunned that all I did was pull the sheet up over me....'

Brett's fingertips, pressed against the table, were white. 'Our time's coming,' Caroline whispered.

'But James was wonderful.' Pausing, Megan shook her head. 'I don't know how he did it, but somehow he got his arms around her so she couldn't move. She was wriggling, struggling ...' Her voice fell off.

'Yes?'

'And then she leaned back, spit in his face, and told him, "I'll kill you for this."'

Thinking of Brett, Caroline felt her stomach clench.

Megan raised her head. 'I'll never forget it,' she said with

421

new clarity. 'James with her saliva on his face, her eyes so green and scary. And then, very softly, she said it again. To be sure he didn't miss it.

' *"I'll kill you."* '

Megan touched her forehead. 'Suddenly, she was gone.'

The last words, slightly tremulous, carried their own resonance: Brett was not gone, the words said. Because she *had* killed him.

'It's all right,' Caroline murmured.

But Jackson let the moment linger – in Towle's subdued, unhappy look, in the reporter, writing furiously, who could not take her eyes off Megan. And, most of all, in Megan herself – so suddenly still, so clearly elsewhere. It was easy to see how she had stolen Jackson's case.

Gently, he asked, 'How did that affect your relationship with James?'

'He kept on seeing her.' Megan sounded drained now, reciting a tragedy she knew by heart but whose end she could not change. 'She'd threatened to kill herself, you see.'

Brett leaned forward. 'Jesus ...'

'Objection.' Caroline stood again. 'Once more, hearsay. And whose state of mind are we talking about now?'

'The victim's,' Jackson said curtly. 'As my next question will show.'

Towle nodded. 'Go ahead.'

Jackson turned to Megan. She waited there, her posture patient, courteous, dispirited: to Caroline, her manner was meant to suggest that she was not taking revenge but keeping faith with a man she loved.

'Did this affect, Ms. Race, the way you and James went about seeing each other?'

Slowly, Megan nodded. 'What James said was that he wanted to be rid of her but that he felt so responsible. I think he really believed that if he broke off with her, Brett might harm herself.' Megan steepled her hands in front of her. 'So we entered this phase which seemed endless to me then and now seems so short – where I was almost like

422

James's mistress, a secret who couldn't be known, and we spent our nights alone at my place.

'We saw absolutely no one – it was like we were safe within our secret. Part of me hated it. But now I remember how he read me poetry, or acted out scenes for a play, and I realize we'd discovered that we needed no one else. That what we had, emotionally and as lovers, was enough to turn my small apartment into a world.' Her head rose again. 'We didn't need anyone.'

Yes, Caroline thought, this is who I expected. For the first time, Jackson looked faintly disconcerted. 'But you stayed together,' he said.

'Oh, yes. Sometimes I thought I was being foolish.' Megan gave a faint, fond smile. 'But then at the end, I knew I had been right to wait.

'The night before he died, James came to me.

'We made love, beautiful love. It had such a desperate quality that part of me was afraid of losing him. That he had come to say that we were over, and it hurt him so much that he needed, one last time, to be as close to me as he could be.'

Caroline saw Brett wince; the description must sound enough like James to her to make her wonder if this was true. The tragedy of Megan, Caroline thought, was a certain ruined sensitivity; her comprehension of others was uncanny, but incomplete. So that her version of these final days had the feel of reality.

Megan turned to Brett now. 'But I was wrong,' she said softly. 'James had come to ask me to go away with him. To California.'

Brett's lips parted, silent. 'What did you say?' Jackson asked softly.

'That I loved him. But that I had an obligation to my mother, and to my father's memory. And that before I tried to pull all that together, he needed to put *us* together.' Her voice grew firm. 'To go to Brett. To tell her what he had asked me and that he would never see her again.'

'And what did he say?'

'That he would.' Megan's stare at Brett was accusing now, but her voice was soft. 'The night he died, Mr. Watts, was the night he promised to tell her.'

Suddenly, Brett's face was less angry than wounded — as if doubting, as Caroline once had made her doubt, the truth of her own memory. Jackson seemed to approach Megan with diffidence, reluctant to interrupt her grief. 'And where were you that night?'

'Alone in my apartment.' Megan's eyes filled with sudden tears. 'Waiting for James, with a bottle of champagne. You see, after he told her the truth, James was coming to me....'

Megan could not seem to go on.

'Perfect,' Caroline murmured.

Chapter 12

Caroline stood, a half smile on her face, gazing at Megan in silence. Megan seemed to square her shoulders, waiting for Caroline to come forward. But Caroline did not move from the defense table.

'Hello, Megan.'

Caroline's greeting, soft and a little sad, seemed to straighten Megan in her chair. Warily, she answered, 'Hello.'

For Caroline, there was no sound, no audience, no one else but the girl in front of her. 'This incident you described, when Brett found you and James in bed together. When did it occur?'

Megan folded her hands. 'April.'

'And how often did you see James after that?'

Megan's mouth tightened. 'As I said, once or twice a week. At my apartment.'

'Did the two of you ever socialize with anyone else?'

'No. We needed time alone.'

'Or go anywhere?'

'No.' Megan's voice was harsh. 'I already testified that James was worried about what Brett might do.'

Caroline tilted her head. 'Were you frightened?'

A delayed nod. 'I couldn't help it.'

'Did you ever talk to anyone about it?'

'James. Of course.'

'Anyone else?'

A slight pause. 'No. It was very painful, and emotional.'

Caroline nodded her understanding. 'Is it fair to say that, at least to this point, James was the love of your life?'

Megan raised her head, prideful again. 'Yes, it is.'

'Then would you also say that when he died, he was the person you were closest to?'

'Yes,' Megan said promptly, and then amended this. 'Except for my mother.'

Caroline nodded again. 'How many times a week do you talk to your mother?'

Megan paused a moment. 'Two or three times a week. Sometimes more, sometimes less.'

'Did you ever mention James to her?'

Megan's eyes narrowed. 'What do you mean?'

'I mean his *existence*.'

Megan seemed to flush. 'Of course.'

'How many times?'

Megan hesitated. In a quiet voice, she answered, 'Two or three.'

'Two or three? What did you tell her about him?'

Megan's mouth compressed. 'I don't remember, exactly. I'm sure she knew that I was seeing him.'

'Not that you were in love with him?'

Megan gave her a long stare of annoyance. 'I really don't remember what I said. My mother and I talk about a lot of things.'

'You must. Did they happen to include that Brett had threatened James?'

Megan hesitated. 'I don't think so.'

'Or was following you?'

'I don't remember.'

Caroline raised an eyebrow. 'After this incident in April, did you mention James to your mother at all?'

For the first time, Megan looked toward Jackson. 'I'm over here,' Caroline said softly. 'And Mr. Watts can't help you. Because he knows exactly why I'm asking these questions.'

Jackson rose at once, to buy his witness time. 'Rather than lecture the witness, Ms. Masters, perhaps you can repeat the question.'

Caroline did not look at him. 'Megan,' she asked quietly, 'after Brett found you in bed with James, did you ever again mention James to your mother?'

426

Megan gazed at her lap. 'I don't remember. As I said, the place I was in with James was embarrassing.'

'Didn't you think your mother could help?'

Megan frowned. 'I didn't want to upset her.'

Caroline looked astonished. 'Surely you must have talked to *someone* about him. Given how important James was in your life.'

Megan hesitated. 'I really don't remember. Being with James was more important than talking about him.'

Caroline was quiet for a moment. 'So am I correct in understanding that after this incident in April, you never mentioned James Case to anyone?'

Megan gave Caroline a quick, hostile look. 'I don't remember.'

'After April, did anyone *see* you together?'

'I don't know.'

'Did you and James ever leave your apartment?'

'No.'

'Did you ever invite people over when he was there?'

'No.'

'When did he come over? Weekends, or weekdays?'

Megan's face was stiff. 'Weekdays. At night.'

'Any particular nights?'

'No. Just when he could, and I could.'

'What did you do, exactly?'

'That's private.' Megan's voice was brittle now. 'I don't see why I have to answer private questions.'

Caroline's voice remained quiet. In the precise same tone, she asked again, 'What did you do, exactly?'

Glancing at Jackson, Megan seemed to gather herself. 'We made love. We were just with each other, and it was beautiful.'

'Did you talk?'

'Of course.'

'What about?'

'Everything. We were each other's best friends.'

Pausing, Caroline felt the door shut on her compassion, the complete and deadly coldness come into her again. In a

427

voice of bored politeness, she asked, 'Where was James from?'

Megan put her hands on the rail of the witness stand. 'I don't remember, exactly.'

'Where did his parents live?'

'I don't remember.'

'Do you know where he was born?'

'No.'

'Or whether he had brothers and sisters?'

'No.'

Caroline looked curious. 'Would you describe James as a closed personality?'

Megan mustered the prideful look. 'Maybe with other people. Not with me.'

'Did he happen to mention to you that he was an orphan?'

Megan's fingers, Caroline noted, clasped the edge of the rail. 'No.'

'Or that he had lived in a series of foster homes?'

'No.'

Next to her, Caroline saw Brett's eyes widen with surprise that Megan knew so little. 'Well,' Caroline said softly, 'I'm sure those subjects were painful for him. Tell me, then, where were you and James planning to live in California?'

Megan glanced at Jackson Watts. 'We hadn't gotten that far,' she said at last. 'The first thing was for him to break it off with her.'

'Did *James* at least have things narrowed down? Like, for example, which city you'd live in?'

Megan sat back, rigid. 'Why are you asking all this? It's like harassment.' Swiftly, she turned, glaring from the judge to Jackson. 'Do I have to answer this?'

Towle took off his glasses, gazing at her narrowly. 'Oh, yes,' he said quietly. 'You do.'

Jackson, Caroline saw, was gazing sharply at his witness. 'Which city?' Caroline snapped.

Megan turned abruptly, lips parted. Then she said, 'We hadn't decided yet.'

'What were you going to do there?'

'If I went? Finish school, of course.' Her voice became scornful. 'But I wasn't sure I'd throw everything over for a man.'

'That would be a big decision, wouldn't it? Did you happen to discuss it with your mother?'

'No. Like I said, it hadn't gone that far.' She paused, modulating her voice to sorrow. 'And then James was dead.'

'And you were waiting for him, at your apartment. With a bottle of champagne.'

'Yes.' It was as if Megan found the question, and her answer, reassuring. 'Yes,' she repeated, and then tears welled in her eyes.

'When James didn't appear, what did you do?'

Megan shook her head. 'I kept calling him, all night....'

'Oh? Did you happen to leave a message on his machine?'

Megan's eyes shut. 'I don't remember. I mean, it was so awful ...'

Slowly, Caroline reached beneath the table and took out her briefcase. She laid it in front of her on the table, releasing the latches with a soft click.

At the sound, Megan's eyes flew open. She stared at the briefcase, then at Caroline. 'Tell me,' Caroline asked softly, 'how did you learn that James was dead?'

Megan looked disoriented. 'On the radio.'

'What did you do?'

Megan went pale. 'I cried.'

'Did you call anyone?'

'No. I couldn't.'

'Or tell anyone?'

'No.'

Caroline paused a moment. 'Not even your mother?'

'No.'

'When *did* you tell her James was dead?'

'I don't remember.'

Quietly, Caroline asked, 'Do you happen to remember when James was buried? Or where?'

The hush in the courtroom had become a pained collective silence. Megan's voice seemed to tremble. 'I couldn't stand –'

'Did you make any effort to find out?'

'I don't remember.'

'Or if there was a memorial service?'

Eyes averted, Megan shook her head. 'No,' she said in a shrill voice. 'Don't you understand how painful this was –'

'Who did you think had killed him?' Caroline snapped.

Megan hesitated. 'It had to be Brett.'

Caroline crossed her arms. 'Knowing that must have been awfully hard to live with.'

'Yes.'

'Unbearable, in fact.'

Megan still looked away. 'Yes.'

'So when did you go to the police?'

Megan put one finger on her mouth, face frozen.

Caroline's voice rose. 'When did you go to the police?'

Megan shook her head. 'I don't remember.'

'Was it six days after James was found?'

Megan looked up. 'I was *afraid* of her.'

'Brett?'

'Yes.'

'Because she might stalk you?'

'Yes.'

Caroline rested one hand on the table. 'Did you ever *see* Brett stalking you?'

'Yes.' Megan's voice was angry now. 'I did.'

'Tell me how she did it.'

Megan swallowed. 'She crept up into the shrubbery beneath my apartment.' Her voice quavered. 'We could see her in the bushes, staring up at us....'

'What did you do?'

'Nothing. James said she had this violent temper....'

'Didn't you call the police?'

Megan flinched. 'No.'

'Or ask your mother for advice?'

'No.'

Caroline was in another zone now; the questions came swift and sure, one upon the other. 'So let me see if I understand you, Megan. James Case and you were lovers, yes?'

'Yes.'

'Brett threatened to kill him.'

'Yes.'

'And to kill herself.'

'That's what James said.'

'And she stalked you?'

'Yes.'

'Hid outside your building.'

'I just told you that.'

'And so, for over two months, you and James never left the apartment?'

'Yes.'

'But in the end, James chose you.'

'Yes.' Megan clamped the arms of the witness stand. 'He chose me.'

'And asked you to go to California.'

'Yes.'

'And on the night of his death, you waited for him to tell Brett Allen and then come to you.'

Megan clasped her hands together, gathering herself again. 'Yes,' she said softly. 'I did.'

Caroline waited for a moment. 'And yet,' she said with equal quiet, 'you never told anyone about any of this. Until the day you went to Mr. Watts and accused Brett Allen of murder.'

For a time, Megan simply watched her. 'No.' Her voice was barely audible. 'I could never talk about it.'

'Not even to your mother.'

'No.'

Caroline paused, then asked, softly, 'Despite all those

telephone calls you made to her ... what was it, at least two or three a week?'

From the stand, Megan seemed to stare at her in desperation, as if trying to read her mind. 'I don't remember now. I already said that.'

'Do you remember whether you called your mother collect or put it on your own phone bill?'

'Objection,' she heard Jackson say. 'This is not only irrelevant, it's petty harassment.'

'Hardly,' Caroline said to Towle. 'It goes directly to this witness's credibility on crucial matters. As I'll show in a moment.'

Towle nodded, grim-faced. 'Go ahead, Ms. Masters.'

Caroline turned to Megan. 'Collect or not,' she snapped.

Megan hesitated, hunched back in her chair. 'Collect, I think.'

'Oh? And who was there to accept your calls?'

Megan's mouth fell open and then closed again.

'It could hardly be your mother,' Caroline asked, 'could it?'

Megan stared at her, new tears in her eyes. 'What do you mean?'

Caroline moved closer. Softly, she said, 'That she's been institutionalized for depression and doesn't speak to anyone. And hasn't for the last five months.'

Megan's face was ashen. 'Did you hear me?' Caroline demanded.

Megan flinched. 'Yes,' she said dully. 'She hasn't been well.'

'So these conversations with your mother – the ones you told us about under oath – never happened. Were, in fact, fabrications.'

Megan's jawline set. 'I was protecting her privacy....'

Pausing. Caroline let the stillness of the courtroom build. From the bench, Towle looked at Megan with open disdain. 'So,' Caroline continued calmly, 'the only thing that *is* true is that you never talked to anyone about James Case. Ever, at any time.'

Megan looked down. 'I can't remember now.'

Eyes still on Megan, Caroline opened the lid of her briefcase. Almost casually, she asked, 'Did you ever *write* about him?'

Megan stared at the briefcase, as if transfixed. In a hushed voice, she asked, 'What do you mean?'

Slowly, Caroline reached inside the briefcase and removed the red journal. She stood it on one end, beneath her fingertips, and looked once more at Megan.

Megan's face seemed to crumble. But except for the fingers of one hand, brought suddenly to her collarbone, she did not move.

Softly, Caroline asked again, 'Did you ever write about your relationship to James Case?'

Megan's fingers pressed against her chest, and then she spun, looking about for Jackson. 'I'd like a recess....'

Caroline watched her. 'Answer the question, please. Then you can have all the time you want.'

Megan stood, voice shrill. 'I won't put up with this....'

'Because you're a compulsive liar,' Caroline said with cutting coldness. 'I know it, you know it, and – in five minutes – everyone in this room will know it.'

Hurriedly, Jackson stepped forward, his own voice taut. 'The witness has been on for most of the day, Your Honor. If she's tired, or upset, no one's served by making her go longer. We can start again tomorrow.'

Towle looked at Megan, staring from the witness stand, and then at Caroline herself. 'Counsel?'

Caroline's eyes still did not move from Megan. Quietly, she said, 'As soon as she admits she lied, I'll be through with Ms. Race for the day. All that she has to say is "I made up everything I told you." It won't even take that long.'

'No.' Megan's look at Jackson mingled fear and betrayal. 'I want to talk with Mr. Watts.'

Towle studied her with something like distaste, and then turned to Caroline. 'It seems to me, Ms. Masters, that this witness should be allowed to consider her own position. Quite carefully. As should Mr. Watts.'

Caroline gave Megan a silent look of pity and contempt. 'Tomorrow morning then, Your Honor. I think I can remember my last question. As, I'm quite sure, will Ms. Race.'

Towle looked from Caroline to Megan. 'Very well,' he said. 'Court is adjourned until nine o'clock a.m.'

There was sudden movement – people stirring, a cacophony of voices. Jackson quickly went to Megan and shepherded her past Caroline. Her face was streaked with tears.

Turning to Caroline, Jackson said tersely, 'I want to see you, Caroline. Five minutes.'

'Take your time,' Caroline answered calmly. 'I think Megan has something to tell you.'

Megan could not look at her. Abruptly, Jackson led her away.

Brett stared at the journal. 'What is it?'

'A kind of diary.' Caroline kept her voice low. 'She lied about almost everything, and it's all in here. James dumped her after you caught them together. She started following you and James, hiding beneath his window. The only way she knew about California is that she went to him, begging for another chance.' Caroline turned to her. 'James said he wanted to leave with you. What you remember, at least about that, is how things were.'

Brett slowly shook her head. 'How did you get it?' she said at last.

Through her weariness and worry, Caroline smiled a little. 'That's what Jackson wants to know.'

Jackson shut the journal and slammed it down. 'What in God's name are you doing?' he demanded.

Caroline shrugged. 'Exposing perjury. She really is quite mad, you know.'

In the spare office Caroline and Brett had used, Jackson stared at her across the tarnished desk. 'You could have come to me with this.'

434

'I could have. But would you have dismissed the case with prejudice? I doubt that, somehow.'

'So instead you let me put on a lying witness and just watch me do it, waiting to destroy her. So that the prosecution seems like such a travesty that we look bad if we even consider pursuing it.'

'You will.' Caroline's voice was steely now. 'Once I'm finished with Megan.'

'Sorry. She's so hysterical now that she's incoherent. I'm withdrawing her as a witness –'

'Too late. She's under subpoena, and she's mine. By noon tomorrow, that girl's going to be far more than a pathetic liar. She'll be the best murder suspect you've ever overlooked.'

Softly, Jackson answered, 'Not unless you use this diary.'

'Which I've every intention of doing.'

Jackson shook his head. 'You've already destroyed her,' he said. 'Use that diary tomorrow, and you destroy yourself. Megan saved you by imploding.'

Caroline was silent for a moment. 'My story is that it came to me in the mail. Which Betty can confirm.'

Jackson's face was stained with anger. 'Don't insult me, Caroline. You mailed it to yourself. Though Betty may not know that.'

'So file a case. But first you have to finish *this* one.' Caroline paused for emphasis. 'I want her back, tomorrow morning. Or I want the case against Brett dismissed with prejudice.'

Jackson's mouth set. 'I can't do that. Megan may be a liar, but that doesn't make Brett innocent. So you'll have to make a public fool of me. And risk your reputation and maybe your career.' His eyes were keen. 'You did it yourself, didn't you? Broke in with a credit card and searched until you found this thing.'

Caroline stood. 'I told you about Larry. I asked you to check Megan out. Asked – no, begged – you to search her place. But you didn't want to *offend* her. Because she was such an *important* witness ...'

'She looked credible, damn it.'

Caroline waved a hand, contemptuous. 'Sorry. I'd forgotten that I'm morally disqualified from throwing this back at you.'

'Fuck you, Caroline. You withheld evidence and used it to set me up. Even though, for you, it's a suicide mission. You should have brought this to me the day that you first had it.' Jackson caught himself, looked at her hard again. 'There's something else to this, isn't there?'

Caroline stood. 'Just have her here tomorrow,' she said, and left.

Chapter 13

Caroline removed the envelope from beneath the seat of her car and spread the sheaf of pictures in her lap.

Joe Lemieux had done well, she thought. Satisfied, she rearranged them: from the top, a close-up of Megan Race gazed up at her, as vivid as in life. And then Caroline replaced them in the envelope.

It was dusk, a little past eight, and Caroline was alone.

Tomorrow would be bad for all of them – Jackson, Megan, Caroline herself. And then, after that, they would each live with the consequences. But that was for tomorrow; before finishing with Megan, there was one more thing to do.

She could have sent Lemieux. But the defense of Brett possessed her now; this was not a task she wished to delegate. She smiled mirthlessly, remembering the young Caroline, the impatient, sometimes impetuous lawyer who did her own investigation. This was far more than that, she knew – more, even, than Brett. Every instinct Caroline had said that she should do this alone.

She turned on the ignition and left Resolve behind.

The road to Heron Lake was, she guessed, much as it had been for Brett that night – winding, tree-shrouded, dusk becoming a film of gray, then darkness. Caroline's headlights cut the dark; a first moon, brightening silver, appeared in the break of trees above the road.

Passing the dirt road to Brett's lot, Caroline slowed but did not turn.

The road became darker, narrower. Perhaps a quarter mile farther, Caroline saw the neon sign of a gas station and convenience store. The successor, no doubt, of the Resolve General Store.

A few yards past it was the head of Mosher Trail.

Caroline turned there.

The road had several switchbacks, twisting among the trees; for a strange, disturbing moment, Caroline remembered the road at Windy Gates; her mother. Then the road opened, and she found herself on a gentle slope of dirt and rock, gazing at Heron Lake.

Caroline got out.

The moon was yellow now, its pale light moving slowly in the water. She walked to the edge.

There was a soft wind; water lapped gently at Caroline's feet. In the swirls of time, it seemed not so very different from some summer night with Jackson, when she had been younger than Brett was now.

Turning, Caroline gazed toward the lot that had once been hers. She could see, in the curve of the lake, a shadow between the lake and trees, the soft grass of the glade.

Perhaps she hoped for too much, or feared too much. There were too many pieces missing. But, standing here, it was not hard to imagine someone silently walking the shallows of the water's edge, moving toward two lovers in the grass.

There were still too many pieces missing, and one that was not – a knife. Unless, in the dark recesses of her memory, she had confused one knife with another.

Megan could have followed them. Assuming that she knew the lake, she might even have found them.

There was a chill in the air, Caroline thought.

She returned to the car, checking the photographs once more. Then she left the lakeside, driving slowly to the trailhead, until she saw the neon light of the gas station.

The building was white and the fluorescent lighting from within gave it a bright, unearthly glow. When Caroline pulled up to the gas tank, a slender man in a baseball cap came out from the store and walked over to her window. He stepped beneath the light above the gas tanks, and Caroline saw that he was barely out of his teens, with a goatee and a ponytail that somehow only made him look younger.

'Fill it up?' he asked.

'Thanks.'

He went to the tank and inserted the hose, and then began cleaning her front window with a squeegee.

Caroline stuck her head out the driver's side. 'There was something I wanted to ask you.'

With a flick of the wrist, he erased a squashed bug. 'Sure.'

Caroline propped her head on her chin. 'I'm a lawyer, working on the murder that happened out at Heron Lake. You've heard about that?'

He stopped, curious. 'A little. I just got back last night – been in Florida, seeing my mother.' He paused a moment. 'Who you working for?'

'Brett Allen, the defendant, who's about your age. I don't think she did it, and I've been trying to figure out if someone in the area saw anything that might help.'

Slowly, he nodded. 'Yeah, my boss said there was a guy out here the other day. I guess the night this other guy was killed was the last night I was on. Before vacation.' He peered more closely at Caroline. 'What you looking for?'

'Anything.' Caroline made herself sound bemused, a woman at sea. 'Like a car, or a person you'd never seen before. Or maybe someone turning down Mosher Trail.'

'Boy.' His show of teeth was reflexive, the surprise of someone asked to find significance in a mundane night three weeks in the past. 'I mean, I was just sort of shuffling between the tanks and in there, thinking more about vacation than anything else. I wasn't really watching the trail.'

The nozzle of the hose clicked off. The boy went back, gave the nozzle a final squeeze, and replaced the hose on the tank. Caroline gave him her credit card and watched him walk to the building.

He returned with a charge slip and a pen. Neatly, Caroline wrote her name and said in a hopeful voice,

439

'Maybe pictures would help. Think you could look at some?'

He paused, reluctant to be involved in this, and then his better nature seemed to overtake him. 'Okay,' he said. 'Sure.'

Slowly, Caroline took the pictures from the envelope. Pausing, she reshuffled them. 'Let's try vehicles first,' she said.

'Okay.'

She flicked on the inner light of the car and handed him three photographs.

The boy leaned inside, squinting at the black-and-white blowups. He went through the pictures, once, then twice. He paused at the last one. 'Where was this taken?' he asked.

'The Connaughton County Courthouse.'

He exhaled softly, puffing out his cheeks. 'Because I've seen this van before. Or one like it, anyhow.'

Caroline kept her voice calm. 'When?'

'That night. When the driver stopped for gas.'

'Man or woman?'

The boy hesitated. 'Woman. I'm pretty sure.'

Don't react, Caroline told herself. *Think of all the witnesses who get things wrong.* 'Is there some reason you remember her?'

Silently, the boy nodded. 'I remember she seemed upset.' His eyes narrowed with the effort of memory. 'I'm pretty sure it was the one in the van.'

Caroline tilted her head. 'Upset ...'

'Yeah. I always like to do a good job on the windows. But this one, she told me to stop, like she didn't have time, and her voice was real sharp.'

What did she look like? Caroline wanted to ask. She stopped herself. 'Could you recognize her from a picture?'

The boy turned to her. 'Is this important?'

Caroline picked up the remaining photographs. 'It could be. Yes.'

The boy scrutinized her another moment and took the

pictures from her hand, leaning back through the window into the light.

He shuffled the first picture, then another, then another. At the fourth one, he stopped.

'What is it?'

The boy's mouth closed, then opened again. 'That's her.'

Caroline's throat constricted. 'You're sure?'

'Yeah. I mean, she looks upset in this picture. Like she did that night.'

Caroline sat back in her seat. 'After that, did you see where she went?'

Her voice, she thought, sounded calm enough. But the boy looked at her with new suspicion. 'Will I have to testify or something?'

'I don't know. I hope not.'

Pausing, he gazed at the picture. 'Well, I don't know where she went, or what direction. But I'd have to say I remember her.'

In the shadows of the car, Caroline collected herself. 'If you wouldn't mind, I'd prefer that you not mention this to anyone. After all, it may be nothing.'

He looked relieved. 'No problem.'

'Thanks. I'll let you know what happens.'

'Sure.' He handed back the picture. 'Have a nice night, okay?'

Caroline placed the picture on the seat beside her. 'Okay.'

Slowly, he turned and walked to the gas station. It was a moment before Caroline started the car.

She drove past Mosher Trail, out of sight of the gas station, and stopped by the side of the road.

She sat in darkness, forcing herself to think. But nothing could dull the ache of guilt and memory, sickness and anger. She could not look at the photograph of Betty.

Chapter 14

When Caroline arrived at Masters Hill, there was a dim glow from the first-floor windows. The upper floors were dark.

The air was quiet, still. When Caroline stepped on the porch, her footsteps sounded hollow.

Softly, she knocked on the door.

Caroline heard a stirring inside, the rattle of a latch. The door opened slightly.

Betty peered at her through the crack. She looked startled.

'Caroline.'

Caroline watched her for a moment. 'Who else is home?'

'Just Larry.' Betty's voice was tight. 'What is it?'

'We need to talk.'

Betty hesitated, glancing over her shoulder. 'Larry's trying to sleep now. Today upset him terribly.'

'Come outside, then. We won't need him for this.'

Still Betty did not move; the tone of Caroline's voice seemed to stop her. Then, reluctant, she stepped out onto the porch.

Caroline walked away from the door. She heard Betty slowly follow her.

'Do you think,' Betty asked, 'that you can discredit this despicable woman?'

Caroline turned to her. 'Which one?'

In the half-light, Betty seemed to blink. Caroline felt a terrible calm come over her. 'Actually,' she said, 'I'm calling you as a witness tomorrow. I think that will help Brett more.'

Betty stiffened. 'Why?'

Caroline ignored this. 'When we discussed the possibility, you seemed concerned. So I thought it might help if we

442

went over a few questions.'

Betty became still again. 'What are they?'

Caroline moved toward her. When she stopped, their faces were two feet apart. Quietly, Caroline asked, 'Why have you been lying to me?'

Betty's eyes widened. 'Lying ...'

'You knew that Brett would take him to the lake that night. Because you listened on the upstairs telephone.' Caroline's voice was chill with withheld anger. 'By the way, I'd suggest not lying to me now. Or on the stand tomorrow. There's only so much nostalgia I can take.'

Betty took one step back, wordless.

'Open your mouth, Betty. And see if it can make a sound. Something like, "Yes, Caroline. I'm an eavesdropper."'

Betty did not move now. 'Caroline,' she said tautly, 'you don't know what you're doing.'

'Oh, I've known for years now.' Caroline's tone was quiet still. 'Did you listen to her, Betty?'

'Yes.' Betty stood straighter. 'Because I love her. I've loved her all these years you were away.'

Caroline felt her fists clench. 'What did you overhear, damn you? That he wanted her to go to California?'

'Yes.' Betty's voice rose in anger. 'And that he was in trouble over drugs –'

'And,' Caroline cut in, 'that there'd been a girl named Megan. You lied about that too, didn't you?'

Betty walked to the corner of the porch.

Caroline's voice became soft again. 'How long after that did you leave the house?'

In the darkness, Betty's profile was still.

Caroline moved closer. 'You left the house, damn it. Just tell me when.'

Slowly, Betty turned to Caroline. With something close to calm, she asked, 'How do you know that?'

'Because you stopped at the gas station,' Caroline paused. 'That wasn't very smart, Betty.'

Betty seemed to slump. She looked thin and tired;

Caroline had a stark, pitiless image of Betty as an old woman.

'I wasn't planning this,' Betty said at last. 'Any of it.'

The admission, so simply stated, drained the anger within Caroline. Suddenly, all she felt was a horror so deep that she wished to erase it. 'My God, Betty.' She heard the tremor in her own voice. 'My God.'

Betty's look became pleading. Tonelessly, she asked, 'So you understand now?'

'Understand?' Caroline stared at her. 'How can anyone understand that?'

Betty came toward her, then stopped abruptly, shock filling her eyes. 'That's what you think of me, Caroline? *That's* who you think I am?' Her voice was thick. 'A woman so deranged she'd kill Brett's boyfriend, then let *her* be blamed for it?'

Caroline could only stare at her.

Betty grasped her collar. 'You're the one who's sick, Caroline – poisoned with guilt and hatred and years of being alone –'

With an awful deliberation, Caroline slapped her sister across her face.

There was a sharp crack; Betty's muffled shriek. Caroline felt a numbness in her wrist, tears in her eyes. Betty stared at her, hand pressed to her cheek.

In a flat voice, Caroline said, 'What were you doing there?'

Betty turned from her. After a time, she murmured, 'I was coming back from Father's fishing camp.'

'Why?'

Betty touched her eyes. 'Because he was so upset. He wanted to be alone.'

Caroline felt a tightness in her chest. She raised a hand, as if to steady herself. 'You told him.'

'Yes.' Betty's expression mingled shame with pride. 'Larry was gone, Caroline. I needed to talk to someone.'

Caroline felt herself shiver. It was a moment before she

could speak. 'Do you have any idea,' she asked, 'what you may have done? *Again?*'

Betty folded her arms, as if against the cold. 'Father and I couldn't tell anyone. If the police had known that Brett and James had been fighting over Megan ...'

She looked away.

Caroline felt a terrible rush of comprehension. 'You think Brett killed him. That you protected her by lying ...'

Betty looked at her steadily now. But she would not, could not, answer.

'What fools we are.' Pausing, Caroline shook her head. 'Brett didn't kill anyone.'

Betty swallowed. 'Who, then?'

Caroline felt a wave of nausea. 'My God, Betty. Have you forgotten who it was that taught us to fillet a fish?'

In the silence, Betty's eyes shut.

'Where is he?' Caroline demanded.

'At his fishing camp.' When Betty opened her eyes, her voice was shaking. 'I'll go with you. It's better if we talk to him together.'

Caroline made herself stand straight again. 'No,' she answered softly. 'This is mine to do. After all, I *am* Brett's mother.'

In the wind and rain, the roiling sea at her back, Caroline had slowly crossed the beach.

She was numb; in her mind, David fought the storm, not knowing the thing that – in the guilt of her betrayal – Caroline could not bring herself to tell him. Mechanically, she went to the boathouse for her suitcase.

The boathouse was stark, empty. She looked vainly about for any sign of him; all that was left were two paperbacks he had forgotten. Unlatching her suitcase, she tucked them in a corner. She would save them for him or, if he wrote to her, send them back.

And then the anguish came over her again – a half hour ago they had faced each other in his room, and now he was gone, and all she had of him was an untold secret.

Turning, she stepped outside and shut the door softly behind her.

Her father's house was dark. She climbed the stairs from the beach, knowing only that she could not tell him that David was gone. And then, in her misery, Caroline saw how she must buy her lover time.

She opened the door and walked silently through the house.

Her father was in the night-shadowed porch. As she stood in the doorway, she saw him pacing distractedly, now and then gazing out to sea.

'Hello, Father.'

He started. 'Caroline,' he said, and then hesitancy entered his voice, and Caroline knew for certain that her father had betrayed them. 'Where have you been?' he asked.

'Boston. You knew that.'

'But you're drenched.'

Caroline did not answer. She fought the impulse to scream at him, to tell him what he had done. But for David's sake, she could not.

Drawing herself up, she said in a calm voice, 'I came back to tell you something.'

In the dim light, she saw the wariness in his deep-set eyes and knew what he expected – that she had come to say she was in love with David and was going away with him. Cautiously, he asked, 'What is it?'

'I'm pregnant, Father.'

'Pregnant?' His voice was hollow, appalled. 'Are you quite sure?'

'Yes. That's why I went to Boston. To see my doctor.'

Her voice sounded civil, Caroline thought, if unapologetic. But her father was quite still; what he knew, and how he felt, kept him from coming close to her. 'You can't have this baby, Caroline.' His tone was soft now. 'Surely that must be clear.'

Caroline raised her hand. 'What I'm going to do, Father,

is go to bed. In the morning, after I've thought more, I'll go see Scott. We're the ones who must decide.'

Her father seemed to blanch. With a satisfaction born of hatred, Caroline saw the terrible emotion cross his face – the knowledge that he had turned in the father of his daughter's child, that David would go to prison. And then, most contemptible of all, Caroline read the hope that she would never know who had betrayed them.

'Caroline.' His voice was rough. 'We must talk about this. Now.'

'I'm sorry, Father. Not now. I seem to be more tired these days.'

'But you're my daughter ...'

'I know,' Caroline said softly. And then, for David's sake, she crossed the room and kissed her father on the cheek. 'I know.'

She could not sleep that night. The windows of her bedroom rattled with waves of rain and howling wind; her mind fought back terrified imaginings, willed David through the storm. The life that he had left inside her seemed barely real.

In the morning, drawn and nauseous, Caroline forced herself to dress.

Her stomach was still flat, she saw. But her body had the first swelling of water retained, and she found that she no longer liked coffee. That, and the sickness, were the small intimations of this living thing that only her sister had craved.

Larry and Betty were in the kitchen. From their expressions – the edgy wariness they had lately assumed for meetings between Channing and the new and unpredictable Caroline – she surmised that Channing had told them nothing.

Yes, she thought, that would be like him. An abortion, then Harvard, and life goes on as it was. With no one but the two of them, and David, ever knowing the truth.

Larry gave her a quizzical smile, Betty a more cautious one. 'How are you?' Larry asked.

But it was Betty whom Caroline looked at. 'Pregnant,' she said.

Betty's mouth fell open. Almost conversationally, Caroline said, 'If you're not feeling nauseous, Betty, it's probably a false alarm. Take it from me.'

Betty half stood. Ignoring this, Caroline walked past them and out into the rear yard.

The morning was sparkling, with that crisp purity of wind and sky that follows a fierce storm. Perfect for sailing, Caroline thought.

Her father was staring at the empty mooring.

Quiet, Caroline came up behind him. 'Oh, yes,' she said. 'David's gone.'

He turned to her: it was a moment before the shock suffused his face. 'Last night,' she said in a tight voice, 'was the hardest thing I'd ever done. But that's almost over for me now. Because this is the last time you and I are ever speaking.'

'Caroline.' He reached out for her, anguish in his face. 'Please ...'

'You made my decision for me. I shouldn't be with David, so you decided to have him sent to jail, letting me think it was just bad luck.' She paused, breathing hard now. 'Well, you've lost me now. And you know the part I hate most? You don't feel sorry for David. You feel sorry for you....'

'Caroline.' Channing drew his hands back, fought for dignity. 'You don't know what it is to love a child.'

'No. But I know the difference between love and ownership.' Caroline fought to control her temper; suddenly what she felt was deeper, and surer, than anger. 'But if you love me, Father, please don't hope for forgiveness. Hope, for my sake, that David Stern is still alive.'

She turned and left him there.

That fall, she stayed alone on the Vineyard.

Her father had given up. She felt him, alone in New Hampshire, waiting out her anger and disaffection. But what he would have known were they still speaking was that Caroline no longer cared.

A life was growing inside her.

Part of this, Caroline admitted to herself with ruthless honesty, was deeply irrational – that the life was part of David, who might already be lost. Were he here, to end this baby might have been possible; perhaps to bear his child was a deep, even twisted, act of anger and revenge. But she could not live with the thought of having killed him and then his child as well.

For that was the crux of it. Caroline had no rules for what other women must do; her rule for society was that women must decide. But she was too unsparing with herself to deny that the decision was to take, or not take, a life. For David, for the child, and, most of all, for herself, Caroline could not do this.

And so, by default, the child remained inside her. Until the choice was only whether to keep it or give it away.

Even as she hoped against hope to hear from David, Caroline began, at last, to imagine a future on her own.

She knew what she would do without the child – move as far from New Hampshire as was possible, put herself through law school, stand on her own. Become the kind of lawyer that Caroline Masters – and no one else – would come to believe she should be. But as hard as it was to imagine life with this baby, it was as hard to imagine the strangers who would become its parents; in that bleak winter on the Vineyard, Caroline had far too much time to consider what a parent might do to a child.

One morning, with a crisp frost on the ground, Larry appeared at the door.

He gave her a small, embarrassed smile. 'I've come to visit you.'

To her surprise, Caroline realized she was glad to see him. She felt grateful that her bitterness had not yet tarnished Larry.

449

'Come on in,' she said. 'These days, I don't have too much company. None, in fact.'

He shot a wry glance at her stomach. 'One,' he amended. 'But I guess he – or she – isn't talking yet.'

Caroline smiled. 'No. But she's walking a little.'

Impulsively, Larry stepped forward and put his arms around her. 'I'm glad to see you, Caro. No one quite knows what to do.'

She pressed her face against his shoulder. 'I don't, either,' she murmured. 'Not about this baby.'

For a while, she just let him hold her. It was strange, she thought, that this made her feel like crying.

'Caro,' he said softly. 'I'm so sorry.'

'I know. I know....'

At last, she led him to the porch, still holding his hand. They sat together on the couch. The seascape before them was stark and gray, and smudges of frost remained on the grass. Caroline hugged herself.

'Have you ever heard from him?' Larry asked.

Caroline shook her head. 'Either he's dead or he's unwilling to forgive me. I hope it's the last.'

Larry fell silent. 'Are you thinking of keeping it?' he said after a time.

'I don't know. I shouldn't, really. But if I don't, it's like throwing a life into the lottery. How do I know who this baby gets?' She turned to him. 'It's not enough that someone wants a child. Look how much my father wanted me.'

Larry looked away, as if gathering himself. 'I don't know how else to say this, Caroline, but to say it. I want you to think about something.'

All at once, Caroline knew why he had come. Coldly, she said, 'What is it?'

Larry could not face her now. 'We'll never have a baby, Caro. The problem's not just me, it turns out. It's Betty too....'

Caroline stood abruptly. 'Never. It's better for our relationship, Larry, if I just pretend to be speechless. But I can't believe that you – the only one I still care about – would come to me for *this*.' Her voice rose. 'Really, what fucking vultures all of you are. But *you* ...'

Larry looked at her now. Quietly, he said, 'Who else could ask you, Caroline? And who else would you want for this baby's father?'

Caroline drew a breath, staring at him. 'You may hate Betty,' Larry went on, 'until the day you die. Although I've got to tell you, for her sake, that she's heartsick and ashamed. But I'm not asking this for her sake. I'm asking for the baby's sake, and mine....'

'This baby thing was Betty's idea, remember?'

'Was,' Larry retorted. 'Until I knew we couldn't have one. And knew you were.' He walked over to Caroline, clasped both her shoulders, and looked into her face. 'Whatever you may think of her, Betty will love this child. And I'll be there to make sure everything goes right. I'll be the father, Caroline. Would you rather trust a stranger?'

Caroline turned from him, walked back to the couch. 'This is just too much,' she said.

Silent, Larry watched her.

Caroline sat with her elbows on her knees, face cradled in both hands, staring at the brick floor. 'It's not just Betty,' she said at last. 'It's my father.'

'Your father's not adopting anyone.'

Caroline looked fiercely up at him. 'My father adopts *lives*. If you're not careful, yours will be one of them.' Her voice turned slow and cold. 'I will not have this child living the life my father sets for her. If it just were you, Larry, this might be possible. But I look at all of you, and I don't believe it *is* possible.'

Larry sat beside her. Finally, he said, 'What would you want from me?'

My God, Caroline thought; for a moment, she had imagined this baby with Larry – with her own home and a father who could separate her life from his. 'What I would want,' she said in a low voice, 'is for you to live away from him – different town, different state. So that he never, ever runs anyone's life again.'

Larry gazed out at the water. 'I can do that,' he said at last. 'One way or another.'

Slowly, Caroline turned to him. To her own surprise, she said, 'Then I'll think about it. Now, please, leave me alone.'

Two days after the baby was born, Larry came to the hospital.

He was alone; Caroline had not had to ask this. With bemusement and wonder, he looked at the baby she held.

'God,' he said. 'All that hair. I didn't know babies came with hair.

'Neither did I.'

Looking down, Caroline studied the little girl's face. It was red, still swollen from birth, but she had the most remarkable eyes. Squinting, the baby stretched an arm, as if reaching out for her. It was strange, Caroline thought, how easy it was for a mother to impose meaning on a baby's simplest reflexes.

'Would you like to hold her?' she asked Larry.

Awkwardly, Larry reached out. Cradling the baby in both hands, Caroline slid her into his arms.

He sat back in the visitor's chair, smiling into the baby's unseeing eyes, until the image of that moment imprinted itself in Caroline's mind, to remain forever – sun streaming through the hospital window, lighting the baby's face and hair as Larry rested his cheek against hers. 'She smells good,' Larry murmured. 'New.'

'I know.'

Larry sat there, holding the baby, until Caroline saw that he could not bring himself to do what must be done. Softly, she said, 'I'm all packed, Larry. There's nothing more for me to do here.'

Slowly, he looked up at her. 'Okay, then.'

Caroline stood. 'I'll carry her.'

'You're all right to do that?'

'Uh-huh.'

For the last time, Caroline took the baby in her arms. She kissed her head and then, because she could not help herself, smelled her skin again.

The first few steps were strange; Caroline still felt wounded, and her stomach seemed a shapeless flap of skin. In time, she supposed, she would be herself again.

As they walked through the corridor, Larry took her arm.

The nurse at the reception desk smiled at them. 'Going home?'

Caroline nodded. 'Going home.'

The nurse brought out a form to sign. Passing the baby to Larry, Caroline could not look at either one of them.

Wordless, she signed the papers.

The nurse patted her hand. 'Enjoy her,' she said.

'Oh,' Caroline said, 'I'm sure I will.' Turning, she saw that, now, Larry could not look at her.

Outside the Vineyard Hospital, it was a clear, cool April day. Caroline stopped for a moment, blinking in the light.

'My car's over here,' Larry said.

They walked there. Betty was waiting across the sound, in Woods Hole, Caroline knew; Larry would drive the baby to the ferry, and within two hours, the three of them would be together.

But Larry did not know how to leave.

'I don't want to hear from you,' Caroline said. 'I don't want to know about any of you. Just, please, take good care of her.'

Baby in his arms, Larry looked at her steadily. 'We will,' he said. '*I* will.'

There was a catch in Caroline's throat. Softly, she asked, 'What will you name her?'

'I don't know yet.' He tried to smile. 'To me, she looks like Baby Allen.'

Caroline gazed at the baby in his arms. At that instant, the little girl opened her eyes.

'To me,' Caroline said, 'she looks like my mother.'

Slowly, Larry nodded. 'Can I give you a ride?' he asked.

'No. Thanks. I'll call a cab.'

With the baby in his arms, Larry came to Caroline and kissed her on the forehead. She could feel the child's small body graze her arm.

'Go, *now*,' she said.

Without answering, Larry put the baby in the car and got inside. As they left, Caroline turned away.

Out of kindness and anger and self-preservation, Caroline did what she thought a birth mother should do. She moved to California, entered law school. She never saw her daughter again.

She had made her own life, and Brett had paid for it.

PART SEVEN

The Final Judgement

Chapter 1

For the first time in twenty-three years, Caroline approached the wooden door of her father's rustic fishing camp, his retreat from the world.

In the cool, still darkness, her childhood came back to her – the soughing of pine boughs in a fitful wind; camping beneath a starfilled sky; eating their catch by the light of a flame in the old stone fireplace. She still knew how the inside would look to her.

Heart pounding, she knocked on the door.

There was silence. And then, with an old man's impatience, her father jerked the latch.

'Caroline.'

He seemed to blink a little, perhaps with surprise, perhaps to adjust his eyes to the light. He wore a robe and slippers; seeing her, he drew himself up, an attempt at dignity. He seemed unsure of whether to ask her in.

'I was sleeping,' he said. 'As you can see.'

Caroline did not answer. Channing hesitated for a moment and then, with a look that mingled resolve and reticence, opened the door.

The living room was not quite as she remembered it. The familiar things remained – the fly rods, the shelf of books on fishing and nature, the pastoral painting of a lake in England – and the sense of order was the same. What startled her was the only photograph, placed carefully on the bookshelf: Caroline at perhaps sixteen, head raised in laughter, hair forming a windblown wave. Caroline recalled the moment precisely: she had just caught a trout and thrown it back. But what she had not seen then was that, captured in that random instant, she looked uncannily like her mother. Uncannily like Brett.

Caroline stared at it.

Her father's eyes followed her. 'I had little else of you,' he said.

Slowly, Caroline turned to him. 'Only Brett,' she answered. 'And the knife.'

He looked pale, she thought. Then he moved his shoulders, steadying himself. 'Yes,' he said at last. 'I could never bring myself to throw it out.'

For the briefest moment, he glanced to his side; on a wooden standing desk, Caroline saw a gray revolver. Her heart still thudded in her chest.

'You followed the shore,' she said in a low voice. 'Just as you described for me.'

With silent dignity, Channing Masters raised his head and looked into Caroline's eyes. His own gaze did not waver.

In that moment, Caroline felt the crushing weight of what she had recoiled from accepting. Sickness rose to her throat. She could not finish. His expression, raw and wounded as he looked at her, was the mirror of her own horror.

'You lost my mother.' Her voice was slow, unsteady. 'And then you lost me. To other men, you thought. You couldn't let another man take Brett –'

'Damn you, Caroline.' Her father's face hardened. 'It's all about that summer for you, isn't it – an evil and possessive man doing in young Lochinvar. I didn't mean for your David to do what he did, though I was willing to accept the consequences as if I had. But don't confuse your trauma with this one, or *that* boy with this one. James Case was narcissistic, manipulative, bent on involving Brett with drugs –'

'So you decided to save her. Just as you saved me.'

'Don't judge me,' her father snapped. 'Just where were *you*, Caroline, when Brett was growing up? Following your own ambitions in California, ignoring your daughter and your family. You were even less to Brett than Nicole was to you.' Channing made himself stand straighter. 'That night, I didn't know what I would do. I knew only that this involvement with James must end, and that no one else could end it – not Betty, and surely not Larry. And so I took the knife and gun, and when I saw them, I saw what I must do.'

His eyes were distant, as if that first sighting were more vivid than this moment. His voice filled with sadness and anger. 'I saw her drinking with him, smoking marijuana, throwing herself away. This beautiful girl, doing gutter things with her body, while this gutter boy invited her to share his gutter life –'

'My God.' A tremor ran through her words. 'Do you know what you've done to her? You are truly insane.'

Channing's face became closed, implacable. 'The doctor gives me a year to live, Caroline. Perhaps two.' He paused. 'There's a certain freedom in that, I find. A certain clarity of thought and purpose. And a distinct lack of sentiment.

'My life – this life we had – is almost at an end. All that remains of it is Brett. Watching from those bushes, I saw that, with what little life was left to me, I might save the rest of hers.'

Caroline felt something in his manner change her. He was calm now, almost detached; she would force herself to be no less. A stillness of heart and mind came over her.

Softly, Caroline said, 'Then tell me what happened. Because, it seems, saving Brett has fallen to me at last.'

The night was dark, shadowed; listening to his sparing words, recalling Brett's passionate ones, Caroline could see it clearly now.

Kneeling behind the bushes, her father watched them. Two silhouettes in the moonlight: the man's head between her legs, the silver-black outline of the woman, softly crying out.

Was that how it had been, he wondered – Nicole and Paul; Caroline and her lover? Part of him wished to look away. But he could not stop watching. The night felt cold to him; the old man's joints ached.

In the moonlight, Brett mounted James.

She moved with a rhythmic frenzy. Beneath her, the man's body became still.

Brett stared down at him. Clumsily, she disengaged her pelvis. And then, to her grandfather's revulsion, knelt to kiss James on the face.

Perhaps it was seeing her at that moment – slavish and lost – that decided him.

Slowly, he took the revolver from his belt.

The air was cool on his face. His fingers felt arthritic, stublike in the leather gloves. The sharp pain in his knees brought tears to his eyes.

Awkwardly, Brett stood, naked against the blackness of the lake.

She paused for a moment. Then, impulsively, she ran toward the water. Channing heard the first splash, her feet and ankles in the shallows, then the awkward slap as she hit the surface of the lake.

Painfully, Channing stood.

He was frightened for her; she seemed too impaired to swim. And then he saw the next, long strokes, as they fell into the rhythm he had taught her, taking her to the platform where they once had sunned themselves.

She had left the two of them alone.

Slowly, Channing put the revolver in his belt.

From the water, the sound of Brett's swimming stopped. There was a splash, the skim of water on her skin as she climbed onto the platform. Even with the lake as a backdrop, Channing could barely see her now – a slightly deeper shadow amidst a moonlit square of boards and nails.

Stiffly, Channing stepped from behind the bushes.

The boy lay on the blanket, arms flung to the sides, like a soldier who had died where he had fallen. Channing's feet were silent in the grass.

Kneeling on the blanket, Channing winced. The only sounds were the hollow crack of cartilage and bone, then the susurrus, barely heard, of James's breathing.

Channing looked into his face.

James's skin was smooth, his lips, slightly parted, were

460

regular and full. As he slept, his look of arrogance slept as well.

But when he awoke, Channing knew, he would envelop Brett in his selfishness and need.

In an act of will, Channing took from its sheath the knife that Caroline had given him.

For a moment, Channing paused, knife held over the boy's sleeping face. In the back of his mind, Channing heard the crickets, felt Brett a hundred feet away.

He breathed in once, closing his eyes. And then, knife angled above James's bare neck, he felt the trembling hesitation of his hand....

Now.

He slashed downward. Numb with age, halt with indecision, his hand betrayed him.

James's eyes flew open. A thin ribbon of blood appeared in a shallow wound.

My God, my God.

'No,' James gasped.

Channing's gloves clasped his throat. Beneath him, James's naked body struggled to free itself from sleep and shock and horror. Channing's heart raced.

His second stroke was swift and sure.

With sickening suddenness, Channing felt the warm spurt of blood on his face and shirt, saw James's eyes, staring up at his in terror and recognition.

Another spurt of blood half blinded him. With a spastic twitch, James reached for Channing's arm.

Channing drove the knife into his heart.

The arm fell back. The first terrible gurgling issued from James's throat.

Channing recoiled in horror.

'James ...'

Brett, calling across the water. Reeling, Channing stood.

On the blanket below him, James writhed in shock and agony. The sound was of someone drowning.

'James ...'

Behind him, Channing heard the splash of Brett's panicky dive.

Throat filled with bile and revulsion, Channing stumbled into the darkness before Brett could see who he was, the thing that he had done.

Chapter 2

'Brett,' Caroline said quietly. 'Yes, there was that, wasn't there.'

In the half-light of his old lamp, Channing's face seemed bloodless; his voice was ashen now. 'I knew it would be terrible for her, as that moment was for me. But it was done. I never thought that she'd be blamed for it. The fingerprints, the mouth-to-mouth, the blood spatter. Taking the knife and wallet. How could I have imagined all those things?' He paused. 'I couldn't even imagine how it would be to kill a man like that.'

Caroline fought back pity and repugnance. 'Could you imagine,' she asked coldly, 'how it is to be charged with a murder you didn't commit?'

Channing turned from the look on Caroline's face. 'I didn't want her to know. And, yes, I did not want to have our family – me – associated with this boy's death.' He paused, voice quiet with shame. 'I thought, knowing she was innocent, that they never would indict her. And when they did, that it would never stand. As to that, at least, I was right.'

Caroline shook her head, numb. 'What perversity made you call *me*?'

Channing seemed to reach within himself. 'Because I knew you'd feel responsible for her. After all, you'd chosen to have her, then to leave her. And because, even from a distance, I could see how gifted you were.' He turned to her again. 'I know how this will sound to you – the way saying it sounds to me. But through all the misery of the last four days, I found a certain pleasure in watching you.' His voice grew softer yet. 'You're a remarkable lawyer, Caroline. But then I always knew you would be.'

Caroline felt the words in the pit of her stomach. 'Then

463

you must have thought I'd find you out. Perhaps hoped I would.'

He shook his head, and then a rueful pride crept into his voice. 'I knew that it was possible. But I never thought you'd recall that knife; I thought I was the only one who remembered your gift, like yesterday.' There was life in his eyes now. 'I believed that you had put everything about those years, and our life together, out of your mind. That all you wished to remember was the last summer.'

For a moment, Caroline could not speak. But when she did, her voice was chill. 'Wasn't part of the pleasure to match wits with me, Father? To re-enact the murder for me and wait to see if I was apt enough to respond to your instruction?'

Channing flushed. 'How can you think that? What I told you was for Brett's sake. She was my responsibility....'

'For *Brett's* sake.' Caroline's voice cracked with anger. 'I don't know how to describe what you've put her through.'

Channing stared at her. Then he turned and went to his bedroom.

Even before he returned, Caroline braced herself.

Inside the clear plastic bag he held was a bloodstained shirt and pants. Taped to it was a letter.

In Caroline's silence, he handed her the bag. 'Read it,' he said.

Caroline stared through the plastic. The spurts of blood, dried thickly on the blue work shirt, were as she knew they must be.

'Read it,' he repeated roughly.

Caroline laid down the bag. Fumbling, she opened the envelope.

The letter was addressed to her.

Swallowing, she made herself read. The voice, she thought, could be no one else's.

The prose was flat, unemotional. In persuasive detail, with little feeling, it explained how he had killed James Case. The letter gave his reasons, but asked no sympathy. Its only excuses were for Brett.

464

Silent, Caroline looked up at him.

'The original is in my safe-deposit box,' he said. 'In case I was suddenly taken.'

'And if you weren't ...?' She let the question die there.

Her father stood taller. 'Then I was prepared to go to Jackson – to go, in fact, if you failed at this hearing. But it seemed you were on the verge of discrediting that wretched Megan.'

'And look at how you let Brett suffer, waiting.'

'Three weeks isn't that long to live with something.' Channing's face was stoic now. 'I know. I've lived with that last summer for twenty-three years.'

Caroline stared at him. 'Lived with *what* ...?'

Her father paused. And then, with quiet simplicity, he said, 'Your David is dead, Caroline.'

Caroline felt herself step backward, heart pounding like an anvil in her chest. 'How can you know that?'

'He was lost on the sound that night.' Her father paused, forcing himself to look at her. 'They found the catboat near Tarpaulin Cove, broken to pieces on the rocks.'

Caroline folded her arms, bent her head. She rocked on her heels, back and forth, to keep herself from writhing. 'You knew.' Her voice was choked. 'All along, you *knew*....'

Channing touched his forehead. 'For three days, Caroline, I hoped – even prayed – that he had somehow gotten through it. I never meant for that to happen.' Slowly, he shook his head, as if reliving the moment of knowledge. 'And then the Coast Guard called.

'The boat was registered to me, you see. They didn't associate it with David. So I simply told them the boat had slipped its moorings....'

'Why?'

'To keep you from knowing.' Channing's face was etched with pain. Softly, he finished, 'I didn't want to lose you, Caroline.'

Helpless, Caroline turned from him. It was as if she could not breathe.

'You know everything now.' Her father's voice was lifeless. 'I'll come to Jackson tomorrow. Please go.'

In front of her, Caroline saw the books, the picture of a laughing girl, the gun. Through an act of will, she faced her father again.

His face was a ghost of what it once had been. Only his eyes, suddenly moist, remained alive to her.

'Caroline ...,' he tried, and for that moment she remembered all there was between them: the hikes, long days on the lake, the death of her mother, talks across the dinner table, their plans for her future, the lawyer she would be. The loss of David. The ways in which, for all the years since and against her will, he still defined who Caroline Masters was.

Whatever he had meant to say, it seemed that he could not.

'You came home again, Caroline. At last, and for whatever reason.' His voice became thick. 'Now, please, leave me here.'

Caroline steeled herself. For a last moment, she looked into his face. And then, unable to answer, nodded.

Blindly, she walked past him, into the night.

She stopped there, a few feet from his door, and then the effort of composure overtook her.

Caroline held her head up. In deep breaths, she inhaled the pine-scented air.

Still she did not leave. She stood there, listening. The night was cool and quiet.

Through the half-open door, Caroline heard a hollow pop.

Her eyes shut. In the aching, awful silence, she could not bring herself to move.

But there was no one else. As she had said to Betty, this was hers to do.

Slowly, Caroline turned and walked back through the door.

She stopped, stiff and silent. No sound came from her throat.

466

Her father had been kind, she saw. His face and head were intact; the wound, fresh blood still spreading, had been to the heart.

The gun lay by his hand, near the letter and the bag of clothes. His eyes stared up at her, unseeing. They would never see her again.

Caroline knelt, and closed them.

As she did this, she looked into his face. Within moments, she knew, the humanity would leave him, and his body would have the waxen otherness of death. But there was color in his face yet, and his skin was still warm.

Slowly, she removed her hand.

She stayed one more moment, the beating of a heart. And then she stood, turning away, and went to call Jackson. She never looked at her father again.

Chapter 3

A few yards from her, the headlights stopped. The motor cut off. A car door slammed, and then Caroline heard the crunch of footsteps on gravel.

In the darkness, Jackson stood in front of her. There was something unready about him, as if he was still startled from sleep. But his eyes were quite clear.

'He's in there,' Caroline said.

Jackson did not move. Silent, he watched her face.

'Please,' she told him. 'Just take care of this for me. I can't do it, anymore.'

But Jackson did not leave her; perhaps he knew that some part of her did not wish him to leave. He took both her wrists, and asked, 'What has all this been about?'

'Too many things.' Caroline paused, then looked into his face. 'Brett's my daughter, Jackson.'

His eyes were still. Softly, he murmured, 'Sweet Jesus Christ.'

He did not let go of her wrists.

When the EMTs came, the two of them had not moved. Behind the ambulance was the flashing light of a police car.

All at once, Caroline thought of Brett. 'Go ahead,' she told him. 'You'll need to see what he left. Before they screw it up.'

He looked at her, understanding now, and slowly nodded.

Motionless, Caroline heard him enter the cabin. Stood there as the EMTs and police, barely noticing her, rushed past in the driveway.

Below the cabin, she remembered, was a bench that faced the lake.

Taking the steps her father had built, Caroline went

there. She sat gazing at the lake, a sheet of glass on the windless night.

There was little sound, only voices from the cabin, sometimes Jackson's. Caroline wished that she could feel something. But all she felt was emptiness, her emotions at bay.

He was dead, she told herself, and Brett was free. Why did she feel nothing?

It was a moment before she heard Jackson Watts behind her. 'I've called the state police,' he said. 'I'm getting you out of here. They can do the rest.'

She did not look up. 'There are others to call,' she answered. 'Betty ...'

'She can wait.'

Caroline did not argue.

The drive to Jackson's fishing camp was perhaps ten minutes. Caroline sat in the passenger seat; Jackson glanced over from time to time, but said nothing. Entering his cabin, Caroline saw the fireplace, registered that they had once made love here. It seemed years ago.

Jackson led her to the screened porch. She sat on a couch; through a clearing in the trees, the lake was a dark oval. Caroline stared at it, unseeing.

'Do you want something?' he asked.

'No. Thank you.'

Sitting in a corner of the couch, Jackson did not touch her. The one sensation Caroline had was of her separateness.

'You can talk to me,' he said at last. 'Or you can go on the way I think you must have, for years.'

Caroline did not look at him; even speaking was an effort. 'I'm not sure I know how,' she answered. 'I don't even know where to start.'

'Anywhere, Caroline. The first thing that comes to you.'

She was too weary for defenses; in silent answer, against her will, Caroline's mind broke free. The first startling image that came to her – black hair swirling in the water – constricted her chest.

'My mother,' she heard herself say, and then she could not finish.

Caroline felt his arms around her. 'Tell me.'

In a monotone, before she could stop to think, Caroline told him everything.

Her mother, and how she had died. Falling in love with David. Her sister's betrayal, and then her father's. How Brett had come to be born, and given up. Why Caroline had returned.

And then, because he must know, the events of the last three weeks. The missing knife. Breaking into Megan's apartment. The pattern, half fact and half intuition, through which she had divined her father's guilt. Their last confrontation. The moment, twenty-three years late, when she learned that David was dead.

When she had finished, Caroline could not look at him.

'Do you know what Father told me?' she asked dully. 'That he was afraid of losing me.'

She felt Jackson's arms close tighter. 'Well,' he said at last, 'you didn't lose me. Just misplaced me for a while.'

Caroline felt something move inside her. She turned to him, looking into his worn, kind face, and then quite suddenly, helpless to prevent this, she began crying, convulsively and uncontrollably, as she never had since the night that David had vanished.

Jackson simply held her.

The first light broke on the lake.

Exhausted, Caroline lay on the couch in Jackson's arms. It was, she thought, cruelly like a normal day.

'What are you thinking?' she asked.

He was quiet for a moment. 'That you were right not to tell me, in a way. I could never have understood, then.'

'And now?'

'I think so, yes.'

If only, Caroline thought, she could stay here with him. And then the image of her father came to her again.

As if knowing this, Jackson said, 'We have things to do this morning. Starting with Fred Towle, who's expecting us in court.'

Through her weariness, Caroline felt the lawyer part of her stir again. She sat up. 'How should we handle that?'

'I will.' Jackson slid away, facing her. 'I'll tell Fred that your father's dead. And that I'm dismissing the case without prejudice....'

'Without prejudice?'

'It's all I can do, Caroline. Until we've had an autopsy and completed our inquiry. I won't tell Fred or the media what's happened until you and I have worked out what to say. But I'll make sure Brett's kicked loose this morning.' Jackson paused, and then finished evenly. 'Your job is to explain all this to her. At least as much as you care to.'

Silent, Caroline nodded.

Jackson watched her. Then, quietly, he asked, 'Does Brett think that she's their daughter?'

Caroline looked away. 'Yes.'

Walking to the edge of the porch, he stood there, gazing at the lake, hands in his pockets. 'Do you mean to tell her the truth?'

Somewhere in her subconscious, Caroline realized, she had asked this of herself. 'I don't know, Jackson. I'm in no shape to do that now. Or even to decide about it.'

Jackson turned to her, studying her face. 'But our world goes on, doesn't it? Perhaps today, that's a mercy.'

Caroline thought of Betty. For a moment, she felt too weary to stand.

Slowly, she walked to Jackson's telephone, to tell Betty that their father was dead.

Chapter 4

Caroline's car was still at her father's camp. Jackson made telephone calls, arranged for its release; when he dropped her there, the yellow tape marking the scene had been cut at the head of the driveway, and a trooper was waiting. Her father's body was gone; for Caroline, the false cheer of morning had a bleak, pitiless quality.

She turned to Jackson. 'Thank you.'

He nodded but did not touch her. They were professionals once more.

'Call me,' he said. 'After you've seen Brett. Among other things, we'll need to work on a statement.'

'Sure.'

She sounded all right, Caroline thought, and she would need to be. But watching Jackson leave, she felt alone.

She walked to her car, got in. Sat there, gazing through the windshield at her father's cabin. And then she remembered the photographs.

They were still on the car seat. Numb, she looked at them again, the faces she had asked Joe Lemieux to capture as they entered the courthouse.

Megan. Betty. Larry. Her father ...

He was climbing the courthouse steps, stiff-gaited, refusing to look down. Gaze straight ahead, the last effort of an old man's dignity.

Caroline's eyes filled with tears again.

Brett, she knew, should never see these. Before she started the car, Caroline placed the photographs beneath the seat.

When the woman trooper brought her to the booking area, Brett looked stunned. Her first steps toward Caroline were tentative.

For a moment, Caroline could not speak. The reality had hit her; the young woman in front of her, David's daughter, had been given back her life.

'It's over,' Caroline said. 'You're free.'

At Brett's first, uncertain smile, Caroline looked away. 'What happened?' Brett asked.

Caroline took her hand. 'Let's go outside.'

As they left, Brett looked over her shoulder. In the sunlight, the large brick building appeared bland, even benign. But its shadow, Caroline suspected, would never quite leave either of them.

Brett turned back to her. 'How did you do this?' she asked.

Silent, Caroline walked ahead of her, and sat on the grass. Brett stopped, looking down at her; Caroline could see her own expression register in the girl's green eyes. She knelt, still watching Caroline.

Caroline drew a breath. 'Your grandfather is dead. He shot himself.'

Brett's face seemed to twitch. And then it fixed in a queer, hurt look, the struggle to absorb and understand. 'James ...'

'Yes. Father killed him.'

It was a day, Caroline thought, for tears.

When Brett's came, they were silent. Even as they ran down her face, her eyes remained on Caroline, as if searching for a reason.

It's been too much, Caroline thought. She took Brett's hands in hers. And to her surprise, Brett asked, 'Tell me how it happened.'

Caroline considered her, and then, without emphasis or inflection, told her as much as seemed right.

'He wouldn't have left you here,' she finished. 'But he couldn't face you, either.'

Brett winced; Caroline imagined her remembering the moment she found James dying. A moment now much farther from healing, or even comprehension.

As if aware of this, Brett's thoughts flickered to Caroline. 'You found Grandfather.'

'Yes.'

'My God ...'

'I'm all right.' Caroline paused, correcting herself. 'No. I'm not all right. But I wanted to tell you myself.'

The answer seemed to push Brett's thoughts back to herself. Where, Caroline thought, they should be. She did not want this girl's compassion, much less when it was not for the truth. It was enough that Caroline was here.

Arms folded, Brett stared at the grass between them. 'I loved Grandfather,' she said at last. Beneath the pain in her voice, Caroline heard the fear of something too enormous to bear. 'I'm sorry ... I don't know what to do. About him, or any of this.'

Caroline felt the words pierce her. It was a while before she spoke. 'Some things – terrible things – are like that. There's no lesson to be learned, no explanation that will help. Sometimes no explanation, period. In the end, all you're left with is yourself. And, if you're lucky, the understanding of a friend or two.'

Tears filled Brett's eyes again. 'You're talking about you, too.'

Caroline hesitated, and then she nodded. 'I'm not even sure when I'll next sleep through the night. But I've been here before, so I know the way back. Perhaps I can help.'

Brett reached out for Caroline's hands again; her fingers, curled in her mother's, felt warm. 'Can we stay here?' she said at last. 'I don't want to see them yet. Or anyone.'

Caroline looked at her, filling with a silent ache. David is dead, she wanted to tell her, your father is dead. But she could not. At least for now, for better or for worse, Brett had a father, the one whom Caroline had given her. Caroline did not know how to replace him with a memory that was hers alone.

'I'll stay with you,' she answered. 'As long as you want.'

Chapter 5

Jackson had been right, Caroline thought: today the law's demands were a kindness.

She had driven Brett to Masters Hill. Larry and Betty waited on the porch; dropping Brett off, Caroline did not go in. As Brett looked back at her, Caroline had the irrational, bitter sense of having deserted her once more. Then Betty pulled Brett into her arms, and Caroline drove away.

Now she worked with Jackson at Carlton Grey's office. Again, Jackson was the consummate professional. His press release required little editing.

Retired Judge Channing Masters, it said, was an apparent suicide. A preliminary inquiry had uncovered substantial evidence – including a written confession – to suggest that he had killed James Case. Pending full investigation, the indictment against Brett Allen was dismissed. A more complete statement would be forthcoming as the facts were known.

Caroline's statement was equally terse. It confirmed that Channing Masters was dead. On her family's behalf, she expressed understanding that the evidence had led to a mistaken judgment, and thanked the Attorney General's Office for Brett's prompt release. Except to state relief at Brett's exoneration and sadness over the circumstances of Judge Masters' death, the family would have no further comment. Now, or ever.

Jackson read it. 'Very gracious. At least to me.'

'Of course.'

He pushed his chair back, gazing at her across the desk. 'I'll do the press,' he said. 'Go hide.'

Afternoon became evening, and then night. Caroline stayed

in her room, not hungry, unable to sleep. Betty was dealing with the prosaic details of a nonprosaic death: scheduling a service, arranging a burial, trying to fathom what a clergyman might say. As she should be, Brett was with them; like Caroline, they were not answering any but the most pressing messages; unlike Caroline, they could retreat into the circle of family. There was nothing for Caroline to do.

Far too tired to sift her own thoughts, she lay there, far from sleep.

There was a knock on the door.

What could it be? Caroline wondered. She had refused to answer any calls from the press; one after another, slips of paper had appeared beneath the door, to be filed in her wastebasket until the moment – if ever – that further comment was helpful to Brett.

Gingerly, Caroline opened the door.

It was the night manager, a shy man with a cowlick and a look of perpetual bemusement. 'It's another telephone call,' he said. 'This man says he's the President. Problem is, the man sounds like the President.'

For a moment, Caroline did not know what to say. 'I'd like to hear this,' she answered. 'Put him through.'

A minute later, the telephone rang in her room.

'Caroline?'

'Mr. President?'

'Well, I'm glad I reached you.' His voice, Caroline realized as he paused, was a mixture of warmth and discomfort. 'They brought me a wire report, not long ago. It's obvious you've suffered a tragedy, and we wanted you to know how much we sympathize. About your father, and about how you must be feeling.' Another pause. 'It's not too early to call, is it? This must just be sinking in.'

Caroline found herself strangely touched. 'No. It's not too early. Actually, this is a help to me.'

'Then there's something else I ought to say, for whatever little it's worth in circumstances like these. That you were right to believe in your niece, and stand by her no matter

476

what.' His voice grew quieter. 'They say a lot of us ought to be disqualified from office for wanting it too much. I don't know about that. But the choice you made reflects well on you, as a person and a prospective judge. And it's sure not any disqualification.'

All at once, the irony of this came over her. There was never any choice but to stand by Brett; not knowing that, the President admired her for something she could not help. But she was far too tired, and too grateful for the misperception, to say this.

She simply thanked him, and got off.

Two nights later, her life in suspension, Caroline ate with Jackson at his fishing camp. It slowly dawned on her that he had remained here, taking a few vacation days, because of her. But she did not know how to acknowledge this.

Caroline ate a juicy piece of T-bone steak, washed it down with Cabernet. 'I just couldn't tell him,' she said.

It continued a conversation dropped before dinner. But Jackson, looking at her over his wineglass, knew at once that she meant the President. 'I expect,' he answered, 'that you didn't really want to.'

Caroline felt defensive. 'As I said before the hearing, I've stopped wanting to be a judge. After all this, why on earth should it matter to me?'

Jackson gazed at the fire. 'Over the years, Caroline, you became someone. You don't stop being that person just because you've had to face the reasons for it.'

Who would she be, Caroline remembered asking herself, if not a judge or a lawyer? 'It's not just that. Or even the time it will take to process what my father did. It's that I broke into Megan's apartment.' Her voice turned flat. 'That's not the kind of thing that judge-type people do.'

Jackson gazed at the fire. 'Megan perjured herself,' he said at last. 'Who'd believe her?'

'No,' Caroline said sharply. 'I can't lie about that.'

Jackson turned to her now. With great calm, he answered, 'You'll never have to. I've made it very clear to your friend Megan that whether she's indicted for perjury is wholly up to me. And that I don't expect to see her charging anyone else with any crimes – whether in the courts or in the media.' He paused. 'She's left college, Caroline, and dropped out of sight. All she wants to do is avoid what last humiliation she can. She's not a problem for you, anymore. And never will be.' He smiled a little. 'After all, I have her diary now.'

Caroline frowned. 'I don't want you to salvage me. Please don't try....'

'You were trying to salvage your daughter, for Christ sake. People do worse every day – I did worse, in this case, without breaking a single law. Which has led to some sobering midnight thoughts. But I very much doubt I'll let them keep me from a judgeship.'

Caroline shook her head. 'You misjudged a witness, Jackson. I broke the law. On the Court of Appeals I'd have to review case after case of other people who broke it, many of whom offer up the most sympathetic of reasons. How can I do that, knowing what I know?'

'Because it would be so colossally stupid not to. You're a brilliant lawyer and, more to the point, a compassionate one. Nothing about this experience makes either of those less true.'

Caroline stood abruptly, walking to the fire. For a time, she watched the flames, flickering orange blue. 'Right now,' she said at last, 'what I do with Brett seems a little more important.'

She felt Jackson step behind her. 'What do you want to do?'

'Want?' She turned to him with sudden intensity, felt the depth of her desire and need. 'Every fiber in me wants her for my daughter. I'm so damned sick of lies. But it's much more than that.' She looked at him intently now, tears coming to her eyes. 'I want her in my life, Jackson. The other day, watching Betty put her arms around her, I was so damned scared of losing her again.'

He looked at her with sympathy and something that, in

her despair, she could not quite identify. 'How would Brett take it, I wonder?'

'I don't know – all right, I think, in time. But the one sure way to keep her is to tell her who I am. If anyone knows the power of parenthood, I do.' With sickening suddenness, Caroline heard herself, and then her voice became almost pleading. 'She's still a young woman, and I could help her. Before, I never believed that. But now I've been with her, and I know I could. How can I just walk off and leave her again?'

Jackson gave her a considering look. He did not reach for her. 'As I just told you,' he said at last, 'you're a compassionate person. Whatever it is, I'm sure you'll know what's right to do.'

Chapter 6

Three mornings later, when they buried her father, Caroline still did not know.

The service was at the chapel at Masters Hill. The family sat in its pew – Larry at the end, Brett between Caroline and Betty. None of them said much; before the service began, Brett touched Caroline's hand. She looked tired but composed.

'Are you all right?' Caroline asked.

Brett could not quite answer. 'He was my grandfather,' she said simply.

The pews were almost filled. Caroline knew many of the faces: people too decent to stay away or to forget who Channing Masters had been to them. Caroline felt the passing of a time. Many who came were old; Channing had been retired for over a decade, and most of his works – large and small – were now a matter of memory. He would surely be the last of them to be buried on Masters Hill.

The service itself was spare and decorous – a soft-spoken minister whom Caroline did not know, simple words from the Old Testament, an expression of hope and redemption. Caroline listened fitfully; she had left this to Betty and Larry. As little as she believed in an afterlife, she believed even less in public pieties, the rituals by which the living, seeking to comfort themselves, obscure the truth about the dead and the act of dying. Her mother's funeral had been enough: Caroline would bury her father, and David, in whatever way her heart might find.

Still, she went to the graveside.

They buried him next to Betty's mother, Elizabeth Brett. What might have happened, Caroline wondered, if Elizabeth had lived? There might have been sons to slake her father's needs; Nicole Dessaliers might still live, an old woman in Paris. Surely there would have been no Caroline, no Brett, and her father would have died as he had meant to, in the fullness of time. And then the earth had covered him, and the four of them were alone.

They stood facing each other, standing around the fresh-turned dirt, Brett between Betty and Larry. What memories of him did they have together? Caroline wondered; in that moment, what she must do became clear to her. Though perhaps she had always known.

She looked at Brett, then at Larry. 'Leave us here,' she asked.

They knew what she meant. Larry nodded, and turned to Brett. Caroline watched them leave, side by side, walking to their house beneath the cool gray sky.

Caroline faced Betty across their father's grave. 'I won't tell her,' she said at last.

Betty's gaze was steady, stoic. 'Why, Caroline? When it's so clear to me that you want to.'

Caroline nodded. 'I do, very much. But no one should have to re-interpret her entire life at the age of twenty-two. That's what you, and Father, made *me* do. I can't bring myself to do the same to Brett.' Caroline's voice filled with emotion. 'Though there have been times, understanding what was done to limit her, that I've quite forgotten how selfish that would be.'

Betty reddened. 'Yes. It would be selfish.'

'But there's a price,' Caroline went on. 'When she was born, I let her go. I can do it again. As long as you do, too.'

'What do you mean?'

'That it's time for Brett to leave here. Leave you, if she wishes. Which, when she comes to terms with this, I'm very sure she will.'

Silent, Betty gazed at their father's grave, and then nodded. 'If she does, I won't try to keep her. *Now.*'

Caroline regarded her. 'Then I doubt you'll see me again. Except, I hope, on Brett's occasions – a wedding, perhaps a baby. But you needn't have me on your conscience, Betty. I think that, now, I'll be able to let you go.' She paused a moment; in the distance, she could see Brett and her father. 'As for Larry, tell him that perhaps I always knew what he would do, and shut my eyes. It was all too much for me, then.'

Betty seemed to look at her across the years, a graying woman who long ago, and at great cost, had gained for herself a daughter. 'Can you really live without telling her?' she asked. 'You won't look at her, or someday her child, and need for her to know?'

Caroline shook her head. 'I've become a very disciplined person, Betty. You should know that much by now.' Caroline paused for a moment, and then told her sister the rest of it. 'It's enough that I came back for her,' she finished softly. 'Brett will never be my daughter. But, for me, I've earned the right to feel like her mother.'

Chapter 7

Alone, Caroline stood by her mother's grave, where Betty had left her.

Well, Caroline said silently, *it's over now. I've done the best I could.*

In the quiet, a few birds calling, she felt someone behind her.

Turning, Caroline saw her daughter, waiting for her.

'Do you mind?' Brett asked. 'My mother said you might be here.'

'No. I meant to see you before I left.' Caroline paused. 'To say how sorry I am that you have to live with this.'

Brett stepped closer now, hands in her pockets, seeming to avoid the sight of Channing's grave. 'I've loved Grandfather all my life. And then he kills someone I care for. How could he have thought that was out of love for me?'

How best to answer? Caroline wondered. 'He was old, Brett. Something happened to him.'

Brett gave a short, dissatisfied shake of the head. 'He wasn't old when you left here. Was that over a boy?'

Her face, Caroline thought, was so very much like Nicole's. Except that the mouth and chin were David's. 'Yes,' she answered simply. 'It was.'

Brett regarded her in silence. 'I'm too old to need protecting, Caroline. From whatever this is about.'

'I know that. But I'm protecting me. And I've got enough to deal with just sorting through this for myself.' Pausing, Caroline searched for a truth that might be helpful. 'Your grandfather was a troubled man. I don't know why; he wouldn't, couldn't, talk about himself ... his own parents, his own hurts, anything. But there was something damaged about him: although he badly wanted to, he didn't know how to love my mother, or your mother, or me, or you, or how to give us what we needed. Because whatever it was he needed kept him from knowing. So that, in the end, all of us were damaged too. You least of all.

'You're young, Brett. You've got a whole life, and now it's yours. There's nothing about you to keep you from living it fully.'

Brett seemed to watch her. 'I'd never met you,' she said at last. 'But ever since you got here, I could sense you weren't going to let anything worse happen to me. At least if you could help it.'

Caroline gazed back at her, the daughter she loved in secret, standing near the headstone of her grandmother Nicole. It made Caroline want to smile, though she did not know why. 'I wasn't,' she answered. 'It didn't matter what you'd done. Though it rather pleases me that it was nothing.'

Brett tilted her head. 'Was that because of Grandfather? Things you thought we had in common?'

'Perhaps at the start. But, in the end, it was because of you.'

Brett hesitated, and then she touched Caroline's sleeve. 'Will I see you again?'

Caroline smiled. 'Maybe you'll come to see me. I'd like that, very much.'

'Would you?'

'Oh, yes. After all, you've never been to San Francisco.'

Brett smiled at this; for an instant, Caroline wanted to hold her, to tell her how she truly felt. Then she saw the fresh grave of her father, and knew once more that the final judgement was hers to make, the wounds of silence hers to bear.

For a last time, Caroline studied her daughter's face.

'I'm ready to leave here,' she said. 'Are you?'

Brett was quiet for a moment. 'Yes,' she answered, 'I am.'

Chapter 8

'So you're leaving tomorrow,' Jackson said.

'Uh-huh. By six o'clock, I'll be in San Francisco.' Caroline's voice softened. 'It's time, Jackson. Before I make some terrible mistake.'

They sat at the end of Jackson's boat dock, each drinking a can of beer and watching the last light of evening fade on Heron Lake. Quietly, Jackson said, 'You did the right thing, you know.'

Caroline turned to him. 'Did I?'

'Sure.' He smiled a little. 'Besides, who ever said you'd be such a great mother? Was yours?'

Caroline gave him a cool look. 'That hurts a bit, you know. But no, she wasn't particularly. In some ways, I suppose, I was my own mother.'

Jackson had stopped smiling. 'Then I take it all back.' He fell quiet for a moment. 'You're a good person, Caroline. To me, you grasped what seems important here: that your father's silence hurt you, but that – at least for now – yours is a kindness. And that there are no rules for this kind of thing, merely the hope of empathy.'

She faced him now, sitting cross-legged on the dock. 'You're the only person I've told all this. Perhaps the only one I'll ever tell.'

He gazed at her a moment, accepting this. 'Then that makes me indispensable, doesn't it? Or maybe just inconvenient.'

Caroline shook her head. 'No,' she said. 'You've helped me a lot. You know that.'

The look that Jackson gave her was tentative, inquiring. 'Because I've wondered, after all this settles in, whether you'd ever want to see me again. Or whether, for your own sake, it would be easier to do what you did before.'

For a long time, Caroline was quiet. 'It's gone too far for that, I think. Although I guess I'd like it better if, like Brett, you came to San Francisco.' Caroline smiled. 'Of course, you'll save hotel fare if you stay with me. I hear civil servants in New Hampshire don't make much money. Even judges.' She touched his hand, finishing quietly: 'I do care for you, Jackson. More than I ever knew.'

After a moment, Jackson smiled again. 'Then do me a favor, okay?'

'What's that?'

'Take the judgeship, Caroline. You don't have to give up everything. And it may make you better company.'

In that moment, looking at Jackson, Caroline saw that this was more than kindness. He was asking her to accept the gift of his generosity. To accept it for herself.

Perhaps she could, Caroline thought. Perhaps she could accept who she was: the daughter of Channing and Nicole, mother in silence to Brett. Flawed, with a life she did not yet understand, but learning still. She could feel Jackson watching her.

That night, Caroline stayed with him.

The next morning Caroline Clark Masters, soon to be a judge of the United States Court of Appeals, flew back to San Francisco to prepare for her confirmation hearings. Her niece, Brett, drove her to the airport.

Acknowledgments

As usual, my task was made easier by a number of friends, old and new.

In San Francisco, I consulted Assistant District Attorney Bill Fazio; defense attorneys Hugh Anthony Levine and Jim Collins; medical examiner Boyd Stephens; homicide inspector Napoleon Hendrix; and private investigator Hal Lipset. And once again, Assistant District Attorney Al Giannini advised me and reviewed the manuscript. For three books now, their help has been invaluable.

Readers devoted to New Hampshire will recognize that Masters Hill and the town of Resolve are fictional locations: a small community in New Hampshire seemed too particular a place to fairly depict here. I hope that I have nonetheless captured the flavor and legal milieu of this unique region. My dear friend and fellow writer Maynard Thomson helped impart to me his deep love and appreciation for the state. Others generous with their time include Assistant Attorney General Janice Rundles; County Attorney Lincoln Soldati; Jennifer Soldati of the New Hampshire Trial Lawyers Association; attorney and writer John Davis; defense attorneys Bob Stein and Paul Maggiotto; Kathy Deschenaux of the office of the New Hampshire Medical Examiner; and Sergeant Kevin Babcock of the New Hampshire State Police. I owe all of them a great debt for whatever success I have achieved; any errors, or simplifications for narrative purposes, are mine.

Special mention should be made of the late Dr. Roger Fossum, chief medical examiner for the State of New Hampshire. In the time that I spent with Roger, I quickly came to appreciate the professionalism, intelligence, humanity, and good humor that endeared him to his many friends.

Martha's Vineyard has a unique charm and history. William Marks — environmentalist, publisher, and writer — was extraordinarily generous in sharing the history of the island, suggestions for locating specific scenes, and advice on sailing. The Vineyard portions of the novel would have been far different without him. Thanks also go to George Manter, a former chief of police of West Tisbury, who helped fill in several gaps in island history. In addition, John Bitzer and his family showed me around their wonderful home and graciously allowed me to use it as a model for the Masterses' summer home.

In assessing the possible impact of drugs and alcohol on Brett's behavior and perceptions, I was kindly assisted by Dr. David Smith of the Haight-Ashbury Free Clinic, and writer Rick Seymour. Dr. Rodney Shapiro helped me consider the potential emotions and motivations of Brett, Channing Masters, and Megan Race. In outlining for me the possible routes through which Caroline Masters might come to be considered for an appellate judgeship, my friend Chief Judge Thelton Henderson enabled me to better posit what might be happening to Caroline. Finally, renowned serologist Dr. Henry Lee graciously responded by telephone to several questions regarding the potential medical evidence in a case such as this. I hope I have done their advice something close to justice.

My wife, Laurie; my friend and agent, Fred Hill; and my wonderful publishers — Sonny Mehta of Knopf, and Linda Grey and Clare Ferraro of Ballantine — commented on the manuscript. And, as usual, Philip Rotner and Lee Zell were generous with their advice.

Most of all, there is my assistant, Alison Thomas. With each new day's writing, Alison helped me pick it apart — looking for weak spots; flaws in characterization; infelicitous language; and flagging plot lines. Writing is a solitary business: without Alison's keen eye and kind encouragement, it would be far more difficult. She has become a dear friend and an integral part of my work. For all those reasons, and more, this book is dedicated to her.

THE OUTSIDE MAN

Richard North Patterson

For Jesse Hill Ford

Murder doesn't round out anybody's life except the murdered's and maybe the murderer's.

Nick Charles, from
Dashiell Hammett's
The Thin Man

We sail with a corpse in the cargo.
Ibsen

Chapter 1

Perhaps the murders were fated when I met Kris Ann, then moved with her here, to Alabama. The move was a change of plans. I'd meant us to live in Washington. We never did, and so three deaths began waiting in the ambush of time.

Seven years passed, and then Cade handed me the envelope. It seemed like nothing at all. I'd come from a Saturday partners' meeting called to set new rates – nineteen southern Protestants and me at a long walnut table buffed so high I could see my face in it – trying to feel like eighty dollars an hour. It took some imagination. So when Cade caught me near the elevator and with a quick, chill glance at my blue jeans asked if I'd drop some papers with Lydia Cantwell, my only thought was to do that much for free.

Outside the morning was hazy from the smokestacks of our clients and the streets looked stale and a little hungover, like a room full of cigarette smoke after a long party. Behind my parking space the neon sign of a dingy department store murmured its fatigue in old-fashioned cursive letters. I tossed the envelope on the passenger seat and drove south with the top down through near-empty streets, then up and over a sudden barrier of green wooded hills until the city behind me dropped abruptly from sight.

Now the road curled downward past immense stone houses sheltered by pine and dogwood and magnolia. The air became clear, damp and heavy, and the feel and blueness of it merged with deep lawns and the bursts of pink and white to create that violence of beauty you can find only in the South, in April. Behind me Birmingham sprawled in a valley of heat and smoke: squat steel mills the corroded color of rust, concrete highways, low-slung warehouses, sinewy towers of glass and steel, sweltering streets. But the road ahead was shady and still. A lone black maid in stretch pants straggled by its side as though on a treadmill to eternity, her slow repeated movements speaking of boredom in the bone and brain, days endlessly the same. I passed her, turning down a road that traced the winding path of a valley in what had once been pine forest, the wind in my face.

There was nothing ahead but shadows. I took the curves fast – shifting and braking, accelerating and shifting – as a smooth radio voice from New York eased into a mass murder, the oil crisis, and a Gallup poll in which three out of four Americans thought things were getting worse. 'Speaking last night in Atlanta,' he went on, 'the chairman of the Federal Reserve Board warned that this country is threatened by permanent inflation which will change the lives of rich and poor alike. . . .' But there was nothing I could do about that, except not smoke my first cigarette. So I didn't, and found myself at the Cantwells'.

Their drive began with a stand of oaks, continuing its gradual climb through magnolia and dogwood until it reached the crest of pines where the house loomed, a white brick monolith with gables and twenty rooms and the sense of weight that time brings. Seventy years before, Henry Cantwell's grandfather had brooded on the site, then built: over time ivy had crept up the walls, hedges had grown, a formal garden had come to surround the slate patio in back, and finally, Lydia Cantwell's roses had lined the walk that led from the drive to the double door. I parked, taking the envelope, and followed it.

The grounds were shrouded in morning silence broken only by a few birdcalls and the rustling of pine boughs. The snarl of the buzzer when I pushed it sounded rude, and got no answer. But when I knocked, the door cracked open by itself.

I looked in, surprised, calling once. No one answered. I hesitated, then stepped inside.

The foyer faced a spiral staircase, with a sitting room to the left and the dining room opposite. Next to me was a low table. I placed the envelope there, turned to leave, stopped in the doorway, and then, turning back, picked it up again.

It was an innocuous manila, sealed only by two splayed

metal fasteners that Cade's secretary had put through the hole in its flap, then pressed down to each side. I pried the fasteners upright and opened the flap. Inside was a typed document of sixteen pages. I riffled it, then read again, this time carefully. When I had finished I checked for missing pages, found none, and reread the twelfth page, twice. Then I placed the papers back in the envelope and took it with me to the sitting room.

It was sparsely decorated, mainly from the past. On polished end tables were porcelain figurines – a sparrow, Marie Antoinette – that Lydia had collected. From above the fireplace stared an oil of her father, framed by candelabra and looking vaguely distressed, as if he smelled smoke. The shelf built-in next to that held portraits of more dead ancestors and a larger one of Henry Cantwell, gray hair neatly parted. The papers in the envelope reminded me that Jason's picture had been removed. Then I noticed that Lydia's was gone.

I called out.

No one answered. I walked past the fireplace through the open door to Henry's library, filled with books: *Lancelot* by Walker Percy, some Aeschylus, much Faulkner and Camus, James Joyce's *Ulysses*, and leaning next to that with a bookmark sticking from it, *Crime and Punishment*. Often I would find Henry in a cardigan sweater, amidst his volumes: the most reliable friends, he'd once remarked, full of consolation. But his half-glasses were on the shelf and his chair was empty. I returned to the sitting room, stopped, and listened.

I didn't like finding the house unlocked, or its silence. Though in the seven years since, I'd been to the Cantwells' perhaps a hundred times, I could still hear the sounds of our engagement party, when the house had been filled with people and laughter and the clink of a barman dropping ice in crystal. I'd begun awkwardly, conscious of Cade and worried that if I moved too quickly I'd slop champagne on the Oriental rugs. I had never met the Cantwells and, while Henry and Lydia were gracious, Jason watched me from one corner with a peculiar bright intensity, never coming forward. The chances of meeting a second northerner were nil and everyone else seemed to have money to burn, even Kris Ann's florid uncle who had backed me to the fireplace denouncing the Berrigan brothers. Then Kris Ann appeared behind him in the crush. For an instant her look seemed probing and uncertain and then, knowing I saw her, she flashed me the dazzling, flirty, self-mocking smile that was an in-joke between us – her southern-girl smile, she called it – until it warmed the darkness of her eyes. I'd felt myself relax, and after that I remembered the moment precisely: her smile, the room, and the sounds of the party – so that now it seemed too quiet.

'Lydia?' I called, and then went back through the foyer to the staircase, glancing toward the dining room as I passed.

I stopped there.

Lydia Cantwell lay sprawled behind the dining room table. Her eyes bulged and her tongue protruded from a smear of lipstick. He throat was circled with bruises.

It was a moment before I knew that I had crossed myself.

I went to her then, kneeling. Her wrist was stiff and cold to the touch. There was no pulse.

My limbs had gone numb and heavy. I stumbled back from her. Her terrycloth robe was pulled to mid-thigh and her legs seemed pitifully thin. Black hair straggled on the Persian rug, and I noticed, foolishly, that she had dyed the gray at her temples.

I felt a moment of awful tenderness, as if I should cover her legs. Instead I went to the kitchen and called the police. When I returned, my throat was parched and my mouth tasted bitter, like half-swallowed aspirin.

It was then I saw her picture.

It had been taken at a formal sitting and placed next to Henry's in the other room. Now it sat on the dining room table. Someone had stabbed out the eyes. I rushed back to the kitchen and vomited.

I raised my head from the sink, breathed deeply, and went back to the dining room. The envelope lay where I'd dropped it, by Lydia's hand. I picked it up and went outside. I didn't look back at the woman, or her picture.

4

The porch was cool. Above the roses a hummingbird hovered in delicate suspension, a picture from a Chinese vase.

I walked to my car and slid the envelope under the seat.

Chapter 2

'Panic is the first enemy of the lawyer,' Cade had once told me. So when the first police came – two uniformed patrolmen in a squad car – I tried to blank out everything but the envelope.

The young man rushed past me through the front door, slamming it behind him. The other stopped in front of me. He was short and paunchy, with pale blue eyes and a creased clown's face so sad it must have always seemed close to tears. 'What happened?' he asked.

'I don't know.'

'Sure.' His voice was patient and unsatisfied. 'Just how you found her.'

I swallowed. 'I got here maybe fifteen minutes ago, on business. Mrs Cantwell's our client –' I paused, deleting the envelope. 'No one answered, and the door was unlocked. That wasn't like her; she was a careful woman. So I stepped inside to check.'

The door opened behind me. 'Called in the body,' the young man said. 'Rayfield's coming himself. You'll want to see this.'

His partner nodded and turned back to me. 'You'd better come inside, Mr Shaw.' I didn't move. 'Come on,' he said, almost gently.

I followed him to the sitting room without looking at Lydia. He pointed me to a sofa across from the fireplace where I couldn't see the dining room or her body. 'You'll have to wait here for Homicide,' he said, and left.

'Jesus Christ,' someone muttered. It was the older man's voice, coming from the dining room, low and close to tender.

'Look at the picture,' his partner said.

There was silence. 'We got a creep maybe – someone who'll do it twice.'

'Might could be rape. It's funny – Rayfield was sending Watkins until I said her name and then he decided to come himself.'

'Look around you,' the older man said. 'She used to be somebody.'

There was no malice in that, just fact and a little kinship, as though Lydia Cantwell had taken a great fall quickly and thus qualified for sympathy. My throat was dry.

The front door opened, there were murmured greetings, and footsteps near the body. A new voice – soft and flat – asked, 'Call the medical examiner?' 'Yessir,' the older man said, and then two plainclothesmen walked into the sitting room.

The thin one had a neat mustache, wire-rimmed glasses, and the meticulous intense look of a demolition expert. But it was the second man who held my attention. He was perhaps fifty, with a large potato face and small cobalt eyes at once pained and bleak and totally absorbed, the eyes of a bitter saint. They lit on me, appraising.

'I'm Rayfield,' he said and inclined his head toward the younger man. 'This is Sergeant Bast.'

I nodded without speaking. Four uniformed police came briskly through the front door with ropes, cameras, and sketch pads, headed for the dining room. The last one carried a black doctor's bag. 'Ready to go, Lieutenant,' he called.

Rayfield glanced over. 'Rope it off,' he ordered, and walked out.

The young patrolman appeared next to a vase of white chrysanthemums, watching me. I didn't look up.

'Feel her armpits?' someone asked. 'She's room temperature.'

Another said, 'She's eight hours old, anyhow. They get this cold no way to tell for sure. Rape test's not much good.'

'Do it anyway,' Rayfield said. Cameras began spitting.

The impersonal noise of strangers – doors opening, footsteps, orders, slamming drawers – came to me like the sound of television through an open window. Someone clambered up the stairs. I lit a Camel, forcing myself to watch Rayfield as he backed into the sitting room. He was around six-two, thick-bodied and awkwardly careful of movement, as if trapped in his own skin. His suit and tie were just something to wear, his gray wavy hair was cut military-style, his stare at the Cantwells' furnishings abstemious and disapproving. He turned to me, asking, 'You're her lawyer?'

'That's right.' My mouth was acrid with vomit taste and I needed some water. Instead I took a deep, harsh drag of cigarette smoke and stood.

Bast materialized with a note pad. Rayfield took out a black notebook and asked, 'Mrs Cantwell invite you?'

I noticed that his hair tonic lent him a not unpleasant whiff of the barber shop: the smell of my father. 'Not exactly,' I answered. 'I was on the way home from the office.'

'Then she wasn't expecting you.' His flat drawl might have passed for witlessness if I hadn't lived in the South, or caught the sharpness of his eyes.

'I'm not sure – she'd talked yesterday with my father-in-law.'

'But you didn't call her.'

'No.'

'Then why'd you come?'

'Private business. Law business, that's all.'

'What was it?'

I shook my head. 'I'm sorry, Lieutenant. That's covered by the attorney-client privilege.'

Bast's eyes rose from his notes. 'Give me the semen slide,' someone said in the living room. Rayfield drawled, 'She's dead now, Mr Shaw,' in a voice so flat and uninflected that his words held the barest trace of irony.

'Not just her. The family.'

His eyebrows raised. 'Dead?'

'No. Clients.'

'Just who are we talking about?'

'Her husband, for one. Henry Cantwell.'

Rayfield paused, head angled to look at me as if revising some impression. His thumb began clicking the ballpoint. I noticed then that his hands were at odds with the rest of him:

8

pale and delicate, with long piano-player's fingers, his nails fastidiously trimmed. In a monotone he asked, 'You a friend of Henry Cantwell's?'

From the side Bast glanced hastily at Rayfield. 'His friend, and lawyer,' I answered.

Rayfield's pen stopped clicking. His tone was cool, accusing. 'Where is he?'

'I don't know.' Then it hit me that Henry might be dead or in trouble. It hit me hard, like sudden knowledge in a man not smart.

'What's the problem, Mr Shaw?'

'Nothing.'

'Then where is he?'

I turned to Bast. 'There's an envelope under the front seat of my car – the Alfa Romeo. You'd better get it.'

Bast looked to Rayfield. But Rayfield was staring at me, voice now taut as he asked, 'Did Henry Cantwell do this?'

'Get the envelope,' I repeated to Bast.

Rayfield kept staring. But Bast nodded and went through the front door. In the minute it took him to come back Rayfield said nothing, his eyes never moving until Bast gave him the envelope. He pulled the document, reading its caption. 'Her will?'

'Her new will. She never got to sign it.'

He flipped its pages as Bast read over his shoulder. He finished, said nothing, and started again more slowly. 'Take another smear,' said someone near Lydia. I reached to stub my cigarette in one of her ashtrays, jabbing twice before it went out. Finally, Rayfield asked, 'Isn't there a son?'

I nodded. 'Jason.'

'But not in here.'

'No. Not in there.'

Rayfield looked up. 'How old's he now?'

'Mid-twenties.'

'Know where he lives?'

'Just that he goes to the university. Sort of a perpetual student.'

Rayfield turned to Bast. 'Better find the boy.'

9

Bast left. Rayfield rolled up the will and began tapping it in his palm. He turned suddenly, walking toward Henry's picture until he stood in front of it. Without turning, he asked, 'Who's your father-in-law?'

'Roland Cade.'

Rayfield turned slowly back to me, eyes widening slightly before they dropped to the will. He stared at it in pensive silence, pen held to his lips. Abruptly, he said, 'We'd better call him,' and went to the kitchen.

The young patrolman still watched me. Police talked near Lydia. An awed voice said, 'Take a man to do like that.'

'Maybe a strong woman,' someone answered.

I went to the window.

The sun had climbed, filtering through the pines in yellow shafts. Beyond the grounds, I knew people were living their same lives, and at the club couples were playing mixed doubles, or drinking. But I couldn't envision it. When Rayfield returned I was staring at nothing.

'You must be worried about Henry Cantwell,' he said softly from behind. 'Would that be like him, being gone?'

His tone seemed strangely kind. But when I played it back I heard a faint, tense undertone. I turned and said in a flat voice, 'I wouldn't know.'

Rayfield watched me for a moment, then looked down at the will again. 'Mrs Cantwell,' he said almost musingly, 'what was *she* like?'

I had no answer.

For me it had never changed from that first engagement party. Mercedes and long Lincolns had eased up the drive as Henry and Lydia greeted each new arrival. Poised and perfectly coiffed, she'd begun as my youthful notion of a great lady, except that I'd watched too long. Guest upon guest, the precise same smile came and went without quite touching her eyes, and her hugs of greeting resembled acts of will. She seemed to play out the party like a role she knew expertly, which stifled her, real only in a quick turn of the head, one sudden worried glance toward Jason. And for seven years after, she kissed my cheek, remembered when we'd last talked and asked how I was, listening closely to my answer with her head slightly tilted – a minuet of courtesy which, when over, left behind nothing but itself. I'd wondered for a while, then just stopped. 'She was our friend,' I said now. 'It's hard for me to talk about.'

The older man from the squad car had appeared next to Rayfield. 'No sign of forced entry, sir,' he put in.

'Upstairs too?'

'Yessir.'

Rayfield seemed almost to smile without changing expression. 'Mrs. Cantwell,' he said to me. 'How'd she get her money?'

'For Christ's sake, Lieutenant, we're not talking about some bird that crashed into a picture window. I *knew* her.'

'That's right,' he said bluntly. 'Past tense. She's been strangled by someone who looks like he could do this again to some other friend of yours. That's why we're talking.'

We stared at each other. 'Her mother was a Maddox,' I finally said. 'Maddox Coal and Steel.'

He jotted that in his notebook. 'What about her father's side?'

I pointed toward the portrait. 'Remember the Grangeville case?'

Rayfield turned to look. 'The one way back, where they executed those two Negroes for rape.'

'He was the judge who sentenced them.'

Rayfield's face was devoid of expression. 'You're not from here, are you?'

I knew where 'here' was. 'No. Cleveland.'

'And Cleveland's where your people are.'

'That's right.'

I'd tracked his thoughts, so I wasn't surprised when he said in a flat voice, 'Grangeville was a long time back,' and shut the notebook. It was then that it struck me that he had asked almost nothing about Henry Cantwell.

'Clean her up,' someone said. I winced, involuntarily, and then Cade walked through the door.

Chapter 3

Cade stopped in the alcove to stare at Lydia Cantwell. No one spoke. Cade's head inclined in the attitude of patience, as if waiting for her to awaken. Slowly, perceptibly, the stiffness went from his back.

'Mr Cade.' It was Rayfield, standing next to me.

Cade turned, ashen, gazing for a moment with vague, frightened blankness as though jarred from sleep by a sudden noise. Then his black hawk eyes settled on Rayfield until they seemed to glare at him from a face all surfaces and angles, like those of some great arrogant bird. Rayfield's pen clicked, once.

'We're in here,' he said.

For several seconds Cade watched Rayfield, refusing to move. Finally, he limped toward us. World War II had left a pin in his hip and he moved with torso canted slightly forward, to ease a pain which seemed etched in the squint of his eyelids and the grooves running like scars from his nostrils to the corners of his mouth and then to the square of his jaw. But his hair was still chestnut and his stomach flat: looking down at Rayfield, he seemed younger than fifty-six.

Rayfield held out the will. 'You know about this.'

Cade gave him a look of repugnance. 'All I know is that an old friend lies horribly murdered in the next room.'

'You did draft this will, though.'

'Yesterday. I said that when you called.'

'Then maybe you could tell me how that happened.'

Cade shot me a hasty glance. 'I'll need to speak with Mr Shaw.'

Rayfield tugged his ear in a distracted, impatient gesture, looking from Cade to me and back again. Then he nodded toward the door. 'You can do that outside.'

We left through the alcove. A white-coated man stood over

the body. Lydia Cantwell's thin legs splayed crazily from behind him like the bottom end of a department store mannequin that had toppled backward. Her toenails were bright red. There was the faint odor of chemicals. I turned away.

We passed the old patrolman at the door and then walked through the roses, a line of police cars, and an ambulance, stopping by the magnolias at the far side of the drive. The blossoms gave a thin, sweet smell. Next to us sun burnt a shimmering patch of asphalt. The white glare of car windows cut into my eyes.

'You found her like that?' Cade was asking.

I nodded.

'Sweet Jesus,' he said softly. A crow cawed. Cade's voice turned harsh. 'What's he want?'

'I don't know.'

'Then why in hell did you give them the will?'

'Because Henry's missing.'

'You don't think Henry –'

'Not me. This man Rayfield. It wasn't a break-in, Roland. She let him in.'

'Who? Jason?'

'Maybe. I don't know. You said once that Jason is a sick man.'

Cade's voice was rough. 'He's scum – for all I care they can electrocute him. But you're stripping the Cantwells in public. You know what the papers will run? That will, and the Cantwells' troubles with it.'

'The will is evidence,' I shot back. 'And there are fewer Cantwells than there used to be.'

Cade flushed. 'What makes you suppose – whatever we might think – that Henry Cantwell wants us pointing at the boy?'

'What makes you suppose,' I said tightly, 'that Henry Cantwell's still alive?'

Cade's mouth opened in an odd, surprised expression. 'Look,' I told him, 'I found Lydia murdered and Henry missing. Jason's supposed to hate them both. The will may be his motive. I had to turn it over. If Henry's in danger – if anything's happened – the police should be hunting for Jason. They'd better do that even if Henry's just gone fishing: Rayfield thinks whoever killed her may do this again. And if I hadn't given him the will, then Henry's his suspect, and by noon every hick sheriff will be looking to bring him back in handcuffs for the six o'clock news – '

'Quiet.' Cade's eyes fixed on some point over my shoulder. I realized my fists were clenched. I relaxed them and turned. Two uniformed police bore a stretcher covered by a white blanket between the roses. Only her outline showed. They carried the stretcher to the back of the ambulance and slid it inside. The door slammed. Someone started the motor. Then the ambulance backed slowly down the long drive and was gone. We listened as the motor sound faded and died, and for a long time after.

Cade slumped with his hands in his pockets. 'Why quarrel?' he said softly. 'It's done.'

We stared at the ground.

'I can't believe this,' I murmured.

He shook his head. 'I've known her so long. And Kris Ann – it will be hard on her, too. I hardly know how to tell her.'

The last was spoken almost to himself. I looked up at him sharply. 'I'll tell Krissy.'

Cade turned to me, arms folded, his face set as if fighting to hold silent. Abruptly, he broke away and called to the man at the door for Rayfield.

A moment later Rayfield appeared amidst the roses, striding toward us deliberately and without hurry. 'You ready?' he demanded.

Cade reddened. 'You'll want to know how that will came to be drafted.'

Rayfield took out his notebook. 'Go ahead.'

Cade paused, breathing deeply, composing himself into a lawyer. 'Mrs Cantwell called me yesterday,' he began, 'to insist on seeing me. I said of course, and she came, around three. Our receptionist can confirm the time, if that's important. In any event, she sat in my office and asked me to

14

change her will.' Cade's voice seemed muted by a kind of buried sadness. 'Her prior will favored her husband and son in equal measure. Now she wanted to leave everything to Mr Cantwell.'

Rayfield's pen skittered across the note pad, face tight with expectation as he watched Cade. Cade continued. 'Jason Cantwell's a deeply troubled boy. He's had psychiatric counseling and fooled with radical politics. There are other things – I'm frank to admit I don't care for him. But Mrs. Cantwell refused to give reasons. I did see that she was quite agitated, to the point that her hands shook when normally she was calm and precise.

'It wasn't a long interview. I asked her if she'd talked with Henry and, when she said no, advised her to. I thought that was best – it was her money, all right, but Jason isn't just *her* son. She said she might, but that she wanted the will revised that day. It wasn't much trouble – just changing some paragraphs – so when she left, I had Miss Millar, my secretary, type it up. I decided to send it to Lydia at home and give her time to consider. If I'd had her come back for it, we could have witnessed the document and the thing would have been done. This way she'd have the weekend and perhaps talk with Henry. So I called her about five and said I'd send it out this morning.' Cade stopped, exhaled, and said, 'You know the rest.'

It had been some moments since anyone else had spoken. Cades' voice had journeyed through calm and sadness in a near-hypnotic rhythm. Rayfield watched him.

'You should be looking for Henry Cantwell,' I said to Rayfield.

He looked over at me strangely. 'Any particular reason why you're this worried?'

'Look, dammit –'

Cade cut in hastily. 'We're his lawyers, Lieutenant. That's all it is.'

I spun on Cade, angry. He was watching Rayfield intently, hand half-raised between them. Rayfield stared back as if choosing his next words. He was interrupted by the whir of a motor. We turned, and then a black Mercedes loomed amidst the dogwood and drove into our silence.

The car stopped and a slight, gray-haired man got out, blinking as if he had stumbled from a darkroom. I hesitated, frozen by pity and relief. But Cade was quickly to him. 'It's Lydia,' he said.

Henry Cantwell's face turned tight and queer. Cade braced his shoulders. 'She's been murdered, Henry.'

Henry's features crumbled, slowly and completely, like ruined putty. He sagged in Cade's hands. 'Henry,' Cade urged.

His tone mixed sympathy and command. Henry stiffened upright as Cade backed him against the hood. He stared emptily ahead. Then he curled and his face dropped into his hands. His shoulders trembled, and then hurt-animal sounds came from between his fingers. I wanted to go to him. But he didn't need my face to remember when he thought of breaking down. So I watched him: a banker in a three-piece suit, sobbing against the hood of his black Mercedes. Rayfield watched next to me, unnaturally still.

After a time Henry cried himself out. Haltingly, Cade walked him to the house, one arm draping Henry's shoulders as he limped beside him. Rayfield followed.

Two cops called to each other as they paced the rear grounds, finding nothing. I leaned against a magnolia tree, smoked one cigarette to the nub, and walked back to the house.

Rayfield was alone in the sitting room, staring at the closed door to Henry's library.

'Where are they?' I asked.

He butted his head toward the library. 'In there.'

'What happened?'

'I asked where he'd been. Cade pulled him into the library.'

'What did you expect?'

Rayfield gave me a long cobalt look. Then he began watching the door again.

It slid open minutes later. Cade came first, and then Henry, following with a glazed expression.

'I'd like to be alone,' he said to no one. Without waiting, he began to shuffle toward the stairway with the steps of an old man. Rayfield reached out toward him, mouth open as if to speak, and then his hand fell to his side and he watched Henry move away.

Henry stopped when he reached me. Without speaking he put his hand on my shoulder and looked toward the dining room. For a moment I felt his weight and Rayfield's silent look. Then Henry dropped his arm and started up the stairs.

I watched him climb as the shape of his future came to me. The quiet he had cherished here would build until it screamed. Gawkers would nose their cars up the drive, and people who didn't would claim to know him – or Lydia or Jason – and to remember some telling incident. And if the killer weren't found, someone, to liven up a party, would mention Henry: 'He was always so quiet, so much to himself. . . .' He reached the top of the stairs, and disappeared.

'You can have him at four,' Cade was saying. 'Assuming it won't be a media event.'

Rayfield's lips were an angry line. 'We'll do what's proper.'

'Good.' Cade was once again crisp. 'I take it you're through here.'

The almost insulting slowness of Rayfield's look at Cade lent the lingering sense of some deeper, more obscure conflict than that between police and lawyer. 'We're through,' he finally answered. Leaving, he snapped, 'Check the neighbors,' to someone at the door, and slammed it behind him.

Cade and I stood alone. 'Henry's in no shape to be questioned,' I said.

He gave me a gelid stare. 'Do you think I like this? But it won't help him to wait and suffer. This way the police will grant us some consideration.'

'Not Rayfield. There's something about him.'

'Yes. He's a policeman.'

I ignored that. 'A couple of times I wondered if he knew Henry somehow, or you.'

'Why would he?' Cade said disdainfully. 'Henry's not a criminal, and I'm not a criminal lawyer.'

'That's a second thing that bothers me. We should bring in the Danelaw firm, someone who does this kind of work.'

'Henry wants us, not some knit-suited showoff.' I sensed Cade trying to regain initiative lost in the matter of the will. 'You needn't participate if you think that's such a mistake. I haven't asked you to.'

We faced each other. Unspoken were the last four years of tacit avoidance, the finding of work with other projects and partners, other clients than Cade's. 'Henry's my friend, Roland.'

Cade shrugged dismissively. 'Meet me, then. Just don't upset Kris Ann.'

There was nothing more – no instructions, confidences, or requests for help. Cade began pacing the sitting room. I said goodbye, got in the car, and drove, past the black Mercedes and away from Cade, the pines, the silent house, the chemical smell of death.

Chapter 4

I reached the street of oaks and sloping lawns and white-trimmed Georgian homes before I knew what I wanted.

Kris Ann's Audi – a gift from Cade to match his own – sat in the rear garage. I parked beside it, walking through the backyard and between the house and the overgrown lot next door until I reached the front porch.

Kris Ann stood beneath the green canvas awning in the way she had, straight like a dancer from her hips through the small of her back. She whirled at the sound of footsteps, black hair flying out and away. Then she came to me. I felt her breathing and the wetness of her face.

'Your father . . .' I began.

Our eyes met and held. As she leaned back I grasped her hand. We went upstairs in a kind of torpor. Undressing, no one spoke. We made love with silent intensity, each without looking at the other. Stiff desperate fingers raked my back, she cried out, and was still.

Afterward she wept, her face turned from me. I held her until it was done.

'Krissy . . .'

She turned to me suddenly. Her eyes were deep and black and brilliant, and seven years had touched only their corners. But in the puffiness beneath them, the slackness of shock still in her face, was the first shadow of age to come. Softly, she said, 'What had he done to her?'

'Does it matter?'

'It matters to any woman. But to Lydia . . .'

Her eyes shut. I could almost see her imaginings: Lydia Cantwell, strangled as close from sex as she was now. Afternoon sun through the leafy tangle outside our window glinted in her hair, thick and soft as I touched it. She shook it free. 'It's like I can feel it.' Her voice turned low and angry. 'Where was Jason?'

'I don't know.'

I felt the line of her body stiffen. 'He could do this.' She slid away from me, rolling on her stomach and pulling the bedsheet over her shoulders.

I bent to kiss her, then stopped. 'Maybe a drink – '

She shook her head. 'You can. But not me. Not now.'

For a moment I watched her. Then I put on a robe and went downstairs.

It was the maid's day off. In the dining room one of Kris Ann's silk blouses lay on the cabinet which held her mother's gold-dipped silver and a lopsided clay ashtray with 'I love you' scratched on it by a small retarded girl to whom she taught art. Next to that was the liquor. I poured some Bushmills, neat, and took that and the blouse upstairs.

The bed was empty. Kris Ann stood in front of her makeup mirror, brushing her hair in a dispirited ritual of something to do. Her skin was tawny and her back straight and slim, with smooth hollows beneath her shoulder blades. My father's wolf-face appeared behind her in the mirror. She leaned back. 'When I was little, Adam – after Mother died – Henry and Lydia would take me to the symphony or the ballet, like *The Nutcracker* at Christmas. I'd sit between them and she'd explain the stories. And Henry – '

'I know.'

She stopped brushing, her reflection grave as she watched mine. 'Adam,' she said quietly. 'Daddy's been a lawyer for a long time.'

I nodded. 'And Henry's my friend.'

'Daddy's friend, too?'

'I think I can help.'

'But how much help will it be if Henry ends up in the middle, between Daddy and you? How do you suppose he'll feel then?'

'I'll watch out for him. You know that.'

She was still, staring into the mirror. With sudden anger she flung a perfume bottle at her reflection. It shattered with the glass. I grabbed her shoulders as shards scattered on the dressing table. 'Baby – I'm sorry . . .'

Her shoulders sagged. 'Worthless.' Her voice was almost dead now. 'I can't *do* anything . . .'

'There's Henry.'

Finally she nodded. 'We can stay with him, if he needs that.'

'I'll find out.' I picked up the drink and finished it in one swallow. 'I think you should go to the Kells' until I get back from the police. Call Rennie and I'll drive you there.'

'I'm okay, now. Really.'

'It's not just that. The police think whoever killed Lydia knew her and might do this thing again.'

She looked away. 'It was Jason,' she said harshly. 'I can feel it.'

'Whoever, Krissy, it was bad. Let me drop you.'

'No. I'll lock the doors.' She didn't look up. I hesitated, watching her. 'Honestly, I'll be all right. I just want to be alone. I can't face anyone yet, that's all.'

I didn't move. Then Kris Ann raised her head in the cool, prideful pose I recognized as Cade's. Softly she finished, 'You'll be late, Adam.'

I let her go.

I went through the house checking locks and windows. When I had done that Kris Ann put on a robe to walk me downstairs. At the door she shook her head, as if trying to dismiss a dream. 'You need to do this, Adam. Even with Daddy there.'

'Even so.'

I touched her cheek and she shivered.

'Poor Henry,' she said.

Chapter 5

As I drove to the police station, it came to me that my talks with Henry Cantwell had begun on a day like this.

It had been a bright spring afternoon, my first months with the firm. Our tax partner had left early to play golf and asked me to drop off Henry's returns. When I got there, late afternoon was falling on the Cantwell place like a gentle mood, muting its colors yet lending them a strange richness that was almost dislocating. So I lingered a moment before pressing the buzzer.

A light-skinned black woman with Indian features answered and led me to the library without a flicker of acknowledgment. But Henry rose from his chair with a bright, surprising smile.

'It's good to see you again, Adam. How long has it been?'

'Almost since the wedding, I think.'

'Too long.' He gave me a firm handshake and gestured toward the window. 'Is that as nice as it looks?'

'I've seen nothing quite like it.' I gave him the papers. 'While I remember, Grayson Fox said to be sure and sign these if you want to keep out of jail. I take it that's a joke.'

He made a rueful face. 'I forgot last year,' he explained wryly. 'Lydia tells me it's premature senility.'

I grinned. 'Then it's catching. Today I walked out of my office and promptly forgot where I was going. Roland caught me in the hallway looking perplexed. He's probably wondering what they've hired.'

'Oh, he knows,' Henry smiled. 'From what Kris Ann told us you could have worked anywhere.' He put on half-glasses, quickly scanned the returns, and signed them in a small, careful hand that was almost like script. 'There,' he said with an air of great accomplishment. 'Let me fix you a drink.'

'You're sure. I don't want to put off your and Mrs Cantwell's dinner.'

'Don't worry, Adam. Lydia's already eaten and gone to bed, so it's just me.'

'I hope she's not sick.'

He looked startled. 'Oh no,' he said quickly. 'Sometimes she gets a bit tired and needs time to herself. I'd be glad of a chance to talk.'

'Then I would too,' I smiled. 'I'll have Bushmills on ice, if you have it.'

He smiled back. 'Irish whiskey. Of course.'

He filled the glass carefully, measuring, stirring, handing me the drink like a proffer of hospitality. When we had settled in our chairs, he asked, 'How goes the job?'

'Pretty well, I guess. Like a lot of things, it takes getting used to.'

'I'm sure. After all, you've changed your entire life in a very little time: first job, new marriage, moving here to Alabama. Some mornings you must wake up and wonder how it happened.'

I had sat back, considering the room, its contents outlined in the evening light: an antique walking stick in one corner, a standing clock, an oil lamp. A blue Miro seemed not so much to hang as to be suspended. 'Sometimes,' I admitted. 'I'll get this strange feeling – just at odd moments of the day – as though I've been exiled. I guess that passes when you've lived somewhere long enough to belong.'

He nodded his understanding. 'Your feeling's not so strange, Adam. The ancient Greeks considered exile the worst form of punishment. Socrates took hemlock instead.' He smiled. 'I expect you won't come to that. The South does take understanding, of course, and some of the people you'll meet may seem complex or even contradictory. But you'll grow to like it – very much, I think. Life here has great beauty, and a permanence most people never find.'

'I'm beginning to see that,' I agreed. 'I'm not sure Krissy could have left.'

Henry's glass stopped at his lips, his look curious and

reflective. He put down the drink. 'Perhaps not. But I've known Kris Ann since she was a child, and the one thing I'm certain of is that she needs affection from someone other than her father. Do try not to get so involved in meeting Roland's standards at the firm that she depends too much on him, or forgets that she married a different man. It's you she needs.' He stopped, faintly embarrassed. 'I apologize, Adam. I seem to be giving you too much advice, and all unasked.'

The whiskey was feeling warm and sudden in me. I waved a deprecating hand. 'It's appreciated, really. The firm isn't the greatest place for candid chats – about Roland or anything else.'

He gave me a long sideways glance. 'I suppose I'm a bit gun-shy, given our troubles with Jason. He's at an age where he resents suggestion.'

His look and tone seemed strangely tentative, apologetic yet questioning. I decided he was in need of reassurance. 'I was nineteen once, too,' I smiled. 'I'm not now.'

'Then there's hope. He seems so angry.'

'You'll be astonished,' I said firmly.

His shy smile of relief was oddly touching. He reached suddenly to the shelf and took down *The Mind of the South*. 'Let me give you a book. I think this might be good reading for a new southerner.'

I hesitated. 'You're sure?' I asked. 'I worry about borrowing things.'

'I'll trust you, Adam.' He held out the book with both hands. 'Please, take it. Perhaps we can talk again when you're through.'

I suppose it was then I first sensed that he was a lonely man. 'Thank you,' I said. I took the volume from his hands. . . .

I lit a cigarette. 'Where were you last night?' Rayfield asked him now.

Henry seemed not to hear. He sat in the middle of a partitioned room with shuttered lights overhead and one window with Venetian blinds slicing sunlight into ribbons on a gray tile floor. Cade and I flanked him, with Bast and Rayfield sitting on two desks in front of us. The stenographer, a young woman with straight black bangs, awaited his answer. I turned, trying to see him as Rayfield would. What I saw was a pallid man with skin almost papery, a ridged nose too large for his face, and crinkled lids that drooped to make triangles of his eyes. They were gray and wasted, and his face seemed drawn in upon itself, as if he had retracted an inch beneath the skin. His normal self showed only in ways that Rayfield might see as too fastidious but now were merely sad – small habits that, one by one, created order. His hair was combed, his suit pressed, and his shoes were shined. A white handkerchief pointed from his breast pocket.

'I was in Anniston,' he said abruptly. He seemed removed from the words, as if recalling some small incident of childhood. 'It was business, with loan customers. They wish to build an apartment complex. I visited the site and afterwards we went to a country club for drinks and dinner. By the time I left it was past ten o'clock, so I turned off at the Holiday Inn and got a room.'

His speech had an eerie precision. Rayfield watched him coldly. 'What happened then?'

'I awoke this morning and had breakfast in the dining room. I remember it was about nine-thirty when I finished. After that I decided to drive back to the apartment site to look at it alone.' He paused, speaking the next four words distinctly. 'Then I came home.'

Rayfield's eyes became slits. 'At the motel – was there someone with you?'

Henry blinked. 'What do you mean?'

Rayfield reached for his pen, still watching Henry. 'Can anyone confirm you were there?'

'No. No one.'

'Did you call anyone from the motel?'

'No.'

The questions came faster. 'You didn't call your wife?'

'Well, yes – Lydia.'

'When was that?'

'Not long after – I don't know exactly.'

'Did she answer?'

Henry flinched. 'Yes.'

'What did you say?'

'I told her where I was. Sometimes, in Anniston, I would stop and drive home the next morning. I told her I might do that before I left.'

'Did she say anything when you called?'

'No.' Henry's voice weakened. 'Not really.'

'She didn't say someone was with her?'

'No, nothing like that.'

'And you didn't ask?'

'No.'

'What *did* you talk about?'

'Just that I was still in Anniston.'

'How long did that take?'

'I don't know – I didn't notice.'

'One minute? Two minutes?'

'I don't know. Perhaps two.'

Rayfield switched tacks. 'Who was the first person you saw this morning?'

Cade's deep-set eyes searched Henry. 'The waitress,' Henry answered in a chastened voice. 'At breakfast.'

Rayfield's cadence eased. 'Anniston's not much more than an hour, Mr Cantwell. Might could be easy for you to check into a motel, drive home, and then back again.' He paused and asked coolly, 'Is that what happened?'

'Is that an accusation?' Cade broke in.

'Are you instructing your client not to answer?'

'No.' Henry had stiffened in his chair. His voice was a rasp. 'I would never harm Lydia.'

Rayfield said nothing. He began stroking his pen between thumb and forefingers, eyeing Henry narrowly. Bast turned to look at him, leaning slightly closer until I sensed him watching over Rayfield in some way I couldn't understand. Rayfield's voice was quieter still. 'The coroner called a while back, Mr Cantwell. He found semen traces in your wife.' Henry's cheek twitched. Rayfield almost whispered. 'Now how do you suppose that happened?'

'That's enough,' I said sharply.

Rayfield's head twisted, eyes slowly moving from me to Henry and back again, almost contemptuous. Then he turned to Cade.

'You want to take Mr Cantwell home?'

'Henry?' Cade asked.

Henry was staring up at Rayfield, his mouth half-open, eyes glittering. The veins of his hands were purple welts. 'Call it off,' I urged Cade.

'No, Adam.' Henry's voice was hoarse. 'It's all right.'

Quickly Rayfield asked, 'Was there trouble with your wife?'

Henry shook his head and looked away.

Rayfield wiped his mouth with the back of his hand. The sun ribbons on the floor had faded. Outside, voices called back and forth – it was quitting time for someone, they would go to a party or watch television, they couldn't decide. 'Y'all have servants?' Rayfield asked.

'Etta, our maid. Etta Parsons.'

'How long you had Etta?'

'Over twenty years.'

'When is she there?'

Rayfield's questions were again rapid. The stenographer shook her wrist and caught Henry's answer: 'Weekdays. Saturdays if we entertain. She was off today.'

'Any other servants?'

Henry leaned on his elbows, hands clasped in front of him. 'We have a new yardman – a Negro.' He sounded embarrassed. 'I never spoke to him, don't know his name.'

'Know anything about him?' Rayfield asked.

Henry shook his head.

'Know anyone who hated your wife?'

'No.'

'Anyone who'd want to kill her, or molest her?'

'No. No.'

'Or mutilate her picture?'

Henry's face was mottled. Without waiting for his answer, Rayfield asked, 'You tell Jason what happened, Mr Cantwell?'

Henry hesitated. 'Yes.'

'What did he say?'

27

'He yelled, about police.' Henry's forehead bent to his hands. 'We've had – '

'Trouble?'

Henry nodded almost indetectably. I moved between him and Rayfield. Cade touched Henry's shoulder and raised his free hand toward Rayfield in a restraining gesture. 'Just two more questions,' Rayfield said.

Cade looked at Henry, then Rayfield, nodded, and said tersely, 'Two.'

I turned angrily to Cade. Rayfield asked Henry, 'You know your wife wanted to cut Jason off?'

'No.' The answer came with seeming effort.

'Know why she would?'

'They fought – last week. I wasn't home.'

'About what?'

'I don't know. She wouldn't say.'

Rayfield stared at the pen. Musingly, he asked, 'Would Jason do this, Mr Cantwell – all of it?'

Henry's face collapsed in his hands and he began crying.

'That's it, Lieutenant.' Cade's tone was final. 'Ask the boy yourself.'

I was certain they already had. But Rayfield merely shrugged. 'There's more questions,' he said. 'We'll want Mr Cantwell again.'

Cade stood. 'He came here voluntarily, sooner than was healthy. You've asked your questions and gotten your answers. Now get out and go to work, because if you want him again you'd better have a warrant.'

Rayfield stared at Cade as if calibrating his power. 'We're working on it,' he said mildly. There was irony in his voice, and clear dislike.

Henry was slumped in his chair. I touched his elbow. 'You okay?'

The stenographer left. Henry raised himself and mumbled, 'Yes,' his face ivory, expressionless.

'All right, Henry,' Cade said. I helped Henry to his feet. Cade took his arm from me and steered him through the partition and toward the door.

'Get them an escort,' Rayfield told Bast, who followed. Rayfield watched them leave. His hair was damp and flat on his head and one shirtsleeve had unrolled until it was longer than the other.

'You didn't need to tell him like that,' I said.

Rayfield turned and looked me up and down with the same expression of curious contempt.

'Why did it bother you so much?'

'Because I've started wondering what you've got in for Henry Cantwell.'

For an instant he looked surprised. Then, in exact, icy mockery of Cade, he said, 'I take it we're through here,' and left.

I walked from the partitioned room through a larger surrounding one jammed with metal desks and plainclothesmen writing reports and answering telephones, then opened the door marked 'Robbery and Homicide,' which led to the corridor. It was jammed with reporters, their shouts echoing off tile floors and walls in a babel of sound. Two bulky police convoyed Cade and Henry amidst the whine of flashbulbs and newsmen jostling with TV cameras. Someone kicked my shin as I shoved to catch up. A voice barked, 'You fucked up my picture.' Near the glass doors in front I saw Henry's head bobbing in the crowd. I elbowed through until I reached the doors and got outside, trying to reach him.

Another crowd of reporters waited in the dusk. 'Mr Shaw,' someone shouted. It was a green-eyed woman, standing at the top of the steps with a bearded man holding a TV camera that blocked my way. 'What did they want to know?'

I stopped, trapped in the crush. Her voice was quick and intense. 'Do they suspect Henry Cantwell?'

The cameras closed in, as they had when we buried my father, twenty years ago. A chill, misting rain had wet my neck. The grave smelled of dirt and wet grass. My mother's face was closed and harsh. She dropped the clump of dirt as Brian clutched at her. The priest chanted. Photographers moved among the black cars, taking pictures.

A flashbulb exploded in my face. 'Will Mr Cantwell be charged?' she was demanding.

'Why don't you rob some graves,' I spat out. 'Maybe take pictures.'

She shrank from me. I grabbed her cameraman by the collar. 'Get out of my way, you sonofabitch.' His mouth fell open. I threw him to the cement and pushed down the steps through the parting crowd.

On the sidewalk police moved Henry toward Cade's blue Audi. They opened the passenger door as I reached his side. He turned to me, voice trembling. 'Adam, you must believe I would never do this.'

His eyes locked mine. Quietly, I said, 'Don't ask again.'

He nodded at the ground. Cade glared at me over the hood of the car. 'If there's anything you need,' I said quickly, 'Krissy and I can move over there, whatever.'

He put his hand on my shoulder. 'It's all right. Roland's called my sister – '

'Let's go,' Cade snapped. Henry Cantwell disappeared into the car and was driven away.

Chapter 6

That night Kris Ann and I put on evening clothes and drove to the country club.

I'd come home to find all the lights on and the telephone off the hook, and no one waiting. No one answered when I called for Kris Ann. I went quickly up the stairs, nerves taut for a long half minute until I heard the shower. I called out, and in the moment of relief when Kris Ann answered knew how frightened I had been. I went downstairs to fix two drinks, and waited.

She didn't come. For a while I watched the ice melt in her drink, then drifted to the porch. It was dark and there were cricket sounds and the whir of a moth near the gaslight, but all I saw was Lydia Cantwell's murdered face, and Henry's as it fell into his hands.

'Are you all right?'

Kris Ann stood near the gaslight in a silk caftan, beautiful without makeup, the shock in her face now become something sadder.

'I was thinking about Henry.'

She nodded. 'Daddy said the police were such bastards.'

'Only when he gave them an engraved invitation.' She watched me carefully, in silence. 'So he called,' I added.

'I called him, to see if I should stay with Henry. His sister's flying in. So I said I'd at least bring a casserole.'

'I'll drive you.'

'It's still baking.' She walked to the end of the porch, staring out. I went to stand next to her.

'There's a drink on the coffee table.'

'No. Thank you.'

I hesitated, then asked, 'Why is the phone off?'

'Reporters kept calling.'

'I might have needed to reach you.'

'It didn't matter. They kept wanting to know things . . .'

I touched her shoulder. She flinched, turning suddenly. 'I want to go out,' she said.

'Out? Where?'

She looked down. 'The club.'

'Jesus Christ –'

'Please.' Her words rushed forth. 'Just for an hour. It's a benefit Lydia put together for the symphony and what with it already planned they've decided she'd want it to go on. You know I'd rather be with Henry but here we are and they need money and dammit I don't want to sit in this empty house feeling sad and afraid instead of seeing friends and at least trying to cope –'

'Sounds perfect,' I cut in. 'Maybe Henry would like a ride.'

She recoiled as though struck. I reached out. 'I'm sorry . . .'

She backed away, gaze steady now. 'I have to, Adam. Please. This afternoon, what we did – afterwards it made me cold.'

My hands fell to my sides. 'That wasn't meant.'

She stood tense and quiet. I felt suddenly drained. 'We'll go then,' I said.

Kris Ann was still quiet on the way to Henry's. When we drove up, the house was dim and massive and Cade almost a shadow as he came to the window. He vanished when Kris Ann got out; then the front door opened and Kris Ann disappeared. I waited outside.

About ten minutes later Kris Ann emerged looking pale. 'Henry?' I asked.

'He's sedated.'

She lapsed into pensive silence as we drove off. 'I'm sorry,' she finally said. 'You found Lydia, not me. I acted hysterical.'

'No matter, Krissy. There's no good form for this.'

'What I mean is that we can go home if you want. Really, it's been so horrible about Lydia that I forgot your father – '

I took her hand. 'It's okay. All that was a long time back.'

She turned to me, questioning. I tried switching subjects. 'I've been missing you all week. When did you get in last night?'

'Not until after midnight. I got the last Atlanta flight and didn't want to wake you. It all seems so long ago.'

'But your cousin's okay.'

'Fine.'

'And the baby?'

She turned back to the window, her profile still. The stab of beam lights on the empty road ahead accented our solitude in the moving darkness. 'He's precious,' she finally said. 'They're very lucky.'

It was quiet as we both thought whatever we were thinking. 'You're sure it doesn't matter?' she asked.

'About the club?' I tried smiling. 'Not really. They can bore me, but they can't make me think.'

We arrived at a staid building of English fieldstone set back from the road with the distance that money buys. There were two prowl cars at the end of the drive and a uniformed officer had replaced the doorman. Leaving the car with an attendant, we took an entrance hall lined with pictures of dead founders to the ballroom. It stretched across the blue hand-loomed rug to a large rectangular mirror on the far wall, two hundred feet from where we stood. Seven chandeliers swept toward it in a crystalline line to be abruptly reflected, the nearest the largest, like stations in society. Beneath a thin haze of smoke men in tuxedos and women in evening dresses drank in small clusters from which the occasional one or two would drift toward the bar, then amble with a fresh drink in search of something new. Usually they would discuss vacations, children, their lake houses, the imbecility of the President and the next party where they would discuss all that again. But tonight there were police inside, and the talk was of Lydia Cantwell.

As we entered, couples turned to stare, their voices lowering. A flashbulb exploded from amidst a clutch of media people about three times too many and too badly dressed to be society editors. Kris Ann blinked, startled. Angrily, under her breath, she said, 'Damn them.'

I took her arm, kept moving as a hard-eyed tractor magnate stopped castigating Jason Cantwell to his willowy lawyer and their plumped wives long enough to announce, 'The little bastard should be executed,' and look to me for an answer. He sounded as if Lydia's death were the ultimate thing that had gone wrong. For him and his friends too many things had gone wrong already – blacks, inflation, their children who couldn't stand them, that first burglary next door – until their pride of place had become mere twitches: harassing waiters, inspecting the greens, reviewing membership with a jeweler's eye as they slid gradually closer to that national nervous breakdown that produced angry shoppers, battered wives, charge-card deadbeats and born-again Christians by the thousands. It was clear from their stares that my finding Lydia's body was common knowledge. 'This is grotesque,' I muttered.

'Adam, Kris Ann.'

I turned to see Ardrey Carr tottering toward us, the fat of soured youth dulling his jawline, face florid to match his hair. Fifteen years ago Carr's forearm shiver had shattered the face of a Mississippi right end before a howling mob at Legion Field, where Alabama played, and brought him fame, a thriving insurance business, and the disgruntled look of a man who has passed his peak and can't remember where. 'We're over there,' he said, jerking his thumb toward a group we hadn't spotted. 'Figured for sure you'd want to be with friends.'

For once Carr watched me instead of Kris Ann, avid with curiosity. I wished fiercely I were somewhere else. But Kris Ann smiled with relief and went toward the circle of expectant faces.

'I'll get drinks,' I told Carr.

The barman was a slight, smooth-faced black with a gray mustache and cautious eyes. 'Evenin', Mr Adam.'

'How're you tonight, Carter?'

A dubious smile crossed his face like trouble. 'Just fine, sir.' He handed me the usual drinks and slipped quickly back into his profession, a small black man in a red jacket, polishing the clean wet glasses from the kitchen with a white towel, snapping the towel and polishing again, until they gleamed. Someone called for a drink. 'Yessuh,' he said.

From the end of the bar a pompous surgeon I knew just well enough to dislike was pushing toward me. Turning to escape, I nearly bumped the fortyish blonde they called West Lounge Winnie, sipping a fresh martini as her restless eyes searched over the rim for a man. For the five years since her husband had died she would arrive at parties in one-strap gowns and an intricate bouffant hairdo and then drink until gin had dulled her features and unwound her hair and psyche, so that by one o'clock she was talking about sex, to no one. Ardrey Carr thought she was very funny.

He was watching Kris Ann as the group talked back and forth. But then most men did. Even me.

It had first happened in a dingy apartment crammed with law students, beer cans, Salvation Army furniture, back copies of *Esquire*, and cigarette smoke that seeped through the screens of the open windows. A paunchy classmate was shouting with a Temptations album in a Mississippi accent, trying to sound black. It was hot and too close and the fall crispness of late afternoon kept looking better. I was about to slide out the door when I saw her.

She was watching the singer from a corner of the room, looking disdainful and a little amused as two first-year law students hovered near her, trying to think what to say. Even at a distance she had an energy of beauty like no one I'd ever seen. Above the chiseled nose and high, strong cheekbones her eyes were wide and black and lambent. Long black hair fell away straight on both sides of her face, and her mouth, full and regular, set off a clean, delicate chin. It was as though the strength in her face had been sculpted to the point of losing that for beauty, but not quite. I took in the cool, easy tilt of the beer to her lips until she ran through me. I went over without thinking.

For an instant her face clouded, as if I had frightened her. But when I introduced myself she mustered a lingering hint of amusement. She was Kris Ann Cade, she told me, a senior and just watching after that rotten game. 'This is terrific anthropology. You've got primitive mating rituals and what with two men to every woman, there's some absolutely vicious social Darwinism.'

'Beats football,' I agreed. 'Vanderbilt may win some year but it'll take legislation.'

The animal white smile came and went so fast it seemed almost a trick. She nodded toward the white soul singer. 'God, he's awful, though.' Her voice was at once smoky and metallic. 'You know, I don't think I've seen you before. Are you a recluse?'

'Almost. I go to law school and work twenty hours a week, so nights and weekends I study.'

She sounded mildly surprised. 'Why do you do all that?'

'Because I'm here in scholarship,' I smiled. 'You've heard of those?'

Her gaze was cool and unembarrassed. 'That was foolish, wasn't it? You must be hell-bent on being a lawyer.'

'I guess I must be.'

She inspected me with mock gravity. 'I think the problem is that you don't look like one. More like Warren Beatty with a mean streak.'

'*Now* you tell me, when I've got student loans to my eyeballs.'

She smiled again, then wrinkled her nose and batted at a near curl of smoke. I stopped reaching for a cigarette. 'Maybe we should find air someplace.'

She raised an eyebrow. 'You don't sing, do you?'

'I don't even hum,' I grinned. 'Plus I'm a virgin.'

Her smile returned. 'It's your schedule,' she said, and allowed that I could walk her home.

We took the gravel path to Branscomb Quad, hands in our pockets, talking back and forth in the pale fall sunlight. Leaves crunched beneath our feet and there was a rich, damp odor of more leaves burning. Her father was a lawyer, she was telling me, which was where she got her notion of how they looked and acted. 'Maybe you should be one,' I remarked. 'You don't look like Warren Beatty.'

She shook her head. 'I don't burn like that – whatever he's got that makes him a brilliant lawyer. I've never been sure I wanted to.' She frowned. 'He needed a son – someone to do what he does. The best I can do for him is *have* one.'

'Is that the program, then? Kids?'

Her shoulders curled downward. 'It's Daddy. He's not always wild about the boys who come home but he wants a son from me.'

I smiled. 'Too bad he can't just start without you.'

'Oh, I want one too, someday. I think most women do' – she looked wryly across – 'no matter what they tell you in the middle of the night.'

I laughed. 'Then you didn't believe me?'

She smiled back. 'About being a virgin? You don't seem the type.'

I shrugged, saying carelessly, 'Easier not to be, these days.'

'Easier to be a man, period.' She became abruptly solemn. 'Sometimes I wish Daddy had gotten what he wanted.'

I was thinking she was funny, flip, and serious by turns, perhaps a little frightened under the cool. 'If you were a man,' I said easily, 'I wouldn't have noticed you. And too many of them are lawyers already. After two years of this I can think of better things.'

'I'm an English major now,' she shrugged. 'Shelley, Keats, and *Adam Bede*, and all functionally useless. But I paint a little.'

The last sounded like more than a throwaway. 'There are things you can do with art. Teach, maybe.'

'Oh, I don't know if I could make it a job. It's more a release – painting to get rid of something until there it is on canvas.'

I nodded. 'I'd like to see what you've done.'

She gave me a sideways look. 'They're kind of private. Maybe sometime.' We reached the dorm. 'The thing is,' she finished, 'I've just been having fun, and I guess I've never wanted to face what comes next.'

'I've had times like that. But something's always happened. It'll come.'

'I guess so.' She looked at me again, suddenly hesitant, as if waiting for something more. Then she shrugged and reached for the door. 'Anyhow, thanks for the walk.'

She turned in the doorway, poised to disappear, a tall, beautiful girl with a voice as stylish as gin and sports cars, eyes as deep and tempting as the things I'd never had. All at once I had to say something, do something.

'About what's next,' I tried. 'Maybe you can start small. Like next Saturday.'

She looked down. 'What's next Saturday?' she asked innocently.

I hung there a moment. Then her eyes raised, and her grin cracked wide and sharp and clean, confirming her joke.

I smiled back. 'There must be a party.'

The party was louder now. The haze had lowered and people drank and smoked in the loose-jointed rhythm that comes with late evening, staring more openly as I moved across the room. Rayfield had materialized near a floral display, watching me. I looked past him. Through the sliding glass doors to the patio I could see only darkness, making the party seem self-contained, as if it were happening on a spaceship. I moved toward Kris Ann.

'Mr Shaw.'

It took me a moment to place the greenness of her eyes: the reporter who had questioned me. 'Back from the cemetery so soon?' I asked.

She placed hands on hips. 'I'd like to know what that was all about.'

She spoke with a trace of Boston accent, its edge matching the knife keenness of her eyes and the quick, kinetic movements of someone who burned off calories just standing around. Her auburn hair was cut short and she had a pert face with no makeup and freckles on the bridge of her nose. Her jawline was square and her skin quite pale and clear. She could have been the girl I'd dated in high school, Mary Moore, who had closed her eyes when I touched her in the dark and had four children now.

'What the hell are you doing here?' I asked.

'This is an important charity event,' she said crisply. 'I'm covering it. What the hell are you doing here?'

'I married well.' I began moving. 'Excuse me.'

'We're not through –'

I turned back. 'What's your name?'

'Nora Culhane. Channel Seven.'

'All right, Ms Culhane. For openers, don't kid me. You're not that wounded and you already know what my problem is: you're scavenging a tragedy so the local voyeurs can get those goose bumps in the night, have their talk a little spicier, their sex a little sweeter. I don't like it.'

A long-necked woman in sequins moved closer, head cocked. Culhane's speech was staccato. 'Murder's news, Mr Shaw. Henry Cantwell's money doesn't change that.'

'No, it just makes them love it more, doesn't it, like with Patty Hearst – vicarious thrills for the mentally unemployed. We both know that if Lydia Cantwell had been a poor black woman no one would give a shit. But here you are, wearing the First Amendment like a Communion dress.'

She flushed. 'I suppose I should be covering the Pillsbury bake-off.'

'Oh God,' I said. 'Not that too. Look, you're not Bacall and I'm certainly not Bogart – I'm not having enough fun. So let's drop it.'

'I've got something to ask you first. Tell me, when Rayfield asked Cantwell how long that last telephone call to Lydia was, what did he say?'

'You tell me.'

'One or two minutes. But it wasn't. It was twelve. Rayfield's got the toll slip.'

'Good for him. It's not hard for a man in shock to make that kind of mistake.'

'Come on, Mr Shaw. What were they talking about? It wouldn't take Henry Cantwell twelve minutes to tell Lydia where he was. He lied about the time, and he lied about what they said to each other. And if he lied about that, chances are he lied about other things.'

I looked quickly around, speaking in a lower voice. 'I'd be damned careful with your choice of words. If Henry wanted to lie, he wouldn't do it about the length of the call – it's too easy to check. He'd admit the length of the call and lie about its substance. Who would know? That he didn't makes my point.'

She shrugged. 'I'm using this on the eleven o'clock. I just thought you could tell me what they really talked about.'

'I wouldn't know.'

From a distance Rayfield watched us intently. He seemed out of place, as if staring through a window. 'And you've got no comment?' she was asking.

'Not a word. Just remember the law of libel. And say hello to Rayfield. It's nice of him to use this to tuck it to Henry Cantwell, and nice of you to help.' I left her there.

Weaving through the crowd, I reached Kris Ann with her drink as she listened to Susie Threadgill talk avidly about Jason: 'And after they threw him out of Phillips for beating some boy half to death, he came home and killed the neighbor's dog with a pistol, just from meanness. Henry had to beg them not to prosecute. He was so ashamed.'

Clayton Kell edged over. 'Adam, I'm sure sorry about this morning. You look ready to kill.'

He said it straight out, not prying, the irony unintended. The usual Clayton, dry-witted and amiably lazy, saw both the world and his role in it as a little bit silly. It was probably a perspective worth having: Clayton puttered around Henry's bank like a large troll who had gone to prep school, getting by on charm. His secret was that, when it mattered, he was better than that. I relaxed for a moment. 'Thanks, Clayt.' I looked around. 'Why all the cops and reporters?'

Clayton gave me a thin smile. 'The police are here because some nervous people want protection from a madman they're afraid knows them already. The reporters are pretending to cover the party so they can snoop. I just hope they don't use Lydia's murder to dog Henry. He's been bad enough.'

'How so?'

'You haven't noticed?'

'Not particularly. I haven't seen him that much. He's been lying kind of low.'

'Well, you all are our counsel – you've seen how he usually

is down there, kind of sleepwalking through business hours like his real life is happening somewhere else. But at least he's always pretty much the same. The last two months, though, he's been almost manic-depressive: hiding in his office with the door shut and then bursting out to insist on something foolish. There was one loan in particular, a high-risk deal with this white-shoe developer out of New Orleans where we ended up under-collateralized and in trouble with the Feds. I mean, Henry's no businessman, but he could usually spot quality.'

'What do you make of it?'

He gave a shrug of vast helplessness. 'You know Henry. Very private. But I figure it's the boy, poor bastard. Henry, that is.' He sipped his drink, asking pointedly, 'How goes it with Roland?'

'Same, same. He looks on me as the son he never had.'

Clayton gave another thin smile, and the talk became general between the eight of us: Susie and Tom Threadgill, half-drunk and riding a kind of crazy animation; Clayton and Rennie Kell, gracious and looking oddly alike; Ardrey Carr and his wife, Sandra, dark and thin, whose nerves had been ravaged by Ardrey and four children and now a murder, and who was looking at me strangely. At the last party, Tom Threadgill had asked brightly if everyone still masturbated and when he closed in on me, I'd said no I didn't have to, I was a hermaphrodite. Clayton had smiled, Tom looked disappointed, and Sandra had clearly been puzzled. From her expression now, she had looked it up.

'Goddamn Atlanta,' Tom Threadgill burst out angrily to Clayton Kell. 'Got stuck again in the screwed-up airport. I swear to God, flush a toilet south of Louisville and even the crap goes through Atlanta.'

Clayton nodded politely as I half listened, wondering why either of us bothered. But with the exception of Ardrey Carr –and me – they had all been born with money and large houses to parents who were friends and then gone to prep school together and met during college vacations until they became part of a context, reminding each other of who they were and had always been. I thought perhaps to Kris Ann they were familiar things, like her mother's crystal or the pictures of Cade she kept. I forgot them and began wondering about Henry's last call to Lydia until I heard her name and picked up the thread again.

'Poor woman,' Rennie Kell was saying.

'Nobody's safe.' Sandra Carr's shrill voice seemed wired to her nerve ends. Next to her Ardrey tottered on his heels. She glanced at him, almost quivering. 'You start out thinking you know how your life is going to be . . .'

Tom Threadgill had forgotten the airport. 'Life plans are stupid,' he pronounced. 'It's all contingent. Lydia lives this decorous kind of life that's supposed to get you loving children and a party for your golden anniversary and instead she ends up murdered, like all along it's been this big fucking joke.'

Clayton frowned. Sandra Carr turned angrily to her husband. 'Let's go home, dammit. We should never have left the children with that girl.'

'I don't know,' Susie Threadgill was saying. 'It's more like these other parts of you reach out so no matter how hard you try, they get you. I just wish Lydia had been more authentic – you know, more in touch with herself. Here she was always doing for other people and never anything but nice, and it makes you think inside maybe she was burning up and that somehow it all came out, and then –'

Ardrey Carr leaned forward, ignoring his wife. 'They say she was bruised something awful,' he said loudly. 'Raped too.'

I realized he was talking to me. The others seemed part of a frieze of rapt-faced people who squeezed their drink in front of them. I took my time lighting a cigarette.

'They're right,' I said.

Awareness that I'd snubbed him stained Carr's face with anger. Sandra Carr turned white. In the silence, Kris Ann turned to me holding out her glass. 'I'm dry, Adam,' she said quietly. 'Could you get me another?'

She looked coolly to Carr until he stopped glaring and

seemed almost to deflate. I waited him out, then took her glass. From a corner Rayfield ran a long appraising look from me to Kris Ann to me again as I went toward the bar.

It was crowded now. There was sweat on Carter's forehead as he worked among angry, competing voices, watching the party for signals from yet other drinkers, the privileged ones who'd slipped him a hundred dollars at Christmas. West Lounge Winnie watched him blankly, hairdo canted dangerously to one side. Next to her a towering woman who'd been flirting with someone else saw her husband moving toward them. 'Here comes Donald,' she drawled. 'My God, I despise that man.' Arriving, Donald looked at the pair with great, tragic eyes. 'What will the symphony do without Lydia?' he asked, and began to weep. I took my cigarette to the verandah.

For a while I leaned on the railing. The swimming pool below was a turquoise rectangle that shimmered with submerged light. I hardly heard the footsteps.

Frenzied hands choked me by the collar. I wheeled with my fist in the air. The woman shrieked: 'Doll lady, fucking doll lady,' in a harsh, crazy voice, over and over.

'Shut up,' I snapped. 'What the hell is wrong with you?'

She stopped, staring at her shoes, abashed. My arm dropped. In the dim light she was just a raddled blonde with overripe hips and the pigeon-toed stance of a drunk. 'Find your husband,' I said, more reasonably. 'You're drunk.'

'No blood.' She nodded ponderously, as if that were very profound. 'No blood.'

She looked at me for approval. Through the window behind her, foolish mouths smiled and lips moved that made no sound. Then there was the sigh of a sliding glass door and a tall man stepped from the ballroom, glancing over his shoulder. 'Joanne,' he called in a low voice.

She stiffened, and as the man came out of darkness I placed them both. Dalton Mooring was the president of Maddox Coal and Steel. The woman was his wife.

He stopped short of her. They looked at each other in dim light from the pool, as if I were forgotten. In a strained, weary undertone, he said, 'Again.'

She looked pasty and about to vomit. 'Better take her home,' I told him.

Mooring spun, eyes angry and luminous, as if he were ready to strike. Subtly, quickly, he reconsidered. 'I apologize for my wife,' he said without feeling.

She began to cry with drunkenness and humiliation. He turned and steered her roughly toward the parking lot, avoiding the party. I went to the bar and got Kris Ann her drink.

Driving home, she said, 'I'm ashamed I asked you to go.'

'Don't worry, hon. It was a chance to think about things.'

Kris Ann lay her head back against the car seat. 'Like what?'

'Like that Tom Threadgill is the biggest waste of time since the Parcheesi board.'

Kris Ann smiled slightly and was silent. I lit a cigarette. 'Was there something wrong with her, Krissy?'

She rolled her head to see me. 'Adam, you can't even be sure what Joanne Mooring was talking about.'

I took a deep drag on the cigarette, its ash an orange circle in blackness. 'Maybe. But Susie made sense for once. Something like this happens and you have to look differently at the woman it's happened to.'

'*I* don't,' she answered, 'and don't want to. Lydia was our friend – my good friend.'

For a moment I listened to the low snarl of the motor. 'I had a friend once at Notre Dame – Eddie Halloran. Eddie was a skinny, sensitive guy with a nice smile. Everyone liked him. He was quick and funny, but when you needed to talk he had this special knack of listening, and somehow you knew that he could slip into your skin and feel exactly what you felt. When Eddie got beaten up one night in a tough neighborhood off campus I was as mad as anyone else. It never occurred to me to wonder why he'd been there.

'Eventually we all forgot it until about a year later, it happens. Same neighborhood, two guys with a knife take Eddie for a ride and kill him. It turned out he was trying to pick them up. You see, anyone could tell him their problems, but he didn't want us to know. So he played it too close to the line.'

Kris Ann touched my arm. 'You never told me – Adam, that's so sad.'

'Sad, and to the point. What I'm wondering is why Lydia seemed so remote. If anyone knows besides Henry, it's you or Roland.'

Kris Ann sat up in the car seat, staring out. 'Whatever,' she said tiredly, 'I don't believe it was anything like I think you're asking. There's only one time I can ever remember her seeming less than perfect and I only understood it later, if I ever did. It was the summer I was twelve, I guess, and Daddy had a cocktail party on a Sunday afternoon. He would sort of let me be hostess and I was there in a blue silk dress he'd bought, feeling like a lady.'

There was memory in her words. She paused as if to puzzle on it, then went on. 'It was around the time that Martin Luther King was here. Claude Acton got drunk out on the patio and started carrying on about how he should be shot. Daddy and Henry and Lydia were there and then she just disappeared.

'A little later I went inside to look at my dress again in the mirror. When I started upstairs I heard someone crying in the first-floor bathroom. It sounded awful. I stopped there on the stairs, and then the door opened.

'It was Lydia. Her face was all tight and drawn so she didn't look herself. I just stared for a minute. Then I ran upstairs. I don't know if she saw me but I couldn't go back outside. The rest of the party I hid in my room – crying too, I'm not sure why. Maybe I was confused about adults.' She shook her head. 'I was confused about a lot of things, then. I remember being angry at King because people always fought over him and it had spoiled the party and my new dress.

'Later Daddy asked where I'd been and I told him about Lydia. He didn't say much, just that he thought Claude's talking like that upset her because of Grangeville and her father. I found out later that was about when the book came out saying those black men were innocent and that Lydia's father had fixed the trial so he could run for governor. I think maybe it just stayed with her all her life, like it was something she'd done or couldn't run from.' She looked sadly ahead. 'Maybe she never even decided who it was that had spoiled *her* party – she was young when it happened, and he *was* her father. But I never really knew.'

Lydia's murder lent the story a horrible poignancy. I wondered at the doubleness that caused her to cry over Grangeville, yet hang her father's portrait on the mantel. Finally I asked, 'Did she ever talk about it?'

'Not that I know of. She probably didn't want to. She must have known how some people felt about her father.'

'Was there anyone she did talk to?'

'Besides Henry? I don't know, unless it was Etta, her maid.'

'That seems odd.'

'Not really. Etta would have been with her more than most. Why is that important?'

'I'm not sure. There's something wrong here – something more than Lydia being murdered. I can smell it even if I can't see it.'

'What you smell is Jason Cantwell.'

I turned to her. 'Sperm and all?'

'Yes. He's twisted enough.' Her voice tightened. 'The only way a man like Jason can touch people is to hurt them. If you want one more reason for Lydia's sadness you can look to Jason. He's a bad seed, Adam.'

Her intensity surprised me. More softly, I answered, 'Even if that's true there's this man Rayfield. There's something off about the way he is with Henry, and how he's using that phone call, with Lydia not twenty-four hours dead. Roland made a mistake today letting him at Henry. He'll make others. He's set on handling this himself.'

'And you?'

'I'm set on keeping Henry alive.'

'So is Daddy.' She looked at me closely. 'For four years now there's been a kind of peace between you, or at least a distance. It's been easier for you both, for all three of

46

us. We've made our adjustments. Please, don't upset that now.'

I inhaled cigarette smoke, playing back what I heard in her voice. 'Is that what you're afraid of? Or is it having to choose?'

She whirled to speak in anger, then bit her lip and looked away. In a low voice, she said, 'It's not just me who has to choose.'

'What does that mean?'

She said nothing for a moment and when she spoke it was not to answer. 'I love you and I love Daddy, and I know he's vulnerable right now. He's older, he's without a wife or son or grandchildren and now some of his investments have gone sour. He's worried and disappointed and maybe even a little frightened, and he's a proud man not used to that. It's not the time, Adam. Leave him be.'

I shook my head. 'Roland's not the point. It's Henry. This is the wrong case for your father to begin a new career in criminal law.'

She faced me now, questioning. Quietly, almost tenderly, she said, 'And your father?'

I stubbed the cigarette. 'He's dead, Krissy.'

She didn't answer. We were silent for the rest of the drive. The house was as we had left it.

That night I couldn't sleep. Kris Ann tossed beside me, restless and troubled. Her face in the darkness was Lydia's.

I smoked three cigarettes and decided to see the maid.

Chapter 7

The light turned red and my car as it stopped spat gravel from the street. Two black girls watched me from the doorway of a dingy corner grocery. Near them, three youths on stripped-down bicycles leaned next to a rusted rain barrel, drinking RC from bottles and ignoring the heat and the girls. The tallest wore sunglasses and an Army jacket, the other two, pea hats, and they stared wistfully at the impossible red curves of the nude woman painted on the cinder-block walls of the 'Night Time Cafe,' across the street. Above the woman the block letters of a loan company billboard spelled out 'Easy Street' below a row of green dollar signs. The air smelled of dirt and gasoline.

When the light changed I drove on toward Etta Parsons'. On my radio Linda Rondstadt gave way to a newsman reading in a tremor of spurious excitement: 'Police continue to investigate the bizarre ritual murder of Birmingham socialite Lydia Cantwell. At a press conference this morning, Lieutenant Frank Rayfield outlined the investigation.'

I found her address and pulled to the curb. Rayfield's radio voice was a monotone. 'Since Mrs Cantwell was found,' he was saying, 'we've reviewed evidence suggesting a possible psychopathic killer as well as questioned members of the family in hope of preventing any further incident. We now believe that the murderer was known to Mrs Cantwell and that his motive was personal.'

'They're already questioning relatives,' Cade had told me a half hour before. 'I don't know what you expect to add.'

We sat drinking coffee in Cade's office amidst the Sunday quiet of a law firm on its day off. Manila folders for the Cantwell estate were spread on the desk in front of him. The dark hollows beneath his eyes became bruises as he leaned back to await my answer, tenting his fingers in an appraising gesture reminiscent of the three years as an associate I had spent in the same armless chair, responding on cue. The window behind him framed the cement tower of the Cantwells' bank, and from over his shoulder stared an iron-faced photograph of Henry Cantwell's father. On a mahogany bookshelf was the portrait of a dark young woman with melancholy gray eyes, Kris Ann's mother. Next to that Kris Ann smiled down at the traces on Cade's desk of his taste for money: a jade vase, a Wedgwood teacup, an antique paperweight of hand-blown glass. Beside that was a morning paper headlined SOCIALITE SLAIN above an old picture of Lydia and a bad one of Henry recoiling from the flashbulbs as he left the police station. 'They talk to Jason?' I parried.

Cade scowled. 'No one's seen him. I gather that when Henry called him yesterday he started screaming about "being trapped." Henry thinks Jason meant that the police had gotten there before he'd broken the news. What *I* think is that Jason knew before anyone. I can't understand why you find that so difficult to grasp.'

'The sperm test. By your theory, Jason would have had to rape his mother, then kill her. Or is it the other way around?'

Cade flushed. 'I don't find incest that amusing.'

'It's not that credible, either, and if Rayfield thought so he wouldn't be leaning on Henry. And that business of the telephone call makes Henry look bad.'

'I take it you're suggesting I mishandled Rayfield.'

'All that I'm suggesting is that we make a few careful inquiries on who Lydia might have seen lately.'

'By stumbling around after the police, looking worried as hell? That's sheer foolishness.'

'Look, when it comes to people like the Cantwells, Rayfield's on foreign ground. We're in better shape to ask questions and understand the answers.'

Cade shook his head. 'I would have thought that anyone who'd found Lydia like that would be damned glad there are police to handle it. And your Stafford Lumber trial is set for

May. You should know by now that defending a five-million-dollar job-discrimination suit is full-time work.'

'You mean especially when your client thinks that manumission was contrary to God's law.'

'Peyton Stafford's eccentricities are beside the point,' Cade snapped. 'You're a lawyer. Sometimes a lawyer's job is not to feel anything.'

Cade raised his head in the prideful pose he shared with Kris Ann. Our eyes locked in a strange, distasteful intimacy, as though whatever we said didn't really matter, that what mattered was something else we never spoke but understood in the way of two animals circling each other in darkness. 'Is it possible,' I asked, 'that Lydia Cantwell had a lover?'

Cade's stare turned hard. 'It would contradict any notion people had of her. What's your basis for that?'

'The sperm. If it's not Jason, then it's rape or an affair, and we'd better start wondering which. And who.'

'Good God,' Cade burst out. 'Try to appreciate what you're saying. Reputation is a fragile thing, lost in strange ways, often small ones and often unfairly. There will always be people now who think Lydia's murder reflects on Henry. You forget that this is basically a small town – society's small here, everyone's known, and no one ever forgets. It's not like the North. Slander Lydia with this kind of nonsense and you'll just add to the gossip.'

I shrugged. 'I'm not so sure that the Suzy Knickerbocker school of criminal defense will work here.'

Cade eyed me carefully. Then he leaned forward, chin resting on his folded hands, as if musing. 'You know, Adam, I begin to see it more clearly. A young man, a little bored with his work, perhaps disappointed with himself, and then suddenly a friend is in trouble and it's only the young man who's sensitive enough to understand the friend, and smart enough to save him. The police are on a witch hunt, and the friend's lawyer is only involved out of ego – he's an older man and the young man can see how others in their firm have indulged him until he's become like a spoiled child, blind to his own limitations.' He paused to give me a look of infinite comprehension. 'Isn't that how it is?'

His grasp of my view of him, the disparaging inversion of my motives until they were those I saw in him, left me off balance. I took a long swallow of coffee. 'That's fascinating, Roland. Maybe you should try it out on Henry.'

Cade's eyes flashed. His mouth opened, then closed. In a cold voice he said, 'You'll do no good with this.'

'You can't know that.'

'It's enough that I *think* it. I you want to survive in this firm you'll do what I tell you and no more.'

'Unless Henry overrules you.'

'He's still in shock, for God's sake.'

'That was my point yesterday. Unlike Rayfield I'm willing to wait until Henry knows what he's saying. We can talk to him tomorrow.'

Cade looked astonished. 'You'd do that, wouldn't you? Even with what he's gone through.'

I sipped some coffee. 'If I have to.'

Cade considered me a moment longer. Then he picked up a file with an air of infinite weariness. 'Go ahead, then,' he answered, suddenly bored. 'I've got real work to do. But it goes no further than the Parsons woman. I want an end to this before you ruin Henry.'

I stood, surprised but ready to leave. 'I'll try not to get him arrested,' I murmured, and closed the door carefully behind me.

I opened the door and got out, looking up and down the street. The ripe morning sun captured its neglect with merciless clarity. The place next to Etta's had boards for windows and a picket fence like a row of bad teeth. But her own house was white-washed, with red roses growing behind the neat square of lawn and honeysuckle near the porch. I went there and knocked.

The door was opened by a light-skinned black woman with processed hair and obsidian eyes which seemed centuries old. A shadow crossed her face. 'You're Mr Shaw.'

It was less question than an affirmation of surprise: I was out of place here, had ventured where I did not belong. 'May I come in?'

She backed reluctantly into a living room whose formal couch and coffee table I recognized as having once been Lydia's. They mixed incongruously with faded brown walls and the faint smell of camphor, as if this were a halfway house between poverty and the Cantwells'. The blinds were drawn and the absence of sun lent the room the brooding sepia tinge of an old color photograph whose tints have blurred. On the coffee table was a miniature of Lydia Cantwell's mutilated portrait.

Etta pointed me to a cane-back chair, arranging herself on the couch with ankles crossed and hands folded in her lap. 'How may I help you, Mr Shaw?'

She had almost no trace of an accent.

The chill I felt was more than roses or a picture. It was her careful movements, the air of courteous interest to match a cool, inquiring voice, even the way she tilted her head like it was something fine. It had all belonged to Lydia Cantwell.

'I'm trying to help Mr Cantwell,' I said at last.

'Mr Cantwell called here yesterday, crying.' Her throat tightened. 'I couldn't understand it any more than him. I'd been with her for twenty years.'

I nodded. 'Perhaps if we could talk about that.'

Her look was sad yet prideful. 'I don't know what good that will do.'

'I know this is hard, Mrs Parsons, but I'm trying to learn why anyone would kill her. You and she must have talked over the years.'

'Some.'

'About Jason?'

Her face set in the impassivity of an Aztec mask. 'I heard they fought last week,' I prodded.

The small shrugging gesture she made was more a curling of shoulders. 'They fought some – off and on.'

Her tone was guarded. 'She's dead now,' I began, then realized that Rayfield had used those words to me. 'What I mean is that she's got no confidences now as important as helping Mr Cantwell.'

She watched me without answering. 'Do you know what they fought about?' I tried.

Her gaze moved to Lydia's picture. 'They were in the library,' she finally said. 'I didn't hear much except that Mrs Cantwell was upset.'

'Exactly what did you hear?'

'Something about politics.' Bitterness pulled at the corners of her mouth. 'I can never make sense out of what Mr Jason says, just a lot of craziness and screaming.'

'What did Jason have to scream about?'

'Money, what she thought or did about things – it didn't matter between him and her. He loved her, and he hated her too.'

There were echoes in the words. 'Enough to kill her?' I asked softly.

Her veiled glance swept the room, returning to the picture. It seemed to check her anger. She folded her arms. 'I don't know.'

I tried switching subjects. 'Did Mrs Cantwell have many visitors? I mean, during the day?'

She seemed relieved. 'Surely,' she nodded, 'what with her committee work and things.'

I hardened my voice. 'Anyone special?'

Her eyes grew large with understanding. Reflectively she said, 'What do you mean?'

I hesitated, suddenly wondering whether Rayfield had been there or was coming later, and then I saw what Cade had meant: 'So Mr Shaw came to see you, Mrs Parsons?' 'Yes, sir.' 'And what did he want to know?' Leaning forward, I asked, 'Have the police been here?'

She stiffened. The fetor of too much bad history came to me in the darkened room: a black woman, cornered; a white man wanting answers. I pushed all that aside. 'Have they?' I demanded.

She shook her head. 'No.'

'They will, Mrs Parsons, and when they do, they'll ask the

same things and you'll tell them, because you have to. All I'm asking is that you do that much for Henry Cantwell.'

She eyed the floor in confusion. For an instant I felt close to something. But when she looked up, her head was tilted in that haunting angle of repose. 'I'll tell them she and Mr Cantwell got on fine, if that's what you mean.'

'It's partly what I mean.'

'Mrs Cantwell was a good woman,' she said coldly. 'It won't help Mr Cantwell or anyone else to try to know everything about her.'

She began smoothing her skirt.

I knew then it was useless. In her reactions – the crumbling poise retrieved by her symbiotic grasp of the dead woman's personality – was an unsettling glimpse of her own life. Over time, she had become half of someone else, until now she protected not just Lydia Cantwell. She protected herself.

I stayed long enough to ask the gardener's name.

Chapter 8

I parked next to the L & N railroad yard and started up the street. On both sides were now shacks painted a flat green that peeled like dried bark. Except for cramped porches there was no shade and the street was pebbled with glass and gravel and lumps of tar and crowded with boys in cut-offs who pitched and batted a red rubber ball. Their parents – men in undershirts and women in cotton dresses – watched me from the porches.

On the third porch to my left a lone black man wearing Army fatigue pants hunched in a metal chair. At his feet were an old coffee can and a bottle of beer which sweated in the heat.

'I'm looking for Otis Lee,' I told him.

The man spat tobacco in the coffee can, took a long, deliberate swallow of beer, and said, 'What you want?'

The preternaturally deep voice seemed to go with the rest of him. He was thick shouldered, with thick wrists and forearms and calloused hands. His face – deep black with large pores and a flat nose that looked broken – sat on a ringed, fleshy neck like some heavy object. But it was his eyes that set him apart. They were a bitter orange-yellow, the left pupil discolored by a white star. I stepped up on the porch, answering. 'To talk about Lydia Cantwell.'

His stare was red rimmed and implacable. 'You the police?'

'Henry Cantwell's lawyer. I'm calling on people who knew Mrs Cantwell.'

'I heard she was dead.' The words were devoid of feeling, as if it were a chance news item: a moon shot, the death of a stranger. 'Workin' for folks, that don't mean you know them. I only worked there a month. Didn't know that lady at all.'

And don't give a damn, his expression said. 'Mind if I sit, Mr Lee?'

He looked me over with stony dispassion and then nodded perfunctorily toward the metal chair next to his. Sitting, I could see only a sliver of his house through the screen door: a worn chair, a television, bare floors, bare walls – a transient's room. 'Been in Birmingham long?' I asked.

He put down the beer and folded his hands, answering in a resentful grunt. 'Maybe six weeks.'

'You from around here?'

'I'm from nowhere. Been in the Army thirty years, bein' a drill sergeant. Just got out.'

I placed his accent then: the low, emphatic chant of a noncom after years of order giving. 'How'd you happen to pick Birmingham?'

'I was born in north Alabama,' he shrugged. 'Served at Fort McClellan. It's a place I knew, so I came here.'

'How did you find the Cantwells?'

The porch was close and hot. A drop of perspiration ran down Lee's forehead to the bridge of his nose. 'How's this gonna help you,' he finally said, 'botherin' me with these questions?'

'I don't know yet.' I loosened my tie. 'You have another beer?'

Lee's strange eyes widened in something like astonishment. 'I'm fresh out. I didn't know you was plannin' on resting here.'

'I thought maybe we could talk.'

'Look here,' he said impatiently. 'I got out of the army with my children growed up, my wife gone off, nowhere to go, and nothin' to do. I got some retirement and I figure this city's as good a place as any to find work, maybe stay outdoors. So I get some temporary quarters and go around where the big houses are at to ask if they need a yardman. I figure I do that awhile, then get some nursery to hire me. I do Mrs Cantwell's yard a couple of days a week and one or two other folks'.' His voice turned thick and sarcastic. 'Now that satisfy you, or you figure I killed the lady?'

'That wasn't what I was asking.'

Lee stroked his chin between thumb and forefinger. 'Well,

56

I figured you was fixin' to ask me that. I know how much white folks always worry about black men rapin' their women.'

'Yeah, well, I thought I'd wait awhile and just sort of spring it on you.'

He grunted, unamused, and turned toward the street. A bat thumped and a tall boy streaked after a fly ball, leaped twisting to hang in the air, and caught it. Lee watched him. 'Mister,' he said slowly, 'the only people I ever killed was in Korea and Vietnam – and they was yellow, not white.'

'Have any idea why someone would kill Mrs Cantwell?'

'No way.'

'Anyone ever visit while you were there?'

He sipped his beer. 'You mean men?'

'If there were any.'

'I wasn't the doorman. Just did the yard. It's the maid you want.'

'I've done that. That's why I'm here.'

He drank more beer, too casually. I imagined his calculations: what had Etta told me, how much did I expect him to know. He finished swallowing. 'Only thing I noticed was a green Cadillac parked there two, three times. Don't know whose it was.'

'What kind?'

'New model,' he said grudgingly. 'Dark green. One of the big ones.'

'Would Mrs Parsons know whose it was?'

'Prob'ly.' It was said with contempt. 'She was hangin' 'round Mrs Cantwell all the time.'

I leaned back. 'Did Mrs Parsons ever talk about Mrs Cantwell's father or the Grangeville case?'

'Didn't talk to me about anything,' he said harshly. 'What the Grangeville case?'

'An old trial. They electrocuted two black men for raping a white girl. I figured you'd heard of it.'

Lee took a contemplative sip. 'How long ago that happen?'

'Forty years or so.'

'That makes me about eight years old, don't it? I wasn't readin' then and killin' black folks wasn't news.'

57

There were cries from the street. The red ball bounced onto the porch followed by a small boy with large, hungry eyes and a head too big for his body. Lee threw it back underhand and watched the boy run away to his game. Without turning, he said, 'You interrupted my peace. Go back where you belong.'

I shrugged, standing. 'Thanks for your time.'

He didn't look up. 'You gonna chase the cops over here?' he asked in a bored, accusing tone.

'Nope. I figure they can find you themselves.'

I started to leave. 'What you say your name was?' he demanded.

I turned. 'Adam Shaw.'

He plucked a wrinkled pouch of chewing tobacco from his pants pocket and stuffed some in his cheek, chewing with a grinding slowness as he looked me up and down. 'Well, Mr Shaw, you been askin' questions like you own this place and me with it. How long you figure I'd last doin' that at white folks' houses?'

The hatred in his eyes was impersonal and years deep. 'Not long,' I answered, and walked back to the car.

I sat there thinking as Lee watched me from the porch. Then I drove toward Henry Cantwell's, stopping at the library for the book on Grangeville.

Chapter 9

When I got there the Cantwell place had lost its magic. The roses looked tired and the house too large and gloomy. It was like revisiting a place you hadn't seen in years but remembered better than it was.

The thin woman who answered had coiffed and lacquered gray-blonde hair, thick glasses, and a bony face whose tension showed in the unnatural tightness of her mouth as she spoke. She was Mr Cantwell's sister, she said tersely. What did I want?

'I'm Adam Shaw. Henry's lawyer.'

Her mouth relaxed slightly, showing age lines on her upper lip. 'I thought you were another reporter.' Her tone was softer. 'Your Kris Ann called just a while ago. She's been very kind – both her and Roland.'

'We're all concerned about Henry. How is he?'

She didn't move from the doorway. Her glasses magnified eyes that even without them would have seemed large and nervous. 'He's as you would expect.'

'I didn't know how bad that might be. Things got rough with the police yesterday.'

Her shoulders drooped. 'He just watches, and you don't know what he's thinking.'

I nodded. She realized that I was still on the doorstep and motioned me inside. 'I'm sorry,' she said distractedly. 'The last day has been very hard. I've been worried over Henry and afraid that whoever killed Lydia might come back. If it weren't for Roland . . .' She shook her head. 'Even when I was small this house frightened me and now there's this business with the police.'

'What business?'

'You haven't talked to Roland? I thought that's why you'd come. The police were here an hour ago.'

59

I tensed. 'Without telling us? Did they talk to Henry?'

'No, it was me they wanted. They called my home in Virginia and traced me here.'

'What did they want?'

Her mouth tightened again. 'What this Lieutenant Rayfield said he wanted was to ask about Lydia. But it all seemed to work around Henry, and finally I asked them to leave.'

'What did he ask, exactly?'

She looked quickly behind her. Henry didn't seem to be downstairs. Our only company was the end table and an empty vase. 'It was more what he implied. The lieutenant wanted to know how Lydia and Henry got on. I think what he meant was whether they were still intimate.'

The old-fashioned word made it somehow more disturbing. 'Did you tell them anything?'

'Nothing. I didn't like the man. There was something cold about him.'

'Did he let on what was behind all that?'

She was unbending now, and the anger showed. 'He wouldn't tell me anything. But I think perhaps Jason. He has a very strange perspective.'

'On what?'

She crossed her arms, hugging herself in a protective, virginal gesture. 'They weren't demonstrative, that's all. There's such a thing as taste.'

I nodded. 'I always thought there was a nice courtliness between them.'

'Explain that to this Lieutenant Rayfield. Or to someone like Jason. We – the family – were all surprised when they had that boy and now I wish they hadn't.'

'Surprised? In what sense?'

'It was just, oh, I don't know exactly, perhaps a little after they were married, Henry told me they'd decided not to have children. Something about Lydia. He wasn't specific.'

'But you don't know what it was?'

'Not really, but Lydia was a tenser person than she seemed. You weren't born here, were you, and of course you wouldn't remember anyway.'

'Remember what, exactly?'

She frowned. 'The Grangeville business. It turned sour on Lydia's father. Some of the Birmingham papers even attacked him. Then he lost for governor and not too long after died of a heart attack when Lydia was only twelve or thirteen.

'We didn't know her then, of course, but when I met her mother after she and Henry were engaged, she told me it was hard on Lydia, that before the executions she'd been quite a happy little girl, very imaginative and a little spoiled by her father – not at all like Henry, whose father terrified him and asked too much. Apparently, she changed. I know there was some unhappy involvement with an older man in Grangeville before she married Henry. But the woman I knew always tried to be perfect. I suppose she thought she wouldn't be perfect as a parent.' Her jaw worked. 'Perhaps Jason proved she was right.'

The last sentence lingered there. Her eyes froze as if shocked by its sound. 'I'm sorry,' she said in a chastened voice. 'That was a terrible thing to say.'

The apology wasn't for me. She held herself tighter, as if afraid of what was inside. I let it drop. 'Henry – would it be possible to see him?'

Interrupted from guilt, she looked pensive. 'I'd just like him to know I was here,' I said.

She nodded slowly. 'He's on the patio.'

Henry Cantwell sat on a bench wearing a thin sweater, staring across the rear grounds at a secluded stand of pines. He was utterly still. His stillness bothered me; it mimed too well the sad, endless patience of those very old who have nothing more to expect. He looked like an old man on a park bench, who shuffled to his mailbox at the same time every day and combed the paper for coupons to clip, painstakingly, and take to cheap groceries to save a quarter on tea. I crossed the patio and stood next to him.

I couldn't tell if he had heard me. His face was ravaged, his eyes bleary and unspeakably tired.

''Lo, Henry,' I said casually.

He moved over on the bench without answering. I sat

down. We watched the grounds in silence. A squirrel rooted at the base of a pine tree, found something, and disappeared up the other side of the tree.

'It's unbelievable,' he said. 'She's here, then . . . no chance even to talk . . .'

I lit a cigarette. I took one deep drag and watched it burn in my hand. 'It was Aeschylus who said, "In our sleep, pain which cannot forget falls drop by drop upon the heart until, in our own despair, against our will, comes wisdom through the awful grace of God." '

He turned to me. 'Do you believe that, Adam?'

I shrugged. 'I don't know. Perhaps it was something to say.'

He seemed to ponder that. Then he shook his head, wonderingly. 'Jason should be here, and instead it's you.'

'I don't mind. I'm thirsty, though.'

He marshaled himself with effort and stood to get me something. I let him.

He returned with a Bushmills on ice.

'Thanks.'

He sat down again. 'It's still peaceful back here,' I said.

He nodded. 'Twenty-eight years – my family's had it for seventy. Not many people last that long in one place.'

'Maybe in the South.'

He thought. 'Maybe here. But it's changing.'

I held the cool, icy glass in my hand. Sun fell through the pines on dark swatches of lawn.

'The funeral's tomorrow,' he said.

'I know.'

We watched together. The squirrel reappeared, scrambling down the tree onto the lawn. Henry's gaze seemed to follow it. 'I've always wondered, Adam, why Roland never taught you to hunt.'

I smoked the cigarette. 'I suppose I was afraid I'd like it too much.'

He nodded silently, seeming to lapse into thought. I didn't mention the green Cadillac or his last talk with Lydia. Finally I stood. 'You know where to find me. If you need to talk, anything at all.'

'Thank you.' He still stared ahead. I started across the patio.

'Adam.'

I glanced back. He had turned. 'I'm pleased you read Aeschylus,' he said.

I smiled. 'You lent me that, remember?'

Henry gave a faint answering smile. 'I remember.' He turned back to the grounds.

I went home. Two reporters with a camera were filming Henry's drive.

Chapter 10

At six o'clock Monday morning I acted out my fear of growing older: running four miles, doing push-ups and sit-ups and lifting weights, punching the heavy bag I'd hung in the basement, and generally battling what Kris Ann had smilingly identified on my thirtieth birthday, before leading me upstairs to forget it all, as the instinct we'd never be back in college. The instinct drove me harder than usual. Then I showered and dressed, kissing Kris Ann hastily as she uncurled from sleep. She awoke suddenly to say that the funeral was at two, as if recalling a bad dream. I checked the locks again on the way out.

The city was hot and drowsy. Bankers and businessmen in lightweight suits ambled toward new glass towers or older cement ones with dime stores, jewelers, and one-story diners squatting in between. I passed a newsstand, saw the headline, DISCREPANCY IN CANTWELL STATEMENT, and stuffed the dollar I'd reached for back in my pocket. In front of our building a wizened black man with no body below the hips lolled in a wagon, begging. I gave him the dollar, pushed through the revolving door, and caught an elevator.

The fifty-one lawyers of Cantwell, Brevard, Winfield, and Cade rented the top two floors of the brown bank building, which had housed them for sixty years. It was the partnership's pride that there was no need to move: as Cade had put it, over bourbon at the club, we were beyond showing off. Our reception area featured oak paneling with the firm name lettered in discreet gold script, a linen-suited receptionist, wing chairs for clients, and *Business Week* to read. Framed oils of the sacred dead – Messrs Cantwell, Brevard, and Winfield – presided over the room like guarantors of probity. Coming off the elevator, I thought again that Cade had worked thirty years to be suitable for framing.

The receptionist looked up at me, vaguely flustered. She was a bony, middle-aged widow with a kind of fading elegance, a proprietary air, and a low, husky voice. I said good morning.

She gave a quick nod, like a hiccup. 'It's horrible about Mrs Cantwell,' she managed.

'Yes, it is. She was here just last Friday, wasn't she?'

She glanced toward a wing chair. 'Right over there, waiting for Mr Cade. It's strange now to think about.'

'Did she say anything to you?'

'Just hello. Usually we'd chat; she always remembered to ask after my son. But Friday she seemed upset.'

'In what way?'

She looked back at the chair. 'I can tell by watching people how they feel about their business here. Mrs Cantwell sat quite straight in her chair, with her ankles crossed and her arms folded, looking at everything and nothing, if you know the look. Once she flipped a magazine and put it down without reading it. She acted as women do when they're here on some upsetting problem.'

'But she didn't tell you what, or why?'

'Oh, no.' She shook her head sadly. 'I didn't know until I read about the will. I suppose that *would* be upsetting. My son would never behave like that.'

'Then you should count your blessings. By the way, I'm not taking calls from reporters. And tell them my wife isn't either. They can try Mr Cade.'

'Very well, Mr Shaw.'

I went toward my office.

The corridors droned with machines and work. In the library a table of shirt-sleeved associates read law books while another associate stood at a computer terminal that could spit out citations to any legal opinion in the last hundred years containing a phrase he wanted, like 'sanctity of contract.' The morning crew in the word-processing center typed on machines that recorded their work on a screen, corrected errors, and replayed the final copy at six hundred words a minute. Their new supervisor, a brisk young woman who went to college nights, waited by the telex for a wire from London or Brazil or wherever steel companies did business. Down the hall more computers were translating the daily time sheets for each lawyer and paralegal into monthly bills to be reviewed by a senior partner and sent to clients. As I passed, Johnny Bentham emerged holding a sheaf of time sheets. 'Morning, Johnny,' I said.

'Morning, Adam.' He stopped, uncomfortable. 'Damned awful weekend you had. Terrible about Lydia, just un-believable.'

'Unbelievable,' I agreed.

He shifted awkwardly, a great shambling man with the owlish look of a tax partner, unsure of what to say. 'That's a mess about Henry being gone,' he ventured, 'and now that phone call. The papers keep bringing that up.'

'Of course they do.'

He scratched his cowlick. 'Yeah, this is all fun to them – the biggest thing to hit Birmingham since Martin Luther King, my wife says. I just hope we can keep the firm off the front page.'

'Henry, too. But it's not easy with that will.'

He looked at me sharply. 'Well, you did what you thought best about that, I'm sure.'

I guessed my handling of the will had been the subject of discussion. 'I couldn't see getting Henry arrested.'

'Sure,' he persisted. 'Still, when it's all said and done it's going to turn out to be some psychopath. I mean, with the picture and all. Some real sickie, you'll see.'

'We all will.' I glanced at the time sheets in his hand, hoping for a change of subject. 'Sending out six years of back bills?'

'Checking on the associates. I want to see who's putting in the hours.' He decided to end on a hearty note. 'I'm sure you'll be glad to get back into some normal work yourself.'

'I'm sure,' I said, and went to my office.

My secretary looked up blandly from her desk. 'Mr Taylor just left word about the Stafford case,' she told me. 'He said to call when it's convenient.'

I stepped inside and dialed. 'Hello, Nate.'

'Adam.' Nate Taylor's black-accented voice was roughly what Otis Lee's would have been after Harvard Law School and enough trial work to give him bleeding ulcers at thirty-three. 'I told your secretary not to rush you to the phone. I figured you might not be in the mood.'

'Consider yourself a diversion.'

'All right. I've been sitting here reviewing the evidence of job discrimination by that fine gentleman of the old school, Peyton Stafford. I thought before I went to the trouble of proving at trial what you know to be true I'd see about talking settlement.'

'I'm always glad to talk. Peyton's a little less flexible.'

'You've got no defense, Adam. Tell him that.'

'It's not quite true, though. Reread my deposition of your lead plaintiff. No jury's going to put some guy with four drunk citations in charge of a lumber mill.'

'Clients lie to you all the time,' he said matter-of-factly. 'Even yours. My other plaintiffs are clean and your man has discriminated. Those are the facts.'

'Okay. We'll sit down next week. I'm just telling you, don't come expecting the sun, stars, and moon. You're not getting them.' I said goodbye and hung up.

'Shit,' I said aloud.

I looked down at the list. Most days I came to the office, drank one cup of black coffee, and went over the list of things to do I'd written the day before. Staring now at Friday's list – eight numbered items with the first three crossed off – I knew with a cold, clear certainty that I didn't give a damn.

I surveyed my office – a framed law license, two shelves of law books, and some comic prints of English barristers – until I came to my grandfather's dartboard on the far wall, pocked with contests between my father and me. I reached in my desk drawer for a dart.

It was wooden, with frayed feathers and weighted in front. I threw it. It struck the seven with a soft thud. I took another and began thinking. Lydia Cantwell's killer had a key, or she had let him in. He had raped her, or they had made love. And then he had strangled her with such intensity of hate that afterward he needed satisfaction from a picture. I threw again. It bounced off the metal ring of the bull's eye and onto the floor.

I snatched a third dart from my desk drawer. There was a quick rap and the door opened. I looked up, surprised.

Nora Culhane's dark green eyes caught the dart in my hand with a sardonic glance. 'Interrupting anything?'

'Any day now. What do you want?'

'I thought we might try having a civil conversation.'

'Why? The last time we tried that you were setting up my client. Now your so-called "discrepancy" is this morning's headline. You people are building pressure to indict Henry Cantwell whether the evidence is there or not.' I threw the dart. 'What the hell do you care – he gets indicted, you get a raise, and by the time he's acquitted, railroaded, or just plain broken you're Birmingham's first anchorwoman. You don't need me for that.'

She hesitated, glancing downward. 'Look, Mr Shaw, we're both trying to find things out. Maybe if you'd quit being so emotional, we could help each other, okay?'

Her voice was cool enough. But her eyes were uncertain. Maybe, I thought, she would know something useful.

Maybe, too, I'd sensed an ambivalence beneath the toughness, as if she were inhabiting a role she didn't yet believe. It didn't make me like her, exactly – I just liked myself less. But two hours later, when she asked why I'd agreed to lunch, all I said was, 'Because I guessed you were Irish.'

We were sitting in a flagstone courtyard bordered by bamboo plants, ferns, and trees in wooden planters. More trees grew from spaces in the flagstone to form a leafy arbor. In the air was the lilting talk of women in silk and the clatter of plates. Black waitresses in print dresses dipped among the tables. 'So you're an ethnologist,' Culhane said dryly.

'It's just that you couldn't be anything else, even if the name weren't yours. Next time you're home – which I'd guess is Boston – look for women with china skin and bright green eyes or maybe freckles, and see that if their hair isn't reddish or black it's the kind of auburn you have. They'll be Irish.'

'You're quite observant.'

'No great trick if you're Irish. Frankly, though, I came to persuade you to lay off Henry Cantwell.'

'He's too logical to ignore,' she said bluntly. 'And I've talked to anyone who'll stand still.'

'Including Jason?'

'Jason slammed the door in my face.'

'I wouldn't fool with him. His problem may be worse than bad manners.'

She nodded. 'He's pretty frightening. But Rayfield doesn't seem to be looking his way.'

'So I gather. And you?'

She took a cigarette from her purse and snapped a lighter at it. 'I think the Cantwells' problems were bigger than just Jason.'

'Based on – ?'

'Several things. To start, there's something I got from a friend of Mrs Cantwell's who's just been divorced. They last spoke just two weeks ago. Lydia steered the conversation around to the divorce: how long it took, whether the woman had to appear in court, that kind of thing. Her friend recalls that she was very curious.'

'From which you surmise what?'

Culhane raised an eyebrow. 'I thought you'd tell me.'

'I couldn't begin to.' She gave me a look of cool disbelief. 'Seriously,' I added, 'if Lydia Cantwell had wanted a divorce she'd have come to the firm.'

'You're telling me she didn't?'

'I'd know if she had. Just who is this woman?'

New arrivals were drifting past us to be matched with name-cards on empty tables. Next to us a plump-armed blonde squealed, 'Marilyn, you look so *thin*,' to a newcomer who didn't at all. Culhane shook her head. 'I told her she'd be anonymous.'

'Anonymous, or nonexistent?'

Her voice cooled. 'What do you mean by that?'

'I mean maybe you fed me a line to see if we were handling a divorce.'

'My source exists,' she snapped. 'You know, you must really hate news people.'

'I prefer "dislike" or maybe "distrust." Whatever made you pick this business?'

'Whatever makes you care?'

'I was cleverly searching for a change of subject.'

She stabbed her half-smoked cigarette into an ashtray. 'Basically because I'd divorced my husband and needed work, if that's any of your business.'

'What happened?'

She shrugged. 'Charles was a heart surgeon I married in Boston when he was still a resident and liked playing his guitar. Then he got a position at the Med Center here and stopped liking anything but cutting chests. Eventually I got tired of begging for attention and asked him to move out. For a while I felt depressed and worthless and jogged five miles a day to keep it together. Finally one of my apartment neighbors who's a cameraman suggested I try news; after all, I was presentable and maybe even bright. By then I was sick of jogging and missing Boston. So I went to the station and asked for a job.'

A thin, silent waitress in shocking blue tennis shoes interrupted with iced tea and a small blackboard with the fare scribbled in chalk. We stopped to order. It was hot even in the shade and our salt was stuck in its shaker. I asked for another one, and the waitress left, undelighted with me and her job.

'So what happened next?' I asked Culhane.

'The news director tried to screw me.' Her voice held a note of warning. 'He didn't, and I began to enjoy the work. It licenses my curiosity – asking questions, meeting people. I even like the hurry. The downside is hassling for air time and never finishing a story; a thirty-second spot is for shit, you tell nothing. So when you get a story you can stay with, like this, you jump on it.'

'One man's tragedy – '

'Is my opportunity. Look, I didn't kill Lydia Cantwell, I'm just covering the story.'

Her role as tough newslady interested me. I was getting an impression of where she stood: a late-blooming new woman, throwing out the makeup with her husband, paying the bills and liking it, but still not quite sure where she fit. 'How long have you done this?'

'News?' She sipped some tea, her gaze growing distant. 'Around two years, I guess.'

I guessed she'd counted back to the divorce and been pulled into the vortex of memory, wondering how it had all happened and who she'd been before. I quoted a line of poetry. ' "I see my life go drifting like a river from change to change . . ." '

She looked up as if troubled. 'You're good at divining mood,' she said. 'Who wrote that?'

'Yeats.'

She smiled fractionally. 'You're quite Irish yourself. Except that "Adam" sounds very Old Testament.'

'My father's idea. My middle name is Francis.'

'Your father had a point. Have you ever been there – Ireland?'

'Once. It was green and beautiful and very poor, and it rained too much and was cold. It felt like I'd been there before.'

Culhane nodded. 'I felt that, too.'

Our waitress brought two crab casseroles that smelled and tasted good. Culhane ate with small, thoughtful bites. As we were finishing she said, 'The next thing is that Henry Cantwell's strange.'

'Is he now?'

'Of course.' She sounded impatient. 'I've talked to the people who should know him best. They start by saying he's a fine gentleman, mention the family – down here they still like to know where you're from and who "your people" are. It gives them a handle on you. But they all end up saying they don't know him very well and that he seems off somewhere, almost secretive.'

'You do understand what that's about?'

She shook her head.

71

'Mother of God, Nora, his wife's just been murdered. They're all preparing for Henry to have sinister secrets. At least try to distinguish between reticence and guilt.'

She was plainly galled. 'We're talking about strangeness, not reticence. People at his bank will tell you the past couple of months he'd be listless, then become totally irrational. Two months ago he threatened to resign if they didn't approve a loan for some shaky project in New Orleans that made no sense, got the bank in a mess, and then he retreated to his office and was hardly seen for days.'

'I've heard all about that. Look, Henry's big problem is being born with money and a bank when he should have been an English professor. I agree with anyone who says he's out of place negotiating loans with some slab-handed wheeler-dealer whose life's dream is to finance trips to Las Vegas and season tickets on the fifty through some real-estate scam. But that's no crime, just a sad incongruity.'

She sloshed the tea in her glass, as if examining it for something important. 'What about affairs?'

I was getting annoyed. 'Henry's never shown the slightest interest in any woman but Lydia, except perhaps the ones in books. You're not dealing with Richard Burton, just a slightly dreamy middle-aged gentleman who likes to read. Nothing strange about him. If you want strangeness, try Rayfield.'

'Why him?'

'Because he's got the look of a classic obsessive-compulsive personality. He began acting like Henry was one of his obsessions before he'd even met him.'

She shrugged. 'Maybe he's afraid Cantwell will do it again.'

'That's droll.'

'I'm serious. There are a lot of scared people out there.'

'And Rayfield's helping to scare them.'

The waitress came with key-lime pie. Culhane took a bite before saying. 'Rayfield *is* sort of a Jesuit: no other interests, no family or friends outside the police and not many of those, no women anyone's heard of. All he wants is to track down sin – you know, "man the hunter." He even told one of our people once that the relationship between him and a suspect is a personal thing, like he almost breathes with the guy. It's a little obsessive, sure. But I don't think he's off about Cantwell. Put together what bits I know: in the last two months Henry begins acting irrational, Lydia shows an interest in divorce and is killed, and then Henry forgets to tell Rayfield about what obviously was a twelve-minute quarrel. You don't have to be brilliant to guess that one of them was having an affair.'

'Just irresponsible. Do yourself and Channel Seven a favor. Watch what you say.'

She looked at me seriously. 'We've got lawyers too. I'm just telling you not to invest too much in this.' She took another bite. 'Incidentally, what does your client say about his little lapse on the telephone call? I'll be happy to report it.'

'I haven't asked him.'

She shot me an incredulous glance. 'I'm glad I don't have your driving lack of curiosity.'

'Yeah, well, I thought I'd wait until after the funeral. I've lived in the South for a while and developed some manners.'

She reddened. 'All right,' she said curtly, then checked her watch. 'I'm late for work. Better eat your pie.'

The check arrived as we finished. We split the bill and hurried silently to the car. She looked wryly across from the passenger seat, as if trying to ease the strain. 'No Holy Mother on the dashboard?'

'I've given all that up.'

'Have you really?' she asked, more serious.

'Haven't you?'

'Yes and no. I still remember things like my first confession: the priest chewed peppermint Lifesavers, I could smell them through the screen. I was too terrified to laugh.'

I started the car. 'You got the whole dose, then.'

'Lord, yes. Mother says the Rosary every day. I remember when a Russian family moved in behind us, poor people. One morning I caught Mother sprinkling holy water in their backyard. She was saving them from communism.'

'Back then you couldn't be too careful,' I smiled. 'Even Ike had it. Anyhow, we all have our mothers.'

'Do we not. Where is your family?'

'Cleveland. My mother, anyhow. My father's dead.'

'What does she do?'

'Works for the clerk of courts. Files things, mostly.'

I turned from the parking lot toward downtown. Culhane's hair rippled in the breeze. 'So how did you get to Birmingham?' she was asking.

'My wife's from here.'

'Is she the tall, dark-haired woman?'

'Uh-huh.'

'I saw her at the party. She's absolutely beautiful.'

'She is that.' We were near downtown. 'Tell me where to drop you.'

She pointed to a parking garage. I pulled over and stopped. 'One thing,' I asked. 'How'd you get past our receptionist?'

'I said I was late for our appointment.' She got out and gave me a fleeting smile. 'Thanks for the time.'

'Sure.'

She walked to her car. I drove off to take Kris Ann to the funeral.

Chapter 11

By the time we reached downtown the dance of bad memory was like tocsins in the brain. 'I know you hate these,' Kris Ann said finally.

I shrugged. 'It's just that Protestant funerals are such dismal affairs. There's no catharsis, just one more dutiful rite of forbearance. No one will cry – not even Henry – and then we'll all go home.'

But then that was all I'd done when they'd buried my father.

The Episcopal church was a large gothic structure, its stone walls blackened by time and weather and a thickening overcast. Inside it was dark and vast, with a high vaulted ceiling. Along both walls intricate stained-glass windows portrayed the life of Jesus in bright, jagged sections. A blood-red carpet declined between pews overflowing with mourners to a marble altar with an ornate silver cross. Toward the right front, my partners grouped in white shirts and gray suits, trying hard to look what they were. We joined them.

Muffled sounds came from the rear of the church. Five relatives and Cade bore Lydia's casket, covered by a white pall and resting on a low metal platform with wheels. A blonde acolyte with the processional cross and two clergy with prayer books preceded it. At the rear, Henry Cantwell stood with his sister.

We all rose. The pallbearers began rolling the casket noiselessly toward the altar. A grim-faced Cade held one handle. I couldn't find Jason. The clergy read in hollow voices:

'I am the resurrection and the life, saith the Lord: he that believeth in me, though he were dead, yet shall he live . . .'

I saw Rayfield standing by the rear door. The voices moved nearer:

'I know that my redeemer liveth, and that he shall stand at the latter day upon the earth: and though this body be destroyed, yet shall I see God . . .'

Henry's eyes fixed emptily on the acolyte's cross. He passed Etta Parsons, face rigid as if fighting tears, then Dalton Mooring, head averted, his blonde wife next to him looking wretchedly hung over. The clergy continued:

'We brought nothing into this world, and it is certain we can carry nothing out. The Lord gave, and the Lord hath taken away . . .'

– 'Deserter,' my mother had shrieked until they pulled her from the coffin and dragged her upstairs.

My father lay in the front hall. 'A fine-looking man, Kieron Shaw,' they kept saying, and him dead and waxy and looking like someone else. Brian babbled the Rosary by the head of the coffin –

The foot of Lydia's casket was placed toward the altar. One of the clergy read over her: 'For I am a stranger with thee, and a sojourner, as all my fathers were. O spare me a little, that I may recover my strength, before I go hence, and be no more seen. Glory be to the Father, and to the Son, and to the Holy Ghost . . .'

– 'In nomine Patri, et Filii et Spiritu Sancti . . .' The old priest chanted over my father amidst the smell of incense. Three candles had lined each side of the closed black coffin. My mother wore black, the priest black vestments. Brian, nine years old, watched him –

I watched the clergyman now as he read: 'Jesus said, let not your heart be troubled: ye believe in God, believe also in me. In my Father's house are many mansions: if it were not so, I would have told you.'

He looked shrunken in his vestments, his gaze through wire-rimmed glasses touched with uncertainty. I sensed his isolation: a middle-aged man repeating an inherited ritual in a reedy voice and doubting his own efficacy.

– Brian wore the priest's collar I could never quite believe. 'Good God, man,' he said, 'you send Mother money instead of visiting, can't bear to see the old neighborhood or anyone in it, and live outside the Church, beholden to a man you despise. For all your beautiful Kris Ann and fine house you've at last no sense of who you are.'

' "Will no one rid me of this meddlesome priest," ' I jibed.

'Don't spar with me, Adam. You can make a sadness of your own life, but our mother deserves better.'

'I'm here now.'

'For our uncle's funeral. That's quite a gesture.'

'Dammit, Bri, since I was twelve all I got from her was "don't be like your father, don't look up to what he did" and all the time knowing she hated him for being killed. Hell, she'd say I looked like him and it was like a curse. So I did as she wanted, and if that's taken me other places, so be it.'

Brian raised a finger to his lips, glancing toward the stairwell. Upstairs my mother had said the Rosary and slept alone, as she had for the twenty years since my father was shot and killed and buried in a spring drizzle like the one that spattered the windows, reminding me of the smell of wet earth. Instead, drinking wine with Brian in the living room, I smelled the same trapped mustiness. A small lamp lit the familiar things of my mother: a Belleek china cup, lace on the couch, the tortured Jesus, the cameo of my father, wolf-faced, with cold blue eyes. I sat in his chair. Brian faced me, a brown-haired replica of the pale sleeping woman. 'I know you paid the price for Da's dying,' he said.

I shrugged. 'At least it didn't make me a celibate.'

He nodded in wry acknowledgment. 'No doubt I found comfort in the Church, if only the sense that someone was looking after me. Who's to say that's a bad thing?'

'Well, what I remember is our dried-out priest mouthing all that cold business of God's will, and me knowing all the time that we were losers in an arbitrary and very nasty lottery. I've not become so weak-minded as to cherish that.'

Brian flushed. 'It's worse than weak-minded to hate your past and neglect your mother,' he came back. 'You've been at war with God twenty years now, and it's left you empty. You're a cynical man, Adam, there's no purpose to your life – '

77

And no purpose in rehashing it, I thought now. It was just that I hated funerals.

I found myself staring at Lydia's casket, ashamed to wonder, yet wondering if my stricken friend in the first pew was a sad, bewildered cuckold with a wife he'd never understood, and shouldn't now. Perhaps better to let it be, and hope that Cade was right, that no one else would come to harm and Henry would go free.

'Unto God's gracious mercy and protection we commit you,' read the clergyman. A little late, I answered silently. 'Amen,' he finished.

We rose again. The pallbearers shuffled to the casket and inched it back up the aisle. Henry trailed, eyes bleak with cold comfort. They rolled the casket to the door of the church and were gone.

Kris Ann took my hand. Mourners edged from their pews looking up or down like strangers in an elevator. We moved in the halting file of reticent bodies, out the door.

Rayfield stood watching in the stone archway. I passed him without speaking. In the street below it was raining and almost dusk. There were newsmen on the other side. Nora Culhane was next to her cameraman, shooting footage for the evening news. Then I saw Etta Parsons.

She stood with her back to me, staring from the top of the steps toward the sidewalk. Joanne Mooring waited there alone. Then a dark green Cadillac glided from the street to stop in front of her. As he pushed open the door Dalton Mooring's face appeared. His wife got inside. Etta Parsons watched the car drive silently away.

I left Kris Ann and walked behind her. 'Mooring?' I said softly.

The single stare she gave me was hard as sculpture. Then she turned and walked away, into the rain.

Chapter 12

The next morning I called on Jason Cantwell.

The night of the funeral I had found Kris Ann in our bedroom, loading a black revolver.

'What's that?' I blurted stupidly.

She gazed at me across the bed, gripping the revolver. It was blunt and smooth and oiled. 'Daddy gave it to me this morning, after you left. To protect myself.'

'From what?'

'Jason Cantwell.' She looked away. 'I'm afraid of him.'

'Why, exactly?'

'Because of Lydia. Isn't that enough?'

She stood framed in the blackness of our window, shoulders curled as if cold. 'I don't like guns,' I said quietly. 'Roland knows that. You know it too.'

Her face burned. 'I just need one until this is over.'

'Krissy, I want you to take it back.'

'Please – '

'I'm here, dammit. Isn't *that* enough?'

Her look across the bed was level and silent. Then she repeated simply, 'I need it, Adam.'

Her eyes held mine without wavering. Softly, I asked, 'Do you know how to use that?'

'I haven't in years. But Henry taught me when I was younger, for target practice. His father was a crack pistol shot.' She paused, then added, 'He taught Jason too.'

For a long time I stared at the gun. 'Put the safety on,' I finally said, 'and stick it in a drawer.'

She silently placed the gun in the drawer of her nightstand and closed it. I lit a cigarette.

'I'm sorry, Adam.'

She turned out the lights and got in bed.

There was nothing more said, or done.

79

In the morning we sat in the sunroom as we usually did, with coffee and the paper. The headline read, CANTWELL FAMILY CENTER OF PROBE. We said little about that or anything else, and nothing about the gun. Riffling the back pages I found Kris Ann's picture above the caption 'Mrs Kris Ann Shaw, Chairman of the Junior League Volunteers for Retarded Children.' In the picture she smiled as she had the day I'd watched her kneeling in a circle of the children she taught, seemingly oblivious to dirty hair or tantrums or runny noses as she helped them shape clay into whatever they imagined. At the circle's edge a small girl with taffy hair and guileless clear eyes had hung back watching her, unnoticed in the clamor of children thrusting lumps of clay toward Kris Ann for the smile she gave. Then the girl had put down her clay and walked to Kris Ann, touching her hair. Kris Ann had looked up, and then her smile had faded and she pulled the girl close, her eyes shut.

'I'm glad you still work with those children,' I told her now. 'You're good with them.'

She took a sip of coffee, her face abstracted. 'Art's something they need, that's all. There are no wrong answers.' She rose, touching my shoulder, and went upstairs.

I stared out the window. Above me Kris Ann started running her shower. I got up abruptly, called the university for Jason Cantwell's address, and left.

In the aftermath of rain, the morning was lush and bright and fresh as Creation. The campus – tan brick buildings with no trees around them – looked scrubbed clean. I found Jason's aprtment at its edge, a worn brick building stuck between an orthodontist and a marriage counselor. I parked, climbed one flight to the end of a dark hàllway, and knocked.

The door was opened by an olive-skinned man with full black beard, flat cheekbones like hammered bronze, and black liquid eyes. His chest strained the dark t-shirt, and his arms were ridged and heavy.

'What do you want?' he demanded, surprised and ready to be hostile.

'I'm Adam Shaw. You remember. I represent your father now.'

'He send you?'

'No. This is my idea.'

The volatile eyes seemed to change like some unstable element. I was recalling more about him than I had thought: a nineteen-year-old boy at our engagement party who seemed somehow uninvited, a stray yet the center of a chemistry that kept Lydia glancing toward him, Kris Ann a careful distance she maintained wherever Jason moved. He had made an impression then, and after that – when I had seen nothing of him and heard nothing good – almost none. But the man who stood now in the doorway had the primal force of a prophet or a Mansonite. 'You've got five minutes,' he said at last, and moved grudgingly aside.

His apartment was cramped – a small living room with a kitchen nook off that and one bedroom – and its contents a riot of confusion. On the far wall a poster of Ho Chi Minh watched from above the color television. A half-finished macrame lay on the couch to the left, there was a cocaine spoon on the coffee table, and I stood on a costly looking Persian rug. A bookshelf of bricks and boards held a revisionist history by Eugene Genovese, some Herbert Marcuse, and a gothic romance, in paperback. In the kitchen, a blue-jeaned girl with long brown hair washed dishes by a spice rack and copper teapot. I figured those, and the paperback, were hers.

'Hello,' I said.

She turned, eyes turquoise and unsure. She was tall and pretty, with tawny skin and small delicate features. Her body stretched with a young girl's leanness to sudden full breasts, and there were tints of honey in her curly hair. 'Hi,' she said in a near whisper and turned quickly back to her dishes.

I felt Jason's eyes warning me off, as clear as speech. He stood in the center of the living room, thumb stroking one side of his beard. 'I hear you found the old lady.' His voice was slow and guttural and half-curious. 'The cops said her neck had these purple welts.'

He could have been discussing a dead hamster. But I couldn't make him out. His neck was bent to the side, his body rigid, and each word seemed molten and heavy. There was something old about him, and terribly young. I nodded. 'That's right.'

Jason stared at his feet. 'Yeah, well, that's how I found out, you know – from the cops. By the time old Henry called, the pigs had been all over me. He must have thought they'd trap me first.'

I caught the edge of hostile pride. 'That's my doing,' I told him. 'They were on the way before Henry got home. I had the will with me when I found her. You did know about the will?'

'No.' The pulse throbbed in his temple. 'The old lady made noises but she never said she'd done it.'

'Well, she had, and that's why the cops came after you. I thought maybe now you could tell me who else might have killed her.'

He gave me a sharp look. 'I don't see how it much matters.'

'Yeah, I noticed you missed the funeral.'

The girl had left the kitchen and moved to the corner of the couch, watching Jason. His eyes turned bright and violent. 'So what? I'm sure you being there was enough for Henry.'

I shrugged. 'Another man might have come, for his father's sake.'

Jason's chest rose. 'You feel real sentimental about him, don't you, Shaw?'

'We've spent some pleasant evenings. He's a sensitive, intelligent man. People could have worse fathers and generally do.'

'Well, I'm just fucking thrilled you've gotten so much out of him. Let me tell you, I used to get a handshake when they sent me off to prep school. Old Henry, the walking secret.'

'None of which explains who killed your mother.'

'I already told that pig lieutenant I was right here with Terry.' He wheeled on her for confirmation. She nodded and Jason turned back with dark satisfaction, as if he'd scored some point about the girl. 'But the pigs wanted to push me around. They asked how I liked Lydia, looked for pieces of her skin under my fingernails – ' His throat began working.

'They were horrible,' the girl broke in.

Her words seemed to draw out his poison. Jason's face relaxed and his breathing eased. 'Maybe they'd heard you'd quarreled,' I said.

'I just reminded her,' he said in a succinct voice, 'that her family were corrupt fascists who got rich exploiting miners. That her father murdered two black men for racist votes. That her little civic works were one pathetic daisy on the family pile of shit.'

It was clear that Jason Cantwell was a wounded man. But he made it hard to care. 'Perhaps your mother was trying, in her own way.'

'Yeah, by taking a busload of black kids to the symphony. Poor Lydia, she had the soul of a fucking Barbie doll – "Give the niggers presents, make them feel better." She didn't like me saying that. I told her whites covered the brown man like thin scum on the surface of the world. You could see her get scared. Hell, she was so paranoid about blacks that the last time I saw her she was all uptight that the fucking yardman was watching her. I said, "Sure, in your dreams." She got pissed and said she'd cut me off, she always did.' Jason kept saying more than he needed, as if he cared more than he wished. He caught himself. 'I didn't do it. I didn't need money or anything else. From her or Henry.'

There was a faint aroma from the kitchen, something boiling I couldn't quite place. 'You tell Rayfield about the yardman?'

'I forgot.' His one-sided smile was no smile at all. 'You're worried about old Henry, aren't you? Well, it wasn't Henry, not that he gives a damn for anything that breathes. Henry likes poetry and vases. He doesn't have the guts for killing.'

'Not to mention that he loved your mother.'

He repeated the same unpleasant smile. 'Who you been talking to, Shaw? Henry? He never even touched her. Hell, they had separate bedrooms. I could never see how they got it up to have me.'

'They probably knew what they could look forward to.'

It was as if I'd struck a match. Jason stepped forward, fists clenched, eyes full of prep-school fights and murdered dogs and all the people who had called him a curse to his parents.

'Jason,' the girl said sharply.

He blinked, stopping in his tracks. I went on as if nothing had happened. 'Maybe she had someone else. Was your mother friends with any men?'

'No.' His voice was low and murderous.

'Ever seen her with Dalton Mooring?'

His body strained. 'Did you?' I prodded.

The girl perched on the edge of the sofa, watching Jason. The room seemed like a cage. Jason stared at his fingernails. 'He was there the second last time I went, sitting next to her on the couch. They were having tea.' His voice rasped. 'Lydia always liked to have tea.'

'What happened?'

'Nothing. They looked surprised, then Mooring started asking about school, how I was doing, bullshit like that – like it was really a big deal to him. He acted strange, kind of embarrassed. She was sitting close to him with her eyes all bright and funny, smiling at me like she didn't know what to do. I got sick of them both and left.'

'Think he and your mother were having an affair?'

His voice lashed out in sudden pain. 'Look, I don't give a shit what Lydia did.'

The smell from the kitchen was tea.

Jason's face was contorted in a torment of hate, instability, and thwarted love. 'Okay,' I said flatly. 'Thanks for the talk.'

'Hang on, Shaw.' Jason's stare brightened with sudden, malevolent curiosity. 'I want to hear how you're making out with Kris Ann Cade.'

His gaze was keen and oddly excited. The girl looked fragile, her eyes deep blue and scared. 'Fine,' I answered.

'I was just wondering. I remember old man Cade was all bent out of shape, you being Catholic and all.'

'That was a while ago.'

The soft answer drew him on. He looked eagerly at the girl,

then to me. His voice seeped adolescent taunting, getting back his own. 'Yeah, I guess you kissed that off to go fuck Kris Ann and live off her old man's money. She must be good. You've really got it made now, don't you.'

The girl turned to me, lips parted in mute appeal. 'As running dogs go,' I answered mildly. 'Of course nothing's perfect. You never come to our parties.'

He moved closer. 'I wouldn't come near you or your cunt wife. You're just a fucking leech.'

All at once I'd had enough. 'Look at you,' I said, 'dancing on your mother's grave and spouting drivel while your girl does the dishes. Christ, you haven't the moral sense or compassion God gave a maggot. Your father's worth ten of you.'

His fist smashed into my forehead.

I wobbled, staggering against the wall. His second punch cracked against my cheekbone. My knees buckled. I ducked by instinct as his next swing crashed into the wall above me.

He yelped, losing a split second. As he grabbed for my throat I spun, still crouching, and hit him in the stomach with a left hook. He grunted, air gasping from his mouth. I hit him in the ribs with a right cross, then sent a left to the stomach that doubled him over and drove him back. The girl screamed. I pivoted and sent a right to his jaw with all the force I had.

Pain shot through my arm as the punch stood him up. He dropped to the floor. The girl sprang from the couch and bent over him.

My face and throat ached and blood was rushing in my head. 'I'm sorry,' I told her, and was. But she didn't answer or even look up. As I left, the sound of Jason's moans came through the hallway like keening.

I made it to the stairs and then down to the car, one step at a time, leaning against the wheel until my head cleared. But I had decided to find Mooring by the time I drove away.

Chapter 13

Dalton Mooring's home was fake antebellum, opulent but without the grace of time. The white brick and pillars were too new, the grounds too crammed with shrubs, the interior, with its porcelain and restored antiques, too clearly decorated. The effect was striking and a little desperate.

I waited in the foyer while the maid went for Mooring. The living room had the glossy heartlessness of new money and no children: silk flowers, deep blue rug, some wire sculpture, a bright asbtract painting in a chrome frame. Above the mantel a smoked-glass mirror inverted the room. Here and elsewhere were small signs of drunkenness: a burn hole in the rug, scratches on a doorknob, rings marring the coffee table.

My head and throat ached and my right hand had swollen. I was feeling it for breaks when Mooring appeared, dressed for golf and looking annoyed. Without preliminaries he asked, 'What do you want?'

'Ten minutes or so.'

He gave his watch an irritated glance. 'I'm due in twenty.'

I hesitated, still shaken, doubtful now that I had come this far. But Mooring's executive crispness seemed less real than calculated. 'Your golf can wait,' I told him. 'This can't.'

He looked me over, taking his time. Then he nodded curtly and led me through the kitchen. His wife sat behind a butcher-block counter sipping a daiquiri. She had circles beneath her eyes and too much lipstick. Her gaze was wary and unsurprised, as if she knew me but had forgotten how.

'Hello,' she breathed, emitting a ragged nimbus of cigarette smoke.

I said hello. Mooring steered me quickly past her, through the family room and down four oak stairs into something unexpected: a greenhouse in the shape of an A-frame, refracting trapped sunlight that made me squint. The room was hot and steamy, its greenery – rubber trees, a ten-foot corn plant, some snake cactus that looked ready to strike – an oppressive jungle of exotica, completed by the babble of a rococo fountain.

Mooring said, 'You could have come to my office,' in a low, flat drawl.

I couldn't square him with the house. He stood by the corn plant about ten feet away, his back to the sun, hands placed on his hips in a pose of impatience. He was trim, though as with slim men in their forties he carried himself carefully around the middle and there was a subtle hardness in the face, a closeness of skin to bone. He had gray eyes set over broad cheekbones, an aquiline nose, and a cleft jaw beneath an angry slash of a mouth whose stamp of drive and temper warred with the vaguely feline look of a cynical diplomat. His overall presence, shrewd and carefully governed, clashed with his surroundings. I guessed there were reasons besides his wife that he didn't want me here: the place embarrassed him. 'You were out,' I answered. 'So I came here.'

'Then tell me what's so important.'

The fountain splashed in an unnerving rhythm. Quietly I said, 'Your relationship to Lydia Cantwell.'

His mouth thinned. 'If you're referring to that scene with my wife, I'll ask you to be gentleman enough to forget it. When she's not' – he searched for the word – 'responsible, she imagines things.'

I realized that Mooring was unsure of what she'd said. 'Then why doesn't she imagine something else?'

His voice lowered and became almost confiding. 'Because she's a jealous woman. Frankly, we started with almost nothing and she feels inadequate next to women like Lydia. It's an old story, one I'm sure you've heard before.'

I paused, wondering when Mooring had begun to speak so well. He had none of the southerner's studied lapses – the 'ain'ts' and 'might coulds' – and his diction was clearly acquired. I guessed that he'd outgrown his wife and her decorator long ago. The house had begun to seem like a prison, with the woman its Mrs Rochester. 'I don't think your wife's insane,' I said finally. 'I have it from other people that you and Mrs Cantwell were close. If I can put that together, so can the police.'

He folded his arms, frowning as if puzzled. But in his stillness I sensed a subcutaneous tension. The conversation had begun oddly enough without my feeling that there was a wordless second conversation stranger than the first: that something he expected me to know kept him from inviting me out. 'I'm a little unclear,' he probed, 'as to what your interest is in this.'

'Roland Cade and I represent Henry Cantwell.'

Mooring's face closed against me. 'What are you after?' he said coldly. 'A boyfriend?'

For a moment it threw me off. But his challenge seemed hollow and too late. 'If you think I should be.'

'I don't think anything. My "relationship" to Lydia, as you put it, was confined to work we did jointly for the symphony. Jason saw us drinking tea. Whatever else he saw exists only in the mind of a confused and unhappy young man.'

'Yeah, I was curious about how that happened – the symphony work, I mean.'

'Lydia asked me.' His voice turned almost bored. 'She was our largest stockholder. I've known her almost since I began at Maddox.'

'When was that?'

'About nineteen fifty-two.' He looked straight at me. 'Please understand, Shaw, I'm sick about what happened. But I'm in no position to help you or the police.'

His voice had thickened. I kept sensing a split in him, a choked undercurrent of real feeling channeled as artifice. 'You can't be sure,' I answered. 'For example, when was the last time you saw her?'

His eyes flickered toward the kitchen. 'What makes that of interest?'

'Several things. Time of death, for instance. The police will be looking for anyone who saw Lydia so much as breathe after three P.M. on Friday.'

His stare turned frank and hard. 'I'd better ask you something first. Does Cade know you're here?'

'Not specifically.'

He placed his hands on his waist. 'If I'd known that, I wouldn't have let you impose like this. How do you think your questions would affect my wife?'

'I don't know,' I shrugged. 'Maybe I should ask her.'

A second persona leapt abruptly from the first, angry and physical. He moved toward me. 'Now hear me well, Shaw, because I'll say this just once: if you make these insinuations anywhere else – anywhere at all – I'll sue you for slander and take your law license in the bargain.'

My hand was throbbing. 'Go ahead. Then you can tell me in open court where you were the night Lydia Cantwell was murdered.'

'I don't have to tell you anything.'

'Not now. But you keep forgetting the police. You do know they found semen traces on Lydia's body?'

'So?'

'So when the lab men take semen smears, they comb the woman's pubic hair. The man leaves his own hair, you see. After that they just keep clipping hairs off suspects until they get a match. And there's not a damn thing you can do about it except wait for them to clip some of yours.'

Mooring straightened as if struggling for control. Then he inhaled, glanced at his watch, and said, 'Get out, Shaw. I'm late.'

His tone was again even. For a moment we stood facing each other. Then I turned and left.

On the way out I passed Joanne Mooring, hunched over the counter with a blender full of daiquiris. She didn't look up. I walked to the car and drove home with one hand.

Chapter 14

I was sitting at the kitchen counter with my hand in a bucket of ice water when Kris Ann arrived from teaching. She smoothed back a damp tendril of hair, glancing quickly around, and saw me.

She started. 'Adam, what happened?'

I raised the swollen hand. 'I fought with Jason Cantwell.'

She turned white. 'Here?'

'No. I went to his apartment.'

She stared at me in silence. Then she took my hand, turning it gently from side to side. 'I think you'd better see a doctor.'

'I'm going to.'

She rested my hand on the counter. 'How did it happen?'

I told her, beginning with Jason's girl and finishing with the fight. She listened without speaking or moving. Then she went to the kitchen table and sat staring out the window, quite still. In an undertone, she asked, 'What else did Jason say to you?'

'That's all, Krissy. It was enough.'

She turned to me, questioning. Finally, she said, 'You should never have gone there,' and lapsed into quiet, unapproachable.

It was strange. Alone at the counter, I began missing her, even though she was four feet away – missing some better time we'd had: staying up in school to smoke dope and smile at old movies, perhaps sitting outdoors at a Paris café inventing lives for passersby, or talking in the beach house late at night with the windows open and heavy gulf air smelling of salt.

The images were freeze frames perfectly captured and imprinted on my mind. Like her eyes the first time we made love. Silver light through my apartment window had crossed her face. Her hair, soft and thick and clean smelling, fell back on the pillow. Just before it happened, she stiffened and then touched my face, eyes large with questions. Slowly, her arms closed tight around me.

It was sweet and intense.

Afterward we lay damp against each other, content to say nothing. Suddenly she grinned. She couldn't stop. I buried my face in her hair and we began laughing out of pure crazy happiness.

When we had stopped, she said, 'You're beautiful.'

'And you.' I was serious now.

She drew some strands of hair over her lip in an absurd mustache. 'And if I weren't?'

I brushed it away. 'Then you'd have to make your own clothes.'

She smiled, knowing how I felt. The newness of things imposed its own wisdom. We didn't talk about it.

Later she was looking around the apartment, not shy. Her walk was lithe and gliding, and I thought then that she carried the South inside her, and in her eyes and the brownness of her skin.

'What are you doing?' she asked.

I was reaching in the closet for a shirt. 'Laying out clothes for tomorrow.'

She looked intrigued. 'Can't you just get up and dress?'

'You're spoiled,' I grinned. 'In the morning you can stumble out to hunt through that mess in your closet for something to wear, and cut English Lit if you can't find it. But my job starts at seven and nine's my first class.'

'Prrretty compulsive.'

'Gets me an extra fifteen minutes sleep.' I turned to see her leaning over my bureau. 'You okay?'

'Uh-huh. Just taking out my contacts.'

She finished and began walking toward me in the semi-darkness with short, myopic steps. I smiled and reached toward her. 'Don't you have glasses?'

'A naked lady in glasses? That's obscene.' Our hands clasped. 'Besides, they're thick.'

I laughed, pulling her to me. 'I think I can live with it.'

I felt her smile against my shoulder. 'I'm not scared now,' she murmured. 'It was good for me, Adam. Gentle. I needed it gentle.'

'I know.'

We went together to the bed, and lay down again . . .

The phone rang. Kris Ann rose from the kitchen table to get it.

'Hello, Daddy. Yes, he's here.' She listened, taut, then asked, 'Can you stay for dinner?' She paused, answered, 'It's fine, really. See you then,' and hung up.

She turned to me. 'He sounds upset.'

'So I gather. Nice you invited him to beard me in our own home.'

'Which he bought us.'

'I'd forgotten that.' I glanced at my hand. It was various shades of purple. 'I'd better have this checked. You father knows where the bourbon is. Just lock the doors until he gets here, okay?'

Her brow knit. 'Don't make a scene with him. Please.'

'I don't think that's up to me.'

Her look at me was long and thoughtful. Then she turned away as if speaking to herself. 'Why are you doing this, Adam? Why are you doing this now?'

Her question lingered in the silence. I left for the doctor's.

When I got there an officious nurse gave me a form to fill out. I did that, still remembering how Kris Ann and I had begun to learn each other, after that first night.

We were together often, doing everything and nothing. I would tease about her debutante party, watching amused as she accepted service at the cheap diner I could pay for with the ease of manner that suggested we had just come in from riding, when more likely we were fresh from making love. Lovemaking left her shamelessly hungry, and she would stalk from our bed to the refrigerator, ripping through my leftovers with noises of mock disappointment until we had to go out. 'This isn't a refrigerator,' she said one evening, 'it's an aluminum mine,' and after that she had stocked the kitchen with food and spices and begun cooking fine dinners of pasta, served by candlelight at my kitchen table, with red wine. She'd learned pasta from a book, she told me, because it wasn't southern, and she was full of questions about the way I'd lived: about my home and father and how I'd made it since, about the steel mill I'd worked in and the ore boat with the drunken captain that I'd served on one summer, running ore from Minnesota to the docks in Cleveland. My job now was our dishes, but sometimes we would look at each other and leave them. One night, afterward, she lay on my shoulder, absorbed in her own thoughts. 'It's funny,' she finally said.

'What's funny?'

'I don't know. It's just that sometimes I think that life is this giant maze, very dark, with people wandering through it bumping into each other and going on, groping for that thing or person that will make the difference – you know, get them to the end – and it's all so much chance. Look at us. We start at different places, you in Cleveland, me in Alabama, from people who are nothing alike, and then enter the maze to go through all the things that make us the way we are now and deliver us by sheer coincidence to a bad party in the middle of twelve thousand people, and by the time we've met maybe these same experiences mean that we're people who can't help each other, that at some point we'll have to go on alone, bumping into more people and things. I mean, it's hard to know when you've gotten to the end, isn't it?'

I looked up at the ceiling. 'For some people, I suppose.'

She rolled over, head propped on her elbow. 'Adam, did any of what I just said make sense to you?'

I grinned. 'Infinite sense.'

'Then how can you sound so *blasé*?'

'Because I know.'

'Know what?'

I turned to see her face. Her eyes were deep and dark and serious. I reached out, touching the nape of her neck, and said softly, 'Because I know the maze ends here.'

For a long time she looked at me, seeming hardly to breathe. Then as if on impulse she stretched to pull me out of bed. 'Come on.'

'Where?'

'You'll see.' She tugged harder. 'Hurry up.'

I began laughing. 'Okay, okay. I'll go quietly.'

We dressed and went down to campus with the key to the stark, unfurnished room that held her paintings, where she had never taken me. Beneath one bare lightbulb was an easel covered with white muslin. She went to it, removed the muslin, and turned.

Beside her was an oil of my face, each feature carefully drawn from memory. It was so much like my father I felt a kind of *frisson*.

Kris Ann studied me closely. 'Do you like it?'

'It's incredible.'

I couldn't move my eyes from the painting. Then she stepped in front of it. Slowly, without speaking, she unbuttoned her blouse until it lay on the floor beside her. 'Make love to me, Adam. Please. Right here.'

We did that. I held her for a long time after.

That Saturday we packed my car with her dishes and dresses on hangers. In the country we found a spool bed and mattress, and for Cade's sake ordered his and hers telephones to go on either side.

The next week Cade called her, to invite us down . . .

When I came back from the doctor's she met me at the front door. 'Daddy's here.'

'I can hardly wait. Incidentally, it's not broken.'

'What isn't?'

'My hand. Where is he?'

'In the sunroom.'

She looked tense and wooden, the look I remembered from when I'd come to Cade's that first time, every southern gentleman's notion of the perfect son-in-law, an Irish Catholic northerner, and broke at that. The pinstripe I'd worn on the flight down was my only suit and I was somehow sure that Cade would know that. He rose from the living-room couch to shake my hand, conveying ease and power in a cardigan sweater. I began feeling like a dress-up doll with sweat glands. Kris Ann stood to one side, watchful and unnaturally quiet.

'That's a long trip,' Cade had smiled. 'Would you like a drink?'

'Yes, thanks. Any kind of whiskey.'

'Good.' He brought two bourbons. We sat at opposite corners of a couch set in front of a Chinese wall hanging and surrounded by antiques I admired for a moment. When I glanced back to the room Kris Ann had disappeared.

'It's good to finally meet you,' Cade was saying.

'And you, too, sir.' I flinched inwardly at the sound of 'sir,' waiting for him to wave it away. He didn't.

'You've done quite well in law school. I'm impressed.'

'Krissy's biased.'

Cade scowled as if he didn't like the sound of 'Krissy.' 'I happen to know she's right. You're fifth in your class and on law review.' He saw my puzzlement. 'The Deans's an old classmate,' he explained. 'I hope you don't mind.' He sounded quite sure I wouldn't, or wouldn't say so.

I shrugged. 'I guess I'd mind more if I were bottom quarter.'

'A good answer. With those grades you can write your own ticket. It all depends on what you want.'

Late sunlight through his window warmed the rich colors of the rug and suffused Cade's bookshelves with a kind of glow. It seemed a good room to discuss good futures. 'The justice department has an honors program, in its antitrust division.' Whiskey warmed me to the subject. 'Antitrust is a growing field, and the government gives you more responsibility, earlier. I think I've got a pretty fair shot.'

Cade balanced his glass in both hands. 'Justice is a useful connection,' he said judiciously. 'But I've seen government ruin young lawyers through lack of training.' He paused, then said abruptly, 'Adam, I'd like you to visit our firm. I can set up appointments tomorrow, if you'd like.'

The warmth turned sluggish in me. Cade raised a

mollifying hand. 'I gather Kris Ann hasn't mentioned this, but you'd be doing me a favor to consider it, and not just because you're seeing my daughter. You've got brains and ambition and those are things no large firm can afford to overlook.' His voice turned easy and comfortable. 'Besides, any interview is good practice.'

'It's just that I never thought to live here.'

Cade nodded as if that were natural and reached for my glass. 'Let me get you a second drink.'

He limped off while I tried to construct an answer. I was still puzzling when he returned with the fresh drink. He paused to look out the window, then jerked the drapes closed with sudden violence, like a man hanging a cat. He handed me the drink, asking, 'How does it stand between you and Kris Ann?'

I hesitated. 'Fairly serious, I think. At least I am.'

Cade settled back in the corner and took one sip, tasting it on his lips and eyeing me thoughtfully. Then he spread his arms in an avuncular, confiding gesture. 'You're adults, of course. I only ask because Kris Ann's always lived here. The South is home to her, and of course she's been spoiled – perhaps more so because her mother died and I've tried to make up for that. But I wonder whether you'd be handicapping yourself were you to ask her to move to a strange place and leave what she's had.'

I was feeling uneasy. 'I guess that's up to her.'

Cade seemed not to hear. 'After all,' he went on, 'there are other differences.'

'Such as?'

He glanced carelessly around the room. 'Just that the two of you are used to different things. And of course there's the Catholic business.'

'The Catholic business?'

He gave me a probing glance. 'You don't think being of different faiths is a problem?'

I wondered why responding was so hard: I only went to Mass at home, and was home rarely. I paused, then said, 'I've sort of let that lapse.'

'I see.' He was cheerful again. 'I don't mean to pry, you understand, but I do worry. Perhaps someday you'll be a father too.'

'I hope so.'

'Then you'll consider my offer?'

I looked past him at the books and antiques. 'I'll talk to Krissy,' I finally said.

'Fair enough.' He broke into the wide-as-the-plains smile I would later see him flash on clients like a sudden gift. 'Let's have another drink, Adam.'

'Let's do this on the porch,' I told him now.

Cade sat drinking in our sunroom, under an antique brass fan Kris Ann had salvaged from an old hotel. He rose with a long upward glare and followed me outside.

Cade took the wicker couch facing the house and set his glass on a low marble table as I sat opposite. Kris Ann's plants hung from the canopy behind him, and beyond that our front grounds sloped gently to the street.

'Dalton Mooring called me.' Cade's voice was soft with anger.

'Did he now?'

Cade leaned slowly forward. The skin near his eyes seemed tight with the effort of self-control. 'Mooring theatened to sue us for slander. What you've done is the single most stupid and irresponsible act ever committed by a member of this firm.'

'Mooring won't sue, Roland, and you know it.'

A vein pulsed in Cade's forehead. 'You can guarantee that.'

'I can. First, because I haven't slandered anyone. Second, because a slander suit only spreads the slander. Third, because to the extent I suggested that he was Lydia's lover it's probably not slander at all.'

'Jesus Christ.' Cade slammed his fist on the table and the drink slopped over. 'Just how do you figure that?'

'It's easy enough. The police found semen on Lydia, Henry was out of town, and Jason's her son, for God's sake. There's no sign of a break-in, which probably means a lover. The Cantwells' yardman saw a car like Mooring's several times in the past month, and Jason found Mooring there alone with Lydia. Mooring's known her for twenty-five years, he's got a wife that drinks and was jealous of her, and, if you believe Jason, Lydia and Henry weren't sleeping together. Yesterday I heard that two weeks before she died Lydia was quizzing a friend on how to get a divorce. Plus, the one civic thing Mooring seems to do gave him an excuse to see her. Which he used.'

'You call that evidence?'

'I call that funny. And when I tried it out on Mooring he did everything but act normal.'

A slight breeze blew the cocktail napkin from Cade's lap. He snatched it back. 'Your theory's a disaster.'

'How so?'

'Because it leads the police right back to Henry, as Mooring was kind enough to point out. You've taken a client with no alibi and found him a motive to go with it: a potential lover.'

'It also gives us at least one more potential killer. We could use one. The police and media have ganged up on Henry, and Jason has an alibi.'

Cade glanced at my hand. 'Yes,' he said coolly. 'You'd better tell me what happened with Jason. And don't leave anything out.'

I described our talk. Cade listened, intent and nearly motionless. When I got to the fight, Cade cut in. 'And that's all he said?'

'That's right.'

'Jesus,' Cade explained. 'And for that you picked a fight with a madman. We don't in this firm go around brawling, or insulting people like Dalton Mooring. We couldn't survive. After seven years you still have no mature concept of your responsibilities. I helped build this firm, dammit, and I won't let you tear it down just because you had the good luck to marry my daughter.'

A retort came to my tongue and died there. 'The point is,' I finally said, 'that without Jason as a suspect, Henry's in trouble.'

'My God, you're fresh from fighting with Jason and you still think he couldn't kill?'

I shrugged. 'I suppose it's possible. He's violent, his feelings about Lydia are a tangle of pathology, and the girl's his only alibi. That has a strange look to it: she's mother, lover, and cheerleader all rolled into one. But incest is hard to accept.'

'I've known Jason since he was a child,' Cade said coldly, 'and I assure you that he could kill his mother and the rest of it too. All it would take is something to make him feel that Lydia had abandoned him. Like that will.'

'That's wading pretty deep in the Freudian slime.'

'Christ.' Cade gave me a slow, disgusted look. 'Did you see Lydia's picture?'

I rested the cold drink on my hand. 'Is that why you gave Kris Ann the revolver?' I asked. 'Or to make some other point.'

'She should be able to protect herself.' His voice was contemptuous. 'With you out stirring up Jason and God knows who else, I'm damned glad I did. He's insane and now you've gone out of your way to draw his attention. Someone has to protect my daughter from your own carelessness.'

I flushed. 'I'll let her keep it, for now. But the next time you want to introduce guns into my house, ask first. Ask *me*.'

Without answering, Cade took a long sip of his drink, watching me over the rim until he put it down. In a tone of polite inquiry, as if continuing another conversation, he said, 'Nothing's worse than being poor, is it?'

I looked at him, surprised. 'I don't know. There are a lot of things I haven't tried.'

'Nothing's worse,' he repeated. 'That's why you came here.'

'I came here for Krissy.'

'But you've stayed, Adam. You didn't like being poor any more than I did.' Cade got up and began pacing stiffly. 'You know how I felt when my daddy lost everything? Like I'd been weeded out. The sad truth is that if you make it, most people don't care how, but if you're poor, well now, they just pity you and shake their heads.' His voice took on a rolling, angry cadence. 'Hell, with money you can even get away with being a liberal. But if you're poor and liberal, people just think you're peculiar. Oh, they'll never be sure whether you're a liberal because you're poor or poor because you're a liberal, but they're damn sure it's one or the other.

'Now you wonder why I tell you this.' Cade stopped to glower at me with a strange, transcendent rage. 'It's because I don't ever intend to see my daughter beholden. I love her more than you could ever understand. I have no wife, no son to call my own, but my God I have Kris Ann. And I've always planned that she not need anything.

'But life has a way of surprising you. You can't plan for everything. Lately some of my investments have gone a little sour. So I might need your help now.' His voice turned sarcastic. 'You might even have to be a little bit of a success. That's why I can't let you ruin Henry Cantwell. Because if you turn up something that gets Henry indicted you'll not only destroy my friend but your own reputation. And then you couldn't find work as a bootblack.'

'Henry's not your ward, Roland. And neither is Kris Ann, like it or not.'

Cade reddened. 'I'm taking you off the Cantwell case. Tomorrow you're going to march to your office, close the door, and start preparing for that Stafford trial.'

'All for Kris Ann and Henry.'

'For them, and for the firm.'

I shook my head. 'No, Roland, it's mostly for you. I've heard that speech about loving Kris Ann one too many times, when you've done your damnedest to leave her without any sense of herself outside of your world. That's not love and never has been. It's ownership.'

Cade was very still, as if holding back. Then, with a thin smile, he said softly, 'But you didn't take her north, did you, Adam?'

I stood. 'You miserable sonofabitch – '

Kris Ann opened the front door to announce dinner, saw our faces, and stopped in mid-sentence. Cade murmured,

'We'll finish this at the firm,' and then looked to Kris Ann and said in a different voice, 'We're coming, honey.'

Dinner was better than the conversation. I ate in silence while Cade asked Kris Ann about her tennis and her cousin's baby. Watching her was painful. Her gestures were sharp and nervous and her smile came late and left nothing behind. When Cade purred, 'The next few weeks Adam's to be quite busy on our Stafford case,' she lapsed into silence, as if at some unspoken punishment for her choice of a husband.

Finally I cleared the dishes, something I did when the maid wasn't there. Kris Ann liked cooking, but hated to clean. When we'd first been married she would throw things in the dishwater still dirty, so that they'd come out with the traces of last night's dinner baked on, like the evidence of some geologic period. When I'd joke that the progress of her cooking would be preserved in layers, for posterity, she'd grinned back and said dirty dishes weren't her *metier*. So I'd taken them on again, while she drank coffee and offered me solemn advice. It had all been very droll, once.

I was alone in the kitchen when the phone rang.

'Adam,' the familiar voice said. 'Can you come by?'

Chapter 15

I left right after Cade, locking the doors behind me. Kris Ann watched me go in silence.

The Cantwell place was almost black. When I knocked, Etta Parsons answered and led me to the library with an air of cool unrecognition. 'Mr Cantwell will be down momentarily,' she said, and left.

For a while I paced the sitting room. It was the same, yet eerily different. Someone had replaced Lydia's picture with one that was older and smaller. The effect was uncannily that of a fading presence. Two sliding oak doors sealed the dining room.

I went back to the library.

The evening paper was folded by Henry's chair. I began riffling the sports section for box scores, as my father had taught me.

'Hello, Adam.'

Henry Cantwell had appeared with two snifters of cognac. I put down the box scores to take one.

'How are you?' I asked.

'Better.'

I wondered. Henry had lost the pallor of the day before, but the hesitance of his movements, a slight dreaminess in the eyes, were like those of a man after his first stroke. There was a rim of loose skin beneath his eyes and the start of slackness in his jawline I hadn't noticed before. The haircut for Lydia's funeral made his ears too large. 'I've been wondering how to help,' I told him. 'Sometimes I think people hover when what they're really doing is relieving their own grief, not a kindness at all.'

Henry gave a thin smile, and his expression turned curious and kind. 'You father was murdered too, wasn't he?'

'Yes. He was.'

I glanced around, unsettled by the familiar surface of things: the cognac and quiet, a space in the bookshelf, something being reread in another part of the house. Henry followed my glance to the space. 'I'm leafing through *Lady Chatterley* again,' he said calmly. 'Lawrence treats the emotions so well, don't you think?'

I flushed, managing to nod. Henry swirled the cognac in his glass, seemingly lost in Lawrence's impotent husband and restless wife. Then he said, 'Jason called this evening.' His eyes rose from the glass. 'He was raving. But he managed to get across that you were asking about Dalton Mooring.'

'I was,' I said flatly. 'Roland called me off. He says it hurts you. I'm afraid I've hurt you already.'

He shook his head. 'Don't be. I've already faced what my life has come to.' He looked slowly around the room. 'When my grandfather built this house, he'd already founded your firm and married my grandmother, whose father owned the bank. He left this house, the firm, and,' he smiled wryly, 'a bank for leftover Cantwells. The way most people see it I was farmed out in my twenties. I've hated that bank ever since, and done badly. Caring for other people's money was a responsibility I never wanted, and now – ' He stopped to look straight at me. 'I failed there, and failed even here. You see, Adam, our marriage was a charade.'

I could think of nothing to say. The light on Henry's face was yellow and pitiless. 'Lydia and I hadn't been truly married for a very long time. Something in the chemistry, I suppose . . .' His voice fell off. 'It's so odd – last night I was trying to remember first being with Lydia and all that came back to me was that her shoes always matched her dress. Imagine remembering Kris Ann for something like that.' He shook his head. 'The void showed up in Jason: love is learned and Jason had little to learn from watching us. I withdrew and Lydia smothered him as if he were her hope in life. It was a problem for the boy. He fought to be free of her, but she was his obsession.'

Henry paused to stare out the window next to him, black and flat and skyless. 'You could see that in his politics and even his girlfriends. It wasn't enough for Jason to sleep with someone. His mother had to know, poor boy.' He turned back to me, voice quiet with embarrassment. 'I failed them both miserably. So there's little now that can hurt me no matter what you find, unless Jason had some part in it. And that I can never accept.'

'You may have to. Roland thinks he killed her.'

Henry's expression was tragic. 'That would be too horrible.' He almost whispered. 'You see, Jason's birth was the only reason Lydia and I stayed married. For it to end like this . . .'

I sipped some cognac. 'He does have an alibi, you know. His girlfriend.'

He nodded. 'What kind of girl is she, Adam?'

'I don't know. She seems quiet and not quite formed. Perhaps I'm getting older. But she clearly cares for him.'

'That's all Jason wanted,' Henry said sadly. 'It doesn't seem much, does it?'

'It doesn't necessarily seem easy, either.'

'He said you fought. How did it happen?'

'He said something. I lost my head.'

'He has an instinct for hurt. It's ruined sensitivity, I'm afraid.'

I shrugged. 'I pushed him too far. I shouldn't have.'

'You're all right, I hope. You look bruised.'

'I'm okay. I boxed some at the CYO when I was a kid and it kind of came back.'

'Stay away from him,' Henry said seriously. 'I mean that. He's an unstable man, full of jealousies you don't know anything about.'

'He managed to get some of that across.'

'So it seems.' Henry's voice was tentative. 'Adam, why did you ask about Dalton Mooring?'

I hesitated. 'Nothing hard. Just little things, times they were together. Is it possible, Henry?'

He rocked back and forth in his chair. 'It's possible,' he finally said. 'It never struck me particularly, but at the club they would always dance.' He closed his eyes, as if to see them dancing. 'He's known her for a long time,' he murmured. His eyes opened. 'Adam, I want you to check this out.'

I shook my head. 'Roland absolutely forbids it.'

'But I have to know.' He pointed at the newspaper. 'You've seen the headlines, I'm sure. All day reporters have called or just pounded on the door. I can't keep on living under this shadow.'

'Rayfield's got toll slips, you know. They prove your call to Lydia was twelve minutes, not two.'

He looked chagrined. 'I suppose I was foolish. We'd fought, you see. Sitting there, I just couldn't talk about it.'

'You shouldn't have been there at all. But now you'd better tell me what was said.'

'Nothing, really. Just' – his mouth twisted – 'accumulated disappointments. Personal things. Nothing about the will.'

'You're sure.'

'Yes.'

'And after that you just stayed there.'

He nodded. 'Yes. Please, Adam, I need your help on this.'

I hesitated. But Henry's voice had a desperate edge. 'You're the client,' I finally said. 'It's your job to tell Roland what you want, and who.'

'I will,' he said flatly. Finishing the cognac, he dabbed his lips with a cloth napkin. 'Is that any better – you and Roland?'

'Worse. We had a blow-up tonight. I've committed heresy by thought, word, and deed.'

'That's a problem with Kris Ann, isn't it?'

'It can be.'

Henry's face hardened. 'What Roland did to Kris Ann was a terrible thing. It was unnatural – I don't mean literally, but psychologically. I remember talking to her after her mother died. She was maybe seven or eight, wide-eyed and a little sad, and beautiful even then. She was talking about Margaret's death like a child does, not quite understanding, and then she said Roland had told her that she could take her mother's place and then they'd never need anyone else. She seemed excited and a little disturbed. God knows it disturbed me.

'Later it disturbed me more. Roland never showed interest in remarrying. Instead he devoted himself to becoming a local power and running Kris Ann's life. He sent her to private schools and all those lessons – piano, dance, everything but art – as if he wanted to starve the thing she really cared about. And more and more he began to substitute her for her mother, using her as hostess, taking her to dinner, making her the central figure in his life, as he was in hers. Love or ego, whatever it was, he was too central. The result was rather sad: at times, Kris Ann would seem self-confident and even precocious, and then she'd shrink in his presence, as if he could turn all that off like a switch. I wouldn't be surprised if on some level she resents him terribly.'

'If she does, I wouldn't know it.'

'But then you're very close to it, and you don't know the background. Kris Ann grew up always comparing young men to her father, who intimidated them. Gradually the local boys learned to shy away. That had to be very difficult for her. One thing Lydia and I agreed on was that we were glad you came along. We thought perhaps you were strong enough to give Kris Ann a chance. I still think that.'

I shook my head. 'It may be too late. I should never have moved here.'

'Roland takes over lives. I wanted to tell you that he needed you close because you were the one he couldn't get rid of. But I didn't know you then.'

'God, Henry, I wish you had.' I fumbled for a cigarette. 'What was her mother like? Krissy hardly mentions her.'

He leaned back, empty snifter cupped in his hands. 'Margaret was very much a lady, pretty in a delicate way and rather passive. That's not an unusual choice in domineering men. She treated Roland like he hung the moon, which is what he wants. As for intellect or vitality, I'm afraid Kris Ann owes those to Roland. In any event, Margaret became ill with cancer and just withered away. And that left Kris Ann with Roland.'

The last was said with clear distaste. 'I've always wondered,' I said, 'how it is that you and he are friends.'

His mouth was a bitter line. 'I suppose we're playing out

something that began when we were young. I admired his sureness then. Perhaps I was even flattered that he seemed to cultivate me. After a time he came here so often he was like family. My father was quite taken with him. Eventually Roland became my father's protégé at the firm, and I was eased out to the bank. I think now that Roland had always had that in mind: he wanted money and power very badly. But he was charming, worked like the devil for his clients, and more and more my father came to rely on him.' Henry sounded almost bemused. 'I still saw him, of course, though not so often. But by the time my father died he'd been handling our family's affairs for several years and it just went on from there. As I said, Roland takes over lives . . .'

The sentence died off. Carefully, Henry added, 'I may ask too much, pitting you against Roland with Kris Ann in between. He'll do anything to keep the upper hand.'

'You should worry about yourself. Roland says I'll end up getting you indicted as a jealous husband.'

'I'll take that chance. It's your career that concerns me, and your marriage.'

I lit the cigarette. 'Our marriage is what we've made it. As for my career, what good has that ever done anyone? We sit down there filling up time sheets so that every month we can send bills to the x-many corporations who pay for big houses we don't really need. Hell, you're one of the few clients I like or even think about.'

He smiled wispily. 'What else would you do?'

I shrugged. 'I used to know, when I was a kid. I don't anymore.'

His smile vanished. 'Permit me, Adam. I've done badly with Jason, I know, but please, don't live one of those lives of "quiet desperation." Find out what it is you want.'

'Right now I want to help you. There'll be time for the rest.'

He gave me a complex look of gratitude, worry, and relief. 'You're certain?'

'Of course. There is one thing, though. About Rayfield, do you know of any reason for him to have feelings about you one way or the other? Run-ins with Jason, even?'

He paused. Then he shook his head and answered tonelessly, 'It makes no sense to me, Adam.'

His voice was tired. I decided he'd had enough. 'I should be getting back to Kris Ann.'

'You should. Especially now.'

I stood, began to leave, then stopped. 'About you and Lydia – '

'Yes?'

'It's just that I'd never have guessed.'

His smile was wan. 'Then I suppose we succeeded – on one level.'

'I'm sorry it wasn't more, Henry.'

'That was never meant,' he said gently. 'Here, let me see you out.'

We walked through the silent house, past the dining room. Opening the door, he said, 'I hope you know, Adam, how much I appreciate this.'

I placed a hand on his shoulder. 'No need. God knows how many reasons I have to help.'

The cool clear look he gave me said he understood perfectly. 'Don't worry about Roland,' he said. 'I'll tell him myself.' We left it there.

I drove off, absorbing what I'd seen and heard. There was something inconsolable about Henry Cantwell that seemed to reach beyond Lydia to the core of his life and steep him in a terrible calm. I figured he had faced the worst, and told me everything.

I began thinking of Henry and Lydia and Jason until, suddenly, I wanted to talk with Kris Ann of my own parents, of Cade and her, and how the flaws of one generation could run through the next like a bad inheritance, if you let them. But I found her sleeping amidst a black tangle of hair almost phosphorescent in the moonlight, the revolver lying next to her. I put it in the drawer, and gently closed it.

Downstairs, restless, I roamed the house until I saw the book I had borrowed, *Grangeville: A Southern Tragedy*, next to a chair in the sunroom. I picked it up and began turning its pages.

After a moment I sat. Fours hours passed in smoking and reading by one dim lamp. I hardly noticed.

It was beautifully written. The author drew me into the warp and woof of the past: Grangeville in the thirties, a courthouse and some red brick buildings in north Alabama, its people embittered by the Depression and the loss of a railroad yard, scratching crops from red clay mostly rock and sand. The town's eccentric Republican past, back through the Civil War. The irony that few blacks had ever lived there, just a handful.

One sweltering summer day in 1937, an old farmer with a shotgun had found one of them in his barn, mounting a white girl with her dress pulled up. A second black was there: the blacksmith, the first man's brother. A man with a wife and son.

They were prodded with shotguns to the small jail, the first man saying he'd paid her three dollars and that his brother, the blacksmith, had come to warn that sleeping with a white girl was no good. The blacksmith swore to that, and it was known that other men had paid her. But the girl said she was raped. A mob gathered in front of the jail shouting for the blacks. Her white customers stopped talking, joining the frenzy of a town whose real enemies could not be punished.

Within two weeks the men were on trial for rape before Lydia Cantwell's father and an all-white jury. Judge Hargrave ruled out evidence of prostitution. Three days later the blacks were found guilty and sentenced to death. In a riptide of publicity, against all reason except politics, clemency was denied. In January 1939, appeals exhausted, both men were electrocuted.

I finished too wrung out to look back at the pictures. But, two cigarettes later, I did.

The trial had been well covered. Judge, jurors, spectators, and accused had been amply photographed, and the writer had chosen with care. White spectators in bow ties or overalls stared from history's fever swamp, dim eyes seeing nothing of how time would view them. Lydia's father presided from his handcarved bench, mouth a dutiful line. Northern newsmen in hats were there for another glimpse of the Sahara of the Bozart. The two black men leaned away from their white lawyer. Outside the spired courthouse the family of the blacksmith, Moses McCarroll, waited. A wife and a small boy.

I stopped there. There was something wrong with the picture. Something else.

I went to the kitchen and pulled a glassine bag of marijuana from the cabinet. Then I got a bowl and strainer and set them with the bag on the kitchen table. I sat down, opening the bag to put some of the brown, dirt-smelling dope in the strainer. I rubbed it back and forth until only seeds were left and the dope was fine powder in the bowl. Then I went to a drawer for the roller, put in powder and paper, licked the paper, and rolled a joint the size of a Lucky Strike. I did that twice. Then I pushed the excess powder from the bowl to the bag, and put away bag, roller, and paper. The two joints went with me to the porch.

There was nothing outside but crickets and a moon and wet, dank air. I lit a joint, lay back on the wicker couch, and smoked and slipped away into the second joint, and then the crickets were all around me . . .

I was trapped. The pictures roared around dark corners in an express train of white streaks and flashes. The back of my eyes and neck hurt like too much whiskey but the pictures wouldn't stop.

Lydia Cantwell's blue shoes matched her dress, but her tongue came from a rictus smile. Then a black man twisted with orange lightning while a small boy watched and I stood back. The man kept on shaking until my father threw me the baseball, beneath the elms in back.

It was all right, I remembered that. I could even feel the stitches as I threw it back to him, though he was quite pale. 'You'll be a pitcher, then,' he said.

But I knew now. 'No sir, I want to be a policeman. Like you.'

My father looked concerned and held the ball. 'But why, Adam?'

'Because I want to know the truth.'

Before he could answer, the police were at the door and my mother screamed that he was murdered. It was funny. It was happening again and still I couldn't cry. Then Cade said I could have the dark-haired woman if I did as my mother said. The champagne turned bitter in my mouth.

It was cold now and there was noise from the gnarled bushes next door. I had to kill the noises, but couldn't move. My vertebrae had snapped. Footsteps stamped the leaves and branches. Henry Cantwell with no eyes quivered with orange lightning that lifted him out of sight as someone laughed. I knew the laugh but couldn't place it. The fish swam away. The black boy followed alone.

The noise came closer. They would kill me now. There was nowhere to go and I had to tell my father I was sorry –

I awoke just before morning when the night is like thin smoke. The sweat had dried cold on my face. There was no one in the bushes.

I got the bag of dope and threw it out.

Kris Ann was still asleep. I laid out some clean clothes on a chair and went for a run. The morning was bright and clear and filled with nothing but facts.

I came home, showered, and drank coffee with Kris Ann without speaking of Henry, or us. Then I crossed the backyard to the car.

I was behind the wheel before I saw the scrap of paper crumpled beneath the rubber blade of my windshield wiper. I got out and lifted the blade to unfold it.

It was Kris Ann's picture, from the newspaper. A pencil had etched harsh age lines by her eyes, nose, and mouth until she was a wrinkled old woman. There were holes where her pupils had been.

Chapter 16

Kris Ann was in the attic, old shirt half-unbuttoned, staring at her easel in shafts of sunlight that came through the window behind her. Resting one hand on her shoulder I glanced dully at the painting, a nightmare of blues and purples surrounding the orange stick-figure of a woman. Then I held the scrap in front of her. 'I found this on my windshield,' I said.

As if by instinct she brushed her fingertips across the surface of her face. Her voice was flat. 'Is that how Lydia's picture was?'

'The eyes. It's probably just meant to scare us.'

'Why?'

'I don't know.' I put the scrap in my pocket and pulled her up to me. 'Krissy, I want you to go to your cousin's for a while. Just until this is over.'

Her lips parted. 'We should call the police.'

'We will. I want you safe. But I'm still not sure you would be. Last night Henry asked if I'd stay on the case.'

I felt her stiffen. 'And you told him you would,' she said tonelessly. 'In spite of Daddy.'

I nodded. 'That's why you've got to leave.'

'But if we've gone to the police – '

'It's not that simple. I'm caught in a vise. I know things that might make Henry look different than he is. Rayfield's going to sense that. Protecting my wife won't be his first priority. You'll be safer out of state.'

She leaned back from me, searching my face. Then she shook her head in a long, slow arc. 'I'm staying, Adam.'

I grasped her shoulders. 'Please, listen. This won't end well, not with you here. Even without this threat you'll be trapped between Roland and me in a case where Henry's overridden him. Those cards are going to be played out this time. You don't want to be a part of that.'

Her stare was long and probing. 'But I am now,' she said quietly. 'Aren't I?'

My palms were damp. 'Think, Krissy. Last night you were so afraid of Jason Cantwell I found you sleeping with a gun. This morning I'm at least that scared. It's not just Henry now. This thing has become part of our lives. Don't make it any worse than it is.'

'And running away would help? How do I know *you* won't be killed?'

I tried smiling. 'I'm too young.'

'You're thirty-two,' she said levelly. 'So was your father. Isn't that beginning to bother you?'

'Why should it?'

'Because of the way you're pushing – '

'Look, I need to find out who's doing this. I don't want you to be hurt before I do. It's that simple.'

She shook her head with finality. 'No, Adam. You've made your decision. Now I'm making mine.'

'But it's senseless – '

'To you.' She stepped back, eyes burning with a low, angry, smoky intensity. 'Look at me, dammit. I'm twenty-nine and it feels like I've spent my whole life waiting for you and Daddy to decide how I'll spend the rest of it. I can't stand by anymore. I can't go cover my eyes while the two of you fight this out.'

Her face had set in a remote determination hauntingly like Cade's. The attic seemed filled with trapped heat and the smell of paint. We faced each other, waiting. 'I'll go see Rayfield,' I said in a low voice. 'Call Rennie Kell. I'll drop you there.'

She watched me another moment, then silently began cleaning up her paints. I went through the house checking doors and windows while she finished and called the Kells. When I dropped her there she turned, said slowly and seriously, 'I don't want you hurt, Adam,' and got out of the car without looking back. I watched until she was inside.

I found Rayfield arranging a deskful of ragged papers ripped from his notebooks, as if trying to make sense of a senseless world. Surprised in thought, he seemed for a moment both old and innocent. Then his face went tough.

'What do you want?'

I tossed the scrap in front of him. 'That used to be a picture of my wife. Someone did the artwork and left it on my windshield.'

He looked at it carefully, turning it once to check the back for marks. 'Know who, or why?'

'Not who. The obvious why is the Cantwell case. I want protection for Kris Ann.'

'And what will you do for us?'

'My job. I'm asking that you do yours.'

He looked at me shrewdly. 'Then tell me who drives the green Cadillac Otis Lee saw at the Cantwells'.'

I paused, glancing at my fingernails, then back to Rayfield. 'I don't know.'

His eyes narrowed. Coldly he said, 'Tell your wife to take a vacation.'

'She won't go without me, and I can't.'

'Yeah.' His face was hard. 'You so busy and all. If you wanted to be your father, Shaw, you should have just been a cop.'

I flushed. 'You've been wasting time.'

'We check backgrounds. After I found you'd been poking around Otis Lee and the Parsons woman I checked yours.' He sounded as though information were power. 'I turned up the usual things. At St Ignatius you were an all-city quarterback but got an academic scholarship for Notre Dame and another to Vanderbilt Law. When you married Cade's daughter you were flat broke.'

'Brilliant work, Lieutenant.'

'And then,' he went smoothly on, 'I dug some more and discovered that of all things your father was a homicide lieutenant. I'm sorry about what happened, Shaw.'

I looked around at the dim hanging lights, gray tile, gray desks with gray faces behind them. 'It's like you said about Grangeville,' I answered. 'That was a long time ago.'

'It's strange, though, how your family has a history of violence. Like your grandfather leaving Ireland because he'd killed a British soldier.'

I shrugged. 'He needed work, unemployment being what it was. Maybe when you quit toying with me we can get back to my wife.'

A telephone rang across the room. Rayfield watched it until someone answered. 'Who else have you been talking to?'

I guessed that he was still looking for a driver to go with Lee's description of the car. A sad, stray thought of Kris Ann went through me as I said, 'No one.'

'Quit playing games,' he snapped. 'You want protection for your wife and you won't tell me shit. You'll end up getting her killed.'

'Is that a threat?' I asked angrily.

'It's an observation.' His face turned curious, analytic. 'It seems you're more interested in protecting Henry Cantwell than your own wife.'

'That's an odd remark.'

He kept staring. 'Is it?'

'Look, Lieutenant, Kris Ann needs protection. I'm not asking for me or Cade or Cantwell, but for her who's got no part in any of this.'

Dislike for me warred on his face with whatever kept him a cop. Finally he scribbled some numbers on a pad of paper. His voice was flat. 'The top one's the police emergency number. The other two are where she can get me or Bast if we're not here. Days I'll have a patrolman look in and if she calls someone will be there. You'll be home nights, I hope.'

'I should.'

He looked down at Kris Ann's photo. 'Tell me, Shaw, how do you know Cantwell didn't do this?'

'That's ridiculous. Henry's known my wife since she was small.'

He paused. 'Thing is, we've never let out what had been done to the eyes. You tell anyone?'

'Just Kris Ann.'

'Then the only other person who knows for sure is the one

who killed Mrs Cantwell. I'd think about that. You in particular should think about that.'

'I already have.'

'Think harder,' he said harshly. 'Because I'm going to get him even if it's Henry Cantwell. You don't want to be in the way.'

We stared at each other. At length, I said, 'Thanks for your help.'

He shrugged. 'They told me your father was a good cop. Except maybe the last.' He looked down at the scraps of paper and began working again.

I shut the office door behind me and slumped in my chair, thinking. Then I picked up the telephone and dialed the main number at Auburn University. Five minutes and four transfers later a deep voice answered, 'Ransom.'

'This is Adam Shaw, Professor, a lawyer, in Birmingham. I've just read your book on Grangeville.'

'Yes?'

'I'd like to ask about your research. It's for a case I'm working.'

There was a pause. 'Grangeville was forty years ago, sir. I don't see what it could relate to.'

'I'm not sure, exactly, but it's about Judge Hargrave's daughter, Mrs Cantwell. She's been murdered.'

'Yes, I saw that.' Ransom's voice – rheumy, ancient, and bourbonous – lent the odd sensation of speaking to history. 'Whom do you represent?' he asked.

'The husband. Henry Cantwell.'

'The papers made it sound like he killed her.'

'Forty years ago, Professor, some of the papers made it sound like two black men raped a vestal virgin.'

'True enough. What do you want?'

'The blacksmith, Moses McCarrolll, had a small boy. Do you know where he is?'

'Nooo,' he said thoughtfully, 'never found him. It was 'fifty-seven whcn I started my research. You can guess how popular it was back then, especially after Little Rock when

Eisenhower sent the troops in. People weren't always helpful. Anyhow, Moses McCarroll's wife had died in nineteen thirty-nine, and the boy just disappeared. Never found any relatives who would talk about it.'

'Know who I might try?'

'Most everyone's dead, Mr Shaw. Except Luther Channing.'

'The assistant prosecutor?'

'That's right. Channing's retired now, but still alive. One of my students tried to interview him not too long ago and got thrown off the porch. He's a steely bastard. Wouldn't talk to me, either.'

'I'll try him anyhow. Thanks, Professor.'

'No thanks needed. Mrs Cantwell was one I always felt sorry for. Tried talking to her once at her house. When I said what I wanted, she began shaking her head. Could hardly talk. Finally she said she was sorry and shut the door. Two weeks later I got a note apologizing. I remember it: small, ladylike writing – I've still got it somewhere. Said she understood my reasons, but she couldn't speak of it and hoped I understood. I never published it, felt too badly for her. She was just a child back then, too.'

'Yes, sir. She was.'

There was a long silence. 'Mr Shaw,' he said slowly, 'that boy, if he's still alive, is over fifty now.'

'I know.'

'If I follow your reasoning, that would be a terrible circle, wouldn't it?'

'Yes, it would. But then people's lives seem to be full of them.'

'Well, let me know if you find him.' He spoke heavily, as if feeling the weight of the past. 'Though I almost hope you don't.'

I said I could understand that, and hung up.

I called the Kells to give Kris Ann the telephone numbers and ask her to stay. Just a few more hours, I promised. Then I went to the car and drove north toward Grangeville.

Chapter 17

Yellow stripes split the two-lane blacktop in a blur racing backward toward Birmingham. Ahead the road ran through fields of crops and rock and harsh red clay, hacked from pine forests and marked by stunted oaks. Amidst a sprawling cornfield the sun-blackened figure of a farmer hoed patiently. Now and then I passed desultory civilization: junkyards, stores, trailers, roadhouses, Baptist churches and cemeteries –the small towns whose people lived, died, hunted, prayed, made love and whiskey, and were carelessly killed in a sun so hot it took the stomach from you at midday. Vaporous heat rising thinly from the road lent the landscapes a cruel, shimmering beauty. Birmingham had ceased to exist.

After an hour or so I passed a blue sweep of lakes nestled in low piny hills and speckled with rowboats and a few shirtless men standing hip-deep with flyrods. Then bait shops began, then gas stations, a small sign marking the turn for Grangeville, two miles of bare asphalt, and I was there.

Past a few stores and a Church of Christ whose sign promised that 'Blessed Are the Optimists,' the road stopped at the town square. It was surrounded by quaint stores and packed with shoppers strolling among sidewalk stands. At its center was a green rolling lawn shaded by oak trees. From their midst the bell tower of the county courthouse rose to a painted gold spire, gleaming in the sun as it had when the black woman and small boy had stood outside, waiting.

I parked and began walking toward a corner phone booth at the end of the crowded sidewalk, weaving among stands and people there from long tradition: Grangeville Trading Day, held for eighty years the first Thursday of the month. Parents and children ambled among handmade quilts and factory-made junk while vendors watched with studied indifference. A sidewalk fiddler in wire-rimmed glasses sawed vigorously and on the grass boys chased a small black dog past shade trees where men sat whittling with keen-edged knives. Their seamed faces spoke of lives spent in harsh sun and the older ones were strikingly the same: sharp chins and noses, spectral eyes, flat cheekbones with cheeks so gaunt they were like grooves. They talked and whittled with utter lassitude, like the fallout from a hundred years of inbreeding.

I got to the phone booth and went through the directory. Then I approached one of the old men, whittling in overalls, wood shavings curled at his feet. 'Help me find something?' I asked.

He spat a brown stream of tobacco juice and looked up with a surprising smile that lacked several teeth. 'Might could.' The words were guttural and half-swallowed. 'What you looking for?'

'Montgomery Street. Luther Channing's place.'

His smile inverted. 'That'd be the old Hargrave place,' he said flatly.

'How do I get there?'

He looked me up and down, then pointed. 'Take Main and turn left at the third street. Big, shadowy white house on the right. Only one like it.'

'Thanks.'

He spat and looked away. I went to the car.

Montgomery Street was lined by maples and haphazard small-town architecture, mainly tan brick houses built close to the street. Two blocks down the right side was a lawn several acres deep with a straight drive running between a quarter mile of parallel oaks. I turned, driving across their shadows until I spotted the white frame house at the end, concealed by more oaks. When I finally parked, I saw that the house was three antebellum stories. Its wide, shady porch had stairs at both ends, and in one corner two empty gliders hung facing each other. Five whitewashed steps rose to it between lilacs a soft mauve color. The grounds were still save for a single orange butterfly jittering among the lilacs. I went to the front door and knocked.

After a moment there were footsteps on the other side of the door. It was opened by an old man with eyes a shocking, opalescent gray.

'Yes?' he demanded.

'Mr. Channing?' He nodded. 'I'm Adam Shaw, a lawyer from Birmingham. If it's all right, I'd like a moment of your time.'

'Without calling? What about?'

'The Grangeville case, partly.'

His eyes glinted. 'I've talked about that once in forty years, and not to a stranger.' He poised to slam the door.

'Also about Lydia Cantwell.' I added quickly. 'You saw she was murdered?'

His hand stopped. 'Go on.'

'Just that it may have something to do with your case.'

'What's your interest in Lydia?'

'I represent Henry Cantwell. The husband.'

I looked past him as he scrutinized me. Through the hallway was a dark living room: two chairs, a lamp, and a standing clock, all antiques, as neatly arranged as if no one lived there. There was something deadly about it: Channing lived in a museum. The clock ticked behind him.

'I'll listen,' he said at last and stepped onto the porch, slamming the door. 'Out here.'

He pointed toward the two gliders, moving toward the far one. He was a tall man and his walk, straight and gliding, held the last vestige of youthful grace. But his vulpine face was ravaged. Two red scrapes on his cheek looked like skin cancer, with a white mark beneath them where more had been removed. Lank, white-yellow hair hung lifelessly over his forehead and to his collar in back. In his linen suit, he looked like a well-bred version of the whittling men, in worse health. I wondered who the suit was for.

'Speak up,' he said harshly.

'I'm sorry. I was wondering if Mrs Cantwell used to live here.'

His eyes riveted me, as though he knew of their effect and used it. 'She did,' he said finally. 'When she was Lydia Hargrave. I bought the place after her mother died. She didn't want it.'

I could see why, though, looking at the shady grounds and

flowers in orderly plots, its air of perfect unreality seemed to match Lydia's. 'You've kept it up nicely,' I said.

'Someone had to. Is that what you came to say?'

'No. I wanted to ask about one of the defendants. Moses McCarroll.'

His voice, rough and old and hollow, held a note of malice. 'What about him?'

'I wanted to know about the trial, and what happened to his family afterwards.'

'Don't know much about the last.' He crossed one leg in a seeming act of will. 'You find that strange?'

'I'm trying to imagine myself in your position.'

'Understand something, then.' He coughed, phlegm rattling in his throat. 'The two nigras weren't the issue.'

'I suppose that depends on your point of view.'

He held a handkerchief close to his mouth and spat into it. 'Where you from?'

'Cleveland.'

'And raised very right-minded, I'm sure. The one thing more certain than that you didn't know any southerners is that you didn't know any blacks.'

'I'm not arguing. I came to ask you things, not tell you.'

'All right.' He looked at me sharply. 'Driving through here, did you look around?'

'Some.'

'Look very wealthy to you?'

'Just this place.'

He ignored that. 'Forty-odd years ago it was worse. The soil had gone from bad to farmed-out. When the Depression hit, Grangeville was so poor that for a while you hardly noticed. Then the L & N shut down the railroad yard. Three hundred men lost their jobs. Stores shut, just flat closed. People starved. They'd sweated and prayed and had nothing to show for it except rain that washed away the topsoil. One farmer hanged himself in his barn. Lucy Vines – the one with those two nigras – turned whore because of it.

'I'd been at law school and came back young and full of ambition, looking to lawyer awhile and then run for state senate. What I found was a town full of angry people and half the legal work in foreclosures where people hated your guts. So I got on at the prosecutor's and started going to meetings, just listening and being seen. And what I heard was anger.

'I hadn't been prosecuting six months – a couple of chicken thieves and a farmer who shot his wife for fornicating and admitted it – and then Roy Cobb found that nigra in his barn, rutting on Lucy Vines. Roy was a man of settled opinions, and right then and there he fetched his shotgun and ran all three of them into the courthouse: Lucy, the nigra, and his brother. It was blazing hot, nothing but fat, lazy flies coming through the windows and the usual bunch sitting on the steps that there'd been since the yard shut down. When they saw Roy prodding the two blacks and Lucy she began screaming rape. News got out fast. Pretty soon a whole crowd of those blank-eyed morons were on the front steps howling for the nigras and some rope, all crazy and excited. Might have done it too. The nigras were something they could reach out and touch.'

He spoke with dispassionate savagery: the McCarrolls seemed hardly to exist and his compassion for the towns-people was mingled with contempt. 'What stopped them?' I asked.

He didn't answer, suddenly absorbed in a black fly that had landed on the glider. It crept nearer his hand. Two inches, then one. The fly stopped. Seconds passed. Channing was perfectly still. The fly turned and began marching back across the cushion. Channing watched narrowly. Two inches, three inches, four . . . I felt a foolish relief. With a sudden snap Channing's palm smacked down and closed. Then, slowly, he brought his fist to chest level and opened it. The smashed fly dropped on the porch. Channing's eyes were like clear ice.

'We've talked enough,' he rasped.

I stared at the fly. 'You haven't told me anything.'

'Why should I? What are you to me?'

'I'm nothing to you. I'm just here.'

He turned toward the grounds. Afternoon shadows were moving toward the house and sluggish winds wafted the scent of lilac. Channing's long fingers rubbed silently together.

There was no sound except the glider creaking under his weight. 'George Naylor was the prosecutor,' he said abruptly. 'He sat there, sweat dripping down his three chins, mumbling, "We never had no nigra problem," which wasn't surprising since we'd never had any nigras except the McCarrolls. By then the lawn was covered with townsfolk and farmers in overalls making that low, ugly mob sound that's not like anything else. Our moon-faced sheriff, Bohannon, is pacing in front of George's desk whining that he can't hold back the crowd. "I know these folks," he keeps saying. "They're my friends." George stares at him without answering. Finally he sucks himself up and steps out on the porch. The sound gets even lower, like some animal. George has his high-pitched voice; I can barely hear him trying to ask the mob for trust. "Just give us the rope," a voice yells back. "Before you do that," George pleads, "stop and think if being part of a mob isn't the lowest thing a man can do. If you men let the law just handle this we'll try these nigras in two weeks." I remember thinking two weeks was pretty fast. But after George promised that, they just milled around without rushing the jail. Finally he came back in, sat down sort of heavy, and said, "We've got work to do, Luther." "Then you'd better find out what your case is," I answered.'

Channing still looked away, voice edged with disdain. 'We went down the hall and had the sheriff bring in Lucy Vines. She sat on a stool, slack-mouthed and not looking up, saying the McCarrolls had raped her – the boy, anyhow. George asked about six different ways if that were true. Lucy wouldn't budge. When she'd left, George just shook his head and mumbled, "Jesus Christ." '

'I guess Lucy couldn't have said anything else.'

Channing turned to stare at me. 'Well,' he said coldly, 'she could have confessed to whoring with nigras.'

He spoke with contempt, I thought for me. 'What about the McCarrolls?' I asked.

'George and I went to look them over. The one that'd had the girl – Lucius – was shaking. Moses stood with both hands on the bars asking in this deep nigra voice to see his woman and boy. "Don't be a fool," I told him. "You want them lynched, too?" Big tears came rolling down his face, and he said, "But I didn't do nothing." "Then you're better off here," I answered, and after that he shut up.'

My stomach felt tight. 'How did he get convicted?'

Channing folded his arms. 'What's that have to do with Lydia Cantwell?'

'I think she may have been killed because of how her father dealt with the McCarrolls. That's what I'm trying to learn about.'

For once someone didn't say that Grangeville was a long time back. 'John Hargrave was an idiot,' he said flatly. 'Handsome in an empty way but vain as a peacock. Even of Lydia: when she was only seven or eight he'd parade her around the court-house in braids and ribbons just to see you smile. She was pretty, too, even then. But that was Hargrave. He looked at you as if your face was a mirror, like he didn't really see you except to wonder how he should feel about himself that day. Hadn't been a judge but one month when he hangs a painting of himself in the courthouse. Let it out he was going to be governor. Three years later he was gone and so was the painting. Only thing he's remembered for is this.

'Morning after they brought the nigras in, Hargrave came to George looking very serious, especially about himself. He sat in front of George's desk and told him in his pompous way that if he and George wanted to stand tall in Monroe County they'd better give this nigra case their best. He didn't have to explain his meaning. George just stares at him, sweating. He'd already turned on the ceiling fan and it had blown half the papers off his desk, but George kept wiping his forehead. Finally he answered, "I understand, Judge." Hargrave gets this peculiar look in his eye, kind of far off. Doesn't say a word more. Just nods and smiles.

'When he's gone, George just sits there with the fan blowing his silly flowered tie in all directions. After a long time he mutters, "Biggest case since the monkey trial," sticks on his hat, and goes home.

'He didn't show until the next afternoon, with purple hollows under his eyes and hair hanging down his forehead. For two weeks he didn't say anything that wasn't business, even about Lucy. She came in to prepare her testimony eating an ice cream cone. George snapped at her to throw it away, not like him at all. Then he drills her on her story and after she's got it down and he's told her how to dress, he throws her out and starts fussing over the next detail. It was the most overprepared rape case in human history. None of that helped. Come the trial, George was a sight.

'The thing was won from when Hargrave appointed C. W. Baxter to defend, who'd been drunk ten years and just wanted to get back to the barn without losing friends. But the court was jammed with townsfolk and Yankee reporters who'd come down by train, and all that plus the heat started making George a little sick.

'Except for Hargrave we were all in suspenders. It was so hot that even with the windows open my shirt stuck to me, and after a spell the crowd settled down to breathing and fanning themselves with this kind of low whoosh. First day they pick a jury of impartial white men and then George puts on Lucy, wearing pigtails and a dress buttoned to her Adam's apple. She swore she'd been raped, real firm like she'd been practicing with George, looking everywhere but at the nigras. On cross Baxter hardly touched her.

'It was going like George planned, except I noticed he was looking worse and worse – almost pasty. They got to where Baxter called Moses to say he didn't do it. Hargrave starts watching real close. The whole trial he'd been playing judge, fresh black robes every day and hair pomaded just so, but he hadn't had much to do. The nigra begins telling his story right along, looking straight at the jury, about how he went looking for his brother and found him with Lucy. Then he gets to the part about Lucy being a whore. Hargrave frowns at George, waiting for him to object. George doesn't say a word. The nigra's still talking when Hargrave bangs his gavel. "Miss Vines is not on trial here," he says, very stern. Baxter starts arguing sort of feebly that the testimony goes to whether there was rape at all. Hargrave orders him to sit down. So he does. All this time the nigra is just watching.'

Channing paused in a seeming trance from the rhythm of his own recall. I loosened my tie. Between Channing and the pictures I'd studied I could see the courtroom. Behind the railing sat twelve white jurors in shirtsleeves. One fanned himself with a long flyswatter. A table full of reporters took notes behind the bank of typewriters they banged at recess. From his hand-carved bench Judge Hargrave peered sternly down at Baxter, half-drunk already, his courage used up. 'What happened then?' I asked.

Channing rasped scornfully. 'After that, cross examination should have been easy. But George can't do it. He whispers to me, "Think you can take cross, Luther?" His eyes are yellow at the rim. You can hear a pin drop. I freeze. They're all waiting. Then someone coughs. Before I know it I'm on my feet walking over to the nigra. "You were there," I say, "weren't you, Moses. There, with your brother on top of Lucy Vines.'

'He was so black he looked almost purple. "Well, sir," he begins, "I was just tryin' – "

' "To rape a white girl?"

' "No, sir."

' "But you didn't stop it."

' "No, sir, but –"

' "Didn't try to pull him off."

'He blinks. "I just got there.'

' "And you were just watching, weren't you, Moses?" His mouth falls open. Almost whispering, I say, "Watching – and waiting."

'He stares at me. Before he can answer I turn my back and say, "That's all, Judge," sort of floating it over my shoulder while I look at the jury.

'But they're all looking past me. Behind, the nigra's stood up and starts shouting. "I been here all my life and never had no trouble. You all know me – got a wife and boy. What I want with that girl? You listen to me, Lawyer Channing." '

Channing paled as though transported. 'I turn and he's

pointing at me. Right quick Hargrave shouts for the sheriff. Two deputies slap cuffs on the nigras and take them off while the newsmen and photographers are scurrying and taking pictures and scribbling notes. All at once half the folks in town are up slapping me on the back.' Channing's words were bitter. 'But that didn't last.'

'How do you mean?'

His eyes turned sharp with malice. 'Oh, it lasted for the trial. George pulls himself together to sum up. Hargrave did the rest. He instructs the jury that if Moses had been there and not stopped it they should find him guilty. They took one hour. Then the sheriff brings the two nigras in handcuffs back in front of Hargrave. He looks past them at the crowd, making a speech on how the law protects the purity of southern women, every posturing inch a judge. Then he asks if the defendants have anything to say.

'Moses sort of gathers himself, standing up slow but straight. "We didn't rape that girl, Judge. You know that." He talks real deep and quiet, so each word drops like a stone. "If you punish us who are innocent, if you take me from my wife and boy, then in his own good time, and his own way, the Lord will punish you and yours." Hargrave turned white. Then he sentenced both nigras to death.

'It didn't go bad until afterwards. George and I are on the courthouse steps in a crowd of reporters when someone asks him what he thinks about both nigras getting the electric chair. For a minute George looks fish-faced. Then he gives this sick grin and says, "Maybe we'll get special rates." It got real quiet, and the smile died on George's face like he'd heard himself. It was stupid, George blustering to cover how he felt. He had no dignity, never did. The Birmingham papers crucified him. And some of it slopped onto me.'

'In what sense?'

Channing fixed me with an angry glare. 'It was over before I knew it. Every time I wanted the senate nomination they had someone else. "It's not your time yet," they'd say at the meetings. Took me a while to see it never would be my time. They were *ashamed*, damn them. I was just there when it needed doing and afterwards the bastards shunned me for it. Oh, they never said right out what it was, but you could feel it – they'd never warm to you. George left office and died. Hargrave was almost comical. He thought he'd be a hero, but when he tried to get backing for governor the party laughed in his face. It near to broke him; the vain stupid fool wouldn't look you in the eyes. He even stopped bringing Lydia downtown, so for a while I hardly saw her. Funny thing is it was all for nothing: everyone but him could see being governor was never in the cards. Two years later he died on the bench probating some farmer's estate. They passed me right over, didn't even ask if I wanted it. Just hung those two nigras like a millstone 'round my neck and walked away.

'Hargrave was dead and so I got stuck here paying for what they'd wanted and he'd wanted to give them: to hang those nigras.' He jabbed a finger at me, voice rising to an angry blast. 'For a hundred years we were all about nigras – hell, we choked on 'em. Got stuck with the tub-thumping trash while quality men like Richard Russell couldn't be President, all because of the nigra. My God, the sheer waste of that – it took someone like Nixon to make Sam Ervin respectable. Now we've got civil rights and air-conditioning and all the sudden we're a fit place for Yankees to live in. That's the biggest joke of all – not long before this goddamned trial a mob of white men in Detroit lynched a nigra for sticking a toe on their beach. And now there's riots in Boston and Yankee companies flocking here like lemmings to get away from snow and nigras. But that's fine: now we've got *civil rights*. And a hundred years of our best men paid for their hypocrisy.'

Channing glowered with dammed hatred. In one terrible moment, I understood: his Grangeville was a white man's tragedy, with Channing its Richard Russell. 'What about the McCarrolls?' I asked quietly.

'They were executed.'

'I meant the wife and boy.'

'Don't know,' he snapped. 'Never saw them again.'

'You mean you saw them during the trial?'

'Outside, maybe.'

'Ever look at them close?'

His stare lit on the glider next to me. 'What does it matter?'

'I was wondering if there was something unusual about the little boy – a discoloration in one of his eyes.'

Channing's face was momentarily thoughtful. 'I think there was.' Brusquely, he added, 'I didn't really notice. You want to know about the boy, check down at the courthouse.'

'I'll do that.' I rose to leave. 'Thanks for your time.'

Sitting, Channing seemed suddenly brittle and disrepaired. 'Wait.' His upward look was furtive, almost shy. 'You were talking about Lydia Hargrave. What's the boy to do with that?'

'I think perhaps he knows about Lydia Cantwell's murder.'

The coldness in his eyes had vanished. 'You found her, Mr Shaw, didn't you?'

'Yes, sir. I did.'

'What – what was she like?'

'She was strangled.'

There was a long silence. Channing looked away to where I'd sat on the glider. In the shadows his face was almost yellow. 'She was beautiful then,' he said softly. 'I tried to tell her, right on this porch – explain how it was. She didn't understand. Said she was leaving to marry someone else. "Please," I begged her. "Don't go. Is it that I'm too old?"' Channing's voice fell. 'She turned her face. "You're dead inside," she answered. I tried to stop her. She pushed me away and ran out into the darkness.'

I left him there.

The courthouse square was still crowded. I angled through mothers and children and vendors selling belts and lamps and old beer bottles, passing a bookstall. A lean young black with cornrows stood thumbing a worn copy of *Soul on Ice*, oblivious to the aching past where Luther Channing lived suspended in bitter memory, like a fly in amber. Three white girls with Cokes and lemonades slid chattering around him. The old men still whittled. I wondered which of them might have milled outside the courthouse forty years before. But it hardly mattered now; the ones touched by it were dead. Except for Channing and perhaps one black man, bound by Grangeville and a murdered woman.

I crossed the lawn, went up the courthouse steps and through its white pillars, inside. The corridors were dim and sleepy. On the way to the clerk's office I passed the double doors of the courtroom. I hesitated, then stepped inside. The jury box was there, and Hargrave's bench. But the room was dark and empty, the way only a stage or courtroom can be empty. It looked like nothing had ever happened there, or ever would. I backed out.

The clerk's office had brown walls and a varnished counter with one swinging door. Behind that were a baldish man with three missing fingers and a strawberry blonde in her twenties. I spoke to the girl. 'I'm Adam Shaw, out of Birmingham. I wonder if you can help me.'

She smiled all the way to her round blue eyes. 'We can try.'

'I need some birth records from the early thirties.'

'Inheritance case?'

'In a sense. The family's named McCarroll.'

'Don't know them.' Her brows knit. 'Family still here?'

'I don't think so, no.'

'White folks?'

'Black.'

'Ummm.' Her mouth made a little bow. 'Let me check in the back room. But don't get your hopes up. Sometimes the records weren't that good.'

'I know.'

She went through a door behind her and closed it. The man frowned at me. I smoked three cigarettes, waiting.

I was stubbing the third when the girl came out, gingerly holding a single worn document. She laid it on the counter, turned toward me so I could read it.

It was a yellowed birth certificate. On May 4, 1930, it said, Moses and Jane McCarroll, Negroes, had a son. Otis Lee McCarroll.

'Is this what you were looking for?' she asked.

'I'm afraid so.'

Outside, I called Kris Ann to say I'd be a few more hours. A van full of teenagers waving beer cans careened around the corner, soul music trailing from their radio. I got in the car and drove south again.

Chapter 18

Perhaps Kris Ann's picture had made it personal. Perhaps I felt the lives of others becoming part of mine. I drove to Lee's shack without calling Rayfield.

Lee wasn't there. His neighbors – women, children, or sullen idle men – didn't know him or where he was. I felt almost relieved. Then the last old woman said sometimes she'd seen him in the park by the county courthouse. Maybe he liked it there, she said. It was quiet and there was all that shade.

The park was a wooded square surrounded by the public buildings of the city and split into quadrants of oak and lawn by narrow stone walks that issued from a central reflecting pool like spokes. I parked and entered, looking to both sides as I walked toward the pool. At its center a gold-painted Statue of Liberty gazed toward the police station, her face in shadows. Old men on benches, wearing hats in the shade, waited for nothing to happen. One got slowly up to study his reflection. He stood over the brackish water, bent and patient and puzzled. I stared down in silent imitation. Beneath me was a dim, dark-haired figure, faceless from a low wind blowing ripples through it. I looked up.

Otis Lee watched from a bench beneath a grove of trees on the far side of the pool. We stared across the water in mute acknowledgment. He didn't run, or move. I circled the pool until I stood over him.

'Did she make it up to you?' I asked.

His gaze upward held a cold curiosity. 'How you find me?'

'A neighbor. Or do you mean how I knew?'

'That.'

'By digging, like the police are now. It would be better to turn yourself in.'

His eyes filled with smoldering bitter resignation. 'I didn't kill that woman.'

'You tracked down Lydia Hargrave and got a job at her house. You had only one reason to do that.'

'You know about Grangeville,' he said flatly.

I nodded. 'They killed your father and uncle. You were about eight then. So was Mrs Cantwell.'

'Always something to keep it fresh.' His voice had an awesome literal quality, as if the forty years since had happened overnight. 'Daddy's in his shop, sayin', "Yes, sir," to white folks so he can come home evenings to hunt for me out back, laughing, "Otis, gonna find you, Otis," in his deep voice because he's pretending not to know where I hide – and then he's gone. My stupid uncle buys the same piece of white ass been peddled all over town and just like that they've locked them both up and Hargrave's walking past us staring straight ahead like the judgment of God. Every week he'd parade that girl by our shop, noddin' and smilin' at us, and now he's killing Daddy by inches. And he knows.'

'Hargrave's dead,' I answered. 'The ones who killed your father are dead or so old and bitter, strangling them would be a mercy. Instead you murdered an innocent woman.'

'I didn't kill no one,' he repeated.

'Then go to the police.'

'You don't know nothing.' He spoke with granite authority. 'The first thing a black man learns is that he's got no *control*, that you can't *decide* things for yourself and make it stick because someone or something can come from nowhere and just wipe you out. A black man can't go asking the police to fix things for him. They taught me that by killing Daddy.'

'That was forty years ago.'

Lee stared through me until I felt the weight of his obsession. 'It was yesterday,' he said tonelessly, 'and so hot Mama brung a jug of water and a rag to cool my face. We're waiting on that goddamned lawn. All around us there's white folks staring but the only one talks to us is Daddy's red-faced lawyer, whining, "It's a hard case," like its something that's happened to him. He breathes liquor; every time he talks, Mama's eyes go dead. I don't understand nothing except that Daddy's in trouble and time's passing so slow I can feel it in my stomach.

'It's the morning of the third day and Mama's holding my hand like if she holds it tight enough he'll be saved. Every hour it gets hotter. Mama starts praying out loud. All at once there's hollers from the courthouse. Mama stops, and then she looks way off, and I can see her shrink. Then there's more shouting and people are running up and down the steps and that fat bag of guts Naylor and the snake-eyed sonofabitch that was with him are gettin' slapped on the back and some man in a straw hat's reached his hand through a car window to blast his horn like he's driving back from a football game. They're bringing my daddy and uncle through the crowd in handcuffs. Daddy's staring straight ahead. He don't want to look at us, don't want to break down. I try running to him. Mama pulls me back. I'm fighting but she won't let go. I just watch them drag him off until I can see him no more.

'I start cryin' in front of those white folks. Courthouse is just a blur, but I don't wipe 'em. Don't want to see nothing. Then through the blur there's Hargrave comin' down the steps. A big redneck farmer shouts, "Praise God, Judge." The blur clears and I see Hargrave turn to the farmer. What's he gonna say, I wonder, this man who's killing Daddy. But he don't say nothing. Just nods and smiles, like he was strollin' past our shop with that girl of his. By the time he slammed his car door and drove off I told myself I'd grow up to kill him.'

Near us an old man in an outsized coat shuffled through lengthening shadows. Lee stared ahead, oblivious. 'Next day Mama takes me to the jail. It's dark. Daddy's in a corner watching the floor. When he sees us he comes to the bars reaching his hand through saying, "Come here, Otis," and bending down. I come, but I can't say nothin'. He takes hold of my hand. I just hold it, thinkin' how rough it is and how my hand almost disappears. He says, "You watch over your mama, Otis," looking so sad it's hardly like him. Then he lets go my hand and calls Mama over to the side. "Don't bring him again," I hear him say. "Can't stand him seeing me like this." Mama's eyes turn wet and she puts her arm around me and sort of shepherds me out. Daddy stands with his back turned until we're gone. That's the last thing I ever saw – his back.

'For two years Mama turns to bone and leather while some white lawyers from New York try saving him from the electric chair. "Just want him alive," she keeps saying. "Just want to know he's breathing somewhere." And after they strapped him in a chair and shot him full of electricity and the lawyers come by to say how sorry they were and went home, she died.' He raised his head, the white star on his pupil like a brand, and finished savagely, 'So now you say let them do to me like they did to my daddy. But I *remember*. They needed a nigger to make themselves feel better and now they'll be needing me.'

The sunlight had faded and the old men gone. Lee and I were alone. 'You followed her here,' I told him. 'No one made you. Twenty years ago a man killed my father. He's in prison now, or dead – I don't know which. It doesn't matter. I won't waste my life on him. You did that with Hargrave and then Lydia Cantwell, who'd done nothing. Don't make this out a lynching. You put yourself in the way.'

Lee's eyes shone with a terrible intensity. 'You talk like things *end*,' he said. 'Like I had no reason to come here. But for all my life Daddy kept coming back to me with a due bill in his hand, asking what I'd done; and I'd done nothing. I knew what he'd told Hargrave, standing up in court like a man. But when Mama died I got moved away to a farm with my aunt and uncle. Hargrave was a judge and I was a ten-year-old black boy with no way to reach him. But I knew I'd grow up to kill him – told my uncle I would. "When you're a man, Otis," my uncle said. I thought about that all the time I watched myself get big. Used to measure myself against an oak tree with a slash I'd cut to mark how tall my daddy was. When I got closer to sixteen, I stopped measuring for a while. On my sixteenth birthday I stepped out back and walked to the tree. The slash was level with my eyes. It was time.' Lee smiled bitterly. 'And then I went inside and my uncle told me Hargrave was four years dead.

'My uncle's face went dark in front of me. I grabbed his throat with my fist raised. His lips started quivering. "God-damn you to hell," I said, and let him go. That night I run away.

'For a while I scrounged and did odd jobs. When I run out of food, I went down to an army depot in Nashville and went in.' His voice was sardonic. 'Nothing else to do but serve my country. Met a woman first stretch at Polk and before I knew it there's a girl and then a boy who looked like Daddy. So I told myself training men was something I could do to take care of my family, even though I hardly saw them. For twenty years I keep Daddy in a corner of my mind I save just for that while I'm drilling and training, training and drilling, over and over until it was like I been asleep.

'I woke up one day in Vietnam with my kids gone and my wife run off, fighting a white man's war in a yellow man's country with a platoon that's half black and all poor, and it come to me: I was helping white men murder niggers they'd needed to do some dying for them, like they'd needed Daddy. We was easy to send there and yellow men was easy to kill – niggers fighting niggers and nobody cares until they started taking white boys after college.' His stare challenged me. 'Wasn't hard to see why they don't come themselves: the jungle's hot and wet and filled with the V.C. cutting up my men and sendin' them back in bags or missing something or maybe just paralyzed from the waist. Month after month we ship out body bags and cripples and they ship more blacks and poor whites to replace them. All I want is to ship some back alive; keep them from getting killed over something foolish or because they're so bored and scared they've turned zombie on the same stuff college boys smoke for fun.

'About two weeks after I learn my wife run off I'm standing with Curtis, my scout. We're near this jungle full of bugs and punji traps with bamboo stakes in them that the slopes rub with their own shit for poison. Curtis is this quick, rabbity kid with sharp eyes good for scouting, and we're trying to figure where the Cong are. All the time he's slipping out there nights to find them and then smelling and groping his way back through the bush. He's got guts, but he gets more scared every time he goes out, so now even when he's back he thinks about it all the time, and never smiles. He's got two months left. I've started makin' deals in my head: if Curtis makes it, don't matter what happens to me. Just want him out alive.

'We're talking. He stops to puff a cigarette kind of nervous like he does, not really pulling the smoke down, and still watching the bush. He's gotten old around the eyes. Scouting's hard, and he's got two months of hard waiting. I try getting him off it. "What you gonna do back in the world," I ask. He puffs and thinks. "Gonna move things," he says. "Get me a truck and move the man's shit all over the country." He's almost smiling. Then his face just disappears. Don't even hear the whine.'

Lee's fingers gripped the wooden bench until veins raised in the back of his hands. 'I brought the rest of him back and put him in a green bag. He was nothin' but a lump of canvas. I lit one of his cigarettes and sat next to it. Looking at the bag I didn't see Curtis no more. I see my daddy, hammering at the forge. "You gonna grow up strong as me," he says. "Better start workin' now." Then he gives me a hammer he's made, just like his only smaller. I take it in my hand. And then Hargrave walks that dark-haired girl by our door like she was a princess, nodding and smiling.'

'I remember what my daddy promised Hargrave and then I understood, sitting there next to Curtis. It didn't matter who killed Daddy. Daddy hadn't raped that girl; they'd killed him for being black. Like Curtis. The V.C. didn't kill him, they just finished him off. It was the white man put him there – for being poor and black. When I'd finished his cigarette I knew I was going to find that woman and kill her like I'd known about Hargrave. For bein' his daughter, and for bein' white.'

I flashed on Lee squatted by the body bag, a blasted-out life staring at a trail of devastation and wasted time. He spoke with an inexorable, pounding anger. 'I thought about it, long and hard until I got out. After that it took time to find where she was. But when I walked up that long driveway, I thought, Isn't this fine. Forty years no one paid for my daddy and she's been living here like it never happened. I knock on the door and that stuck-up maid answers and looks at me like I was trash. I had to beg and shuffle on the front steps to get the white lady even come to the door.

'Finally she steps out, closing the door behind her so I can't look in. She's older but it's Hargrave's girl all right, and dressed real nice; you can see the money in the way she stands, straight and lookin' at you like you better speak up. 'Well, ma'am,' I say, 'I'm going around to some houses hopin' for yardwork. I don't drink and I pack my own lunch so the maid don't have to make me a sandwich. Maybe one, two times a week you might need me, and I'd sure appreciate it."

'The whole time I'm looking her over. She's tight, not like that girl at all, and she don't say nothin', just stares. It's sure she don't need no help with the yard and I figure she's gonna tell me that. Finally, she says, "I don't know your name." I say, "Otis Lee." She keeps staring like she don't hear. Then she says, "You can come Tuesday and Friday, in the afternoon." Don't ask me what I charge or nothing. Just backs through the door and closes it.

'When I come back next Tuesday she answers the door herself. There's shadows under her eyes like she hasn't been sleeping and I notice white hairs at the side of her head. "You're here," she says. "Yes, ma'am." She just nods. Finally she asks me to prune her roses and slams the door shut. I go to the rose bed, wondering how I'll know when the time comes. Then I see her come to the window, to watch.

'It goes on like that, every Tuesday and Friday. I knock on the door. She answers – quick, like she's been waiting. She gives me money and orders and shuts the door again. Then there she'd be, staring at me through the window – five, ten, fifteen minutes without moving. Pretty soon I can sense when she'll come out. She always does that, the same every time. She waits until I'm away from the front door. Then she'll open it and walk to some far corner of the yard, pretending to garden while she watches me. Sometimes I can feel her staring before I ever know she's there. It's just the two of us then, and quiet. Anytime I could have walked over and wrung her neck like a chicken. But I just waited. I liked *deciding* about her. Every Tuesday and Friday, I decided for that day.

'She never went out the whole time I'm there and nobody comes except the gray-haired man with the Cadillac. Only time I see her smile was one time he drove up. Before the car has even stopped she's opened the door, smiling with her head held up. But not with me. She just keeps staring. She's looking tired now. But every time I'm there she comes outside to watch, until it's like being near a flame.

'The time it happened I was digging out the rose bed. It was cool and cloudy and I wasn't thinking about her for once but about Germany and how the sky was there when it rained, flat and gray and different from anywhere else. I hear the front door open. She's standing in the doorway. Then she walks out toward the roses until she's stopped right near me. It's time, I think, like it's taken me by surprise. I watch her out the corner of my eye. She starts pruning the roses. I hear the clippers snapping next to me. Then they stop. She gives a little cry. I look over and she's staring at a fingertip she's pricked on a thorn. On the end there's a round drop of blood. She keeps staring at it. Then she looks up at me and her eyes get real big. She don't say nothing. Just stands there with her mouth half-open. I stare back. Without saying a word she turns and walks back to the house, slow and sort of brokenlike. Don't even close the door.

'That's when it came to me. She *knew* – maybe knew inside the first time she saw me. She hadn't forgotten.

'I didn't go through the door. Just stood in the yard, waiting. Nothing happened. I went home and for three days and nights I waited. The police never came. She never did nothing about it.

'Friday I went back and knocked on the door. When she opened it, all I saw was this scared, skinny white woman with dyed hair, holding my money in one hand and not able to talk. I took the money and went to the rose bed without saying a word.

'It was finished. I didn't want to kill her anymore. It was enough I could decide.

'End of the day I knocked to say I'm quitting. She nods with her head down. "Do you want anything?" she asks. Her voice is shaking. "No," I says. "I don't want nothing." Her face gets real funny. "Thank you," she says. I just turn my back on her and start walking down the driveway. When I get to the end, the green Cadillac passes me going the other way. I don't even look back.

'I was sitting around the next day wondering what to do when it come on the radio she'd been murdered. It was crazy. Whole time I was workin' there I wondered how it'd be when I'd killed her and the police came. I never decided – imagined it all kind of ways. Then she was dead and I hadn't killed her, and I thought, "They're comin' like they came for Daddy. And now I'm not ready." '

For a moment I could almost imagine it: Lydia's death as fate's last trick, turning what redemption had passed between them into a tragic joke. I stopped myself. 'What about the picture of my wife?'

He looked up, as if surprised I had spoken. 'Mister,' he said indifferently, 'I don't know what you're talkin' about.'

'The person who killed Mrs Cantwell threatened my wife.'

Lee's eyes grew careful. 'You going to the police, then.'

I nodded. 'There's too much on one side. Mrs Cantwell. My wife. My friend and client. And what's to balance that? Your word, and white man's guilt.'

'Then why'd you come here?'

'I'm not sure. Maybe I've come too far to not look you in the face.'

I sensed his weight shifting from his haunches to the heel of his boots. His eyes took me in, measuring, judging the distance. 'That was stupid,' he said softly. 'All this talk, all this *tellin'* you how things was, and now I may have to kill you.'

'I wonder if you want that.'

Lee shrugged. 'Won't bother me none. Already done that to a V.C. with the knife I got in my back pocket. Come up behind him on the balls of my feet and hook his neck. For a second we're so close I feel the pulse in his throat. Then I draw the knife across it. He don't even scream. Just flops back quivering against my chest until I let him slip down me into the bush. Never thought their eyes could get that big. He was already dead.' He stood, 'I killed that yellow man just because he was in the same stinking patch of jungle. But I got reason to kill you.'

'Then you'd better decide about *me*. Now.'

For a long moment we faced each other. Neither of us moved. Then I turned and began walking toward the police station.

It was near dusk and the park was silent. Between me and the police station was fifty yards of lawn, some steps down, and the street. The fastest route was to cut straight across the grass. Instead I took the walkway where I might hear Lee's footsteps. My strides lengthened. Forty yards to the steps, then thirty. I listened. In one swift movement Lee's imagined knife-edge crossed my throat. Shock as warm blood spurted down my neck, quick, searing pain, then blackness. I loped from the park, across the street and up the steps to the glass doors. By the time I got inside I was breathing hard. There was no one behind me.

'What's wrong with you?' Rayfield asked.

I leaned on his desk with both palms. 'Moses McCarroll's son is across the street. The gardener.'

Rayfield moved quickly from behind his desk, calling, 'He's in the park,' to Bast. Bast slammed down his telephone.

'How did you know?' I asked.

'Army records,' Rayfield said curtly over his shoulder and rushed out the door behind Bast.

By the time I reached the steps they were across the street running into the park. I followed them to its edge. Perhaps part of me hoped he was gone. But he wasn't. He sat like a carving as they trotted up with drawn revolvers.

I turned and walked slowly to my car.

Chapter 19

That night I refused calls from reporters until Kris Ann left the phone off the hook. I had several drinks and no dinner. I felt drained. When I called him, Henry sounded the same. 'Do you really believe it's the black man?' he asked.

'It has a certain demented symmetry. But right now all you should think of is that you're free.'

'I suppose I am.' For a free man he sounded oddly dispirited. 'You sound tired, Adam.'

'I'm okay. We'll both be better when it hits this is over.'

'Over.' The word fell emptily. 'Yes, I suppose so. I should thank you.'

'Just get some sleep. I'll call you in the morning.'

'In the morning. Surely.'

I said goodnight and put the phone back on the kitchen table.

Kris Ann was stretched out on the couch in blue jeans, staring up. I sat on the floor with another drink. She said, 'It's this man Lee that's bothering you, isn't it?'

I nodded. 'He could have killed me, Krissy. Why lie about Lydia's murder and then just watch me go to the police?'

'I don't know.' She propped on her elbow to look at me. 'I don't know why you were there at all.'

'I was afraid for you.'

'The police could have found him.' She sat up, her gaze long and penetrating. 'What you did was almost suicidal, like you have a death wish or something to prove – and I'm not even sure to whom. It scares me.'

I slid next to the couch. 'I'm here now.'

'You don't understand.' She looked away. 'I'm scared of *you*.'

I reached out. She whirled in sudden anger. 'Who are you, Adam? Are you a lawyer, a policeman, my husband, what?

This afternoon I could have lost you to something I don't understand. I look at you now and I don't know you. What do you want for us? Can you tell me that? Can you even tell me what you want for yourself?'

My hand froze in midair. 'I want you.'

'Oh God, Adam, that's not an answer. That's just something you say.'

'But it's the only answer I've got. I can't sit here and tell you "What I Want from Life" like it's some sophomore exercise. I don't know anymore and even if I did it might not be true five years or even five days from now. All I know is that I want you. That's true no matter what.'

'But *why* do you want me?' She held up her hand as if to prevent an answer. Then she ran it across her face, murmuring, 'I need time to think things out.'

She rose and walked to the stairwell, paused, and turned to watch me, head angled and still. 'What happened to Lee is terrible, Adam. But once you found him there wasn't any choice. You can't feel guilty now.'

I glanced down at my drink. 'Guilt's out, anyhow. Now they're selling books like *Kicking Ass for Number One* and *How to Be a Shit to Your Friends and Like It*. It's just that sometimes I think that guilt is the only thing that keeps us human.'

She shook her head. 'That's conscience, Adam. Guilt just keeps you looking back.' She hesitated, then added softly, 'But I'm grateful he let you go,' and went up the stairs.

I stared after her. Then I finished my drink and turned on the eleven o'clock news.

The screen crackled and then the white dot at its center widened to become Nora Culhane, standing in front of the police station. 'It's quiet here now,' she was saying, 'and police spokesmen have not yet released the information leading to Lee's arrest. But it follows by less than twenty-four hours an apparent threat against Kris Ann Shaw, wife of attorney Adam Shaw, who discovered Mrs Cantwell's body five days ago. There is no word yet on whether Lee has confessed to the murder. But this first break means that the intense police efforts to find the killer may be drawing to a close. For TV Seven, this is –'

'Nora Culhane, girl reporter,' I said aloud, and switched her off.

I went to the kitchen for the fifth of Bushmills and stayed up killing it. It was like going through a wall. The last three drinks didn't touch me. I walked into the kitchen and tossed the bottle in the garbage with a heavy thud.

I leaned against the kitchen door and smoked two cigarettes. Then I picked up the telephone.

'Hello?' It had taken Culhane five rings to answer and she sounded sleepy.

'Laid it on pretty thick tonight, I thought.'

'Who is this?'

'Adam Shaw.'

'Adam. God, I tried to reach you all night.'

'I had the phone off the hook. Listen, I think you missed something. They should have run a test. Clipped some of Lee's pubic hairs to match with those they found on Lydia Cantwell.'

'I didn't miss it.' She sounded annoyed. 'They just didn't have results by air time. There's a problem with that. The hair they found on Mrs Cantwell isn't Lee's. He may have strangled her but he didn't rape her.'

All at once I felt drunk. 'Oh, Christ,' I blurted and hung up.

At seven-thirty the next morning, five minutes after I put the phone on its hook again, Culhane called back. 'Were you really that surprised?' she asked.

'Just tired.' I leaned against the kitchen wall, rubbing my eyes. 'When I'm tired I like things to make sense.'

'And this doesn't.'

'Maybe it will when I've thought awhile. It's just that rape-murder was logical. Anyhow, Rayfield owns the problem now.'

'Unless you turned in an innocent man.'

'In which case it's still his problem. That's what cops are for, and juries.'

'You're very tough this morning,' she said tartly. 'When it was Henry Cantwell's ass Rayfield couldn't be trusted.'

'Henry's my client. Lee isn't.'

'That's the trouble, isn't it? You thought you'd wrapped this up and now it still might be Cantwell.'

'It's not Henry. Lee still looks good.'

'So does whoever raped Lydia Cantwell.'

I stared out the window. It was sunny and the world had a mean, clear-edged, hungover brightness. 'Last night I celebrated,' I told her. 'This morning I haven't shaved yet and even my hair hurts. Catch me later at the office. I'll be charming. I'll tell you everything. I'll even have brushed my teeth.'

'Two-thirty, then. And quit smoking. It makes the morning worse.' This time it was she who hung up.

I took three aspirin and arranged some orange juice and black coffee on the kitchen table in front of me, downing the coffee in stiff gulps. Then I got up and called Rayfield.

'I want to talk to you,' he said. 'Lee keeps saying he didn't kill Mrs Cantwell.'

'What can I do about that?'

'Give me a statement: say how you found him, what he said to you.' His voice turned edgy and aggressive. 'You might even figure out who Lee's gray-haired man is – the one he says visited her. That man's gone important on him since he landed in jail.'

'Then you're not sure Lee's the one who killed her.'

'For sure not the one who had her. Tell Cantwell not to go on vacation.'

'Why? You going to charge him with rape?'

Rayfield laughed for the first time I could remember. It was short and unpleasant. 'Maybe he sent someone.' I didn't understand that, and didn't answer. 'Maybe the black man killed her,' he went on, 'and then maybe Cantwell didn't want to lose her money.'

'He has enough to live on.'

'She had more. Rich people have strange ideas of enough.'

'Some do. Henry doesn't.'

'We're wasting time. I want you to come down.'

'In the afternoon,' I parried. 'I need time to think on your question, try and come up with a name. And I still want Kris Ann looked after until you're sure that Lee killed Mrs Cantwell, or find someone better.'

I heard him inhale. Finally he said, 'We'll do that – for now. You'd just damned well better be here at four. And think about that man.'

'Fair enough. There's one thing more, though. When you arrested Lee, was he carrying a knife?'

'Big one. Why?'

'Just that he could have used it on me.'

'Could have,' Rayfield said, and rang off.

I leaned back against the wall. Then I called Nate Taylor and told him about Lee. 'I don't know if he's got a lawyer,' I finished, 'but you might want to ask.'

'Thanks. I'll go down there.'

I said goodbye without telling him Mooring's name.

My coffee was cold. The cigarette I took one puff of tasted bad and smelled worse stubbed in the ashtray. I poured fresh coffee, letting its aroma rise to my nostrils as I rubbed the back of my neck.

When the phone rang I let Kris Ann answer in the bedroom. After two or three minutes she called down the stairs. 'Pick up the phone, Adam. It's Daddy.'

I went to the stairs. She was in a silk peignoir, long hair falling over her shoulders. 'I'll see him at the office,' I said.

'He's upset and worried about me. Please talk to him.'

I went reluctantly to the kitchen phone. 'What the hell are you doing?' Cade demanded.

My ears rang. 'Talking to you.'

'With my daughter, damn you.'

'Trying to keep her safe. Trying to find the man who killed Lydia. Trying to handle the police. Trying to get off the fucking telephone, frankly, and get some time to think.'

'As if you were capable. I'm through with you, Adam.'

'Not through with me. Stuck with me. We're stuck with each other.'

'Only as long as Kris Ann wants.'

I paused. 'No, Roland. Only as long as you live.'

There was a long silence. Almost whispering, he said, 'By the time I die, Adam, you'll be past fifty and your balls the size of raisins. I promise you that.'

I lit another cigarette. 'You called. There must be a reason.'

'All right. I want it clear that you're no longer on the Cantwell case. Your sole job is to protect Kris Ann.'

'I mean to. And Henry. I assume he's talked to you.'

'That changes nothing. I won't be undercut by a junior partner, particularly you. If Henry doesn't wish my advice the firm will drop him as a client.'

'But he's your oldest and dearest friend, remember? Besides, the partners won't let even you do that. The Cantwells pay those whopping fees that line our various pockets. The trips to Europe, the beachhouses, the new Mercedes –'

'Don't talk to me of greed.' He bit off the words. 'Not you. Not ever.'

There was a click, like someone hanging up. Cade said, 'I'm coming over.' His phone slammed down.

I went to the stairs. Kris Ann stood above me on the landing, face streaked with tears.

'Why did you do that?' I asked.

She didn't answer. I stood looking up. It seemed a long way. 'He's coming,' I said finally. 'At least there'll be someone here. I have to go.'

'Where?' She said it absently, indifferently.

I shook my head. 'He'll ask you, sure. Better to keep out of it.'

'You're so selfless.' Her voice was drained of feeling. 'From moving here, to this – all for me. I never have to ask.'

I climbed the stairs to grasp her shoulders. 'What he said, Krissy – that's not right. You know it isn't.'

She turned her face, squirmed free, and ran to the bedroom. I started after her, then stopped myself. There was no way to reach her, now. I had to finish it. I went slowly to the kitchen and stood over the phone, thinking. Then I dialed.

A singsong voice answered, 'Maddox Coal and Steel.'

'Mr Mooring, please.'

'I'm sorry, sir. Mr Mooring is on another call now. Can you hold?'

I was already heading out the alley for Mooring's place when Cade's dark-blue Audi turned in from the street. His mouth opened to shout. I passed him without stopping.

Chapter 20

It was only nine-fifteen when I got there. But when Joanne Mooring answered the door I knew it didn't matter.

Leaning on the doorframe, she was half-drunk already. For a moment we shared a kind of recognition. Perhaps I looked as bad as she did. 'Yes?' she said thickly.

'I'm Adam Shaw. Remember me?'

'Doesn't matter.' Her voice, tinged with empty gaiety, seemed dragged up from the floor. 'You're welcome, any-how.'

I followed her inside. She motioned me carelessly toward the kitchen. It was done in instant French country, with new copper pans hanging on the near brick wall next to some butcher knives and assorted utensils that I guessed had never been used. She sat behind a butcher-block counter with an ashtray and the same blender full of daiquiris, patting the barstool next to hers. 'Sit,' she commanded.

I sat, surveying the damage. With the blue beneath her eyes not quite purple, the veins of her nose not quite burst, she was a wreck-in-process, not quite finished. She tapped some ash off a cigarette that lay burning in the ashtray – the ladylike gesture of some thinner, more fastidious person trapped within the sagging body – and peered at me. 'Want a drink?'

I nodded reluctantly. 'Sure.'

She pointed toward the cupboard. I took the smallest tumbler and half filled it, sitting back down beside her. She watched my drink until I took a sip. It tasted sick-sweet. Her smile was bemused, as if summoned by instant laughter. 'I've always hated the taste,' she said. 'You hate it too, don't you?'

'When it makes me feel like less.'

She nodded solemnly. 'You mean the waves. You have to keep drinking 'til the tide comes back in.'

'It always goes back out though, doesn't it?'

'Yes, dammit.' She stared at the blender. 'Why did you come?'

'To talk.'

'What's there to talk about?'

I turned to her. 'You.'

The smile she managed seemed stolen from time, the almost flirtatious smile of a pretty girl with a present behind her back. Thirty years ago the smoke of early womanhood would have shown in her hazel eyes, and the delicate nose and chin have made her pretty. But now harsh sunlight through the window exposed bleached hair and the puffiness of drink, and her smile was the last relic of a widowed sexuality, sad as a stained-glass window in a slum. 'More daiquiris?' she asked.

'Sure. I was wondering why you drink so much alone.'

'Or drink so much, period.' She filled my glass. 'It's not by choice.'

I raised my drink. I would have hated myself even without the hangover. 'What were we talking about?' she asked.

'Your husband.'

Her smile faded. 'It wasn't always like this. Not at the start.'

'Then you've been married a long time.'

She nodded. 'Twenty-nine years – thirty next June thirteenth. We were both eighteen and ran away just out of high school. I put him through school at Alabama.' She looked joylessly around their overdone kitchen. 'It's funny. The hardest times are the best. He was so straight and serious and handsome then, and we were together.'

'That's too bad – that it changed, I mean.'

'*He* changed.'

I tried for a note of mystified empathy. 'Why'd that happen, I wonder.'

Her mouth made a scornful *O*. 'What's your name?'

'Adam. Adam Shaw.'

'Well, Adam, talk about something else.' She smiled out of some vagrant mood, running both hands along the ruined line of her hips. 'I'm out of cigarettes,' she said, a pretty girl again, prettily annoyed at her own foolishness.

I offered her one. She placed it carefully between her lips, bending her head toward mine for a light. When I lit it, her head stayed close. 'You're a nice man, Adam Shaw.'

'You're an easy woman to be nice to.'

'But not a lady.'

'Of course you are.'

She shook her head. 'Not enough of one.'

It was as though we were continuing a conversation she had begun with someone else. I took a chance. 'I think I know what the problem was.'

'What?' She clasped my hand. 'What was it?'

'Lydia Cantwell.'

Blood splotched her cheeks. 'But why?'

'I'm not sure, Joanne.'

'Just the goddamned way she walked? That she could have babies?'

She was almost screeching. I shook my head in feigned bewilderment. 'I don't know. It was Lydia, though, wasn't it?'

Her cigarette burned forgotten in the hand she waved at her cold, sparkling kitchen. 'Hell, it was always her – for the twenty-eight years Dalton's been with her goddamned company. Poor Dalton, he's been waiting and waiting all these years, hanging on with me for appearance's sake until Lydia Cantwell made up her mind.'

'How did you find out?'

'He made it too damned obvious,' she said scornfully. 'It was only later he got sophisticated. The second year he was there they put him on one of her charity things. He was so excited: her the biggest stockholder, he said, and him almost an office boy. He started coming home each night full of Mrs Cantwell this and Mrs Cantwell that: how pretty she was, how poised. I only half listened; I'd lost the baby and wasn't all there. All I knew was he was working harder. Then one night at dinner he called her Lydia. I started listening closer. The next night it was Mrs Cantwell. Then, just like that, he stopped. Never said her name again. That was when I knew.'

'Knew what?'

She smiled bitterly. 'Why it was so boring for him to touch me. And why he spent nights listening to those speech records so he could talk better.'

'Was he seeing her back then?'

'I don't know how you could think about someone so much and not be with them. And he volunteered for every symphony thing she did.'

'Then why did you stay with him?'

'He was the boy I loved,' she said simply. 'The smartest boy in Clio, Alabama, and he was mine. We were going to do everything together.' Her hand tightened. 'Am I boring to you, Adam?'

She caught me thinking ahead to the next question. 'Of course not.'

I said it hollow and too late. Her hand loosened. She squinted up at me and then recognition came into her face. I could almost read its stages: who I was; why she had lunged at me that night on the porch; why I was here.

'Joanne –'

'I know you.' She stood, backing away. Her festering smile was no smile at all. 'You don't want me. You poor stupid bastard, you think Dalton killed Lydia Cantwell.'

'Didn't he?' I managed.

'Oh, my God.' She laughed shrilly. 'And you're Henry Cantwell's lawyer. Dalton didn't kill his precious Lydia. He just did everything else.'

'What does that mean?'

Her eyes lit. 'I was *there* – the same night he killed her.'

I tried to show nothing. 'The black man?'

'No.' Her smile was unpleasant. 'Your precious client, Adam Shaw. Henry Cantwell.'

I felt a chill. 'How can you know that?'

She stopped to pour a diaquiri, stretching it out. She had all my attention now. 'I followed him – Dalton. He thought I was asleep. But I knew who he was running to. I could see him dressing in the bathroom, smiling a little to himself in the mirror. He thinks I can't do things by myself, but I dressed and waited until he drove out of the garage. Then I followed him. To *her* house.'

'Mrs Cantwell's?'

'*Lydia's,*' she corrected. 'Precious Lydia. I parked down by the road where they couldn't see me, trying to pull myself together in the dark. Ever since he'd met her he'd stopped wanting me and still I'd waited all those years, hoping he'd change, decorating each room so he would like coming home; and now here he was, with *her*. I thought of them inside and me alone in the goddamned car he gave me instead of himself. And then I decided to take every rotten minute of every rotten year and cram them down her fucking throat.'

'By killing her.'

'Don't you wish. No, I sat and waited, like always. I don't know how long I was in the car, thinking about it. I sat too long. How will I look to her, I thought. She'll laugh at me and Dalton will turn away. I didn't want him to see us together, her like she was and me . . . I was sitting there crying when Dalton's Cadillac came back down the driveway and left.'

'Then it was Dalton.'

'Wrong.' She was gleeful now. 'Lydia Cantwell was still alive.'

'Because that's Dalton's story?'

'No.' She was circling now around the counter where I sat, waving the drink and cigarette butt and talking with the stagy intensity of an actress at her moment of triumph. 'Because I heard her voice.'

'You heard her,' I repeated. 'Through a quarter mile of pine trees and a closed door.'

'The door was open.' She spoke clearly now, as if anger and excitement had made her sober. 'When Dalton left I decided to face her. I got out of the car and began to walk up the drive. There was almost no moon. I had to feel my way by the dogwood trees. Once a branch snapped in my face and I nearly fell. The drive was so steep I started panting. But I kept on and when I got closer the light from her living room helped me see a little. I wanted her. I wanted to spoil her face.'

I had stopped doing anything but listen. 'I was almost to the top,' she continued. 'There was a noise. Headlights came toward me from the bottom of the drive. I jumped back. My shoe caught on the edge of the drive and I fell backwards over the hedge and landed on my face behind it.

'When the car passed I stayed pressed down in the grass and brush where he couldn't see me. I could smell the dirt under my face but I didn't move. A car door slammed and I heard footsteps on the walk. Then they stopped. The front door opened. From inside comes a voice: Lydia Cantwell, society and very cool. "I wasn't expecting you," she said. And then the door shut behind them.

'I peeked out over the hedge. There was no one on the porch. The car was in front of the garage. But I could see it. It was a black Mercedes – Henry Cantwell's car.'

I lit a cigarette, trying to collect my thoughts. 'But you never saw this person. For all you know it could have been a woman.'

'I saw the car. It was Henry Cantwell.'

'Sure it was. You could tell because he rang the doorbell of his own house. He wanted to make things hard on himself.'

'I didn't say he rang. I said the door opened.'

'Then why did you hear Lydia's voice?'

'She was still up. Dalton had just left.'

'How long before? Fifteen minutes? Twenty? Two hours? Maybe you fell asleep in the car. Maybe you'd been drinking.'

'He suffered,' she said stubbornly. 'Like me. So he killed her.'

'Of course he did. After deciding not to park in his own garage. I'll tell you what makes better sense. Your husband had an affair with Lydia Cantwell. Six days ago tonight, with Henry gone, he went to her house. They fought. Maybe he wanted a divorce and she didn't. It doesn't matter. He lost control: I've nearly seen that twice. By the time he got a grip on himself he was alone in the house with a dead woman. So he mutilated her picture, wiped his prints off everything he could think of, and left her there, the victim of a psychotic killer.

'You followed him, and saw him leave. Perhaps you saw the

murder. Maybe you heard about it later. But you had him back now. Because if he ever leaves you, you'll tell the police he killed Lydia Cantwell. And that's exactly what you've told him, isn't it?'

'No.' Her face twisted in horror – at me, or at herself. 'It's not like that.'

I rose and walked toward her. 'Then it's like this. You killed her.'

She backed away, shaking her head with a child's vehemence. 'No. That's not true.'

'Isn't it? Maybe when he left, you crept up the driveway, just as you've said. Every step in the dark you're thinking about how you lost the baby and how through all the years since, he's wanted her. How you put him through school so he could shuck you for a woman who made you shrink, a woman he wanted like he wanted to be powerful, and someone else. All that churned inside you. By the time you made it to the house, you wanted to kill her. And Henry Cantwell wasn't there to stop you.'

'He was,' she insisted.

'No. It was Lydia who answered. She was surprised, but she let you in – she'd do that. You were filled with crazy energy, like now. You quarreled over Dalton. Probably you pushed her to the floor and began banging her head. Maybe she just fell that way. But then you strangled her until the tongue came from between her lips. And when that wasn't enough you took her picture and made it ugly.'

'You fucking bastard.' She stumbled back against the brick wall, knocking the carving knife to the floor. She picked it up, staring at it for an instant. Then she bean waving it wildly in front of her. 'Don't come any closer,' she warned.

I circled until the counter was between us. 'Get hold,' I urged. 'Think.'

She looked puzzledly down at the knife. I edged toward her. She glanced up, starting. In one frenzied motion she reached for the blender and flung it at me. I jumped sideways, feet tangling in the barstool as the blender flew past me and shattered against the sink. I fell, palms open to catch myself.

She rushed forward and lunged at my face with the knife. With one hand I flailed at her arm. There was slicing pain as flesh tore beneath my eye. I fell on my side, arms raised in front of me. She stood with her mouth open. The knife she held had blood on it. Without looking she dropped it clattering to the floor and ran.

I staggered up and ran after her, warm blood down my face and neck. There were footsteps in the greenhouse. The door at its rear was open. Then she was outside running pigeon-toed across the lawn, arms flying upward as she stumbled and fell. I caught up to her crawling forward on her hands and knees, hurt sounds coming from deep in her throat. 'You bastard,' she was saying. 'Look at what I am, you bastard.'

She was no longer talking to me, or about me. I walked in front of her to stop her crawling. Her face bent over my shoes as she began weeping helplessly.

'Come on,' I said.

She looked up, face shiny with sweat and tears. I reached down. She took my hand, struggling upright. 'You're cut,' she said blankly.

'It's under my eye. You missed.'

Her whole body seemed to wilt and her head lolled. 'It was Henry Cantwell,' she mumbled. 'I saw his car.' She turned and began stumbling toward the house.

I let her go.

I walked slowly to the car, handkerchief held to my face. When I looked in the rearview, blood trickled from a one-inch gash. It didn't matter. I was thinking of Henry Cantwell.

Chapter 21

At the emergency room a mustached young doctor in cowboy boots took six stitches and made jokes while a nurse sponged the blood off my face and neck. When they finished I drove to my office, told people who asked that I'd tripped at home, and shut the door behind me without returning a message from Cade that ordered me to call. I felt trapped and shaken.

I was pulling a fresh shirt from my credenza when the telephone rang.

'Mr Shaw.' Mooring's voice was strained. 'We're going to need a precise understanding.'

'I have one, Mooring. You're a liar, and maybe worse.'

There was a long silence. 'Meet me at the club,' he said finally. 'Twelve-thirty.'

I hesitated, tracing the stitches with my finger. 'Make it noon.'

He hung up.

I looked at my watch. It was eleven-thirty. At four o'clock Rayfield would ask for Mooring's name.

I began pacing. But I could talk to no one about Joanne Mooring – except Cade. I would have to meet Mooring.

When I arrived the club was teeming: golfers in bright shirts, overdressed matrons with sullen mouths, bankers come to lunch with borrowers and look into their faces. Parking-lot boys eased long cars to rest, chrome gleaming in the sun. On the far tennis court two figures in white scrambled amidst money-green trees.

Entering, I passed a doorman in spit-shined shoes, coat, and a military cap. Down the hall, in small fussy corners, dowagers played bridge. In the men's grill it was darker and the game was gin, played tight-mouthed, for money. A barman brought drinks. Cards slapped and were shuffled again. Dim wreaths of smoke hung over the center table where a steel company chairman, the senior federal judge, a bank president, and the owner of a newspaper held the same four chairs they'd held for years. Their heads butted forward like prows. No one else played, or asked to play.

'Mr Shaw.' At my side was Lewis, the headwaiter. 'Please follow me.'

He led me out of the grill and down a side hallway. Three years before, when the club president had collapsed on the last tee, Lewis had been a pallbearer. He had always called the dead man Mister. After the funeral, the man's friends came to the club to drink. Lewis had served them. He motioned me through the doorway of a small private room. 'In here, please, Mr Shaw.' He made a point of not noticing my face.

The room had green walls and a worn Oriental rug. Mooring sat beneath a crystal chandelier, next to the portrait of some half-forgotten plutocrat. His table was covered in white linen. Two places were set. Lewis whisked out my chair. When he was gone I said, 'Isn't this a little baroque?'

Mooring inspected the gash under my eye. 'I've hired a nurse for Joanne,' he finally said.

'Like with Martha Mitchell?'

He shrugged. 'The result's the same. You can't see her.'

In the doorway a red-jacketed barman was waiting to be noticed. Mooring's nod summoned him. 'Bloody Mary,' I said. Mooring ordered Dry Sack. The waiter thanked us and left.

Mooring sat straighter, as if buoyed by the ritual of service. I sensed that he was part romantic: a man who'd redefined himself, selecting the elements of his new persona and the trappings to go with them, leaving his wife earthbound. 'You know,' I told him, 'I've sometimes wondered why I came to despise this place – besides the obvious. It's that people like you find such comfort in it.'

For an instant someone else lived behind his eyes, vulnerable and angry. 'You're fresh from bullying my wife, Shaw, and in no position to offend.'

'I am, though. I'm an Irish Catholic whose father was a cop.

Twenty-five years ago you were listening to elocution records. So forget where we are. As far as I'm concerned this conversation's happening in the street. What you told me before was lies. Either tell me the truth about Lydia Cantwell or I go to the police.'

Mooring looked at me, expressionless and appraising. A cough came from the doorway. The barman served my drink, then Mooring's, from a silver tray. Mine was tangy with lemon and Tabasco. Mooring sipped his sherry, passing it beneath his nostrils. 'There's not much to tell,' he said softly. 'Lydia and I had an affair. I might be with her now.'

'When did that start?'

He ran his index finger down the side of the glass. 'Three years ago, whatever Joanne thinks. The details are none of your business. You need to understand only two things. The first is that Lydia wasn't raped.' He looked away. 'What the police found was mine.'

I lit a cigarette, still watching him. 'And the second?'

'That when I left, Lydia was still alive.'

Laughter came from the hallway, clubmen walking to lunch in pairs. 'He's not worth the money,' someone was saying. 'You could fit the entire Republican party down here into one room and wipe 'em out quicker than the St Valentine's Day massacre.' To Mooring, I said, 'What happened that night?'

'I was only there an hour. She was high-strung, but laughing. We celebrated.'

'Celebrated what?'

He gave me a quick sideways glance. 'Being together. It was hard to arrange.'

'Is that what made her high-strung, or was it Jason and the will?'

'No,' he said flatly. 'She didn't mention that.'

'Wouldn't she?'

His eyelids dropped. Scowling, he said, 'I'm not sure. Did you draft that?'

'Cade did. And he knows only what Lydia told him: not much.'

He took a pensive sip. 'I can't help with Jason. That night we didn't talk about him. We made love and said foolish things. Personal things, that's all. We made plans. When I left, she was smiling in the window.'

'Or dead on the floor.'

He flushed. 'I had no reason, Shaw. Lydia was a rare woman – refined, yet real. There are no women like that, now.'

The words had the tinny ring of cheap sentiment. I wondered if Lydia were another fine thing he'd wanted, a mirror in which to see himself, the new aristocrat. 'Life is unfair,' I said with a shrug.

His face hardened. Between his teeth he said, 'It wasn't meant like that. She was kind; it wasn't practiced, it just was. There are things I can't explain to anyone. With Lydia I never had to.'

'Where did your wife fit in?'

'Badly.' He put down his drink. 'Most people have two lives, perhaps three. You start as one person, and then – you can't expect a man and woman to keep fulfilling each other, not without children, something to build on.' His gaze grew pointed. 'Perhaps you understand that.'

I shook my head. 'Kris Ann's still the woman I want. That's one thing *you* should know: that if I find out who threatened her I won't invite him to the club and quote *Passages*. I'll kill him.'

Mooring stared at me fixedly. 'Bravely spoken.'

'Lunch, gentlemen?' A waiter had slipped into the room and stood at a middle distance. Light from the chandelier made his face shiny. Carelessly, Mooring said, 'You don't eat here, do you. You might try the Coquilles St Jacques.'

'Roast beef,' I told the waiter. 'Medium rare.'

'Thank you, sir.' He was a grizzled, crease-faced man old enough to be my father. Mooring ordered prawns and the waiter shuffled out, stiff and careful in the joints.

Mooring's eyes had stayed on me through the byplay. 'I've had enough condescension now,' he said evenly. 'You think you're different from me. The only difference is that your marriage made things easier. You see, I've known you since you first came here for parties, without ever being introduced. The first dance you stared at the floral display. You were wondering what it cost. I knew that. I knew that your tuxedo tie fastened in back because you hadn't learned to knot one. Your hands kept groping for pockets. When your wife talked to other men, you watched as though one might steal her. You felt out of place. Like me. And like me you kept coming back.'

His insight startled me. For a moment I recalled feeling always about to select the wrong fork. 'Once I thought Fitzgerald characters were interesting,' I told him. 'They are – in books.'

Mooring lit a cigarette. Narrowly he watched it burn, taking one deep drag with the cigarette still between his lips. 'It's ironic. Lydia understood that in you; she used to worry over your marriage, what would happen when you knew yourself. She understood it in me, that it was part of why I loved her. Not her money. Her sense of entitlement. You and I will never have that if we live to be a hundred.'

I didn't answer. Mooring was a surprising man. His voice turned crisp. 'About your wife. I know nothing of threats. You can accept that or not. But Joanne you leave alone. You're not to come near her or the house. The nurse on duty has instructions.'

'You're incredible, Mooring. This morning I got a good look at your wife. She's feverish drunk and violent and crazy from neglect, and all you want is to lock her up.'

Mooring's face closed against me. 'There's too much you don't understand. I'm not asking your advice. You haven't quite caught on, have you?'

'Draw me a picture.'

'I've told you all this so you would understand one thing: you're not going to the police.'

'You're forgetting that I know Otis Lee may be innocent. And you or your wife, guilty.'

'It wasn't rape, Shaw. That means in theory it could be anyone: me, Jason, Joanne, this man Lee – or Henry Cantwell.' He pronounced the name bitterly.

'No one will believe your wife.'

His look was keen. 'Think about what she told you. She didn't see Cantwell, although that makes the best story. She saw his car. The police say there was no break-in. After Cantwell called Lydia no one saw him until the next morning. Except Joanne. Her testimony could send Henry Cantwell to the electric chair. And that's why you'll leave us out of it and the black man in jail. Because it's practical.'

'That's already been done,' I shot back. 'To Lee's father. You're a bloodless prick and your wife's story is horseshit. If it weren't, you'd be tripping over me to nail Henry Cantwell for killing the woman you were supposed to love.'

'Don't judge me, Shaw.' Mooring's eyes turned bright and angry. 'I hate Henry Cantwell more than you can dream. But Lydia's gone now. I have other obligations – things that don't concern you. There's no one, ever, who can truly judge another person's life, and I won't have you judge mine. All you need to know is that your friend's a murderer. You see,' he finished softly, 'we *are* at the country club. You've come here, and we've just made a deal.'

A golfer laughed in the hallway. Mooring's stare was utterly composed. I stood without speaking, and left.

Chapter 22

I left the parking lot driving too fast until I forced myself to slow down and and think. But it was almost by instinct that I stopped at a telephone booth and called Jason Cantwell's.

No one answered. Cradling the still-ringing phone, I checked my watch and read one-thirty. I had less than three hours to decide what I could tell Rayfield. Nora Culhane would have to wait. I drove to Jason's and parked a half-block away.

An hour passed in the heat of the car before the girl appeared, striding loose-limbed with a grocery bag slung on her hip, hair bouncing as she walked. I waited until she was inside the building, then took the stairs up and knocked.

When the door unlatched, her wide, turquoise eyes peered frightenedly through a three-inch crack with a chain across. 'I need to talk to you,' I said.

She shrank back. 'Jason might come home.'

'I won't take long. Please, you might save someone from being hurt. Maybe you.'

She hesitated for what seemed minutes. Then she unhooked the chain to let me in. She had changed to cutoffs and a thin t-shirt that showed her nipples. Her legs were long and tan, and she reminded me of when I was fourteen and read Erskine Caldwell, and the southern girls of my imagination were ripe and knowing and carried mysteries inside them. I was older now and hadn't read Caldwell for a while; the girl seemed young.

'What's your name?' I asked.

'Terry Kyle. What happened to your face?'

'Nothing with Jason.'

She watched me from in front of the door. I moved away from her to the couch and sat looking up. Softly I said, 'There are things about this I don't understand. I'm afraid.'

She waited silently. 'I'm afraid of Jason,' I said with more emphasis. 'For you and for my wife.'

Her mouth parted. 'Why your wife?'

'Before we fought he said things about Kris Ann. The way he said them – how he looked and sounded – was more than getting back at me.'

She turned away as if hurt. Then she went to a chair across the living room and sat with the coffee table between us. 'He hates you,' she said sadly.

I stared at her. 'He hardly knows me.'

'It doesn't matter.' She kneaded one slim wrist with the fingers of the other hand, staring at a half-finished needle-point cat which lay by the chair. 'He has this thing about Kris Ann Cade.' She looked at me with unhappy candor. 'People are never with the people they want, are they?'

'Not always.'

'Not Jason, always. Maybe sometimes. I think with Kris Ann it's just from being messed up when he was young.'

'What do you mean?'

She shook her head. 'Look, I'm telling you this so you'll leave, okay? It's not good you being here.'

'I can't leave yet. There are things I have to know, for my wife's sake and for Jason's father.'

'But that makes it worse.' Her frightened voice ran words together. 'I know "Old Henry's" your friend and all, but he was no good for Jason – almost shunned him. Jason even used to pretend Henry Cantwell wasn't his real father, that the real one was a tall man who watched him whenever he went outside, to see that he was safe.'

'He told you that?'

She nodded shyly. 'He tells me everything.'

'How does that relate to Kris Ann?'

Her glance ran to the door and then back to me. 'You're all mixed up in it, don't you see? After that fight he told me Henry saw you as a son, not him.' The words rushed out now. 'It's all a mess. One night when we were smoking dope with the lights turned out he started telling me, like he could only say it when I couldn't see him and he was stoned. About how when he was fourteen, looking at Kris Ann made him feel tight in his throat, all strange. He would think about her alone in his room – like maybe he did things to himself.' She blushed. 'I shouldn't say that. It's just that he wanted to believe they were close somehow – like she had no mother and he didn't really have a father so they should have each other. But then she did something to spoil it, he said, something about a garden, I don't know what. I've been afraid to ask – you know, when he was straight.' She looked at me. 'Kris Ann loves you and so does his daddy. So he's got to hate all of you, understand? He can't handle it any other way.'

'That doesn't scare you?'

She gazed down at the needlepoint cat, catlike herself: darting eyes clear, then opaque. In a low voice, she said, 'Sometimes I hate her, too.'

'Krissy's no one to hate,' I answered gently. 'She's as confused as you or I, only her looks don't ask for help. That makes it harder.'

She seemed suddenly not to hear me, but to be listening outside. Footsteps echoed in the tile corridor, moving toward us. We listened like mutes as they came closer and stopped outside. Keys jangled. She turned to me, pleading. I rose, and then the neighbor's door opened and shut.

In silence like a caught breath I asked, 'For God's sake, why do you stay with him?'

She sagged in her chair. 'He loves me,' she said finally. 'I'm not from fancy people. I'm no one special. But I can help him. He's not like he seems; the reason his daddy hurt him so is that he's a gentle boy who went begging for love. That's all he needs.'

It sounded like a litany of faith. 'The Florence Nightingale route is a hard one, Terry.'

'What's that?'

'The notion that if you just love someone a little more, ignore what they are, you'll undo things that happened so young that they're part of them.'

'But you don't understand.' She said it with youthful stubbornness, clinging to what she hoped she knew. Her face

– soft, unlined, yet to be written on – was still that of a woman yet to happen. In a fierce, scared undertone, she pleaded, 'Let me alone with him. Please, just leave.'

'I can't. The night before last, someone left a picture of Kris Ann on my windshield. It was mutilated like Jason's mother's.'

She stiffened. 'Jason wouldn't have done that to his mother.'

'But what if she weren't raped, if she'd slept with someone first: a lover. Jason could have killed her.'

'He couldn't have,' she insisted.

'Terry, if you were alone that night then he might not only have killed Lydia, he may kill Kris Ann, or you.'

She shook her head, looking away. 'I told the police he was here with me, remember?'

'Then you may be accessory to a murder.'

She stood abruptly and went to the door. 'Please, go before he comes home.'

I got up, catching her by the wrist. 'Terry, he might kill someone. You have to tell the truth.'

She turned, frightened, and then her eyes went blank. I heard footsteps again, becoming louder, felt her trembling. When the door opened I still held her wrist.

Jason stood in the doorway.

'Jason. It's all right.'

Terry's voice was a thin wire of fear. He looked from her to me almost glassily, flushed and swallowing. I dropped her arm. 'Hold on, man.'

His face went rigid. He threw the door closed behind him and stalked between us to the bedroom. We froze watching the bedroom door. Jason came through it pointing a black revolver.

It followed me as I moved away from Terry. 'I don't like guns,' I said in a low voice.

'Jason.' She was panicky now. 'Don't.'

He didn't seem to hear. As he came closer the small black hole of the revolver moved upward toward my face, stopping two inches from my mouth. His black eyes watched me over the gun. Terry moved next to him. 'Jason, please . . .'

His boot jackknifed into my groin. I doubled retching as sickness numbed me and the girl screamed. Then the gun butt smashed my temple.

I was crawling on my stomach through a black hole with white flashes and a wooden door at the end while someone grappled behind me. A girl's voice panted, 'Don't shoot him.' My head swelled and shrank. With two hands I reached grasping toward a doorknob and wrenched myself up. I couldn't walk. A long dark moment later I fell face first down a flight of stairs, out of the universe.

Chapter 23

I reached in the darkness. My face brushed his overcoat, mildew-smelling. His revolver lay on the closet shelf above me. Teetering on the stool, I grasped the shelf with one hand and stretched. My fingers splayed. The tips felt cold steel . . .

'Adam!'

My hand fell away as the stool tipped clattering to the floor. I caught the shelf, hanging amidst his clothes. Her fingers clutched the back of my shirt. I lost my grip, fell, landed off balance. Hangers rattled as I stumbled against the closet wall and turned.

Her face was ivory, the blood gone from her lips. Brian cowered behind her. I stood straight. 'I have to hold it, Mother.'

She began shrieking and then her palm cracked across my face . . .

Ice water ran down my face and neck. 'Can you hear me?' she asked.

I heard myself moan, tasted blood, warm and salty. 'Let me take you to the hospital,' she was saying.

'Where am I?' The words came slurred to my ears.

'Your car. You crawled here.'

I tried opening my eyes. Terry leaned through the window with a rag and a green jug of water, her features swimming.

'No time . . .'

'Please, you're not seeing me, I can tell. There was this crack when he hit you.'

She sounded scared. I rolled my neck on the car seat, trying to focus until I could make out the building. From upstairs a bearded man looked down with his palms pressed on the window. 'Get out,' I said. 'Go to the police.'

'I can't. Not now.'

White sun cut into my eyes. I propped myself against the

wheel and jabbed at the ignition with my key until the motor snarled. The world had shrunk to the size of my windshield, with Terry pleading from the side. Her face fell away.

My car was crawling onto Twentieth Street as horns blasted and my head screamed. In slow motion I drove to the police station, to sleep . . .

Rough hands shook me. 'Drugs and whiskey,' he rasped. 'You look for poison in your sports car instead of Jesus in your heart.'

It was no dream. I raised my head, squinted into the red worn face of a wrinkled stranger with rotten teeth and craziness in his eyes. He stopped waving his Bible up and down. 'Give me a hand,' I murmured.

I cracked open the door and fell sideways until he caught me. I let my feet slide out, pulling up by his lapels. His breath stank. 'So you're who he's got left,' I said.

His eyes, clear, white, and glassy, seemed only to see distances. 'He's coming, brother.'

'Come on,' I managed. 'Help me inside.'

He clutched my elbow as I walked up the stairs, stopping every few steps, his breathing a low asthmatic whistle. At the top I rested on the glass door. 'Thanks.'

He looked through me. 'He's coming,' he wheezed, and teetered away, shouting at passersby.

I walked leaning forward through a long tunnel toward a door I remembered. I opened it, falling. Rayfield disappeared.

I awoke lying on a metal desk with my suit coat folded under my neck and a paramedic watching me. I could smell iodine, felt explosions in my skull. 'I fell,' I said absently.

The paramedic answered, 'You were hit.'

'You stupid bastard,' said Rayfield.

The colloquy came to my ears with detached lucidity, as when you're prattling at a cocktail party and suddenly hear the sound of your own emptiness so clearly it seems someone else's. But now there was numbness in my feet, nausea, a ringing skull. My crotch felt swollen. 'Get me a chair,' I mumbled.

Bast slid one over. I pushed off the table and sat. But I couldn't retrieve the pounding of my subconscious, why I awoke believing that I shouldn't be here, that I couldn't tell Rayfield about Jason. Better to stick with Lee. 'Listen –'

'Where you been?' Bast demanded.

'Searching –'

The paramedic broke in. 'You're concussed, man. You're slurring words.'

'He's a stupid fuck,' Bast said, 'who's going to get himself killed.'

'I don't think it was Lee –'

'Who's the gray-haired man?' Rayfield cut in.

'What man?' Then I remembered Mooring.

Rayfield's face reddened. Bast leaned over me. 'If anyone's killed out of this, asshole, it's on you.'

The place smelled of raw nerve ends. 'Better take him to the E.R.,' the paramedic said nervously.

'Get Bast out of here,' I told Rayfield.

Rayfield's jaw worked. He pulled the ball-point pen from his shirt pocket as he nodded toward Bast. Bast and the paramedic disappeared. A fluorescent ceiling light blinked above me. In the open room silent figures moved at the corners of my eyes. Rayfield seemed distant, on the wrong end of a telescope. He shoved coffee at me. I drank some and lit a cigarette, constructing a small manageable world where I did the same things, smoke and drink coffee. Rayfield's pen began clicking. 'What about Lee?'

'He didn't kill me. He didn't rape Mrs Cantwell . . .' My voice fell off.

'So you say to let him go.' The question was taunting, silken.

I tried to concentrate. 'I don't think you can hold him.'

'You don't see the mayor, my captain, or all those people who need a killer. Just the idea of who Lee is makes people anxious. Some people want him burned.'

My teeth ached. The pen noise was like dripping water. 'I don't.'

'But you'd do that to protect Henry Cantwell.'

I couldn't answer. I righted myself and tried reaching for my jacket.

'You know, I've wondered.' He said it behind me, musingly. 'I guess the worrying over your wife was crap.'

I turned back to his long, speculative look. The look and something new in his voice kept me there. He placed a chair with its back to me and straddled it leaning forward, eyes curious and disdainful as he said quietly, 'You're queer, aren't you?'

It was like falling in a dream. I wasn't sure where I was or how the fall would end. 'Aren't you?' he spat.

'Just graceful.'

'No, you don't look queer. But you can't go by that.' His silent stare gauged me until he seemed to decide something after a long while. 'You really don't know, do you? He's got you running like a rat in a maze, getting beat up and lying for him, and he hasn't told you.'

'Who? Told me what?'

'Henry Cantwell.'

'What about him?'

Rayfield smiled slightly. 'He's a faggot, Shaw.'

'Bullshit.'

'Seven years ago,' he spoke over me, 'the vice squad raided a gay motel. Your good friend Henry Cantwell was in bed with a sixteen-year-old boy. He likes them young, Shaw; he just doesn't like getting caught. He was crying when they brought him in.'

I closed my eyes. 'Who told you this?'

'I saw him. He was begging – it would ruin him, couldn't they understand – weak, like a fairy.' His voice thickened. 'It made me sick to watch him. He shivered while they read his rights and told him he had one phone call. He got up, pacing in a little circle like he couldn't decide. When he reached for the telephone his hands were shaking.

'It was over in an hour. Someone called the captain who ran vice. The records were destroyed. Cade walked into the station, looked around like we were dirt, asked the captain for Cantwell, and dragged him off without speaking. Cantwell wouldn't even look at him. But the boy was a stray and Cantwell had money. It never made the papers, never went to court. It never happened. Except it did.' His voice shook now. 'I hate queers, Shaw. But even worse I hate Cade and Cantwell buying us like whores. It won't happen twice. This isn't some sweet little boy getting cornholed and some vice-squad politician. It's a murder. It's mine.'

There was thin sweat on his forehead. From my subconscious welled the reason I hadn't turned in Jason. The room shimmered as I stood, said, 'See you, Lieutenant,' and tried moving toward the door.

'Where were you?' he called out.

I didn't turn. 'Nowhere.'

His pen clicked behind me.

Chapter 24

A slim, silent black man gave me a sideways glance as he walked past the house. I knocked again, resting my hand on the doorframe. The porch was cool, but the dirty, sweet honeysuckle smell made me sicker. I took the deep, rhythmic breaths I used while running. My ears echoed with their sound.

The door opened and then Etta Parsons' mouth. 'We need to talk,' I said.

'Why?'

'Because you've known about Jason Cantwell for twenty-seven years and told no one. Now it's time.'

Her surprise became shock. I stepped in front of her. 'Look, whoever killed Mrs Cantwell threatened my wife. If anything happens to her . . .'

She backed stiffly from the door to the living-room couch without answering or dropping her gaze, and sat. She looked smaller, older, less today like Lydia Cantwell than a lone black woman strip-mined of dreams. Through the sepia gloom, she asked, 'What do you want?'

'The truth about Jason, from the beginning.'

Her eyes moved sadly to Lydia's picture, as if saying that it was only she who had lived to know the end of things. 'I don't see it matters now.'

'It matters to me. I think Lydia's murder began long before she died, perhaps with Jason. Or don't you give a damn?'

Her face toughened. 'They've arrested Otis Lee.'

'Yes, and maybe he killed her. Maybe that's a chance you'd like to take.'

The sound of my own hypocrisy echoed in the room. But only I heard it. Her hardness dissolved in doubt. I had the sense of a long ago secret, hoarded inside until its sadness was hurtful to the touch. More gently, I asked, 'Jason isn't Henry Cantwell's son, is he?'

173

She looked at the pictue. Then, slowly, she nodded.

My knees were buckling. I sat heavily across from her. 'How do you know that?'

Her legs were crossed, thin shoulders drawn in. 'It's all complicated,' she finally murmured. 'I came to the Cantwells' after she'd married him, when I was just past being a girl, like her. Clifton – the one I'd meant to marry – he was killed in Korea.' She paused, swallowing, and her words came faster. 'After that I didn't know what I'd do. My godmother got me a place with the Cantwells because she'd been maid to the family. It was such a big house I was scared when I came there, not knowing my duties, my mind still with Clifton. At first I didn't see much and I don't know about before, except what she told me later.'

'What was that?'

'Nothing to start with. It was more a feeling things weren't right. Oh, they talked some; every night I'd bring them Manhattans in the sitting room after he'd come home. But something was left out. You know how a man watches a woman when she's new to him – sort of follows her with his eyes – like the way she's made, or even that she's there, surprises him?'

I nodded, for a moment almost smiling. 'I think so.'

'Well, Mr Cantwell wasn't like that.'

'How was he?'

'I don't know,' she said, 'I guess close to cowed, like when he talked to her his eyes would slide away and mornings sometimes he'd even look down when he saw me, like he was fixing to apologize.' Etta spoke in a rush now, as though speech were catharsis. 'I remember once they were in the dining room, talking real low, and then she got up from the table and left him there. He went to the liquor cabinet for a bottle of brandy. I saw him staring in at his library with the bottle in one hand, like he couldn't decide what to do. Then he just stepped inside and closed the door behind him. I should have felt sorry for him, he seemed so lonely. But I saw what was happening to her.'

'What was that?'

'It was like she was falling apart. She was pretty and so *young*.' Etta spoke the word feelingly, almost in anger, her hands becoming small fists. 'She should have been laughing, going out with someone who wanted her, not wasting in a dark house, day by day and year after year just drying up, not being loved or touched. It's a waste that should happen.'

My head was pounding. 'Sure, now. It is.'

Etta nodded fiercely. 'She'd walk from room to room, looking around like it was all strange and she was a prisoner. You don't have to be in jail to be in prison: I already knew that. She began staying in bed until he'd gone. One morning I brought breakfast to her room, hoping she'd eat. She was still in bed, holding a man's framed picture in both hands. She looked up and gave me a funny smile, like, "It's no use pretending, is it?" ' Etta's own smile was slight and sad. 'That was the first time she really noticed me – *me*, not a maid. After that we began to talk.'

'Do you know who the man was?'

'She never said, but I think maybe a man from Grangeville. From the picture he was pushing forty, good-looking except for his eyes: clear enough to see through and cold as a snake's. It chilled me to look at them. But all she told me was that she'd run from loving him, that he was a part of her but evil and that he wanted to put her on a shelf away from people to make up for things he couldn't have. It didn't make sense, all of it. But I think he was the reason she married Mr Cantwell.'

'Did she say that?'

'She just said she married him thinking he'd never lie or hurt her, and then moved her shoulders like she'd been wrong. She didn't say it angry; it was sadder than that, and surer. A few days later she started going out.'

'In what sense?'

'Disappearing.' Etta's eyes turned vague until I guessed that Lydia Cantwell had become more real than me or where she was. 'She'd be gone three or four hours and then come back late afternoon jittery and absentminded, like she was part scared and part somewhere else. I started making tea to settle her down. She'd never liked it but she got to taking it at the kitchen table where she would look out the window. She'd ask me to sit with her and then start talking about all sorts of things, wild almost, everything except about where she'd been or who she'd seen. Something in her couldn't say that. I never asked. I didn't want to press things.'

I said nothing. But silence and my face gave my thoughts away. 'Things were understood,' she insisted. 'Oh, they'd have their Manhattans and weekends they might give dinner parties for his parents or the Summers or Cades, and she'd smile or even laugh, like nothing was wrong. But when I served them drinks I could tell how alone she was. *I* was the one who really saw her.'

'You, and at least one other.'

Understanding came into her eyes. 'Yes,' she said coldly. 'One.'

'When did you learn that?'

Her lids dropped and she placed her palms flat on the couch, speaking without emphasis or inflection. 'One morning as soon as Mr Henry was gone she dressed in a hurry and left. She was out longer than normal – five, six hours. I was dusting the staircase when she burst through the door looking flushed and half-crazy. Right away I ask if she wants tea. She flings down her red silk scarf, runs past me up the stairs, and slams the door behind her without answering. I wanted to go up after her. But I couldn't. I just dusted.' Etta's eyes were still hooded, her flatness of speech lending the trancelike quality of literal recall. 'At four o'clock she came to the kitchen where I was, and says, "I'd like tea now," real quiet, like she's sorry. I put one tea service in front of her. She looks up at me, then toward the other chair. "Please," she says.

'I sat down with my cup. You could see she'd been crying but her eyes were dry now. She looks at me very steady and says, "I'm pregnant."

'She doesn't say anything about Mr Henry. She doesn't have to. "What will you do?" I ask.

'She looks sad. "I don't know," she says. "It's all hopeless. He's married; I'm married. I'm not even sure I want him. He was just there."

' "What does he say?" I ask.

'She looks out the window. "He loves me, in his way: at least I'm part of a life he's wanted. But it would be impossible for him at work, and his career has really just begun. He knows that."

'I can't think of what to tell her. After a time she says in a low voice, "Etta, it's like I'm being punished."

'The way she looks and sounds I feel like shivering. "Why would you be punished?" I ask.

'She shakes her head. "For many things."

'I feel so bad that without thinking I reach out to touch her hand. As soon as I touch her I feel like it's wrong and pull back. But she just looks at her hand, smiling a little.

'We sit like that across the table, neither one of us talking. Then we hear Mr Henry coming through the front door. She looks at me and says very quiet, "Thank you, Etta." Then she stands, sort of squares her shoulders, and walks out to meet him.

'I stayed in the kitchen. She said something to him and then I heard the library door close. I waited, pretending to work. They didn't come out for over an hour. Then the door slid open and she called out that her and Mr Cantwell would be having their Manhattans. When I brought them to the sitting room, they were in their same chairs, talking polite, like usual, except he was so pale. "Thank you," he says, and she smiles and tells me, "You should go home now, Etta. It's late." It was always strange how she could do that. From her face I couldn't have told anything at all.

'I thought about her all night. But when I came back the next morning she was still in her room. When she finally came down I was in the kitchen, polishing silver. Her hair was just so, and there was powder beneath her eyes, as though she were hiding circles. She looked hardly alive, more like a doll. "I'll be staying home now," she said.

' "Is that what you want?" I asked.

'She stared out the window. "We've come to an understanding." I didn't say anything. Then she looked straight at me and said, "You're the only one who knows, Etta" And then she asked for tea.'

Etta's face had begun fading in front of me. 'Did the man try to see her?' I managed.

'I don't know. Right away she shut herself in, reading up on babies, picking names, trying to be the best mother she could after Mr Jason was born by smothering him with love. She saw the father only once I'm sure about, when Mr Jason was about to turn six. It was afternoon and I was in the dining room and she was upstairs. The telephone rang. When I picked it up, she said through the extension. I didn't know who was calling. But a few minutes later she was dressed and hurrying out the door. Two hours later she came back looking tired. She sat down in the kitchen and said, "He wants to marry me."'

'She didn't need to say who. "Can you?" I asked.

'She shook her head. "Not now," she answered, and for a long time after there was only the birthday presents.'

I rubbed my temple. 'I don't understand.'

Etta blinked as though she had forgotten that, her glance moving from piece to piece of the Cantwell's hand-me-down table and chairs. 'He made her do that. Just before that same birthday she gave me ten dollars and asked if I'd stop on my way across town to get a toy gun for Mr Jason, one of those that shot caps. She said she hated them but the father said if he couldn't have her or a son he'd at least be part of his birthday. She told me it was something that had to be. I wish it hadn't. Mr Jason always liked guns too much.'

I shrugged. 'It wouldn't have mattered. Take them away and a kid just makes one with his finger and pretends.'

'Well, it wasn't always guns,' she allowed. 'But every year until his fifteenth birthday, she'd hand me money – his money, she said – and tell me what present he wanted to give.'

'And after that?'

'It just stopped. She never said anything about it.'

'Did she ever say who it was?'

'No,' she said firmly. 'She never would have done that.'

I took a deep breath and asked, 'But you know it was Mooring, don't you?'

Etta's face was cold. She looked down at her skirt, smoothed it, and nodded curtly.

'How?'

Her voice turned scornful. 'Because he called once or twice, just before she started going out, even came by once on his way home – to drop something, he said, when I could see he didn't need to and just wanted to stare at her. He looked awkward, out of place.' Grudgingly she added, 'She seemed to like him and I guess I could see why in the state she was in. He was good-looking enough.'

'But that's not all of it.'

'No.' She said it quickly, as if embarrassed. 'Three years ago he started turning up again. It was like she didn't care about the secret anymore. She'd run to the door every time he came. I felt strange. We'd gotten older together, caring for the house and Mr Jason, and I hadn't seen her act like that since before he was born. She looked younger. I didn't like how he'd gotten so smooth but to her it didn't matter. It was a second chance, she said: Jason was grown, for worse or better, and she didn't want to be with Mr Henry anymore.'

'Was she divorcing him?'

'She never said.' Her forehead creased. 'One day Mr Mooring and her had a long talk out back and after that she stopped leaving the house to meet him. He still sneaked by – she was still glad to see him – but they acted more careful.

'It was like that the last time he came. He dropped by the day after the fight with Mr Jason, just before she went to see Mr Cade. He was there maybe fifteen minutes. They talked out back looking real serious and then he went this way and she went downtown. She told me she had an appointment to see Mr Cade and that I could leave.'

'But you don't know what she and Mooring talked about?'

Etta looked at me gravely. 'I never saw her again.'

In the silence that followed, my head filled with metronomic pounding. Finally, I asked, 'Who do you think killed her?'

She stared at me. 'I guess Otis Lee had reason,' she said evenly. 'And he watched her all the time.'

179

'Would she have let him in?'

'I don't know.'

'But she would let in someone she knew, like Mooring. Or Jason.'

'I don't see why Mr Mooring –'

'But you do see Jason, don't you.'

Etta looked back at Lydia's picture. After a long time she said, 'Lord knows she tried. But all that caring didn't seem to matter at the end. He had a terrible temper and Mr Henry always pretty much ignored him. And they'd had that fight. Still, it would be so wrong. I mean, she gave up everything for that one child.'

Until the end, I thought, and even then, when she wanted more, she had never quite made it. 'Did she ever ask you to go with her if she left Mr Cantwell?'

Etta's head snapped up. 'She didn't have to. I was the only one who really saw her.'

But did she see you, I wondered. Etta read my thoughts. 'She understood me,' she said sharply. 'She understood about Clifton. She gave me part of her own life to make up for that.'

Her words were tense, angry. I realized what she had sought from me was not release from secrets, but something more: an affirmation that the service to which she had given her life was not just that of a maid. They had been friends, she said, but what she meant was that was all she had.

'I know,' I told her. 'That was why I came.'

She nodded fractionally. I rose, feeling dizzy. 'Thank you for helping,' I managed.

She didn't answer. My part of witness was over. As I silently left, she smoothed her skirt again, still staring at Lydia's picture.

Henry Cantwell opened the door. His head seemed to get smaller, then larger. 'Good Lord, Adam, what have you done?'

I steadied myself. 'I got pistol whipped by Jason Cantwell. You know, the son who isn't yours.'

Henry blanched. 'What happened?'

I told him curtly, then snapped, 'I need your phone,' and passed him in the doorway. From behind he said thinly, 'I'll be in the library.'

I went to the kitchen, sat by the window at the table with two chairs, and called Kris Ann. 'Where are you?' she asked somewhere beyond anger.

'Henry's.' There was no way to explain. 'I'll be home right after. Lock the doors and don't go anywhere.'

'Whatever,' she said coldly. 'I can always call Daddy, can't I?'

'Krissy, I don't think Otis Lee killed her –'

She hung up.

For a moment I sat listening to the dial tone. Then I stood, got my balance, and walked to the library.

Chapter 25

Henry sat in his chair. On the table beside him were a snifter of cognac, his half-glasses, and the copy of *War and Peace* he read for consolation. 'Should you begin fearing death,' he had told me once, 'pick up *War and Peace* and after a time all that will melt away.' That much was familiar. But the way he looked had changed, and the way I saw him.

'How did you know?' he asked tonelessly.

I lit a cigarette and gazed down at him. He wore a three-piece suit with his father's gold chain across the vest. His eyes, shiny and translucent, stared back with shamed insistence.

'Rayfield told me part. He enjoyed that.'

Henry winced. 'And what did you think?'

'That I've never known you.'

His mouth opened, closed, opened again. 'Adam, we – my feeling for you isn't because –'

'Oh, God, Henry.'

'I mean, you're almost a son.'

I took a deep, harsh drag. 'Then I can see Jason's point.'

He shut his eyes. 'Sit down, please.'

I didn't move. His eyes opened. 'Sit down, damn you. I won't have you hovering like that.'

I took a long time sitting. Wisps from my cigarette twisted between us, then disappeared. Twilight and his reading lamp cast thin silver in the room. 'Is it – what I am?' he asked.

'Don't make it so easy on yourself.'

His eyebrows raised. 'You think that's easy.'

'Easy, and not the point.'

'You're hurt then,' he said gently.

'Don't be sentimental. There's a black man in jail who maybe shouldn't be. I've taken on Cade and Rayfield and Mooring, been beaten up by Jason, put my marriage in jeopardy and now Kris Ann, and you've been content to let me do that, not knowing the truth. I'll get that now if I have to shake it out of you.'

He raised a hand to stop me. 'Adam, please –'

'*Hurt* is a trivial word, Henry. I want to know what you're really after. Your marriage was a fraud and you don't give a damn about Jason. I'm a cat's paw you've played against Roland.'

'Has that been too hard for you?'

There was sudden steel in his voice. Softly, I answered, 'Not too hard.'

'I hope not.' He spoke without apology. 'Because I couldn't tell you.'

'Just Roland.'

'There were reasons for that.' I shrugged my indifference. 'Please,' he urged. 'Hear me out. I'll explain as much as I can.'

I sat back to light a second cigarette, watching him. His chest looked small, his breathing shallow and rapid. In pale light the skin of his face – too slack beneath the eyes, drawn tight across his cheeks – made him look like a dying man. He stared fixedly away. 'That boy I was with wasn't the beginning, Adam. I'd had those feelings – wanted to touch and be touched – long before, from when I was young. They made me sick. I tried believing I wasn't like that. My father, Roland – they were the men they wished to be. There was no one I could tell.'

I rubbed my forehead to fight the ache inside, and for a moment Henry was Eddie Halloran, smiling, listening, telling no one, winding up dead. 'I married Lydia hoping to be different,' he went on. 'There was someone else, I knew, but we had things in common, and I thought somehow . . .' His voice flattened out. 'The wedding night was a disaster. I was what I had feared. Afterwards she lay awake in her pink nightgown. I could hear her breathing. Finally I couldn't stand it. I told her about the feelings. It was as though she went into shock. She began shaking her head, saying, "Oh God, no," over and over and asking why, why had I married her. Then she broke down. When I closed the door behind me she was still sobbing.

183

'The next morning I couldn't face her. Neither of us – it just went on like that. We talked of annulment, finally. It wasn't fair to keep her but I didn't know what to do. I was so damned afraid of being found out. Then she told me she was pregnant. It was odd: I was shocked and then that wore off, and I was relieved. I had something to forgive now, too, and she needed me.' Henry paused, finishing in a hollow voice, 'And God help me, I knew people would think it was mine.'

He looked up – for a question, something to keep him going. I just watched him. His face fell and he lapsed into a drone. 'Lydia made it easier, in a sense. I asked who the father was. She tilted her chin in that pose she had, sitting right where you are now, and told me never to ask again. When we stepped from this room, the lie began, and grew until it cut across all our life. We were faithful in our way: she played the gracious hostess and I the contented husband and father. But there was little between us except appearances and less between me and Jason. She mothered him as if to say, "Look: here's someone I care for." But when I looked at him, I saw my failure: the weakling, the one who'd let down his wife and father, the closet homosexual.' His voice was bleak. 'And still I wanted to know how that would be.

'For years I wondered, playing out my part. I'd never – I'd never had a man, never had sex with anyone. The evening it happened I was driving back from a business trip. The boy was thumbing by the shoulder of the road: a tall, slim boy in blue jeans. I stopped for him. He was hungry and dirty and needed money.' Henry's voice turned raw. 'When I put my hand on him, he didn't move. My throat was tight. He was young and empty-looking. I drove to a motel with a smirking nightman. It was dirty and there were stains on the sheets. But that blank-faced boy was exactly what I needed.

'At the moment they burst through the door I was the happiest I could remember. And then they were pulling us apart and calling me an "old queer." It was like being trapped inside someone else's body. I rode to the station in the back of a prowl car with the boy chewing gum and a fat policeman in between. All I could think of was to be free. When we reached the station they took the boy somewhere and dragged me inside. I never saw him again.

'When they booked me I broke down, begging. They just looked away, all except for that policeman, Rayfield. He was staring at me from a corner like I made him sick. He wouldn't stop.' A purple vein throbbed in Henry's temple. 'I imagined our friends looking at me like that. I saw Roland's face, the contempt in it hardening. It came to me then. Of all of them, Roland was the one I'd sell my soul to keep from knowing. And only Roland could help.'

'So you called him.'

He nodded dejectedly. 'He fixed it. I don't know how. I didn't want to. I was just grateful, then.'

'And later?'

'Later, it was done.'

I was silent. Henry's eyes raised from the floor. 'You do understand about not telling you, at least a little? I'd failed with Jason, and you at least respected me. It didn't seem relevant to Lydia.'

He leaned forward as though reaching. I ground my cigarette as smoke died in acrid curls, lit another, and said, 'Did you kill her, Henry?'

He went white. 'I suppose I deserve –'

'Because Joanne Mooring says you did.'

'That's insane –'

'Specifically, she says she waited here that night spying on Lydia and her husband. She swears that when Mooring left Lydia was still alive. So she started toward the house to confront her. And then, while you say you were sixty miles away, your black Mercedes turned up the driveway and scared her off.'

Henry seemed to shrivel in his chair. Faintly he inquired, 'Why hasn't she gone to the police?'

'That puzzled me until I learned about Jason. If Mooring's his father all that would come out. And Joanne drinks. The police might not believe her and suspect Mooring instead. Not bad reasons. The one I believe is more complex. For years Jason received anonymous birthday presents from his real father. Suppose Mooring wants to protect Jason. Perhaps he thinks that if the police learn that it was he who made love to Lydia, they'll suspect Jason of killing her. Jason wouldn't have to be Oedipus then. Just a murderer.'

Henry's hands twisted together. When I finished, he looked up, mumbling as if it didn't matter, 'But she lied, Adam.'

'How would you know?'

He flushed. 'I never left Anniston. I was with someone that night.'

'With whom?'

His gaze was level. 'A man.'

'A man,' I repeated.

He nodded. 'Yes.'

'If that's true, then you perjured yourself to Rayfield.'

'I suppose I did.'

'You suppose. Does Roland know?'

'He knows.'

I felt the pain in my skull leeching strength from the rest of me. 'And he sat there with Rayfield and let you lie.'

'I'd do anything to hide this,' he said miserably. 'That was something Roland already knew.'

'You commit perjury, a jailing offense, to put yourself closer to the electric chair, and Roland watches.'

Henry's hands trembled. 'You talk about something you don't understand. I'd go to cocktail parties, pretending to be happy, and all the time I'm hoping, looking for someone whose eyes don't slide away. Furtiveness becomes a way of life.'

'That's no answer.'

He looked across at me. 'I'd found someone, Adam. A man with a wife and three children.'

I pulled out a cigarette and began tamping one end on my wristwatch. 'Who is he?'

'I can never tell that.'

I looked up. 'Rayfield would find that convenient.'

'It doesn't matter.' For a moment Henry's face was almost serene. 'I love him,' he said simply.

I lit the cigarette and smoked half of it. Night had fallen. Henry sat in a circle of lamplight as if cornered by darkness. Finally I said, 'Tell me what happened, leaving out his name.'

'You won't try to find him, Adam.'

'I won't even assume that he exists.'

'Then you don't believe me.'

'Just tell it,' I said angrily.

Henry checked his cuffs and tie knot with quick, nervous gestures. 'There's not much to tell,' he said reluctantly. 'We'd arranged to meet. He told his wife he was going on a trip. I got the room and called Lydia to say I was too tired to drive home. I'd used that excuse before; she knew what it meant. Usually she treated it with weary, almost tolerant, contempt. But this time she was intrusive, tense sounding. Who was I with, she asked. When I wouldn't say, she grew angry. There was something we had to discuss, right now. Couldn't it wait, I asked. She hesitated, then said, "It's waited too long already." But I didn't want to know. I just wanted to get off the phone.' His voice was hoarse. 'I just wanted to be with him. So I told her I'd be back in the morning and hung up.'

'Then you never learned what she wanted.'

He shook his head. 'Jason and the will, perhaps. But I didn't return to find out. If I had, she might have lived.'

'And now you wonder.'

'Yes.' He spoke intently. 'But there's something more. I have this terrible sense of buried connections, that what's happened to all three of us – even Lydia's death – is entwined with what I am. I have to know, Adam.'

In the bad light his face seemed etched with guilt and questions. I wondered how much of him I knew, how far the hidden parts had taken him, how much good there was between us. 'There was a girl once,' I said, 'in Florence. I was there for two weeks on a college tour, with money I'd saved working. It was good and it wasn't. I got a *pensione*, spent most of my time at the Uffizi and the like. I saw the paintings. Then, the evening before I was to leave, I looked out my window to the alley below which led to a *piazza*. The sun was setting and for a moment before nightfall the walls of the city were dusty pink. It became dark. I was turning away when I saw her through a window across the alley. She was slim, with long dark hair like Kris Ann's, though I didn't know her then. She was packing. She began to undress, carefully folding her things in the suitcase, one by one until they were all folded. I watched her. When she was through she came naked to the window and for a moment looked out at the city, as I had. Then she pulled the blinds.

'The next day I looked for her in the *piazza*, hoping to buy her a glass of red wine. I never found her and at noon our bus left for the airport. Perhaps I wouldn't have recognized her. But I always wondered.'

Henry listened, thoughtful. 'It's different,' he said when I was through.

'Perhaps.'

'I have to know,' he repeated. 'Maybe none of this has ever meant anything. Maybe life doesn't. But a man has to live as though it does. *I* have to. Especially now.'

'Why me? Why not Roland?'

'Because I trust you.' He looked at me directly. 'And because you need answers too.'

I shrugged. 'I guess we'll see.'

The depression in his face seemed to ease. 'You believe me then, Adam.'

'We'll see.' I stubbed my cigarette. 'We'll see what I do.'

I got up without waiting for an answer. My legs were rubbery, my head light. I felt foolish, surprised. Henry rose, reaching for me. 'You're pale, Adam. Let me drive you to the hospital.'

I waved him back. 'I need to get home to Kris Ann. Just stay there. Please.'

He slumped, arms falling to his sides. I got to the library door, hesitated, then turned, propping one hand in the doorway. He watched me in the dimness. 'Men,' I said. 'Jesus, Henry, how did you get stuck with that one?'

He shook his head. 'I don't know, Adam. It just was.'

I nodded slowly. When I turned to leave he was reaching for *War and Peace*.

I awoke panicky with the sense of lost time. It was dark. Seconds passed as I recognized my garage, replayed the surreal drift of the drive home, a collage of strobe-light beams, curves that shifted and distances that shrank abruptly, leaping shadows. The luminous blur of my wristwatch became numbers again. I relaxed; I had lost perhaps fifteen minutes.

I got out, moving from muscle memory through the garage and into the backyard. The night moved. Fluorescent moonlight yellowed the grass and oaks and the pathway of mossy stones leading to the sunroom. Its windows were dark. Inside the house was total darkness.

Stumbling from stone to stone I ran toward the house, slipping, falling palms forward on the slippery moss of the stone in front of me, smelling its dankness. Crablike, I pushed at the slimy rocks and then the whine came and bits of rock flew into my face.

The second bullet struck the tree behind me. Kris Ann, I thought frenziedly. I came up running off balance with the third shot, headed for the sunroom window. Ten feet, five feet. A fourth shot. Arms across my face, I hurtled through the window amidst a hail of shattering glass and hit the floor, blacking out for the last time.

Chapter 26

I awoke staring up at the antique fan. Stinging cuts covered my hands. The house was dark and silent and no one stood over me. I couldn't remember Kris Ann's Audi parked in the garage.

I got up.

Glass crunched beneath my first step. The step took too long. My brain was a box of light unable to send signals through its walls. Inside the box I knew someone could kill me, but my feet were stone.

I took a slow second step. My head felt melon soft.

The third step was easier, and the fourth. I got used to the numbness and to making noise that they could hear.

The living room was empty.

I stopped to let my eyes adjust. In the dining room ahead, moonlight caught the hard polish of mahogany. Its corners were stained by darkness. But when I went there nothing happened. The windows were cracked open and through the screens came cricket sounds in a chorus of rising and falling, moving like the night had moved. The lot next door, tangled and overgrown, was full of them. I realized that the shots had come from there. Still I heard no footsteps but mine.

I edged to the kitchen door, back to the wall until my head turned the corner.

Nothing. Nothing but two barstools at the counter, a coffee cup and dirty ashtray, thin shadows on the wall. Slowly, silent now, I moved to the drawers for a carving knife.

It was smooth, balanced in my hand. I began reaching for the light switch, then stopped. Light would help them.

A pen clicked behind me. I froze, heard nothing, felt nothing except fear that tricked the brain. Fear now at the base of my spine and between my shoulder blades. The sound of my own steps came to me from some great distance.

Suddenly I was tripped, falling forward, losing the knife. My palms hit as it clattered across the tile. I turned on my knees to fight.

Kris Ann's shoes lay where I had stumbled. The knife slid against the far wall and stopped. I was dead if they heard me. I crawled sweating toward the knife, grasped it, rose again.

Still nothing.

I began up the dark staircase to the bedroom, breathing harder. Perhaps they would be there. I moved faster to the second floor, hurried down the dark hallway past empty bedrooms, toward ours. It was dark. I gripped the knife tighter, found the light switch, pushed down.

Our bed was made and inside there was no one dead or living. I went to Kris Ann's nightstand and opened it.

The gun was missing, 'Kris Ann,' my brain began chanting, faster and faster in a terrible rhythm. I went down the hallway to the stairs, holding the knife in my left hand, feeling and not feeling the smooth banister. 'Kris Ann . . .'

Footfalls. I was trapped in mid-stairway. No trick of the nerve ends but footfalls moving from the kitchen below me toward the dining room, real as the acid in my mouth. Coming closer.

A shadow moved into the alcove. I raised the knife.

Something clicked. The lights turning on. Shock as the knife dropped from my hand. 'Thank God,' I blurted. 'You're all right.'

I told them about Jason. Bast took notes. Rayfield asked questions. He seemed backed away from me, just a police-man, and his thumb stroked the pen without clicking it. I didn't tell him about the Moorings, or Henry's lover. Jason used a gun, I said: it had to be him.

Rayfield shrugged without comment. When I ventured that it couldn't have been Lee, he answered coldly that I was wrong: my friend Nate Taylor had sprung Lee an hour after I had left. There wasn't enough to hold him, Rayfield added: they'd just wanted to see what I'd do.

I stared at him. 'Like get shot.'

This time it was Bast who shruggled. 'If that's what you want,' he said, and closed the notebook. Kris Ann watched in silence.

They went. A bespectacled doctor and two nurses came and went, leaving Kris Ann and me alone. Everything – the walls and sheets, even the bed frame – was white. Kris Ann still wore her white tennis dress.

'You shouldn't have left,' I said. My voice sounded tinny. 'He might have shot you.'

'I was too angry to wait.' She looked away. 'And I had the revolver.'

'So you could drill Jason Cantwell at fifty paces.'

'Yes.' She didn't smile.

I watched her. She sat against a cinder-block wall, the right strap of her dress blood-speckled from helping me to the car. 'Next time,' I said, 'just tell me to fuck off. Something simple.'

She said nothing. After a moment she rose and took a cool rag from the nightstand, running it across my face. Her finger gently traced the stitches beneath one eye. 'What's happened to us, Adam?'

I tried smiling. 'You cheat at backgammon –'

'The baby?'

'Krissy, stop –'

'I mean it's not coming here and Daddy, is it?'

'Not now.' I reached up, my fingers disappearing in her hair. She closed her eyes.

'I don't know who you are.'

I looked away. 'When my father died I stopped thinking about that. My mother needed someone and I was there. Then she wanted a lawyer – someone who wouldn't desert her by being killed – and I became one. I don't know – I don't like talking this way.'

'But why?'

'Because words don't make any difference. You string them all together and in the end people define themselves by what they do.'

She shook her head. 'Word games, Adam. There's too much we never say.'

I looked up again. 'Like what happened between you and Jason Cantwell?'

She stiffened. 'What do you mean?'

'The way you avoided him at our engagement party, how afraid you are. Roland giving you that gun and how desperate you were to keep it. You've been trying to tell me ever since Lydia was murdered, and I haven't listened.'

'He killed Lydia –'

'What happened in the garden, Krissy?'

She looked startled. In a muted voice, she said, 'It doesn't matter now.'

'Krissy, you've been threatened and now I've been pistol-whipped and shot at. It matters.'

She stared at a spot beside my head. 'All right.' She said it bluntly, angrily. 'He tried to rape me.'

'How?'

'How do you suppose?' When I didn't answer, she spoke hurriedly, getting it over. 'One Sunday when I was sixteen Daddy took me by to visit after church. Sometimes he'd do that. That day Henry and Lydia got to talking with Daddy, and Jason said why didn't we go out back. He was talking too fast and wouldn't look at me but I thought it was mostly shyness. I didn't know until it was too late.'

'Easy,' I said. 'I know that. Just tell me what happened.'

Her eyes were wide with memory. 'Is this really necessary?'

I took her hand. 'Yes. It is.'

'If you want, then.' Her voice was harsh. 'We were walking across the lawn toward the back. I was chattering on about people we knew, anything because he was so awkward. We got away from the house and then he stops and turns to me with his hands in his pockets. His face is contorted and then he started talking so fast to the ground that at first I hardly heard him. It was insane, things he'd dreamed up. We're close, he keeps saying, he knows I must feel it too. He looks so twisted up and lonely that I feel sorry for him, as if I'm his mother or something. I begin telling him it's all right, sure, we're friends and can talk. "But I love you," he says, and begins coming towards me with this strange expression. His eyes were so dark.

'I knew before he touched me. I looked around but couldn't see the house for the pine grove we were in, like he'd wanted. He began kissing me. I said, no, it wasn't like that. He just shakes his head and then he's pushing me against a pine tree. He's too strong. His hands are up my skirt and I start wriggling and begging him not to. Then his fingers came inside me. I began screaming.' Her voice fell off. 'No one had done that before.'

'It would matter anytime –'

'I was still screaming when he got my pants down. I hurt inside and no one could hear me. He kept panting, "Fuck me," and pushing his fingers deeper in me with the other hand on my throat. I began punching and kicking and then suddenly his fingers came out and he was bent over holding his groin and looking up at me wide-eyed like I'd hurt his feelings. I was bleeding where he'd touched me. "Kris Ann," he moaned, and reached out for me. I ran into the house.'

I felt sick and angry. 'What happened then?'

She breathed out and her voice became less strained. 'I told Daddy I didn't feel well and wanted to go home. Lydia looked at me strangely but Henry got me some soda water and then I left with Daddy. On the way home, I told him.'

'What did he say?'

'Nothing. All the way home he stared straight ahead. It was his face.' She looked down at me. 'It's the same face you have for him sometimes: so filled with hate that I almost believe you could kill him. His eyes were like diamonds. And the quiet. The way he was quiet scared me almost worse than Jason. It was like he felt too much to speak.

'When we got home he sat me down across from him and began asking questions in a voice that never changed no matter what I told him. He made me tell him everything. I don't remember him even blinking. He must have seen the way he frightened me because suddenly his face changed and he put his arms around me and began telling me things would be all right, that he'd take care of it.'

I reached up. There were chill marks on her arms. 'You frighten me now,' she murmured.

'No need. It's just that it still matters. It matters to you.'

She shook her head. 'I learned better, with you. It wasn't like that and mostly I forgot.'

'What did Roland do?'

'He sent me away for a couple of weeks, but he never really said what else. I do know that the Cantwells never brought Jason by again and that somehow he was kept pretty much out of my way. I saw him once or twice a year; Birmingham's a small place and sometimes you have to get by. But he always looked away. It just died.'

But now I knew it hadn't. 'Does Henry know?'

She looked thoughtful. 'He must. I'm sure Lydia did, because for a while she seemed embarrassed, almost over-solicitous. But no one ever mentioned it. I knew it wasn't *their* fault, and if anything they were kinder to me than before. It seemed better to pretend it hadn't happened.'

'But it did.' I shook my head. 'Why didn't you tell me – at least after Lydia was killed?'

She gazed at me steadily. 'Because I was afraid of what you'd do.'

'Jesus –'

'Adam, look what you've done *without* knowing.'

'Yes. Get shot at. Ever since I found Lydia I've heard nothing but lies and secrets and half-truths, and now it's you and your father. I'm sick of it.'

Her eyes still held mine. 'I'm sorry, Adam. I thought it was best.'

I realized that my feet and legs felt numb, disconnected from my nervous system. I closed my eyes, almost floating. More softly, I said, 'I'm sorry, too. For everything.'

She took my hand again. A nurse appeared with something to swallow. Kris Ann promised to stay. In five minutes I fell asleep.

I dreamed, but not of Jason. We were in Paris, four years prior. It was spring and Kris Ann sat on the porch of the *pensione* with a view of the Tuilleries up a narrow side street of small shops, a patisserie, sidewalk cafés. Her dress was white and simple. She still held herself carefully from the baby, as if her body were strange to her. In the dream I knew that later she would exercise and her shape would return, but now she was pale and thin and stretched and emptied out.

I brought our breakfast, black coffee and croissants. The croissants were flaky and soft. When I told her that, she nodded but took nothing. Sun crept down the side street as she stared out and beyond to where tourists walked at a relaxed, almost ceremonious, pace among the hedges of the Tuilleries, as though it were Sunday even for them. Coming down the alley a plump Frenchman with a poodle and newspaper whistled to himself. She watched it all gravely, disinterestedly. 'What will happen,' she asked, 'in time?'

Her face hadn't moved from the street and her monotone made the question no question at all. 'Nothing,' I answered. 'Or the same things. We'll have the same quarrels and joys and disappointments, and food will cost too much and I'll keep on loving you. I'll still like sex in the morning, you'll like it at night, and sometimes I'll come home at noon to work out a compromise –'

'Seriously.'

'Seriously, I didn't marry you to provide an heir.'

Her voice was still flat. 'Then why did you?'

'Because I love you. It's that simple.'

'But you wanted a son.' She said it accusingly, or self-accusingly.

'I did, Krissy. So did you.'

'But he was the only chance we'll ever have.' She turned to me in wonderment. 'When they told us that I watched your face before I even thought of me. It was like you were listening to a weather report. I spent three days crying. You never cried.'

'I can't cry, Krissy. I never could.'

Her eyes blazed. 'Damn you,' she said fiercely. 'Damn your father for getting shot.'

I reached her as she started sobbing and held her to me,

face buried in my shoulder. 'Too early,' I said softly. 'It's okay, baby, it's all right. I brought you here too early, that's all.' Her shoulders shook with sobbing. 'It's all right,' I wanted to say now. 'A son just has to be a boy. There's no magic in being *our* boy.' But when I awoke, Kris Ann was gone.

She returned in the morning with two books I liked. I didn't tell her about the dream.

They weren't allowing visitors, she said, just her and the police. But friends called and some of my partners. Nora Culhane called, trying to sound angry about being stood up, trying more seriously for a story: I referred her to the police, and did that with all the reporters who called after. The Kells called. Cade called saying he'd hired private police to guard our house; I didn't thank him and he didn't ask how I was. Nate Taylor called, but when I asked him where Lee had been last night he didn't know.

Then Henry called.

He sounded tense. 'They won't let me visit.'

'They're like that. I'm no worse than when you saw me.'

He paused. 'What I said, about going on: I want you to stop.'

'I'm not sure I have that choice anymore.'

'Adam, this is my responsibility. It always was. I realize I never should have involved you. Please, believe this is for your own good.'

'Not until we've talked.'

'We'll have time. Just take care of yourself and Kris Ann.'

'Henry, there's something I have to know –'

'Goodbye, Adam. Rest.' He hung up.

I held the phone for a long time after.

Kris Ann returned with the doctor. There was no fracture, he said: I could go home Monday if I remembered that a second blow to the head could cause brain damage. Kris Ann promised to remind me.

I kept wondering about Henry, and Jason.

But Rayfield had Jason now and I was hurt, fearful of the

wounds and hatreds I felt reaching from the past toward Kris Ann and me. They gave me another pill.

Then Rayfield called to say Jason was out free.

Chapter 27

'The girl swears Jason was home all night,' he said Monday morning, 'and their neighbors don't know different.'

He sat flatfooted in the armless chair, thumbs gripping his notepad like a hat he didn't know where to put. Burst veins like faultlines in his eyes made him look sleepless and volatile.

'What about the gun?' I asked.

Rayfield put the pad in his lap and began rubbing the tips of his fingers. 'She says she made him drive to the Cahaba River and throw it in.'

'So you let him go.'

He looked sharply up. 'We booked him for assault. If you'd told me the truth downtown we'd have pulled him in with the gun and you wouldn't have been shot at. Assuming it was him.'

'Jesus Christ, forget the gun. The will is good enough now.'

Rayfield stood. 'Oh, it's the will that killed her. It's just not Cantwell's boy.' He walked to the end of the bed. 'Let me tell you what I think happened. Lydia Cantwell had a boyfriend she wanted to marry. Cantwell knew, or guessed. For years she'd been his cover and now he stood to lose both that and her money. Then, the night he called from Anniston, Mrs Cantwell told him about the will. It came to him: by killing her before she signed that will, he could pin it on the boy. So he drove back that night and strangled her. It all fits. He's got no alibi, he lied about the phone call, and there's no one in town believes Cantwell gave a shit for his son. All you have to do is think about how he could use that will.' He leaned forward, speaking intently. 'I'm almost there, Shaw. All I need is her boyfriend's name.'

It hit me with the force he had intended: Rayfield had Henry Cantwell one witness from a death sentence, with me in between. Find Mooring, I thought, and he had Lydia's lover, Jason's father, and the final proof that would convict Henry Cantwell: Joanne Mooring to say Henry had come home that night. 'I'm curious, Lieutenant. Why did Henry shoot at me? I forget.'

'Because you know the boyfriend or some other detail that convicts him. It's good you're starting to think about it.'

I shook my head. 'It doesn't compute. I was coming from his place the night I was shot at. I'd just seen him.'

Rayfield leaned still closer. 'Cantwell was alone, Shaw. Nothing to keep him from following. He's a crack shot, you know, and what with you blacked out in the garage he'd have time to see the lights weren't on and set up in the bushes next door. It's a perfect blind.'

'It's perfect bullshit.'

'You know it isn't. He killed Mrs Cantwell, played you off against Cade, and then threatened your wife when you got too close. Who did you see the night before you were shot at? What did you tell him that can't come out?'

I said nothing. 'You want your wife killed?' he kept on. 'By the time we cull all of Mrs Cantwell's friends for gray-haired men it may be too late. But you can stop it. Just tell me who Lee saw visit Mrs Cantwell. Lee's not lying, is he?' His voice rose. 'Tell me, Shaw. Tell me before that fairy kills you too.'

His face was rapt and excited. I felt concerned. In a low voice I answered, 'You might be better off looking to your own fears.'

A sick, trapped look drained the keenness from his face. 'You're obstructing justice,' he said tightly. 'Withholding evidence, lying. I can have you disbarred.'

'Maybe.'

'It's your last chance. Make me leave the room without her boyfriend's name and I start working on you.'

I shrugged.

In the instant before leaving he looked almost lonely. Then he straightened and walked out, closing the door with fearful gentleness.

*

Kris Ann smiled behind me in the bathroom mirror. 'Like what you see?'

'Not particularly.' For a moment my image had blurred. I squinted, shaking my head, and my features reappeared. The stitches were gone, leaving a thin scar the doctor said would turn white. But the bruise near my temple was blue and yellow and still swollen enough that my left eye was half-closed. I didn't mention the blurring. 'I take it Henry hasn't called.'

'No. Should he have?'

'I guess not.'

'How do you feel?'

'My head's kind of light.'

'You're home now,' she assured me. 'You can relax.' But when I'd finished toweling off and followed her to the bedroom she was loading Cade's revolver. She took it with us to the living room, secreting it behind a vase on the mantel. Cade's bulky rented policeman paced the porch outside.

I listened for the telephone.

Kris Ann brought two mineral waters. 'I think you should talk with him.'

'Henry?'

'Daddy. Maybe if you discuss this face to face . . .' Her voice trailed off.

I got up and began pacing with the policeman on the other side of the window. 'How good was Henry with guns?'

She looked at me curiously. 'Good enough to teach me, remember? Jason, too.'

'I've got to see him.'

Her eyes widened. 'Jason?'

'Henry.'

The policeman's footsteps sounded from the porch in monotonous rhythm. Kris Ann looked silently up at the mantel. In a flat voice she said, 'So now you think it's Henry.'

'I just need to talk to him.'

The telephone rang.

Kris Ann went to answer it. 'Oh, hi,' I heard her say. 'He's fine, just resting . . . No, Daddy's not here. I think today's his board meeting . . . Yes, he's up . . . You're sure? . . . All right, just a minute.'

She reappeared in the living room. 'It's Clayton,' she said almost sadly. 'He says he has to see you.'

The taxi dropped me in front of the fifty-year-old building I thought of as Henry's bank.

The Cantwell-Alabama Bank and Trust was a cement-pillared structure with marble floors and oak-paneled rear offices of which Henry's was the largest, a commodious rectangle with high ceilings, a brass chandelier, and a green rug so deep it muffled my steps like a prowler's.

He wasn't there. Neither was any piece of him – plaques or portraits or family pictures – except the sense of a man passing silently through. I wasn't sure why the room made me sad. I didn't stay to think about it.

I stopped in the wide marble lobby as customers passed and employees in white shirts or blouses glided around me at such a uniform pace they seemed run by remote control. I'd wanted enough to find Henry, imagined it so clearly, that I seemed unable to do what I had come for.

'Adam.'

I turned to see Clayton Kell hurrying towards me. 'I'm sorry,' he said. 'You look terrible.'

'I'm okay. It sounded important.'

'It is.'

I trailed him to his office, a windowless square he'd worked years for, sitting while he shut the door behind us and reached for ice in the small refrigerator he hid in his credenza with a fifth of bourbon. He filled two glasses, slid mine across the desk, took a hasty gulp of his, and blurted. 'It's all a mess.'

I stopped the drink an inch from my mouth and watched him until he stammered, 'Adam, the police were here.'

'What did they want?'

'They had a warrant. There was nothing I could do. I

tried calling Roland and he wasn't in. Henry either – he just hasn't been around –'

'For Christ's sake, Clayton, spit it out.' I caught myself. 'Look, no one's saying you fucked up. Just tell me what happened, okay?'

'All right.' He nodded silently, repeatedly. 'Okay. It's just that Rayfield –' He looked up and said, 'Lydia's bank account is total hash, Adam. It's all wrong.'

'How wrong?'

'Eight hundred thousand fucking dollars.'

'How could that be? You're computerized, you get daily balances –'

'I don't know.' He slammed down his drink. 'I mean, I do and I don't. They made me go through the records and it's gone.'

'What records? What did they show?'

He pushed a low stack of papers at me. 'I copied what they took.'

'Good.'

'The top one's Lydia's last statement of account, all right? Now the earlier ones show that for years she kept her balance at around a million –'

'Just lying around at six percent?'

'Christ, Adam, I'm not her investment counselor. Henry is. That's the problem.' He jabbed his finger at the top sheet. 'Look here. On March fifteen, there's an entry showing that Lydia's account was debited eight hundred thousand dollars. Now she could have withdrawn that much, though I don't know why she'd want to. But there's no withdrawal slip, not a goddamned thing with Lydia's signature to show she got the money. I know. Rayfield made me go through them twice. There has to be a slip. Money doesn't leave here without one.'

'Or shouldn't.'

He nodded, collapsing in his chair until his chin doubled into folds and his small round belly strained his shirtfront. His face sagged with the unexpectedness of it. 'What about the auditors?' I asked. 'You've got a daily audit. Wouldn't they pick this up?'

'No.' Clayton wiped his face. 'What they look at is whether the records for all our accounts square with the cash we actually have on hand. That part's okay; Lydia's statement shows eight hundred thousand dollars withdrawn and we've got eight hundred thousand dollars less money. The problem is that the money went out and there's no signed withdrawal slip. The auditors don't check slips. It would take too long.'

Clayton took off his glasses, wiping an imaginary smudge. My head began to throb. 'Let me ask you something, Clayton. You don't keep people's money segregated, right? I mean, you don't have some special place for Lydia's and another for mine and Krissy's.'

'Uh-huh.'

I reached for my glass and drank, the whiskey burning down. 'So,' I finished slowly, 'what really happened is that eight hundred thousand dollars of the bank's money disappeared and Lydia's statement of account kept the auditors from catching on.'

Clayton's cheeks blotched. 'What are you saying?'

'Clayton, how many people know about this?'

'Just us. Why?'

'I think someone's embezzled eight hundred thousand dollars.'

His mouth fell open. 'Who?'

'Who could alter Lydia's account statement?'

'The computer programmer, clerks – I suppose anyone at the bank. Hell, I could have. But to do that to cover embezzlement wouldn't work. Lydia – the customer would raise holy hell as soon as we mailed out her interest statement. She'd open that sucker and –' His lips stopped moving.

'Unless she were dead,' I finished.

'Oh, my God.'

'We can't let this out.'

'We've got to.' His voice rose. 'There's Rayfield, reports to the Feds –'

'I mean just until we get to Henry. Maybe there's some reason. We can't go running off.'

'Sure.' Clayton nodded and dabbed his forehead. 'Sure.'

The word fell emptily into the long silence that followed and then Cade walked in.

Chapter 28

When he saw me Cade stared in anger and surprise. Then he limped to a chair in front of Clayton. From his pallor the shattered hip was hurting.

'Well,' he demanded, 'what's the problem?'

The question was for Clayton, its rough edge for me. Clayton hung between speech and the dread of speaking. 'There's eight hunderd thousand dollars missing on Lydia's account statement,' I cut in, 'and no withdrawal slip.'

Slow comprehension leeched the anger from Cade's face and voice. He turned to me. 'Do the police know?'

'Yes. And Henry's out of pocket. Clayton tried finding him and couldn't.'

'You've told no one else, Clayton?'

'No, sir. I wanted your advice.'

'Then I'd better see the account statement.'

Clayton passed the single paper and Cade gripped it tightly in front of him while he scanned. 'Rayfield's got that,' I told him.

'Good God.' He looked up at Clayton. 'Adam and I need to talk somewhere. Please, you just stay put and don't say a word to anyone. We'll be back.'

Cade led me down the hall toward Henry's office. It was past five and the bank was empty, but Cade shut the door before taking Henry's chair. He leaned over the desk, staring moodily past me, fingers drumming silently, uncharacteristically, on the glass top. 'You're wondering why I never told you about Henry.'

The irrelevance of that surprised me. But I nodded, saying, 'At least I'd have understood the tension between you and Rayfield.'

'It was Henry's place to tell you, not mine.'

'So you let him commit perjury.'

'This isn't ethics class,' he said sharply. 'When Henry told me he'd been with a man we were in the library, with Rayfield waiting outside. He swore he'd perjure himself before giving his friend to Rayfield. What was I supposed to do, come out and tell him Henry was going to lie? I couldn't abandon him, not then, and knowing what I knew I couldn't turn him over to someone else. It was a dilemma. My one hope was to get the questioning done with and then keep Rayfield away until he found another suspect. Besides' – Cade paused, speaking slowly now – 'you're not sure this man even exists, are you?'

It hadn't been irrelevant at all. 'No,' I answered. 'But Henry told you about his lover that morning, not later. That argues he didn't make it up.'

Cade smiled with humor. 'You asume that Henry was too shocked to lie. That's your flaw, Adam. It's fatal in a lawyer to be so tangled in his own emotions that he can't think like someone else. Think like Rayfield. His Henry Cantwell is a clever man who killed Lydia and then reappeared the next morning ready to play a part. His Henry spins sympathetic lies about loyalty to a friend to make his failure to confide in you sound noble. Rayfield's Henry Cantwell ruined the lives of both Lydia and Jason to conceal his own sexual transgressions. Rayfield's Henry is a virtual schizophrenic.'

I felt sick. 'And yours, Roland?'

He slumped for a moment, trapped-looking and for once intensely human, worry eroding the hard angles of his face. 'I don't know anymore. I think about Kris Ann . . .'

I was almost sorry for him. Reluctantly, I said, 'There's something worse.'

'What could be worse?'

I told him about Joanne Mooring.

As he listened, Cade's fingers stopped drumming. His eyes became intent, expressionless. When I finished, he drew himself up, took an audible breath, and asked, 'She saw him?'

'No. His black Mercedes.'

Cade stared at me. Then he murmured, 'That's enough for Rayfield,' paused with his hand over his forehead, and added, 'So you think Mooring's the father.'

'That's right.'

'Did you tell all this to Henry?'

'I'm afraid so.'

Cade began rubbing his temple. 'It's too much,' he protested. 'Do you appreciate in all of your busyness that I've known Henry Cantwell for over forty years?'

'I appreciate that, yes.'

'Do you?' he lashed out. 'Do you know what you've done? You've trapped your own client so that Rayfield can break him like an egg. By now Henry's a desperate man.'

I felt too weak to argue. 'Clayton's waiting,' I said tiredly, 'and we're getting nowhere.'

Cade flung out his arm. 'Then tell me what to do, why don't you. Your Mooring discovery puts me in a hopeless conflict. One client, the bank, is out eight hundred thousand dollars which it appears that another client, my friend, murdered his wife to conceal.'

'To believe that, Roland, you have to believe that Henry strangled Lydia, set up Jason, threatened Kris Ann, and shot at me – all because he's a thief, which is as incredible as the rest.'

'Who else, dammit. Show me who. Otis Lee, Mooring, Mooring's wife, even Jason – none of them could take this money. Only Henry could and then keep that from Lydia. Say she *did* want a divorce. The first thing she'd do is take stock of all her assets. If he'd stolen her money, and not told her, he could never let that come out. Think what he might do –'

'We have to talk to him.'

Cade shook his head. 'But that's where the conflict is. Until now I've looked at this like he's innocent. Now I have to consider, what if he confesses? We're barred by the attorney-client privilege from telling the bank.'

'But we can't be sure there's a conflict until we talk to him.'

'God.' Cade looked at me resentfully. 'I need time to think what to do.'

'Maybe the morning,' I tried. 'We can think overnight and see him then.'

'It won't work. Clayton can't hold off telling his board that long.'

'He told *us*. If we ask him to keep quiet until tomorrow, then we've assumed the burden.'

Cade leaned back. 'That would leave the night to figure how to handle Henry, and maybe by noon tomorrow we'd know what to tell the bank.'

'Right.'

'Very well.' Cade began snapping decisions. 'We'll see Henry tomorrow morning, at his place. I don't want anyone else around. And you're to come with me. I may want a witness.' He snatched the telephone, stabbing out numbers.

'What's this?'

'Henry.' Cade's mouth was a tense line as he held the phone out so I could hear it ring. 'Not in.' Then there was a click and Henry's voice, thin and reedy and faraway sounding, said, 'Hello.'

Cade clamped the phone to his ear. 'Hello, Henry. How are you feeling? . . . Good.' I watched Cade maneuver his face to match the smoothness of his voice. 'Adam and I are here at the bank. He's found something, and we both think it's important we meet with you tomorrow morning, early.'

Cade began listening. I wondered how Henry felt and sounded. Cade was telling him, 'It's better at your place.' He listened again, nodding, then casually answered, 'Eight will be fine. Bye, now,' and hung up. Henry would never imagine Cade's hand shaking as it put down the phone. His forehead glistened with the beginnings of sweat. 'Eight o'clock,' he said tiredly. 'God, I hated that.'

'How is he?'

'I don't know.' Cade shook his head. 'I just don't know.'

'Think he'll call one of us tonight?'

'If he does we can't talk to him. I want both of us there, especially me.' He looked at me, bursting out, 'It's you who's made this disaster, letting Henry manipulate you until you've built a case against him by accident and then baited Rayfield into coming here to finish it.'

'Look, Henry asked me to help.'

'Did he? Or did you force him to pretend to want that while trying to scare you off with Kris Ann's picture and then gunshots, so that he could ask you to stop helping for your own good. Think – you're not clever enough. Not once since the killing has he told you anything you haven't forced out of him. He's maneuvered you until he couldn't anymore –'

'Save it, Roland. This is hard enough.'

Cade looked incredulous and then his face became blurred in front of me. 'Do you think I like it?' he was saying.

My skull was a blinding ache. I blinked once, saw Cade again. 'Clearly not.' I answered. 'But whether's that's on Henry's account I wouldn't know.'

Cade gave me a long, wintry glare before asking, 'Now what does that mean?'

'You probably hate Jason Cantwell more than I do. More, even, than you hate me.'

He stared until he was sure what I meant. 'She told you?'

'Yes. I understand now why you gave her that gun. It would have been simpler to tell me about Jason.'

'*That* was between *us*.' Cade's fist crashed down on the desk. 'Damn you, you're like a skin graft, stuck where you don't belong. For two cents I'd rid us both of you –'

He stopped, eyes narrowing as I stood, dug in my pocket for two copper pennies, clinked them in the cup of my hand before I tossed them underhand so that they hung for an instant above the desk, fell, hit his chest, dropping silently on the soft rug. 'They're yours,' I said. I turned my back and went to find Clayton.

By the time Clayton dropped me off it was dusk and I was having trouble with balance. I passed the guard on my porch without speaking. Kris Ann's face as she met me was a double image. 'Are you all right, Adam? Let me call the doctor.'

I leaned in the doorframe. 'No need. I'm just tired.'

She took my arm. 'There's a problem at the bank, isn't there?'

Something in her voice made me turn. 'Henry called,' she said reluctantly. 'He sounded upset.'

'I'd better call him.'

Her face became one, then two, then one again. 'It can wait until morning,' she urged. 'You look like a ghost.'

I stared past her from the hallway toward the kitchen telephone. It was a blur. I put my hand on the railing and walked slowly upstairs.

Henry never called back. After a time I fell asleep. But in a dream my father died again, and only Brian wept.

Chapter 29

Cade knocked before eight, grim-faced and hostile, staring over my shoulder at Kris Ann. We drove to Henry's without speaking.

This morning I saw clearly. Sunlight fell through the pines like yellow dust. A slow wind stirring their needles felt like wetness hovering and the dogwood were wilting or fallen and smelled faintly of decay. A bird called. No one answered when Cade rang the doorbell.

We stood with hands in our pockets, waiting. After a moment Cade began pounding the door. I went to the garage and saw the black Mercedes through the window, and Lydia's Lincoln. Cade kept pounding as though transfixed. When I came back and said, 'Their cars are here,' he jabbed angrily at the doorbell without answering.

I began circling the house.

I saw nothing through the left front window but an empty living room. Cade hit the doorbell again. I went around to the side.

Henry's library window was level with my chin. I edged through the bushes and hydrangeas, stretched but could see only part of the room: the standing gold ashtray, the chair where I often sat, but not Henry's chair. His copy of *War and Peace* lay facedown on the floor.

I went to the rear of the house, more quickly now. The lightheadedness returned.

Double glass doors led from the patio to the living room. They were locked. From the front Cade's hollow pounding came again.

Decorative stones lay scattered in the garden. I snatched one and tossed it through the windowpane nearest the doorknob.

The sound of shattering glass made me flinch. I reached to

turn the knob and stepped inside. Cade rang the doorbell with the staccato bursts of a madman.

I went to the library.

Henry slumped in his chair, staring out.

The book lay at his feet, and near that the revolver. Dried blood came from his mouth where the bullet had gone. There were blood and brains and fragments of skull on the chair and the shelves behind it and on one corner of the blue Miro. The reading glasses were in his lap and his arm had fallen over the side of his chair. He still wore his cardigan sweater.

His hand was white and cold-feeling. Time stopped as half-forgotten fragments tumbled through my mind: 'Hail, Mary, full of grace . . . The Lord is with thee . . . Holy Mary, Mother of God, pray for us sinners now and at the hour of our death.'

It was quiet. Cade had stopped ringing.

I dropped Henry's hand and stared at him. His gray eyes seemed frozen in eternal disappointment.

'Why?' I asked him.

Cade rang the doorbell again. I turned away, walked slowly to the front door, and opened it.

Cade stood back, surprised. 'He's in the library,' I said.

Cade brushed me aside. I sat on the front steps.

Time passed. Things happened that I half noticed and didn't care about. Two police came, like before, and, like before, a team with doctor bags. They glanced at me and hurried on.

Then Rayfield came. When I followed him mechanically he looked away. But when he looked at Henry Cantwell there was pity on his face, and something like relief.

From around me came now-familiar noises: orders, doors opening, footsteps. 'Just blew his fucking brains out,' someone said.

My brain began screaming.

I went back to the steps and sat. Someone stood over me. I gazed stupidly up.

Cade's face was filled with hate. 'I hope you're satisfied, Adam.' His voice was barely controlled. 'Because you as good as pulled the trigger.'

I sprang up.

From the side, Rayfield moved quickly between us, snapping, 'Drive him home,' at Bast. But as Cade stared past him there was still only hate.

Chapter 30

The next two mornings I went to the firm, burying myself in trial strategy. I avoided Cade. When word seeped back that he had asked that I be fired, I did nothing except work harder. The dizziness came and went.

The media were full of Henry's suicide and guilt: 'The quiet man who exploded,' wrote someone who had never met him. Otis Lee left town unnoticed. Mooring's role remained hidden.

The second morning, Cade began meeting secretly with senior partners. There was nothing I could do, or cared to do. I was drafting a motion to throw Nate Taylor out of court when Culhane knocked on the door.

'Aren't you returning phone calls?' she asked.

'I've got nothing to say.'

She leaned in the doorway, considering me. 'You look awful,' she said seriously, paused, and then asked, 'How is your wife taking it?'

I couldn't explain Kris Ann's face when I told her: not shocked or even bewildered, but like that of a hunted animal. And then without speaking she had walked upstairs and closed the door behind her. 'He was our friend,' I told Culhane now. 'So was Mrs Cantwell. Kris Ann's life was threatened. It's hard for us to talk about, or even know what to feel.'

'Still, there must be things you want to say about him.'

'Only to myself.'

Her look wavered between hesitant and bold. 'It's not your fault,' she finally said.

'Sure. I know.'

She shook her head with a small, doubting smile, and was gone.

I stared down at the motion. Halfway through the fourth

page I flung my pencil against the wall and went to the police station.

Rayfield and Bast sat stirring coffee, torpid and diminished-seeming, like actors without roles. 'What do you want?' Bast demanded.

'To be certain it was suicide.'

'Suicide,' came his sardonic answer, 'or self-defense.'

'Even without a note?'

Rayfield swiveled to stare at a window blocked by venetian blinds. 'Two-thirds don't leave any,' Bast said.

'It's hard to believe that Henry Cantwell would do that.'

'Well, you'd better get used to it. Suicides are tough to fake. You have to get every detail right: the victim's fingerprints not only have to be on the trigger but the cylinder. Cantwell's prints were on both, his wound was a contact wound like suicides have usually, and the bullet looks to be from the same revolver that was fired at you.'

'Was it registered to Henry?'

In profile Rayfield's jawline worked. 'Look,' Bast said, 'Alabama's full of unregistered guns, especially over fifteen years old, like Cantwell's. They didn't start registering them until after Kennedy was shot. The first one, that is.'

'Then you're not troubled that he used a gun you can't trace.'

Bast shrugged. 'Not really. There were no strange prints in the house and no one had broken in. Plus, for a murderer to get everything right, Cantwell would have to be a very cooperative victim. It's time to start living with it. Henry Cantwell stole his wife's money, then killed her and tried to kill you. You're lucky to be alive.'

'But someone could have –'

'Let it be,' rasped Rayfield. His face, still turned to the window, was slate gray. 'He killed himself, now let it be.'

Bast rose from his chair to stand between Rayfield and me. 'It's done with,' he said.

His voice was final. Nothing remained except Henry's funeral.

Cade and I went, separately, Cade because Henry's sister

had asked it, me for reasons of my own. Kris Ann stayed home. 'I can't go,' she told me. 'I can't resolve this yet.' She had said almost nothing else about Henry. But there was still a strange alertness to her, a sense of watching and listening, and the revolver remained hidden on the mantel. I had decided to give her time, and to go to the funeral alone.

It was sparsely attended. The people who knew Henry Cantwell had fallen away, leaving reporters and Clayton and scattered others, blinking from the afternoon sun as they entered to sit by themselves. I chose the front row. The funeral party gathered at the back of the church. Behind Henry's casket his sister and Roland Cade followed four pallbearers who seemed to lean outward in silent dissocation. In the far corner stood a short, balding man I didn't know; a relative, I supposed. But when they began rolling the casket toward the altar, he hung back watching it, and I forgot him.

They came slowly down until they were next to my pew and for a moment frozen in time Cade's stare riveted me across the rolling casket. And then it was past and Cade and the rest were sitting, and the funeral began.

The clergyman mumbled the prayers in haste. An air of sad embarrassment settled on the mourners and when the service was over and the casket gone, they left quickly. I stayed, not following to the grave. The church emptied and it was silent, and I lost track of time.

The quiet turned oppressive. I stood finally and began walking up the aisle.

The balding man remained at the rear of the church. I passed him without speaking and went outside.

Jason Cantwell waited on the steps in front of me. 'I've come for you,' he said.

The reporters were gone and there was no one else near. Jason's face was sullen and defiant. 'It's not time,' I answered. 'They're burying him now.'

He shrugged. 'It doesn't matter. He was never my father.'

'He was never anyone's father, and Kris Ann was never yours to have. It's past and all in your mind. Let us be.'

He shook his head. 'It isn't settled.'

He was moving closer. 'Don't do this,' I said quietly. 'You've no gun now.'

He flushed. 'I don't need one.'

'Then I'm telling you, Jason – once. This is nothing you want to happen.'

He stopped, searching my face, and then took one slower step forward. I waited.

There were footsteps behind us. We turned. The bald man stood framed in the door of the church, as if to call us back.

Jason stared at him, and then, slowly, his face became irresolute. I moved to pass him on the steps, stopping so that our shoulders brushed and our faces were inches apart. 'It's over,' I said softly. 'Touch Kris Ann and I'll kill you, sure.'

His face went rigid. I waited, letting the moment pass between us. Then I went down the steps without looking back.

I walked to my office and sat alone with the door closed and no lights on. Through the window a late afternoon sun died slowly among the high-rises of the city, its cast in the room thinning to light and shadow. I didn't move.

The rap on the door was so soft and tentative that I had to listen before saying, 'Yes?'

The door opened. The man from the funeral peered in. He was round and owlish in his glasses, one hand jammed awkwardly in a pocket. 'Mr Shaw?' he asked.

I stared at him. 'Who are you?'

His smile was more nervous tic, shy and self-hating. Then he closed the door behind him and said simply, 'I'm Henry Cantwell's lover.'

Chapter 31

I watched him across the room. Finally I asked, 'Why are you here?'

His mouth twitched again. 'Henry spoke of you often.'

'But why now?'

'I had to trust someone.' He looked down. 'You see, we were together that night. The only person Henry killed was himself.'

'Oh, my God.'

'You see how it is, then.' He said it almost tenderly.

'Yes,' I murmured. 'I see.'

He walked to a chair in front of my desk and grasped it. 'I could have come forward. But he knew how afraid I was. I'm a banker in Anniston, with a wife and three teenagers who know nothing of this. I couldn't face becoming a different sort of man.'

For a long time I just looked at him. 'How did it happen, you and Henry?'

'We found each other, that's all. For two years I thought I loved him. But not enough.' He shook his head. 'Perhaps I was too hurt.'

'Hurt?'

His eyes were small and tortured. 'Before the night she was killed I hadn't seen Henry for over two months. When he called I scrambled for any excuse to get away. We were together all night. At six o'clock I got ready to sneak out. Henry took my hand and began talking very fast. He couldn't see me anymore, he said. He loved me, I should never doubt that, and this was for my own good. I was shocked. Why, I asked him. He kept shaking his head and saying he was sorry, that he'd wanted us to have one last night and could I understand that. But I didn't, I couldn't, there was no reason and he looked so miserable. I wanted to stay and make him tell me why. But,' he smiled bitterly, 'it was nearly morning and getting light outside. I drove away.'

I ran a hand across my face. 'What's your name?'

He hesitated. 'Calvin Bayles.'

'Did you ever see him again?'

'No.' Bayles' face seemed almost to decompose. 'I called him when I read about his wife. I asked if he was all right, if things were too hard. He said no, that you were helping him. I hardly listened. What I really wanted to know was whether he'd exposed me to the police. I hung on the line, afraid to ask and afraid to hang up. He knew. "Don't worry, Calvin," he said, very quiet, "you'll be all right too." Then he hung up. I almost cried. But after that I didn't talk to him until the night he died and then I let him down again.'

Bayles' fingers were white on the chair. 'Look,' I said. 'You're not alone in caring for Henry, or deserting him. Just tell me.'

He gave me a strange pitying look: sadness and community and comprehension. 'This last will hurt you, too.'

'Then that has to be.'

Bayles' voice was raw. 'The night he died, Henry called me at home. He'd never done that before. I took it in the den so no one could hear. I was angry at him for calling there but when he began talking his voice trembled so much I forgot that. He said that my name might come out now, that he couldn't help it anymore, but we were all tangled up in things at the bank he couldn't explain. I didn't understand any of it. Please, I begged him, please protect me. He said he'd tried to, that he'd called you, but you hadn't called back and probably weren't going to and he had nowhere else to turn –'

'Oh, Jesus . . .'

' "Do anything," I told him. "Please, anything else at all. Please, if you love me." For a long time he didn't answer and I thought maybe he was crying. Then he said, "Forgive me," and the line went dead. The next day I saw his picture in the evening paper. He was gone.'

We faced each other across the desk. Bayles said hoarsely,

'I pushed him to it. I was his last chance and he shot himself to save me.'

I closed my eyes. 'Why tell me this now, when he's dead?'

'You were part of it too. I want you to know what I did.'

My eyes opened to his strange expectant look. 'For what? To share the guilt? I've earned that. But you'll have to find absolution somewhere else. I don't qualify to give it.'

He flushed. 'That's not what I want. You can decide whether the police should learn what I've told you. Henry's dead, I know. But if it will help clear his name I won't run from him anymore.'

I shook my head angrily. 'I won't play God. You passed that buck to Henry and he's dead. I won't decide for you what kind of a man you are.'

He shrank back. 'Please . . .' The word died on his lips.

'God help him,' I mumbled.

His shoulders sagged. 'I loved him.'

I turned away. 'Go home,' I finally said. 'I'll do what I can. Just go home.'

He was crying now, his 'thank you' close to a whisper. He paused as if searching for other words, found none, and shuffled to the door. He turned there with a last silent look of pity and thanks and then disappeared into the long corridor. I listened until his footsteps made no sound.

The firm was almost empty now. The receptionist had left and the phones had stopped ringing. Two silent janitors drifted by like ghosts with dustmops. I sat motionless.

After a long time I reached in the drawer for my father's darts. I threw them mechanically, retrieving and throwing again until my mind was washed blank. Then I sat back and reviewed everything I knew about Lydia's murder, and everyone involved, from the beginning. When I finished my hands were shaking.

I held them in front of me until they stopped. Then I picked up the telephone and called Clayton Kell.

Chapter 32

At eight the next morning I met Clayton at his office. The papers I'd asked for were stacked on the desk in front of him. 'Maybe,' he said carefully, 'you can sort of explain this, so I can pretend to know what I'm doing.'

'Pretend to who? You're a bank officer, we're your counsel.'

He frowned. 'Roland's our counsel.'

'Then you'd better tell me straight out.'

'All right.' Clayton paused to rub the bridge of his nose. 'Roland called after Henry shot himself. He said that until reports were made to the feds, we should say nothing to anyone except him or people he sent. He specifically mentioned you.' He looked embarrassed. 'Somehow he managed to float across the notion that you were on the way out.'

'Then I need your help.'

He looked down at the stack of papers. 'What do these have to do with Henry's suicide?'

'I won't know until I see them. Please, it's important to me.'

Clayton grimaced. 'You're buying trouble, Adam.'

'No,' I said flatly. 'It's a favor I'm asking. Really.'

Clayton hesitated, searching my face. Then he pushed the papers across the desk.

The top packet was headed 'Loan File: Rue Napoleon Center.' I began reading hurriedly through its pages. 'At the cocktail party you said this got the bank into trouble. How?'

Clayton leaned back in his chair. 'Okay,' he sighed. 'Three months back this man Broussard came to us wanting a loan for Rue Napoleon Partners. They'd bought an area of old warehouses in New Orleans and were renovating it as condominiums and a shopping mall. The project was going bad; the area's shabby and they've had overruns on construction that left them cash-short. Their problem was that they'd borrowed several million already and without more money from us they'd have to stop building. If that happened they'd be forced to sell the property at less than they'd borrowed, and paying back the rest might have wiped out Broussard and his partners. So it was a salvage loan and I didn't like it.'

'Why'd Broussard come to you?'

'He came to Henry. That bothered me too. Broussard's a "New South" hustler, one cut below nouveau riche. I didn't understand why Henry wanted the business.' He winced. 'It turned out there was a lot about Henry I didn't understand.'

I finished the first file. 'This says the bank loaned Broussard four-and-a-half-million dollars on January sixth.'

Clayton nodded. 'Henry pushed it through over everyone's objections. Our only collateral was the propery. As I said, that's no collateral: if Rue Napoleon Partners were forced to sell it they couldn't have paid off what they'd already borrowed, let alone us. About two weeks after we made the loan a federal bank examiner came to audit our loans and said the same thing. He gave Henry a choice: nine hundred thousand dollars more collateral, or nine hundred thousand dollars less loan. Henry looked ill.'

'Which way did he go?'

'There wasn't any choice. They had no more collateral. We had to reduce the loan by nine hundred thousand dollars.'

'What did Broussard do?'

'It's in the next file. He threatened to sue on the grounds that we'd committed the extra money and then ruined him. That went on for over a month. Henry became totally irrational, tried everything to save the loan and couldn't. But Broussard never sued and the partnership's finishing the project. Maybe he found money somewhere else.'

I lit a cigarette. 'I think he did, Clayton.'

Clayton's face went slack with comprehension. 'Lydia?'

'The sequence fits. Look: in early January Henry brought Broussard to the bank and got him a loan you should have never made. Late that mouth the examiner forced you to reduce it by nine hundred thousand dollars. For over a month thereafter, Broussard fought to get the loan restored and Henry tried to help him. They gave up in early March. And on March fifteenth Henry stole eight hundred thousand from Lydia's account.'

'So you're saying that Henry had a cut in Napoleon Partners, and was bailing himself out.'

'That's consistent with what he did. Do you have papers showing who the partners are?'

'No.' Clayton frowned again. 'Henry was supposed to get those, and never did.'

'Then I'll try to find out.'

He shook his head. 'What difference could it make? Henry killed Lydia and stole the money, and now that he's dead his reasons don't matter anymore. You should be looking to Roland and your job, and to getting it together with Kris Ann before it's too late.'

I stood. 'I'll be all right, and Krissy too. Just don't tell anyone what I've asked you. Not yet.'

Clayton's round, troubled face gazed up at me. 'Rennie and I like you both, Adam. Why would I make this worse?'

I nodded. When I closed the door to return to my office he was still staring after me.

A clean copy of the motion waited on my desk. I sat, reading and not seeing, and then snatched the telephone to call Nora Culhane.

She wasn't in. I left messages and spent the day waiting. She returned the call around five. 'I'm surprised,' she said.

'I need your help.'

'Why?'

'Your boss, people at the station – they can't know.'

'You sound crazy, Adam.'

'Look, are you interested or not?'

'Yes, okay – off the record. What is it?'

'I think I know why Henry Cantwell stole the money.'

'Go on.'

I explained what I learned at the bank. When I was through she asked, 'Why are you telling me this?'

'I want you to fly to New Orleans.'

'For what?'

'Go to the parish recorder's office and check the name and address of each partner. Make copies. Do whatever you have to do to find out who they are. After that you can use the information any way you want.'

'Why can't you do your own errands,' she said tartly.

'I can't leave now. There's something else I have to do.'

'Then if you want my help, be honest. Does all this relate to Lydia Cantwell's murder?'

'I'm not sure. It depends on what you find.'

'Adam, the station can't send me unless I at least tell them something.'

'Get sick then. Charge the ticket and I'll pay for it.'

'You're serious.'

'Yes.'

'Then let me think about it.' She hung up.

I paced and smoked cigarettes. An hour later she called to say that she would fly out in the morning. 'I hope you find what you're looking for,' she said.

Chapter 33

Kris Ann was quiet that night, the deep and inward silence of someone brooding on a hard decision. She glanced at me occasionally, distant and thoughtful. I tried reading until she picked up her sketches of the children she taught, done to distract her since Henry's death. She began drawing with deft, short strokes, lips parted as they were when sleeping, so that she looked always about to speak, or even smile. I watched her, remembering how I'd watched her seven years before, memorizing her movements and expressions so that I could hold them in my mind like photographs. She had known that, and it had quickened her smile and the things she did in my apartment. She had cooked and I cleaned and she spent her spare time painting and reading the books I liked then, Joyce's *Portrait of the Artist As a Young Man* and essays by Camus, talking about them later. 'It's strange,' she once said of Camus. 'I don't think he's sure why he hopes for so much, or even if he should. But he does.' I had smiled then. We were going to Washington. . . .

The next morning I went to Maddox Coal and Steel.

Mooring's office was at the end of a carpeted hallway lined by pictures of foundries, open hearths, and blast furnaces. A short-haired woman in her forties sat next to his closed door. 'Do you have an appointment?' she asked.

'No. But tell him Adam Shaw is here. I think he'll see me.'

She frowned, pressed the intercom button, and said, 'There's a Mr Shaw outside.' Her frown deepened and she hung up looking betrayed. 'Go on in,' she said.

Mooring sat at his desk. His drapes were drawn, his office spare, neat, and dark. 'What is it?' he asked.

'Our deal is finished.'

His lids dropped. 'You wouldn't be here,' he finally said, 'if you didn't want something.'

'I've got two questions. I want the answers.'

'And if I won't give them?'

'Then I'll help the newspapers grub through your affair with Lydia Cantwell until you wish it had never happened.'

He looked up at me, curious and almost detached. 'What's in that for you?'

'The pleasure of it.'

His eyes flickered. 'That's unnatural.'

'It's natural as breathing. Push too many people too far and one of them is going to watch you, and wait. It's my turn.'

He folded his hands on the desk in front of him, appraising me. 'All right,' he said at length. 'I'll listen to your questions.'

I sat, leaning forward over his desk to ask quietly, 'Whose son is Jason Cantwell?'

Mooring looked away. Finally, he said, 'I've never known.'

'That's hard to believe.'

He turned back. 'Why, because you think he's mine? He couldn't be. She had someone else then, I don't know who. If she hadn't it might all have been different. But then the most I could do was be *around* her. Being *with* her was something I grew into.'

For the first time he spoke with feeling, as if seeing the pattern of his life. For a moment I thought of Kris Ann. 'Then how does it seem now? I asked. 'The rest of it.'

Mooring watched my face, pondering whether to answer. 'It's a habit,' he said at length. 'I've gotten used to who I've become. But you didn't come to ask that.'

'No. I didn't.'

'Then tell me your other question.'

I lit a cigarette, still watching him carefully. 'Did Lydia ask Cade to get her a divorce?'

His face stiffened. Then he nodded, once.

'When?'

He winced. 'Just before she was killed.'

'You mean the afternoon she went to see him.'

'Yes.'

'Is that what you visited her about, just before she left?'

227

'Yes.' He looked at me steadily, miserably. 'I was leaving Joanne.'

'Why didn't you tell me that before?'

'At first I thought you knew. I was sure you'd come to the house because Cade had told you. When I realized you knew nothing I was amazed and then I began thinking it was better you didn't. After I called Cade I was convinced he was acting to protect his client and perhaps others from needless hurt, and that you were irresponsible. And' – Mooring's voice fell off – 'there was no point in hurting Joanne, now.'

'Did you believe she had killed Lydia?'

'No.' Mooring shook his head. 'That would be too grotesque. I don't think she could, even with what I'd done. I just didn't want – after Lydia died, the only thing left was simple decency. I owed her that.'

He grimaced at the sound of it. I took a deep drag of cigarette smoke. 'About Cade: are you sure she actually told him?'

'He didn't say so exactly.' Mooring looked as though a sudden light had hurt his eyes. 'But she must have. When I came back that night Lydia was a different woman. Her first smile seemed to come from deep within her, and then all at once she was smiling and crying and leaning against me. When she looked up, her face was streaked with tears. I brushed her cheek, and asked, "Is that what I'm getting?" She shook her head. "It's just that I'm free," she answered, and then she told me I made her feel delivered to herself, after being lost. I couldn't imagine how I'd done that. But I felt delivered too. She was all I'd ever wanted.' Mooring turned from me. His voice was thick. 'She wouldn't lie, Shaw. Not about that.'

'No,' I said quietly. 'Lydia wouldn't lie.'

He didn't move. 'Why do you want to know this?'

'That doesn't concern you, anymore.'

'Then I've answered you now.' His profile was utterly still. 'Please, go.'

I let myself out.

His secretary peered up, ready to pass the messages spread

in front of her. 'Hold his calls,' I told her. 'Just ten minutes or so.'

She looked at my face, and slowly took her hand off the telephone. I went to my office and waited for Culhane.

It was midafternoon before she called.

'Where are you?' I asked.

'Here. Home.'

'Already?'

'I was done by eleven. I got a twelve-thirty plane.'

'You should have phoned from there.'

She hesitated. 'I could have. I didn't want to.'

My head was pounding again. 'There's no problem, is there?'

'I got what you asked for, the partners' names.'

'And?'

'Adam, there's one of them you're not going to like.'

'Who. Cade?'

'No.' I heard her inhale. 'It's your wife, Adam. Kris Ann Shaw.'

Chapter 34

Culhane lived on the second floor of a two-story building in a complex twenty minutes from town. As I drove there the skies lowered and darkened and then light rain spattered on my windshield and the road turned slick and shiny. It was raining harder when I knocked on her door.

'You're wet,' she said awkwardly.

I stepped into her living room: white walls and sliding glass windows opening to a porch where Swedish ivy hung. Culhane stood to one side, watching me, her expression stiff and cautious. 'You'd better show me the papers,' I said.

She was still for a moment. Then she went to the kitchen and brought back a small pile of Xeroxes. The top paper was headed: 'Napoleon Partners – Certificate of Partnership,' with signature lines for five partners. The last name was signed in a small, careful hand. The *i* in *Kris Ann* was dotted with a circle. 'Is it hers?' Culhane asked.

'It's hers.'

She looked small and serious. 'I'm sorry, Adam.'

'No need. It's nothing you did.'

'But you still love her, don't you?'

'At least the idea of her. Maybe that was never fair.'

'Please, tell me what this means.'

'It means that Henry Cantwell didn't kill his wife.'

She stared. 'Then you're going to the police.'

I shook my head. 'This is mine to do, Nora, like the story is yours. Surely you see that.'

She stood taut. 'Call Rayfield. You've already been hurt. You're begging for something worse to happen.'

I handed her the paper. 'Then you'd better keep this for your story.'

'For Christ's sake, Adam, don't you see what you're doing?' I started for the door. She grabbed my arm. 'Damn you, you're acting out the case that killed your father.'

Her face when I turned was pale and intense. 'Just where did you dredge up that?' I asked softly.

'It's so fucking obvious. The chances you've taken, this obsession to prove who killed her – it's more than saving Henry Cantwell or your wife. It began making sense when Rayfield told me how your father died. So I got the clippings from when it happened and then called police who knew him. They told me everything. It's incredible. He was thirty-two, like you are now, and a homicide lieutenant. The wife of a policeman – your father's closest friend – was found raped and murdered. Your father was assigned to the case. He found out that the dead woman had been sleeping with a police captain named Tyrell, a man he'd never liked. His friend's wife had broken it off –'

'I know the facts, Nora. He *was* my father.'

'Then let me finish. For almost a year your father tried to prove Tyrell had killed her, until they hated each other. Tyrell spied on your father and tried to have him busted. Each time Tyrell interfered, your father documented that, for evidence. It became obsessive. Tyrell stopped doing anything but worry about Kieron Shaw. Your father never got a warrant: Tyrell was over him, and made sure of that. But when your father was very certain, he went to Tyrell's house alone to face him. He told Tyrell what he had. Tyrell pulled a gun and shot him through the heart. They sentenced Tyrell to life. Your father was buried, with photographers and newsmen everywhere. His picture ran in all the papers. You look exactly like him.' Culhane's eyes were sad and knowing. 'Adam, you're not doing this for Henry Cantwell. The man you've done this for was murdered twenty years ago. You've given him too much already.'

I waited. 'Are you through now?'

'Yes.'

I opened the door. Then I paused, turning back in the doorway. 'You left something out, Nora. Things I haven't let myself remember for years. My father was a good and decent man. He never made a promise – no matter how small, or how busy he was – that he didn't keep. He never lied, and hated lies and liars. We played baseball. He was tall and slim and had this way of looking at people, even the priest, that said he saw them through their words. He was proud. He even walked proud into Mass, kneeling so quick and graceful by our pew that he was up in an instant. He seldom smiled, but when he did it was bright and sudden, and without knowing it he made people want to be like him. We – my mother, Brian, and I – lived on his strength. And when he died, my mother found her strength in hating him for that, and Brian in God, and I became someone I was never meant to be and made a mess of Krissy's life, and now that's mine to face. But there's the other thing.'

Nora looked up. 'What's that?' she asked.

'My father was right. Tyrell killed the woman.'

'Oh God, Adam.'

I touched her cheek. Then I turned and walked to my car through the rain, to find Kris Ann.

The skies had turned black and slantwise rain battered my hood in the metallic beat of the night seven years ago, when I knew how I'd begun to lose her.

We had come back late from a movie and parked at the end of Cade's driveway in a cocoon of rain and darkness, not wanting to go in. Thin vapor from our breathing glazed the windshield. Through it, the house was vague and dark and massive, its single light a blur of yellow from Cade's bedroom. Kris Ann and I slid down in the seats, faces turned to each other, debating whether she would come to my room again. 'But it's unnerving,' she said, 'like making love in a fire drill.'

I grinned in the dark. 'It develops intense concentration and singleness of purpose. Someday our children will be banging on the bedroom door demanding water, and we'll have either learned to concentrate or else –'

'Our children,' she smiled 'are one thing. My father is something else.'

'He is that.'

Her smile faded. 'What are you going to do about his offer?'

'I don't know. We've been planning on Washington, after

232

all. Of course it's a fine firm and a better start in some ways: more money, a good practice if I make partner. I suppose our life might be easier.'

'What about that apartment in Georgetown we were going to find?'

There was something in her tone I couldn't place 'It still sounds good. I just wonder whether Birmingham might have more of a future for us. And it is where you've grown up.'

She looked away. 'Of course Daddy's here,' she said slowly.

'I've thought of that. The other way you wouldn't see him very much.' I smiled. 'Fortunately, once we're married he won't be sleeping next door. What do you think?'

She turned to face me. 'It's up to you, Adam. Please, just think about what you really want. I need to know that.'

I nodded. 'Then I'll consider what your father said.'

For a long time she was silent. 'If you like.'

She sat straighter, facing toward the windshield so that her face was in shadows. The rain beat down. 'Let's go in now,' she said abruptly. 'I'm getting tired.'

She didn't come to my room that night. The next morning she said nothing about it, nor in all the years since, living in the house her father bought us . . .

When I got there, Cade's car was next to hers.

Chapter 35

I parked and circled the house to the front. Rain soaked my clothes and hair and ran down my face. I reached the porch, slowed, and went noiselessly up its rain-slick steps.

Cade and Kris Ann were framed in the living room window, close together on the couch, their backs to me. Cade talked urgently, index finger jabbing his palm. Kris Ann's face in profile was strained and attentive. Their lips moved, but on the other side of the glass I heard only rain beating on the canopy and the steps and the leaves of trees. I moved to the front door, opened it, and walked inside.

Cade stood quickly. Kris Ann turned pale. 'I know about New Orleans,' I told her.

Her mouth opened. Cade moved between us, eyes hooded and watchful. I looked past him. 'We're going to the police, Krissy.'

Her glance moved between us. 'For what, Adam? Why?'

'Lydia Cantwell's murder.'

She shrank from me in horror. Cade was still, almost expressionless, watching me with his back to the mantel where Kris Ann's revolver was. 'We have to go,' I told her softly.

Cade's voice was tight. 'I can't let you do that, Adam.'

I shook my head, speaking to Kris Ann. 'I've got no choice, Krissy. Maybe you can explain to Rayfield why you got home so late the night Lydia was killed. But now I know that Henry never left Anniston, and that the black Mercedes Joanne Mooring thought she saw in the Cantwell's drive was a navy blue Audi like yours.'

'Adam, that's not right –'

'I wish it weren't. From the time I started looking into Lydia's murder you tried to stop me – for Roland's sake, you said. And when I wouldn't, I found your picture on my windshield. You're an artist, after all.'

'You can't believe that.'

'I can't believe you. When I asked you to leave town you refused and tried persuading me to quit. The night I was shot at, you'd switched off every light in the house, your revolver was in your purse. This partnership finished it. You hid that from me, damn you, and now Henry and Lydia are dead. I'm giving you to Rayfield.'

I moved towards her. Cade's face as he stood between us was hard, determined. 'I won't permit this. They'll try Kris Ann for murder.'

'They'll do that anyhow. The news people know about Napoleon.'

Cade stared at me. 'Then you sent the Culhane woman.'

'That's right. By nightfall Rayfield will be here looking for Kris Ann. It's already done.'

Kris Ann looked to Cade, pleading. He stepped forward. 'You've ruined everything, Adam. I always knew you would. God, how I hate you.'

'For what, Roland? Finding Lydia's murderer?'

'You're such a fool.' He shook his head. 'Sweet Jesus, to have lived through this for seven years and remained so stupid.'

'Not quite so stupid.'

A strange smile of contempt turned the ends of his mouth without touching his eyes. 'But you are. You see, Kris Ann didn't kill anyone.'

I stopped to face him as he awaited my answer. After a moment I said simply. 'I know.'

Cade stared at me in the long silence that followed. I broke it, speaking softly. 'I counted on you, Roland. You do love her, in your way.'

Cade's eyes widened as if admitting light. Kris Ann bolted up, staring wildly at both of us and backing away until we formed a triangle, the couch between us, Cade to one side. The mantel and gun were still behind him. 'How did you know?' he finally asked.

'Bayles came to see me.'

'I wouldn't have thought that.'

'Love is strange. But then you know all about that. It all comes back to the three of us: you, me, and Kris Ann.'

Cade's head tilted. 'How long have you wanted me for this?'

'I suppose since the beginning, on some level.'

'Why so soon?'

'I started sensing the connections. You've hated me ever since Kris Ann brought me home. At first I tried believing you were a protective father. I didn't want to face the fact that we were rivals. The job offer, the house, the talks with me – all these were ways of keeping Kris Ann for yourself. She knew that, inside. I didn't, or didn't want to.' I turned to Kris Ann. 'I never wanted to be a lawyer, so how I did it never really mattered. Maybe I was dazzled by things I'd never had. All the time you wanted me to take you away from him. You sensed how unhealthy it was. Instead I used you as an excuse and kept you here. God help me, it was you I wanted, not the rest.'

Her face was blank and wounded. She shook her head, over and over. 'But look at what you've done –'

'Please, Krissy, understand what *he* did. Roland meant to destroy our marriage. Over time he planned to cut me down in front of you and then wean you with money until you didn't respect or need me. But he invested badly. Another man would have given up. Your father is a different sort of man. He learned Napoleon was in trouble and promised them financing in return for a share in your name. He didn't have that kind of money himelf. But Henry had the bank's money and Lydia's, and Roland knew that he was homosexual. My guess is that he put detectives on Henry until he found his lover. Then he threatened to expose the other man unless Henry arranged a loan. The details aren't important. What I have to know is why you took that partnership.'

'It was a present from Daddy,' she burst out bitterly.

I shook my head. 'Why didn't you just tell me?'

'It was between me and Daddy. I thought maybe it would hurt your pride. I didn't know about Henry –'

'It was *ours*,' Cade cut in. 'You don't need to explain anything.'

I turned. 'Then you can, Roland. You can tell her about Jason.'

Cade turned to her, face suffused with blood. I went on. 'Ask him, Krissy. Ask him if you have a brother.'

They faced each other in terrible silence. Then Cade nodded mutely, and reached toward her. She recoiled, crying out, 'Why, Adam? Why do this now?'

'Because we have to face the truth or there's been no point to any of this. Your father was young when his family lost their money. It humiliated him. He despised Henry for his "weakness," and for what he had. So piece by piece he took what was Henry's: his father's affection, his place at the firm, and then Lydia. Roland wanted her and had her, and she had a son. But they couldn't marry because of the scandal it would cause and perhaps for fear he'd lose you. After your mother died he proposed. Lydia refused and denied him Jason, but it was you who paid the price. He became fixated on you, pouring all his hate and disappointment into keeping you his –'

'Stop.' Cade's face and voice filled with torment. 'How can you know anything of me?'

I turned on him. 'Before Henry died you told me that I couldn't think like someone else. You were wrong. I've learned to think like you. You'd taken Henry's place but now he had your son. At first you tried to reach Jason through Lydia, forcing her to buy Jason presents. But Jason grew up warped. When he tried to rape Kris Ann the conflict tore you apart: *your* son, touching the daughter you wanted for yourself. It ate through you until you hated all of them. Did you ever tell Henry, Roland?'

'Why should I have? He was *our* son. Henry was a weakling –'

'So you destroyed him.'

'I warn you, Adam.'

I shook my head. 'Krissy has to see what you are. You blackmailed Henry for more than just money. You enjoyed it. When Broussard's loan was reduced you forced him to use Lydia's money to cover the difference. You hoped she'd never find out. But she was in love with Mooring. She must have despised coming to you. But you knew the Cantwells' finances and could minimize the involvement of outsiders. In a way she began her own murder. The will is a fake, isn't it, Roland?'

He nodded reflexively. 'How did you learn that?'

'It has to be. When Lydia came to your office you must have found out she'd fought with Jason and that only Mooring knew she was asking for a divorce. You would have asked when she intended telling Henry and learned she wasn't expecting him back that night. You knew a divorce would uncover your blackmail of Henry. Everyone would learn what you are – me, your partners, even Kris Ann. You couldn't let that happen. So when Lydia left, you had your secretary type a new will to cover Lydia's reason for coming. But you had a second purpose. You could use it to revenge yourself on Jason.

'Late that night you called on Lydia. She let you in: after all, you were Jason's father. But she was set on Mooring. All the years of hate and jealousy overwhelmed you. I wonder what she felt when she realized you meant to kill her, and how –'

Kris Ann's hands clutched her throat. In one continuous motion Cade leaped to the mantel and whirled on me with the revolver. 'No,' Kris Ann screamed.

Cade turned to her. 'He means to put me in prison. I can't let him live to see that.' His voice became rhythmic, compelling. 'Please, baby, you have to choose. How can you think he loves you? He used you to get my money, left you here alone when he thought you might be harmed. Now he's accused you of killing Lydia to get at me. He knew I loved you. Everything I've done was for you. He used you –'

'Tell her the rest, Roland.'

'Stop,' she screamed.

'Please, baby –'

'Tell her how you strangled Lydia.'

Cade started toward me with the revolver. 'She'll choose, in time. She'll understand what I did –'

'She'll understand what you are. You took Lydia's picture and mutilated it with her dead at your feet hoping the police would think her killer was insane, like Jason. It was no deception. You're more psychotic than Jason ever dreamed of. You liked killing her.'

'No.' Cade's voice was anguished. 'She looked so *new*. All those years I'd wanted her, her elegance, even her distance, and then she says she's free at last – free of Grangeville and all of Henry's secrets, and ours –'

'Maybe she was just happy, Roland. She'd almost made it.'

He shook his head. 'She insulted me. When I began moving toward her she started to beg, told me she'd do anything to please me as long as she could have Mooring. It was all for *him*. She was crying when I touched her.' His arm raised until he faced me over the sight of the revolver.

'It's no good. You can't believe Kris Ann will forget watching you kill me. You'll go to the electric chair.'

Cade's mouth was a harsh line. 'I'm going either way. You've seen to that. At least now you'll die first and I'll have time alone with Kris Ann, to explain –'

'Daddy – no.' Kris Ann ran to him, grasping his free arm and falling to her knees. 'Don't do this.'

She looked up. Cade reached to stroke her hair. 'Do you choose me, baby? I want you to choose me.'

'Don't touch her, Roland.'

Kris Ann's eyes closed. Her face was white and frozen. Cade kept the gun on me as he stroked her hair and the back of her neck. 'She's mine, Adam. There's nothing you can do to stop me now.'

I moved toward him. 'Let her go.'

'No.' He shook his head. 'Not again.'

'Then let her hear first. You can't be afraid, not the way you've maneuvered me.'

The gun didn't move. Only the keenness of his look disclosed interest. 'So you understand that, too.'

'I understand it all. You gave me the will so that I'd be the one to find Lydia. You knew I'd give it to the police to protect Henry. The will provided them Jason as a suspect and you an excuse to force yourself on Henry and control me. You counted on that: you'd run my life for seven years. And you wanted one last contest with Krissy as the prize.'

Kris Ann covered her face. A close volley of thunder exploded, rattling the windows. I talked through it. 'It began falling apart when Henry came home. You knew he would be gone that night, but you must have been sick to find out *where* he had been, and with whom. So you helped him commit perjury, knowing – as he did not – that Bayles' exposure would reveal you as the murderer.

'Rayfield made it harder. He hated you and knew Henry was gay. Then they discovered Mooring's semen. Rayfield didn't know whose it was, but you must have. You were almost caught. But your interest and Mooring's were identical: he didn't want to be uncovered and although he didn't know why, you couldn't withstand it. For twenty-eight years since, you changed the course of his life, and he never knew.

'When *I* uncovered Mooring I wanted to protect Henry. So like a fool I hid what I knew from Rayfield and protected you instead.'

Wind and rain began howling on the porch behind me. Kris Ann wept at Cade's feet. His stare over the gun sight was filled with rage and loathing. I spoke faster. 'Henry and you were locked in a terrible contest. Henry didn't want Bayles exposed and you'd concealed the link between your blackmail and the murder by covering her divorce plans with the fake will. But he had enough suspicion to ask me to investigate and enough guts to insist on that to you. It wasn't my favor to him. It was *his* favor to me. We were friends –'

'Likes attract,' Cade said contemptuously. 'The weak and the envious.'

'I don't envy the strength it took to mutilate Krissy's picture.' Her face raised from her hands. 'That was him, too,' I told her. 'All through this he's tried to make me afraid of losing you to a murderer, or to him. I didn't know that they were the same man.'

Cade looked down at Kris Ann. His gun wavered slightly.

I calculated the distance between us. 'Please,' Cade was saying. 'He never cared for you. I proved that with the picture.'

She rose, looking from Cade to me. Reason – cold and certain and unforgiving – came into her face. 'You bastards.' She turned to me. 'Both of you. I've been the battlefield where you could prove who was the biggest man –'

'Baby, I had to show you he didn't care –'

I began moving toward him. 'Bullshit, Roland: by then I'd found Mooring. You were trying to save yourself. When I talked to Joanne Mooring, I began closing in on you, except that I didn't understand what she was telling me. Instead I suspected everyone: the Moorings, Otis Lee, and finally Jason. You were willing to sacrifice Lee and I was caught between Lee and Henry. But when Rayfield told me about Henry's arrest and then Henry admitted what had happened I was closer yet. How did you find out fast enough to shoot at me?'

Cade still watched Kris Ann. 'Coincidence,' he said absently. 'I called Kris Ann right after you did and found out where you were.'

He nodded. Kris Ann stared at him. 'But people's lives. Lydia's and Henry's. Ours.'

'Baby.' Cade's voice was soft, crooning. 'You're the only one who mattered. The rest . . .' He looked back to me.

I stopped six feet from him. 'The rest were expendable, like Henry. When Clayton told me that Rayfield had found eight hundred thousand dollars gone from Lydia's account, all I needed was to lean on Henry until he told me who Bayles was and what you'd done. You knew how close I was: when you talked about Henry – how trapped and desperate he must feel – you were talking about yourself. I swear it, Roland, even if I could forgive you the rest I can never forgive what you did next. You maneuvered me into giving you time to think while believing I'd bought time for Henry. Then you went to work. You implied that he had no lover. You blamed everything you'd done – Lydia's murder, Krissy's picture, your shots at me – on Henry. You had to break my faith in him for just a few more hours. You succeeded. I didn't return his call that night. God damn you, I could have saved him.

'The appointment you made wasn't for eight the next morning. It was for eight that night. You made sure he never called again. It wasn't suicide, Roland. You killed him.'

'No, Adam.' Cade's smile flickered eerily. 'You killed him, by not calling. When I put the gun in his mouth he just looked at me. He wanted to die.'

'But you're insane.' Kris Ann's voice was broken. 'To kill Lydia and Henry. To think that was for me –'

'There's more, Krissy. Roland planned to use Henry's murder to have you for himself. He meant to burden me with guilt and have me fired. He was in the clear now and had the partnership to give you. I was to be the irrational ex-partner. That was the choice he meant to give you. You were going to be his.' I began moving toward Cade. 'You killed my friend, Roland, but I survived. I'm taking you in.'

'No.' Cade raised the gun, bracing his shooting wrist with his left hand. 'That's one thing you will never do.'

Kris Ann reached toward him. 'Daddy –'

'I have to.' Cade straightened with an insane ravaged dignity. 'Perhaps it's better that you know what I've done for you. Now you can truly choose.'

'Don't make me.' She reached out for him. 'Please.'

'There's nothing else left.' Cade squinted, aiming at the center of my face as I moved closer. 'You have to choose now.' His finger tightened on the trigger.

Kris Ann lunged as he fired.

The gun jerked upward. Cade stared at me, astonished, amidst falling plaster. Kris Ann fell past him in the bullet's echo. I jumped.

My head drove into his stomach and knocked him against the mantel. He bounced back, cracking his gun on my skull. I doubled, stunned, hugging his waist tightly as his momentum pushed me backward and my knees collapsed and I pulled him down on top of me. As we fell my arm lashed up at his wrist and knocked the gun to the floor, and then Cade landed on me with his full weight, fingers grasping my windpipe.

They tightened, shutting off air. There was ripped tissue in my mouth and the taste of blood. Rhythmically, he began smashing my head on the floor. My skull exploded. His face, intense and rapturous, broke into pieces in front of me. Then it went dark and there was only his sweat and weight and panting, the sourness of his breath, iron fingers as I choked for air. My left hand flopped on the wooden floor, touched steel, groping. The trigger curled against my finger. His thumbs pressed toward the back of my throat. My hand closed. In a blind reflex I jammed the gun between us and fired.

His fingers dug fiercely. I gagged, and then they twitched and loosened and I swallowed air, raw and tender in my throat, and retched it up. There was light. Cade's face was inches from mine. His eyes seemed great with surprise, a last, profound disappointment. They made his expression softer, almost gentle. 'Lydia,' he murmured, and then they went blank, and he was dead weight, and his face fell against my shoulder.

His body trembled. I lay down the gun and pushed him off me. He flopped on his back, staring emptily at the ceiling, a dark stain near his heart. Kris Ann was crawling toward us. I couldn't speak. There was no rain or wind or thunder.

In the aching, awful silence I got up and stumbled toward the telephone. I turned in the hallway. Kris Ann knelt over Cade, tear streaked, holding his head in her hands. Her hair fell across his face.

I went to the telephone and told them to send Rayfield.

When I returned, Kris Ann was chattering at Cade, crying and asking him why. Blood tricked from the corner of his mouth. I let her go until she wasn't speaking or sobbing. Then I went to her side.

'They're coming,' I said softly.

She looked up at me. Her eyes were burnholes. 'You had to kill him, didn't you?'

'Krissy, it's time now.' I reached out.

She turned away. When I took her hand it was lifeless. She didn't struggle, or help. I pulled her up and led her to the porch as she looked back at Cade.

It was quiet outside, and cool. The rain had stopped, and there was the shine of wetness on the grass and the fresh smell of ozone. Sirens wailed in the distance coming closer. Kris Ann wept. I pulled her to me. She was stiff in my arms, resisting. My eyes turned wet, and then I began silently to cry, for Henry and Lydia, and for my father, for what I had done and all the things between us Kris Ann and I would have to face.

She shivered. I held her close.

NO SAFE PLACE
Richard North Patterson

YOU CAN RUN – BUT YOU CAN'T HIDE

Kerry Kilcannon's future looks golden, but in an election campaign seven days can be a dangerously long time.

NO SAFE PLACE is Kerry's story — an electrifying novel that follows the campaign trail, where death and the undying past haunt the most charismatic presidential candidate in a generation, where violence and scandal threaten to erupt, where public image and private life collide with explosive effect.

SILENT WITNESS
Richard North Patterson

Two brutal murders.
Two dead high school students.
Two families bereaved.
Two men suspected of killing their lovers ...

Twenty-eight years separate the crimes that link Tony Lord and Sam Robb.

In 1967 Tony Lord is suspected of killing his girlfriend Alison, but the case never comes to trial, and Tony has never officially cleared his name in a case that is still open.

In 1995, Tony is a successful San Francisco attorney and receives a desperate call from Sam's wife: Sam has been accused of the murder of one of his students. Reluctantly, but inevitably, Tony agrees to defend his boyhood friend.

At once, Tony is plunged into the unfinished business of his past. And in the merciless arena of the murder trial, he must face not only his fear that Sam is a killer, but also the dark, buried truths that surround Alison's death all those years earlier ...